T0038433

HIGH PRAISE FOR
THE THIN RED LINE

"James Jones's best!"

—*The New York Times*

"One of the strongest and most effective war novels ever written."

—*The Nation*

"One step away from sheer, howling madness!"

—*New York Post*

"*The Thin Red Line* is a fitting companion to . . . *From Here to Eternity*. . . . Future generations will look back on both of them as definite statements of human combat in our time."

—*Life*

BY JAMES JONES

From Here to Eternity
Some Came Running
The Pistol
The Thin Red Line
Go to the Widow-Maker
The Ice-Cream Headache and Other Stories
The Merry Month of May
A Touch of Danger
Viet Journal
WW II
Whistle

THE
THIN
RED
LINE

THE THIN RED LINE

A Novel

JAMES JONES

DIAL PRESS TRADE PAPERBACKS

NEW YORK

The Thin Red Line is a work of fiction. Names, characters, places and incidents are the products of the author's imagination or are used fictitiously. Any resemblance to actual events, locales, or persons, living or dead, is entirely coincidental.

2012 Dial Press Trade Paperback Edition

Copyright © 1962 by James Jones

Copyright © renewed 1990 by Gloria Jones, Jamie Anthony Phillipe Jones, and Kaylie Anne Jones

Foreword copyright © 2012 by Francine Prose

All rights reserved.

Published in the United States by Dial Press Trade Paperbacks, an imprint of The Random House Publishing Group, a division of Random House, Inc., New York.

DIAL PRESS is a registered trademark of Random House, Inc., and the colophon is a trademark of Random House, Inc.

Originally published in hardcover in the United States by Scribner, a division of Simon & Schuster, Inc., in 1962. This edition reprinted by arrangement with the Estate of James Jones.

ISBN 978-0-385-32408-3

Printed in the United States of America

www.dialpress.com

FOREWORD

Francine Prose

My father fought in the Philippines during World War II. When I was little, I pictured the Pacific theater as a huge, chaotic Radio City Music Hall where soldiers slogged through mud, slept in tents, and scanned the sky for enemy bombers. My father used to tell us stories about his army days. Oddly, I can't remember a single one of his stories, but only that he told the same ones over and over. We used to roll our eyes and say, Stop! We already heard this!

I do remember hearing that he'd been sent home from the front with hepatitis: an eighty-pound skeleton by the time his ship docked in New York. I suppose that story stuck in my mind because it suggested a different ending, an alternate future, or a lack of one, an alarming parallel history in which I, born after the war, would never have existed. I think that's why my brother and I discouraged our father from talking about the war: his stories were all too threatening, we couldn't bear to hear them.

My father-in-law spent the war in Okinawa, doing construction work with the Seabees. By the time I met him, I knew the difference between "theater of operations" and the music-hall stage where the Rockettes danced. He too had a limited repertoire of memories from that time, but unlike my father, he left behind a snapshot of two men hunkering on the ground, looking at the charred corpse of a Japanese explosives expert pinned under a large fragment of an airplane wing.

Though I often think about my father and father-in-law, only rarely do I think about the fact that they both fought in the Pacific. But for days after I'd read James Jones's *The Thin Red Line,* I could think of little else, and both men seemed intensely present to me in a way that they hadn't for a long time.

The Thin Red Line is, both as a tribute and as an act of virtuoso ventriloquism, channeling the spirit—the voices—of the men of that generation, as they told and retold the stories of how they got through the war. As I read the novel, I realized something I could never have understood when I was a child, first listening to my father and later teasing him about himself. Nor did it occur to me when I listened to my father-in-law, though I was already an adult by the time I met him. What struck me now was the most simple and, one might think, obvious fact: They were young when those things happened to them: they were hardly older than boys.

First published in 1962, *The Thin Red Line* was one of the simultaneously popular and "serious" novels to come out of World War II. Eleven years earlier, *From Here to Eternity* had established Jones's popular and critical reputation; *The Thin Red Line*—whose title, like that of the earlier novel, is taken from a line of Rudyard Kipling's—was meant to be the second book in a trilogy about the war.

The book begins when a group of soldiers—the C-for-Charlie company—are belowdeck in the transport carrier that has brought them to Guadalcanal. Soon they will be off-loaded to take (mile by mile, though it more often seems to be inch by inch) a small corner of the tropical landscape distinguished by two hills. The topographical features of these natural formations have been named, with appropriate absurdity, after the anatomical parts of an elephant and a boiled shrimp.

Caught up in the tension affecting the men who are preparing to disembark, and then in the wave of relief, shock, disorientation, and fear that washes over them when the waiting is over and they've finally made land, we may not notice, for fifty pages or so, that this deceptively conventional and straightforward novel is actually a model of complex literary technique.

Within one long opening chapter, Jones manages to introduce us to, let's say, twenty men, all of whom are on the same ship charged with carrying out the same mission on the same Pacific island. Already they are suffering the stench, the humidity, the heat, and the discomfort of the transport. Yet there isn't one of them who doesn't know that they are enjoying something like a moment of grace, after which their suffering is about to get worse.

Despite the commonality of their psychic state and their precarious situation, each is an individual. With astonishing rapidity Jones introduces and establishes each character so that the reader can keep them clearly in mind, immediately identifiable and distinguished from one another. Anyone who imagines that something like this is easy to do should try it: working with a large, all-male cast, all of them sharing a uniform, some military training, a sensible anxiety about the future—and somehow separating them out into distinct and nuanced fictional creations.

Would we be able to tell them apart in a group photograph? Though Jones tells us how the men look, he offers us something more important. We learn who each one *is*, not just in his quirks of behavior and speech, but in his secret heart. In some of the most memorable scenes, the eye of the narrative moves like the eye of a camera, panning from face to face as the men regard an object or an event that has commanded their full attention.

One such scene occurs not long after their arrival on the island, when the men discover a bloodstained khaki shirt that has obviously belonged to a severely wounded American soldier. At first their responses to the relic blend together to form a sort of chorus. "There was a peculiar tone of sexual excitement, sexual morbidity, in all of the voices—almost as if they were voyeurs behind a mirror watching a man in the act of coitus; as though in looking openly at the evidence of this unknown man's pain and fear they were unwillingly perhaps but nonetheless uncontrollably seducing him" (66).

But then one detail seen in closer focus—the sleeves of the shirt have been shredded to make a stylish cowboy fringe—inspires a more specific response in the mind of Corporal Queen, otherwise known as Big Queen:

The sight gave Big Queen, who had owned and worn a buckskin jacket during his two years as a hand, a peculiarly painful twinge. A twinge of odd loneliness—and of something else. It was that American love of cowboy fringe. It brought Queen closer in understanding to this other, unknown man that Queen liked to be. It was such a ridiculous, boyish gesture; and, intuitively, Queen understood it all too well. Much better than he wanted to understand it consciously. Because the gesture hadn't worked. It hadn't protected him at all. That much was obvious (67).

The soldier who exerts the most immediate claim on the reader's attention is a lanky young Virginian, Private First Class Doll. "A quiet, freshfaced youth with considerable naivete, who talked little and shyly, Doll had always remained pretty much in the background; but lately, in the past six months, something had been slowly happening to him, and he had been changing and coming forward more. It did not make him more likeable" (6).

Just before the soldiers disembark, we see Doll obsessed with the idea of stealing a pistol, a bad-boy act that nonetheless reveals an anxious interest in self-protection. As Doll sneaks around the hold of the ship on his secret errand, he bounces past the others, some of whom are introduced to us and defined by the way in which they view Doll.

First Sergeant Welsh has no use for him. Or for anything, really. The most cynical—and privileged—of the men, possessed by private demons, "amused" by politics, integrity, ideals, and "most of all human virtue," Eddie Welsh has joined the army as an elaborate scam to avoid being drafted to serve in a war. But he has stayed to fight the war because, as we come to see, the military allows him to walk an impulsive, furious, psycho edge that might not be tolerated in peacetime. "Welsh was mad. He was insane. Truly a real madman" (12). Leading C-for-Charlie is Captain James "Bugger" Stein, a lawyer from Cleveland, a decent guy who wants to do a good job and keep his men from being slaughtered. As they prepare to disembark, Stein believes "that officers should be with their men on a day such as this, should share their hardships and dangers, rather than staying up topside in the club cabin where they had remained for most of the trip, and Stein had so informed his juniors. While none of them had looked too pleased about it, no one had commented . . . And Stein was convinced that it could not help but aid morale" (11).

Private Bell, a former officer who has been demoted because he couldn't stand to leave his beloved wife, is the most meditative in the group, at once the most reflective and objectively intelligent about the war. As the novel progresses, we move deeper into Bell's psyche, until his sensibility begins to seem like the likeliest stand-in for that of the author.

Though the soldiers possess wildly unequal shares of social skills and cardinal virtues, there are—strictly speaking—neither heroes nor villains, but only human beings in an impossible situation, capable of bravery and generosity at one moment, cowardice and callousness the next. Indeed one of the most "experimental" aspects of this apparently conventional novel is that its real hero is not any particular individual but rather the group, C-for-Charlie.

The population of this group keeps changing as men transfer out and return. Men with names like Mazzi, Nellie, Big Un, Fife, Whyte, and Storm, men we become attached to and invested in, so that we want them to stay alive and are sorry when they are frightened or hurt or killed. And just in case we are in any doubt about how mature they are, we need only watch them playing like puppies as they attempt to set up shelters in the "thin sea of mud":

> It was so bad, everything was so miserable, that suddenly the whole thing turned itself into a lark. A hollow and pathetic lark, to be sure, when associated with the dead, dying and wounded from the air raid whom they could not forget;—but perhaps for that very reason the clowning and laughter rose to an even higher pitch, one that in the end resembled hysteria. Some men, less cautious and able to forget that even combat fatigues had to be washed, were not above sitting down and sliding themselves around in the mud like children playing in snow. In the end, however, it did not lessen their painful new tension (55).

Even as we watch them at play, we are, like the men themselves, waiting nervously for the good times to end. An enemy is out there, a war is going on. The men have learned this, though from a slight remove; they've taken fire during the landing, and they've seen a soldier killed. As the days and weeks progress, they will each learn the harsh truths about war, intimately and first hand. In the process the reader learns about men—how men talk to each other, tease and joke, how they fear or succumb to the terror of not looking brave and manly in front of other men.

It cannot be easy for a writer to ratchet the tension up and keep it pitched so extremely high as we anticipate the inevitable escalation of horrors: the first dead body, the first explosion, the first bullet, the first soldier wounded or killed. It's a measure of Jones's skill that we suffer so little combat fatigue even when, for so much of the novel, what occurs (or doesn't occur) is nothing less than a matter of life and death.

Not only does the point of view nimbly shift from man to man, from outside to inside the minds of this large and various population, but the principal characters change in the course of the book, as we would expect them to, given the extremity of what they are undergoing.

At moments, the movement of time in the novel seems to re-create "real time." We may feel, as the soldiers must, as if several weeks have passed, only to be told that just a few days have elapsed. We may imagine we are watching a slow-motion marathon race in which each contestant must pass certain milestones: the first killing, the first flush of remorse over having killed someone and the subsequent subsiding of that guilt, the initial jolt of manic bravery or paralyzing terror. Consider how time seems to slow down and nearly stop in the following passage, a fraction of the long scene in which Doll prepares to throw his first grenade:

He had spread the cotter pins so widely for reasons of safety that he had to bite its ends together before it would pull out, sending a sharp drill of pain through an old bad tooth. Perhaps that was what undid him. He remembered movies where men pulled the pins of grenades with their teeth, and realized with a shock of inadequacy that his teeth would never be able to stand it. In any case, he had waited too long. He now had the pin out and was standing looking at this heavy orange corrugated castiron object in his hand. As long as he clenched it and kept the tin lever down it was not dangerous, but already his hand felt slippery. Even if he had not already dropped the pin on the ground, he knew it would be impossible to reinsert it, dangerous to attempt. He had activated it, and now here he was with it, and if he did not want to go on carrying it forever while his hand slowly weakened or cramped itself and relaxed, he was going to have to throw it; but what he really wanted to do was simply drop it on the ground and turn and flee (162–63).

Few human emotions don't surface in the course of the novel. James Jones seems unafraid and at ease not only with men at their best but with their less admirable feelings and responses: competition, envy, resentment, schadenfreude, impatience. There is also affection, admiration, even tenderness, though not much. The fact that some of the soldiers are gay is accepted as a matter of course, and one of the novel's saddest sections focuses on Doll's pain and confusion when he finds himself attracted to a fellow soldier.

One of the things that make the book so memorable and successful is Jones's consistent refusal to moralize, preach, or judge. He's not turning thumbs up or thumbs down on these men, he's just telling you what occurred. These are the men who went to war, and this is what happened to them on Guadalcanal.

Two films have been made from *The Thin Red Line*, one in 1964 (directed by Andrew Marton) and one in 1998. Certainly, both have their strong points; the more recent of the films, directed by Terrence Malick, is characteristically lush, ambitious, personal, and uninterested in making things easy for the viewer. But neither can do what the novel does, which is to completely and unerringly avoid glorifying war. The minute we put something on a big screen, or in glorious color, it begins to look pretty good, even the violence and gore. The fear, the mud, the tension, the boredom, the hard work, and the exhaustion of battle are more readily communicated in print, on the page—without the cosmetic improvements effected by the fact of the camera.

The intimacy of the reading experience brings the action extremely close, even as we're denied the visual pleasure of watching the attractive mists rising in the beautiful jungle. What Jones is describing is terrible, and he knows it; there's nothing "pretty" about it.

We never feel that James Jones has set out to write an "antiwar novel," and it's certainly not a "prowar novel." So, you might ask, what is it? What was he trying to do? His aim, as far as I can tell, was simply to tell the truth, to create art out of what he saw, to make war look as awful and overwhelming as it is in life.

We may find ourselves thinking: If only everyone in the world would read *The Thin Red Line,* together with *The Red Badge of Courage, The Charterhouse of Parma, War and Peace,* and *The Things They Carried!* Do I believe that reading these books would prevent future wars? I would like to think so, but the truth is, I don't. In any case, if all wars were to suddenly stop, and no new wars begin, we would still want novels like this to remind the peaceful future of the bullets they dodged. If there *are* wars, as there are as I write this, as there probably always will be, then we will always need novelists to tell us what war feels and looks like from the outside and from within, what it does to those caught up in it, and how it affects us all, the children and the grandchildren of those boys playing in the mud of a jungle in the Pacific.

FRANCINE PROSE is the author of sixteen books of fiction. Her novel *A Changed Man* won the Dayton Literary Peace Prize, and *Blue Angel* was a finalist for the National Book Award. Her most recent works of nonfiction include the highly acclaimed *Anne Frank: The Book, The Life, The Afterlife,* and the *New York Times* bestseller *Reading Like a Writer.* A former president of PEN American Center and a member of the American Academy of Arts and Letters and the American Academy of Arts and Sciences, Francine Prose lives in New York City.

THE
THIN
RED
LINE

DEDICATION

This book is cheerfully dedicated to those greatest
and most heroic of all human endeavors, WAR and
WARFARE; may they never cease to give us the
pleasure, excitement and adrenal stimulation that
we need, or provide us with the heroes, the presi-
dents and leaders, the monuments and museums
which we erect to them in the name of PEACE.

Then it's Tommy this, an' Tommy that,
An' Tommy, 'ow's your soul?
But it's 'Thin red line of 'eroes,'
When the drums begin to roll—

—KIPLING

There's only a thin red line between the
sane and the mad.

—OLD MIDWESTERN SAYING

SPECIAL NOTE

Anyone who has studied or served in the Guadalcanal campaign will immediately recognize that no such terrain as that described here exists on the island. "The Dancing Elephant," "The Giant Boiled Shrimp," the hills around "Boola Boola Village," as well as the village itself, are figments of fictional imagination, and so are the battles herein described as taking place on this terrain. The characters who take part in the actions of this book are also imaginary. It might have been possible to create a whole, entirely fictional island for the setting of this book. But what Guadalcanal stood for to Americans in 1942–3 was a very special thing. To have used a completely made up island would have been to lose all of these special qualities which the name Guadalcanal evoked for my generation. Therefore I have taken the liberty of distorting the campaign and laying down smack in the middle of it a whole slab of nonexistent territory.

And naturally, any resemblance to *anything* anywhere is certainly not intended.

"Styron's Acres"
Roxbury, Conn.
Thanksgiving Day
1961

COMPANY ROSTER

(Partial)

"C" CO, UMTH INF

9 Nov 1942

—Stein, James I, Capt, "C" Co Cmdg
—Band, George R, 1st Lt, Exec
—Whyte, William L, 2d Lt, 1st Pl Cmdg
—Blane, Thomas C, 2d Lt, 2d Pl Cmdg
—Gore, Albert O, 2d Lt, 3d Pl Cmdg
—Culp, Robert (NMI), 2d Lt, 4th (Weapons) Pl Cmdg

E M

1st Sgt
—Welsh, Edward (NMI)

S/Sgts
—Culn, Guide 1st Pl
—Grove, Ldr 1st Pl
—Keck, Ldr 2d Pl
—MacTae, Supply
—Spain, Guide 3d Pl
—Stack, Ldr 3d Pl
—Storm, Mess

Sgts
—Beck, Sqd Ldr Rfl
—Dranno, Co Clk
—Field,   Sqd Ldr Rfl
—Fox,   "   "   "
—McCron, "   "   "
—Potts,   "   "   "

—Thorne,   "   "   "
—Wick,   "   "   Mtr

Cpls
—Fife, Fwd Clk
—Jenks,   Asst Sqd Ldr Rfl
—Queen,   "   "   "   "

Pvts 1cl
—Arbre, Rflmn
—Bead, Asst Fwd Clk
—Cash, Rflmn
—Dale, 2d Cook
—Doll,   Rflmn
—Earl,   "
—Fronk,   "
—Hoff,   "
—Land, 1st Cook
—Marl, Rflmn
—Park, 1st Cook

Pvts
—Ash,   Rflmn
—Bell,   "
—Carni,   "
—Catch,   "
—Catt,   "
—Coombs,   "
—Crown,   "
—Darl,   "
—Drake,   "
—Gluk,   "
—Gooch,   "
—Griggs,   "
—Gwenne,   "
—Jacques,   "
—Kline,   "

—Kral,   "
—Krim,   "
—Mazzi,   Mtrmn,
—Peale,   Rflmn,
—Sico,   "
—Stearns,   "
—Suss,   "
—Tassi,   "
—Tella,   "
—Tills,   Mtrmn,
—Tind,   "
—Train,   Rflmn,
—Weld,   "
—Wills,   "
—Wynn,   "

REPLACEMENTS
—Spine, Morton W, Lt Col, 1st Bn Cmdg
—Bosche, Charles S, Capt, "C" Co Cmdg
—Creo, John T, 1st Lt, "C" Co
—Payne, Elman W, 2d Lt, "C" Co
—Tomms, Frank J, 2d Lt, "C" Co

OTHERS
—Barr, Gerald E, Rear Adm, US Navy
—Grubbe, Tassman S, Lt Col, Rgtl Exec
—Tall, Gordon M L, Lt Col, 1st Bn Cmdg
—Roth, Norman M, Lt Col, Asst Div Srgn
—Haines, Ira P, Maj, Rgtl Srgn
—Gaff, John B, Capt, 1st Bn Exec
—Task, Fred W, Capt, "B" Co Cmdg
—Carr, Frederick C, Capt, Rgtl S-1
—Achs, Karl F, 2d Lt, "B" Co
—Gray, Elijah P, 2d Lt, "B" Co
—James, Sgt, Bn Hq
—Hoke, Pvt, of Cannon Co
—Witt, Pvt, of Cannon Co

DON'T MONKEY AROUND WITH DEATH

Lyric by James Jones
Music by Arnold Black

Tempo di March

Don't Mon-key a-round with death It will on-ly make you dir-ty Don't futz a-round with the reap-er He will on-ly make you smell Have you got B.O.? Then do not go fid-dl-ing with that

© 1962 by James Jones and Arnold Black. All rights reserved.

CHAPTER 1

The two transports had sneaked up from the south in the first graying flush of dawn, their cumbersome mass cutting smoothly through the water whose still greater mass bore them silently, themselves as gray as the dawn which camouflaged them. Now, in the fresh early morning of a lovely tropic day they lay quietly at anchor in the channel, nearer to the one island than to the other which was only a cloud on the horizon. To their crews, this was a routine mission and one they knew well: that of delivering fresh reinforcement troops. But to the men who comprised the cargo of infantry this trip was neither routine nor known and was composed of a mixture of dense anxiety and tense excitement.

Before they had arrived, during the long sea voyage, the cargo of men had been cynical—honestly cynical, not a pose, because they were part of an old regular division and knew that they were cargo. All their lives they had been cargo; never supercargo. And they were not only inured to that; they anticipated it. But now that they were here, were actually confronted with the physical fact of this island that they had all read so much about in the papers, their aplomb deserted them momentarily. Because though they were from a pre-war regular division, this was nevertheless to be their baptism of fire.

As they prepared themselves to go ashore no one doubted in theory that at least a certain percentage of them would remain on this island dead, once they set foot on it. But no one expected to be one of these. Still it was an awesome thought and as the first contingents came struggling up on deck in full gear to form up, all eyes instinctively sought out immediately this island where they were to be put, and left, and which might possibly turn out to be a friend's grave.

The view which presented itself to them from the deck was a beautiful one. In the bright, early morning tropic sunshine which sparkled off the quiet water of the channel, a fresh sea breeze stirred the fronds of minute coconut palms ashore behind the dun beach of the nearer island. It was too early yet to be oppressively hot. There was a feeling of long, open distances and limitless sea vistas. The same sea-flavored breeze sifted gently among the superstructures of the transports to touch the ears and faces of the men. After the olfactory numbness caused by the saturation of breath, feet, armpits and crotches below in the hold, the breeze seemed doubly fresh in their noses. Behind the tiny cocopalms on the island masses of green jungle rose to yellow foothills, which in turn gave place in the bright air to hulking, blue-hazed mountains.

"So this is Guadalcanal," a man at the rail said, and spat tobacco juice over the side.

"What the fuck you think it was? Fucking Tahiti?" another said.

The first man sighed and spat again. "Well, it's a nice peaceful morning for it."

"Jeez, my ass is draggin," a third man complained nervously. "All this gear." He hitched up his full pack.

"Mor'n your ass'll be draggin soon," the first man said.

Already little bugs which they recognized as LCIs had put out from shore, some circling scurryingly about, others heading straight out for the ships.

The men lit cigarettes. Slowly they assembled, shuffling about. The sharp cries of junior officers and noncoms cut through their nervous conversation, herded them. Once assembled, as usual they waited.

The first LCI to reach them circled around the leading transport about thirty yeards off, bouncing heavily on the wavelets under its own power, manned by two men in fatigue hats and shirts with no sleeves. The one not steering hung on to the gunnel to keep his balance and looked up at the ship.

"Well, look at what we got here. More cannonfodder for the Nips," he shouted up cheerfully.

The tobacco-chewing man at the rail worked his jaws a moment, ruminating, and then without moving spat a thin brown stream down over the side. On the deck they continued to wait.

Down below in the second forward hold the third company of the first regiment, known as C-for-Charlie company, milled about in the companionway and in the aisles between its allotted bunks. C-for-Charlie had chanced to be assigned as the fourth company in line to go over on the third forward cargo net on the port side. Its members knew they had a long time to wait. They did not as a result feel as stoical about it all as the first wave already up on deck, who were getting off first.

In addition to that it was very hot in the second forward hold. And C-for-Charlie was three decks down. Also there was no place to sit. Tiered in fives, and sometimes even sixes where the ceiling was higher, the bunks were all strewn with items of infantrymen's equipment ready to be put on. There was no place else to put it. So there was no room on them to sit; but even had there been, the bunks were unsittable anyway: hung on pipes bolted to deck and ceiling they barely left room for one man to lie below another, and a man attempting to sit on one suddenly would find his rump sinking into the canvas laced over the pipe frame, with the result that the base of his skull would come up sharply against the frame of the bunk above. The only place left was the deck strewn with nervous cigarette butts and sprawled legs. It was either that or be left to wander in and out through the jungle of pipes that occupied every available inch, picking a way over the legs and torsos. The stench from the farts, breath and sweaty bodies of so many men suffering from the poor elimination of a long sea voyage would have been brain-numbing had not the nostrils mercifully deadened themselves to it.

In this dimly lighted hellhole of exceedingly high moisture

content, whose metal walls resounded everything, C-for-Charlie scrubbed the sweat from its dripping eyebrows, picked its wet shirts loose from its armpits, cursed quietly, looked at its watches, and waited impatiently.

"You think we'll catch a fucking air raid?" Private Mazzi asked Private Tills beside him. They were sitting against a bulkhead clutching their knees up against their chests, both for moral comfort and to keep them from being trampled on.

"How the goddam hell do I know?" Tills said angrily. He was more or less Mazzi's sidekick. At least they often went on pass together. "All I know, them crew guys said they dint catch no air raid last time they made this run. On the other hand time before last they almost got blew up. What do you want me to tell you?"

"You're a big help. Tills: nothin. Tell me nothin. I'll tell you somethin. We're sittin out here on this great big wideopen ocean like a couple big fat fucking ducks in these here boats, that's what."

"I already know that."

"Yeah? Well, brood on it, Tills. Brood on it." Mazzi hugged himself tighter and worked his eyebrows up and down convulsively, a gesture of nervous release which gave his face an expression of pugnacious indignation.

The same question was uppermost in all of C-for-Charlie's minds. Actually C-for-Charlie was not the last in any line. The numbers ran up as high as seven and eight. But this did not give consolation. C-for-Charlie was not concerned with the unlucky ones that came after it; that was their problem. C-for-Charlie was concerned only with the lucky ones who came before it, and that they should hurry, and as to just how long it itself was going to have to wait.

Then there was another thing. Not only was C-for-Charlie fourth in line at its assigned station, which was resented, but it also happened for whatever reason to have been set down among strangers. Except for one other company far away in the stern C-for-Charlie was the only company of the first regiment to be assigned to the first ship, with the result that they did not know a single soul in the companies on either side of them, and this was resented too.

"If I'm gonna get blown-fucking-up," Mazzi mused gloomily, "I dont wanta ged my guts and meat all mixed up with a bunch of strangers from another regiment like these bums. I had much ruther it's be my own outfit anyway."

"Don't *talk* like that!" Tills cried, "for fuck's sake."

"Well—" Mazzi said. "When I think of them planes up there maybe right now . . .

"You just aint a realist, Tills."

In their own way other C-for-Charlie men coped with the same imagination problem as best they could. From their vantage point against the companionway bulkhead Mazzi and Tills could see the activities of at least half of C-for-Charlie. In one place a blackjack game had been started, the players indicating whether they would hit or stay between peerings at their watches. In another place a crapgame proceeded in the same oscillating fashion. In still another Private First Class Nellie Coombs had pulled out his everpresent poker deck (which everyone suspected—but could never prove—was marked) and had started up his near-perennial five-card stud game, and was shrewdly making money off the nervousness of his friends despite his own.

In other places little knots of men had formed, and stood or sat talking earnestly to each other with widened, consciously focused eyes while hardly hearing what was said. A few loners meticulously checked and rechecked their rifles and equipment, or else merely sat looking at them. Young Sergeant McCron, the notorious motherhen, went along personally checking each item of equipment of each man in his squad of nearly all draftees as if his sanity, and his life, depended on it. Slightly older Sergeant Beck, the professional martinet with six years service, occupied himself with inspecting the rifles of his squad with great preciseness.

There was nothing to do but wait. Through the locked glass of the portholes along the companionway a few faint sounds of scrambling and some shouts came in to them, and from up on the deck a few even fainter still, to let them know that debarkation was moving ahead. From the hatchway beyond the open water-tight door they heard the clangor and muffled cursing of another company toiling up the metal stairs to replace a company already taken off. At the closed ports a few men who could get close enough, and who felt like watching, could see portions of the dark hulking figures of fully equipped men climbing down the net which hung outside the ports; now and then they would see an LCI pull away in the water. They shouted out progress reports back to the rest. Every so often an LCI, caught wrong on a wave, would bang against the hull and reverberate through the closed space of the dim hold the clang of tortured steel.

Private First Class Doll, a slender, longnecked southern boy from Virginia, was standing with Corporal Queen, a huge Texan, and Corporal Fife the orderly room clerk.

"Well, we'll soon know what it feels like," Queen, an amiable giant several years older than the other two, said meekly. Queen was not usually meek.

"What what feels like?" Fife said.

"To be shot at," said Queen. "To be shot at seriously."

"Hell, I've been shot at," Doll said, drawing up his lip in a supercilious smile. "Hell, aint you, Queen?"

"Well, I only just hope there arent any planes today," Fife said. "That's all."

"I guess we all hope that," Doll said in a more subdued tone.

Doll was very young, late twenty, possibly twenty-one, as were the majority of C-for-Charlie's privates. He had been in C-for-Charlie over two years, as had most of the regulars. A quiet, freshfaced youth with considerable naivete, who talked little and shyly, Doll had always remained pretty much in the background; but lately, in the past six months, something had been slowly happening to him, and he had been changing and coming forward more. It did not make him more likeable.

Now, after his subdued remark about the planes, he put back on his lip-lifting supercilious smile. Very consciously he lifted an eyebrow. "Well, I reckon if I'm goin'a get me that pistol, I better get with it," he smiled at them. He looked at his watch. "They ought to be about primed, about nervous enough, by now," he said judiciously, and then looked back up. "Anybody want to come along?"

"You'll do better on your own," Big Queen rumbled distantly. "Two guys after two pistols'll be just twice as noticeable."

"Guess you're right," Doll said, and sauntered off, a slender, small-hipped, really quite handsome young man. Queen stared after him, his Texas eyes veiled with dislike of what he could only see as affectation, and then turned back to Fife the clerk as Doll went out from between the bunks into the companionway.

In the companionway against the far bulkhead Mazzi and Tills still sat hugging their legs up, talking. Doll stopped in front of them.

"Aint you watchin the fucking fun?" he asked them, indicating the more or less crowded portholes.

"Aint interested," Mazzi said gloomily.

"I guess it is pretty crowded," Doll said, with a sudden lessening of his superciliousness. He bent his head and wiped the sweat out of his eyebrows with the back of his hand.

"Wouldn't be interested if they weren't," Mazzi said, and hugged his knees up more closely.

"I'm on my way to get me that pistol," Doll said.

"Yeah? Well have fun," Mazzi said.

"Yeah; have fun," Tills said.

"Dont you remember? We talked about gettin a pistol one day," Doll said.

"Did we?" Mazzi said flatly, staring at him.

"Sure," Doll began. Then he stopped, realizing he was being told off, insulted, and smiled his unpleasant, supercilious smile. "You guys'll wish you had one, once we get ashore, and run into some of them Samurai sabers."

"All I want is to *get* ashore," Mazzi said. "And off of this big fat sitting fucking duck we all sittin on out here on this flat water."

"Hey, Doll," Tills said, "you get around. You think we're liable to catch an air raid today before we get off this damned boat?"

"How the fucking hell would I know?" Doll said. He smiled his unpleasant smile. "We might, and we might not."

"Thanks," Mazzi said.

"If we do, we do. What's the matter? You scared, Mazzi?"

"Scared? Course I aint scared! Are you?"

"Hell no."

"Okay then. Shut up," Mazzi said, and leaned forward and thrust out his jaw, working his eyebrows up and down pugnaciously at Doll with what could only be called comic ferocity. It was really not very effective. Doll merely threw back his head and laughed.

"See you chaps," he said and stepped over through the watertight door in the bulkhead they leaned against.

"What's all this 'chaps' shit?" Mazzi said.

"Ahh, there's a bunch of Anzac Pioneers on this boat," Tills said. "Guess he's been hangin around them."

"That guy just aint hep," Mazzi said decisively. "He's as unhep as a box. I can't stand people who aint hep."

"You think he'll get a pistol?" Tills said.

"Hell no he wont get no pistol."

"He might."

"He wont," Mazzi said. "He's a jerkoff. 'Chaps!' "

"Right now, I couldnt care less," Tills said. "Whether he ever gets a pistol, or whether anybody ever gets a pistol, including me. All I want is to get off this here fucking boat here."

"Well you aint by yourself," Mazzi said as another LCI clanged against the hull outside. "Lookit over there."

Both men turned their heads and looked over into the bunk area and, hugging their knees nervously, observed the rest of C-for-Charlie going through its various suspension-of-imagination exercises.

"All I know," Mazzi said, "I never bargained for nothin like this here when I signed up in this man's army back in the old fucking Bronx before the war. How did I know they was gonna be a fucking war, hanh? Answer me that."

"You tell me," Tills said. "You're the hep character around here, Mazzi."

"All I know, old Charlie Company always gets screwed," Mazzi said. "Always. And I can tell you whose fault it is. It's old Bugger Stein's fault, that's who. First he gets us stuck off on this boat clean away from our own outfit where we dont know a fucking soul. Then he gets us stuck way down in fourth place on the list to get off this son of a bitch. I can tell you that much. Churchez old Bugger Stein. Whatever it is."

"There's worse places than fourth, though," Tills said. "At least we aint in seventh or fucking eighth. At least he didnt get us stuck down in eighth place."

"Well it aint no fault of his. He sure didnt get us in no first place, that's for sure. Look at the son of a bitch down there: pretending he's one of the boys today." Mazzi jerked his head down toward the other bulkhead, at the other end of the companionway, where Captain Stein and his exec and his four platoon officers squatted with their heads together over an orders map on the deck.

"So you see, gentlemen, exactly where we will be," Captain Stein was saying, and he looked up from his pencil at his officers with his large, mild, brown eyes questioningly. "There will of course be guides, either Army or Marines, to help us get there with the least amount of trouble and time. The line itself, the present line, is, as I've shown you, up here." He pointed with the pencil. "Eight and a half miles away. We will have a forced march, under full field equipment, of about six miles, in the other direction." Stein rose, and the other five officers rose too. "Any questions, gentlemen?"

"Yes, sir," said Second Lieutenant Whyte of the First Platoon. "I have one, sir. Will there be any definite order of bivouac when we get there? Since Blane here of the Second and I will probably be in the lead, I wanted to know about that, sir."

"Well, I think we shall have to wait and see what the terrain is like when we get there, dont you, Whyte?" Stein said, and raised a meaty right hand to adjust his thick-lensed glasses through which he stared at Whyte.

"Yes, sir," Whyte said, suitably chastised, and reddening a little under it.

"Any further questions, gentlemen?" Stein said. "Blane? Culp?" He looked around.

"No, sir," Blane said.

"Then that's all, gentlemen," Stein said. "For the moment." He stooped and scooped up the map, and when he straightened back up he was smiling warmly behind the thick lenses. This was an indication that the official solemnity was over, that everybody could relax. "Well, how goes it, Bill?" Stein asked young Whyte, and slapped him warmly on the back. "Feel all right?"

"Little nervous, Jim," Whyte grinned.

"How about you, Tom?" Stein asked Blane.

"Fine, Jim."

"Well, I guess you better all of you have a look at your boys, dont you?" Stein said, and stood with his exec, First Lieutenant Band, watching the four platoon officers go off.

"I think they're all good boys, dont you, George?" he said.

"Yes, Jim; I do," Band said.

"Did you notice how both Culp and Gore were taking everything in?" Stein asked.

"I sure did, Jim. Of course they've been with us longer than the youngsters."

Stein removed his glasses and in the heat polished them carefully with a large handkerchief, and then replaced them firmly on his face, adjusting and settling them over and over again with the thumb and fingers of his right hand on the frame, while he peered out through them. "I make it about an hour," he said vaguely. "Or at most an hour and a quarter."

"I just hope we dont get any of those high level bomb groups before then," Band said.

"I rather do too," Stein said and made his large, mild, brown eyes grin behind their lenses.

Whatever Private Mazzi's criticisms, and however valid or invalid they might be, Mazzi had been right about one thing: It had been Captain Stein who had given the order that C-for-Charlie's officers would stay in the hold with the men this morning. Stein, whose nickname "Bugger" among his troops had come from the oft-quoted remark by a nameless private upon seeing his com-

mander walk across a parade ground that he "walked like he had
a cob up his ass," felt that officers should be with their men on a
day such as this, should share their hardships and dangers, rather
than staying up topside in the club cabin where they had remained
for most of the trip, and Stein had so informed his juniors. While
none of them had looked too pleased about it, no one had commented, not even Band. And Stein was convinced that it could not
help but aid morale. As he looked out across the crowded, sweating jungle of bunks and piping, where his men worked quietly
without hysteria at checking and inspecting their equipment, he
was even more convinced that he had been right. Stein, who was a
junior partner with an excellent, large law firm in Cleveland, had
taken ROTC as a lark in college, and had been caught early, over
a year before the war. Luckily, he was unmarried. He had spent
six months of astonishment with a National Guard outfit, before
being shipped off to this regular division as a First Lieutenant and
a Company Commander, after which he had been once passed
over and had an old wornout Captain shipped in over him before
he himself got his captaincy, during which terrible time he could
only say over and over to himself, "My God, what will my father
say," because his father had been a Major in the First World War.
Settling his glasses again, he turned to his First Sergeant whose
name was Welsh and who was in fact of Welsh extraction, who
had been standing nearby all the time, during this briefing, wearing a look of sly amusement which Stein did not fail to notice.

"I think our outfit looks pretty capable, pretty solid, dont you,
Sergeant?" he said, putting a certain amount of authority in his
voice, without overdoing it.

Welsh merely grinned at him insolently. "Yeah; for a bunch of
slobs about to get their fucking ass shot off," he said. A tall,
narrow-hipped, heavily-muscled man in his early thirties, his
Welsh blood advertised itself in every part of him: in his dark
complexion and black hair; in his dark, blue-jowled jaw and wild,
black eyes; in the look of dark foreboding which never left his
face, even when he grinned, as now.

Stein did not answer him, but neither did he look away. He felt
uncomfortable, and he was sure his face showed it. But he didn't

really care. Welsh was mad. He was insane. Truly a real madman, and Stein never had understood him. He had no respect for anything or anybody. But it didn't really matter. Stein could afford to overlook his impertinences because he was so good at his job.

"I have a very real sense of responsibility toward them," he said.

"Yeah?" Welsh said softly, and continued to grin at him with his insolent look of sly amusement, and that was all he would say.

Stein noticed that Band was watching Welsh with open dislike, and made a mental note to take this up with Band. Band must be made to understand this situation with Sergeant Welsh. Stein himself was still looking at Welsh, who was staring back grinning, and Stein who had deliberately not looked away before, now found himself in the silly position of being engaged in a battle of stares, that old, ridiculous, adolescent business of who is going to look away first. It was stupid as well as silly. Irritably he cast about for some way of breaking off this childish deadlock with dignity.

Just then a man from C-for-Charlie walked past in the companionway. Easily, Stein turned to him and nodded brusquely.

"Hello, Doll. How's it going? Everything okay?"

"Yes, sir," Doll said. He stopped and saluted, looking a little startled. Officers always made him uncomfortable.

Stein returned the salute. "Rest," he murmured and then grinned behind his glasses. "Feeling a little nervous?"

"No, sir," Doll said, with great seriousness.

"Good boy." Stein nodded, halfway dismissing him. Doll saluted again, and went on out through the water-tight door. Stein turned back to Welsh and Band, the silly locked stare broken, he felt, without indignity. Sergeant Welsh was still standing grinning at him, in insolent silence, but with an asinine look of petty, sly triumph now. He really was mad. As well as childish. Deliberately, Stein winked at him. "Come on, Band," he said brusquely, with shortened temper. "Let's have a look around."

Private First Class Doll, after he stepped through the water-tight door, veered right and crossed the hatchway area to the forward hold. Doll was still looking for his pistol. Since leaving

Tills and Mazzi, he had made the long trip back to the stern, covering the entire rear of the ship on this deck, and he was beginning to wonder now if he had not done it too hurriedly. The trouble was, he did not know exactly how much time he had.

What did Bugger Stein mean, stopping him and asking him if he was nervous! What kind of shit was that? Did Bugger know he was out after a pistol? Was that it? Or was Bugger trying to make out that he, Doll, was yellow or something. That was what it looked like. Anger and outraged sensibilities rose up in Doll.

Furious, Doll stopped in the oval water-tight doorway to the forward hold to look this next hunting-ground over. It was very small, compared to the area he had already covered. What Doll had hoped, when he started out, was that if he simply went wandering around with an open mind and open eyes, the proper moment, the right situation, would eventually present itself, and that he would be able with inspiration to recognize and seize it. That was not what had happened, and now he was desperately beginning to feel that time was running out on him.

Actually, in his entire circuit of the whole stern, Doll had only come upon two loose pistols which were not being worn. That was not very many. Both pistols had presented him with a decision to make: Should he? Or shouldn't he? All he had to do was pick it up belt and all and put it on and walk away. Both times Doll had decided against. Both times there had been quite a few men around, and Doll could not help but feel, quite very forcefully, that a still better opportunity would show up. None had however, and now he could not help but wonder, with quite equal force, if he had not perhaps erred on the side of caution because he had been afraid. This was a thought Doll could hardly bear.

His own company might begin to move upstairs at any moment now. On the other hand, he was tormented by the thought of Mazzi and Tills and the rest, if they saw him come back now without a pistol.

Gingerly, Doll wiped the sweat from his eyes again and stepped on through the doorway. He went on up the starboard side of the forward hold, working his way in and out amongst this crowd of strangers from another outfit, searching.

Doll had learned something during the past six months of his life. Chiefly what he had learned was that everybody lived by a selected fiction. Nobody was really what he pretended to be. It was as if everybody made up a fiction story about himself, and then he just pretended to everybody that that was what he was. And everybody believed him, or at least accepted his fiction story. Doll did not know if everybody learned this about life when they reached a certain age, but he suspected that they did. They just didn't tell it to anybody. And rightly so. Obviously, if they told anybody, then their own fiction story about themselves wouldn't be true either. So everybody *had* to learn it for himself. And then, of course, pretend he hadn't learned it.

Doll's own first experience of this phenomenon had come from, or at least begun with, a fist fight he had had six months ago with one of the biggest, toughest men in C-for-Charlie: Corporal Jenks. They had fought each other to a standstill, because neither would give up, until finally it was called a sort of draw-by-exhaustion. But it wasn't this so much as it was the sudden realization that Corporal Jenks was just as nervous about having the fight as he was, and did not really want to fight any more than he did, which had suddenly opened Doll's eyes. Once he'd seen it here, in Jenks, he began to see it everywhere, in everybody.

When Doll was younger, he had believed everything everybody told him about themselves. And not only told him—because more often than not they didn't tell you, they just showed you. Just sort of let you see it by their actions. They acted what they wanted you to think they were, just as if it was really what they really were. When Doll had used to see someone who was brave and a sort of hero, he, Doll, had really believed he was that. And of course this made him, Doll, feel cheap because he knew he himself could never be like that. Christ, no wonder he had taken a back seat all his life!

It was strange, but it was as if when you were honest and admitted you didn't know what you really were, or even if you were anything at all, then nobody liked you and you made everybody uncomfortable and they didn't want to be around you. But when you made up your fiction story about yourself and what a great guy you were, and then pretended that that was really you, everybody accepted it and believed you.

When he finally did get his pistol—if he did get it—Doll was not going to admit that he had been scared, or unsure of himself, or indecisive. He would pretend it had been easy, pretend it had happened the way he had imagined it was going to happen, before he started out.

But first he had to get it, damn it all!

He had gone almost all the way forward when he saw the first one, up here, that somebody was not wearing. Doll stopped and stared at it hungrily, before he bethought himself to look around at the situation. The pistol hung from the end of a bed frame. Three bunks away in the heat a group of men clustered around a nervous crapgame. In the companionway itself four or five other men stood talking about fifteen feet away. All in all, it was certainly not any less risky than the two he'd seen in the stern. Perhaps it was even a little more so.

On the other hand, Doll could not forget that maddening sense of time running out. This might be the only one he would see up here. After all, he had only seen two in the entire stern. In desperation he decided he had better chance it. No one was taking any notice of him as far as he could tell. Casually, Doll stepped over and leaned on the bunk frame for a moment, as if he belonged here, then lifted the pistol off and buckled it around his waist. Stifling his instinct to just up and run, he lit a cigarette and took a couple of deep drags, then started leisurely toward the door, back the way he had come.

He had gotten halfway to it, and, indeed, had begun to think that he had pulled it off, when he heard the two voices hollering behind him. There was no doubt they were aimed at him.

"Hey, you!"

"Hey, soldier!"

Doll turned, able to feel his eyes getting deep and guilty-looking as his heart began to beat more heavily, and saw two men, one a private and one a sergeant, coming down toward him. Would they turn him in? Would they try to beat him up? Neither of these prospects bothered Doll half so much as the prospect of being treated with contempt like the sneak-thief he felt he was. That was what Doll was afraid of: It was like one of those nightmares everybody has of getting caught, but does not believe will ever really happen to them.

The two men came on down toward Doll ominously, looking indignant, their faces dark with outraged righteousness. Doll blinked his eyes rapidly several times, trying to wash from them the self-conscious guilt he could feel was in them. Behind the two, other faces had turned to watch, he noticed.

"That's my pistol you're wearin, soldier," the private said. His voice held injured accusation.

Doll said nothing.

"He saw you take it off the bunk," the sergeant said. "So dont try to lie out of it, soldier."

Summoning all his energy—or courage, or whatever it was— Doll still did not answer, and forced a slow, cynical grin to spread across his face, while he stared at them, unblinking now. Slowly he undid the belt and passed it over. "How long you been in the army, mack?" he grinned. "You oughta know fucking better than to leave your gear layin around like that. You might lose it some-day." He continued to stare, unflinching.

Both men stared back at him, their eyes widening slightly as the new idea, new attitude, replaced their own of righteous indig-nation. Indifference and cheerful lack of guilt made them appear foolish; and both men suddenly grinned sheepishly, penetrated as they had been by that fiction beloved in all armies of the tough, scrounging, cynical soldier who collects whatever he can get his hands on.

"Well, you better not have such sticky fingers, soldier," the sergeant said, but it no longer carried much punch. He was trying to stifle his grin.

"Anything layin around out in the open that loose, is fair game to me," Doll said cheerfully. "And to any other old soldier. Tell your boy he oughtn't to tempt people so much."

Behind the two, the other faces had begun to grin too, at the private's discomfiture. The private himself had a hangdog look, as if he were the one at fault. The sergeant turned to him.

"Hear that, Drake?" he grinned. "You better take better care of your fucking gear."

"Yeah. He sure better," Doll said. "Or he wont have it very goddam long." He turned and went on leisurely toward the door, and nobody tried to stop him.

Outside, back in the hatchway area once more, Doll stopped and allowed himself a long, whooshing sigh. Then he leaned against the bulkhead because his knees were shaking. If he had acted guilty—which was what he really had felt—they would have had him. And had him good. But he had carried it off. He had carried it off, and it was the private who had come out as the guilty party. Nervously, shakily, Doll laughed. And it had all been one big lie! Over and above his scare he had a sense of high elation and of pride. In a way, he really was that sort of guy, too, he thought suddenly: that type of guy he had pretended he was back there. At least, anymore he was. He hadn't used to be.

But he still hadn't got a pistol. For a moment, Doll looked at his watch wondering, and worrying, about time. He hadn't wanted to leave this deck, hadn't wanted to get that far from C-for-Charlie. Then, on legs still a little shaky, but feeling triumphant, he began to mount the stairs to the deck above with a high sense of his own worth.

From the moment Doll stepped into the bunk area on the deck above, everything played for him. He was still a little shaky, and certainly he was considerably more skittish than before. It didn't matter. Everything worked perfectly for him, and for his purpose. It could not have worked more perfectly if he had requested this exact sequence of events personally from God. Doll did not know why, he did nothing himself to cause it, and had he been a minute earlier or a minute later, it might certainly have been different. But he wasn't earlier or later. And he did not intend to stop to question fortune. This was the perfect situation and set-up that he had originally imagined himself seeing and, in a flash, recognizing, and he did recognize it that way now:

He had not taken three steps inside before he saw not one but two pistols, lying almost side by side on the same bunk, right on the edge of the companionway. There was not a man in this entire end of the bunk area except for one, and before Doll could even take another step, this man had gotten up and gone off down to the other end where, apparently, everyone was congregated.

That was all there was to it. All Doll had to do was step over, pick up one of the pistols, and put it on. Wearing the stranger's pistol, he walked on through the bunk area. At the other end he merely went out and down the hatchway stairs, turned back left, and he was back safe in the midst of C-for-Charlie. The company had not yet begun to move and everything was just as when he left it. This time he made a point of passing close by to Tills and Mazzi, something he had deliberately avoided before, when returning empty-handed from the stern.

Tills and Mazzi had not moved, and still sat against the bulkhead with their legs clutched up against their chests, sweating in the heat. Doll stopped in front of them with his hands on his hips, his right one resting on the pistol. They could not fail to notice it.

"Hello, lover-boy," Mazzi said.

Tills, on the other hand, grinned. "We seen you sneakin past a while ago. On your way back from the stern. When Bugger caught you. Where you been?"

Neither of them, of course, was going to mention it. But Doll didn't really care. He raised the holster and flapped it at them a couple of times against his leg. "Around," he said, raising his lip and eyebrow in his superior smile, "around. Well, what do you think of it?"

"Think of what?" Mazzi said innocently.

Again Doll grinned his unpleasant smile, his eyes brilliant. "Nothin. The war," he mocked, and turned on his heel and went on inside among the bunks, toward his own bunk and the rest of C-for-Charlie. It was the reaction he had anticipated. He still didn't care. He had the pistol.

"Well, what do you say now, hep guy?" Tills said looking after Doll.

"Just what I fucking said before," Mazzi said, unperturbed. "The guy's a jerkoff."

"But he's got a pistol."

"So he's a jerkoff with a pistol."

"While you're a hep guy, without a pistol."

"That's right," Mazzi said stoutly. "What's a fucking pistol? I—"

"I'd like to have one," Tills said.

"—could get me one any time I want," Mazzi went right on unshaken. "That guy goes wanderin around lookin for a fucking pistol while we're all waitin here to get our ass bombed off."

"At least when we get ashore he's got a pistol," Tills insisted.

"*If* we get ashore."

"Well if we dont, it aint gonna matter anyway," Tills said. "At least, he was doin something. Not just sittin here like you and me, sweating it out."

"Leave it, Tills; leave it," Mazzi said stoutly. "You wanna do somethin, go do somethin."

"I think I will," Tills said angrily, getting up. He started off, then suddenly turned back, a strange look on his face. "You know, I aint got a single friend?" he said. "Not one? You aint, I aint?" Tills rolled his head around on his neck in a mad, wild circle to include the company behind him, "not a single guy in this outfit has? Not one? An' if we get killed?—" Tills stopped, abruptly, still on the questioning note, which continued to hang, loudly and uncompleted, about his head in the air, very like the periodic long-echoing clangs of tortured steel when the LCIs struck the ship. "Not one?" he added inconclusively.

"I got friends," Mazzi said.

"*You* got friends!" Tills cried wildly; "*you* got friends! Hah!" Then his voice fell off and away, drooped: "I'm goin over and get in a poker game." He turned away.

"Long as I dont borrow money off them. Or loan it," Mazzi said after him. "You want money? You want money, Tills?" he shouted after him, and burst out laughing. He clutched his knees to his chest again, laughing loudly, his head thrown back with violent appreciation of his wit.

The poker game Tills came to first was little Nellie Coombs's. Nellie, slight and blond and frail, was as usual dealing and cutting the game ten cents to a quarter a hand. In return for this, he furnished cigarettes to the players, and he never allowed anyone

to deal except himself. Tills did not know why anybody ever
played with him. Tills did not know why he himself did. Especially when he was suspected of a crooked deal. There was another, normal game, with a passing deal, just a few steps further
on, but Tills got out his wallet and took some bills out of it and
sat down in Nellie's game. If only this damned waiting would get
over with.

Doll was thinking the same thing. Getting his pistol had occupied him so fully that for the moment he had forgotten all about
the possibility of air raids. After leaving Mazzi and Tills, he had
hunted around among the crowded aisles until he found Fife and
Big Queen again, and had shown it to them. Unlike Mazzi and
Tills they were both satisfactorily impressed with his feat,
and also with how easy it had been when he described it to them.
Even so, Doll's pleasure could not rid him of that gnawing
thought about the possibility of air raids. If, after getting a
damned pistol, and all of that, they were to get bombed out anyway—He could hardly bear the thought. Hell, he might never
even get to use it. It was a very distressing idea, and it left Doll
with a bottomless feeling of the uselessness of everything.

Both Queen and Fife had mentioned that they might go out and
try to get a pistol for themselves, since it seemed so easy. Doll
however did not encourage them: because of the time element, he
said. He pointed out that they should have started sooner. He did
not tell them about the second pistol he had seen upstairs, either.
After all, he had had to find his own; why shouldn't they? And
anyway, if the men upstairs found one pistol missing, they would
certainly be on the lookout; so it might be dangerous for his
friends. He was really doing them a kindness not to tell them.
After discouraging them, Doll had started back for his own bunk,
to check over his equipment for lack of anything else to do. It was
then that he suddenly found himself confronted by the wild hair
and looming figure, and the sly, mad, brooding face of First Sergeant Welsh.

"What are you doing with that fucking pistol, Doll?" he demanded grinning crazily.

Before those eyes Doll's new-found confidence wilted, and his perceptions melted down into a mishmash of confusion. "What pistol?" he mumbled.

"This pistol," Welsh cried and stepping forward, seized the holster at Doll's hip. With it he pulled Doll slowly to him until they were only inches apart, grinning a cunning, insolent grin, right down into Doll's face. With gentle violence he shook Doll back and forth by the holster. "This is the pistol I mean," he said. "This pistol." Very slowly, the grin faded from Welsh's face, leaving a look of black, ominous violence; a piercing, murderous scowl which was nevertheless somehow sly.

Doll was fairly tall, but Welsh was taller; it made for a disadvantage. And even though Doll knew the slow disappearance of the grin was deliberate, a theatrical bit of dramatics, it still affected him with a mild paralysis.

"Well, I—" he began, but was interrupted. It was just as well. There were no words in his head.

"—And what if somebody comes around here to Bugger Stein and wants to search this outfit for a stolen pistol? 'Ey?" Slowly Welsh raised Doll up to him by the holster, until Doll was standing on tiptoe. "Have you ever thought of that day? 'Ey?" he hissed with sinister gentleness. "—And what if I then, knowin who had it, was forced to tell Bugger Stein where it was? 'Ey? Have you thought of that, too?"

"Would you do that, Top?" Doll said feebly.

"You bet your fucking sweet ass I would!" Welsh bellowed with startling suddenness right into his face.

"Well—Do you think anybody'll come around?" Doll said.

"No!" Welsh roared in his face. "I dont!" Then, as slowly as it had disappeared, the sly ominous grin came back over the Sergeant's face. After forcing this in his face a moment, Welsh let Doll down off his toes and all in the same motion flung the holstered pistol away from him as if it were not attached to anyone. Doll was carried back half a step with it, to see Welsh standing before him, hands resting easily on hips, and grinning his sly, mad grin. "Clean it," Welsh said. "It's probly dirty. Any man'd leave it layin around's a fuckass soldier anyway." He continued to stand grinning insanely at Doll.

Once again unable to meet those eyes, Doll turned away toward his bunk, which was some distance away, filled with a mad rage. He was, in effect, retiring from the field, and his ego was badly bruised. Worst of all, it had happened in the midst of the crowded bunk area, and this was acutely painful to Doll, even though it had happened so suddenly and swiftly that hardly anyone had noticed it except the men nearby. Goddamn him, he had eyes like a hawk; he saw everything. Actually, the single idea remaining uppermost in Doll's mind, above everything else, was what Welsh had said about cleaning it. It had left Doll startled. He would never have thought of it. Curiously, Doll could not find it in him to be angry at Welsh, even though he wanted to be, and this filled him with even greater rage. Objectless, and therefore frustrated, rage. But then who could be angry at an insane man? Everyone knew he was crazy. A regular madman. His twelve years in the army had debrained him. If Welsh had wanted to jump him about the pistol, then why hadn't he gone ahead and followed it through and taken it away from him? Any *normal* noncom would have; that in itself proved he was crazy. On his bunk, Doll commenced to take down his new pistol, just to see if it *was* dirty. He would love to prove The Welshman wrong. What he found, triumphantly, was that it was not dirty at all. It was clean as a whistle.

First Sergeant Welsh continued to stand grinning slyly in the aisle after Doll retreated. He had no particular reason to, he had already dismissed and forgotten Doll, but he enjoyed doing it. For one thing, it made all the men near him uncomfortable and Welsh liked that. Hands still on his hips, shoulders hunched ever so slightly, feet apart; in short, in exactly the same position he had assumed after shoving Doll away from him; Welsh decided arbitrarily to see how long he could stand without moving anything except his eyes. He was allowing himself his eyes. He couldn't raise his arm to look at his watch, that would be moving, but there was a big navy clock high up on the bulkhead and he could tell how long by that. Immobile as an iron jockey on a lawn he darted his eyes this way and that above his sly grin and beneath his black, brooding brows, and wherever his glance fell, the nearby men beneath it would stir uneasily and drop their eyes and fall to doing something: adjusting a strap, checking a tie-rope, rubbing a riflestock. Welsh watched them all with amusement. They were a sorry lot, any way you took them. Almost certainly, nearly all of them would be dead before this war was over, including himself, and not a damn one of them was smart enough to know it. Maybe a few did. They were getting in on virtually the very start of it, and they would continue all the way right on through it. Hardly any of them were able or willing to admit or see what an alarming drop in chances this gave them. As far as Welsh was concerned, they had coming to them and deserved everything they would get. And that included him himself. And this amused him, too.

Welsh had never been in combat. But he had lived for a long time with a lot of men who had. And he had pretty well lost his belief in, as well as his awe of, the mystique of human combat. Old vets from the First World War, younger men who had been with the Fifteenth Infantry in China, for years he had sat around getting drunk with them and listening to their drunken stories of melancholy bravery. He had watched the stories grow with the years and the drinking sprees, and he had been able to form only one conclusion and that was that every old vet was a hero. How so many heroes survived and so many non-heroes got knocked off, Welsh could not answer. But every old vet was a hero. If you did not believe it, you had only to ask them, or better yet, get them drunk and not ask them. There just wasn't any other kind. One of the hazards of professional soldiering was that every twenty years, regular as clockwork, that portion of the human race to which you belonged, whatever its politics or ideal about humanity, was going to get itself involved in a war, and you might have to fight in it. About the only way out of this mathematical hazard was to enlist immediately after one war and hope you would be too old for the next; you might just make it. But to accomplish that you had to be of a certain age at just exactly the right time, and that was rare. But it was either that, or enlist in the Quartermaster Corps or some such branch. Welsh had already understood all this when he enlisted in 1930 exactly between wars at the age of twenty, but he had gone ahead and enlisted anyway. He had gone ahead and enlisted, and he had enlisted in the Infantry. Not in the Quartermaster Corps. And he had stayed in the Infantry. And this amused Welsh, too.

The way Welsh chose to see it, he had beaten the Depression in his country and had outsmarted the nation, and now, today, November 10, 1942, he was preparing to begin paying for it. Welsh found this amusing also.

Everything amused Welsh. Or, at least, Welsh hoped it did. The fact that he had stayed in the Infantry amused him—although, if asked, he could not exactly have articulated why he had, except that it amused him to. Politics amused him, religion amused him, particularly ideals and integrity amused him; but most of all, human virtue amused him. He did not believe in it, and he did not believe in any of those other words. If pressed, as he often had been by irate friends, and asked to say just what he did believe in, he would have answered promptly, as he often had done, "Property." This generally infuriated everyone, but that was not Welsh's only reason for saying it, although he enjoyed infuriating everybody. Born of a highly Protestant, genteel family, whose Protestantism and gentility were both false even though the family owned much real estate, he had observed the principle of property in action all his life, and he saw no reason for changing his opinion because of some squeamish humanity lover. Property, in some form or other, was, in the end, what always made the watch tick. Whatever words people chose to call it. That much he was sure of. And yet Welsh had never tried to acquire property himself. And in fact whatever property came his way as by-product, he threw away or else got rid of, almost hastily, as soon as he could. This amused Welsh, too; as did the haste with which he watched himself get rid of it.

Behind him in the corridor Welsh heard footsteps approaching his back and then a voice.

"Sergeant, can I ask you a question?" It sounded like one of the draftees. Obsequious.

Welsh did not move or speak, and put his eyes up onto the big bulkhead clock. It had only been just a little over a minute, and that certainly wasn't long enough. Welsh remained immobile. After a while, the voice and footsteps went away. Finally, when the clock showed he had been at it two minutes and thirty seconds, he bored of it and decided to go and needle his clerk Fife for a while. Around him, as he moved off toward the area where the company headquarters had been bunked, there was among the men something like a soundless sigh of relief. Welsh did not fail to notice and relish it with his sly, insolent, mad grin.

Welsh had no use for Doll, and he had no more use for Corporal Fife, his forward echelon clerk. Doll was a punk kid who, up until his fight with Jenks six months ago, at least had pretty much kept to himself and out of the way and kept his mouth shut. Now, after his so-called 'triumph,' he had begun to think he was a big grownup man and had become a complete and obnoxious ass, getting in everybody's hair. Fife, on the other hand, while also being a punk kid and an ass, was a coward. Welsh did not mean coward in the sense that he would shit his pants and run away. Fife wouldn't do that; he would stay. He would be trembling like a dog shitting peach seeds and scared within an inch of his life, but he would stay. And as far as Welsh was concerned, that was an even worse kind of coward. When he said coward, what he meant to say was that Fife had not yet learned—if he ever would—that his life, and himself, his He, didn't mean a goddamned thing to the world in general, and never would. Whereas Doll was too dumb to understand such a concept, or even be able to conceive of such an incredible idea. Fife was smart enough to know it, or at least learn it, but he wouldn't let himself admit it. And in Welsh's dictionary, that was the worst kind of coward there was.

He found the small but broad-shouldered Fife sitting amongst the headquarters bunks with a group of the kitchen force, and approached him wearing his sly, cunning—and remarkably hateful—grin.

Corporal Fife was sitting with the cooks and listening to their talk to take his mind off the unpleasantly nervous thought of being bombed. He saw Welsh coming, and what was more, recognized from his face and from considerable past experience what sort of mood the first sergeant was stoking up. Fife's first impulse was to get up and saunter away before Welsh arrived. But Fife knew it wouldn't do any good. Welsh would only follow him; or worse, order him to come back. So Fife simply sat, feeling acute discomfort growing on his face, and watched Welsh descend on them. If there was anything Fife hated, it was being made conspicuous; and that was what Sergeant Welsh, as if he slyly realized this, was always doing to him.

Fife had let Doll talk him out of going out to try and steal a pistol. So had Big Queen, the Texan. Both were sure there wouldn't be enough time. So, when Queen had left him, in an effort to dispel, or at least cope with his own growing nervousness over an air raid, Fife had gone around through the bunk area looking for a particular friend of his to talk to, one of the only two friends in fact that Fife felt he had ever had in C-for-Charlie Company.

One of these two friends had been transferred out of the company and was not even on this ship. The other, and by far the most spectacular of the two as far as Fife was concerned, was a massive, quiet-voiced, big-handed private named Bell. Fife had found him sitting quietly with three or four other privates, waiting, and had joined them. But it had been pretty unsatisfactory. They hardly talked at all. And after a little while Fife had left them and come back here to where the cooks were chatting nervously. The, to Fife, spectacular Bell had offered him very little solace, and Fife was disappointed in him.

Bell, who was a new draftee, talked very little and kept to himself a lot, and there certainly was nothing about him that appeared to be at all unusual. The reason Bell was spectacular, however, was that he had a secret; or at least he had had; and the twenty-year-old Fife knew what it was. Bell was a former army officer. He had been a First Lieutenant in the Corps of Engineers in the Philippines; back before the war; and he had resigned.

Fife would never forget the feeling of first awe and then surprised delight with which he had, in the orderly room, read this information in Bell's 201 file, when Bell had first come into C-for-Charlie three months ago with a group of other draftees. Such an adventurous story, as far as Fife's two and a half years' army experience had shown, existed only in the pages of *Argosy* or some other such magazine. The Officers as well as the Men whom Fife had known had had pretty prosaic careers; only a few of the Men were ex-criminals or anything adventurous like that. Naturally Fife was delighted to find a Bell. As for the awe, all Officers awed Fife. Fife did not like Officers as a class, but he was awed by them, even when he knew they didn't deserve awe, simply because they exercised over him the same authority that his parents and his teachers back at school had had, and exercised it over him in much the same way, too. That any man would voluntarily give up that authority to have it in turn exercised upon himself, seemed to Fife to be both very romantic, and very dumb.

Fife was really quite intelligent, although by his excitability he more often than not gave the impression that he wasn't, and he had decided afterwards that he must have shown what he knew by his face that day, when he had looked at Bell in the chowhall. Anyhow, Bell had approached him later in the afternoon and, after giving him a quiet but rather careful scrutiny, had taken him aside and asked him not to say anything to any of the men about what he had seen in his records. Fife, who at least as yet had not consciously thought of telling anyone, agreed eagerly, although regretfully. Perhaps too eagerly, he thought afterwards: It made him look as though he was enjoying entering a conspiracy with Bell, apparently, and to Bell's evident distaste. And Fife hadn't meant that; it was just that damned excitability of his again. But how could he explain that to Bell?

Anyhow, after having granted Bell his request, Fife had been emboldened to ask Bell eagerly and excitedly to tell him the story of it. Maybe it was a dirty trick. Anyway Bell, after giving him another long, careful, quiet scrutiny, apparently had decided he must do it and had sat down on his bunk and kneading his big hands together with a curious desperate patience and staring at them fixedly, had told him. It was all because of his wife. They had graduated from Ohio State together, himself with an engineering degree. Naturally he had taken ROTC, and he had been called up in 1940 and sent out to the Philippines. Of course his wife had gone with him. But after getting there and being assigned, he had been sent off into the jungle on another island to work on a dam being built there that the army had its fingers in for defense reasons. Wives were not allowed there because the jungle was bad and she had stayed in Manila, and they had been separated. He had got the dirtiest job simply by being the newest man.

"You know what those pre-war officers' clubs were like," Bell said, kneading his big hands and staring at them. "And she didnt know anybody in Manila. We'd never been separated before, you see. Not overnight. I took it for four months and then I quit. Resigned."

"Yeah," Fife had said, with eager encouragement.

"We were always very sexual together," Bell said.

Fife waited for him to go on. "Yeah," he smiled encouragingly.

Bell looked up at him almost angrily, with that curious desperate, sad patience, bottomlessly deep. "That's all." He appeared patiently resigned to Fife's inability to comprehend what he was saying. And perhaps in a way it was true, Fife had reflected eagerly, since he'd never been married. But he couldn't honestly see what was so terrible, why so much fuss.

"We both are the kind of people who need lots of physical aff—" Bell broke off, perhaps to try another tack. "It's undignified," he said stiffly. "It's undignified for a married man my age to be separated from his wife."

"Yeah," Fife said sympathetically.

Again Bell merely stared at him. "Anyway, I worked in Manila until we had enough money to come back to the States, and we came back, and I went back to my job." He spread his hands. "That's all. They told me I'd never get another commission, they said they'd see to it that I got drafted, and what was more that I'd for damn sure be in the Infantry. And here I am," and again he spread his hands. "Took eight months to get drafted. We had eight months."

"Why the fucking sons of bitches!" Fife said loyally.

"Oh, you can't blame them. It's their way of life, you know. And I was thumbing my nose at it, I guess. From their point of view anyway. That isn't their fault."

"But the dirty bastards!"

Bell would not be moved. "No. I dont blame them."

"Where is she now?"

Bell looked at him again with that curious, strange look. "She's home. Back in Columbus. With her folks." Bell continued to stare at him, his eyes veiled with a deep and, to Fife at least, curiously adult reserve, behind which lay that impressive, tremendously deep, tremendously painful, hopeless patience. "How old are you, Fife?"

"Twenty."

"Well, I'm thirty-three. You see? Well, there's your story."

"But why dont you want any of the guys to know?"

"Well, for one thing, because EM dont like officers and it would be embarrassing. And for another," Bell said, his voice sharpening, "it embarrasses me to talk about it, Fife."

"Oh." Fife flushed, rebuked.

"The only reason I've told you is so you'll know why I dont want it mentioned." Bell had stared at him with that curiously reserved—now almost commanding—look.

"Well, dont worry about me telling anybody. I won't," Fife had promised.

Fife had kept his promise. He hadn't mentioned it to anyone. But it hadn't made much difference. It all came out finally, anyway. Within a week the entire company knew about Bell's former status. No one knew how. But things always had a way of doing that. Nobody ever talked, but the word always got out anyway, somehow. The officers had all known about it of course, so had Welsh, and so had the rest of the office staff. Bugger Stein had called Bell in, in fact, and had had a long private talk with him, the subject of which Fife knew nothing about. All in all, it created quite a little furor, and in one way Fife was sorry, and a little jealous, to see it come out in the open. As long as it remained a secret Fife had felt he owned a personal stake in Bell. He had, of course, gone to Bell as soon as it became public knowledge, and had explained that the leak had not come from him. Bell had merely thanked him, staring at him with that same curious reserved, desperate patience.

Thinking it over later on, Fife had decided that it was not nearly as adventurous a story as he had imagined. He had hoped for something more dramatic, such as a fist fight with a general. Fife's own experience with women had not, of course, been legion. He had had two serious girlfriends in his life, one back home, the other at the university in the town where the division had been stationed and where he had taken a few courses. Fife had never been able to sleep with either of these, but he had slept with a lot of whores on payday at various times. He could not help but feel that it was rather a show of weakness, to do what Bell had done, just because of wanting to be with his wife. On the other hand, he had to give it to Bell on one thing: he was certainly true to her. He had gone on pass with Bell several times, later on, after they finally became friends, and he had never seen Bell with a woman, or even go after one. When the rest went off to get laid, Bell would stay by himself and drink. Fife had to hand it to Bell on that, and he could not help but wonder if Bell's wife was being as faithful at home? And he wondered if Bell wondered about that too. Probably he did.

Which would be worse, Fife wondered academically: To have her write and tell you honestly that she was going out and screwing some guy or guys although she still loved you? Or to have her go ahead and do it, screw somebody, but *not* tell you, and keep right on writing you as though she was faithful on the theory that if you never learned it it wouldn't cause you pain? Fife couldn't make up his mind which he would prefer. Both choices made his heart jump leaving him a little sick in the stomach, although he could not say just why. Could a woman actually love one man and enjoy screwing another, if the old man wasn't available? Fife supposed she could. But he certainly didn't like the idea. It left a man feeling pretty naked and unprotected, and it made Fife uncomfortable when he thought about a woman doing it. And they were back home where it was possible to have a lover; Christ, out here in this God-forsaken place there wasn't even anything available. And Bell had said his wife was the kind that needed a lot of physical affection, hadn't he? Fife decided that he was glad he wasn't married.

Actually, there had been almost no reaction at all to Bell's former status, when it became public; and all the concern expressed by everybody beforehand was wasted energy. The men eyed him curiously for a while, when they thought about having a former officer in their midst; and soon it was apparently forgotten. In any case, it was Sergeant Welsh's reaction to Bell which most inflamed Fife and Fife's very strong sense of fair play. Welsh had glanced at the 201 file and then tossed it down on his desk contemptuously, making one of his caustic, supremely cynical remarks which could be so inhumanly devastating, and infuriating, to anyone who believed in humanity as Fife did: "Well, here's a real assbreaker. I sure can collect them. Probably figured out for himself there wasn't going to be any war so why waste a couple years. Bet you ten, Fife, he won't wait five days before he starts givin orders." That he proved to be completely wrong did not bother Welsh in the least. And this was the man who at the moment was bearing down on Fife with that crazy, sly glint in his eye. Fife prepared himself as stoically as he could to endure the flaying that was coming. Unhappily, he glanced around at the cook force clustered nervously around their mess sergeant while they all waited. Fife at least was glad he had never told the son of a bitch about Bell's wife. That really would have given him something to sneer about. At least that was one thing Welsh didn't know.

Mess Sergeant Storm, sitting in the middle of his cooks, did not fail to notice the look on Sergeant Welsh's face, also. Storm, who was twenty-six and in his third enlistment, was acquainted with the First Sergeant's moods fully as well as Fife his clerk, and he was just as much aware of what was coming. In his eight years of service Storm had known a number of first sergeants, but never one who resembled Welsh. Most of them were pretty stolid, solid gentlemen, accomplished in their main business of paperwork, used to commanding and being obeyed. A few were drunken old thieves, getting by on a record of past performance, or else carried along by the services of an efficient staff sergeant who would one day succeed them. And here and there among these two types you might find one who was a little bit wacky on some particular point or other. But never anything like Welsh.

Personally, Storm got along with him quite well. Their association, if not quite actually what could be called armed truce, was that of two suspicious dogs eyeing each other warily in the street. Storm did his job and did it well, and Welsh left him alone. And Storm was aware that as long as he did his job well, Welsh would continue to leave him alone. That was enough for Storm. If Welsh wanted to be crazy, that was his own business.

On the other hand, Storm could not see what advantage to efficiency or organization could be gained from giving a clerk a verbal hiding for no reason at all except that you yourself felt in the mood for it. Storm could, and often did, give a man an oral flaying when it was necessary; but never when there wasn't a specific reason for it. About the only thing to be gained from Welsh's raking little Fife over the coals was that it would take the minds of Storm's cook force off the prospect of being bombed in an air raid and relieve their nervousness a little, which was what Storm himself had been trying to do. But Storm knew Welsh well enough to know that that was not Welsh's only reason for doing it, or even his main reason. He had seen him do it too many times before. He could even give the first line of Welsh's routine before it was said.

"All right, fuckface! Where's that fucking platoon roster I told you to fix up for me?"

The fact that it was already done and handed in, and that Welsh himself knew this, made no difference at all.

"I already did it," Fife said indignantly. "I made it up and turned it in to you, Welsh."

"You what! You did no such a fucking thing, Fife. I dont have it, do I? Christ, of all the . . ."

Storm sat silently and listened to the First Sergeant's elaborations. Welsh was really a master craftsman at the art of imaginative insult. Some of the comparisons he could think up when inspired were fantastic. But when was Fife ever going to learn not to get mad or indignant? Storm's kitchen were grinning and enjoying themselves.

Storm looked around at them, covertly. Land, the tall, thin, silent one; efficient when he was sober, but without the initiative to do anything for himself unless specifically ordered. Park, the other first cook, fat, lazy, petulant; loving to give orders but hating to take them; and always complaining that his authority was being flouted. Dale, the little second cook, muscular and hard as a rock, a constant worker who never stopped; but doing it with a scowling, nervous, angry intensity that could not be anything but abnormal; and always more than willing, too willing, to take on every bit of authority given him. These three were the main personalities of Storm's gang.

Storm could not help but feel an outwardly hard, but inwardly melting and near tear-starting, sentimentality for all of them, the slobs. He had gathered them here, sensing their nervousness, and only partly because he wanted them where he could keep an eye on them, and had got them started in a bull session and begun regaling them with comical stories out of his past eight years' service. All to keep them, as best he could, down off that too-high pitch of nervousness which the whole outfit was beginning to suffer from with all this waiting. And it had worked, at least partially. But now Welsh had taken over with his verbal skinning alive of poor little Fife, and so Storm didn't need to bother now, for a while. He could think about himself.

Storm had done just about everything he could think of to set his own personal affairs straight. In the staging area, before shipping out, he had made a large allotment of almost all of his pay to his widowed sister and her large family back in Texas. She was his only living relative and his army insurance was already made out to her, and where he was going to be from now on for quite a while there wasn't going to be much use for money. Before leaving he had written her a long letter, explaining that he was going; and he had also written two other letters which he had given to friends on the other transport with instructions to mail them only if the ship he was on got sunk or bombed out and himself killed. If either letter reached his sister, it would explain to her to start checking into the insurance and deviling the government even before the final telegram arrived. It would almost certainly take her a long time to collect it in any case, and with that big family of kids to feed she would need it once the allotment stopped. It wasn't a very satisfactory or efficient way of handling it, but under the circumstances it was the best Storm could do. And once he had done it, he felt he had done all he could, and that he was ready. Ready for anything. Storm still felt the same way now, despite his own rising squeamishness over possible air raids. It amused him that he kept continually wanting to raise his arm and look at his watch. He was forced to exercise the whole of his will power in order not to.

Welsh was still raucously deriding Fife, who by now had become quite red in the face and very angry. Storm debated whether he should say something that would stop it, shift the subject. Storm had no particular liking, or even sympathy, for Fife. He was a good enough kid. He just hadn't been away from home long enough. And Storm, who had started off bumming during the Depression when he was only fourteen, couldn't find kids like that very interesting. But Welsh was a man who often didn't know when to quit; he would get something like this going, which could be fun, but then he would keep on with it until it passed beyond the point of being funny. And even though it was keeping Storm's cooks amused and thinking about something other than air raids, Storm felt it was time to call a halt. He was saved from having to do anything about it, though, by the great, vibrating belch of the klaxon horn which resounded through the clanging, overheated hold, deafening everybody. The immense sound caused everyone to jump, even Welsh.

It was the signal for the inhabiters of this particular hold to prepare to disembark, and with its sounding everything that was taking place ceased to be important, or even to exist. The dice and poker games stopped in mid-play, everybody grabbing back his share of the pot, and a little extra if he could. Conversations died soundlessly in mid-word, their very subjects no longer remembered; and Welsh and Fife simply stared at each other without recalling that Welsh had just been insulting Fife to make him angry. After so much waiting of such high intensity, it was as if life itself had crossed a line with the sounding of the klaxon, and that whatever had happened or existed before had not and would never have, any connection with whatever would come after. Everybody had turned hastily to their equipment, and cries of "All right! Off and on!" and "Drop your cocks and grab your socks!" rose up from the throats of noncoms to bounce off the steel ceiling; and in the one moment of total, complete silence which had somehow got mixed in with this jumbled stew of noise and then emerged out of the middle of it, nobody would ever know how, could be heard one nameless man's single voice, high and shrilling, and intensely elucidating some declaration of faith to a neighbor with the words: "I guaran-fucking-tee you!" Then the noise closed back over as everybody went on struggling into their equipment.

Bulging in all directions under full field equipment, they found the narrow steel stairs difficult to navigate; and after three nervous flights of them each man was winded. And as they emerged into the now hot, midmorning sunshine and fresh sea air on deck, Captain Bugger Stein their commander, standing by the hatch in musette bag, map case, glasses, carbine, pistol and canteens, stared into each of their helmet-shadowed, intense faces and chokingly felt tears rising up in him, tears which of course as an officer and commander he must hold back and never show above a stiff upper lip. His sense of responsibility was monumental, a near holy thing. He treasured it. Not only that, he was very pleased with himself that he felt it. If the old man could only see him now!

And beside him stood his first sergeant, no longer looking like Welsh an individual, now that he was in full gear and had his helmet on. He too watched the faces, but in a different way: in a sly, cunning, calculating way, as if he knew something none of the rest of them knew.

By squads and by platoon they went over the side and clambered down the four-storey-high side of the ship on the nets and into the endless chain of LCIs still shuttling back and forth from shore. Only one man fell, and he got no more than a slightly wrenched back because he lit on two other men already in the barge, all three crashing to the steel floor in full equipment with loud grunts and curses. But they heard from the barge pilots that the list of injured, for this ship, had already reached fifteen: par for the course, the barge pilots, who had the experience, said with dry, cheerful cynicism. C-for-Charlie heard this news with the awed realization that these injured were first casualties: the division's first casualties in a combat zone. They had expected at least bombs, or machineguns, to account for that. But to fall into a barge? By standing up, while digesting this, they could see the shore and the sand beach and cocopalms gradually coming closer, and closer, to them. As they got closer to it, they could see where the tops of a number of the coconut trees had been shot away.

In the barge in which Doll's squad found itself the assistant pilot, who was Army Transport Corps like all the others, quipped grinning, in best Naval officer style: "Glad to have you aboard, gentlemen!" then added with matter-of-fact cheer: "Your outfit's lucky. Old Nippy'll be comin along in—" he looked at his waterproof watch—"in about another fifteen minutes."

"How do you know?" Doll's squad sergeant, whose name was Field, asked.

"We just got the news from the air strip," the assistant pilot smiled.

"But, well wont they try to get the ships out?"

"Cant. Not enough time. We'll just have to go on unloading." The information didn't seem to bother the assistant pilot much, but Doll, who was wearing his new pistol proudly, gripped the gunnel to keep his balance in the jouncing, swaying barge and looked back at the dwindling ship with the greatest sense of relief he had ever felt in his life. He devoutly hoped he would never see that old tub again in his lifetime, or any other ship—save one; and that was the one that would take him off this island.

"In this business you take them as they come," the assistant pilot said.

"But wont the fighter planes—" Field started to say.

"They'll try. They always get some of them. But some always get through."

"Hey, Terry, jerk the lead!" the barge pilot called in a harassed voice.

"Aye, sir," the assistant called back dryly. He went aft.

Ahead of them in the barge the island had got steadily larger, and now they could make out individual men scurrying around huge piles of stores. Doll stared at them. They got slowly bigger. Doll continued to stare. He was fascinated by something he could not even put a name to. What made men do it? he wondered suddenly, awed. What kept them there? Why didn't they just up and leave, all go away? All he knew was that he was scared, more scared, and in a different way, than he had ever been in his life before. And he didn't like it, any of it.

"Grab holt and prepare to land!" the barge pilot shouted at them. Doll did. In a couple of moments the barge grated, cleared and rushed on, grated again, lurched, ground on noisily a few more feet and stopped, and Doll was on Guadalcanal. So were the rest of the men in the same barge, but Doll did not consider that. The front ramp, handled by the talkative assistant pilot, had already begun to fall almost before the barge was stopped.

"Everybody out!" the barge pilot shouted. "No transfer slips!"

There still remained two feet of water beyond the end of the ramp, but it was easy enough to jump; and only one man, who slipped on the metal of the ramp, landed in the water and got one foot wet. It wasn't Doll. The ramp was already rising, as the barge went into reverse and pulled back out to go for another load. Then they were trudging through the sand up the long beach, trying to pick their way across it through the streams of men, to where Bugger Stein and Lieutenant Band were assembling the company.

Corporal Fife had, of course, been in the barge which brought off the company headquarters. Their barge pilot had told them substantially the same thing Doll's had: "Your outfit's lucky. The Jap's on his way." The transports must have been spotted, he said. But they were getting off just ahead of time, he said, so they'd be safe. The main thought uppermost in Fife's mind was that everything was so organized, and handled with such matter-of-fact dispatch. Like a business. Like a regular business. And yet at the bottom of it was blood: blood, mutilation, death. It seemed

weird, wacky, to Fife. The air strip had got the news, by radio
from a plane apparently, and had transmitted it to the beach,
where the barge pilots were all informed—or else informed themselves and each other—and presumably the crews as well as the
army commanders, if not the troops themselves, on board the
ships were told, too. And yet there was nothing anybody could do
about it, apparently. Except wait. Wait and see what happened.
Fife had looked around at the faces in the barge covertly. Bugger
Stein betrayed his nervousness by continually adjusting his
glasses, over and over, with the thumb and fingers of his right
hand on the frame. Lieutenant Band betrayed his by repeatedly
licking his lips. Storm's face was too impassively set. The second
cook Dale's eyes were snapping bright, and he blinked them over
and over. Welsh's eyes, through the narrow slits to which they
were closed in the bright sun, betrayed nothing of anything. Neither amusement nor anything else, this time; not even cynicism.
Fife hoped his own face looked all right, but he felt as though his
eyebrows might be too high up on his forehead. Once they got
ashore, and the guide had led them to their assigned spot in the
edge of the coconut trees which came right down to the beach
itself, Fife kept saying over and over to himself what the barge
pilot had told them on the way in: "Your outfit's lucky. You're
getting off ahead of time."

And in a way, it was quite right too. When the planes came,
they were after the ships, not the shore. As a result, Fife, and all
the rest of C-for-Charlie had a perfectly safe grandstand, ringside
seat for the whole show. Actually Fife at least, who loved humanity, was going to find that he wished he hadn't had a seat at all,
after it was over. But he had to admit it fascinated him, with a
morbid fascination.

Apparently the news had not affected the beach very much at
all. The LCIs and a welter of other types of barges still came
roaring, jamming in to unload their cargoes of men or supplies,
while others were in process of pulling back out to rejoin the
shuttle. The beach was literally alive with men, all moving somewhere, and seemed to undulate with a life of its own under their
mass as beaches sometimes appear to do when invaded by armies

of fiddler crabs. Lines, strings and streams of men crossed and recrossed it with hot-footed and apparently unregulated alacrity. They were in all stages of dress and undress, sleeveless shirts, legless pants, no shirts at all, and in some few cases, particularly those working in or near the water, they worked totally stark naked or in their white government issue underpants through which the dark hairiness of their genitals showed plainly. There were no women anywhere around here at all anyway, and there were not likely to be any either for quite some little time. They wore all sorts of fantastic headgear, issue, civilian, and homemade, so that one might see a man working in the water totally naked with nothing adorning his person except his identity tags around his neck and a little red beany, turned-up fatigue hat, or a hat of banana leaves on his head. The supply barges were unloaded by gangs of men immediately, right at the water's edge, so that the barge could go back for more. Then lines of other men carried these boxes, cases, cans back up the beach into the trees, or formed chains and passed them from hand to hand, trying to clear the space at the water's edge. Further away down the beach the heavier matériel, trucks, anti-tank guns, artillery, were being unloaded, driven by their own drivers, or hauled up by Marine tractors. And still further away, this whole operation was being conducted a second time for the second transport, anchored quite a few hundred yards behind the first.

All of this activity had been going on at this same pace since very early morning apparently, and the news of the impending air raid did not appear to affect it one way or the other. But as the minutes crept by one after the other, there was a noticeable change in the emotional quality and excitement of the beach. C-for-Charlie, from its vantage point at the edge of the trees, could sense the tautening of the emotional tenor. They watched a number of men who had been calmly bathing waistdeep in the sea in the midst of all this hectic activity, look at their watches and then get out and walk naked up to their clothes in the edge of the trees. Then, just a few moments after this, someone at the water's edge flung up an arm and cried out, "There they are!" and the cry was taken up all up and down the beach.

High up in the sunbright sky a number of little specks sailed
serenely along toward the channel where the two ships lay. After
a couple of minutes when they were closer, a number of other
specks, fighter planes, could be seen above them engaging each
other. Below on the beach the men with jobs and the working
parties had already gone back to their work; but as the others,
including C-for-Charlie company, watched, about half the engaged fighter planes broke off and turned back to the north, apparently having reached the limit of their fuel range. Only a
couple of the remaining fighters started out to chase them, and
they almost at once gave it up and turned back, and with the
others began to attack the bombers. On they all came, slowly
getting larger. The tiny mosquitoes dipped and swirled and dived
in a mad, whirling dance around the heavier, stolid horseflies,
who nevertheless kept serenely and sedately on. Now the bombers
began to fall, first one here, trailing a great plume of smoke soon
dissipated by the winds of the upper air, then another one there,
trailing no smoke at all and fluttering down. No parachutes issued
from them. Still the bombers kept on. Then one of the little mosquitoes fell, and a moment later, in another place, another.
Parachutes appeared from both, floating in the sunbright air. Still
the mosquitoes darted and swirled. Another injured horsefly fell.
But it was surprising, at least to C-for-Charlie and the other newcomers, how many did not fall. Considering the vehemence and
numbers of the attack, it appeared that they must all go down. But
they didn't, and the whole concerted mass moved slowly on
toward the ships in the channel, the changing tones of the motors
as the fighters dived or climbed clearly discernible now.

Below on the beach the minutes, and then the seconds, continued to tick by. There were no cheers when a bomber fell. When
the first one had fallen, another new company nearby to C-for-
Charlie had made an attempt at a feeble cheer, in which a few
men from C-for-Charlie had joined. But it soon died from lack of
nourishment, and after that it was not again attempted. Everybody
watched in silence, rapt, fascinated. And the men down on the
beach continued to work, though more excitedly now.

To Corporal Fife, standing tensely in the midst of the silent company headquarters, the lack of cheering only heightened his previous impression of its all being like a business. A regular business venture, not war at all. The idea was horrifying to Fife. It was weird and wacky and somehow insane. It was even immoral. It was as though a clerical, mathematical equation had been worked out, as a calculated risk: Here were two large, expensive ships and, say, twenty-five large aircraft had been sent out after them. These had been given protection as long as possible by smaller aircraft, which were less expensive than they, and then sent on alone on the theory that all or part of twenty-five large aircraft was worth all or part of two large ships. The defending fighters, working on the same principle, strove to keep the price as high as possible, their ultimate hope being to get all twenty-five large aircraft without paying all or any of either ship. And that there were men in these expensive machines which were contending with each other, was unimportant—except for the fact that they were needed to manipulate the machines. The very idea itself, and what it implied, struck a cold blade of terror into Fife's essentially defenseless vitals, a terror both of unimportance, his unimportance, and of powerlessness: his powerlessness. He had no control or sayso in any of it. Not even where it concerned himself, who was also a part of it. It was terrifying. He did not mind dying in a war, a real war,—at least, he didn't think he did—but he did not want to die in a regulated business venture.

Slowly and inexorably the contending mass high up in the air came on. On the beach the work did not stop. Neither did the LCIs and other barges. When the planes had almost reached the ships, one more bomber fell, crashing and exploding in smoke and flames in the channel in full view of everybody. Then they began to pass over the ships. A gentle sighing became audible through the air. Then a geyser of water, followed by another, then another, popped high up out of the sea. Seconds later the sounds of the explosions which had caused them swept across the beach and on past them into the coconut trees, rustling them. The gentle sighing noise grew louder, carrying a fluttery overtone, and other geysers began to pop up all over the sea around the first ship, and then a few seconds later, around the second. It was no longer possible to distinguish the individual sticks of bombs, but they all saw the individual stick of three bombs which made the hit. Like probing fingers, the first lit some distance in front of the first ship, the second coming closer. The third fell almost directly alongside. An LCI was just putting off from the ship, it couldn't have been many yards away, and the third bomb apparently landed directly on it. From that distance, probably a thousand yards or more, one faint, but clearly discernible scream, high and shrill, and which actually did not reach them until after the geyser had already gone up, was heard by the men on shore, cut off and followed immediately by the sound wave of the explosion: some one nameless man's single instinctual and useless protest against the taking of his life and his own bad luck at being where he was instead of somewhere else, ridiculous, pointless, but not without a certain dignity, although, ironically, it was not heard, and appreciated, until after he himself no longer existed. His last scream had lived longer than he had.

When the spout of water had subsided so that they could see, there was nothing left of the LCI to be seen. At the spot where it had been a few figures bobbed in the water, and these rapidly became fewer. The two barges nearest them came about and made for the spot, reaching them before the little rescue boat that was standing by could get there. Losing way, they wallowed in the trough while infantrymen stripped off equipment and dived in to help both the injured and uninjured who had had no time to strip equipment and were being dragged under by it. The less seriously wounded and the uninjured were helped aboard the barges on little rope ladders thrown over the side by the pilots; the more seriously hurt were simply kept afloat until the rescue boat, which carried slings and baskets and was already on its way, could get there.

On shore, the watching men—the lucky ones, as the barge pilots had said, because they were out of it—tried to divide their attention between this operation and the planes still overhead. The bombers, having made their run, turned out toward the channel and headed back north. They made no attempt at strafing, they were too busy protecting themselves from the fighters, and the antiaircraft crews on the ships and shore could not fire either for fear of hitting their own fighters. The whole operation, except for the dropped bombs themselves, had taken place up there, high up in the air. Slowly, sedately, the bombers headed back into the north to where a protective blanket of their own fighters would be waiting for them, growing slowly and steadily smaller, as before they had grown slowly and steadily larger. The fighters still buzzed angrily around them, and before they were lost to sight a few more fell. All during the action the defending fighters had been hampered by having to break off and streak back to the air strip to renew fuel or ammunition. Replenished, they would return. But the number of fighters actually engaged was never as large as it might have been. Apparently the bombers were allowing for this factor. At any rate, slowly they dwindled to specks again, then to invisibility. Then finally, the fighters began to return. It was over. On the beach the work of unloading, which had never ceased during the attack, went right on.

Men who had been here longer and who were standing nearby to C-for-Charlie, which still waited—and watched—from the edge of the coconut grove, told them that there would probably be at least two more attacks, now, during the day. The main thing was to get the damned ships unloaded so they could get out of here and thus let things settle back peacefully to normal. The unloading was the most important thing of all. But it had to be finished by nightfall. The ships had to be out of here as soon as it got dark, fully unloaded or not, rather than risk night air attacks. If they weren't fully unloaded, they would leave anyway.

Already, long before the retreating bombers were out of sight, word had circulated around the beach that the first transport had been damaged by the same bomb which had destroyed the bargeful of infantrymen. This was an even more important reason for the ships to get out. The damage was slight, but the bomb had sprung some plates and she was taking water, though not enough that the pumps could not handle it. There had been some casualties aboard the ship, too, caused by bomb fragments or pieces of flying metal from the barge among the densely crowded men on deck; and one man, word had it, had had his face smashed in by a helmet blown from the head of some man in the barge: a complete, solid helmet, undented, undamaged. Such were the vagaries of existence, the word had it. Pieces of meat and chunks of shattered equipment had also been blown up onto the ship's deck from the barge, the jagged riflestocks causing some little further injury. Apparently, word from the ship said, the bomb had not landed directly in the barge itself, but had hit right alongside its gunnel, between it and the ship. This was the reason for the blast damage to the ship. On the other hand, had it landed on the opposite side of the barge away from the ship, or even in the barge, the men on deck would have been bombarded with a great deal more meat and metal than they had been. As it was, the most of it had—because of the bomb's position—been blown away from the ship across the water. The casualties on board the ship, the word said, had been seven dead and twenty-two injured, amongst which injured was the man who had had his face smashed in by the helmet. All of these were being cared for aboard in the ship's hospital.

C-for-Charlie heard this news with a strange feeling. This had been their ship, these men now dead and injured their sailing companions. The spot where the bomb fell had not been at all far from their own debarkation position. They listened to the word-of-mouth reports with a sort of mixture of awe and imaginative fear which they found completely uncontrollable: If the bombers had been a few minutes earlier. Or if they themselves had been only a few minutes later getting up on deck. Suppose one of the companies ahead of them had been much slower getting off? Suppose, for that matter, the bomb hadn't landed some yards off in the water? Suppose it had landed that number of yards toward the rail? This sort of speculation was, of course, useless. As well as acutely painful. But a strong awareness of this uselessness did not seem to help to make the speculation cease.

The survivors of the destroyed LCI were landed from the two barges and the rescue boat which had picked them up, not far away from C-for-Charlie company; so C-for-Charlie got to observe this action, too. With practical comments as to the extent of the various injuries in their ears from the nearby men who had been here longer, C-for-Charlie watched round-eyed as these men were tenderly led or carried up from the beach to where a field dressing station had been set up at dawn. Some of them were still vomiting sea water from their ordeal. A few were able to walk by themselves. But all of them were suffering from shock, as well as from blast, and the consummate tenderness with which they were handled first by their rescuers and then by the corpsmen was a matter of complete indifference to them and meant nothing. Bloodstained, staggering, their eyeballs rolling, the little party faltered up the slope of the beach to sit or lie, dazed and indifferent, and acquiescently allow themselves to be worked on by the doctors.

They had crossed a strange line; they had become wounded men; and everybody realized, including themselves, dimly, that they were now different. Of itself, the shocking physical experience of the explosion, which had damaged them and killed those others, had been almost identically the same for them as for those other ones who had gone on with it and died. The only difference was that now these, unexpectedly and illogically, found themselves alive again. They had not asked for the explosion, and they had not asked to be brought back. In fact, they had done nothing. All they had done was climb into a barge and sit there as they had been told. And then this had been done to them, without warning, without explanation, perhaps damaging them irreparably; and now they were wounded men; and now explanation was impossible. They had been initiated into a strange, insane, twilight fraternity where explanation would be forever impossible. Everybody understood this; as did they themselves, dimly. It did not need to be mentioned. Everyone was sorry, and so were they themselves. But there was nothing to be done about it. Tenderness was all that could be given, and, like most of the self-labeled human emotions, it meant nothing when put alongside the intensity of their experience.

With the planes which had done this to them still in sight above the channel, the doctors began swiftly to try to patch up, put back together, and save, what they could of what the planes had done. Some of them were pretty badly torn up, others not so badly.

Some would yet die, so much was obvious, and it was useless to waste time on these which might be spent on others who might live. Those who would die accepted this professional judgment of the doctors silently, as they accepted the tender pat on the shoulder the doctors gave them when passing them by, staring up mutely from bottomless, liquid depths of still-living eyes at the doctors' guilty faces.

C-for-Charlie, standing nearby, and already counted off again into its true structural unity of platoons, watched this action at the aid station with rapt fascination. Each of its platoons and its company headquarters instinctively huddled together as though for warmth against a chill, seeking a comfort from the nearness of others which was not forthcoming, five separate little groups of wide-eyed spectators consumed with an almost sexual, morbid curiosity. Here were men who were going to die, some of them before their very eyes. How would they react? Would some of them rage against it, as they themselves felt like raging? Or would they simply all expire quietly, stop breathing, cease to see? C-for-Charlie, as one man, was curious to see: to see a man die. Curious with a hushed, breathless awe. They could not help but be; fresh blood was so very red, and gaping holes in bared flesh were such curious, strange sights. It was all obscene somehow. Something which they all felt should not be looked at, somehow, but which they were compelled to look at, to cluster closer and study. The human body was really a very frail, defenseless organism, C-for-Charlie suddenly realized. And these men might have been themselves. So might those others, out there now under the water over which the LCIs still scurried, and who would not be searched out and raised until the cessation of the unloading offered time and opportunity.

The wounded men, both those who would die and those who would not, were as indifferent to being stared at as they were to the tenderness with which they were treated. They stared back at their audience with lacklustre eyes, eyes which though lustreless were made curiously limpid by the dilation of deep shock, and if they saw them at all, which was doubtful, what they saw did not register. As a result, the whole of C-for-Charlie felt it, too: what all the others, with more experience, knew: These men had crossed a line, and it was useless to try to reach them. These had experienced something that they themselves had not experienced, and devoutly hoped they never would experience, but until they did experience it they could no longer communicate with them. An hour ago—even less than that—these had been like themselves; nervous, jumpy, waiting with trepidation at how they would behave, to be disembarked. Now they had joined company with—and had even gone beyond—those strange, wild-eyed, bearded, crazily dressed Marines and soldiers who had been fighting the Japanese here since August and who now stood around matter-of-factly, discussing professionally which of these wounds they thought might be fatal, and which might not.

Even the army itself understood this about them, the wounded, and had made special dispensations for their newly acquired honorary status. Those who did not die would be entered upon the elaborate shuttling movement back out from this furthermost point of advance, as only a short time back they had been entered upon the shuttle forward into it. Back out, and further and further back, toward that amorphous point of assumed total safety. It was as though, if each man's life in the army were looked upon as a graph, beginning at the bottom with his induction and rising steadily to this point, then this moment now—or rather the moment of the explosion itself, actually—could be considered the apex from which the line turned downward, back toward the bottom and his eventual discharge: his secret goal. Depending upon the seriousness of his condition and the amount of time required to heal him, his graph line would descend part, or all of the way, to the bottom. Some, the least injured, might never even get as far back as New Zealand or Australia, and might end their downward course at a base hospital in the New Hebrides and from there be sent back up again. Others, slightly more wounded, might get to New Zealand or Australia, but not back to the States, and so be sent forward again from there. Still others, more serious yet, might get to the States and yet not be discharged, so that they might be sent out again from there, toward this moving danger point of the front, either back this way, or to Europe. All of these graph lines would rise again, perhaps to an even higher apex. The dead, of course, would find that their graph lines stopped; at the apex itself, like those out there under the water, or else a little way below it like these men dying here.

It could all be worked out mathematically, young Corporal Fife thought suddenly when he discovered these thoughts running through his mind, and someone ought to do it. It would require a tremendous amount of work though, with all the men there were in all the armies of the world. But perhaps an electric brain could be constructed that would handle it.

At any rate, clearly the best way to be wounded, if one must be wounded at all, was to have a wound so bad that you would almost die, one that would leave you sick long enough for the war to get over, but which when you recovered from it would not leave you crippled or an invalid. Either that, or receive a minor wound which would incapacitate or cripple you slightly without crippling fully. Fife could not decide which he would prefer. He didn't really prefer any, that was the truth.

In the end, C-for-Charlie got to see three men die in the aid station, before the jeep with its route guide from regimental head-quarters arrived to lead it to its bivouac. Of these three, two died very quietly, slowly sinking further and further into that state of unreality brought on by shock and by the ebbing of the functions so that the mind mercifully does not comprehend what is happening to it. Only one man raged against it, and he only for a moment, rousing himself briefly from his steadily encroaching hallucination to shout curses and epithets against what was happening to him and against everything which contributed to it, the doctors, the bomb, the war, the generals, the nations, before re-lapsing back quietly into the numbing sleep which would pass over into death with scarcely a transition. Others would die too here, certainly—as well as almost certainly still others on the plane out, or in the base hospital—but C-for-Charlie was not there to see them. They were already off on their six mile route march to their new bivouac.

It was a march the like of which none of them had ever experi-enced before, and nobody had really prepared them for it. Though they had read newspaper accounts of jungle fighting. As they moved back inland through the coconut groves, the aid station near the beach was quickly lost to sight, though not to memory, and they found themselves coming suddenly into those tropic conditions they had heard so much about. Here where the sea breeze of the beach could not reach them, the moist humidity was so overpowering, and hung in the air so heavily, that it seemed more like a material object than a weather condition. It brought the sweat starting from every pore at the slightest exertion. And unable to evaporate in it, this sweat ran down over their bodies soaking everything to saturation. When it had saturated their clothing, it ran on down into their shoes, filling them, so that they sloshed along in their own sweat as if they had just come out of wading a river. It was now almost midday and the sun blazed down on them between the widely spaced trees, heating their helmets to such temperatures that the steel shells actually burned their hands and for simple comfort had to be removed and slung from packs, leaving them wearing only the fiber liners. They tramped along through a strange, heavy quiet caused by the humidity which damped the air with moisture so that sound waves did not travel but simply fell dead to the ground. There was so much water in the heavy, hanging air that the marching men had to gasp for breath, and then got very little oxygen or relief for their extra exertion. Everything was wet. The roads used by the transport were seas of soft mud churned up by the traffic, axledeep on the big trucks. It was impossible to march on—or *in*—them. The only possible way for marching men to move at all was to travel in two lines, one on either side, picking their way over the great rolls of drying mud, turned back as though by a plow, and the lumpish hummocks of grass between them. Clouds of mosquitoes rose from the disturbed grass hummocks to plague them in the quiet, heavy air. Several times they came upon jeeps mired down, with their smaller wheelbase, to their belly plates, vainly trying to extricate themselves; and their own jeep which was leading them had to pick its way very carefully through the worst of the muddy places.

Everywhere around them as they moved along were great piles

of stores and supplies of all kinds, stacked in great dumps thirty and forty feet high, and into which and out of which moved a constant traffic of the big trucks. They had to march quite some little time, before they got far enough inland for the supply dumps to cease.

Trudging along the road edge on this incredible march and moving directly behind Captain Stein and Lieutenant Band, First Sergeant Welsh, betweentimes wiping the sweat out of his eyes, could not stop thinking of the little band of wounded animals— because that was what they were, had been reduced to—that he had seen back at the aid station, and he kept muttering softly to himself over and over while grinning slyly at Fife: "Property. Property. All for property." Because that was what it was; what it was all about. One man's property, or another man's. One nation's, or another nation's. It had all been done, and was being done, for property. One nation wanted, felt it needed, probably did need, more property; and the only way to get it was to take it away from those other nations who had already laid claim to it. There just wasn't any more unclaimed property on this planet, that was all. And that was all it was. He found it immensely amusing. "Property," Welsh muttered to himself too softly for anyone else to hear, "all for property," and frequently he would take from his first sergeant's musette, where he kept the Morning Report and other reports, a large Listerine bottle full of straight gin, from which he would pretend to take loud gargles for a non-existent sore throat. He had three more full bottles, carefully and separately wrapped up in his blankets in his full field pack, which now hung heavily on his back. It was precious stuff. Because in a new, unknown terrain it would take him probably two whole days, possibly three, to ferret out and find a new source.

Behind Welsh and Fife trudged Storm and his cook force, marching with their heads hung down in order to pick their way, and saying little. They were thinking about the wounded too, but none of them had a coherent philosophy about it such as Welsh had. Probably that was why they marched in silence. At any rate, only the muscular, intense, small second cook Dale, with the perpetual snapping eyes, made any comment.

"They should of let them have it with the anti-aircraft from the ships!" he said suddenly in an intensely furious, brooding voice to the tall, thin Land who marched beside him. "Fighters or no fighters! They could of got a lot more of them. A lot more. If I'd been there I would of. If I'd been there, and had my hands on one of them forty millimeters, I'd of let them have it orders or no orders. That's what I'd of done."

"You'd shit, too," Storm said shortly from in front of him; and Dale subsided with the look of hurt pride of an inferior who feels his boss has accused him unjustly.

The enlisted men were not the only ones who were thinking about the division's first real wounded. Directly in front of Welsh Captain Bugger Stein and his exec Lieutenant Band had marched for a long time in silence. In fact, after getting the company out and moving, neither had said a word. They had nothing much to do now, really, except follow the jeep that was leading them. So there was no need to talk. But the real reason they were silent was because they too were thinking of the bloody, numb little party of wounded.

"Some of those boys were pretty badly chopped up," Band said finally, breaking the long silence as he picked his way over another grass hummock.

"Yes," Stein said, stepping around a big mud roll.

"Jim," Band said, after a moment. "Jim, did you know how many officers were with that barge?"

"Why, yes, George. There were two," Stein said. "Somebody told me that," he added.

"That's what I was told," Band said. After a moment he said: "Did you notice that they were both with the wounded?"

"Why, yes," Stein said. "Yes, I did."

"Did you notice that neither one of them was hit very bad?"

"Didn't appear to be. Did they?"

Fumbling with his pocket a moment, Band said: "Have a stick of gum, Jim. I got two left."

"Why, thanks, George. I will," Stein said. "I'm all out."

Further back in the column, and on the other side of the road, Pfc Doll marched—exhaustedly, gasping for breath, as everybody did—with his right hand resting on the holster flap of his new pistol, but the only feeling that was in him was one of a gigantic and gloomy sense of depression. He too had been affected by the sight of the wounded, and the effect upon him had been to diminish his recent acquisition of a pistol to total meaninglessness, nothingness, complete unimportance. Obviously, whether a man had a pistol or not, it was not going to mean a thing under the blast of an aerial bomb like that. Of course, up on the front lines later, where most of the fighting would be done with small arms, it might be different; but even there, there would be the big mortars, and artillery fire. Doll felt completely defenseless. As well as exhausted. How the hell much further was this march?

At that moment, in point of fact, the six mile march still had five miles to run; but had anybody told Doll this, or told any other man in C-for-Charlie company, it would not have been believed. There were men in this company who, back before the war in the peacetime regular army, had made forced marches upwards of fifty miles and lasting more than twenty-four hours. But never had any of them experienced anything like this. Slowly, very slowly, as they progressed through the coconut groves along the edges of these rivers of mud called roads, the terrain began to change a little. Fingers of matted jungle began to be visible, reaching down into the coconut trees, and every now and then yellow hills of kunai grass could be seen far back in the distance above the jungle. Wearily, exhaustedly they trudged and stumbled on.

To cover that six miles took them most of the afternoon, and by the time they reached the place they had been assigned more than a third of the company had given up and fallen out along the way. Those who made it were staggering, gasping from sheer airlessness, and almost senseless with exhaustion. The company kitchen equipment and the men's duffel bags, as well as one of the company's jeeps, had already been delivered to the spot; but nobody could do anything about it for more than half an hour after they arrived and collapsed when told that they were home. Then the jeep was sent out to collect the stragglers along the route, and Sergeant Storm, with a weary detail to help him and his cooks, set about putting up the kitchen tent and fly and putting up his field stoves so that he could serve a meal that night. Other details exhaustedly, sickly, went about putting up the supply tent and orderly room tent. Before any of these jobs could be completed, it began to rain.

CHAPTER 2

There was a long line of jungle about a hundred and fifty yards from the bivouac. Off through the coconut trees and through the steaming, chill curtain of tropical rain it looked more like a massive wall than anything else. Dense, solid, sweeping away to the foothills and a hundred feet high, it might have been an ancient green lavaflow laid down by some volcano centuries ago to form this flat-topped plateau: up whose steep green slope one could climb, to walk away over the top on a surface at least as solid as the wet earth on which they stood. Almost invisible in the rain, it loomed there, alien, supremely confident, making them aware of it even when they could not see it, a fact of nature like a mountain or an ocean and equally as ominous to the human ego.

In the coconut grove they worked doggedly to set up their camp. The rain came straight down, unbreathed upon by any wind. A quarter of a mile away they could see the humid sun shining brightly down into the apparently endless cocopalms. But here it came down in bucketsful—in huge, fat drops so close together that it seemed to be a solid sheet of water which was pouring down on them from the sky. Everything not already accidentally covered up was soaked through in a matter of seconds. In minutes it had flooded the area. To think of raincoats was ridiculous, this rain would have gone right on through them. Soaked to the skin, still worn out by the march, C-for-Charlie company sloshed around through the area, churned it into a thin sea of mud with their feet, did whatever had to be done to make a camp. There was no other choice.

It was so bad, everything was so miserable, that suddenly the whole thing turned itself into a lark. A hollow and pathetic lark, to be sure, when associated with the dead, dying and wounded from the air raid whom they could not forget;—but perhaps for that very reason the clowning and laughter rose to an even higher pitch, one that in the end resembled hysteria. Some men, less cautious and able to forget that even combat fatigues had to be washed, were not above sitting down and sliding themselves around in the mud like children playing in snow. In the end, however, it did not lessen their painful new tension. When they had worn out their clowning, they found the nervousness still there. All their howling and laughing and sliding about had not in the slightest bit diminished that. Meanwhile, the rain did not cease.

In the kitchen tent which had been on the way up when the rain started, Storm, cursing and swearing, tried to light his field stoves with wet matches. No one had any that were dry, and if he did not get them lit there would be no hot meal tonight; and Storm was determined that there would be one. Finally he managed it with a borrowed Zippo, knowing beforehand that if he succeeded he would burn his hand rather badly, and which in fact he did do. Stoically, he wrapped his hand in a towel and after giving orders to dry out some matches over the lit stove went on with his work, considerably prouder of himself than he would have admitted aloud. He would show these bums who it was kept them fed. Nobody'd ever say Storm didn't feed his people.

Outside in the rain it appeared upon closer inspection that the company's allotment of eight-man personnel tents had not arrived from the ship; nor had the folding cots which were supposed to go in them. When Sergeant Welsh grinning with great relish brought him this news, Captain Bugger Stein did not know what to do. This was one of those little inefficiencies that could always be expected, wherever large groups of men tried to carry out a complex operation together. But on this particular day, and in this rain, it was an especially bad one to have inflicted on him, Stein felt. Logically there was only one order to give, which was for the men to break packs and put up their sheltertents, and that was the order Stein gave. Logical or not, it was still an absurd order, and Stein was painfully aware of that. He was sitting bareheaded in the newly risen, comparatively dry orderly-room tent, drenched and cold, and rummaging around in his own barracks bag trying to find a dry uniform, when Welsh came to him; and when he saw the grinning contempt on Welsh's wet face at the order, he became so incensed that he forgot his policy of parental tolerance toward his crazy first sergeant.

"God damn it, Sergeant, *I* know it's a ridiculous order, *too!*" he shouted. "Now go and *tell* them! That's an order!"

"Yes, sir!" Welsh grinned, saluting him insultingly; and did. With sardonic relish.

The men heard the order with stolidly set faces and little comment, standing with hunched shoulders in the rain. Then they set about it.

"He's nuts!" Private Mazzi snarled to Private Tills, wiping the water from his face as he coupled their tentpoles together, "plain fucking nuts!" They were bunking together, and Tills was sitting on a five gallon watercan buttoning their shelterhalves together in the rain. He did not answer.

"Well, aint that right?" Mazzi demanded, as he finished the poles and started unwinding the rolled ropes. "Aint that fucking right, Tills? Hey, Tills!"

"I don't know," Tills said and relapsed into silence. Tills had been one of those who had got carried away into playing in the mud, and now he was regretting it. At the height of the clowning, sitting in the mud, he had even daubed streaks of it across his face. By now the rain and simple usage had washed most of it from his hands and, with some help from himself, from his face; but the rest of him was one great concerted smear of the foul, evilsmelling tropical mud. "What else could he do?" he asked spiritlessly after a moment.

"How the goddam hell do I know what he could of done? I aint the company commander." Mazzi gathered their combined ten tentpegs, having stretched the wet ropes as best he could, and began laying them out.

"You think these goddam little old pegs going to hold in this muck?" he demanded. "I was compny commander of this compny, there'd be a lotta changes around here, and pretty damn fucking quick. And up yours, Tills. You about finished there?"

"I'm sure there would be," Tills said. "Yeah, I'm finished." He stood up, letting the joined mass of soaked canvas fall from his lap to the muddy ground, and wiped the rain from his face.

"Well come on then." Mazzi tossed out the last two pegs. "He's a jerkoff. A goddam mothergrabbing jerkoff. That's what he is. He don't know his ass from third base and he aint about to ever. Come on, damn it."

"Everbody's a jerkoff," Tills said. But he remained standing where he was. Furtively he made a couple of useless swipes at his face, then wrung his hands and rubbed them together. It was futile. Fine lines of the thin, glutinous mud remained in all the wrinkles and grooves of his hands, rolls of it under his fingernails and in the angles of the cuticles. Only the ridges were clean, giving his hands a curious two-tone effect, as if he were trying to imitate his own fingerprints. He still did not move his feet. "To hear you tell it."

By contrast Mazzi looked extraordinarily clean. Even though he was wet to the skin. He had not joined in the mudplaying, although he had been willing to laugh and yell with the rest, and had cheered on the ones who did.

"That's right," he agreed. "Except for me and a couple my better acquaintances around here who are the ony ones around here who are hep. Come on I said goddam it. Let's get this fuckin thing up."

"Look, Mazzi." Tills still did not move. "I want to ast you somethin. You think there's any fucking germs in this mud?"

Mazzi stared up from where he squatted by the tentsite, momentarily surprised into speechlessness. "Germs?" he said finally. "Germs." He too wiped the water from his face again, thinking. "Sure there's germs. All kinds of germs."

"You really think so?" Tills said in a worried voice. He looked down at himself. For the moment imagination had made him totally defenseless.

Mazzi continued to stare up at him sensing this, his face beginning to take on a pleased look. He grinned maliciously. "Why, hell yes. Dont you read the papers? This island's loaded with all kinds a germs. Any kind a germ you want this island's got it. And where do you find germs? In dirt, dopehead. What kind a germs you want?" He held up a hand and began ticking splayed fingers. "Malaria germs—"

"—Malaria germs are in the mosquitoes," Tills interrupted sullenly.

"Sure but where do they get them? From the dirt. There's—"

"—No," Tills interrupted again. "They get them from other people who got malaria."

"Okay, sure. But where they come from first? Everybody knows that. Germs come from dirt and bein dirty." He went on ticking his fingers. "And then there's dinghy fever germs, and jaundice germs, black water fever germs, jungle rot germs, dysentaria germs—" Mazzi was onto the other hand by now. Still grinning up at Tills, he stopped and threw both hands away into the air expressively. "Hell, what kind of a germs you want? You name it this island's got it." He paused.

"Christ," he said looking pleased with himself. "You'll probly be sick as a dog tomorra, Tills."

Tills regarded him defenselessly. "You're a son of a bitch, Mazzi," he said after a moment.

Mazzi raised his mobile eyebrows, together with his expressive shoulders. "Who? Me? What'd I do? You ast me a question. I answered it for you. Best as I could."

Tills did not make any answer and continued to stand looking at Mazzi in an attentive, defenseless way, the wet muddy canvas draped around his feet. Still squatting by the tentpegs Mazzi grinned back at him.

"You dint see me down and slidin around in that mud, did you? Sure, I laughed and hollered and cheered them on. That never cost me nothin. Trouble with you, Tills, you're a jerkoff. A born jerkoff. You're awys gettin sucked into somethin. Take a lesson, kid. You dont see me gettin sucked into somethin, me and my better acquaintances around here who are hep.

"Right, Tills?"

Smug complacency dripped from his use of the word "kid." Mazzi was several years the younger. Tills did not answer him.

"Now come on. Let's get this thing up," he said. His face squinted up again: "before you get so sick you can't even help me. One guy can't put up a puptent by himself. Hell, if you get real sick, I'll have the whole tent to myself. Hell, maybe you'll get so sick you'll be lucky and they'll ship you out—if you dont die."

Without speaking Tills stopped and gathered up the stiff, wet mass of canvas and started with it over to the tentsite where Mazzi, still grinning at him complacently, rose to help him spread it.

"Look at them goddamn blankets," Mazzi said pointing at them. They had stuffed them under a tarp covering some equipment. "Would you mind tellin me, Tills, how a man is gonna sleep in blankets like that tonight? Would you? Hunh?" he demanded. But when Tills did not answer he did not bother to repeat the question as they fell to stretching the canvas over the first pole.

Around them other men were working in the rain and other sheltertents were going up in the long, even lines. Everyone tried to avoid walking where the little tents would sit but it did not help. The force of the rain itself was enough to turn the ground into a mire. Without cots they would have to spread their soggy blankets on this quagmire, and then on top of them protect what halfdry clothes they could find. It was going to be a miserable night for everyone but the officers whose sleeping tents, cots and bed rolls were always carried with the company, and it would not be pleasant for them.

This was the last chore and since it was not yet nightfall, naturally a number of the more adventuresome wanted to have a look at the jungle. They had nothing to lose, they could not get any wetter. One of them was Big Queen, the huge Texan. Another was

Private Bell, the former Engineer officer. A third was Pfc Doll, the proud pistol thief. In all they were twenty.

Doll swaggered over to his pal Corporal Fife, his rifle slung from his left shoulder with his thumb hooked in the sling, his right hand on the butt of his pistol. He was ready to go. His helmet and ammunition belt completed him. Everyone had already put away his stupid gasmask. They would have thrown them away, but were afraid they might have to pay for them.

"You comin with us to have a sweat at the jungle, Fife?"

Fife had just finished putting up his own sheltertent which he shared with his assistant, an eighteen-year-old from Iowa named Bead. Bead was smaller yet than Fife with large eyes, narrow shoulders, big hips, small hands, and was a draftee.

Fife hesitated. "I don't know if I ought to. The Welshman might need me around here for something. We're not all set up yet." He looked off at the distant green wall. It would be a long walk in this rain, and a muddy one. He was tired, and he was depressed. His toes squelched in his shoes. Anyway, what would they find? Lot of trees. "I guess I better not."

"I'll go, Doll! I'll go!" This from Bead, large eyes larger than usual behind his hornrimmed glasses.

"You aint invited," Doll drawled.

"Whada you mean I aint invited? Anybody can go that wants to go, can't they? Okay, I'll go!"

"You'll do no such a goddam thing," Fife said curtly. "You'll get your fat ass in the orderly tent and do some work, schmuckface. What do you think I fucking pay you for? Now git." He jerked his head. "Go on."

Bead did not answer but stumped off sourly in his customary slump-backed gait.

"You just can't treat them decent," Fife said.

"Better come along," Doll said. He raised his lip and his eyebrow. "No tellin what we may run into or find."

"I guess not." Fife grinned. "Duty, you know." But he was glad to get out of it so easily.

Doll raised his eyebrow and his lip further. "Fuck duties!" he

said from the side of his mouth looking very cynical and knowl-
edgeable. He turned and marched off.

"Have fun!" Fife called after him cynically. But once having
decided he regretted that he was not with them as he watched
them move off in the rain.

The coconut trees ended just beyond the edge of the bivouac.
Beyond them there was nothing except flat open ground all the
way to the jungle. Across this open space the distant green wall
looked even more menacing than it had from within the groves.
At the edge of the trees the men stopped to look at it. Then, still
without raincoats but so soaked now they no longer thought about
that, they approached the high wall of jungle curiously and gingerly in the rain. Rolls of mud formed on their feet, and they kept
kicking them off.

They had all read about it for months now in the papers, this
jungle. Now they were seeing it at first hand.

At first they only skirted it, cautiously. From a distance they
made a funny sight: groups of wet men in the rain, moving skit-
tishly up and down along the jungle edge, bending and looking
and peering in here and there. It really was a wall; a wall of
leaves; meaty green leaves jostling and elbowing each other, with
hardly a minute opening anywhere between them. Peering at them
Big Queen felt you might almost expect one of them to bite back
at you if you shoved it. Spreading these—finally—and stepping
through, taking the plunge as it were, they found themselves immediately enveloped in a deep gloom.

Here the rain did not fall. It was stopped high above by that
roof of green shingles. From there it dripped down slowly, leaf to
leaf, or ran down the stems and branches. Despite the heaviness
of the downpour which now purred loudly in their ears from just
outside, here there was only a low rustle of slow occasional dripping. Everything else was supremely quiet.

As their eyes adjusted, they became able to see huge vines and
creepers hanging in great festooning arcs, many of them larger
than young trees at home. Giant treetrunks towered straight up,
far above their heads to the roof, their thin bladelike roots often
higher than a man's head. Every-where, every-thing, was wet.

The ground itself was either bare dirt, slippery, slick, with wet; or else impenetrable tangles of deadfall. Here and there a few stunted straggly bushes struggled to maintain an almost lightless life. And saplings, totally branchless with only a few leaves at the top and hardly bigger around than the width of a pocketknife, strained to stretch themselves up, up, always up, to that closed roof and closed corporation a hundred feet above, where they could at least compete, before they strangled here below. Some of them that were no bigger around than the base of a whiskey shotglass had already attained a height equal to twice that of a tall man. And in all of this, nothing moved. And there was no sound save the rustle of the dripping moisture.

The men who had slipped through the protecting wall and come in here to see, stood rooted before the enormity their adjusting eyes disclosed. This was more than they had bargained for. Whatever else you could call this teeming verdure you certainly could not call it civilized. And as civilized men, it made them fearful. The toughest barroom brawler among them was fearful. Gradually, as they continued to stand without moving, vague, faint sounds began to make themselves heard again. High up in the foliage leaves rustled or a branch vibrated and there would be a twitter or a mad, raucous shout as some invisible bird moved. On the ground a bush would shake furtively as some minute animal moved away. And yet they saw nothing.

By entering the jungle they had been as suddenly and completely cut off from the bivouac and the company as if they had closed a door between two rooms. The suddenness and completeness of the shutting off dismayed them all. But by peering out between the leaves they could see the tall brown tents still standing among the white shafts of the cocopalms in the rain: see the distant greenclad figures still moving casually and securely about among them. This sight reassured them. They decided to go on.

Big Corporal Queen moved along with them saying nothing, or at least very little. Queen was aware of a strong reluctance to be separated from the others. This jungle wasn't his meat. Back at the bivouac in the pouring rain Queen had been in his element and exultant. He had snorted and grinned and rubbed the rain into himself and his chest and clothes, and laughed loudly at the more reluctant ones who looked like drowned cats. Rain was something he knew about. Back home he had worked for a while as a hand on a ranch; he had been caught out in many a summer rainstorm, been forced to ride all day in them. He hadn't liked it then; but when he remembered it now, he remembered it as though he had liked it, that it was manly, that it showed great endurance and strength. But this jungle was something else again. The indignant thought kept coming back to him that no American would ever let his woodlot get into any such condition as this.

Big Queen would not have admitted this mild fear of his to anyone, and in fact he did not actually admit it to himself. Instead he changed it around, made it acceptable, by saying to himself that he was on unfamiliar ground here and naturally would be uneasy until he learned his way around. But it could not have anything to do with fear because Big Queen had a reputation to maintain.

Big (just over six feet, with a 56-inch chest and arms and legs to match) and exceptionally strong even for this size Big Queen was one of the sights of the organization; a myth had grown up around him in C-for-Charlie company. And once Queen discovered it (he was rather slow about certain things which concerned himself) he had—with a strange welcoming sense of having at last found his identity—done everything he could to live up to it. Searched for, the origins of this myth would almost certainly be found among an amorphous collection of small men in the outfit, men who adored and longed for a size and strength they themselves would never have, and who in their admiration had let their creative imaginations run away with them. Whatever its source, it was now established as fact rather than myth, and believed by nearly everybody including Queen, that Big Queen was invincible both in heart and physique.

His reputation imposed certain obligations on Queen. For example, he must never do anything that even remotely resembled bullying. He no longer had fights, principally because nobody cared to argue with him. But there was more to it than that because he himself could no longer argue either. Not without looking like a bully imposing his opinions by force. He no longer expressed his opinion in discussions unless it was something of really great importance to him. Such as President Roosevelt whom he worshipped; or Catholics whom he hated and feared. And then he voiced it quietly and without insistence.

Remembering how to act required a great deal of Queen's time and energy. He found himself having to think almost all the time. It tired him. And it was only when dealing with feats of strength and endurance that he any longer could let himself go and act without thinking. Sometimes he longed for them.

Right now he had another problem. Another obligation imposed by his reputation was that he must never seem to be scared. Thus he found himself in a position where he was forced to clump ahead through this damned undergrowth with an impassive face for the benefit of the others, while at the same time his imagination was cramming every footfall with all sorts of horrible results. Having an important reputation was sometimes harder than people thought. Terrible things.

Snakes, for instance. They had been told there weren't any poisonous snakes on Guadalcanal. But Queen had acquired a more than healthy respect for rattlesnakes during his two years out in northwest Texas. His snakefear if anything was more unhealthy than healthy, carrying with it an almost uncontrollable tendency to freeze into a panicstricken target. And in the jungle his imagination kept presenting him over and over with a picture of his own shod, leggin'd foot falling heavily on a coiled mass of muscular life which would erupt into a writhing, clattering, jawpopping viciousness squirming under his boot, capable of striking completely through the canvas leggin, or through the shoe leather itself for that matter. He knew them. He had killed at least a hundred of them during his two years out there on that ranch, most of which had not bothered him. Only twice had he come upon them close enough to be struck at. All the others had merely lain there, coiled and suspicious, watching him beadily, tasting him with those forked tongues, while he got his pistol out. He hated them. And the fact that the Army said there weren't any here didn't prove it; he had never seen a more likely looking place for them.

Thus equipped, Big Queen lumbered on skirting the tangles of deadfall, hoping nobody could read from his face what he was thinking, silently cursing his imagination and wishing he did not have any, remembering the snakes of his past.

It was just then, about twenty yards in, that somebody discovered the bloodstained shirt. The man raised a shout and stopped. Instinctively they had spaced themselves out at five yard intervals as if in a skirmish line, although nobody had unslung his rifle. Now they converged. As they congregated the finder simply stood, a surprised look on his face, and pointed to a spot between two narrow, shoulderhigh roots of one of the huge trees. The rest clustered around and peered excitedly. Queen, having been the far right end of the line, was one of the last to arrive.

Another of the last to arrive was Private Bell, the former Engineer officer from the Philippines. He had been near Big Queen on the right. Heavily muscled himself, Bell nevertheless looked frail alongside Big Queen. Bell, however, was no stranger to jungles. After four months of living in the Philippine jungle (without wife) that eerie, other-planet look common to all jungles held no new emotional experiences for Bell. He had come along, taciturn and retiring, keeping his own counsel as was his way, more for purposes of botanical comparison than anything else; and he had none of the trepidity or excited compulsion to look, to see, which afflicted the others. It was an interesting thing which Bell had noted before about the American Army that wherever they went, and no matter what dangers they expected to encounter, they went prepared to look and, if possible, to record. At least a third of every outfit carried cameras, lens filters and light meters tucked away somewhere. The fighting tourists, Bell called them. They were always prepared to record their experiences for their children, even though they might be dead before they could have any. Bell himself, painful as the memory was for him—and for that very reason—wanted to see the similarities between this jungle and his own so-well-remembered one (without wife) of the Philippines. It was as predictable—and in his memory as exquisitely painful—as he had expected. But when he came up to the group and looked down at the cause of the excitement, he was on the same unfamiliar ground as the rest. He, like them, had never before seen material remains of a man killed in infantry combat.

It had taken sharp eyes to spot it. A crumpled ball of khaki the same color as the dirt lay at the apex of the angle of the roots. It did not look as if someone had deliberately deposited it there, but more as though somebody had stripped it off, wadded it and flung it—either the wearer himself or someone looking after him—and it happened to land there. A crusty, black stain camouflaged it even further into the jungle floor.

There was a spate of pointless, rather nonsensical comment, all of it oddly breathless, excited.

"Where you think he got it?"

"Is it American?"

"Fuck yes it's American. The Japs dont wear khaki like that."

There was a peculiar tone of sexual excitement, sexual morbidity, in all of the voices—almost as if they were voyeurs behind a mirror watching a man in the act of coitus; as though in looking openly at the evidence of this unknown man's pain and fear they were unwillingly perhaps but nonetheless uncontrollably seducing him.

"That's chino! That's not even Marine khaki! That's Army chino!" A hollow voice.

"Well, the Americal Division's here. Maybe he's one of them."

"Whoever he was he was hit pretty bad," Queen said. It was the first time he had spoken. Queen felt curiously, but strongly, ashamed of himself for looking at the hurt man's shirt, and for the nervous excitation which possessed him in doing it.

"Wonder just where it did hit him?" A guilty voice, this one; trying to sound offhand.

It was the second time this had been mentioned. One of the men nearest it—not the finder—leaned down silently and picked it up with thumb and forefinger as if afraid he might catch a terrible disease from it.

"Here," he said, and looked pleadingly at the man next to him.

Between them they stretched it out, turned it around, turned it back—strangely like two lady clerks in a dress shop holding up a new model for prospective buyers. From within the group there was a sudden high constrained hysterical giggle.

"Now this here's from our new Spring-of-'43 collection, just out. Fits any type a figure. Wouldja like to try it for size?"

Nobody acknowledged the remark. The giggler subsided. The two men turned the shirt back and forth a few more times while the others looked in silence.

Like so many of the shirts they had all seen here it was without sleeves. It was not entirely sleeveless however, like some. The sleeves had been lopped off halfway up the upper arm, then meticulously shredded to the shoulder seam with either a very sharp knife or a razorblade to look like the oldfashioned buckskin fringe of the plainsmen.

The sight gave Big Queen, who had owned and worn a buckskin jacket during his two years as a hand, a peculiarly painful twinge. A twinge of odd loneliness—and of something else. It was that American love of cowboy fringe. It brought Queen closer in understanding to this other, unknown man that Queen liked to be. It was such a ridiculous, boyish gesture; and, intuitively, Queen understood it all too well. Much better than he wanted to understand it consciously. Because the gesture hadn't worked. It hadn't protected him at all. That much was obvious.

The bullet had entered at the bottom of the flat plane of the pectoral muscle just above the nipple and had struck bone and keyholed downward, coming out flatways below the left shoulderblade. There was not much blood around the neat hole in the front. Most of it was on the back. The fringewearer had been very unlucky. Had the bullet caromed upward it might have missed the lung. As it was, it had torn its way down and out through the center of it, moving flat instead of by the point and thus insuring even greater tissue damage.

Once again the two men, after pausing, turned the shirt back and forth a few times, its wet homemade fringe fluttering heavily. Still nobody said anything.

Bell, peering between the helmeted heads of the two men in

front of him, blinked suddenly as if struck in the face by a sea wave while swimming. Quite without preparation he had found himself staring at a horrible, halucinatory double-image of himself and that shirt. He was both standing upright wearing that pierced, lifesoaked shirt and at the same time lying pierced and lifesoaked himself on the ground after having flung it away from him, while somewhere up behind him out of eye range he could nevertheless see a weird, transcendental image of his wife Marty's head and shoulders superimposed among the foliage gloom of the trees looking down at the two images sadly. The blink did not help. The images did not go away. *Oh, I'm sorry,* he clearly heard her voice say. In an infinitely, exquisitely sad tone. *I'm so sorry. So sorry for you.* It was said with all of that vitality and force-of-life lifeforce Marty had so much of in her. *Go away!* he frantically wanted to shout at her. *It isn't real anyway! Go away! Dont make it real! Dont look! Do not pass Go! Do not collect two hundred dollars!* But he could no longer even blink, let alone shout. *Oh, I am sorry,* she called down to him, *really and truly so sorry.* And Bell knew without thinking it, without daring to think it, that half of her sorrow was because she knew as well as he that that powerful, perpetually affirming, female force for life that was in her would require her to go on living, even when she might not want to; require her to go on needing to be loved by a male, another male, even when she might have preferred not. It was in her, that female puissance; was her nature; as unstoppable as water running downhill. *So sorry, John. So sorry for you.* It faded away softly in the dripping jungle gloom, infinitely sad. Frantically, in a sheer terror at having to face sheer terror, Bell forced his eyes to blink. Then he blinked them wildly several more times. Perhaps seeing the jungle again today, after the Philippines, after so long? . . . But the most terrifying of all was that Bell knew, again without daring to think it, that if he had been alone at this moment he would have found himself wearing an erection. Out of his pain, out of the agony of his knowledge, the surety of his intuition, he would have had a full sexual erection. This at least trebled his terror. Again he blinked; desperately, this time. The two men were once again holding the shirt, that death shirt, and still not a soul had spoken a word.

"Well, what'll I do with it?" the man who first had picked it up said.

As if released from his responsibility by these first words spoken into the bellying silence, the second man immediately let go and stepped back. His half of the soggy, muddy shirt fell heavily toward the first man. The first man straightened his arm out, so the shirt would not touch him, and continued to hold it. And there it dangled, like some forever windless flag symbolic of the darker, nether side of patriotism.

"Well I mean it dont seem right— . . ." he began, and stopped. The end of the statement trailed off into conjecture.

"What do you mean it dont seem right?" Queen demanded in a suddenly furious, almost squeaky voice. He managed to pull it down into its normal deepness before finishing: "what dont seem right?"

Nobody answered.

"It's only a shirt, aint it? It aint the guy who was in it, is it? Whatta you want to do? Take it back to the compny? What'll you do with it there? Bury it? Or give it to Storm to clean stoves with?"

This was a great deal of talking for Queen. But at least he regained control of his voice, was speaking in the deep voice everybody expected from Big Queen. Again, nobody answered.

"Leave it where you found it," he said with ponderous authority.

Without a word the man (who still held it by thumb and forefinger as if it might contaminate him) turned and swung it and let it go. It fluttered back down into its angle between the roots, no longer wadded.

"Yeah, leave'm lay where Jesus flung'm," someone else said. No one answered him.

The breathless, curiously sexual look had disappeared from the faces. It had been replaced by a sullen look of sexual guilt. Nobody seemed to want to meet anybody else's eyes. They looked curiously like a gang of boys caught masturbating together.

"Yeah. Let's look around a little more," one said.

"Yeah; maybe we'll find out what happened here."

Everybody wanted to leave.

And so it was that, in such a mood, they found the battlefield and nearby to it, afterwards, the trench grave.

A curious sense of unreality had come over all of them with the discovery of the shirt. The dripping, gloomy, airless jungle with its vaulted cathedral-like ceiling far above did not serve to lessen it. Fighting and killing, and being struck by death-delivering bullets which keyholed through you, were facts. They existed, certainly. But it was too much for them to assimilate, and left them with a dreamlike nightmare feeling which they couldn't shake off.

Mutely (because of course nobody wanted to admit this essentially unmanly reaction to anybody else) they moved off through the green air of the arm of jungle in a conspiracy of silence. Their minds had balked. And when the mind balked like that, the reality became more dreamlike than the nightmare. Each man each time he tried to imagine his own death; tried to conjure up the experience of that bullet keyholing through his own lung; found himself being tricked by his own mind. The only thing he was able to picture was the heroic, brave gesture he would make when dying. But the rest was unimaginable. And at the same time somewhere in the back of each mind, like a fingernail picking uncontrollably at a scabby sore, was the small voice saying: but is it worth it? Is it really worth it to die, to be dead, just to prove to everybody that you're not a coward?

Tacitly they had resumed almost exactly their same places in the line. Instinctively and without apparent reason they all moved off to the left, leaving the line anchored in the person of Queen. And it was there, at the other, the far left end, that they found the first abandoned, tumbledown emplacements. They had entered the jungle perhaps thirty yards too far to the right to see them. Had they not found the shirt, and then had they not reasonlessly extended their line to the left, they might never have known the place was there.

The position was unmistakably Japanese. It was also clear that

it was a lost position. They had had a line here along the edge of
the jungle at some time or other, and C-for-Charlie's men had
come upon it just where it turned in from the edge to wind its way
tortuously back into the depths of the jungle. It was in acute
disrepair. Mounds and humps and ditches and holes which once
had been dugouts, trenches and parapets twisted in and out in a
continuous band of raw earth between huge tree boles and clumps
of undergrowth until they lost themselves in the dim light of the
jungle interior. Total silence hung over it everywhere except for
the occasional loud cries of birds. Eagerly in the dim light, more
than glad to forget the shirt, the men hurried over and began to
clamber up onto the mounds to inspect—with a sort of painful,
almost lascivious masochism—what they one day soon would be
up against themselves. It was beyond these mounds, where it had
remained hidden from their view because of them, that the mass
grave lay.

From the top of the mounds a look at the terrain was enough to
show that the Marines and, as evidenced by the shirt, elements of
the Americal Division had attacked or else counterattacked this
line. Slowly (that much was apparent) and perhaps several times,
they had come across the same ground which C-for-Charlie's
men had themselves just traversed. Stumps of saplings, torn undergrowth, cut vines, pitholes all showed the volume of mortar
and machinegun fire to which the ground in front of the position
had been subjected. Already, new growth had effectively hidden
most of these signs and they had to be searched for, but they were
there. Only the scarred, bullet-hacked forest giants, standing impassively like rooted columns, seemed to have survived this new
type of tropical storm without crippling effects.

Like a band of energetic ants the men spread out, poking here,
peering there, looking at everything. Souvenirs had now become
their preoccupation. But no matter how greedily they hunted,
there was almost nothing left for them to find. Quartermaster
Salvage units had been over the ground with fine-tooth combs.
Not a piece of equipment, not a single strand of barbed wire, not
even an empty Japanese cartridge casing or old shoe remained to
be picked up by scavengers like themselves. Once they had disap-

pointedly assured themselves of this, as if by a common accord they turned their rapt, still somewhat awed attention to the long mass grave.

It was here that the delayed emotional reaction to the death shirt caught up with them in the form of a sort of wild horseplay of bravado. Big Queen was the leader of it. The grave itself ran for perhaps forty yards along the very edge of the jungle, just inside the tight skin of leaves. It had been made by widening the former Japanese trench. Either it was very shallow or there was more than one layer of bodies, because here and there undecayed appendages or smaller angular portions such as knees and elbows stuck up out of the loose dirt that had been shoveled back over them.

Obviously it had been a sanitary arrangement more than anything else. Which was quite understandable, if one contemplated the acrid, bronzegreen odor that hung over the position and became slowly stronger the closer one came to the edge of the ditch. It must have been hellish before they buried them. They were of course all Japanese. An ex-undertaker, after examining a greenishcolored, half-clenched hand found sticking up near the edge, gave it as his opinion that the bodies were a month old.

It was up to the edge of this ditch, not far from where a stocky, uniformed Japanese leg thrust up out of it at an angle, that Big Queen advanced and stopped. Several men before him already had somewhat incautiously stepped out onto the grave itself in their eagerness to see, only to find themselves slowly sinking kneedeep into the dirt and dead. For men whose feet were still sinking and not resting on anything solid they all had leaped back out with astonishing nimbleness. Cursing savagely and smelling strongly they provided, to the guffaws of the others, a sterling object lesson. So Queen ventured no further.

Standing with the toes of his combat boots exactly at the edge of the solid ground, sweating a little, grinning a strangely taut, fullwidth grin which made his large teeth resemble a dazzling miniature piano keyboard in the green light, Queen looked back at the rest challengingly. His face seemed to say that he had suffered enough personal indignities for one day and by God now he was going to get even.

"Looks like this one was a healthy spec'men. Ought to be somethin worth takin home on some of them," he said by way of preamble, and leaning forward seized the shod foot and jiggled it around tentatively to see how well it was attached, then gave it a solid heave.

The surface of the ditch quivered seismically, and along it tranquil flies rose buzzing in alarm, only to settle back in the quiet that followed. In the late afternoon jungle light everyone watched. Queen still held the leg. The leg itself still remained in the ditch. After a time-dead second in which nothing moved or breathed, Queen gave the foot another, even more tremendous heave; and again the flies buzzed up in panic. The leg still held.

Not to be outdone another man standing by the ex-undertaker stepped forward and took hold of the greenishcolored half-clenched hand. This was Pfc Hoff, an Indiana countryboy from the second platoon. Clasping the hand as if in a handshake, as though he were wishing its former owner a bon voyage on his journey, Hoff took the wrist with his other hand and pulled too, grinning stupidly. In his case too nothing happened.

As though taking these two actions as their key, the rest began to spread out around the grave edge. They seemed seized by a strange arrogance. They pushed or poked at this or that exposed member, knocked with riflebutts this or that Japanese knee or elbow. They swaggered impudently. A curious Rabelaisian mood swept over them leaving them immoderately ribald and laughing extravagantly. They boisterously desecrated the Japanese parts, laughing loudly, each trying to outbravado the other.

It was just then that the first souvenir, a rusting Japanese bayonet and scabbard, was found. It was found by Pfc Doll. Feeling something hard under his foot, he reached down to see what it was. Doll had taken a quiet backseat at the finding of the blood-stained shirt, and had not said a word. He did not know exactly what it made him feel, but whatever it was was not good. He had been left feeling so depressed that he had not even bothered to hunt for souvenirs among the mounds with the rest. The trenchful

of dead Japanese made him feel even worse but he felt he must
not show this so he had joined in with the others; but his heart
wasn't in it, and neither was his stomach. Finding the bayonet by
sheer luck like that restored his spirits somewhat. Cleaned up and
shortened it would make him a better belt knife than the cheap
one he had. Feeling considerably better Doll held it up to be seen
and called out his find.

Further up the ditch on the other side Queen was still staring
fixedly at his Japanese leg. He really had had no intention of
disinterring the leg or the body at the other end of it. He was only
showing off. He only wanted to show them, and himself, that
dead bodies—even Japanese ones afflicted with God knew what
horribly dirty Oriental diseases—held no terror for him. But with
Hoff getting into the act, and trying to top him like that—And
now that punk Doll had to go and find a Jap bayonet—

Tightening his mind and his grip on the foot, clamping his jaws
even tighter in their piano-keyboard grin, Queen jiggled his leg
around tentatively once more, issuing to it as it were the final
definitive personal challenge. Then, grinding his exposed and
grinning teeth together, he began to pull on it with every ounce of
his great strength.

Standing back on the perimeter of all of this, taking no part,
Bell was nevertheless watching it all with a horrified fascination.
Bell still could not free himself from that earlier illusion that he
was in the midst of a nightmare dream, that he would soon wake
up home in bed with Marty and push his face between the soft-
nesses of her breasts to forget it. He would slide his face down
her to inhale the lifecreating, lifescented womanperfume of her
which always reassured and soothed him. At the same time Bell
knew he was not going to wake up; and once again his mind
tricked him with that weird transcendental image of Marty's presence somewhere nearby watching this. But this time instead of
seeing him as the leg in the grave, as before she had seen him
wearing the shirt, she now stood somewhere up behind him
watching the scene with him. *Brutes! Brutes! Animal brutes!* he
could hear her cry. *Why dont you do something? Brutes! Dont
just stand there! Stop them! Is there no human dignity?*

Bru-u-u-tes! It rang in his head, fading away eerily in the high gloom of the trees, as he continued to stand, watching.

Big Queen was now in the midst of making his main effort. His face was beet-red. Great veins stood out on his neck under his helmet. His big teeth, totally exposed now, dazzled whitely in his face. A high, semi-audible keening sound resembling one of those silent dog whistles came from his throat as he strained his strength beyond even his capacity.

It was clear enough to Bell that the leg was not going to pull off its body. Therefore, only two possibilities remained. Bell understood, not without sympathy, that Queen had publicly committed himself. He must now either pull the corpse out of the grave bodily, or admit he wasn't strong enough to do it. Fascinated by a great deal more than just simply what he was seeing, Bell watched quiescently while Queen fought to win his selfimposed test.

What could I have done, Marty? Anyway, you're a woman. You want to make life. You dont understand men. Even in himself there were elements of pride and hope involved; he didn't want to see Queen lose. Numb and sick as he was. Come on, Queen! Bell suddenly wanted to yell wildly. Come on, boy! *I'm* for you!

Across the ditch Doll was having an entirely different reaction. With all his heart and soul, furiously, jealously, vindictively, he was hoping Queen would *not* win. His new bayonet dangled from his hand forgotten and he held his breath, his belly muscles tensed with the effort of helping the corpse resist Queen's strength. Damn him, Doll thought with clenched teeth, damn him. Okay, so he's stronger than us; so what?

Queen couldn't have cared less about either reaction. He stared down with bulging eyes, teeth bared, his breath whistling through his nose as he strained. He was furiously convinced that the leg was stretching. Heavily muscled in the calf, wrapped in its wool leggin, bandylegged and cocky even in death, it seemed as self-confident of its supreme Japanese superiority as its former owner must have been in life. Queen was dimly aware that the others had stopped what they were doing and were watching. But he had already used all his strength. In desperation he called upon a reserve beyond his capacity. He couldn't quit now, not with them all watching. Once on a fatigue detail he had lifted a whole tree down off its freshly cut stump on his back. He concentrated on remembering that. And miraculously, the leg began to move.

Slowly, dreamily, mercifully mudcovered, the body drifted up out of the grave. It was like some mad, comically impure travesty of the Resurrection. First came the rest of the leg; then the second leg, flung out at a grotesque angle; then the torso; finally the shoulders and stiff, spreadeagled arms which looked as though the man were trying to hold on to the dirt and keep himself from being dragged out; and lastly the mudcovered head. Queen released his grip on the foot with a great gasp and stepped back—and almost fell over. Then he simply stood, looking down at his handiwork. The helmeted head was so covered with mud it was impossible to distinguish its facial features as such. Indeed, the whole body was so mudsmeared that it was impossible to tell whether it wore any equipment in addition to its uniform or not. And Queen had no inclination to get closer. He continued to look at it, breathing heavily.

"Well, I guess I was mistaken," he said finally. "I guess there's nothin worth keepin on this one after all."

As if released from their rapt state by his words a sudden spontaneous, if feeble, cheer-for-Queen broke out from among the watchers. Overhead, birds fluttered, squawked in panic and fled. Attacked by modesty, Queen smiled back shyly, sweating heavily. But the cheer, as well as any subsequent action, was suddenly choked off by a new development. From the grave a new smell, as distinct from the former greenishcolored one as if they derived from different sources, rolled up like an oily fog from around the muddy body and began to spread. With dismayed curses and astonished, pained exclamations of consternation the men began to back off, then finally just simply turned and fled, jettisoning their dignity and everything else. Anything with a nose must retreat in rout from that odor.

Bell, escaping with the others and laughing as senselessly as they, ran breathlessly. He felt curiously surrealistic, and found a new popular-song title was running through his head over and over.

"Dont Monkey Around With Death"

It ran over and over in his mind to the tune of some real song whose title he could not remember, as he made up words for it.

> *"Dont monkey around with death,*
> *It will only get you dirty;*
> *Dont futz around with the Reaper,*
> *He will only make you smell.*
> *Have you got B O?*
> *Then do not go*
> *Fiddling with that Scythe-man;*
>
> *(optional break:)*
> *Because . . .* (upbeat; pause)
> *Your best friend will not tell you;*
>
> *Dont monkey around with death;*
> *You will only wind up soiled."*

Bell reached the top of the mounds with the others, whistling his little melody between his teeth soundlessly and staring off blankly, then turned around to look back. The mudcovered Japanese man still sprawled stiffly and all spraddled out atop the ditch beside the pit his enforced disinterment had opened down into the depths of the grave there in the jungle gloom. Nearby Bell saw Doll still holding his souvenir bayonet and looking back also, with an odd faraway look on his face.

Doll was trying very hard not to throw up. That was the reason for the faraway look; it was one of intense concentration. There was a strong urge in his throat to swallow repeatedly, and Doll was trying to control it. It was not enough to refrain from vomiting; if he kept swallowing, someone would be sure to notice it whether he threw up or not. And that was unthinkable. He couldn't allow it. Especially with Queen standing not far from him.

When Queen first had stepped back from his labor, his heel had struck something metallic behind him. Wild hopes had risen in him that he might find a Japanese .31 caliber heavy machinegun or some such item, buried in the mud. He discovered instead that it was a mud-daubed helmet. He had seized it and retreated to the top of the mounds with the others.

But he got no chance to inspect his find there. It became apparent quite quickly that the top of the fortifications was not going to be far enough. By the time the last fleeing man reached the mounds, the smell like some invisible cloud had arrived too, right on his heels. There was no choice but to retreat again.

There was no fighting that smell. It was as different in kind and texture and taste from the earlier one as two smells could be. The earlier had been mild, was greenishbronze in color, acrid, dry, only slightly unpleasant. The second smell was wet and yellowwhite. It was not mild. No man who was sane and at liberty to leave was going to stay around to smell it.

They did not go back to the place of the shirt, but headed out toward the edge. Everybody had had enough exploring. At the tight skin of leaves they paused, still laughing senselessly, and looking back like Hallowe'en pranksters who have just upset the outdoor toilet of a farm. It was there that Queen finally got time to inspect the helmet.

It made a pretty poor souvenir. They all had heard that Japanese officers had stars of gold or silver on their helmets. Real gold, or real silver. If that was so, this was the helmet of a junior private. Its star was iron—and very thin iron at that, and badly bent. The outside of the helmet was covered with mud, but inside though badly sweatstained it was curiously clean.

Looking at it, this gave Queen a sudden inspiration. He had had a curious sense of oppression after dragging that poor damned muddy Jap corpse out of its final resting place—as though he knew he had done something bad and would be found out and punished for it. The oppression had abated somewhat during the stumbling, laughing, breathless trek back out to the jungle edge.

And, instinctively in a way he could not have formulated, Big Queen sensed he had at hand the means of vanquishing it completely. By making himself laughable and ridiculous he could both atone and at the same time avoid admitting he needed to. Removing his own GI helmet Queen put the Japanese one on his head and struck a pose, throwing out his great chest with a silly grin.

There was a burst of uproarious laughter from the others. Queen's head was too big even for an American helmet, which rode high up on his head like a hat. The Japanese one, made to be worn by small men, did not come down over his head at all; it sat up flat on top of it. The chinstrap did not even come down to his nose, but hung in front of his eyes. From behind it Queen peered out at them. He began to caper.

Even Doll laughed. Bell was the only one who didn't. He grinned, and gave a short bark, but then his face sobered and he eyed Queen shrewdly. For a second they looked into each other's eyes. But Queen would not meet his gaze and looked away and unwilling to meet Bell's eyes after that, went on with his farce for the others.

It had stopped raining while they were in the jungle. But they had not known it. The falling moisture, trapped high above and retarded in its descent, had continued to drip down—and would continue to long after—just as if it still rained outside. With surprise they stepped out to find the sky was blue again, and the washed air clear. Almost instantaneously, as though Storm had been watching with binoculars for them to reappear through the green wall, the chow whistle sounded clear and shrill across the open ground from within the grove. It was an intensely familiar, curiously heartwringing sound to hear here, studded with memories of secure evenings. It rose and then fell away to silence in the late clear island air which carried a feel of the sea. And it shocked the explorers. They stared at each other, realizing that those dead Japanese men were really dead Japanese men. From the hills the mortarfire and small-arms fire of some struggle came down to them clearly, faintly, reinforcing the opinion.

They returned to the bivouac with Queen in the lead, clumping along and capering in his tiny enemy helmet. Doll dangled his new bayonet, showing it first to one then another. The others trooped along, and laughed and talked again after their shock. They were anxious now to tell their adventure to the rest of the company who had missed it. Before morning Big Queen's forcible disinterment of the dead Japanese man had been added to the company's annals of myth and legend, as well as to Queen's own.

That night at supper C-for-Charlie received its first dosage of atabrine. It had been decided not to dose the new troops until arrival because of the large number of jaundice cases the atabrine was causing. The pills were brought down in the bulk in cans from battalion medical.

Storm took over the administering of it himself, ineptly assisted by the company's first medic, whose job it really was. Standing at the head of the chow line by the Lister bag so the men could draw water, with the mild, bespectacled, unauthoritative medic standing helplessly behind him, Storm doled out the yellow pills, chaffing everyone goodnaturedly, but belligerently determined that nobody was going to avoid taking his pill. If a cynic threw back his head with dramatic abandon and brought down a closed hand, Storm would make him open it and show it. Only a few tried to deceive a second or third time. In the end, before he got his hot food, each man knew the gagging, bitter taste which made them all retch.

Because the meal *was* hot. Storm, sporting his singed, wrapped hand, had succeeded in that if in little else. All he had to serve was fried Spam, dehydrated potatoes, dehydrated sliced apples for dessert. But in the chill wet the men were grateful, even if only the coffee was real. The coffee, and the atabrine.

"What the fuck do you bother so hard for?"

The tall blackbrowed Welsh spoke coldly from just behind Storm's elbow as the last man was force-fed his pill and sloshed away down the line in the mud. Storm had no idea how long he had been there. He had come up and elbowed the selfeffacing medic out of the way in silence. Storm refused to turn around or be startled.

"Because they going to need all the fucking help they can git," he said, just as coldly.

"They going to need a lot more than that," Welsh said.

"Than help?"

"Yeh."

"I know it."

"And as for that shit," Welsh said.

"Least it's somethin." Storm looked down at the box of pills and shook it. He had counted them out carefully, so as to make sure each man got one. A few remained.

The last man in the line had stopped and was looking back at them, listening. He was one of the draftees and his eyes were large. Welsh glanced at him.

"On your way, bud," he said. The man went on. "Ears stuck out a foot," Welsh said with a thin look.

"Some of them so dumb they actu'ly wouldn't take them," Storm said. "If I didn't make them."

Welsh stared at him expressionlessly. "So what? They don't take them maybe they'll get asshole malaria so bad they'll get themself shipped out and save their fucking useless life."

"They aint learned that yet," Storm said. "They will."

"But we'll be ahead of them. Won't we? We'll make them fucking take them. Won't we? You and me." And Welsh grinned his sudden mad, evil grin; then as quickly and suddenly he removed it. He continued to stare at Storm somberly.

"Not me," Storm said. "When it gets down that low, I let the officers take over."

"What are you, a fucking revolutionary anarchist? Dont you love your country?"

Storm who was a Texas Democrat and loved President Roosevelt almost as much as Queen did not bother to answer such a silly question. And as Welsh said nothing further, the two men simply stood and stared at each other.

"But we know the secret, dont we? You and me," Welsh said in a silky voice. "We already know about not taking them, dont we?"

Again Storm didn't answer. The stare seemed to go on and on.

"Gimme one," Welsh said at last.

Storm held out the box. Without taking his eyes from Storm's face Welsh reached down, got a pill, popped it into his mouth and swallowed it dry. He continued to stare at Storm.

Not to be outdone Storm got one himself and swallowed it as Welsh had, dry, and stared back. He could taste the yellow gall of it spreading in his throat, incredibly bitter. Luckily, when he had first learned to drink whiskey he had also learned the trick of pressing your tongue against the roof of your mouth and not letting in any air. Also, as he had seen the astute Welsh do, he had thumbed the surface chemical dust from the pill as he picked it up.

With all the expressiveness of a stone Welsh stared at him another twenty seconds, apparently hoping to see him gag. Then he turned on his heel and strode off. But before he had gone thirty feet he executed an accurate aboutface and came striding back. Everyone was off eating. They two were alone.

"You know what it is, dont you? You realize what's happened, what's happening." Welsh's eyes brooded across Storm's face. "There aint any choice. There's no choice left for anybody. And it aint only here, with us. It's everywhere. And it aint going to get any better. This war's just the start. You understand that."

"Yeh," Storm said.

"Then remember it, Storm; remember it." It was all very enigmatic. Welsh turned and strode away again.

Storm stared after him. He had understood it. Or at least he thought he did. But what the hell? If a man's government told him he had to go and fight a war, he had to go, that was all. The government was bigger than him and it could make him. It wasn't even a matter of duty; he *had* to go. And if he was the right kind of a man he would want to go, no matter how much he didn't really want to. It didn't have anything to do with freedom, for Christ's sake. Did it? Storm looked down at his box again. He could still taste the incredible bitterness of the dry pill and repressed a desire to gag. There were nine left, three for his cooks on shift and six for the officers. If only it hadn't had to go and rain on them like that, God damn it, the very first thing. Storm slapped at a mosquito on his bare elbow, perhaps the fiftieth within an hour. Well, at least the rain had stopped.

Storm was being optimistic. Whether the rain had stopped actually made very little difference. It was perhaps nicer not to have to eat standing in the rain, but the main damage was done. In this humid, saturated air their soaked uniforms were only just beginning to dry on their bodies. It was next to impossible to clean a rifle in so much mud. And after supper, with their blankets wet and their sheltertents nearly awash, there was nowhere to go and nothing they could do. Then night fell. One moment it was full daylight in the coconut groves—late light it was true but still full day; the next moment it was full, black night and everyone was groping around surprised, as if they had all gone suddenly blind. Soon after this novel experience they had another. They got their first taste of the nocturnal air raids.

At the moment that night fell upon them like a huge flat plate young Corporal Fife was sitting in the corner of the orderly tent. He was trying to arrange his files and his portable typewriter without getting mud on them. He had one small portable table upon which to attempt all this. The job was doubly hard because whoever designed the table did not foresee that it might be used on a mud floor. One or another of its legs was continually sinking slowly into the mud and throwing the top off level, threatening to spill everything. When the swift, sudden fall of night blinded him, Fife gave up in despair. He simply sat, his grimy hands placed flat upon the unlevel tabletop, one on either side the little typewriter like tools put away upon a shelf. And during the five minutes it took to get a hooded blackout lantern lit and going, while other people groped around him trying to get this job done, he did not move. Now and then he rubbed his muddy fingertips against the grained wood of the tabletop.

Fife was suffering from a deep depression of an intensity he had never known before. Even his eyelids seemed immobilized by this slumping awareness of his total inability to cope. All the little dirts of life were attacking him en masse, threatening to destroy him, and they terrified him because there was nothing he could do. He could not even keep his files clean. He was wet and filthy

dirty. His toes squished in his wet socks in his shoes, and he had
not heart or energy to go and change them. Tomorrow he would
probably be sick. Mosquitoes swarmed around him in the dark
and bit his face and neck and the backs of his hands. He did not
even attempt to dislodge them. He simply sat. Temporarily he had
ceased to function. He stagnated in the close darkness, consciously rotting toward some indefinite future death, and the most
painful thought of all was knowing that eventually he would have
to move again. He continued to touch the mudgritty tips of his
fingers against the tabletop.

Undoubtedly part of Fife's distress came from not going off
with them to see the jungle when Doll asked him. If he had gone,
it might just as easily have been himself who found the bayonet
instead of Doll. But he hadn't thought it would be exciting. It
seemed to Fife that he was always missing out on all the exciting
things simply because he couldn't tell beforehand which ones
would be. But he had pretended Welsh might need him. He hadn't
had the guts, and had been too lazy. And so he not only missed
finding the bayonet, he also missed being in on Big Queen's
unbelievable feat—which had been the topic of every conversation since their return.

Fife himself had approached his old friend Bell, who had been
there and had seen it, wanting to learn the visual details truly
firsthand. But Bell had only stared at him with blank eyes as if he
didn't know him, muttered something incomprehensible, and
walked away. It hurt Fife's feelings after all the things he felt he
had done for Bell.

But with everybody else it was the only thing they could talk
about. Even here, before the night had fallen upon them bodily so
suddenly, the officers—all of whom were hanging out in here as
if this were their club—had been discussing it among themselves.
And when the shaded lantern was finally lit and got to going, they
went right on talking about it. Just as if, in the interval of darkness, nothing devastating had happened to Fife, still sitting there
in his corner.

"God damn you, Fife!" Welsh bawled at him, outraged, as
soon as there was light, turning from the lantern. "I told you to

get over here and fucking help me with this goddam thing! And all you did was sit there! Now get up off your ass and get to work around here!''

"Yes, Sergeant," Fife said. His voice was utterly toneless. He neither moved nor looked up.

From across the tent Welsh sent him a sudden sharp glance. It penetrated through the tobacco smoke and renewed din of conversational voices, straight into his face. Even when he wasn't looking Fife felt it. He tried to prepare himself for a tirade. Then, curiously, Welsh turned back to the lantern without a word. Fife continued to sit, grateful to him, but too numbed in what he thought of as his mudcaked soul to think further, and listened to the officers discuss Big Queen and his feat.

It was unnecessary to record in his mind the words they said. It was enough to watch their expressions and catch their inflections. Without exception they all laughed with a constrained embarrassment when they spoke about it. Without exception they were all proud of Queen—but they could not be proud of him with the same raucous, cynical amusement of the men, so that their pleased amusement carried a slight overtone of shame. But they were proud. Corporal Queen'll be making Sergeant very soon, Fife thought absently, you watch. Well, he didn't mind. Big Queen deserved it if anybody did. And it was just then that somewhere far away down the long aisles of the groves in the night the klaxons began their mournful, insistent belching.

Panic and an objectless fright seized Fife and he surged up off his watercan blindly. By the time he reached the tent door the panic had changed to normal apprehensiveness and a morbid curiosity to see. He was not alone at the tent flaps, he realized, as he came to. Everybody else had done the same thing and he was in the midst of a crowd.

"Wait!" Welsh bawled behind them. "Wait, God damn it! Wait'll I shut this fucking lantern off! Wait!"

The man in front of Fife—whoever it was; Fife never did find out—hesitated with the tie ropes, as if caught in a monumental indecision. Then the tent was plunged into blackness. There was more fumbling and cursing in front of Fife. Then everybody, officers and men alike, surged outside through the opened flaps past the hanging blanket into the clear, fresh, star-scattered night. They carried Fife along with them in the press. He couldn't have stayed inside if he had wanted. All of them looked up at the sky.

They were not alone. Every other member of C-for-Charlie had come out too, from wherever they had retired to nurse their chilled damp bodies. They had all been told to dig slit trenches, but in actual fact only six holes—the six for the officers; which were dug by details under orders—had been made by the entire company. If anyone regretted it now (and Fife, for one, did) nobody said so out loud. They stood in the mud in a straggling uneven crowd among the three big tents alongside the rows of smaller ones, talking little and craning their necks up at the sky, trying to see something. Anything.

What they saw was two or three weak searchlight beams feebly fingering the sky and finding nothing, and now and then the single quick blink of an antiaircraft shell exploding.

They could hear a lot more than they could see. But what they heard told them exactly nothing. There were the klaxons, which kept up their long, monotonous, insane growling protest all through the raid. There were the machinelike, repetitious reports of the various-sized antiaircraft guns pumping their useless shells up into the night sky. And finally there was the stuttering, thin sound of the motor, or motors, up there in the dark. It was impossible to tell from the sound whether there was one plane or were several.

Everyone tried—not very successfully—to conceal his nervousness. This was Washingmachine Charley, or Louie the Louse as he was also called with less wit. All of them had heard about him of course: the single plane who nightly made his single nuisance raid, and who had been nicknamed by the stouthearted American troops. This information was in all the news communiques. And in fact, because of the great height, the sound did resemble the noise made by an antiquated, onelung Maytag washer. But the nickname proved to be generic; it was applied indiscriminately to all raids of this type, whatever the number of planes, or the number of raids per night. The news communiques tended to minimize this point. Anyway, it was much funnier to read about Washingmachine Charley in the communiques than it was to discuss him here as they stood looking up into the unfamiliar tropic constellations of the night sky, listening, and waiting, and slapping absently at hordes of feasting mosquitoes.

Finally there came that almost inaudible sighing sound which their hearts had memorized this morning. There was an instinctive ducking motion among them, like the passing of a breeze over a wheatfield, but nobody went to the ground. Already, their ears had learned enough to know these were too far away; and the ground was muddy. From far away down the groves in the direction of the airfield came the ca-rumping explosions, walking slowly toward them in great giant strides. They counted two sticks of five each, one stick of four (perhaps with a dud). If Washingmachine Charley was one plane, he was certainly a big one. In the profound silence that seemed to follow, the laughable antiaircraft guns kept on sturdily pumping their ridiculous shells into the sky for several minutes more. Then the klaxons all down the line began sounding their short, sad, barking belches which signaled the allclear.

C-for-Charlie began to laugh and snort and pound each other on the back. Down the long aisles of cocopalms the klaxons kept on with their short, maniacal barks. Officers and men alike, they appeared to be congratulating each other on having personally ended the raid. This lasted almost a minute, then the officers remembered their dignity and separated themselves. The klaxons stopped. Within the two groups the laughter and backslapping went on for several minutes more. Finally this too wore itself out, and with halting steps because of the darkness they straggled back to their places of shelter looking sheepish and hoping no real veterans had seen their violent display, and once again began trying to protect themselves against the chill and wet.

That was the way they spent the night. Nobody slept. There were five more raids during the course of the night and if Washingmachine Charley was one single man, he certainly was an energetic one. He was also sleepless. So was C-for-Charlie. In one raid the last bomb in the last stick landed a hundred yards in front of them damaging an antiaircraft position and killing two men—all quite by accident, of course. It was close enough (that huge earfilling impersonal rushing flutter descending like an express train) to put them all down on the ground and wet and muddy them up again and next day two chesthigh rents were found in the sides of the supply tent. Everybody speculated upon the fact that if there had been one more bomb in that particular stick it might well have landed very close to the center of their bivouac. In the morning when they all came out into the warm, revivifying safety of the sun and looked into each other's stubbled, dirtcaked faces from which human eyes still peered, they found they all were looking at changed men.

During the next two weeks they changed more. Labeled "acclimatization period" by the division's plans and training section, this two weeks sifted itself down into a peculiar double rhythm. There were the hot sunny days of comparative safety on the one hand, and on the other nights of wet chill, mosquito clouds, klaxons and terror. And the two really had nothing at all to do with each other, had no continuity between them. There was a great deal of joking laughter about fear during the days, because in the sunshine the nights did not seem believable. But when dusk came, that swift purple tropical dusk, whatever had happened during the day was laid aside, not to be taken up until the morning, as they prepared themselves for the night. The days might be ones of work or loafing or perhaps a little training. The nights were always the same.

Daily everyone bathed in the nearby stream, whose official name was Gavaga Creek they learned. Every evening they shaved, with stream water heated in their helmet shells over little fires. There were—in the daytime—further excursions to the jungle and to the site of Queen's feat. The swiftly moldering Japanese man still sprawled on top the trench. This position they had discovered in the jungle marked the site of the final phase of the Battle of Koli Point. A large Japanese force had been surrounded and destroyed here, and it was possible to trace the entire perimeter of the Japanese fortifications in and out of the jungle along Gavaga Creek. They did this. It did not affect the nights. There were excursions to other points of interest. They went to the beach, to Koli Point itself, to the big home of the plantation manager, now full of shell holes and abandoned. A couple of groups, on different days, even ventured as far as the airfield, which was several miles away, bumming rides on trucks along the soupy roads through the endless groves of coconut. At the airfield in the hot, lazy sun bombers took off and landed. Mechanics worked in the shade of the cocopalms bare to the waist. The groups bummed rides home again. And everywhere they went or looked, both coming and going and all along their route, trucks and men were busily laying up great caches of stores for the coming offensive. The offensive of which, they remembered, they themselves were going to be a part. All of this still did not affect the nights.

The hot tropic sun was marvelous to sit and soak in, after one of these nights. It rejuvenated and refreshed, bringing with its heat and its daylight the daily return to sanity. There was always a slight breeze to rustle the fronds of the palms. They made a dappled, swaying shade on the ground. From it the fetid smell of the tropical mud rose with warm, humid, overpowering force.

It was not all play however. Almost daily new ships arrived to unload troops and supplies. Details of platoon strength, commanded by their own sergeants, were requisitioned to help with the unloading. It was the same work they had watched with awe on the day of their arrival, and they became veterans of it, and of the occasional daylight raids. On the days when no ships arrived the same details were needed to help move the supplies away from the beach, back to the huge caches within the groves. Every morning there was an hour of intensified calisthenics, ridiculous to everyone but required by division order. They made a few tentative little practice marches, hardly more than walks. One whole day was spent on an improvised rifle range testing and firing weapons. None of this affected the nights.

Nothing affected the nights.

It was always the same. There would be supper. Then there would be an added half hour, perhaps, of reprieve. Then the dusk would come while they sat and watched helplessly, powerless to prevent it. Then it would be night. On the morning of the second day they all had dug slit trenches without further orders or urging. They now slept ready to leap into them with increasing proficiency, wet or not, whenever the klaxons sounded. To stumble up half awake and fight your way out of your mosquito netting. (Never fully to sleep, only half sleep, in the first place.) Then to grope your way out to that hole outside the tent. To lie there numb and dumb and nervous, scared, target for millions of mosquitoes, if not for bombs. To fumble your way back inside afterward in the darkness and try to laugh it off while in fact you were embarrassed. These were the nights. It was not heroic. It was merely undignified. Nightly they acquired more and more the aspect of suspicious, sullen cats. Faces glowered and eyes burned. Finally it would be day and they would take up their lives once more.

This strange schizophrenic life, this separation of nights and days, was enhanced when they were ordered to move their bivouac. They had spent three days hunting down their lost tents, cots and mosquitobars, a fourth day getting them set up, and two days living with them. Then they had to move and do it all again—a hard job entailing a long trek by truck, manhandling of the canvas, redigging all of their slit trenches. Making it even more difficult was the fact that at least one and usually two platoons were absent every day at the beach. Probably the reason for it was to put them closer to the unloading area to make them more available for work. But they did not know, because no one told them. Some logistics expert worked it all out on a chart. The result was to put them much closer to the airfield, so that now instead of having only one bomb land near them occasionally, they were right in the middle of it and the personnel bombs, known as daisycutters in the trade, were exploding all around them every night. And while such a move for such a reason might have its ironic, funny side from a certain point of view, it was not laughed at much in C-for-Charlie.

Back at the old bivouac there had been an element of decision available. It was possible to ask yourself whether to go out to your hole, or not to go and be brave and stay in bed. Generally it was answered in the affirmative. Most went. But at least indecision was possible. At the new bivouac no such choice existed. You got out and you lay in your hole. And you were glad.

It was strange that only one man was wounded. A distinct impression existed that there should have been many more. And of course there were, in other outfits around them. The one man wounded in C-for-Charlie was Pfc Marl, a Nebraska cornball and dry-dirt farmer. Long and work-gnarled, a draftee who had not wanted to leave his father's farm, he had never much liked the army anyway. A piece of a daisycutter whistled into his hole as he lay in it during a raid and cut off his right hand as neatly as a surgeon could have done with a knife. When Marl yelled, two men nearby leaped in with him and put a tourniquet on him until the medic could get there. The bomb had landed thirty yards away and by this time the giant strides had already marched on anyway.

Marl thus became the first actual wounded casualty in the company. It was bad luck for him. He was treated with the same upsurging consummate tenderness as the wounded at the beach had been, but he did not like it any better than they. Everything was done for him that could be, but Marl became hysterical and began to blubber. Never very bright, he could not get it through his head that he would still be able to work.

"What'm I gonna do now, hey?" he cried at his helpers fretfully. "How'm I gonna work, hey? How'm I gonna plow, hey? I mean it. What'm I gonna do now, hey?"

Sergeant Welsh tried to soothe him by telling him how he was all through now, how he could go home, but Marl would have none of it. "Take it away!" he cried at them. "Get that damned thing out of here! I dont want to look at it, goddam it! It's my hand!"

The hand was taken away by one of the two company medics, who was supposed to be trained at this kind of work but actually was not as yet, and who stopped to vomit behind a tree. Because no one knew what to do with it, since all felt it deserved an obscure respect, it was later buried by Storm out behind the mess tent under a log. But its absence did not aid Marl to bear his misfortune. He refused to be placated by descriptions of what marvelous artificial hands they made nowadays.

"Goddamn it, it's easy for you!" he cried. "But how'm I gonna work?"

"Can you walk?" the medic asked him.

"Sure I can walk, goddam it. Fuck yes I can walk. But how'm I gonna work, hey? That's the point."

He was led off into the darkness to the battalion medical station and C-for-Charlie saw him no more.

The increased bombing affected different people in different ways. Fife, for instance, discovered he was a coward. Fife had always believed he would be as brave as the next man, if not perhaps a little more so. He realized with surprise and dismay after two raids that he not only was not more brave, he was actually less so. This was fierce news but there was no way out of facing it. When he laughed and joked after a raid, it was plain to him that his laughter was more shaky and less sincere than the others' laughter. Doll, for instance. Obviously they did not shiver and shake in their holes as he did, did not cringe without dignity in the mud. Obviously they were only scared; whereas he was terrified, would have given anything he possessed in the world— or anything he did not possess, if he could get his hands on it— not to be here defending his country. To hell with his country. Let somebody else defend it. That was how Fife honestly felt.

Fife would never have believed he could react like this, and he was ashamed of it. It affected the way he regarded everything in life—himself, the sunlight, the blue sky, the trees, skyscrapers, girls. Nothing was beautiful. A desire to be somewhere else constantly trickled up and down his back in vague muscular spasms, even in the daytime. Worse was the knowledge that these violent, raging twinges did him no good at all, did not change anything, affected nothing. It was awful to have to admit you were a coward. It meant he would have to work harder at not running away than the others. It was going to be a hard thing to live with, and he knew he had better keep his mouth shut about it and try to hide it.

Pfc Doll on the other hand—he whom Fife envied—discovered

two good things about himself and was pleased by both. One of them was that he was invulnerable. Doll had suspected this, but had not been willing to trust his intuition until he had proved it beyond shadow of doubt. Twice now—one of them the night Marl lost his hand, when Doll had been not far away—he had forced himself to stand up in his hole when he heard the bombs start down. The muscles of his back were jumping as though trying to buck a rider, but there was a testicletingling, excited pleasure in it too. Both times he went untouched—although the one time Marl had got his close by. Doll felt this proved it. And he felt twice was enough to prove what he desired to know. Especially since in the other raid the bombs had landed even closer than the ones that got Marl. Both times, afterward, he had sunk down in his hole triumphant if exhausted, his knees trembling in a strange way and he had not done it more than twice because it took too much out of him. But he was glad that he had proved it.

Doll also found out he could convince everybody he had not been afraid. It all went back to that thing he had learned in his fight with Corporal Jenks. You acted out your fiction story and everyone accepted it. Thus he could laugh and josh about the raids, pretending he had been scared, yes, but not really terrified. And whether it was true or not didn't matter. Doll was almost as glad to learn this as he was to prove he was invulnerable.

A third reaction was that of Sergeant Welsh. Welsh discovered something, too. What Welsh discovered, after all these years of wondering, was that he was a brave man. He reasoned this way: any man who could be as terrified during these raids as he was and not either roll over and die or else just get up and walk away forever—that man had to be brave; and that was him. Welsh was glad, because he *had* wondered; and when Welsh sacrificed himself to United States property and to the properties of the world, he wanted to be able to do it grinning sardonically. And he now felt that he could.

There were other reactions. There were in fact as many various reactions as there were men under the whickering bombs. But however various, there was in all of them one constant: Everybody wished these nightly air raids would stop. But they didn't.

There was one night of relief for them in the two weeks. Regimental Headquarters, functioning as a unit now after its separation into echelons for the sea voyage by transport, opened up a post exchange. C-for-Charlie only learned of this at all through the loyalty of their regular company clerk (a sergeant; Fife was only the forward clerk) an Italian boy from Boston named Dranno (and of course universally known as "Draino") who being stationed with the personnel section knew about it and came and told them. The entire stock of this new PX consisted of two things, Barbasol shaving cream and Aqua Velva shaving lotion. But this information was enough to cause a run on the store. Inside of seven hours the entire stock of Aqua Velva was sold out, although there was plenty of Barbasol left for those who wanted it. The trouble was that the other company clerks were just as loyal to their outfits as Draino was to C-for-Charlie. Nevertheless, members of the company managed to buy enough bottles of Aqua Velva so that everybody was able to get solidly drunk for one night.

Mixed with canned grapefruit juice from Storm's kitchen supply, the shaving lotion did not taste at all. Grapefruit juice seemed to cut all the perfume out of it. It made a drink rather like a Tom Collins. Everyone loved it. There was a number of cases of men stumbling into the wrong slit trenches during the raids. There were several sprained wrists and ankles. And there was one bad incident where a drunk dived into the latrine by mistake when the klaxons sounded. But for one night at least, one glorious memorable night, there was relief from the spraying daisycutters. Many men went right on sleeping through every raid. And those who did not didn't give a damn that night—about air raids or anything else—and trooped out to their slit trenches laughing and sportive.

Meanwhile, life in the daytime went right on. Two days after the Aqua Velva party there occurred the most important thing to happen to C-for-Charlie since their arrival. This was the discovery, in a tent near the airfield, of a cache of Thompson submachineguns which they were able to send a raiding party after and steal. This triumph was largely due to little Charlie Dale, Storm's belligerent little second cook, who not only found the guns but also—if he did not actually organize the raid—certainly stumped for it and was its sparkplug.

Dale did not like working in the kitchen and never had. A lot of this was due to having to work for Storm whom Dale considered too authoritarian. Dale might ride his shift of KPs overhard, and was noted for this, and secretly was proud of it; but that was only because you couldn't make them work any other way. But Storm—Storm was in the habit of demanding an instantaneous and unquestioning obedience from his own cook force which not only seemed to imply he didn't trust their abilities, but also that he did not even trust their motives, their good faith. Dale resented this. Also, for a long time now, he had felt Storm did not like him personally for some reason. Twice Storm had passed over him for promotion to first cook. Both times Dale should have had the job. And yet Storm had not said a word to him. Dale had not forgiven him for this, either.

Like many others Charlie Dale had come into the Army from a career of two years in the CCCs, enlisting as soon as he became eighteen. He had not cooked in the Cs—or anywhere else—beyond frying himself a couple of eggs once in a while. He had come into Storm's kitchen after six months as a rifle private because on regular duty—contrary to his expectations—he had remained lost in the shuffle and mass of khaki ciphers. If he left the kitchen, he would lose his rating and his authority and go right back to that. And Dale had no intention of getting lost again. He stayed in the kitchen. But he did not have to like it.

Because he didn't like the kitchen, and because on Guadalcanal cooks naturally were exempt from the unloading details when off shift, Dale had taken to going off by himself on exploring trips whenever he was off duty. It was on one of these trips one hot still afternoon, while wandering along the edge of the dust-blown airfield under that drowse-producing, perpetually midsummer sun, that he found the tent full of guns.

Dale did not at first know what was in it but he was struck by the fact that it was isolated. There was a bivouac perhaps thirty yards away in the cocopalms, deserted and lazy under the heat of the sun. The tent itself had all its flap ropes tied shut. But it wasn't locked; how could you lock a tent? His curiosity aroused, Dale lifted a loop from one of the wall stakes and slipped inside. It was stifling hot in the tent and in that dim, peculiarly pleasant, lazy-making light of hot sun shining through tentage canvas, rack after wooden rack of guns filled the interior like rows of pews. Seven of these worshippers, all in their own row, were Thompson submachineguns. At the front the altar was a raised platform stacked with drums and clips of .45 ammunition and their canvas carriers. Both clips and carriers bore the Marine Corps stamp.

The rest of the congregation were .30 cal Springfields, and a few of the new .30 cal carbines which had only gotten to C-for-Charlie recently. All mused at their devotions in the dim hot air while Dale stared at them. A closer inspection revealed that the working parts showed no signs of wear. They were all brand new. Yet they had the grease cleaned off them and stood ready for immediate use, freshly oiled. There they were. In the tent, as outside, the hot stillness of Sunday revival meeting reigned.

Dale was overjoyed. Here was any old soldier's dream of a perfect piece of thievery. It was too good to be true. And from the Marines, yet! One for himself, of course. But what about the other six? And those carbines? Greedily and with chagrin Dale realized he couldn't possibly carry all of the Thompson guns even. Let alone enough .45 ammo to supply them. It was a shame to waste them.

Then there was another thing. If he took just one—for himself—and some ammo, what would he do with it? The moment he showed it at the company he would be in danger of having it confiscated. And it was then that the idea of not taking any now, but instead coming back on a raid, struck him. With enough guys maybe they could even take some of those delicious carbines.

If he could get any of the officers interested, enough to come along for one themselves, then they wouldn't dare to confiscate his. At the same time it would be a big boost to the reputation of the guy who found the guns and thought of the idea—namely, Dale. Him. Me. Young Lt Culp of the weapons platoon, who was a former Dartmouth football player and was always laughing and kidding around with the men, would be the one. Or maybe he would go to Welsh. Welsh would always be game for anything like this. In either case, he was not going to say anything to that bastard Storm, who if he wanted a Thompson gun could go and find it for himself.

Having figured it out to his satisfaction, Dale ducked back outside and carefully replaced the wall loop over its stake. But then he stopped. He could not help but feel he was leaving behind an opportunity which was too good to let go. Maybe they had sentries on this place, he would have, and the sentry was just goofing off somewhere asleep. They might come back to find the place guarded, out of reach. And Dale wanted one of those tommy guns so bad it made his hands itch. Especially since Storm had announced publicly that he was going up into the line with the outfit, and would take with him any cooks who wanted to go. Well, when he put it that way, who would dare to say he didn't want to go? Certainly not Dale. Even though the pit of his stomach felt hollow when he thought of it.

After a minute of standing lost in thought in the hot sunny afternoon with his hand resting on the warm tent seam, Dale loosened the loop, ducked back in, selected one of the Thompsons. With it and all the drums and clips he could cram into two of the canvas carriers, he ducked back out, refastened the loop and walked away into the cocopalms. He headed back toward the bivouac. A few of the men he met stared at him but seemed not to think his equipment odd, even though he was carrying his rifle as well. He did not enter the bivouac but instead turned off toward the jungle where it came closest to the company area. Inside the jungle he left the new gun hidden and went to the bivouac for a shirt, returned and wrapped the gun in it carefully, then hid it and the ammo in a hollow beneath the tall roots of one of the giant trees. Only then did he saunter into the bivouac, whistling innocently with his hands in his pockets, to look for either Welsh or Culp.

It was Culp that he found. And the Lieutenant's broad fleshy face with its broken pugnose wreathed itself in a happy acquisitive smile, when in his hoarse belligerent voice Dale told him of the find.

"How many are there?"

"Seven. I mean, six."

"Six Thompson guns," Culp savored it slowly and gave a low whistle. "And you say all the drums and clips we can carry?" He paused, and appeared to be licking his chops. "This will require thought and planning, Dale. Yes sir. Yes, *sir!* Thought and planning." Culp rubbed his footballplayer's hands together. "Three men would be enough, if it was just the guns. But with the ammo—We're going to need that ammo, Dale," he said nodding; "we're going to need it. Every bit of it and every clip we can get. Because can you imagine me going up to Regiment and asking for an issue of .45 ammo for six Thompson guns we aint even supposed to have? Yes, sir! Now let me think a minute," he said but did not pause more than a second. "We're going to have to take this to Captain Stein, I'm afraid. Yes, I think we'll have to take it to Captain Stein."

"Well, will he go along?" Dale said. He stared at Culp stonily out of his flat, narroweyed face. He did not like the idea of bringing Bugger Stein in at all.

"If he gets one for himself out of it?" Culp made a wise smile. "I wouldn't see why not. I would myself, I know that. Wouldn't you?"

"I aim to," Dale said flatly.

Culp nodded, but absently, a faraway greedy look in his eye. "Yes, sir. Yes, sir. And anyway, he'd find out soon enough when he saw us sporting those tommyguns around here; and then what? Yes sir, if I had anything to say about it, Dale, you would get the first medal of the war to go to old C-for-Charlie. We need more men like you, Dale."

Dale flashed him a pleased smile. But he did not relinquish his point. "Well, what about takin Sergeant Welsh in on it, instead?"

"We'll take him, too. We'll take him, too. But we've got to tell Captain Stein. Dont you worry. He'll go along. You just leave it to me. Leave me worry about everything, Dale." He slapped his big hands down on his knees and pushed himself up. "Come on, Dale. We got things to do, things to do. Now, what do you think? I think mid-afternoon tomorrow. Just the same time you went there, you see. Night's too dangerous; might get shot. And evening's bad because that's when everybody in the outfit's home for supper.'' He was already striding off toward the orderly tent and Dale with his much shorter legs had almost to run to keep up.

In the end they took seven men. Dale could not say exactly how much .45 ammunition there was—except that there was a lot—and Culp wanted to be sure and get it all. As it turned out, they could have taken nine or ten and still not have carried off all of it.

Perhaps Stein would have refused them permission, except for the loud enthusiasm of Culp. Certainly Stein was not very hot on the idea. But there was no stopping Culp. Culp did everything, including convincing Stein. He even thought of borrowing pistols for them so they would not have to carry their rifles and thus could porter back more loot. He waved his bighanded arms around the orderly tent like windmill blades. Dale stood against the wall of the tent in silence, his flat face a careful mask, and let them talk.

Culp and Welsh chose the personnel. Naturally membership did not get very far outside the club. Dale was the only man below staff sergeant in the party. And Dale had the feeling they would not have invited him if they could have found an honorable way out of it. But it was Welsh, not Culp, who suggested taking Storm.

Dale was furious. But he daren't tell them that the reason he had gone to Culp and Welsh in the first place was in order to keep Storm out. He continued to stand against the tent wall in silence and watched half his own reason for the raid go down the drain. Storm, when called in, said nothing. But he gave his second cook a glance which showed he understood. And Dale knew Storm would not forgive him soon.

So they had their personnel. They were Culp, Welsh, Storm, Dale, MacTae the young draftee supply sergeant, and two of the platoon sergeants: one officer, five sergeants, and Dale.

They were very nearly six sergeants and Dale. Bugger Stein—even after he allowed the raid, and accepted one of the Thompson guns—still did not feel he should allow an officer to go. What if they should get caught? How would that look at Battalion? And at

Regiment? An officer leading an organized raid to steal guns! On the other hand Stein had before him the example of what he thought his father the Major would have done in the First War. It was a difficult decision, and Stein took quite a while in making it.

Stein had been confused and rattled by the air raids, too. He did not know whether as an officer and commander he should stay up in the open or get down in his hole like everybody else. It was a constant battle every night, and every raid. It was heroic to walk about and disdain to take shelter as officers had done in Napoleon's time. And he could have done that. But it was common sense, in this war, to take care of yourself and protect your government's investment in you, not get yourself killed pointlessly in some air raid. Every raid made an exhausting decision for him before he finally went to his hole, and it was the same sort of thing now with this decision.

In the end he let Culp go. Culp was damn near irrepressible, that was the truth. But it was Stein's father the Major and his example that finally decided the issue. Stein could remember stories of his father's about the thieving expeditions they had carried out in France. These were what gave him a mental picture he could follow as a policy. He did not want to look like an old maid, a wet blanket who ruined all the fun with overcautious advice. It was easy for Culp who was young and without responsibilities to go around yelling and enthusiastically waving his arms. Culp did not have this company to run, and to answer for. When Stein looked at Culp he found himself realizing the price he unwittingly had paid for the command of a company which he once had wanted so badly. Brusquely, in a way which he felt effectively covered up his sad, sagging sense of age, he gave his consent.

"There's only one thing," he said again; "officially. Officially I dont know anything about it. What you men do without my knowing about it isn't my responsibility. When you go, you're on your own."

He thought that was a rather well-rounded, powerful statement of his position. He thought he had stated it boldly and well, and he was pleased by this. But his pleasure was negated by the sentiment which attacked him when he remembered he would soon be leading these same exuberant men into battle—battle in which some of them would surely die, very possibly including himself.

But with Culp Stein drew the line. None of the other officers could go. That was a flat-out order by Stein, and the faces of the other three young platoon officers fell. All of them wanted to take part in the raid.

The only officer who didn't want to go was George Band, the exec—who nevertheless did want one of the submachineguns, and got it.

First Lieutenant Band did not agree with, or like, the way his superior had handled this whole matter of the gun raid. Band was a tall, stooped, emaciated high school teacher, an OCS graduate whose spine had not been straightened by close order drill, a possessor of strange bulging eyes which looked as though they ought to require glasses and did. But Band felt he knew the Army. If you were going to command a company, you had to command it. You simply could not give the impression that you were letting your subordinates sway you in your decisions. Only by avoiding that, or even the semblance of it, could you truly command. And only by commanding could you stimulate and cause to grow that intense and closely knit working relationship of true comradeship, which should exist between the souls of men who had shared the rigors and shocks of combat, and which was the greatest human value of combat. Any other course led to fractionization, not unity. And that unity was what differentiated human men from the various beasts of the world.

There was, for Band, a mysterious quality of deepest, most manly friendship which could exist between men who shared the pain and death, the fear and the sadness of combat—and the happiness, too. For there was happiness. Happiness in doing your best, happiness in fighting by the side of your friend. Band did not know where this powerful, manly friendship came from, or what exactly caused it, but he knew that it existed and there were times when Band felt closer to the men in his outfit than he had ever felt to his wife.

But Band knew that the closeness could not be achieved as

Stein was trying to do it: by giving them their head and letting them have their way. You had to let your men know where they stood. You had to make it plain to them what they were allowed to do, and what they weren't allowed. Your men wanted to know that. If Stein wanted Culp to go, he should have said so at first, not let himself be talked into it—or else he should have refused and stuck by it. Just as he should sit down on that insolent Welsh and bring him to heel, and should have done it long ago.

Band said nothing of all this, however. It was not his place to interfere—especially with junior officers and sergeants present. All he said out loud was his modestly murmured request for one of the guns—which he knew Stein would let him have, as soon as he asked for it. And Stein did.

With two Thompson guns siphoned off the top by the element of command, that left four. It was decided to apportion these beforehand to avoid argument after. Culp of course got one. Dale, who continued his cautious silence and did not mention the one he had hidden in the woods, was allowed one as the finder. And Welsh and Storm, being the next two men in line of rank, got the other two. MacTae, the young supply sergeant, didn't want one anyway, because he was not going to go up with the company; he was only going along on the raid for the lark. The two platoon sergeants had to be content with carbines, but both were glad enough to have the chance to go.

All this was decided the afternoon of the raid, with the seven raiders standing excitedly around the orderly tent wearing their borrowed pistols, shortly before taking off.

The reason Dale had not mentioned the seventh gun was because he did not fully trust in the successful completion of the raid. With his country suspicion of authority, he feared his Thompson might wind up in the possession of Bugger Stein or Brass Band (as Tall George was sometimes called) before the raid ever commenced—in which case, if the raid was unsuccessful, he would be out of luck. After the raid was over and successful, he brought it out of its hiding place in his slow deliberate way, pretending to grin sheepishly at his own dishonesty—thus elevating it to the plane of humor, where everyone was forced to laugh.

The extra, unexpected gun went to MacTae—who had changed his mind and decided that, when the time came, he too would go up and see what combat was like, as Storm and all the cooks were going to do.

The time came much sooner than any of them had anticipated or expected.

The sounds of mortar and small arms fire off in the hills had grown steadily louder, growling more angrily, day by day. The excited little jeeps scurrying along the mud roads bearing highranking officers with mapcases had gradually increased in number, and in their speed. This much C-for-Charlie knew. And yet, when their orders finally came to go up, everybody was astonished and surprised. Partly of course it was because they somehow had never quite believed this time would come, this moment arrive. Their own orders to move seemed to burst upon them suddenly and resoundingly—echoing in their ears like an explosion in a cave.

Corporal Fife was sitting on a watercan in the sun outside the orderly tent when Bugger Stein and his driver, Stein with his mapcase across his knees, roared up in the company jeep. Before either of them jumped out Fife knew by the look on their faces what they were coming back to say. Fife realized then that the hollow echoing he was hearing was not an explosion in a cave after all, but the slow bumps of his own heart perched beneath his swallowing mechanism. Reluctance and anticipation pulled him excitedly in two directions. If his excitement got the least bit stronger, he was afraid it might turn to open fear, perhaps uncontrollable.

Fife had been a bystander at the conferences over the submachinegun raid only a few days before. He had not yet forgiven Welsh for that. He had wanted one of those guns, and to go on that raid, so badly that it made his face twist into a gargoyle mask whenever he thought about it.

He had even broken his solemn promise to himself never to ask Welsh for anything. He had asked Welsh outright. During a lull, of course; when nobody else was around to hear. He didn't even ask for a gun. All he wanted was to go along. The darkbrowed sergeant had merely stared at him—stared with a deliberately feigned astonishment, while his black eyes kindled murderously.

"Kid," he said; "I want that sickbook with them three new malaria cases in five minutes. Flat."

That was all. Fife did not think he would forget the shame of it during the rest of his life. He did not believe even the terrible demands of combat could erase this brand. The thought of it made his flesh itch, still.

During those two days while the event of major importance which was the gun raid was happening to the company, something of minor importance had happened to Fife. He had been visited by his second friend—second counting Bell, that is, Fife's other friend. Though lately Fife was about ready to give up and stop counting Bell. This second friend of Fife's was a man named Witt, and he had been transferred out of the company two months before the outfit sailed.

This man Witt was a small, thin, Breathitt County Kentucky boy, an old Regular, a former Regimental boxer. He had been in C-for-Charlie several years. His transfer had been a fine object lesson to Fife, an interesting study of the ways in which armies worked.

Shortly before its troops were hurled bodily into what was officially called Final Training Phase, a new company had been created in the Regiment. Existing first on paper as a directive from the War Department, and dreamed up for reasons largely technical and uninteresting to anyone not a student of tactics, this new unit was called the Cannon Company. There already was an Anti-Tank Company. But in addition to using its new type guns as antitank defense, Cannon Company was to be able to elevate them for use as artillery, and was to serve as a tiny artillery force within the Regiment, capable of putting heavy fire down quickly onto targets of platoon- or company-size.

Admirably conceived on paper, and existing only on paper, men were still needed to make Cannon Company an actuality. This was accomplished within the Regiment, by a strange process which might well have been named "shunting the crud." Fife observed how it worked. A Regimental memorandum was sent out ordering each company commander to donate a certain number of men. The commanders complied and the worst drunkards, worst homosexuals, and worst troublemakers all gathered together under one roof to form Cannon Company. This command was then given to the officer in the Regiment whom the Regimental Commander liked least. Witt was one of the men donated by C-for-Charlie.

Witt, though a drunkard (like most), was not one of the worst drunkards, and neither was he a homosexual. He could perhaps, by a loose application, be classed as a troublemaker—since he had been busted several times and twice had gone to the stockade on a Summary Court Martial. All this made him something of a romantic hero to Fife (though perhaps not on a level with Bell) but it did not endear him to Stein or Welsh. Still, he was not unique, and other men who were not sent to Cannon Company had had similar careers. Witt's trouble was that he had earned the personal enmity of Welsh by arguing back, because he did not like Welsh. Welsh did not like him, either. In fact, each thought the other stank, totally and abominably, without relief or reservation.

Though he refused to go and ask to stay, Witt was unhappy at being transferred. All his friends were in C-for-Charlie, and he liked the reputation he had there. As Witt saw it, everybody knew he loved C-for-Charlie and for Welsh to transfer him out while knowing this only proved his total contempt for Welsh correct, thus making it even more impossible for him to ask to stay. So he was transferred in silence, along with several real drunkards, and two homosexuals. And now he had come back for a visit.

Cannon Company along with other elements of the Regiment had arrived almost a month earlier with the first echelon of the Division. They had had a good deal more time to become "acclimatized," and Witt now had malaria. He looked wan and there was a yellowish tinge to his skin. Never heavy, he was now even thinner. He had kept his ears open for news of the old company and whenever a transport arrived with troops had tried to find them. He must have repeated this process twenty times. Finally he had been rewarded. He had been on the beach with a work detail the day they arrived, but had missed them because he was up at the other end unloading the other ship. So he had started out to find them. It was harder than it sounded. The island was jammed to boiling with men and matériel. After persistent inquiry he finally found someone who knew where they were bivouacked—only to find when he arrived (after slipping off and going AWOL and making the long walk up the island) that they had moved. He had had to start the whole thing over again. The feat was indicative of Witt's stubborn patience. It was a quality Fife wished he had more of himself.

Fife was overjoyed to see him, especially after the downhill route his friendship with Bell had taken lately. Also, Fife was not unaware that—for another reason—Witt admired him as much as he admired Witt. Fife admired and heroized Witt for all of the manly, tough, brave qualities he had; but Witt secretly admired Fife for his education. Fife was not above playing to this flattery.

As it happened, Witt showed up on the very afternoon of the gun raid. Fife had, only just a short time before, stood and watched the seven raiders depart without him. Perhaps that had something to do with what happened between him and Witt, afterward. At any rate, it was a half hour after his sour observation of the raiders' departure that he went outside for a break and heard himself hailed by a man standing some distance off near the supply tent and leaning against a cocopalm. It was Witt, who had made up his mind not to come near the orderly tent where his archenemy Welsh would be, and so had decided to wait here until his friend came out. Fife couldn't make out who it was at the distance. He went over to him.

"Well, Witt! By God! How are you! Christ, it's good to see you!" he cried as soon as he recognized him, and rushed to shake hands.

Witt grinned, not without some triumph, in his taciturn way. But he looked tired and worn. "Hi, Fife."

For Fife, on this miserable disease- and death-ridden, frightening island, it was like finding a longlost brother. Witt allowed himself to be pumped by the hand and pounded on the back, grinning triumphantly all the while. Then they went off and sat down some distance away on a downed cocopalm log.

Mostly, Witt wanted to know about the company, and when it was going up on the line. He had seen Big Queen, and Gooch, his special pal, and Storm (who fixed him some hot Spam sandwiches, for the lunch he'd missed) and some of the others he used to know. But while he was happy to see them all, still nobody could tell him anything about the company. He thought perhaps Fife could. Though he was glad to see him, too, of course, naturally. He had, in fact, been waiting more than half an hour, and wouldn't have left without seeing him.

"But aren't you AWOL?"

Witt shrugged, and flashed his shy—but proud—grin. "They won't do nothin to me. Not in that stinking outfit."

"But why didn't you come on in and get me?"

Witt's face hardened, almost as though someone had modeled his features in quicksetting cement and Fife was watching it dry. His eyes took on a curiously flattened, deadly look—with which he stared at Fife. "I aint goin noplace where that fucking, poorly son of a bitch is."

Fife suffered a trace of spinechill. There was something oddly snakelike about Witt at certain times such as this—like a coiled rattler ready to strike and certain it is right and, although this was only instinct, or perhaps because of that, completely satisfied in its own tiny mind. You know it is useless to argue with it. Also— because Witt was staring at him—Fife could not escape a feeling that Witt was personally insulted by his suggesting Witt might be willing to go where Welsh was. This made him uncomfortable.

"Yes, well," he said. He shifted on the log. "Well, you know, I think maybe he's changed some, Witt. Since we got here." He did not really believe this.

"That son of a bitch aint never going to change. Not in no way," Witt stated.

Fife believed he was right. Anyway, he could never argue with statements. "Well, I tell you. It just won't be the same old company, Witt," he explained. "Going up there without you in it. It just won't, that's all. I wish you were goin with us." He fidgeted on the log. "And I guess that's why I said that." He essayed a pleasantry he did not entirely feel. "How's the old shootin arm?" Witt was a crack shot.

Witt ignored the compliment. "Fife, I tell you. When I think of old C-for-Charlie goin up there into them Japs without me, it like to breaks my heart. I mean it." His eyes became all right again as he leaned forward to talk seriously. "I been in this compny— what now?—four years. You know how I feel about this compny. Everybody does. It's my compny. It aint right, that's all. It aint. Why, who knows how many of the guys, how many of my old buddies, I might save if I was there. I belong with the compny, Fife, old buddy." Suddenly he slumped back on the log, his say said, his face morose. "And I don't know what I can do about it. In fact, there aint a fucking damn thing I can do."

"Well," Fife said cautiously, "I think if you went around to Stein and told him how you feel, he'd arrange a transfer back for you. Old Bugger knows how good a soldier you are. It never was a question of that. And right now he's feeling pretty warm and sentimental about the compny, you know, leading them into combat and all."

Witt was leaning forward again, his eyes shy and warm as he listened eagerly. But when Fife stopped he sat up straight and his face stiffened again.

"I cain't do that," he said.

"Why not?"

"Because I cain't. And you know it."

"I honestly think he'll take you back," Fife hazarded, cautiously.

Witt's face darkened, and undischarged lightnings flickered in his eyeballs. "Take me back! Take me back! They never should of made me go! It's their fault, it aint mine!" The storm receded, passing away inward. But the cloud, sullen and dark, remained. "No. I cain't do that. I won't go to them and beg them."

Fife was irritated now, as well as uncomfortable. Witt had a habit of making you feel that way—without ever meaning to, of course. "Well—" he began.

Witt interrupted. "—But I want you to know how much I appreciate you tryin to help." He smiled warmly.

"Yeh."

"I mean it," Witt said urgently.

"I know you do." There was always this fear of disagreeing with Witt, for fear you might make him mad. "What I was about to say was this. Just how bad do you want to get back into the compny?"

"You know how bad."

"Well, the only way you're going to do it is to go to Stein and ask him."

"You know I can't do that."

"Well, God damn it," Fife shouted, "that's the only way you'll ever get back in! And you might as well face it!"

"Well, then I guess I just won't get back in!" Witt shouted back.

Fife was tired of it. Here it was the first time he had seen him in months. Also, he could not help thinking about his own encounter with Welsh, and of the seven departing raiders. But mostly it was just general irritation.

"Then I guess you'll just have to stay out, won't you?" he said, thinly and in a provoking way.

"I guess I will," Witt said, glowering.

Fife stared at him. Witt was not looking at him, but was staring moodily at the ground. Somberly, he cracked his knuckles one by one.

"I tell you it aint fair," Witt said looking up. "It aint fair, and it aint square. Any way you look at it. It aint justice. It's a traversty of justice."

"It's travesty," Fife said precisely. He knew how careful Witt was of his words. Witt was very self-conscious about his vocabulary, having taught it to himself by working crosswords. But Fife was irritated. "Tra-ves-ty," he repeated, as if teaching a child.

"What?" Witt was staring at him disbelievingly. He had been still thinking about his martyrdom.

"I said you pronounce it tra-ves-ty." Anyway, he had an ace in his sleeve. He knew Witt would not hit him. Witt would not hit a friend without giving him one free warning. It was against his goddamned, stupid Kentucky code.

But if he did not expect to get hit, Fife was astonished by the reaction he did get.

Witt was staring at him as if he had never seen him before. The storm cloud with its flickers of impending electrical discharge had come back on his face.

"Take off!" he barked.

Now it was Fife's turn to ask: "What?"

"I said take off! Leave! Get out! Go away from here!"

"Shit. I got as much right here as you have," Fife said, still startled.

Witt did not move. But it was more ominous than if he had. Calm murderousness flamed in his face. "Fife, I never hit a friend before in my life. Not without givin them fair warnin they aint friends no more. I don't want to start now, either. But I will. If you don't take off right now and go, I'll beat the livin hell out of you."

Fife attempted to protest. "But what the hell kind of talk is that? What the hell did I do?"

"Just go. Don't talk. You and me aint friends any more. I dont want to talk to you, I dont want to see you. If you even try to talk to me after this, I'll knock you down. Without a word."

Fife got up from the log, still startled and stunned, still confused. "But, Christ, for God's sake. I was only kidding with you. I only—"

"Take off!"

"Okay, I'll go. I don't stand a chance with you in a fight and you know it. Even if I am bigger than you."

"That's tough. But that's life," Witt said. "I said, go!"

"I'm going. But you're crazy, for God's sake. I was kidding you a little." He walked off a few steps. He could not quite make up his mind whether he was being cowardly or not, whether it was more manly to go back and stand on pride and get beaten up. After a few more steps he stopped and turned back. "Just remember the only way you'll ever get back in the compny is like I told you."

"Take off!"

Fife did. He was still unsure whether he was acting cowardly or not. He thought maybe he was. He felt guilty about that. He felt guilty about something else, too, terribly guilty, though he could not say exactly what it was. He was willing to accept that Witt was right and that he had done something terribly mean, vicious and insulting, something destructive to Witt's manhood. At any rate, he felt as he had when he was a child and had done something he knew was terribly wrong. General guilt loomed over him like a mustardcolored cloud. Halfway to the camp he stopped again and looked back. Witt was still sitting on the downed coconut tree log.

"Go on! Beat it!"

The words came to Fife faintly. He went on. At the door of the orderly tent he stopped and looked back again. Witt was gone, nowhere to be seen.

Now he had lost his other friend, as well as Bell—to whom he must have done something also, although despite his guilt for that too, he could not figure out what it was. Two real friends, Fife thought, out of all these guys—and now he had lost them both. At a time like this. All he had left now was Welsh. And that was something, wasn't it?

He brooded about it, about Witt, trying to construct in his mind other ways it might have ended, for several days—every day, in fact, up to the day that he sat outside the tent on a watercan and looked across the strapped-down windshield at Stein and his driver, and knew what they were coming back to say. And it was essentially a friendless Fife who watched them clamber out and come toward him—which was no way to be to receive the news they brought.

"Corporal Fife," Stein said briskly. He was being formal, official and efficient today. As well he might be, Fife thought, considering the news.

"Yes, sir?" Fife tried to make his voice smooth and unshaky.

"I want every officer and platoon grade noncom who isn't out on a detail here in five minutes. Get them all. Dont miss anybody. Get Bead. Send him around too." Stein paused and took a breath down into his chest deeply. "We're moving out, Fife. We're moving out for the line. We leave this time tomorrow. In twenty-four hours."

Behind him the driver was nodding his head at Fife vigorously in a nervous, or perhaps sad confirmation.

CHAPTER 3

Along the route of march the arteries of runny mud were clotted with stalled trucks. All faced in the direction of the march. Sometimes two or three or four were lined up one behind the other. Most were abandoned, sitting silent in the mud, waiting for the big tractors to come haul them out. Now and then there was one which had a knot of men around it who still struggled with it hopelessly, swarming kneedeep in the black soup. All of them were loaded with either the wirebound cases of C ration, three-handled jerrycans of water or brown chests of small-arms ammo, cases of grenades, or the clusters of black cardboard tubes containing mortar shells. Obviously supply by the big trucks was failing, or had failed.

The foot marchers picked their way over drying mud rolls and mosquito-laden hummocks along the edges. The stalled trucks were no problem to them. Loaded down with full packs and extra bandoliers, they couldn't have waded out to them if they had tried. Each company marched in a ragged single file, strung out to its fullest length, at one place bunched up to the point of having to stand still, at another spread out so that the gasping men must run to catch up. In the heavy sun the heat and humidity bore down on them, leaving them sweatdrenched, with stinging eyes, and gasping for air where there seemed only to be moisture.

In some ways it was not unlike a gala, allout, holiday parade.

As far as the eye could see in both directions the two lines of overladen overheated greenclad men picked and stumbled their way along the edges of the river of mud. A Fourth of July excitement spread electric tentacles everywhere. Working parties, when they paused to ease their muscles, looked always toward the road. Men with nothing to do came out from their bivouacs to watch, and stood in clusters in the edge of the coconut trees, talking. Only a very few, possessors of more brass than the majority of men, ventured out to stare more closely. These marked the individual faces of the gasping marchers, as if wanting to memorize them. But except for the ghouls there was a curious respectfulness.

Occasionally, rarely, some watcher would call out an encouragement. His answer, if he got any at all, would be a half wave of a hand, or a quick dark look and a forced grin. The marchers needed every spark of concentration they possessed simply to keep going. Any thoughts beyond that remained their own. After an hour's marching, even such private thoughts were displaced. The infantry forgot where it was going in the urgent immediate problem of getting there, of keeping going without dropping out.

Not all solved it. Slowly a new line was forming on each side, between the watchers and the road. Suddenly a marching man would turn aside and step out of line and sit or fall down. Others simply fainted. These were generally dragged aside by the men behind them. Sometimes the already exhausted pulled them over.

Almost always all of this was done in silence. Once in a while some still-marching man might call out hopefully to a beaten friend. But that was all. The watchers in the halfshade of the trees did not offer to help. And the stricken themselves seemed to prefer it that way. Few even attempted to crawl into the shade. They simply sat, dulleyed and lolling back in their packs as if sitting in armchairs; or lay in their packs on their sides facedown; or, if they were able to shuck out of their packs, stretched flat on their backs with fluttering eyelids.

C-for-Charlie Company's march was one of seven and a half miles. At eleven in the morning, with a last look back at the slit trenches, kitchen fly and tied-down storage tents which served them as home, they moved out for the road edge to await a gap in the stream of moving men. They arrived at their assigned guide point at seven-thirty and nearly dusk, half dead, and by eight were encamped there in the jungle beside the road. Over forty-five percent of them had fallen out; and the last of the stragglers, heat prostrations and breakfast vomiters did not cease coming in till after midnight.

It was an incredible march. No one in C-for-Charlie, including the old timers who had hiked in Panama and the Philippines, had ever experienced anything like it. Early in the morning Bugger Stein had had hopes—had dreamed—of bringing his company in full strength without a man missing; of being able to go up to the battalion commander and report to him that he for one was all present and accounted for. When the head of the column, with Stein still shakily in the lead, turned in off the road, Stein could only laugh at himself bitterly.

Tired and shaky and still sweating after checking the platoon areas, he walked alone along the road to the battalion CP further up ahead nearer the river, to report.

He had had a strange hystericky encounter with his clerk Fife on the march. It had upset Stein, then had made him hotly furious with injured ego. Now it colored his blue mood as he walked along the road in the gathering twilight. The whole thing was strange. To take eight and a half hours to march seven and a half miles was strange enough. Add to that the terrain and it was stranger still: that march through the coconut groves with those people standing around watching like a bunch of frustrated gravediggers: after that striking the Trail and marching inland always between two crowding, gloomgreen, bird-chattering walls of jungle. They had been marching almost six hours by then, and everyone was near-hysterical. At the front of the column four of the cook force had already fallen out, and two of the company headquarters: little Bead and a new man, a draftee named Weld who because of his age had been attached to the headquarters group as a sort of combination runner and assistant clerk. All these were somewhere behind. Overhead, birds squawked or made piercing, ironic whistles which seemed specifically directed at the marchers.

Fife had been complaining for some time in a gasping, painful, wildly emotional voice that he didn't think he could go on. Then, after a ten break, he had not gotten up right away with the rest. Stein had turned to him thinking to help, to encourage.

"Up you come, Fife. Come on, boy. You dont want to give up now. Not after you've made it this far. On those poor old aching feet."

The reaction he got was startling. Fife did not get up. He leaped up. As if stabbed in the ass with a needle. On quivering legs, quivering all over, he broke out in a mad fit of rage and abuse.

"You! You tell me! Whadda *you* tell me! I'll be walking when *you're* on your back! I'll be going when *you* and all these other guys—" his head described a wild arc—"are on your knees and out! *You* and any other goddamned *officer!*" With trembling fingers he was getting back into his pack.

"Shut up, Fife!" Stein had said sharply.

"Any goddamned fucking officer in the world! I'll walk till I drop dead—and when I do, I'll be ten feet in front of *your* dead body! Don't *you* ever worry about *me* quitting!"

There had been more of this sort of talk. Staggering in his pack, Fife had lurched out onto the edge of the road. He did not shut up.

Stein had not known what to do. It was up to him to make an issue or not make one. Fife was past the point of caring. Stein knew the theory of slapping an hysterical man back into his senses, but he had never actually done it himself. He was a little hesitant to try it, fearing that somehow it might not work. Or of course he could have put him under arrest and charged him. He had plenty of charges. Stein decided to do neither. In silence he walked to his place at the head of the column and raised his arm and the company moved out.

They were marching in two lines now, here on this narrower road in the jungle, one line on either side. Two files behind him Stein could hear Fife as he continued to curse and rage. Nobody else seemed to care, or paid much attention, they were all too tired. But Stein could not be sure he had not lost face with his company by deciding to ignore Fife. This tormented him and inside his helmet his ears burned. He maintained his silence. After a while Fife ceased of himself. The column marched in silence. On the other side out of the corner of his eye Stein could see Sergeant Welsh. (He had sent Band to the rear to try to cut down the straggling.) Welsh marched along with his head down, communing with some element of himself, and looking as though he were out for a walk and had felt no fatigue all day. He took frequent gargles from his Listerine bottle of gin, which infuriated Stein. As if Welsh was fooling anybody. At the side of the road in the thick leaves, almost in Stein's ear, some mad tropic bird screamed at them irritably, then whistled shrilly as though it had seen a woman.

His anger when it came on him, marching, had not come until some little time after Fife subsided. But when it came it was potent. His neck swelled and his whole head burned inside his helmet. He was so furiously angry it blurred his eyes until he feared he would trip and fall down and lie there and howl senselessly. He hated them, all of them. You break your ass trying to look after them, be a father to them. And all they do is hate you for it, and for being an officer, with a hard, ignorant, stubborn endurance.

Fife had not fallen out.

Stein continued along the twilit road. He was sunk in a morose melancholy. To be honest, he had to admit he carried a certain guilt about Fife. He had always had rather mixed feelings about him. That he was an intelligent boy he had no doubt. And he had made him corporal nine months back because of this, and because he did his work well—even though this meant an assistant squad leader had to remain a Pfc. In addition to this, Stein had allowed Fife two mornings a week off to attend some courses at the university in the town where the division was stationed, when the new law giving free tuition to servicemen first came out.

He liked the boy. (And he thought he had proved that.) But he could not help feeling Fife was emotionally unstable. He was flighty, and inclined to be overimaginative. Highly emotional, he lacked the ability to control his emotions which might have given him good judgment. Of course he was still only a boy. But after all he was twenty. Stein did not know his background in detail, but he felt that somewhere along the line (mother feelings; defeated father competition; suchlike) Fife had become a case of arrested adolescence. There were so many like that in America today. In the Civil War men of twenty had led regiments, even divisions. In practice in the company none of this made any difference. The boy did his work and except for an occasional angry flare-up at Welsh (for which nobody could be blamed!) kept his mouth shut. But it was because of all this that Stein had felt he could not wholeheartedly recommend Fife for Officers' Candidate School.

Back when War Department was deep in its campaign to get talent entered in the ninety-day OCS, Stein had encouraged a number of his high school graduates and more intelligent noncoms to apply. Almost all were accepted and all but two graduated with commissions. One day in the orderly room, in a moment of inspiration coupled to a misdirected desire to do good works, he had suggested to Fife that Fife apply for the Administrative School—as distinct from the Infantry School, because given Fife's personality as Stein read it, Stein did not believe Fife would make a good infantry officer. Fife's first reaction was to balk and refuse; and Stein should have left it at that. But to Stein it was obvious that Fife was imitating his hero Welsh who, whenever he was approached about OCS, merely snorted and looked as though he were going to spit on the floor. So later Stein tried again; because he felt it was for the good of the Army, as well as Fife.

The second time was what tore it. It still made Stein angry to think about it. The second time he was asked Fife said he had changed his mind, that he would apply, but that he would not apply to the Administrative School; if he was going to be an officer at all, he said with some highly tragic emotionality Stein did not clearly understand, he wanted to be an infantry combat officer. Stein did not know what to do. He did not want to come out and tell Fife to his face he didn't believe he would make a good infantry officer. This was the position he had got himself in by trying to do good works, to help the Army and Fife.

In the end he helped Fife fill out his application and signed it and sent it in. After all, every soldier had a legal right to apply. But Stein did not feel he himself had any moral right to be dishonest in his recommendation. He sent in his character analysis of Fife and his honest opinion, which was that he did not think Fife would make a good infantry officer. It was the only thing he could see to do.

The application came back immediately. To it was affixed a note from the Regimental S-1 saying: *What the hell? Don't give me all this Pro and Con crap, Jim. If you don't think a soldier will make a good Officer, why the hell send me his application? I got more papers than I can take care of now.* Stein was again angered, as well as embarrassed, this time. If the son of a bitching S-1, whom Stein knew well as a drinking buddy at the club, didn't know every soldier had a legal right to apply, he was stupid; and if he did know it, he was immoral. Once again Stein was placed in the position of not knowing what to do. He filed the application away without mentioning it to Fife, and once again tried to get him to apply for the Administrative School. Fife refused. He said he preferred to wait until he heard from the first one, and that was what he proceeded to do: wait, angering Stein yet again.

The worst of it all was that Fife found the application, with Stein's character analysis of him, and the S-1's note. Two weeks before they were to leave they cleaned out all their papers. Fife, cleaning out Stein's personal files, found it in a bunch of other papers. Stein, sitting at his desk, had reached out and grabbed it, saying it was something of his, and had locked it away. But not before, Stein was sure, Fife had had a good chance to run through it. At any rate Fife had looked at him with a very odd look on his face. As usual Welsh was there grinning, missing nothing. But then, with another of those high—and usually tragic—emotionalities which Stein could never fully understand though he could sense them, Fife went on with his work and said nothing. And he had not said anything, from that day to this. Had never mentioned it. But of course it didn't take any great feat of brainwork to know that this was basically what was behind his outburst of today. The enlisted man's viewpoint! It was this unfairness which angered and so infuriated Stein.

Now, though, he felt only blue. It was always a shock to rediscover how much enlisted men hated you, because you tended to try to forget it. And tomorrow he would be taking them in. He felt very inadequate. Especially when he recalled how badly the march had gone today. He had been horrified and shocked by what had happened. None of his officers or platoon sergeants had fallen out on him. They knew better than to. But when Stein thought about the number of big, tough men in his outfit who had given up, or for that matter simply fainted dead away, it left him with a dark foreboding for the future. When an undermuscled, essentially puny man like himself could keep going and these guys could not, it did not speak well for the conditioning of his company, physical *or* mental. He had tried to do the best he could by them in training, God knew. Great God, what would the heat and exhaustion and tension of combat itself do to them! He did not, of course, when he reported, say anything to the battalion commander about any of this; and when he did report, he discovered to his surprise that his forty-five percent straggling was in fact the best mark made in the battalion. It did not make him feel any better. He accepted the battalion commander's rather sour congratulations with a tired grimace. Then he walked back along the darkening road looking slowly and with thoughtful care at the tall trees and fat-leafed jungle undergrowth.

With a flashlight Stein held a briefing for his officers and platoon sergeants in front of his little sleeping tent. It made his heart feel funny in his chest to be doing it. First Battalion would be in reserve most of the morning unless called. In the afternoon they would move forward to take over the positions on the hills which 2d Battalion was supposed by then to have gained. In the reflected glow of the flash on the map Stein studied their faces. Welsh was there of course, but the clerk Fife who should have been on hand in case Stein needed him, was nowhere to be seen. Probably he was embarrassed. Well, it didn't matter. He didn't need him. And there was no tactical reason why Fife should hear the dispositions. Stragglers were still coming in. Stein had already resigned himself to the fact that he was not going to get much sleep tonight.

The reason Fife was not present at Bugger Stein's briefing was because he had gone for a walk in the jungle. It had nothing to do with embarrassment. Not only was Fife not embarrassed by his outburst of the afternoon, he was rather proud of it. He had not thought he was that brave. And the reason he had gone for a walk in the jungle alone had to do with the fact that, having pleased and surprised himself with his own courage like that, he had then discovered that it was all meaningless anyway.

When compared to the fact that he might very well be dead by this time tomorrow, whether he was courageous or not today was pointless, empty. When compared to the fact that he might be dead tomorrow, everything was pointless. Life was pointless. Whether he looked at a tree or not was pointless. It just didn't make any difference. It was pointless to the tree, it was pointless to every man in his outfit, pointless to everybody in the whole world. Who cared? It was not pointless only to him; and when he was dead, when he ceased to exist, it would be pointless to him too. More important: Not only would it *be* pointless, it would *have been* pointless, all along.

This was an obscure and rather difficult point to grasp. Understanding of it kept slipping in and out on the edges of his mind. It flickered, changing its time sense and tenses. At those moments when he understood it, it left him with a very hollow feeling.

Because from somewhere down in the lowest bottom of his mind there had risen a certain, sure knowledge that tomorrow, or at least within the next few days, he would be dead.

This had filled Fife with such a huge sadness that he forgot all about the dispositions conference and simply walked off by himself, into the jungle to look at all the things which would continue to exist after he had ceased to. There were a lot of them. Fife looked at them all. They remained singularly unchanged by his scrutiny.

It really made no difference what he did, or whether he did anything. Fife did not believe in God. He did not disbelieve in God. It was just that it was a problem which did not apply to him. So he could not believe he was fighting this war for God. And he did not believe he was fighting it for freedom, or democracy, or the dignity of the human race. When he analyzed it, as he tried to do now, he could find only one reason why he was here, and that was because he would be ashamed for people to think he was a coward, embarrassed to be put to jail. That was the truth. Why it was the truth, when he had already proved to himself that it made no difference what he did or whether he did anything, he could not say. It was just the fact.

Fife had unslung his rifle when he left the camp, because they had been warned there might be Japanese infiltrators this close to the front. He had not seen anything move anywhere, but as the dusk in the jungle deepened he began to get a little bit edgy. He knew this ground had been fought over only a week ago, but from the look of it he might have been the first man ever to set foot here. And yet some man, another American, might have been killed here where he himself now stood. Fife tried to imagine it. He gripped his rifle tighter. The eerie stillness of the jungle thickened around him as the daylight failed. Quite suddenly Fife remembered they would be posting sentries around the camp tonight. Hell, he might get shot by some triggerhappy sentry. Without waiting longer, and forgetting about his conviction that he would be dead soon so that nothing mattered, he turned and started legging it back to camp, glad to be returning to the presence of his own breed.

The sentries had not yet been posted. The sergeant in charge of the guard was just rounding them up. Fife stared at them a moment wildly, as if they were not real, thinking how narrowly he had escaped being killed by one of them with his foolish emotionalism, then reported to Stein's sleeping tent. There he was told by Welsh, who was preparing to bed down nearby, to take the hell off and go to bed.

For a moment, just for a moment, Fife thought of asking him for something, some assurance. He wanted to. But then he realized he did not know what to ask him for, or how to phrase what he wanted to say, or even what that was. After all, what assurance could be given? He didn't want anyone to think he was a nervous sissy, or a coward. So instead of speaking, he shrugged elaborately at Welsh, though feeling that his face did not look right, looked too scared, and turned and walked away.

Welsh, who was sitting crosslegged in front of his tent with his rifle across his knees, stared after him with crinkled eyes until the boy limped from sight around a tree. From beneath the black brows the eyes themselves glinted. So the kid was finally learning how important he was to the world. Welsh sniffed. Taken him long enough. It was a concept any intelligent child ought to understand readily. Only, they just didn't like to. So now he was learning it the hard way. Hurts, don't it. Scares you a little bit, hunh. Shock to the system. Make anybody constipated. In a way Welsh sympathized with him. But there was nothing he could do about it. Nor anybody else. Except advise him to go back and get born dumb. Property, kid; all for property. Everybody dies; and what's it all about? In the end, what's everything about? What remains? Property. Welsh went back to cleaning and checking his rifle. He had aleady gone over his new Thompsongun and the pistol he had pre-empted from MacTae's supplyroom. And if they had handed out sawed-off shotguns, he would have had one of those. He had to hurry with the rifle, it was almost too dark. Satisfied finally, he held it up in both hands and sighted along it off through the trees. Give him the Garand anytime. Let the romantic kids have the Springfields and spotweld BAR clips on them. The Marines had to do that. He'd take the Garand. Give him the firepower, and you could keep your pinpoint accuracy. This was going to be the age of firepower, not accuracy. Welsh dropped the rifle back onto his thighs and dangled his hands from his knees. He wished he had something to fuck tonight. A goat would do. Or a clean old man. Crosslegged, his rifle across his lap, Welsh sat and stared off into the dark trees.

Fife did not sleep much either. But it was for a different reason than either Stein or Welsh. When he left Welsh, he hunted up a ration stack. His conviction that he would be dead tomorrow or the day after did not stop hunger. He ate a cold can of C ration Meat & Beans sitting on the ground outside his tent, mashing the solid food between his jaws with relish. Then he crawled in and lay down, his heart pounding when he suddenly thought about tomorrow. Die? Why, he had never seen Nice and Monte Carlo. It was twenty minutes after this little Bead, who had fallen out on the march today, came crawling in.

Fife had seen him earlier, down by the first platoon, visiting some kid draftee friend of his. When he heard him now, he rolled over with his face to the wall and pretended to be asleep. Bead scrambled in under the net without a word, and turned to his own side ignoring Fife in return.

They lay like that for a long time, in silence, while the camp settled down around them. Then they lay for an even longer time in the quiet that followed. The air in the tent was stiff with pretended sleep. Finally Bead moved. He rolled over and said in a hoarse voice:

"Well, what about it?"

Fife made no answer, and continued to pretend he was sleeping.

"I said, well what about it?" Bead said again finally, more harshly.

Fife did not answer.

"I don't see that either one of us's got anything to lose. Not by now. And it might be the last time of anything for both of us." Bead's voice was hoarse, as though it were being pulled out of him, and was not without a bitter undercurrent. His breathing was loud in the tent.

Fife still did not answer or move, and Bead said nothing further. He had rolled over and was now facing Fife's back. He did not roll back. His breathing continued loud.

"I got one on, and you do too," little Bead from Iowa said finally, with a kind of fierce honesty.

It was true. In a way that was answer enough. Slowly Fife rolled over toward him. They were now lying face to face, about a foot between them. Fife could just barely make out Bead's face in

the dim light. Bead's pale blue eyes seemed to collect the meager
light and illuminate his face with it.

"Well?" Bead said.

"Well what?" Fife said irascibly. "One of us has got to turn
end for end." What the hell? Bead had brought it up, let him do
the turning. There was a rustle and Bead's face disappeared from
in front of him. Fife waited. Thoughtfully he ran his tongue over
his unbrushed teeth. First Bead's shoes, then his knees, appeared
in front of his face.

Curiously enough, Fife during the next minutes was thinking
about his girlfriend at the university in town whom he had never
been able to seduce, remembering her vividly, almost physically.
She was a large girl with heavy breasts, big thighs, muscular
buttocks, and a protuberant mons Veneris, all of which he had felt
through her clothes just once one passionate night, but never had
seen. He had not been able to seduce her, but he had received
four fervid love letters from her since the division left for combat.
He had answered two, with appropriately tragic letters for a
young infantryman about to die soon, but after the third the effort
was too painful. It was easy for her to write that she now regretted
she had not given herself to him when she had the chance; but for
Fife to read it was almost unbearable. And long-range sympathy
gained him nothing. Still, on occasion he liked to remember the
way she had felt, through her clothes, better, richer, *juicier*, than
any whore he had ever been to bed with.

Fife did not, on the other hand, like to remember how this
business with Bead had got started. But there were times, like
tonight, when he could not avoid it. It had started the second
night on the island, in fact. The first night was the night of the day
it rained so hard, also the first they had ever bunked together in a
sheltertent. The second night was much drier; more comfortable.
Bugger Stein still had not found the company's big tents. It was
Bead who broached the subject. He had come crawling in at a
moment when Fife, already disrobed to his underwear, had been
thinking ardently about girls. Fife was embarrassed, but Bead
made no comment. However while he undressed he began to
complain about what a hardship it was for him to be where he

was denied the services of women. They had often been on pass together, Fife and he, and had gone up to the whorehouses together in the town where the division was stationed, and had Fife not noticed it? Well, he was a very horny type, little Bead said, and he needed lots of sex. At eighteen this may well have been true; and Bead had stated it many times before; but Fife could not help feeling Bead perhaps bragged a little. Anyway, for Bead, the worst thing about this whole war was that, he said. And what the hell could a guy do? Nothing, that was what. Beat it. Or do without. Unless guys helped each other out now and then. It was either that, or find yourself a queer cook or baker someplace, or it was nothing. Guys could help each other out, Bead supposed.

"You know, like the things you used to do together when you were kids in school," he grinned, shyly.

That was all he said. He had finished undressing down to his shorts. Then he lay down on his own side of the tent, and went on talking about girls and whores in that almost childish tenor which at eighteen he had not yet lost. Finally he stopped talking also. There was a long pause. Then he rolled over to face Fife.

"Well, what do you say?" he said cheerfully. "Shall we help each other out? I'll do it to you if you'll do it to me."

Fife had divined what was coming. Nevertheless he pretended surprise and confusion. But he already knew that he was going to accept. And Bead, finding that he was not rebuffed, now became more confident in his voice and in his salesmanship. Apparently it made no difference to him and did not worry him that he was suggesting something homosexual. And perhaps, being eighteen and just out of school, he didn't see it that way. But that could not be entirely true, Fife speculated later, because as he started to crawl over to Fife's side of the little tent he stopped and said:

"I just dont want you to think I'm no queer, or nothing like that."

"Well, dont you get the idea I am, either," Fife had answered.

Fife thought about his lost girl that time, too. He thought about her every time. There weren't many more times. There was that first night, the second night on the island, and the following night which was the third night on the rock. On the fourth day the company's tents were found, the puptents were struck, and every-body moved into the larger eight-man tents. After that, opportu-nity was lacking. Once, one single time, on an afternoon when Welsh was gone and there was no work for them to do, they had gone off for a walk in the jungle, knowing beforehand what they were going to do but not mentioning it, so that when it happened off there alone in the massive, high-arching jungle, it seemed to both of them to come as a complete surprise. But that was all, just those three times and this last one.

It had of course changed their relationship. Fife to his own surprise found himself becoming more and more authoritarian with his little assistant than he had ever dared be with anyone in his life. He gave him curt orders, cursed him out for the slightest thing, criticized him constantly, insulted him more and more fre-quently, used him as his perpetual butt; in short, more and more treated Bead as he himself hated to be treated by Welsh. Bead on the other hand seemed to understand this, and moreover accepted it as though he felt it in some way to be his due. He accepted Fife's insults in silence, carried out his repeated orders as best he could, and received his constant criticism quietly without anger or answering back. And yet all this time Fife was not really angry at him for anything. Bead seemed to know this. Fife knew it, too. But his reaction was an emotional response he could neither un-derstand nor control.

After Bead had gone off into a relaxed, profound sleep Fife lay wide awake staring into the darkness. He had given up trying to sort it all out. All he knew was that he did not feel guilty about what he did with Bead. He felt he ought to feel guilty. But the truth was that he didn't. After all, what was the difference be-tween doing the same things now that you did as a kid, and doing them when you were a freshman or sophomore. Only all the talk you had heard in the meantime about fairies and queers. Fife knew there were oldtimers in the army who had their young boy-friends whom they slept with as with a wife. In return, the young soldiers received certain favors from their protectors, not the least of which was more money to spend on women in town. None of this buggering was considered homosexual by anyone and author-

ity turned a blind eye to it. But that was buggering. On the other
hand there were the overt homosexuals, much increased since the
drafting of civilians, whom everybody disliked, though many
might avail themselves of their services. This was the type company commanders tried to get rid of whenever a levy of men was
demanded. These two types constituted the extent of Fife's
knowledge. He could not honestly place himself among them, but
was terrified that someone else might. On this night before his
outfit went into its first combat he lay awake a long time, wondering whether he was a homosexual. Every now and then his heart
would jump suddenly when he remembered he had never seen
Nice or Monte Carlo. Anyway, he knew he liked girls.

Almost everyone was up at dawn. At the very first light which
filtered down to them from the high trees men began crawling
out, taking down their tents, rolling their packs. No orders had to
be given them. Some, still afflicted with the American cleanliness
complex, poured water from their canteens onto their tooth-
brushes to brush their teeth. Most did not. A few others remembered to powder their feet. There was very little horseplay, and a
subdued air hung over everything in the dim green jungle light.
Breakfast was a simple affair. There were C ration stacks around
everywhere, and each man simply went to one of them when he
felt like eating and took what he wanted. After eating, they settled
down on their packs to wait.

Dawn had come shortly before five o'clock. It was after eight-
thirty when an out-of-breath guide appeared with orders for them
to move. While they had waited they could hear if not see other
outfits moving invisibly into or out of other positions all around
them in the jungle. Gasping infantry companies kept straggling
past on the road. Now, led by the guide (who had regained his
breath) they moved out onto the road behind a company from
their own third battalion whom they recognized. They themselves
knew nothing about what was happening.

The guide led them half a mile in half an hour. There he
stopped, and pointed to a grassy place under some trees at the
roadedge. This was where they were supposed to wait. They were

supposed to drop their rolls and form combat packs, sit down and wait. He turned on his heel and left, going toward the front.

"But hey!" Stein protested after him. "There must be more instructions than that. I know what the dispositions are. I know what we're supposed to do."

"I dont know nothin about none of that, sir," the guide called back. "All I know I was suppose to bring you here and tell you what I tole you."

"But won't they send another runner for us?"

"I reckon they will. I dont know. All I know is what I tole you. You'll excuse me, sir, but I got to get back up there." He turned and went on, disappeared around a bend in the road.

It was as though C-for-Charlie Company suddenly had dropped completely out of the world. With the disappearance of the guide they did not see another living soul. There had been companies marching both in front of and behind them. Now there were none. The one in front had gone on, the one behind evidently some other way. There had been jeeps loaded with supplies bucking through the mud. There was now nothing, not a vehicle. The road stretched before them totally deserted. And nothing came along it either. Even sound seemed to have ceased. Except for the normal jungle noises, they seemed to have dropped into a vacuum; and the only sound they could hear, one which their ears gradually became aware of, was the distant splashing and faint voices of men moving something up or down the river somewhere off behind the screen of jungle.

They unslung their packs and dismantled them, then settled down to wait. They waited another hour and a half—from nine to ten-thirty—before they saw another human, listening to the splashing and faint shouts from the river, staring at their neat, stacked rolls.

There was not much discussion of the situation while they waited, largely because nobody knew what it was. But they didn't want to talk about it anyway, and preferred not to think about it. What little discussion there was employed a new word; simply, "Elephant." During the past two days whenever the group of treeless hills C-for-Charlie's regiment had been assigned to attack was mentioned, it was called The Elephant, or simply Elephant. Everyone was quick to pick the word up and use it, but nobody knew where it came from or what it meant.

In actual fact, the complex of hills had been named "The Dancing Elephant" by a young staff officer while studying an aerial photograph. Outlined on all sides by dark jungled valleys, the group of grassy hills did somewhat resemble an elephant standing on its hind legs with its forelegs up and its trunk above its head. The hind legs up to the belly were already held by the Marines, and the regiment's attack (less the 3d Battalion, which had been given another objective) was to commence there and work its way up and across the rest of the group of hills to the Elephant's Head. The Japanese had been felt out by reconnaissance and were known to hold at least two strong points in the Dancing Elephant from which it was believed they would contest vigorously any attack. One of these was a high, steep ridge running across the Elephant's body at about the shoulder; the other was the Elephant's Head itself, the highest point in the entire hill mass. From it the Elephant's Trunk tapered down to the low jungled country, affording the Japanese a good supply route—and a good escape route, if they needed it. It was the high ridge at the Elephant's Shoulder, which had been labeled Hill 209, that the 2d Battalion was supposed to be attacking today. But sitting on their suddenly deserted road, C-for-Charlie had no idea if they were doing it or not, and if they were, how they were faring, and—except for the officers and platoon sergeants—did not even know the hill's designated number. Nor did many of them very much care.

John Bell was one of those who did. Bell had had enough infantry strategy and tactics to be interested generally. Besides, if his life was going to be in jeopardy because of this action, he wanted to know as much about it as he could. Anyway, sitting on this weirdly deserted road was singularly unnerving, and Bell wanted something to do. Discussing the action was as good as anything else.

Bell was in the second squad of the second platoon, which was the squad of young Sergeant McCron, the notorious motherhen.

McCron was great when it came to looking after his draftee charges, but he knew next to nothing about tactics, and cared even less. Bell approached his platoon sergeant, Keck. Keck was an old Regular who had been sergeant of this same platoon since 1940. Bell learned nothing from him. Keck merely sneered at him irritably and told him that 2d Battalion was attacking a hill called 209 today at some place called The Elephant (Christ knew why), that beyond it was another hill called (appropriately enough) Hill 210 which they themselves would probably have to attack tomorrow provided 2d Battalion did not bog down today and, since they were in reserve today, what the hell difference did it make? All of this Bell already knew. Keck was one of those toughened field noncoms who preferred to leave the maps and planning to the officers until he himself could get on the ground and see just what little jobs his platoon would have to do. Bell appreciated this, but it didn't help him any.

His own platoon officer Lieutenant Blane was sitting close by but Blane had always been distant to Bell. Undoubtedly this was because of Bell's former status and Bell did not feel like asking Blane. Then he saw Culp of the weapons platoon sitting on a hummock further on. Culp the typical uncomplicated happy-go-lucky college football player had always been kind to him. Bell decided to ask him.

Culp appeared to be a little unnerved himself by the strangely deserted road and the waiting, because he seemed glad to talk. He was able to tell Bell that some bright young staff officer (who would probably make Lt Colonel out of his feat) had conceived the poetic name of The Dancing Elephant, and with a stick drew him a rough map on the damp ground showing The Elephant's salient features. When they had exhausted the topic—exhausted it to the point of mutual embarrassment, in fact—Bell went back to his squad, thinking it over. He decided there would be at least two rather nasty jobs of work in securing The Elephant. He had consumed twenty minutes. He sat down with his squad, thinking about his wife Marty and wondering what she was doing right now. It would be night now back in Columbus. Wouldn't it? Suddenly a physical desire for her, a desire to take her and undress her and spread her out and look at her and mount her, so strong that it made his head begin to burn with a hot fever of flushed blood, passed over him and gripped him. It was so impossibly painful that he thought he must scream. Almost delirious with the fever of it, he could not make it go away. Immediately afterward he had a severe chill. Bell was not so delirious that he did not know what that meant. He made the tenth man in three days.

Malaria was not considered a hospitalizing ailment except in the most extreme cases, and Bell was not the only man present with beginning malaria when finally a solitary figure appeared around the bend of the still-deserted road in front of them. At the spot where they sat the road bore a slight upgrade to the bend ahead. At the bend it turned sharply downhill to the right. The figure trudged uphill around the bend breathing heavily, stopped momentarily on the level ground to breathe, then stopped a second time when he saw them. After a couple of deep gasps for air, the man came on at a quickened pace, already shouting.

"Where the fuck have you guys been? I been lookin all over hell's half acre for this outfit! What the hell have you been doin? You're supposed to be on the other side the river, not here! What the fuck happened?" He continued to come on, shouting other plaintive statements.

"All right," Bugger Stein called disgustedly to his company. "Fall in, men, fall in."

The new guide did not cease his nervous exhortation even when he came up to them and, once they had fallen in, began to lead them onward.

"Honestly, sir, I been lookin all over. You're suppose to be clear over on the other side the river. That's where they tole me you'd be."

"We were just exactly where the other guide left us, and told us to stay," Stein said. All his many pieces of equipment, dangling from their various straps, suddenly did not seem to be able to be kept in time and kept knocking against each other and against himself as he walked, ruining his balance.

"Then he must of made some kind of a mistake," the new guide said.

"He was very positive about what he told us," Stein said; "and quite definite."

"Then somebody up there gave him the wrong orders. Or else they told me wrong." The guide thought. "But I know I'm right. Because the rest of the battalion's all over there."

Not a very auspicious beginning. But Stein was even more concerned with some other things. He waited a full fifteen seconds before he spoke.

"What's it like up there?" He could not fully disguise in his voice the guilt he felt for asking.

But the guide didn't notice. "It's a—" he searched for a word—"a crazyhouse."

Stein had to be content with that. The guide didn't elaborate. George Band was marching just alongside Stein, and they exchanged a glance. Then, suddenly, Band grinned at him a wolfish grin. Wondering what the hell that meant, Stein put his mind on the job at hand, because they had reached the bend.

From the bend the road ran almost straight down to the unnamed river, and the slope was steep. The road itself, churned by traffic, was a mudslide, a gloomy descending tunnel between impenetrable jungle walls. The only way to take it was to turn sideways like a man running down steep steps, and then dig in with the sides of the feet. At least half of the company took wet pratfalls going down, but there was very little laughter. What laughter there was was highpitched and nervous, and did not sound truly sincere.

The pontoon bridge, wide enough and with wood tracks for the jeeps to cross, was directly at the bottom. Groups of traffic control men and bridge tenders watched them from both ends of it with curious but sympathetic eyes. After their scrambling, sliding, falling trek down, jerky, too fast and out of time like an early Chaplin movie, their momentum carried them right on across.

In crossing, they saw for the first time the cause of the splashing and faint shouting they had heard earlier. Groups of naked or nearnaked men were wading in the river pushing boats ahead of

them, one line coming upstream another going down, an improvised supply line replacing the stalled trucks. The boats coming
upstream carried supplies. And in the ones going down C-for-
Charlie got its first look at infantry wounded by infantry: dulleyed men most of them, lolling against the thwarts and wrapped
here and there with the startlingly clean white of bandages,
through which on many the even more startling red of fresh blood
had soaked. From the bridge every eye in C-for-Charlie turned
toward them whitely, as the company crossed. Not all of the
returning boats carried wounded men, only about half.

As soon as they reached the other side they began to climb as
steeply as they had come down, but the climb was longer. Many
more men could be seen now everywhere, running back and forth
and up and down and talking. To C-for-Charlie after an hour and
a half alone the sight was comforting. They saw D-for-Dog, their
battalion's heavy weapons company, sitting all together in the
jungle on the slope with their big mortars and .50 cal machineguns. There were some waves and greetings. Able and Baker had
already gone up, they were told. Then they came out of the jungle
onto the grassy slopes. As if there were a manmade demarkation
line, the mud ceased suddenly and became hard, packed dirt
which dusted their faces. They climbed on.

It was here that S/Sgt Stack, platoon sergeant of the third lead
platoon for an even longer time than Keck had been sergeant of
the second, a lean hardfaced tough old drillmaster and discipli-
narian, was found sitting by the trail with his legs pressed tightly
together and his rifle in his lap, crying in agony at them as they
passed: "Don't go up there! you'll be killed! dont go up there!
you'll be killed!" The entire company had to pass him, one at a
time and man by man in single file as if passing in some macabre
review, as he sat pressing his legs and shouting at them. Most of
them hardly saw or heard him in the intensity of their own excitement, and they left him there. It was as close to the front as Stack
ever got, and they did not see him again. They were about two-
thirds up.

Nothing they heard or saw on the way up prepared them for the
pandemonium they entered when they came over the crest.

Climbing with the wind behind them they had heard no battle noises; then, rounding the last bend and coming out onto the open hilltop suddenly, they found themselves immersed in infernal noise and tumult. Like a river running into a swamp and dissipating its current, the line of files trudged over the crest and disappeared in a mob of running or standing, shouting and talking men who struggled to make themselves heard above the din.

Invisible but not far off, 81mm mortars fired off rounds with their peculiar gonglike sound. From further off came the monumental crashes of artillery firing sporadic salvos. Further off still .50 cal machineguns, chattering in bass voices, punctuated the intervals. And much fainter, but coming clearly across the rolling unjungled terrain in front, there were the sounds of small-arms fire and grenades, and the explosions of the mortar shells and artillery rounds landing. All of this, compounded by the excitement, shouting and rushing about, created a demented riotous uproar whose total effect could only be mad confusion. C-for-Charlie had arrived on the field, at just a few minutes after eleven.

They were on a high knoll overlooking a series of grassy hills and draws rising out of the surrounding sea of jungle. To their front the slope fell to a smaller knoll upon which the jungle encroached more closely, forming in effect a narrow deck of untreed land leading to the wider areas beyond. On this knoll, too, stood or ran groups of Americans in their green combat fatigues, a lesser number than up here, thirty perhaps. Beyond the second knoll the slope dropped again, not so steeply but much further, to a broken ravine covered with sparse grass; and beyond this low point the land rose again, steeply this time, to a high ridge which dominated the area and made invisible anything beyond it. On this slope, perhaps a thousand yards away and higher even than the original vantage point, infantrymen were fighting.

To a few men like Bell who were informed about The Dancing Elephant's terrain, it was clear that the knoll they occupied was The Elephant's hind foot. The lower knoll in front, which was obviously 2d Battalion's command post, thus became The Elephant's knee leading to the wider areas ahead which formed the torso. And the high ridge where the infantrymen now fought was the Elephant's Shoulder, the strong point labeled Hill 209.

A fire fight was obviously in progress. Several groups of squad or platoon size, tiny at this distance but plainly visible, were trying to get close to the crest and take it. The Americans, too far down the slope to lob grenades up to the crest, had to content themselves with riflefire. The Japanese, also clearly visible from time to time among the trees which rose above the crest from the jungled reverse slope, were under no such handicap; they could simply drop them down, and the black explosions from the Japanese grenades kept bursting out here and there, from the hillside. One American, receiving such a grenade near him, was seen to turn and simply jump out from the side of the hill like a man jumping off a ladder. He hit and rolled, the grenade exploded black behind him, and after a moment he rose and began to work his way back up to his group.

C-for-Charlie had arrived just at the climax. As they stood in the milling mob on the knoll trying to see and taking all of this in for the first time, the several groups on the slope rose into a concerted line and rushed the crest, lobbing grenades ahead of them and firing. They got to within perhaps fifteen yards of the top before they were repulsed. The machinegun fire, clearly heard on the knoll, was too much for them. They broke and began leaping and scrambling back down the hill where they went to ground as before, having left a number of their men, perhaps ten percent, behind them on the uphill slope. There were exclamations of dismay and a number of angry groans on the hilltop around C-for-Charlie.

The chorus of groans was not the only action on the knoll as a result of the repulse. Runners and junior staff officers began to push their way out through the crowd and go various places. The center of all this activity was a small group of seven men standing together in grand isolation on the knoll's peak. They were almost the only men present wearing any insignia, and all of them wore stars or eagles on the collars of their green fatigues. They were further distinguished from the others by their cleanliness. All of them were older men. From time to time they looked through binoculars or pointed at the terrain, talked to each other or into one of three telephones which they held. Occasionally one would also talk into a wireless radio packed on a much younger man's back. C-for-Charlie was able to recognize among them their battalion commander, their regimental commander and, from their photographs, their division and corps commanders.

One of these men now yelled irately into one of the sound power phones. Below on the second knoll the 2d Battalion's Colonel shouted back at him into its mate. The one above, tall and spare, listened intently, nodding his helmeted head. Then he turned to the wireless radio, looking angry and unsatisfied. Completing his call, he began to speak apologetically to three of the others who wore stars. He wore eagles. Below, the 2d Battalion's Colonel was now speaking into still another phone in his other hand.

Across the valley eight hundred yards in front of him the company CP of the repulsed platoons was located behind the crest of a subsidiary ridge growing out of the side of the main ridge. Off to one side of this small group two smaller clusters of men went through motions which could only mean that they were the company's mortar section plying the tubes of their 60mm mortars, invisible from here. As the Colonel talked, a figure detached itself from the CP group and dropped over the crest and went forward in rushes toward the groups which had been repulsed and which now were sporadically firing uphill at the Japanese. Before he reached them, he tumbled, shot. Immediately another dropped over the crest in his place. The moment this one reached them the groups began to withdraw along the ridge, again in rushes, firing in groups to cover each other, all the way back to the command post, where they lost no time in diving back over the crest of the subsidiary ridge. In the high-ranking group of older men on the hill, one was now waving his arms angrily and pounding himself furiously on the leg. Below, the 2d Battalion's Colonel was doing the same thing. Seconds later artillery shells began to fall in great mushrooming clusters on the Japanese-held ridge.

Whatever other manifestations occurred on the hilltop in connection with this operation, C-for-Charlie did not see them. They now were too involved in themselves and their own forthcoming part in the drama to care about watching the internationally famous command group. During the action Bugger Stein had gone over to report to his battalion commander, who was more a student observer there than an integral part of the group. Stein now returned to them. 1st Battalion less D-for-Dog was ordered as regimental reserve to occupy and hold the main ridge behind and to the left of the F-for-Fox CP which they had just been watching. The main ridge here, lower than Hill 209 on the right, had been labeled Hill 208 and formed, so to speak, The Elephant's middle and lower spine. The Japanese had never occupied it, but there was fear of a flanking counterattack. A-for-Able and C-for-Charlie were to man the line with B-for-Baker in reserve in the ravine, Colonel Tall's orders. Since Able and Baker were already moving down right now, this meant that C-for-Charlie would have to pass through Baker—always a difficult maneuver, and they should watch it. There was a crinkly look of painful preoccupation around Bugger's eyes behind his glasses as he spoke. His own dispositions were: 1st and 2d platoons on the line, 3d in reserve; Culp would set up his two MGs at optional points of choice along the line, the mortars to be set up near the company CP. Order of march would be 1st Platoon, 2d Platoon, Company HQ, Weapons Platoon, 3d Platoon. They were to move out right away.

In the fact, as they formed up by platoons, it was discovered that they could not move right away. Their front was being crossed by E-for-Easy, the 2d Battalion reserve. Easy was being committed to the right wing of 2d Battalion's attack where G-for-George, invisible from here around the corner of jungle, had also bogged down. C-for-Charlie knew many Easy Company people, and some of them called greetings. But Easy Company, going to certain attack instead of to a safe defensive position, preferred to ignore them and stared at them with a mixture of nervousness and hateful envy. Slowly they plodded across and disappeared down the righthand slope of the hill into the woods. It took them fifteen minutes to cross. Then C-for-Charlie began to move down the slope, 1st Platoon in the lead.

It was during this fifteen minute wait that First Sergeant Welsh suddenly came to the fore. Up to now Welsh had been very carefully taking a back seat. He had no intention of becoming conspicuous or committing himself until he knew where he stood. He had tried to prepare himself, and two of the three canteens on his belt were filled with gin. In addition, he had his Listerine bottle. He could not say exactly what the experiences of today made him feel. All Welsh knew was that he was scared shitless, and at the same time was afflicted with a choking gorge of anger that any social coercion existed in the world which could force him to be here. In addition the tremendously intense excitement on the hilltop affected him powerfully. It was not unlike the feeling in a stadium generated by a crowd rooting at an important college football game. It was this outrageous comparison which gave him the idea to do what he did.

Standing with Stein and the Company HQ while E-for-Easy jogged past their front, Welsh spied a whole stack of unopened hand-grenade cases on the edge of the hill, and simultaneously realized somebody had fucked up somewhere along the line in not issuing grenades to C-for-Charlie. Grinning his sly, mad grin, he decided to issue them himself. But in such a way that the cheering-section emotional tenor of the day should be properly honored. Without so much as a word to anyone, he suddenly crouched with his palms on his knees and at the top of his command voice bellowed: "Hup! Twenty-six, thirty-two, forty-three; *hike!*", whirled like a halfback, and ran over to the stack of cases drawing his bayonet and began splitting the soft pine cases open through the middle. The grenades inside were in black cardboard cylinders, their halves held together with yellow tape. Welsh began to draw them out and to bellow.

"Eggs! Fresh eggs! Nice fresh yard eggs! Who wants eggs!"

The enormous, booming command voice was easily heard despite the racket and tumult. The men of his company began to turn and look. Then hands began to shoot up out of the crowd. And Welsh, still bellowing, and still grinning crazily, began to forwardpass the canned grenades into the crowd.

"Eggs! Eggs! Footballs! Footballs! Sammy Baugh! Sid Luckman! Rah rah rah! Who wants footballs! Bronco Nagurski!"

His bellow rang magnificently over the entire hilltop. While men everywhere turned and stared as if he were insane, Welsh bellowed on and continued to forwardpass grenades to his company, a perfect caricature of the classic football passer's stance: left arm out, right arm cocked, right leg bent, left leg forward.

In the grandly isolated command group one of the seven older men heard him. He turned to look, then slowly grinned his approval. With his elbow he punched a companion to look, too. Soon the entire group were watching Welsh and grinning. This was the type of American soldier these generals liked to see. And across fifteen yards of hilltop crammed with American soldiers and matériel Welsh grinned back at them murderously, his insolent eyes crinkled slyly, and continued to bellow and to throw.

Perhaps only one man really understood it, if anyone did, and this was Storm. An ironic grin began to spread across Storm's cynical, broken-nosed face and drawing his own bayonet he ran over and began hacking open the cases and feeding Welsh the cylinders.

"Sammy Baugh! Sid Luckman! Jack Manders! Sammy Baugh!" they bellowed in unison. "Rah rah rah!"

They went through the entire stack of cases in very little time. By this time E-for-Easy had passed. Taking the last two each for themselves, and laughing idiotically in a moment of rare understanding, they rejoined the Company HQ. With the men stripping off the yellow tapes and opening the cylinders, spreading the cotter pins and buttoning the pull rings down under their pocket flaps as they'd seen the Marines do, C-for-Charlie moved off down the slope.

If Bugger Stein had hoped for an orderly advance by elements, he was out of luck. 1st Platoon led off, and did it properly: scouts out, double line of skirmishers. But before they had gone ten yards, all order vanished. It was impossible to keep any sort of formation on this slope which was so crowded with men. Some were simply watchers, standing and looking. Others in straggly lines sweated and panted horribly in the heat, carrying supplies forward. A number of walking wounded were given a wide berth by everyone; and there were three groups sweating impossibly in the tropic sun to carry back seriously wounded who groaned or whimpered every time their stretchers were jerked or raised or lowered. By the time they reached the 2d Battalion CP on the knoll they had become a resolute gang. What little semblance of order remained was lost passing through the CP personnel.

Beyond the command post it was less crowded, but the damage was already done. They were too mixed up to be able to reform into any sort of formation without making a long stop. Stein could only curse with frustration and try to keep the sweat off his glasses. He was painfully aware of all the brass that was watching him today. His only consolation was that Able and Baker ahead of him and now crossing the brushy bottom, were in no better shape. Around him his own men moved forward steadily with set, curiously covert faces in which the eyes seemed to be trying to betray no expression which might ever be used against them. The men in front, without having to be yelled at by Stein, veered left after Able and Baker according to instructions. Stein was glad of that.

One of these men in front was Pfc Doll, who was from the 2d Squad of the 1st Platoon. Doll didn't know how he happened to be in front and it made him feel nervous and peculiarly exposed, but at the same time he was proud of his position and jealous of it. Whenever someone behind seemed to be narrowing the gap, Doll would quicken his pace for a moment so as to stay the same distance in front. It was he who, remembering Stein's instructions, began the veering movement after Able and Baker, both of whom had now disappeared in the bottoms. Doll was carrying every bit of armament he had been able to get his hands on. His stolen pistol dangled on his hip fully loaded, cocked and on safety, and on his belt hung two knives now instead of one: his old one from home and the new bowie-type knife he had made from the Jap bayonet. Two grenades hung from his pocket flaps and two more reposed in his side pockets. He had not been able to get in on the Thompsonguns, like Charlie Dale, but he still had hopes of being able to get one later on, perhaps from a casualty. He walked steadily ahead with his stomach tingling very unpleasantly, almost sickly, glancing to left and right to make sure no one behind caught up to him.

They were receiving very little fire. Now and then a single bullet would strike the ground in amongst them and bury itself or go shrieking off without touching anyone. Nobody could tell whether they were spent ricochets from Hill 209 or deliberately aimed fire. These hurt nobody, but the men blinked and jerked away from them. Every now and then a man would go to ground when one struck near him and commence to crawl until embarrassed by the fact that the others were still up walking.

As they advanced down into the dry, treeless ravine they were able to see around the angle of The Elephant's belly. Here G-for-George was having another go at the right side of Hill 209. Like Fox on the left they had set up a CP and base of fire on a lower subsidiary ridge and were now plugging away at the main crest with their mortars and machineguns, while receiving heavy mortar fire from the hill in return. Under cover of their fire two platoons of George were creeping close to the crest past the huddled bodies of their former attempts. C-for-Charlie slowed down to watch, then stopped entirely as the two platoons leaped up, their tiny black bayonets visible on their rifles against the dun hillside, and rushed the crest. This time they went almost all the way. And a few of the men in front, perhaps a half dozen, actually got in among the Japanese who rose to meet them bayonet to bayonet. Here on the right side of the long ridge, where the reverse slope was not jungled and there were no trees along the crest, their struggle was clearly visible. Once again the heavy fire of the powerfully placed Japanese machineguns was too much. The two platoons broke and fled. Left alone, the little group engaged hand to hand attempted to break off their engagement and escape also, leaping and jumping and tumbling head over heels down the slope after their mates. Two however did not succeed. They were seen to be dragged alive and still struggling back over the crest by the Japanese.

Below in the dry narrow valley C-for-Charlie stood watching this action open-mouthed. Pfc Doll, for one, felt his heart pounding slowly and thuddingly in his throat. With a raw honesty that was almost insupportable Doll wondered to himself how men could bring themselves to do such things, and what must it feel like when they did. To find yourself face to face with a screaming Jap bent on killing you and engage with him with naked bayonets. That was George Company up there. Doll knew a great many of them. He had a number of good friends in George Company. He had got drunk with them. But to find yourself being dragged back over the crest into the midst of those jabbering, Emperor-worshiping savages. Furtively his right hand sought his pistol. He meant to keep one round in at all times for his own head. But those guys there, they wouldn't have had time to use a pistol if they had it. If he was using his rifle or bayonet, how could he keep his pistol ready in his hand. He couldn't. Doll decided he would have to give this problem more thought, serious thought.

Above on the slope the remnants of the two platoons had gone to ground and were hugging the earth under the mortar and MG fire being thrown at them.

Behind them C-for-Charlie heard a shout. Turning to look, they saw a man standing on the 2d Battalion knoll waving his arms at them. At first they simply stared. The man continued to shout and wave his arms. Slowly they came out of their trance. Bugger Stein who had been as guilty as the rest suddenly cleared his throat and said, "All right, men, let's move out." Glancing stealthily at each other, because no one wanted to betray what he was feeling, they began to move again and Doll, still in the lead, jumped to move out in a sudden fear that somebody might pass him.

Sighing loudly, the artillery shells were still arching overhead to crash against the ridge. 155 and 105 shells were bursting on the crest and on both sides of it with an almost continuous roar. Underneath them C-for-Charlie walked on nervously. There seemed to be so many potentially dangerous objects floating around loose everywhere today.

One of the most nervous was young Corporal Fife. Fife had gotten away late because Stein had sent him to Battalion HQ with a message about the spot Bugger had chosen for his CP. Except for the two Signal Corps men stringing the wire for the company's sound power phone some distance behind him, Fife was the last man in the crowd. Because he was moving so slowly he remained the last man. Ahead of him he could see Storm marching along with his big jaw set, carrying his Thompsongun in one hand with his rifle slung from his shoulder and surrounded by Dale with his Thompson and the other cooks. Not far from them walked Welsh, Stein and Band and the two clerks Bead and Weld. Fife wanted to catch up to them, but he found it hard to move any faster when he was looking this way and that all the time to see if there was something or someone about to shoot at him.

When Fife had come over the lip of the hill down onto the slope, he had experienced a singular feeling of exposure. Only once before in his life had he had a similar sense of such total exposure and that was one time on a patrol on maneuvers when he stood on a mountaintop and looked down to see how far he could fall if he should lean over too far. But today the feeling of exposure was accompanied by another of total isolation and helplessness. There were too many things to watch out for. One man simply could not take care of them all to protect himself. It was about as easy to get killed by accident as by enemy deliberation. Trying to look everywhere at once, he stumbled ahead tripping now and then on the tough grass stems or on rocks. When first one bullet and then moments later a second kicked up puffs of dust in front of him, he went to ground and began to crawl, convinced some Japanese sniper had signaled him out to shoot at. The crawling was hard work. The kneehigh grass made it hard for him to see where he was going. Sweat poured down his forehead and over his glasses. He had to stop repeatedly to wipe them. Finally he tied his grimy handkerchief across his forehead. This helped a little. But there was something else bothering him: his grenades. Fife had caught two of the handgrenades Welsh had passed into the crowd and had spread the pins and buttoned them under his pocket flaps. Now as he crawled they bounced and bumped along the ground, catching on grass stems. Terrified by the aspect of one of them pulling off and igniting its three-second fuse underneath him, ashamed of himself for what he considered his cheap cowardice, but not so ashamed that shame could wash away the imagined picture, Fife unbuttoned his pocket flaps from over them and rolled them away from him, left them and crawled on. But when he raised up his head to look around he could see that the company, all of whom appeared to be standing up walking, was alarmingly far ahead of him, and gaining.

It was then that Fife had had to make a heroic decision. Terrified as he was of standing up and being shot at by some invisible party, he was more terrified of being accused for his cowardice. His back muscles crawling, he stood up and took one tentative step, then another. Nothing happened. He began to jog toward his company trotting bent over at the waist and carrying his rifle at high port. When another bullet kicked up dirt in front of him and went screaming off, he shut his eyes, then opened them and trotted on.

It was just then that the entire company had stopped to witness George Co's attempt on the crest, and Fife was able to catch up to them. He too saw the attack. He stood with the others, wide-eyed, slack-mouthed, disbelieving, until the arm-waving shouter on the knoll reminded them that they were not here simply as spectators. Then he picked himself a spot in amongst the Company HQ and stayed with them, comforted unreasonably to be in a crowd. The brushy bottom of the ravine was just in front of them.

When they emerged from the brush of the bottom and began to climb, they were not far from the protection of the subsidiary ridge which held Fox's command post. In a very few minutes they would pass into complete cover behind it, out of view of Hill 209 entirely. And it was just here that the first man in the company was wounded. Whether deliberately or by accident no one could tell, because no one could tell whether the desultory fire they were getting was aimed or was simply stray bullets from the ridge.

The man's name was Peale and he was an older man, perhaps thirty-five, one of the draftees. He was moving in the middle of the crowd, not far from John Bell and not far from Fife and the Company HQ either, when he suddenly clapped his hand to his thigh and stopped, then sat down holding his leg, his lips trembling, his face white. Bell ran over to him pulling at his first aid pack.

"Are you all right, Peale?"

"I'm hit," Peale said thickly. "I'm wounded. I'm hit in the leg."

But before Bell could get his first aid packet out one of the company's medics was there with a gauze compress and looking very serious at this first opportunity of exercising his trade in combat. While Bell and Peale watched he tore open the pantsleg and inspected the wound which was bleeding only superficially. A little rill of dark blood ran down the white leg. Peale and Bell stared at it. The medic salted the compress with sulfa powder and wrapped it onto the wound with a roll of gauze. The bullet had gone in but had not come out.

Peale had begun to grin stiffly. His face still white, his lips still trembling, his mouth was nevertheless stretched into a stiff but happily cynical grin.

"Can you walk?" the medic asked him.

"I dont think so," Peale said. "I think my leg hurts pretty bad. You better help me. I think it's goin to be a long time before I can walk good again."

"Well, come on. I'll take you back," the medic said and grunting, hoisted him up onto his one good leg.

Behind them, coming up with the Company HQ, Bugger Stein was already calling to the men who had stopped to move on, keep going, don't stop. First one then another they began to turn away back to the climb.

"So long, Peale."

"Take it easy, Peale."

"Good luck, Peale."

"So long, you guys," Peale called after them, his voice rising as they moved away. "So long. You guys take it easy. So long. Good luck, you guys. Dont worry about me. It'll be a long time before I can walk good. No doctor's goin to tell me I can walk on this leg. Good luck, you guys!"

All of them had passed him now moving up the slope and he suddenly stopped calling as though he knew it was futile and stood looking after them, his grin fading. Then with his arm around the neck of the medic he turned to descend. Fife, who was one of the very last to pass him, heard what he said as he turned away.

"I got me a Purple Heart," Peale said to the medic, "and I been in combat. I never even seen a Jap; but I dont care. No doctor's gonna tell me I can walk on this leg for a long time. Come on, let's get out of this. Before I get hit again and get killed. That'd be hell, wouldn't it?"

Fife, too dumbfounded by the events of the day and still in a state of shock, did not know what to think of this and, in fact, did not think anything. His ear simply recorded it.

A little further in front John Bell, as he climbed on, knew only that he had about Peale a curious double feeling of grinding envy and at the same time a great relief that it was not himself who had been injured, hurt, like that.

Whether Peale made good his promise about the doctors or not no one ever found out, but C-for-Charlie did not see him again.

They had now passed behind the subsidiary ridge. The sense of relief it gave them was enormous, unbelievable. From the look on their faces they might have just been removed clean away, all the way back to the real safety of Australia. In front of them B-for-Baker in battalion reserve, and equally relieved, had spread out over the only level space available on the slope and were already digging their slit trenches for the night. C-for-Charlie passed through them with an exchange of greetings that was near-hysterical in its happy relief to be out of the line of fire. Behind them and out of sight now on Hill 209, though not out of hearing, the fight went on.

The spot Bugger had picked for his CP was a tiny spur a hundred yards below the crest. Here the Company HQ and the mortar squads dropped off, Culp going on up with the rifle platoons to place his two machineguns. While they waited for him to come back and place the mortars, Mazzi and Tills, who were members of the same mortar squad, engaged in a discussion with Fife and Bead about the day's events and the walk the company had made under their first fire.

The overly gay mood of relief and safety still prevailed in everybody. But underneath it lurked the unspoken awareness that today had not been tough at all, that this protection was only temporary, that eventually the good luck would run out and people would die. It was visible in the dark depths of everyone's eyes.

"This Tills," Mazzi sneered squatting by the 60mm baseplate that he carried. "He spent more time on his belly on the fuckin ground than he did up on his feet. I dont see how he managed to keep up with the rest of us."

Tills, looking sheepish, did not answer.

"Aint that right, Tills," Mazzi said. "Didn't you?"

"I guess you never hit the dirt any, did you?" Tills said.

"Did you see me?"

"No, I never," Tills admitted lamely.

"You fucking A you never, Tills. What was the use, I say? Anybody could tell that fire wasn't aimed fire. It was stray stuff from the ridge. So it could hit you just as well layin down as standin up. Maybe better."

"And I guess you wasn't never scared even once?" Tills said angrily.

Mazzi merely grinned at him without answering, his face crinkled up around his eyes, his head on one side.

"Well, I was," Fife said clearly. "I was scared shitless. All the time. From the moment I stepped onto the slope till I got here. I was crawlin around on my belly like a snake. I never been so scared in my life."

But it did not help him to tell it. He found that no matter how he overstated it he could not convey the true extent of his fear. It became only funny, when you said it. It wasn't the same thing at all.

"So was I," little Bead put in in his child's voice. "Scared to death."

Bugger Stein happened to be standing not far away, with Lt Band and one of the platoon lieutenants who had come down from the ridge to ask something, and Fife saw him stop what he was saying and look over straight at him, Fife, with a surprised look of reluctant approval. It was as though Bugger would have liked to have said the same thing himself but couldn't, and at the

same time had not expected anything so honest to come from
Fife. For a moment Fife felt a fleeting resentment. Then taking
Bugger's look of approval as his cue, he began to elaborate his
adventure of the walk under fire. He had not meant to tell anyone
about the grenades, but now he did, making himself the buffoon.
Before very long he had all of them laughing hard, even the three
officers and Mazzi the New York hep guy. He was the 'honest
coward.' If you wanted to make people like you, play the buffoon
whom they could laugh at without having to admit anything about
themselves. It still did not make him feel any better: did not
alleviate his shame, did not cause to cease the misery of fear he
felt right now.

"As a matter of fact," he said, utilizing even this point, "I'm
still scared shitless, right now."

As if to prove him right, there was an instant's fluttering sound
in the air, not unlike a man blowing through a keyhole, and three
geysers of dirt spouted into the air thirty-five yards away, followed instantly by one loud clap of sound. There was an antlike
scramble on the little spur as everyone tried to hit the dirt on the
slope away from the surprise. Private Mazzi, if not the foremost,
was certainly not the last among them, and Tills had the last
word.

"Not even once you weren't scared?" he asked loudly, as they
all began to get up with sheepish faces when no more shells
arrived. Everyone was glad to laugh at Mazzi and turn the ridicule away from their own sheepishness. But Mazzi did not laugh.

"And I guess you stood up there like a big fat fucking hero,
fuckface," he said and glowered sullenly at Tills.

There was some muttering about short rounds, but it was soon
stopped by Stein. Everybody knew that the Japanese had a habit
of dropping their heavy mortar shells in, to upset the troops,
whenever there was an American artillery barrage. However, the
arrival of the mortar shells did put a stop to the discussions.
Everyone decided at the same time to unship their entrenching
tools and start digging their slit trenches, the heavy work of
which they had been putting off. Bead and Weld were designated

to dig the holes for Stein and Band, who decided it was time they inspected the ridge. Corporal Fife was put in charge of them.

During his little comic routine of the 'honest coward', Fife had noted that Welsh was the only one who had not laughed. Instead the First Sergeant, who was standing with Storm (who was roaring), only eyed him shrewdly with screwed-up knowing eyes. Now, when Fife had put his assistant clerks to work on the officers' holes, he went over to Welsh and Storm who, after a prolonged discussion about night infiltrators, were preparing to dig their holes together at a certain spot.

"Hey, First, is this where you guys've decided to dig in?" he said cheerfully.

Welsh, in the act of detaching his shovel from his combat pack, did not look up or answer.

"Because I thought I'd dig in over here with you guys if it was," Fife said.

Welsh ignored him.

"I mean, I guess it's as good a place as any," Fife said. "This is where you're gonna dig, aint it?"

Welsh continued to ignore him.

"Is that okay?" Fife said. He unslung his pack.

Welsh stopped his unbuckling of straps and looked up at Fife with eyes of stone and a face as expressionless as unchiselled granite. "Take off," he barked. "Get the fuck away from me. And stay away from me, kid."

Storm had stopped his work to watch.

Fife was carried back a step by the sheer viciousness of the sergeant's retort. "Well, tshooo!" He attempted a sarcasm which did not come off. "I certainly didn't mean to inflict my presence on anybody."

Welsh stared at him, silent, refusing to be drawn into any carping discussion.

"Well, I guess I know when I'm not wanted," Fife said with a lame try at airiness. Visibly crestfallen, unable to hide it, he turned and moved off carrying his pack by its straps.

"Why don't you ever treat the kid decent once in a while?" Storm said. His voice was dispassionate.

"Because I don't mean to wind up playin nursemaid and havin to mother some kid, that's why. I got enough problems to occupy me." Welsh straightened from his pack. "Here. You got some dirt. Take the shovel and gimme the mattock."

Storm didn't answer and exchanged the tools. Behind and above them Lt Culp was coming down the slope in the great leaping strides of a fullback on vacation. Hardly pausing at the CP he collected his mortar section and carried them on down to a nearly level spot almost a hundred yards below. From here they could lob shells over the crest onto the precipitous jungled slopes beyond. After setting up their mortars, they would dig in their own perimeter defense for the night.

For quite a long while everyone was occupied with digging.

Private Mazzi was still infuriated at Tills for having given him the finger when the mortar shells dropped in. It was an unfair advantage because everybody had ducked for cover. On the other hand during the walk across Mazzi had not hit the dirt one time. While he had seen Tills go down on at least three occasions. So Mazzi had every right to ridicule Tills. While Tills had no right to ridicule Mazzi. Him and Tills was supposed to be buddies, but Tills was always doing something like that.

Mazzi had not picked Tills for a buddy. He did not like to be buddying with a cornball hick from Hicksville who was not hep. But in this mortar squad there had not been no choice. In this mortar squad Tills was only an ammunition carrier. Mazzi was designated as the second gunner and carried the baseplate. But he was really only an ammunition carrier, too, because Sergeant Wick and the first gunner, who carried the tube, did everything together and handled all the firing between them. Mazzi hardly got to touch the sights. And the other ammunition carrier Tind was only a punk kid draftee. So there wasn't nothing left but Tills. Mazzi treated him kind and gave him lots of good advice, and was always right, and Tills always ignored it and did something else, and was always wrong. But he wouldn't never learn, and wouldn't never admit Mazzi was always right. That was what come of trying to be buddies with a cornball hick from Hicksville.

But this time Tills had tore it. Mazzi made up his mind he wasn't having no more to do with Tills. Fullback Culp had ordered them to dig two-man holes and double up, one awake and one sleeping, and ordinarily Mazzi would have dug with Tills. This time instead he asked Tind in a loud voice to dig with him, without saying a word to Tills, leaving Tills to dig alone. And after digging in, he got permission from The Fullback to go up to the crest for a while. All his good buddies who were hep, a whole gang of them from The Bronx and Brooklyn, Carni, Suss, Gluk, and Tassi, were all up there in the 1st Platoon. He could feel Tills looking after him, but he ignored him. Let him do his own damn fucking thinking. See how he liked it. The fact that he had been scared on the walk across didn't have nothing to do with it. He hadn't hit the ground, had he? Everybody was scared.

As Mazzi climbed past the CP on his way up, a loud roar of laughter wafted down the steep fall to them from the crest. By standing up and leaning their heads far back the CP men could see the platoons on the ridge, seemingly almost straight above them, small but sharp in the sunlight.

"What the hell's going on?" somebody yelled up.

"Nellie Coombs's got a hard on," a voice yelled down. "Is that horny or not? Waitin here to get his ass shot off."

"It's a lie," the man below yelled up.

"Like hell it's a lie!" the voice above cried. "I just seen it. It's no lie."

Mazzi, as he climbed on, laughed. Nellie Coombs's sexual propensities were almost legend, as well known as his improper practices at cards. Everyone knew them. And those were all Mazzi's bunch of hep pals up there in the 1st Platoon. Mazzi would be interested to see how many of them had hit the dirt on the walk across.

The line of slit trenches curved along the military crest of the ridge in a parallel line a few yards below the true crest. On the other side tall jungle trees strung with lianas towered above it. From up here, above the subsidiary ridge and only a few yards lower than the highest point on Hill 209, it was possible to view the entire bowl of the battle area. The officers had climbed up to inspect the company's line before the work on the holes was done, and Captain Bugger Stein had stood for a long time looking down at this panorama of a military operation. Now, the work of digging done, the platoons could sit on the sides of their holes and have grandstand seats.

Not all of them wanted to, however, and soon a blackjack game which included Mazzi and his New York friends as players, was under way on the edge of Nellie Coombs's hole. Cries of "Hit me!" and "I'll stay" competed with the battle noises from 2d battalion. And John Bell though invited to play preferred to sit on the edge of his slit trench and look down into the basin.

It was a formidable sight. Except for the slopes of Hill 209 still under Japanese fire, the entire area was aswarm with American troops carrying supplies and wounded. 2d Battalion still battered at the hill, trying to take it. When Bugger Stein had stood for so long looking down at it, the situation was static. But now, as the first afternoon shadows began to creep out from the deepest hollows down there, a new artillery barrage began to crash down onto the right side of the long ridge where George Co had attacked before. Minutes later a roaring came from the west, growing in volume to a piercing shriek until seven P-38s carrying depth-charges appeared in the sky, then flashed by overhead. The planes made two preliminary passes for looking, then on the third pass dropped the big black drums which threw up oily gouts of flame as they burst along the ridge. Not one landed on the Japanese forward slope toward the Americans. Dipping their wings, the planes flew off. The infantry watched them wistfully. The artillery continued to gnaw at the ridge.

The Japanese, without either planes or artillery to support them, were fighting back toughly. Bell, knocking the flat of his mattock against the edge of his dangling foot with rhythmic thoughtfulness as he sat and watched, could not help feeling, along with his fear of them, a little sorry for them. On the other hand it was a purely intellectual sorrow. They would not feel sorry for him, so to hell with them. Still, he was glad he was on his side instead of theirs. He was also glad he was here and not there, with the 2d Battalion. Intellectually, he felt sorry for almost everyone. His wife Marty, for instance. In a way this war was tougher on her than it was on him. Bell knew how much a need she had of physical affection, its reassurance, its re-establishment of—of existence, of personality. In a way it was much harder for her to be back there where there were lights, nightclubs, booze, people than it was for him to be here where there was nothing to be tempted by. Much harder. But all of this was intellectual. Emotionally, Bell felt sorry most of all for himself.

Something had happened to him today with the wounding of Peale. Perhaps it was the sheer accident of it. There was no earthly reason why that bullet should have struck Peale and not someone else. But whatever it was, when he saw that little hole in Peale's leg with its trickle of blood running down the white thigh, the actuality of his own death, perhaps sometime soon, perhaps not, had become a reality to Bell. It terrified him. Bell understood the superstitious talisman he had made of never having anything to do with any other women after being called up; he would not even have conversations with them for fear of feeling some desire. Now he added to that first superstition a second which was that if he and Marty both remained true to each other, he could make it back with his genitals intact. Continuing to tap his pickmattock against his shoe, he continued to watch the basin, wondering if that first light shot of malaria he'd had this morning would come back on him tonight. Everybody who had it said evening seemed to be the worst time for attacks.

The planes had claimed everyone's attention, even that of the blackjack players, and when the barrage lifted everybody who was up high enough was watching. From up here the distance to the right end of Hill 209 was greater and the tiny greenclad figures harder to see. They seemed to pass in and out of visibility as they moved up the slope. Much closer, though still far, the small figures of Fox Company's mortar section could be seen on the reverse slope of the subsidiary ridge, working their mortars like fury. And indeed, all across the basin, as the shadows in the hollows continued to creep outward, wherever there were weapons men served them furiously, putting down fire on the ridge.

This time they went all the way. The tiny greenclad Americans met the tiny Japanese chest to chest on the crest, pushed them back and disappeared over the top. Others followed them. After a moment, when they did not reappear running backward, feeble cheers broke out faintly all across the basin on the rearward slopes, sounding more stimulated by a sense of duty than by any real happiness. Undoubtedly the others, like C-for-Charlie whose cheering was quite light, were thinking more about what might be in store for themselves tomorrow, than about what 2d Battalion had accomplished today.

But the morrow was not to be so bad. 2d Battalion had been ordered to renew the assault at dawn, this time against Hill 210, The Elephant's Head and the regiment's main objective. This good news reached them by evening together with the details of today's fight. The regimental commander had dictated a bulletin which was copied down in longhand on the spot by clerks and sent forward to all companies. It said that American arms had triumphed. All of Hill 209 was now in American hands. Easy Company (whom C-for-Charlie had watched cross their front so woodenly and uncommunicatively) had made a march of eleven hundred yards along the edge of the jungle while receiving fire from two directions, and with twenty-five casualties and the aid of G-for-George had completed the envelopment of the Japanese position. They had killed fifty Japanese, captured seventeen machineguns, eight heavy mortars, and a host of smaller arms. They took no prisoners; the Japanese who had not escaped back to Hill 210 preferred to die. 2d Battalion's losses had been 27 killed and 80 wounded, many of whom were picked up on the slopes after the battle. The majority of the Japanese dead were not in good physical condition and many appeared to have suffered from malnutrition.

This was the official news, would be written into the Regimental Papers. C-for-Charlie couldn't have cared less. They were glad 2d Battalion had won the hill, of course. But they were more glad to learn that 2d Battalion was continuing the attack. That the Japanese were hard up for food did not interest them at all. The casualty numbers interested them, though it seemed to them that after what they'd witnessed the numbers were astonishingly light.

There seemed some hope in that. If, of course, they were being told the truth.

But the news that interested them most was unofficial. It was not contained in the regimental commander's bulletin, but it was in the mouth of every messenger who carried the bulletin forward. This was the story of what happened to the two men from George Co whom they had watched the Japanese drag back over the crest in the earlier assault. Their bodies had been found on the reverse slope after the Japanese retreat. Both bodies had sustained numerous bayonet wounds, and one of them had been beheaded alive with a sword. He was found by the advancing E-for-Easy with his hands tied behind his back and his head sitting on his chest. And as a gesture of defiance, or hatred, or something, the Japanese after beheading him had severed his genitals and stuffed them into the mouth of the severed head. That this occurred after death was clear from the lack of blood on the ground near the mutilated crotch. That he had been beheaded alive was equally clear from the amount of blood which had soaked into the earth near the severed neck.

The sheer barbarity of the thing swept through C-for-Charlie like a cold water shock. A cold knifing terror in the belly was followed immediately by a rage of anger. These men they were fighting were veterans of Burma and China and Sumatra. That they professed to hate all white men was well known. That they had perpetrated this sort of outrage in China and the Philippines on their own dark-skinned races was known too. But that they would dare to do the same sort of thing to civilized white American infantry, and specifically the—Regiment of the—Division, was almost too much to believe and certainly too much to be borne. There was a storm of promises never to take a by God prisoner. Many swore they would henceforth coolly and in cold blood shoot down every Japanese who came their way, and preferably in the guts.

The official sources were trying to keep the thing hushed up. Perhaps they felt it might overly frighten the troops. More likely they felt that to let it out would be to allow the entrance of basic human problems into what official sources hoped to keep an essentially simple, uncomplicated military situation. That was what Bugger Stein felt, and he disagreed. Official sources always wanted a clean, clearcut, easily understood military campaign, easily explainable afterwards in terms of strategy and tactics which the generals of the world could write about cleanly, and this sort of thing was embarrassing to that concept. But in spite of official sources the story had swept around the front like wildfire, and Stein did not intend to be a party to the suppression of it. The troops should know what they were in for. Perhaps those two poor bastards hadn't felt much. After all, with the adrenaline and rage and shock of fighting hand to hand, they were probably half crazed. That was all that Stein could see to hope for.

When the messenger who brought the bulletin delivered his other, unofficial news at the CP on the spur, there was almost a riot of murderous reaction. Storm, Bead, Culp, Doll who had come down from 1st Platoon with a message, and Lt Band all made sanguinary promises. Storm looked particularly killerish. Only Welsh with his sly eyes said, and showed, nothing. Little Dale the second cook with his stooped shoulders and intense, tough, flat-eyed face was almost beside himself and swore to gutshoot every Jap who tried to come to him to surrender, after toying with him five minutes first. Young Corporal Fife's reaction on the other hand (though he said not a single word) was one of fear, disbelief and finally a massive horror (as he enviously watched these others) that any creatures who spoke a language, walked upright on two legs dressed in clothes, built cities, and claimed to be human beings could actually treat each other with such fiendish animal cruelty. Obviously the only way really to survive in this world of humansocalledculture we had made and were so proud of, was to be more vicious, meaner and more cruel than those one met. And Fife, for the very first time in his life, was beginning to believe he did not have the toughness of character which this demanded.

It was Pfc Doll who carried the news up the slope to the platoons on the line. John Bell, when Doll on his way back to the 1st Platoon stopped off to tell the 2d, was standing with his squad leader Mother McCron and Big Queen and another man named

Cash. Queen, made sergeant after the defection of Stack, and
Cash were both 1st Platoon. Queen's and McCron's squads
linked the two platoons, and Bell's and Cash's holes were the
actual joining point. The two sergeants were just in the act of
telling the two men to buddy up for the night, one sleeping and
one awake, to facilitate liaison between the platoons, when Doll
reached the crest, breathing heavily, with his news.

Bell had never seen such reactions on men's faces. Big Queen
turned red as a beet with rage, and muttered something about
cracking skulls, flexing his big fists. McCron's eyes got vague
and faraway and his face took on an unwilling, shamed look as if
he did not want to hear as he muttered, "Oh, the dirty fuckers,"
sadly. Cash, a tall powerfully built Ohio draftee who had been a
cab driver in Toledo and was known in the company simply as
"Big Un," on the other hand grinned. He had a cold, gleefully
tough face anyway, as hard and of the same texture as an un-
cracked walnut, and when he grinned and licked his lips like that,
his blue eyes squinted, he looked positively and spinechillingly
murderous. All he said was "Okay" in a very soft, breathed
voice. He said it several times. Bell's own reaction was one of
sickness. He felt sick all over, physcially sick. He said nothing.
But he thought. He thought about the new talisman he had made
just today, and he thought about his wife Marty. Ah, Marty. He
hoped if anything ever happened to him like that, that nobody
would ever write or tell her how this cock and these balls of his
which she had loved so had finally wound up.

The evening itself that night, in cynical contrast to the news,
was very lovely. Up here in the hills night did not fall so swiftly
as it did down below in the groves. The twilight lingered on
turning everything including the air itself to rose, seeming as
though it were reluctant to leave and plunge them into the blackness of their first night in combat. It did not depart until, apparently diabolically, it had given them a lovely striated tropic sunset
to look at in the western sky. It was a time to think of peacefulness and women.

Shortly before dark, when it came time to eat, it was found that
there was no water. There was plenty of C ration around. But

ration details coming down from the platoons on the crest wanted water much worse than food. The sun, the heat, the sweltering, and the sweating had been enormous and every canteen was empty.

All of them had seen jeeploads of watercans on the way up from the river. But wherever these were, diverted into the back areas, or poured out on the ground, they were not at the front. Finally, after much haggling and arguing on the sound power phone and much sending back and forth of messengers, Stein was able to obtain enough water to allow each man half a canteen, which was to last him all through tomorrow. Supper was eaten dry and cold, choked down without any liquid to wash it down.

In the night it rained twice. No one slept much. Many useless grenades were thrown. And every now and then flaming bursts of riflefire lit the night, betraying positions, hitting nothing.

And at dawn, bearded, mudstained, grimy and greasy, rising in their blue holes to watch 2d Battalion take off over the top of Hill 209, the whole of C-for-Charlie looked as though they had been living here for months.

In the chill mists of first light, from this far away, it was difficult to see them as one by one, crouching and carrying their rifles in both hands or one, they hopped over the last foot of ridge and disappeared. A sort of ragged cheer rose briefly and fell away. After that those who remained watched in silence. With The Elephant's Shoulder and Hill 209 now secured, the line snaked along for a thousand yards and more, following the contours of the several ridges which formed the Dancing Elephant's spine. As the attacking companies of 2d Battalion were pulled out and sent forward a gap was opened up between the two battalions, and twice during the morning C-for-Charlie was forced to move.

Breakfast had been choked down dry, also. After that there was nothing to do but sit and wait. The moves, when the orders for them came, were not difficult to make. The left platoon simply pulled out, passing to the rear of the right one, and took up positions at the appointed spot. Then the former right platoon, now the left, joined them. To C-for-Charlie's left Able Company was making the same maneuver and to the left of Able a battalion of the division's reserve regiment was moving in.

Even with the two moves, they had not moved far enough right to see into the battle area proper. They were now almost to the actual Elephant's Shoulder, and they could now hear the mortar and machinegun fire. But just here, as though The Dancing Elephant to keep its balance had hunched its massive shoulders, the ridge curved inward forming an angle of jungle which cut off the view. They were now on the same slope where yesterday, while they watched, F-for-Fox had made its try for the crest and been repulsed; and recognizing it with a sense of squeamishness, they settled down again to wait. They were not unaware that each time they were moved, it was closer to the fight, never farther away from it.

During one of the moves Fullback Culp had seen something move in the brush below, or thought he had. At that moment they had been above and just in front of the side ridge which the F-for-Fox CP had occupied yesterday, and at the foot of its forward slope a small brushgrown draw fell steeply to the main ravine. Culp stopped and whistled softly and pointed. Far down below them in the basin, so recently secured from the enemy, lines and groups of men were moving everywhere with supplies, but up here on the forward slope of the subsidiary ridge there was no one. Nobody else could see anything moving in the brush, but a sort of gleeful manhunt was organized anyway. Increasingly since yesterday and irrespective of rank the seven men who carried the new Thompsonguns had begun to see themselves more and more as a sort of private club. Welsh, Storm, Dale, MacTae, the officers Stein and Band, all of them except Culp were part of the Company HQ anyway, and Culp as commander of the weapons platoon was almost always with the HQ. And it was now the club which took over the manhunt. Spacing themselves so nothing in the little draw could get past their combined fire, while the rest of the CP and the reserve platoon stopped to watch, they waited while two of them, Culp and MacTae, came down the draw like beaters. When they had come halfway and with everyone watching intently, still nothing had moved.

"Watch out," Culp called from above, grinning with all his teeth. "I'm gonna give 'em a burst or two, if they're in there. Hold on." Turning the gun in its side in the approved manner, he sprayed the brush with two short bursts. When he released the trigger he looked surprised. "Damn things really do kick. More'n I thought."

Still nothing moved in the brush. "Come on, let's look." MacTae said. The two of them disappeared into the brush, which swayed above their heads as they moved. They came out looking sheepish.

"Nothin," Culp said. "But you never can tell. Might of been. You know, infiltrators."

He was quite right. There had been infiltration last night in 2d Battalion's area. But there was a good deal of nervous laughter at his expense, anyway, as they all climbed back up to the platoons on the line. There had been some rather extreme nervous tension there for a moment, and now it relieved itself in laughter at Culp. None of them, they found to their surprise, were at ease in the use of their weapons. They had been trained too well and too long in the restrictive safety precautions of the rifle range to feel relaxed shooting over the heads of friends.

Shortly after noon they sustained a counterattack. After the firing all stopped, and they began to compare notes, it was discovered that not one of them could honestly say he had seen a Japanese during the firing. Later it was found that D Company on their right actually had repelled what was probably a patrol in force and had killed several. But when D had begun firing, the firing had spread all along the line until everybody, including the battalion from the reserve regiment on the far left, was heaving grenades and firing over the crest into the jungle whether they saw any Japanese or not. And even afterward when it was over, at least half of the firers still believed they had repelled a major Japanese attack. The others, who knew better, momentarily looked sheepish in the midst of their excitement, but were unable to refrain from rejoining the wild celebration. A few perhaps wondered what the Japanese patrol must have thought, to see a line a thousand yards long suddenly blaze up firing at nothing; they must have laughed heartily.

Corporal Fife, curiously enough, was one of these cynics. With the rest of the Company HQ he had rushed to the line when the firing started. He had fired a whole clip of eight and reloaded, intending to fire more, before common sense attacked him in the form of a deep depression at the uselessness of it all. All around him men were hollering happily and throwing their grenades and firing. A few feet to his left Welsh, cursing joyously and grinning ecstatically, was spraying everything in sight with his Thompsongun. And in front of them the empty jungle underbrush swayed and rustled as though in a rainstorm and chunks of bark and wood popped from the trees. Nursing his depression and setting his safety, he crept back away from the line a few feet and sat down by himself, cradling his rifle between his knees and leaning on it. What the hell was the matter with him? Even in a happy blowoff of useless firing he could not take part. But what depressed him most of all was the awareness of all these new situations he was being thrown into, which he could neither evaluate nor understand. It was like being blind.

It was during this 'counterattack' that Pfc Doll threw his first live grenade, and it was a traumatic experience. Doll lost his nerve. At the point where Doll stood the ridge made a slight dip and there was a chest high clay bank (whether manmade or not it was impossible to tell) behind which one could stand as though in a trench, though the back of it was open to all the basin. The firing when it started was feeble and sporadic and spread slowly, but when it thickened and the dull booming of grenades began to be heard among the chattering of riflefire Doll who had already fired a clip pulled one of his four grenades from a side pocket and pulled its pin. He had spread the cotter pins so widely for reasons of safety that he had to bite its ends together before it would pull out, sending a sharp drill of pain through an old bad tooth. Perhaps that was what undid him. He remembered movies where men pulled the pins of grenades with their teeth, and realized with a shock of inadequacy that his teeth would never be able to stand it. In any case, he had waited too long. He now had the pin out and was standing looking at this heavy orange corrugated castiron object in his hand. As long as he clenched it and kept the tin lever down it was not dangerous, but already his hand felt slippery. Even if he had not already dropped the pin on the ground, he knew it would be impossible to reinsert it, dangerous to attempt. He had activated it, and now here he was with it, and if he did not want to go on carrying it forever while his hand slowly weakened or cramped itself and relaxed, he was going to have to throw it; but what he really wanted to do was simply drop it on the ground and turn and flee. That of course was crazy, insane. If it did not kill him, it would certainly kill the men around him. Why oh why had he ever pulled the pin out? Clenching his teeth until his jaws ached, spacing his feet with great care, oblivious to the noise and firing around him and staring with bulging eyes at the object in his hand as though it were a lighted bomb he was holding, which in fact it was, he threw it with all his strength into the jungle and ducked shaking behind the bank, the 'splatt!' of the igniting fuse as loud in his ears as an explosion. When he had first pulled it out of his pocket, he had meant to watch it light and explode. There was no thought of that now. He could no more have stayed up and watched it than he could have flown after it. He heard a low boom from across the bank, then immediately after it two others. He would never know which was his, and he didn't care. Shattered, he crouched quaking against the bank for several moments more, then blushing furiously, rose and commenced firing his rifle angrily into the empty jungle, hoping nobody had seen him. He fired three clips one after the other, but he did not try to throw any more grenades. When the whole thing was over, he simply turned in his tracks and sat down with his knees drawn up and his back against the bank, breathing in a kind of convulsive groan and staring furiously at nothing.

Somehow during the firing session a dead man had appeared behind C-for-Charlie. In the excitement he went unnoticed at first. Then everyone seemed to discover him all at once. Whole groups turned simultaneously to stare with startled faces. Nobody knew how he had got there or where he came from or who he was. He could not be from C-for-Charlie because nobody in

Charlie had been hurt. He could not have been killed just now in the 'counterattack' because he was obviously already stiff. He had just sort of appeared. Ten yards back from the crest down the slope which was not as steep here as at other places, on a little clay ledge about two yards wide, he lay on his side in an almost fetal position, his knees drawn up against his chest, his half clenched hands up on either side of his face but not touching it. His helmet still on his head, his rifle belt still fastened around his green fatigue blouse, he appeared to be trying to hide from what had already overtaken him. Just below his little clay ledge the slope steepened sharply, and if he could only have rolled over once he could have slid all the way to the bottom of the basin. Many in C-for-Charlie wished that he would.

It was established later that he was a 2d Battalion man who had been killed yesterday but who had not been found until just now because he had fallen a few feet over the crest. D Company had found him while pursuing the Japanese patrol and had placed him on the ledge behind C-for-Charlie for safekeeping at a time when C-for-Charlie was too engrossed in its firing to notice. In the meantime, here he was. The flush of excited talking and laughter had all died quietly away. Angry frowns began to appear. There was muttering. C-for-Charlie did not feel they had done anything to deserve him, and they resented his being palmed off on them. Several men who cautiously approached to within six or seven yards of him returned to say that he smelled. Not strongly yet perhaps, but enough to be upsetting. Soon cries were heard: "Medic! Medic!" "Where the hell's the goddam medics!" "Tell the medics to get that stiff out of here!" Everyone was indignant.

They came for him. Whether or not C-for-Charlie's griping was the cause, they came for him. Two harassed-looking men climbed up from below carrying a folded stretcher. They were obviously tired and looked very short-tempered. Seizing him by a stiffened arm and leg as if they were handles, they deposited him on their stretcher on his back; but when they tried to lift it, he threatened to roll off. They put it down and turned him on his side. This time when they lifted he did roll off. The men dropped the stretcher and putting their hands on their hips, stared at each

other with the air of men who have had about all they can support. Then, bending and seizing him by the handles of his arms
and legs, they moved off with him that way, angling down the
steep slope, one of them dragging the stretcher by a strap. They
had said not one word to anyone.

C-for-Charlie had watched all this action wide-eyed and with
sheepish faces. They could not help feeling the two men were a
little irreverent in their treatment of this newly dead man; at the
same time, they were aware that their own reaction smacked of
irreverence too. Nobody wanted the poor bastard, now. Well,
whatever he had accomplished for 2d Battalion in the last moments of his life, which apparently was not much, he had certainly accomplished something after his death. He had solidly and
effectively put the quietus to C-for-Charlie's short-lived mood of
high, laughing confidence.

It was now after two-thirty. While these experiences were oc-
cupying C-for-Charlie's attention, the battle round the bend
which they could hear but not see had continued unabated. Now
for the first time whole groups began to return from it. The attack
had failed. Running, they would drop gasping over the crest and
lie breathing in hysterical sobs with eyes like drilled holes dark in
their outraged, furious, unbelieving faces. More and more groups
kept coming in, haphazard, piecemeal, rarely even with their own
squads. Everything was going to hell, they gasped. C-for-Charlie
was close enough now to The Elephant's Shoulder, where the
main ridge turned and angled down to the forelegs and barrel,
that as more and more men returned and spilled out along the
interior slope, some of them spread over into C-for-Charlie's
area. A few even came dashing in through the extreme right of
their line, hollering to them not to shoot, for God's sake don't
shoot. Once inside they simply collapsed. One boy, sitting in a
row of five or six, wept openly like a child, his forehead and hand
resting on the shoulder of the man next to him, who patted him
absently while staring straight ahead at nothing with smoldering
eyes. None of them knew what the overall situation was, or had
any idea of what was taking place anywhere except where they
themselves had been. C-for-Charlie, feeling shamefaced, watched

them quietly with a wide-eyed, awed hero worship, which no one could honestly say he wanted to lose, if it entailed—as it would—sharing their experiences.

What they themselves felt was illustrated by an incident most of C-for-Charlie witnessed. It was not an intellectual reaction, nor could it honestly be called the reaction of a student of war. The division commander had been observing the day's fighting from the crest of Hill 209. Of course his career was involved in this offensive. When the groups began returning pellmell and shaken, he strode among them smiling and talking, trying to bolster them. "We're not gonna let these Japs whip us, are we, boys? Hunh? They're tough, but they're not as tough as we are, are they?" One boy, young enough to be the general's son, if not his grandson, looked up at him from where he sat with distended eyes. "General, you go out there! You go out there, general, you go out there!" The general smiled at him, pityingly, and walked on. The boy did not even look after him.

Half way down the main ridge the battalion aid station was filled to overflowing with more wounded than the three doctors could take care of, and more were still coming in. Along the rearward slopes of the basin leading to Hill 206, where just since yesterday the jeep road had been extended forward, jeeps were coming as far out onto the steep slope as they dared to pick up the hand-carried litter cases, and red-and-white-splashed walking wounded tottered rearward in groups, trying to help each other.

Finally the correlated news reached C-for-Charlie, as well as the other companies. The plan had called for two companies to attack abreast after artillery preparation. Fox and George, the workhorses of yesterday, were given the dirtiest work. They were to assault Hill 210, on the left. E-for-Easy was to attack right, into the area of the Elephant's Forelegs labeled Hill 214. Beyond Hill 209 on the left the short, fat Elephant's Neck rose slowly to the eminence of Hill 210, a U shaped ridge with its open end toward the attackers; to go up there was like walking down a bowling alley toward the bowlers, and before the battle was over that was what it came to be called: The Bowling Alley. This area, as well as the couple of hundred yards of open ground immediately in front, was cut by numerous low ridges and hills which might afford protection to attacking troops. On the right, divided from The Elephant's Head by a low-lying salient of jungle, the broader, lower, more level area of The Elephant's Forelegs spread itself. This was the terrain, still as yet never seen by C-for-Charlie, which 2d Battalion had had to attack.

Everything had begun to go wrong almost immediately. First of all there was very little water, hardly half a canteen per man. Fox had led off, followed by George, who were to come abreast of them later for the assault up both sides of The Bowling Alley. But almost at once Fox was caught in a narrow impasse between two of the preliminary ridges. Heavy fire from in front stopped them. Jammed in the narrow space they were hit repeatedly by mortars which apparently had the ranges all taped out. When they tried to maneuver and work out of it, heavy flanking machinegun fire from hidden emplacements forced them back. George, immediately behind them, could do nothing either and suffered their own mortar casualties. The two companies had remained there through most of the morning and through the early afternoon. Fox Co's commander was hit by mortar fire around twelve-thirty and was evacuated, but died on the way back to Regiment's aid station. Squeezed in together under the hot tropic sun and the heavy fire many men, still exhausted from yesterday and waterless today, passed out. When the battalion commander gave the order to retreat, the two companies had broken in rout and returned in bunches.

E-for-Easy's attack was likewise a failure. The lead platoon, moving out onto the broader, but flatter area of The Elephant's Forelegs, had been caught in a withering crossfire from the jungle on its right and left. Easy's commander, trying to send up an attached machinegun platoon from H, had them almost annihilated. And after that the rest of the company did not try to move and remained just a few yards in front of the crest of Hill 209.

That was the story. By three-thirty all those who were able had returned. Medical parties, at considerable risk, were searching out the others. There was no dictated bulletin that night by the regimental commander. Casualties for the day were 34 killed and 102 wounded. Speculations as to why, with this holocaust, today's casualties were only slightly higher than yesterday's, were left without any answer. The only reasonable thing to say was that yesterday there had been more hours of actual fighting. But more important than all of this news was the news that the regimental commander had ordered the exhausted 2d Battalion back to Hills 207 and 208 into regimental reserve. This meant that tomorrow 1st Battalion would take over the attack. The battalion from the division's reserve regiment on their left would then, undoubtedly, take over their lines on Hill 209.

This was exactly what happened, and their orders reached them soon enough. There had existed a remote possibility that the regimental commander might order the battalion of the division reserve to make the attack, and C-for-Charlie clung to this hopefully, but nobody really believed it. Their orders, which reached them around six o'clock, confirmed their wisdom.

Colonel Tall's plan was not radically different from the 2d Battalion's colonel. Two companies would attack abreast; C-for-Charlie would be on the left and would capture The Elephant's Head, Hill 210, and A-for-Able on the right would move into The Elephant's Forelegs, Hill 214, and hook up there with the 3d Battalion who were encountering less resistance. Baker would be in reserve behind Charlie. The plan was really no different from today's. The only difference was that tomorrow there would be water and whatever casualties 2d Battalion may have inflicted today, if any.

C-for-Charlie had drawn the worst assignment: the Bowling Alley. They believed the drawing of the worst assignment to be their perpetual destiny. And that evening when a company of the divisional reserve battalion moved in to take over their slit trenches so that they might rest up for tomorrow, C-for-Charlie received them without friendship. They came smiling and talking, filled with flattering hero worship and eager to please, because they believed C-for-Charlie to be veterans and themselves green; and C-for-Charlie treated them to the same morose silences which yesterday morning they themselves had received from E-for-Easy going up to attack.

But some time before any of this had happened, young Pfc Bead had killed his first Japanese, the first Japanese to be killed by his company, or for that matter by his battalion.

It was, Bead reflected about it later, when indeed he was able to think about it at all, which was not for some time, typical of his entire life; of his stupid incompetence, his foolish idiocy, his gross mismanagement of everything he put his hands on; so that whatever he did, done so badly and in such ugly style, gave no satisfaction: action without honor, travail without grace. A man of a different temperament might have found it funny; Bead could not laugh.

At just about five o'clock he had had to take a crap. And he had not had a crap for two days. Everything had quieted down on the line by five and at the aid station below them the last of the wounded were being cared for and sent back. Bead had seen other men taking craps along the slope, and he knew the procedure. After two days on these slopes the procedure was practically standardized. Because every available bit of level space was occupied, jammed with men and equipment, crapping was relegated to the steeper slopes. Here the process was to take along an entrenching shovel and dig a little hole, then turn your backside to the winds of the open air and squat, balancing yourself precariously on your toes, supporting yourself on the dirt or rocks in front of you with your hands. The effect, because of the men below in the basin, was rather like hanging your ass out of a tenth floor window above a crowded street. It was an embarrassing position to say the least, and the men below were not above taking advantage of it with catcalls, whistles or loud soulful sighs.

Bead was shy. He could have done it that way if he'd had to, but because he was shy, and because now everything had quieted down to an unbelievable evening peace after the terror, noise and danger of the afternoon, he decided to have himself a pleasant, quiet, private crap in keeping with the peacefulness. Without saying anything to anyone he dropped all of his equipment by his hole and taking only his GI roll of toilet paper, he started to climb the twenty yards to the crest. He did not even take an entrenching tool because on the other side there was no need to bury his stool.

Beyond the crest he knew that the slope did not drop precipitously as it did further to the left, but fell slowly for perhaps fifty yards through the trees before it plunged in a bluff straight down to the river. This was where D Company had caught the Japanese patrol earlier in the day.

"Hey, bud, where you going?" somebody from the 2d Platoon called to him as he passed through.

"To take a shit," Bead called back without looking around and disappeared over the crest.

The trees began three yards below the actual crest. Because the jungle was thinner with less undergrowth here at its outer edge, it looked more like the columnar, smooth-floored woods of home and made Bead think of when he was a boy. Reminded of times when as a Boy Scout he had camped out and crapped with peaceful pleasure in the summer woods of Iowa, he placed the roll of paper comfortably near, dropped his pants and squatted. Half way through with relieving himself, he looked up and saw a Japanese man with a bayoneted rifle moving stealthily through the trees ten yards away.

As if feeling his gaze, the Japanese man turned his head and saw him in almost the same instant but not before, through the electrifying, heart stabbing thrill of apprehension, danger, disbelief, denial, Bead got a clear, burned in the brain impression of him.

He was a small man, and thin; very thin. His mud-slicked, mustard-khaki uniform with its ridiculous wrap leggins hung from him in jungledamp, greasy folds. Not only did he not wear any of the elaborate camouflage Bead had been taught by movies to expect, he did not even wear a helmet. He wore a greasy, wrinkled, bent up forage cap. Beneath it his yellowbrown face was so thin the high cheekbones seemed about to come out through his skin. He was badly unshaven, perhaps two weeks, but his greasy looking beard was as straggly as Bead's nineteen-year-old one. As to age, Bead could not form any clear impression; he might have been twenty, or forty.

All of this visual perception occurred in an eyewink of time, an eyewink which seemed to coast on and on and on, then the Japanese man saw him too and turning, all in one movement, began to run at him, but moving cautiously, the bayonet on the end of his rifle extended.

Bead, still squatting with his pants down, his behind still dirty, gathered his weight under him. He was going to have to try to jump one way or another, but which? Which side to jump to? Am I going to die? Am I really going to die now? He did not even have his knife with him. Terror and disbelief, denial, fought each other in him. Why the Japanese did not simply fire the rifle he did not know. Perhaps he was afraid of being heard in the American lines. Instead he came on, obviously meaning to bayonet Bead where he sat. His eyes were intent with purpose. His lips were drawn back from his teeth, which were large, but were well formed and not at all protruding as in the posters. Was it really true?

In desperation, still not knowing which way to try to jump, all in one movement Bead pulled up his pants over his dirty behind to free his legs and dove forward in a low, shoestring football tackle when the Japanese man was almost to him, taking him around the ankles, his feet driving hard in the soft ground. Surprised, the Japanese man brought the rifle down sharply, but Bead was already in under the bayonet. The stacking swivel banged him painfully on the collarbone. By clasping the mudcaked shins against his chest and using his head for a fulcrum, still driving hard with his feet, the Japanese man had no way to fall except backward, and Bead was already clawing up his length before he hit the ground. In the fall he dropped the rifle and had the wind knocked out of him. This gave Bead time to hitch up his pants again and spring upward once more until, kneeling on his upper arms and sitting back on his chest, he began to punch and claw him in the face and neck. The Japanese man could only pluck feebly at his legs and forearms.

Bead heard a high, keening scream and thought it was the Japanese begging for mercy until finally he slowly became aware that the Japanese man was now unconscious. Then he realized it was himself making that animal scream. He could not, however, stop it. The Japanese man's face was now running blood from the clawing, and several of his teeth had been broken back into his throat from the punches. But Bead could not stop. Sobbing and wailing, he continued to belabor the unconscious Japanese with fingernail and fist. He wanted to tear his face off with his bare hands, but found this difficult. Then he seized his throat and tried to break his head by beating it on the soft ground but only succeeded in digging a small hole with it. Exhausted finally, he collapsed forward on hands and knees above the bleeding, unconscious man, only to feel the Japanese immediately twitch with life beneath him.

Outraged at such a display of vitality, alternately sobbing and wailing, Bead rolled aside, seized the enemy rifle and on his knees raised it above his head and drove the long bayonet almost full length into the Japanese chest. The Japanese man's body convulsed in a single spasm. His eyes opened, staring horribly at nothing, and his hands flipped up from the elbows and seized the blade through his chest.

Staring with horror at the fingers which were cutting themselves on the blade trying to draw it out, Bead leaped to his feet and his pants fell down. Hiking his pants up and standing spraddlelegged to keep them from falling, he seized the rifle and tried to pull it out in order to plunge it in again. But the bayonet would not come loose. Remembering dimly something he had been taught in bayonet practice, he grabbed the small of the stock and pulled the trigger. Nothing happened. The gun was on safety. Fumbling with the unfamiliar, foreign safety, he released it and pulled again. There was a flesh-muffled explosion and the bayonet came free. But the fool of a Japanese with his open eyes went on grasping at his chest with his bleeding fingers as if he could not get it through his thick head that the bayonet was out. My god, how much killing did the damned fool require? Bead had beaten him, kicked him, choked him, clawed him, bayoneted him, shot him. He had a sudden frantic vision of himself, by rights the victor, doomed forever to kill perpetually the same single Japanese.

This time, not intending to be caught in the same trap twice, instead of sticking him he reversed the rifle in his hands and drove the butt down full force into his face, smashing it. Standing above him spraddlelegged to keep his pants up, he drove the rifle butt again and again into the Japanese man's face, until all of the face and most of the head were mingled with the muddy ground. Then he threw the rifle from him and fell down on his hands and knees and began to vomit.

Bead did not lose consciousness, but he completely lost his sense of time. When he came to himself, still on hands and knees, gasping, he shook his hanging head and opened his eyes and discovered his left hand was resting in a friendly way on the Japanese man's still, mustard-khaki knee. Bead snatched it away as though he had discovered it lying across a burning stove. He had an obscure feeling that if he did not look at the corpse of the man he had killed or touch it, he would not be held responsible. With this in mind he crawled feebly away through the trees, breathing in long painful groans.

The woods were very quiet. Bead could not remember ever having heard such quiet. Then faintly, penetrating the immensity of this quiet, he heard voices, American voices, and the casual sound of a shovel scraped against a rock. It seemed impossible that they could be that close. He got shakily to his feet holding up his pants. It also seemed impossible that anything could ever again sound as casual as that shovel had. He knew he had to get back inside the lines. But first he would have to try to clean himself up. He was a mess. He had no desire to finish his crap.

First of all, he had to go back to the vicinity of the dead man to get his roll of toilet paper. He hated that but there wasn't any choice. His pants and his dirty behind were what bothered him most. Horror of that was inbred in him; but also he was terrified someone might think he had crapped his pants from fear. He used most of his roll of toilet paper on that, and in the end even sacrificed one of his three clean handkerchiefs which he was saving back for his glasses, moistening it with spittle. In addition he was spattered with blood and vomit. He could not remove every stain, but he tried to get enough so that nobody would notice. Because he had already decided he was not going to mention this to anybody.

Also, he had lost his glasses. He found them, miraculously unbroken, beside the dead man. Searching for his glasses, he had to go right up to the body, and to look at it closely. The face-less—almost headless—corpse with its bloody, cut fingers and the mangled hole in its chest, so short a time ago a living, breathing man, made him so dizzy in the stomach that he thought he might faint. On the other hand, he could not forget the intent look of deliberate purpose on the man's face as he came in with the bayonet. There didn't seem to be any reasonable answer.

The feet were the saddest thing. In their hobnailed infantry boots they splayed outward, relaxed, like the feet of a man asleep. With a kind of perverse fascination Bead could not resist giving one of them a little kick. It lolloped up, then flopped back. Bead wanted to turn and run. He could not escape a feeling that, especially now, after he'd both looked and touched, some agent of retribution would try to hold him responsible. He wanted to beg the man's forgiveness in the hope of forestalling responsibility. He had not felt such oppressive guilt over anything since the last time his mother had caught and whipped him for masturbating.

If he'd had to kill him, and apparently he had, at least he could have done it more efficiently and gracefully, and with less pain and anguish for the poor man. If he had not lost his head, had not gone crazy with fear, perhaps he might even have taken him prisoner and obtained valuable information from him. But he had been frantic to get the killing over with, as if afraid that as long as the man could breathe he might suddenly stand up and accuse him. Suddenly Bead had a mental picture of them both with positions reversed: of himself lying there and feeling that blade plunge through his chest; of himself watching that riflebutt descend upon his face, with the final fire-exploding end. It made him so weak that he had to sit down. What if the other man had got the bayonet down quicker? What if he himself had tackled a little higher? Instead of merely a bruise on his collarbone, Bead saw himself spitted through the soft of the shoulder, head on, that crude blade descending into the soft dark of his chest cavity. He could not believe it.

Settling his glasses on his face, taking a couple of deep breaths

and a last look at his ruined enemy, he got up and started clumping up out of the trees toward the crest. Bead was ashamed and
embarrassed by the whole thing, that was the truth, and that was
why he didn't want to mention it to anybody.

He got back through the line all right, without questions.
"Have a good shit?" the man from the 2d Platoon called to him.
"Yeah," he mumbled and clomped on, down the slope toward the
CP. But on his way he was joined by Pfc Doll, on his way down
from 1st Platoon with a message to ask again about water. Doll
fell in step with him, and immediately noticed his damaged hands
and the blood spatters.

"Christ! What happened to your knuckles? You have a fight
with somebody?"

Bead's heart sank. It would have to be Doll. "No. I slipped and
fell and skinned myself," he said. He was as stiff and sore all
over as if he *had* had a fistfight with somebody. Horror welled in
him again, suddenly, ballooningly. He took several very deep
breaths into a sore rib cage.

Doll grinned with frank but amiable skepticism. "And I spose
all them little blood splatters come from your knuckles?"

"Leave me alone, Doll!" Bead blazed up. "I dont feel like
talking! So just leave me alone, hunh? Will you?" He tried to put
into his eyes all the fierce toughness of a man just returned from
killing an enemy. He hoped maybe that would shut him up, and it
did. At least for a while. They walked on down in silence, Bead
aware with a kind of horrified disgust that already he was fitting
the killing of the Japanese man into the playing of a role; a role
without anything, no reality, of himself or anything else. It hadn't
been like that at all.

Doll did not stay shut up, though. Doll had been a little taken
aback by Bead's vehemence, a forcefulness he was not used to
expecting from Bead. He could smell something when he saw it.
And after he had delivered his message, receiving the answer he
expected which was that Stein was doing everything he could to
get them water, he brought it up again, this time by calling it to
the attention of Welsh. Welsh and Storm were sitting on the sides
of their holes matching pennies for cigarettes, which were already

beginning to be precious. They would match four best out of
seven, to lengthen the game and cut down the expense in cigarettes, then both pull out their plastic pack holders which everyone had bought to keep their butts dry and carefully pass the one
tube between them. Doll went over to them grinning with his
eyebrow raised. He did not feel, at least not at the time, that what
he was doing had anything to do with ratting on someone or
stooling.

"What the fuck happen to your boy there? Who the hell he
beat up with them skinned knuckles and all them blood splatters
on him? Did I miss somethin?"

Welsh looked up at him with that level gaze of his which, when
he wasn't pretending to be crazy, could be so penetrating. Already, Doll felt he had made a mistake, and guilty. Without answering Welsh turned to look at Bead, who sat hunched up by
himself on a small rock. He had put back on his equipment.

"Bead, come over here!"

Bead got up and came, still hunched, his face drawn. Doll
grinned at him with his raised eyebrow. Welsh looked him up and
down.

"What happened to you?"

"Who? Me?"

Welsh waited in silence.

"Well, I slipped and fell down and skinned myself, that's all."

Welsh eyed him in silence, thoughtfully. Obviously he was not
even bothering with that story. "Where'd you go a while ago?
When you were gone for a while? Where were you?"

"I went off to take a crap by myself."

"Wait!" Doll put in, grinning. "When I seen him, he was
comin down from the 2d Platoon's section of line on the ridge."

Welsh swung his gaze to Doll and his eyes blazed murderously.
Doll subsided. Welsh looked back at Bead. Stein, who had been
standing nearby, had come closer now and was listening. So had
Band and Fife and some of the others.

"Lissen, kid," Welsh said. "I got more problems than I know
what to do with in this screwy outfit. Or how to handle. I got no
time to fuck around with kid games. I want to know what hap-

pened to you, and I want the truth. Look at yourself! Now, what happened, and where were you?''

Welsh apparently, at least to Bead's eyes, was much closer to guessing the truth than the unimaginative Doll, or the others. Bead drew a long quavering breath.

''Well, I went across the ridge outside the line in the trees to take a crap in private. A Jap guy came up while I was there and he tried to bayonet me. And—and I killed him.'' Bead exhaled a long, fluttering breath, then inhaled sharply and gulped.

Everyone was staring at him disbelievingly, but nevertheless dumbstruck. ''Goddam it, kid!'' Welsh bellowed after a moment. ''I told you I wanted the goddam fucking *truth!* And not no kid games!''

It had never occurred to Bead that he would not be believed. Now he was faced with a choice of shutting up and being taken for a liar, or telling them where and having them see what a shameful botched-up job he'd done. Even in his upset and distress it did not take him long to choose.

''Then god damn you go and *look!''* he cried at Welsh. ''Dont take my word, go and look for your goddam fucking *self!''*

''I'll go!'' Doll put in immediately.

Welsh turned to glare at him. ''You'll go nowhere, stooly,'' he said. He turned back to Bead. ''I'll go myself.''

Doll had subsided into a stunned, shocked, whitefaced silence. It had never occurred to Doll that his joking about Bead would be taken as stoolpigeoning. But then he had never imagined the result would turn out to be what it apparently had. Bead killing a Jap! He was not guilty of stooling, and furiously he made up his mind that he was going along; if he had to crawl.

''And if you're lyin, kid, God help your fucking soul.'' Welsh picked up his Thompsongun and put on his helmet. ''All right. Where is it? Come on, show me.''

''I'm not going up there again!'' Bead cried. ''You want to go, go by yourself! But I aint going! And nothin's gonna make me!''

Welsh stared at him narrowly a moment. Then he looked at Storm. Storm nodded and got up. ''Okay,'' Welsh said. ''Where is it, then?''

"A few yards in the trees beyond the crest, at the middle of the 2d Platoon. Just about in front of Krim's hole." Bead turned and walked away.

Storm had put on his helmet and picked up his own Thompson. And suddenly, with the withdrawal of Bead and his emotion from the scene, the whole thing became another larking, kidding excursion of the "Tommygun Club" which had held the infiltrator hunt that morning. Stein, who had been listening in silence nearby all the time, dampened it by refusing to allow any of the officers to leave the CP; but MacTae could go, and it was the three sergeants and Dale who prepared to climb to the crest. Bead could not resist calling a bitter comment from his rock: "You won't need all the goddamned artillery, Welsh! There's nobody up there now but *him!*" But he was ignored.

It was just before they departed that Doll, his eyes uneasy but nonetheless steady, presented himself manfully in front of the First Sergeant and gazed at him squarely.

"Top, you wouldn't keep me from goin, would you?" he asked. It was not begging nor was it a try at being threatening, just a simple, level, straightforward question.

Welsh stared at him a moment, then without change of expression turned away silently. It was obviously a reprimand. Doll chose to take it as silent acquiescence. And with himself in the rear the five of them started the climb to the line. Welsh did not send him back.

While they were gone no one bothered Bead. He sat by himself on his rock, head down, now and then squeezing his hands or feeling his knuckles. Everyone avoided looking at him, as if to give him privacy. The truth was nobody really knew what to think. As for Bead himself, all he could think about was how shamefully he and his hysterical, graceless killing were going to be exposed. His memory of it, and of that resolute face coming at him, made him shudder and want to gag. More times than not he wished he had kept his mouth shut and let them all think him a crazy liar. It might have been much better.

When the little scouting party returned, their faces all wore a peculiar look. "He's there," Welsh said. "He sure is," MacTae said. All of them looked curiously subdued. That was all that was said. At least, it was all that was said in front of Bead. What they said away from him, Bead could not know. But he did not find in their faces any of the disgust or horror of him that he had expected. If anything, he found a little of the reverse: admiration. As they separated to go to their various holes, each made some gesture.

Doll had hunted up the Japanese rifle and brought it back for Bead. He had scrubbed most of the blood and matter from the buttplate with leaves and had cleaned up the bayonet. He brought it over and presented it as if presenting an apology offering.

"Here, this is yours."

Bead looked at it without feeling anything. "I dont want it."

"But you won it. And won it the hard way."

"I dont want it anyway. What good's it to me."

"Maybe you can trade it for whiskey." Doll laid it down. "And here's his wallet. Welsh said to give it to you. There's a picture of his wife in it."

"Jesus Christ, Doll."

Doll smiled. "There's pictures of other broads, too," he hurried on. "Filipino, it looks like. Maybe he was in the Philippines. That's Filipino writing on the back, Welsh says."

"I dont want it anyway. You keep it." But he took the proffered wallet anyway, his curiosity piqued in spite of himself. "Well—" He looked at it. It was dark, greasy from much sweating. "I dont feel good about it, Doll," he said looking up, wanting suddenly to talk about it to someone. "I feel guilty."

"Guilty! What the hell for? It was him or you, wasn't it? How many our guys you think maybe he stuck that bayonet in in the Philippines? On the Death March. How about those two guys yesterday?"

"I know all that. But I can't help it. I feel guilty."

"But why!"

"Why! Why! How the fuck do I know why!" Bead cried. "Maybe my mother beat me up too many times for jerking off when I was a kid!" he cried plaintively, with a sudden halfflashing of miserable insight. "How do I know why!"

Doll stared at him uncomprehendingly.

"Never mind," Bead said.

"Listen," Doll said. "If you really dont want that wallet."

Bead felt a sudden clutching greed. He put the wallet in his pocket quickly. "No. No, I'll keep it. No, I might as well keep it."

"Well," Doll said sorrowfully, "I got to get back up to the platoon."

"Thanks anyway, Doll," he said.

"Yeah. Sure." Doll stood up. "I'll say one thing. When you set out to kill him, you really killed him," he said admiringly.

Bead jerked his head up, his eyes searching. "You think so?" he said. Slowly he began to grin a little.

Doll was nodding, his face boyish with his admiration. "I aint the only one." He turned and left, heading up the slope.

Bead stared after him, still not knowing what he really felt. And Doll had said he wasn't the only one. If they did not find it such a disgraceful, botched-up job, then at least he need not feel so bad about that. Tentatively he grinned a little wider, a little more expansively, aware that his face felt stiff doing it.

A little later on Bugger Stein came over to him. Stein had remained in the background up to now. The news of Bead's Japanese had of course spread through the whole company at once, and when messengers or ration details came down from the line, they looked at Bead as though he were a different person. Bead was not sure whether he enjoyed this or not, but had decided that he did. He was not surprised when Stein came over.

Bead was sitting on the edge of his hole when Stein appeared, jumped down in and sat down beside him. Nobody else was around. Stein adjusted his glasses in that nervous way he had, the four fingers on top of one frame, the thumb beneath, and then put his hand on Bead's knee in a fatherly way and turned to look at him. His face was earnest and troubled-looking.

"Bead, I know you've been pretty upset by what happened to you today. That's unavoidable. Anybody would be. I thought perhaps you might like to talk about it, and maybe relieve yourself a little. I dont know that what I would have to say to you about it would be of any help, but I'm willing to try.''

Bead stared at him in astonishment, and Stein, giving his knee a couple of pats, turned and looked sadly off across the basin toward Hill 207, the command post of yesterday.

"Our society makes certain demands and requires certain sacrifices of us, if we want to live in it and partake of its benefits. I'm not saying whether this is right or wrong. But we really have no choice. We have to do as society demands. One of these demands is the killing of other humans in armed combat in time of war, when our society is being attacked and must defend itself. That was what happened to you today. Only most men who have to do this are luckier than you. They do their first killing at a distance, however small. They have a chance, however small, to get used to it before having to kill hand to hand and face to face. I think I know what you must have felt.''

Stein paused. Bead did not know what to say to all of this, so he did not say anything. When Stein turned and looked at him for some answer, he said "Yes, sir.''

"Well, I just want you to know that you were morally justified in what you did. You had no choice, and you mustn't worry or feel guilty about it. You only did what any other good soldier would have done, for our country or any other.''

Bead listened incredulously. When Stein paused again, he did not know what to say so he didn't say anything. Stein looked off across the basin.

"I know it's tough. You and I may have had our little differences, Bead. But I want you to know—'' his voice choked slightly—"I want you to know that after this war is over, if there is anything I can ever do for you, just get in touch with me. I'll do everything I possibly can to help you.''

Without looking at Bead he got up, patted him on the shoulder and left.

Bead stared after him, as he had done after Doll. He still did not know what he really felt. Nobody told him anything that made any sense. But he realized now, quite suddenly, that he could survive the killing of many men. Because already the immediacy of the act itself, only minutes ago so very sharp, was fading. He could look at it now without pain, perhaps even with pride, in a way, because now it was only an idea like a scene in a play, and did not really hurt anyone.

He was not given much time to speculate on this point, however. By the time Stein, in leaving Bead's hole, had arrived back at his own, the messenger with tomorrow's dispositions had arrived and was waiting for him. They were to move out immediately, down into the basin and around the curve of the ridge, as soon as the reserve battalion could take over for them.

They already knew of course that 2d Battalion was being pulled out. They had watched the battered and broken companies moving back along the slopes. There was only one logical answer to this. C-for-Charlie however had preferred not to believe it. Now it had come.

The relief platoons began to come in fifteen minutes later, smiling and obsequious, somehow guiltyfaced. C-for-Charlie was already packed and was glad to get away from them quickly. There was no point in talking about it. One by one the squads came down from the top past the CP and continued on down, angling off across the steep slope toward the bottom. At the head of the basin where Hill 209 cut across the fall of the land like a dam, the bottom was much less deep than further down, perhaps only fifty yards from the crest, and this was where they were to congregate. The HQ and the mortars left last, following the platoons. There had been very little to pack. The incoming platoons still carried their combat packs, complete with meatcan, entrenching tool, raincoat, etc. C-for-Charlie had already dispensed with these. Instead each man carried his spoon in his pocket, and had his entrenching tool hooked to his belt. A few lugged their raincoats along over one shoulder.

Bugger Stein and his opposite number, when Stein made the official turnover, reacted exactly as their troops had. The other captain, a man of Stein's age, smiled apologetically and offered his hand which Stein took perfunctorily. "Good luck!" he called softly as Stein moved off after his men. Stein, with a lump of excitement and tension filling his throat, did not think it worth the effort to swallow one half and cough up the other in order to make a pointless answer, and only bobbed his head without looking back. He, like his men, only wanted to get away quickly, and especially without having to talk.

But down in the bottom they found others who wanted to talk to them. Bars of D ration chocolate were pressed upon them by the reserve platoons stationed there. They were given first pick at the C rations for their suppers. The best places to sleep were offered them. By now it was almost dark, and over an hour was consumed in making sure each man had two full canteens of water. Stein and the officers went off for a flashlight briefing in a small ditch with Colonel Tall, an older man though not as much older as the generals, lean and boyish and burrheaded, a West Pointer. He had been trained in all this as his life work. They came back looking solemn. Tall had told them the corps commander as well as the division commander would be watching tomorrow. Men spread themselves out in holes dug by other, unknown men or in little erosion ditches and tried to force sleep upon bodies which kept shooting messages of reluctance along humming nerves.

In the night it rained only once, but it was a very hard rain which wet everyone to the skin, and woke those who had managed to doze.

CHAPTER 4

Dawn came, and passed, and still they waited. The roses and blues of the dawn light changed to the pearl and misty greys of early morning light. Of course everyone had been up, and nervously ready, since long before dawn. But for today Colonel Tall had requested a new artillery wrinkle. Because of yesterday's heavy repulse, Tall had asked for, and got, an artillery time-on-target "shoot." This device, an artillery technique left over from World War I, was a method of calculating so that the first rounds of every battery hit their various targets simultaneously. Under TOT fire men caught in the open would suddenly find themselves enveloped in a curtain of murderous fire without the usual warning of a few shells arriving early from the nearest guns. The thing to do was to wait a bit, play poker with them, try to catch them when they were out of their holes for breakfast or an early morning stretch. So they waited. Along the crest the silent troops stared across a silent ravine to the silent hilltop, and the silent hill stared back.

C-for-Charlie, waiting with the assault companies on the slope below, could not even see this much. Nor did they care. They crouched over their weapons in total and unspeakable insularity, so many separate small islands. To their right and to their left A-for-Able and B-for-Baker did the same.

At exactly twenty-two minutes after first daylight Colonel

Tall's requested TOT fire struck, an earthcracking, solidly tangible, continuous roar on Hill 210. The artillery fired three-minute concentrations at irregular intervals, hoping to catch the survivors out of their holes. Twenty minutes later, and before the barrage itself was ended, whistles began to blow along the crest of Hill 209.

The assault companies had no recourse except to begin to move. Minds cast frantically about for legitimate last minute excuses, and found none. In the men themselves nervous fear and anxiety, contained so long and with such effort in order to appear brave, now began to come out in yelled exhortations and yelps of gross false enthusiasm. They moved up the slope; and in bunches, crouching low and carrying their rifles in one or both hands, they hopped over the crest and commenced to run sideways and crouching down the short forward slope to the flat, rocky ground in front. Men in the line shouted encouragement to them as they passed through. A small cheer, dwarfed by the distant mountains, rose and died. A few slapped some of them toughly on the shoulder as they went through. Men who would not die today winked lustily at men who, in some cases, would soon be dead. On C-for-Charlie's right fifty yards away A-for-Able was going through an identical ritual.

They were rested. At least, they were comparatively so; they had not had to stand watch one half of the night, and they had not been up on the line where jitters precluded sleep, but down below, protected. And they had been fed. And watered. If few of them had slept much, at least they were better off than the men on the line.

Corporal Fife was one of those who had slept the least. He still could not get over little Bead's having killed that Jap like that. What with that, the rain, the total lack of shelter from the rain, and his nervous excitation about the morrow, he had only dozed once for about five minutes. But the loss of sleep did not bother him. He was young, and healthy, and fairly strong. In fact, he had never felt *healthier* or in better shape in his life; and earlier in the day, in the first gray of early light, he had stood forth upon the slope and, exuding energy and vitality, had looked a long time

down the ravine as it fell and deepened toward the rear until he
wanted to spread wide his arms with sacrifice and love of life and
love of men. He didn't do it of course. There were men awake all
round him. But he had wanted to. And now as he dropped over
the ridge and into the beginning of the battle, he shot one swift
look behind him, one last look, and found himself staring headon
into the wide, brown, spectacle-covered eyes of Bugger Stein,
who happened to be right behind him. What a hell of a last look!
Fife thought sourly.

Stein thought he had never seen such a deep, dark, intense,
angrily haunted look as that which Fife bent on him as they
dropped over the ridge, and Stein thought it was directed at him.
At him, personally. They too were almost the last to go. Only
Sergeant Welsh and young Bead remained behind them. And
when Stein looked back, they were coming, hunched low, chopping with their feet, sliding down the shale and dirt of the slope.

Stein's dispositions had been the same today as in the two
previous days. They had done nothing much and he saw no reason to change the march order: 1st Platoon first, 2d Platoon second, 3d in reserve. One of the two machineguns went with each
forward platoon; the mortars would stay with the Company HQ
and the reserve. That was the way they had moved out. And as
Stein slid to the bottom of 209's short forward slope he could see
1st Platoon pass out of sight beyond one of the little folds of
ground which ran across their line of advance. They were about a
hundred yards ahead and appeared to be deployed well.

There were three of these little folds in the ground. All of them
were perpendicular to the south face of Hill 209, parallel to each
other. It had been Stein's idea, when inspecting the terrain with
Colonel Tall the evening before, to utilize these as cover by shoving off from the right end of the hill and then advancing left
across them and across his own front—instead of getting himself
caught in the steeper ravine immediately between the two hills, as
had happened to Fox Co. Tall had agreed to this.

Afterward, Stein had briefed his own officers on it. Kneeling
just behind the crest with them in the fading light, he pointed it
all out and they looked it over. Somewhere in the dusk a sniper's

rifle had spat angrily. One by one they inspected it through binoculars. The third and furthest left of these three folds was about a hundred and fifty yards from the beginning of the slope which became the Elephant's Neck. This slope steepened as it climbed to the U-shaped eminence of the Elephant's Head, which from five hundred yards beyond commanded and brooded over the entire area. This hundred and fifty yard low area, as well as the third fold, was dominated by two lesser, grassy ridges growing out of the slope and two hundred yards apart, one on either side of the low area. Both ridges were at right angles to the folds of ground and parallel to the line of advance. With these in their hands *plus* the Elephant's Head, the Japanese could put down a terrible fire over the whole approach area. Tall's plan was for the forward elements to move up onto these two ridges, locating and eliminating the hidden strong points there which had stopped 2d Battalion yesterday, and then with the reserve company to reinforce them, work their way up the Elephant's Neck to take The Head. This was the Bowling Alley. But there was no way to outflank it. On the left it fell in a precipitous slope to the river, and on the right the Japanese held the jungle in force. It had to be taken frontally. All of this Stein had lined out for his officers last evening. Now they were preparing to execute it.

Stein, at the bottom of the shale slope, could see very little of anything. A great racketing of noise had commenced and hung everywhere in the air without seeming to have any source. Part of course was due to his own side firing all along the line, and the bombardment and the mortars. Perhaps the Japanese were firing too now. But he could see no visual signs of it. What time was it, anyway? Stein looked at his watch, and its little face stared back at him with an intensity it had never had before. 6:45; a quarter to seven in the morning. Back home he would be just—Stein realized he had never really seen his watch. He forced himself to put his arm down. Directly in front of him his reserve 3d Platoon were spread out and flattened behind the first of the three little folds of ground. With them were the Company HQ and the mortar section. Most of them were looking at him with faces as intense as his watch's face. Stein ran crouching over to them, his equipment bouncing and banging on him, shouting for them to set up the mortars there, motioning with his hand. Then he realized that he could only just barely hear his own voice himself, with all this banging and racketing of doom bouncing around in the air. How could they hear him? He wondered how the 1st Platoon—and the 2d—were doing, and how he could see.

The 1st Platoon, at that particular moment, was spread out and flattened behind the middle of the three little folds of ground. Behind it the 2d Platoon was spread out and flattened in the low between the folds. Nobody really wanted to move. Young Lt Whyte had already looked over the area between this fold and the third and seen nothing, and he already had motioned for his two scouts to proceed there. Now he motioned to them again, using an additional hand-and-arm signal meaning "speed." The booming and banging and racketing in the air was bothering Whyte, too. It did not seem to come from any one place or several places, but simply hung and jounced in the air, sourceless. He too could see no visual end results of so much banging and exploding. His two scouts still not having moved, Whyte became angry and opened his mouth and bellowed at them, motioning again. They could not hear him of course, but he knew they could see the black open hole of his mouth. Both of them stared at him as though they thought him insane for even suggesting such a thing, but this time, after a moment, they moved. Almost side by side they leaped up, crossed the crest of the little fold, and ran crouching down to the low where they flattened themselves. After a moment they leaped up again, one a little behind the other, and ran bent almost double to the top of the last fold and fell flat. After another moment and a perfunctory peek over its top, they motioned Whyte to come on. Whyte jumped up making a sweeping forward motion with his arm and ran forward, his platoon behind him. As the 1st Platoon moved, making the crossing as the scouts had: in two rushes, the 2d Platoon moved to the top of the middle fold.

Back at the first fold of ground Stein had seen this move and been a little reassured by it. Creeping close to the top of the fold among his men, he had raised himself to his knees to see, his face and whole patches of his skin twitching with mad alarm in an effort to call his insanity to his attention. When nothing hit him immediately, he stayed up, standing on his knees, to see 1st Platoon leave the middle fold and arrive at the crest of the third. At least they had got that far. Maybe it wouldn't be so bad. He lay back down, feeling quite proud, and realized his flattened men around him had been staring at him intently. He felt even prouder. Behind him, in the low of the fold, the mortar squads were setting up their mortars. Crawling back to them through the infernal racketing still floating loose in the air, he shouted in Culp's ear for him to make the lefthand grassy ridge his target. At the mortars Private Mazzi, the Italian boy from the Bronx, stared at him with wide, frightened eyes. So did most of the others. Stein crawled back to the top of the fold. He arrived, and raised himself, just in time to see 1st Platoon and then 2d Platoon attack. He was the only man along the top of the first fold who did see it, because he was the only man who was not flattened on the ground. He bit his lip. Even from here he could tell that it was bad, a serious tactical blunder.

If tactical blunder it was, the fault was Whyte's. First Whyte, and secondly, Lt Tom Blane of the 2d Platoon. Whyte had arrived at the top of the third and last fold of ground without a casualty. This in itself seemed strange to him, if not highly overoptimistic. He knew his orders: he was to locate and eliminate the hidden strong points on the two grassy ridges. The nearest of these, the righthand one, had its rather sharply defined beginnings about eighty yards to his right front. While his men flattened themselves and stared at him with intense sweating faces, he raised himself cautiously on his elbows till only his eyes showed, and inspected the terrain. Before him the ground fell, sparsely grassed and rocky, until it reached the beginnings of the little ridge, where it immediately became thickly grassed with the brown, waist-high grass. He could not see anything that looked like Japanese or their emplacements. Whyte was scared, but his anxiety to do well today was stronger. He did not really believe he would be killed in this war. Briefly he glanced over his shoulder to the ridge of Hill 209 where groups of men stood half-exposed, watching. One of them was the corps commander. The loud banging and racketing hanging sourceless in the air had abated somewhat, had raised itself a few yards, after the lifting of the barrage from the little ridges to the Elephant's Head. Again Whyte looked at the terrain and then motioned his scouts forward.

Once again the two riflemen stared at him as though they thought he had lost his mind, as though they would have liked to reason with him if they hadn't feared losing their reputations. Again Whyte motioned them forward, jerking his arm up and down in the signal for speed. The men looked at each other, then, gathering themselves on hands and knees first, bounced up and sprinted twenty-five yards down into the low area and fell flat. After a moment in which they inspected and found themselves still alive, they gathered themselves again. On hands and knees, preparing to rise, the first one suddenly fell down flat and bounced; the second, a little way behind him, got a little further up so that when he fell he tumbled on his shoulder and rolled onto his back. And there they lay, both victims of well placed rifle shots by unseen riflemen. Neither moved again. Both were obviously dead. Whyte stared at them shocked. He had known them almost four months. He had heard no shots nor had he seen anything move. No bullets kicked up dirt anywhere in front. Again he stared at the quiet, masked face of the deserted little ridge.

What was he supposed to do now? The high, sourceless racketing in the air seemed to have gotten a little louder. Whyte, who was a meaty, big young man, had been a champion boxer and champion judoman at his university where he was preparing himself to be a marine biologist, as well as having been the school's best swimmer. Anyway, they can't get all of us, he thought loyally, but meaning principally himself, and made his decision.

"Come on, boys! Let's go get 'em!" he yelled and leaped to his feet motioning the platoon forward. He took two steps, the platoon with their bayonets fixed since early morning right behind him, and fell down dead, stitched diagonally from hip to shoulder by bullets, one of which exploded his heart. He had just time enough to think that something had hurt him terribly, not even enough to think that he was dead, before he was. Perhaps he screamed.

Five others of his platoon went down with him almost simultaneously, in various states of disrepair, some dead, some only nicked. But the impetus Whyte had inaugurated remained, and the platoon charged blindly on. Another impetus would be needed to stop it or change its direction. A few more men went down. Invisible rifles and machineguns hammered from what seemed to be every quarter of the globe. After reaching the two dead scouts, they came in range of the more distant left ridge, which took them with a heavy crossfire. Sergeant Big Queen, running with the rest and bellowing incoherently, and who had only been promoted two days before after the defection of Stack, watched the platoon sergeant, a man named Grove, throw his rifle from him as though he feared it, and go down hollering and clawing at his chest. Queen did not even think about it. Near him Pfc Doll ran too, blinking his eyes rapidly as though this might protect him. His mind had withdrawn completely in terror, and he did not think at all. Doll's sense of personal invulnerability was having a severe test, but had not as yet, like Whyte's, failed. They were past the dead scouts now. More men on the left were beginning to go down. And behind them over the top of the third fold, suddenly, came the 2nd Platoon in full career, yelling hoarsely.

This was the responsibility of 2d Lt Blane. It was not a particularly complex responsibility. It had nothing to do with envy, jealousy, paranoia, or suppressed self-destruction. He too, like Whyte, knew what his orders were, and he had promised Bill Whyte he would back him up and help him out. He too knew the corps commander was watching, and he too wanted to do well today. Not as athletic as his fellow worker, but more imaginative, more sensitive, he too leaped up and motioned his men forward, when he saw 1st Platoon move. He could see the whole thing finished in his imagination: himself and Whyte and their men standing atop the bombed out bunkers in proper triumph, the position captured. He too died on the forward slope but not at the crest like Whyte. It took several seconds for the still-hidden Japanese gunners to raise their fire, and 2d Platoon was ten yards down the gentle little slope before it was unleashed against them. Nine men fell at once. Two died and one of them was Blane. Not touched by a machinegun, he unluckily was chosen as target by three separate riflemen, none of whom knew about the others or that he was an officer, and all of whom connected. He bounced another five yards forward, and with three bullets through his chest cavity did not die right away. He lay on his back and, dreamily and quite numb, stared at the high, beautiful, pure white cumuli which sailed like stately ships across the sunny, cool blue tropic sky. It hurt him a little when he breathed. He was dimly aware that he might possibly die as he became unconscious.

2d Platoon had just reached the two dead 1st Platoon scouts when mortar shells began to drop in onto the 1st Platoon twenty-five yards ahead. First two, then a single, then three together popped up in unbelievable mushrooms of dirt and stones. Chards and pieces whickered and whirred in the air. It was the impetus needed either to change the direction of the blind charge or to stop it completely. It did both. In the 2d Platoon S/Sgt Keck, watched by everyone now with Lt Blane down, threw out his arms holding his rifle at the balance, dug in his heels and bellowed in a voice like the combined voices of ten men for them to "Hit dirt! Hit dirt!" 2d Platoon needed no urging. Running men melted into the earth as if a strong wind had come up and blown them over like dried stalks.

In the 1st Platoon, less lucky, reaction varied. On the extreme right the line had reached the first beginning slope of the right-hand ridge, long hillock really, and a few men—perhaps a squad—turned and dove into the waisthigh grass there, defilading themselves from the hidden MGs above them as well as protecting them from the mortars. On the far left that end had much further to go, seventy yards more, to reach dead space under the lefthand ridge; but a group of men tried to make it. None of them reached it, however. They were hosed to earth and hiding by the machineguns above them, or bowled over stunned by the mortars, before they could defilade themselves from the MGs or get close enough to them to escape the mortars. Just to the left of the center was the attached machinegun squad from Culp's platoon, allowed

to join the charge by Whyte through forgetfulness or for some
obscure tactical reason of his own, all five of whom, running
together, were knocked down by the same mortar shell, gun and
tripod and ammo boxes all going every which way and bouncing
end over end, although not one of the five was wounded by it.
These marked the furthest point of advance. On the extreme left
five or six riflemen were able to take refuge in a brushy draw at
the foot of Hill 209 which, a little further down, became the deep
ravine where Fox and George had been trapped and hit yesterday.
These men began to fire at the two grassy ridges although they
could see no targets.

In the center of 1st Platoon's line there were no defilades or
draws to run to. The middle, before the mortars stopped them,
had run itself right on down and out onto the dangerous low area,
where they could not only be enfiladed by the ridges but could
also be hit by MG plunging fire from Hill 210 itself. Here there
was nothing to do but get down and hunt holes. Fortunately the
TOT barrage had searched here as well as on the hillocks, and
there were 105 and 155 holes available. Men jostled each other
for them, shared them. The late Lt Whyte's 19th Century charge
was over. The mortar rounds continued to drop here and there
across the area, searching flesh, searching bone.

Private John Bell of the 2d Platoon lay sprawled exactly as his
body had skidded to a halt, without moving a muscle. He could
not see because his eyes were shut, but he listened. On the little
ridges the prolonged yammering of the MGs had stopped and
now confined itself to short bursts at specific targets. Here and
there wounded men bellowed, whined or whimpered. Bell's face
was turned left, his cheek pressed to the ground, and he tried not
even to breathe too conspicuously for fear of calling attention to
himself. Cautiously he opened his eyes, half afraid the movement
of eyelids would be seen by a machinegunner a hundred yards
away, and found himself staring into the open eyes of the 1st
Platoon's first scout lying dead five yards to Bell's left. This was,
or had been, a young Graeco-Turkish draftee named Kral. Kral
was noted for two things, the ugliest bentnosed face in the regiment and the thickest glasses in C-for-Charlie. That with such a

myopia he could be a scout was a joke of the company. But Kral had volunteered for it; he wanted to be where the action was, he said; in peace or in war. A hep kid from Jersey, he had nevertheless believed the four-color propaganda leaflets. He had not known that the profession of first scout of a rifle platoon was a thing of the past and belonged in the Indian Wars, not to the massed divisions, superior firepower, and tighter social control of today. First target, the term should be, not first scout, and now the big glasses still reposed on his face. They had not fallen off. But something about their angle, at least from where Bell lay, magnified the open eyes until they filled the entire lenses. Bell could not help staring fixedly at them, and they stared back with a vastly wise and tolerant amusement. The more Bell stared at them the more he felt them to be holes into the center of the universe and that he might fall in through them to go drifting down through starry space amongst galaxies and spiral nebulae and island universes. He remembered he used to think of his wife's cunt like that, in a more pleasant way. Forcibly Bell shut his eyes. But he was afraid to move his head, and whenever he opened them again, there Kral's eyes were, staring at him their droll and flaccid message of amiable good will, sucking at him dizzyingly. And wherever he looked they followed him, pleasantly but stubbornly. From above, invisible but there, the fiery sun heat of the tropic day heated his head inside his helmet, making his soul limp. Bell had never known such eviscerating, ballshrinking terror. Somewhere out of his sight another mortar shell exploded. But in general the day seemed to have become very quiet. His arm with his watch on it lay within his range of vision, he noticed. My God! Was it only 7:45? Defeatedly he let his eyes go back where they wanted: to Kral's. HERE LIES FOUR-EYES KRAL, DIED FOR SOMETHING. When one of Kral's huge eyes winked at him waggishly, he knew in desperation he had to do something, although he had been lying there only thirty seconds. Without moving, his cheek still pressed to earth, he yelled loudly.

"Hey, *Keck!*" He waited. "Hey, *Keck!* We got to get out of here!"

"I know it," came the muffled answer. Keck was obviously

lying with his head turned the other way and had no intention of moving it.

"What'll we do?"

"Well . . ." There was silence while Keck thought. It was interrupted by a high, quavery voice from a long way off.

"We know you there, Yank. Yank, we know you there."

"Tojo eats shit!" Keck yelled. He was answered by an angry burst of machinegun fire. "Roozover' eat shit!" the faraway voice screamed.

"You goddam right he does!" some frightened Republican called from Bell's blind right side. When the firing stopped, Bell called again.

"What'll we do, Keck?"

"Listen," came the muffled answer. "All you guys listen. Pass it along so everybody knows." He waited and there was a muffled chorus "Now get this. When I holler go, everybody up. Load and lock and have a nuther clip in yore hand. 1st and 3d Squads stay put, kneeling position, and fire covering fire. 2d and 4th Squads hightail it back over that little fold. 1st and 3d Squads fire two clips, then scoot. 2d and 4th fire covering fire from that fold. If you can't see nothin, fire searching fire. Space yore shots. Them positions is somewhere about half way up them ridges. Everybody fire at the righthand ridge which is closer. You got that?"

He waited while everyone muffledly tried to assure themselves that everybody else knew.

"Everybody got it?" Keck called muffledly. There were no answers. "Then—GO!" he bellowed.

The slope came to life. Bell, in the 2d Squad, did not even bother with the brave man's formality of looking about to see if the plan was working, but instead squirmed around and leaped up running, his legs already pistoning before the leap came down to earth. Safe beyond the little fold of ground, which by now had taken on characteristics of huge size, he whirled and began to fire cover, terribly afraid of being stitched across the chest like Lt Whyte who lay only a few yards away. Methodically he drilled his shots into the dun hillside which still hid the invisible, yammering MGs, one round to the right, one to the left, one to center, one to the left . . . He could not believe that any of them might actually hit somebody. If one did, what a nowhere way to go: killed by accident; slain not as an individual but by sheer statistical probability, by the calculated chance of searching fire, even as he himself might be at any moment. Mathematics! Mathematics! Algebra! Geometry! When 1st and 3d Squads came diving and tumbling back over the tiny crest, Bell was content to throw himself prone, press his cheek to the earth, shut his eyes, and lie there. God, oh, God! Why am I *here?* Why am I *here?* After a moment's thought, he decided he better change it to: why are *we* here. That way, no agency of retribution could exact payment from him for being selfish.

Apparently Keck's plan had worked very well. 2d and 4th Squads, having the surprise, had gotten back untouched; and 1st and 3d Squads had had only two men hit. Bell had been looking right at one of them. Running hard with his head down, the man (a *boy,* named Kline) had jerked his head up suddenly, his eyes wide with start and fright, and cried out "Oh!", his mouth a round pursed hole in his face, and had gone down. Sick at himself for it, Bell had felt laughter burbling up in his chest. He did not know whether Kline was killed or wounded. The MGs had stopped yammering. Now, in the comparative quiet and fifty yards to their front, 1st Platoon was down and invisible amongst their shell holes and sparse grass. Anguished, frightened cries of "Medic! Medic!" were beginning to be raised now here and there across the field, and 2d Platoon having escaped were slowly realizing that they were not after all very safe even here.

Back at the CP behind the first fold Stein was not alone in seeing the tumbling, pellmell return of the 2d Platoon to the third fold. Seeing that their Captain could safely stand up on his knees without being pumped full of holes or mangled, others were now doing it. He was setting them a pretty good example, Stein thought, still a little astonished by his own bravery. They were going to need medics up there, he decided, and called his two company aidmen to him.

"You two fellows better get on up there," Stein yelled to them above the racket. "I expect they need you." That sounded calm and good.

"Yes, sir," one of them said. That was the scholarly, bespectacled one, the senior. They looked at each other seriously.

"I'll try to get stretcherbearers to the low between here and the second fold, to help you," Stein shouted. "See if you can't drag them back that far." He stood up on his knees again to peer forward, at where now and then single mortar shells geysered here and there beyond the third fold. "Go by rushes if you think you have to," he added inconclusively. They disappeared.

"I need a runner." Stein bawled, looking toward the line of his men who had had both the sense and the courage to climb to their knees in order to see. All of them heard him, because the whole little line rolled their eyes to look at him or turned toward him their heads. But not a single figure moved to come forward or answered him. Stein stared back at them, disbelieving. He was aware he had misjudged them completely, and he felt like a damned fool. He had expected to be swamped by volunteers. A sinking terror took hold of him: if he could be that wrong about this, what else might he not be wrong about? His enthusiasm had betrayed him. To save face he looked away, trying to pretend he had not expected anything. But it wasn't soon enough and he knew they knew. Not quite sure what to do next, he was saved the trouble of deciding: a wraithlike, ghostly figure appeared at his elbow.

"I'll go, Sir."

It was Charlie Dale the second cook, scowling with intensity, his face dark and excited.

Stein told him what he wanted about the stretcherbearers, and then watched him go trotting off bent over at the waist toward the slope of Hill 209 which he would have to climb. Stein had no idea where he had been, or where he had come from so suddenly. He could not remember seeing him all day today until now. Certainly he had not been one of the line of kneeling standees. Stein looked back at them, somewhat restored. Dale. He must remember that.

There were now twelve men standing on their knees along the little fold of ground, trying to see what was going on up front.

Young Corporal Fife was not, however, one of these. Fife was one of the ones who stayed flattened out, and he was as absolutely flattened as he could get. While Stein stood above him on his knees observing, Fife lay with his knees drawn up and his ear to the soundpower phone Stein had given him care of, and he did not care if he never stood up or ever saw anything. Earlier, when Stein had first done it with his stupid pleased pride shining all over his face, Fife had forced himself to stand straight up on his knees for several seconds, in order that no one might tag him with the title of coward. But he felt that was enough. Anyway, his curiosity was not at all piqued. All he had seen, when he did get up, was the top two feet of a dirt mushroom from a mortar shell landing beyond the third fold. What the fuck was so great about that? Suddenly a spasm of utter hopelessness shook Fife. Helplessness, that was what he felt; complete helplessness. He was as helpless as if agents of his government had bound him hand and foot and delivered him here and then gone back to wherever it was good agents went. Maybe a Washington cocktail bar, with lots of cunts all around. And here he lay, as bound and tied by his own mental processes and social indoctrination as if they were ropes, simply because while he could admit to himself privately that he was a coward, he did not have the guts to admit it publicly. It was agonizing. He was reacting exactly as the smarter minds of his society had anticipated he would react. They were ahead of him all down the line. And he was powerless to change. It was frustrating, maddening, like a brick wall all around him that he could neither bust through nor leap over and at the same time— making it even worse—there was his knowledge that there was really no wall at all. If early this morning he had been full of self-sacrifice, he now no longer was. He did not want to be here. He did not want to be here at all. He wanted to be over there where the generals were standing up on the ridge in complete safety, watching. Sweating with fear and an unbelievable tension of double-mindedness, Fife looked over at them and if looks of hatred could kill they would all have fallen down dead and the campaign would be over until they shipped in some new ones. If only he could go crazy. Then he would not be responsible. Why couldn't he go crazy? But he couldn't. The un-stone of the stone wall immediately rose up around him denying him exit. He could only lie here and be stretched apart on this rack of double-mindedness. Off to the right, some yards beyond the last man of the reserve platoon, Fife's eyes recorded for him the images of Sergeants Welsh and Storm crouched behind a small rock outcrop. As he watched, Storm raised his arm and pointed. Welsh snaked his rifle onto the top of the rock and checking the stock, fired off five shots. Both peered. Then they looked at each other and shrugged. It was an easily understood little pantomime. Fife fell into an intense rage. Cowboys and Indians! Cowboys and Indians! Everybody's playing cowboys and Indians! Just as if these weren't real bullets, and you couldn't really get killed. Fife's head burned with a fury so intense that it threatened to blow all his mental fuses right out through his ears in two bursts of black smoke. His rage was broken off short, snapped off at the hilt as it were, by the buzzing whistle of the soundpower phone in his ear.

Startled, Fife cleared his throat, shocked into wondering whether he could still talk, after so long. It was the first time he had tried a word since leaving the ridge. It was also the first time he had ever heard this damn phone thing work. He pushed the button and cupped it to his mouth. "Yes?" he said cautiously.

"What do you mean, 'yes'?" a calm cold voice said, and waited.

Fife hung suspended in a great empty black void, trying to think. What had he meant? "I mean this is Charlie Cat Seven," he said, remembering the code jargon. "Over."

"That's better," the calm voice said. "This is Seven Cat Ace." That meant 1st Battalion, the HQ. "Colonel Tall here. I want Captain Stein. Over."

"Yes, Sir," Fife said. "He's right here." He reached up one arm to tug at the skirt of Stein's green fatigue blouse. Stein looked down, staring, as if he had never seen Fife before. Or anybody else.

"Colonel Tall wants you."

Stein lay down (glad to flatten himself, Fife noted with satisfaction) and took the phone. Despite the racketing din overhead, both he and Fife beside him could hear the Colonel clearly.

When he accepted the phone and pushed down the button, Bugger Stein was already casting about for his explanations. He had not expected to be called upon to recite so soon, and he had not prepared his lessons. What he could say would of course depend on Tall's willingness to allow any explanation at all. He could not help being a guilty schoolboy about to be birched. "Charlie Cat Seven. Stein," he said. "Over." He released the button.

What he heard astounded him to speechlessness.

"Magnificent, Stein, magnificent." Tall's clear cold calm boyish voice came to him—came to both of them—rimed over with a crust of clear cold boyish enthusiasm. "The finest thing these old eyes have seen in a long time. In a month of Sundays." Stein had a vivid mental picture of Tall's closecropped, boyish, Anglo-Saxon head and unlined, Anglo-Saxon face. Tall was less than two years older than Stein. His clear, innocent, boyish eyes were the youngest Stein had seen in some time. "Beautifully conceived and beautifully executed. You'll be mentioned in Battalion Orders, Stein. Your men came through for you beautifully. Over."

Stein pressed the button, managed a weak "Yes, Sir. Over," and released the button. He could not think of anything else to say.

"Best sacrificial commitment to develop a hidden position I have ever seen outside maneuvers. Young Whyte led beautifully. I'm mentioning him, too. I saw him go down in that first melee. Was he hurt very bad? But sending in your 2d too was brilliant. They might very well have carried both subsidiary ridges with luck. I dont think they were hurt too bad. Blane led well too. His withdrawal was very old pro. How many of the emplacements did they locate? Did they knock out any? We ought to have those ridges cleaned out by noon. Over."

Stein listened, rapt, staring into the eyes of Fife who listened also, staring back. For Fife the calm, pleasant, conversational tone of Col Tall was both maddening and terrifying. And for Stein it was like hearing a radio report on the fighting in Africa which he knew nothing about. Once in school his father had called him long distance to brag about a good report card which Stein had thought would be bad. Neither listener betrayed what he thought to the other, and the silence lengthened.

"Hello? Hello? Hello, Stein? Over?"

Stein pressed the button. "Yes, Sir. Here, Sir. Over." Stein released the button.

"Thought you'd been hit," Tall's voice came back matter-of-factly. "I said, how many of the emplacements did they locate? And did they knock any of them out? Over."

Stein pressed the button, staring into the wide eyes of Fife as if he might see Tall on the other side of them. "I dont know. Over." He released button.

"What do you mean you dont know? How can you not know?" Tall's cool, calm, conversational voice said. "Over."

Stein was in a quandary. He could admit what both he and Fife knew, or perhaps Fife did not know, which was that he knew nothing about Whyte's attack, had not ordered it, and until now had believed it bad. Or he could continue to accept credit for it and try to explain his ignorance of its results. He could not, of course, know that Tall would later change his opinion. With a delicacy of sensibility Stein had never expected to see at all in the army, and certainly not on the field under fire, Fife suddenly lowered his eyes and looked away, half turned his head. He was still listening, but at least he was pretending not to.

Stein pressed the button, which was a necessity, but which was beginning to madden him. "I'm back here," he said sharply. "Behind the third fold.

"Do you want me to stand up? And wave? So you can see me?" he added with caustic anger. "Over."

"No," Tall's voice said calmly, the irony lost on him. "I can see where you are. I want you to do something. I want you to get up there and see what the situation is, Stein. I want Hill 210 in my hands tonight. And to do that I have to have those two ridges by noon. Have you forgotten the corps commander is here observing today? He's got Admiral Barr with him, flown in specially. The

Admiral got up at dawn for this. I want you to come to life down there, Stein,'' he said crisply. ''Over and out.''

Stein continued to listen, gripping the phone and staring off furiously, though he knew nothing more was forthcoming. Finally he reached out and tapped Fife and gave it to him. Fife took it in silence. Stein rolled to his feet and ran crouching back down to where the mortars were periodically firing off rounds with their weird, other-world, lingering gonglike sound.

''Doing any good?'' he bellowed in Culp's ear.

''We're getting bursts on both ridges,'' Culp bellowed back in his amiable way. ''I decided to put one tube onto the right ridge,'' he said parenthetically, and then shrugged. ''But I dont know if we're doin any damage. If they're dug in—'' He let it trail off and shrugged again.

''I've decided to move forward to the second fold,'' Stein yelled. ''Will that be too close for you?''

Culp strode three paces forward up the shallow slope and craned his neck to see over the crest, squinting. He came back. ''No. It's pretty close, but I think we can still hit. But we're running pretty low on ammo. If we keep on firing at this rate—'' Again he shrugged.

''Send everybody but your sergeants back for fresh ammo. All they can carry. Then follow us.''

''They dont any of them like to carry them aprons,'' Culp yelled. ''They all say if they get hit with one of those things on them . . .''

''God damn it, Bob! I can't be bothered with a thing like that at a time like this! They knew what they were gonna have to carry!''

''I know it.'' Culp shrugged. ''Where do you want me?''

Stein thought. ''On the right, I guess. If they locate you, they'll try to hit you. I want you away from the reserve platoon. I'll give you a few riflemen in case they try to send a patrol in on our flank. Anything that looks like more than a patrol, you let me know quick.''

''Dont worry!'' Culp said. He turned to his squads. Stein trotted off to the right, where he had seen Al Gore, Lt of his 3d

Platoon, motioning at the same time for Sgt Welsh to come over
to him. Welsh came, followed by Storm, for the orders conference. Even Welsh, Stein noticed parenthetically, even Welsh had
that strained, intent, withdrawn look on his face—like a greasy
patina of guilty wishful thinking.

While 3d Platoon and Stein's Company HQ were trooping forward in two parallel single files in their move to the second fold,
the 1st Platoon continued to lie in its shellholes. After the first
crash and volley and thunder of mortars they all had expected to
be dead in five minutes. Now, it seemed unbelievable but the
Japanese did not seem to be able to see them very well. Now and
then a bullet or a burst zipped by low overhead, followed in a
second or so by the sound of its firing. Mortar rounds still sighed
down on them, exploding with roaring mushrooms of terror and
dirt. But in general the Japanese seemed to be waiting for something. 1st Platoon was willing to wait with them. Leaderless,
pinned down, pressing its hands and sweating faces to the dirt, 1st
Platoon was willing to wait forever and never move again. Many
prayed and promised God they would go to church services every
Sunday. But slowly, they began to realize that they could move
around, could fire back, that death was not a foregone conclusion
and inevitable for all.

The medics helped with this. The two company aidmen, given
their orders by Stein, had moved up amongst 2d Platoon along the
third fold, and had begun little sorties out onto the shallow slope
after wounded. In all there were 15 wounded men, and 6 dead.
The two aidmen did not bother with the dead, but slowly they
retrieved for the stretcherbearers all of the wounded. With insouciance, sober, serious and bespectacled, the two of them moved
up and down the slope, bandaging and salting, dragging and half-
carrying. Mortar shells knocked them down, MG fire kicked up
dirt around them, but nothing touched them. Both would be dead
before the week was out (and replaced by types much less admired in C-for-Charlie), but for now they clumped untouchably
on, two sobersides concerned with aiding the sobbing, near-help-
less men it was their official duty to aid. Eventually enough 1st
Platoon men raised their heads high enough to see them, and

realized movement was possible—at least, as long as they did not all stand up in a body and wave and shout "Here we are!" Not one of them had as yet seen a single Japanese.

It was Doll who saw the first ones. Sensing the movement around him as men began to stir and call softly to each other, Doll took his bruised confidence in hand and raised his head until his eyes showed above the slight depression into which he had sprawled. He happened to come up looking at the rear of the little lefthand ridge, just where it joined the rocky rim slope up to Hill 210. He saw three figures carrying what could only be a machine-gun still attached to its tripod start across the slope back toward Hill 210, running bent over at the waist in the same identical way he himself had run up here. Doll was astounded and did not believe it. They were about two hundred yards away, and the two men behind ran together carrying the gun, while the man in front simply ran, carrying nothing. Doll slid his rifle up, raised the sight four clicks and, lying with only his left arm and shoulder outside his little hole, sighted on the man in front, leading him a little, and squeezed off a shot. The rifle bucked his shoulder and the man went down. The two men behind jumped sideways to-gether, like a pair of skittish, delicately coordinated horses, and ran on. They did not drop the gun, and they did not lose a stride or even get out of step. Doll fired again and missed. He realized his mistake now: if he had hit one of the men with the MG, they'd have had to drop it and leave it or else stop to pick it up. Before he could fire a third time they were in among the rocks on the rim, beyond which the steep precipice fell to the river. Doll could see their backs or heads from time to time as they went on, but never long enough to shoot. The other man remained where he had fallen on the slope.

So Doll had killed his first Japanese. For that matter, his first human being of any kind. Doll had hunted quite a lot, and he could remember his first deer. But this was an experience which required extra tasting. Like getting screwed the first time, it was too complex to be classed solely as pride of accomplishment. Shooting well, at anything, was always a pleasure. And Doll hated the Japanese, dirty little yellow Jap bastards, and would gladly have killed personally every one of them alive if the US Army and Navy would only arrange him a safe opportunity and supply him the ammo. But beyond these two pleasures there was another. It had to do with guilt. Doll felt guilty. He couldn't help it. He had killed a human being, a man. He had done the most horrible thing a human could do, worse than rape even. And nobody in the whole damned world could say anything to him about it. That was where the pleasure came. Nobody could do anything to him for it. He had gotten by with murder. He watched the figure on the slope. He would like to know just where he had hit him (he had aimed for the chest), and whether he died right away, or if he was lying there still alive, dying slowly. Doll felt an impulse to grin a silly grin and to giggle. He felt stupid and cruel and mean and vastly superior. It certainly had helped his confidence anyway, that was for sure.

Just then a mortar shell sighed down for a half-second and ten yards away exploded a fountain of terror and dirt, and Doll discovered his confidence hadn't been helped so much after all. Before he could think he had jerked himself and his rifle down onto the floor of his little depression and curled up there, fear running like heavy threads of quicksilver through all his arteries and veins as if they were glass thermometers. After a moment he wanted to raise back up and look again but found that he couldn't. What if just as he put up his head another one exploded and a piece of it took him square between the eyes, or knifed into his face, or ripped through his helmet and split his skull? The prospect was too much. After a while, after his breathing had quieted, he again put his head up to the eye level. This time there were four Japanese preparing to leave the grassy ridge for the uphill road to Hill 210. They came into sight from somewhere on the ridge already running. Two carried the gun, another carried handled boxes, the fourth had nothing. Doll pulled his rifle up into position and aimed for the gun-carriers. As the party crossed the open space, he fired four times and missed each time. They disappeared into the rocks.

Doll was so furious he could have bitten a piece out of his own arm. While cursing himself, he remembered he had now fired six rounds. He released the clip and replaced it with a fresh one, sliding the two unused rounds into his pants pocket, then settled down to wait for more Japanese. Only then did he realize that what he was watching might have more implication and importance than whether he got himself another Jap.

But what to do? He remembered Big Queen had been running near him when they hit the dirt.

"Hey, Queen!"

After a moment, there was a muffled answer. "Yeah?"

"Did you see them Japs leavin that left ridge?"

"I aint been seein much of nothin," Queen called with muffled honesty.

"Well, why dont you get your fuckin head up and look around?" Doll could not resist the gibe. He suddenly felt very powerful and in command of himself, almost gay.

"Go fuck yourself, Doll," was Queen's muffled answer.

"No, Sarge," (he used the title deliberately), "I'm serious. I counted seven Japs leavin that lefthand grassy ridge. I got me one of them," he added modestly without, however, mentioning how many times he'd missed.

"So?"

"I think they're pullin out of there. Maybe somebody ought to tell Bugger Stein."

"You want to be the one?" Queen called back with muffled sarcasm.

The idea had not occurred to Doll. Now it did. He had already seen the two aidmen moving about on the slope, and apparently nothing had happened to them. He could see them now, simply by turning his head a little. "Why not?" he called cheerfully. "Sure. I'll carry the message back to Bugger for you." Suddenly his heart was beating in his throat.

"You'll do no such a goddam fucking thing," Queen called. "You'll stay right the fuck where you are and shut up. That's an order."

Doll did not answer for a moment. Slowly his heart returned to normal. He had offered and been refused. He had committed himself and been freed. But something else was driving him, something he could not put a name to. "Okay," he called.

"They'll get us out of this in a little bit. Somebody will. You stay put. I'm ordering you."

"I said okay," Doll called. But the thing that was driving him, eating on him, didn't recede. He had a strange tingling all through his belly and crotch. Off to the right there was a sudden burst of the MG fire his ear now knew as Japanese, and immediately after it a cry of pain. "Aidman! Aidman!" somebody called. It sounded like Stearns. No, it wasn't all that easy. In spite of the two aidmen moving all around. The tingling in Doll got stronger and his heart began to pound again. He had never in his life been excited quite like this. Somebody had to get that news to Bugger. Somebody had to be a—hero. He had already killed one man, if you could call a Jap a man. And nobody, not a single soul in the world, could touch him for it, not a single soul. Doll raised his left eyebrow and pulled up his lip in that special grin of his.

He did not wait for Big Queen, or bother with his permission. When he had squirmed himself around facing the rear, he lay a moment lifting himself to the act, his heart pounding. He could not quite bring himself to begin to move. But he knew he would. There was something else in it, also. In what it was that was driving, pulling him to do it. It was like facing God. Or gambling with Luck. It was taking a dare from the Universe. It excited him more than all the hunting, gambling and fucking he had ever done all rolled together. When he went, he was up in a flash and running, not at full speed, but at about half speed which was better controlled, bent over, his rifle in both hands, even as the Japanese he himself had downed. A bullet kicked up dirt two feet to his left and he zigged right. Ten yards further on he zagged left. Then he was over the third fold into the 2d Platoon, who stared at him uncomprehendingly. Doll giggled. He found Capt Bugger Stein behind the second fold where he had just arrived, ran almost headon into him in fact and did not even have to hunt. He was hardly even winded.

1st Sgt Welsh was crouching with Stein and Band behind the crest of the second fold, when Doll came trotting up, bent over, giggling and laughing, so out of breath he could not talk. Welsh, who had always disliked Doll for a punk, and still did, thought he looked like a young recruit coming giggling out of a whorehouse after the first real fuck of his life, and he eyed him narrowly, wanting to know why.

"What the hell are you laughing at?" Stein snapped.

"At the way I fooled them yellow bastards shooting at me," Doll gasped, giggling, but soon subsided before Stein's gaze.

Welsh, with the others, listened to his story of the seven Japanese and two guns he had seen leaving the left ridge. "I think they're pullin completely out of there, sir."

"Who sent you back here?" Stein said.

"Nobody, sir. I came myself. I thought it was something you'd want to know."

"You were right. It is." Stein nodded his head sternly. Welsh, watching him from where he crouched, wanted to spit. Bugger was acting very much the company commander, today. "And I won't forget it, Doll."

Doll did not answer, but he grinned. Stein, on one knee, was now rubbing his unshaven chin and blinking his eyes behind his glasses. Doll was still standing straight up.

"God damn it, get down," Stein said irritably.

Doll looked around leisurely, then consented to squat, since it was obviously an order.

"George," Stein said, "get a man with glasses and have him spot the back of that ridge. I want to know the second anybody leaves it. Here," he said, removing his own, "take mine."

"I'll do it myself," Band said, and bared his teeth in a brilliant-eyed, weird smile. He took off.

Stein looked after him a long moment, and Welsh wanted to laugh. Stein turned back to Doll and began to question him about the attack, casualties, the present position and state of the platoon. Doll didn't really know very much. He had seen Lt Whyte die, knew Sgt Grove was down but not whether he was dead. He had—they all had, he amended—been pretty busy when the first big bunch of mortars began to hit. He thought he had seen a group of about squad size go into the deep grass at the base of the right ridge, but wasn't sure. And he had seen the machinegun squad run far out ahead and all go down together with one mortar burst. Stein cursed at this, and demanded what they were doing there in the first place. Doll of course didn't know. He thought that the center, ensconced in their U.S.-made shellholes and depressions in the bottom, were safe enough for the moment, provided the Japs did not lay a heavy mortar barrage on them. No, he himself had not been very scared the whole time. He didn't know why, really.

Welsh hardly listened to them. He was looking over the crest at the 2d Platoon flattened out in a long line behind the crest of the third fold, and thinking his own thoughts. 2d Platoon was as flattened as it could get, cheeks and bellies pressed tight to the earth, faces scarred with the white of staring eyeballs and bared teeth, all looking back his way, watching for their Commander, who conceivably might order them to go over this crest again. 2d Platoon would make a great photograph to send back home, Welsh's eyes told him—without in the least disturbing his thinking—except that of course when the newspapers, government, army, and *Life* got ahold of it, it would be subtly changed to fit the needs of the moment and probably captioned: TIRED INFANTRYMEN REST IN SAFETY AFTER HEROIC CAPTURE OF POSITION. THE FIRST TEAM AT HALFTIME. BUY BONDS TILL IT HURTS YOUR ASSHOLE.

But all of this more or less visual thinking had nothing to do with what Welsh was thinking on another, deeper level. Mostly, he was thinking about himself. He found it satisfying to contemplate the fact that if he got it, got knocked off, the government wouldn't have anybody to send a Regrets card to for him. He knew how those fuckfaces of government whitecollar workers loved their jobs and their authority. When he first enlisted, he had given a false first name and middle initial. He and his family had not heard from each other since. On the other hand if he only got crippled, maimed, his enemies the government would have to take care of him, since they had no next-of-kin for him. So he had the bureaucracy fucked both ways. His view of 2d Platoon misted over slightly with a vision of himself in one of those horrible Veterans Hospitals across the country, an aged man in a wheelchair, with a pint bottle of gin hidden in his cheap flimsy robe, cackling and quacking at the weight-lifter lesbian Napoleons of nurses, at the pinheaded, pipsqueak, hard-jawed Alexander-the-greats of doctors. He'd give them a hard time. . . .

"You're not really pinned down, then," he heard Stein say. "I was told—"

"Well, we are, in a way, sir," Doll said. "But, like you see, I got back all right. We couldn't all come back at once."

Stein nodded.

"But two or three at a time could make it, I think. With 2d Platoon firing covering fire," Doll suggested.

"We dont even know where those goddamned fucking emplacements are," Stein said sourly.

"They could fire searching fire, couldn't they?" Doll suggested professionally.

Stein glared at him. So did Welsh. Welsh wanted to boot the new hero in the ass: already giving the company commander advice—about searching fire, yet.

Welsh interrupted them. "Hey, Cap'n!" he growled. "You want me to go down there and get them men back up here for you?" He glared murderously at Doll, whose eyebrows went up innocently.

"No." Stein rubbed his jaw. "No, I can't spare you. Might need you. Anyway, I think I'll leave them there a while. They dont seem to be getting hurt too bad and if we can get up onto that right ridge frontally maybe they can flank it." He paused. "What interests me is that squad on the right that got into the deep grass on the ridge. They—"

He was interrupted by George Band who, bent over, came running down the little slope. "Hey, Jim! Hey, Captain Stein! I just saw five more leaving the left ridge, with two MGs. I think they really are pulling out."

"Really?" Stein said. "Really?" He sounded as relieved as if he had just been told the battle had been called off until another time. At least now he could act. "Gore! Gore!" he began to bellow. "Lt Gore!"

It required fifteen minutes to summon Gore, instruct him, assemble his 3d Platoon, and see them off on their venture.

"We're pretty sure they're pulling out completely, Gore. But dont get overeager; like Whyte. They may have left a rearguard. Or maybe it's a trap. So go slow. Let your scouts look it over first. I think your best approach is down the draw in front of Hill 209. Go left behind this middle fold here till it hits the draw, and then down the draw. If you get hit by mortars like they did there yesterday, you got to keep going, though. If there's a waterhole in that brush at the foot of the ridge, let me know about it. We're running very short of water; already. But the main thing. The main thing, Gore, is not to lose any more men than you absolutely have to." It was becoming an increasingly important point to Stein, almost frantically so. And whenever he was not actually occupied with something specific, that was what he brooded over. "Now, go ahead, boy; and good luck." Men; men; he was losing all his men; men he had lived with; men he was responsible for.

It required another half hour for Gore's reserve 3d Platoon to reach its jumpoff point at the foot of the grassy ridge. He was certainly following orders and going slow, Stein thought with impatience. It was now after 9:00. In the meantime Band had come back from the crest of the fold with a report that he had counted three more small bodies of men leaving the left ridge with MGs, but had counted none in the last fifteen minutes. Also in the meantime little Charlie Dale the second cook had returned, his narrow closeset eyes snapping bright, and at the same time dark and thunderous. He showed Stein where he had brought the stretcher bearers to the low between the first and middle folds, four parties of four, sixteen men in all, who were already starting to collect the first of the eight litter cases which had by now accumulated. Then he asked if there were any more little jobs for him to do.

Corporal Fife, lying not far from the Company Commander with the sound power phone which had more or less become his permanent responsibility, thought he had never seen such an unholy look on a human face. Perhaps Fife was a little jealous because he was so afraid himself. Certainly there wasn't any fear in Charlie Dale. His mouth hung open in a slack little grin, the bright and at the same time lowering eyes darting everywhere and filmed over with an unmistakable sheen of pleased selfsatisfaction at all this attention he suddenly was getting. Fife looked at him, then sickly turned his head away and closed his eyes, his ear to the phone. This was his job; he'd been given it and he'd do it; but he'd be damned if he'd do anything else he wasn't told to do. He couldn't. He was too afraid.

"Yes," Bugger Stein was saying to Dale. "You—"

He was interrupted by the explosion of a mortar shell amongst the 2d Platoon on the rear slope of the third fold. Its loud thwonging bang was almost simultaneous with a loud scream of pure fear, which after the explosion died away continued until the screamer ran out of breath. A man had thrown himself out of the line back down the slope and was bucking and kicking and rolling with both hands pressed behind him in the small of his back. When he got his breath back, he continued to scream. Everyone else hugged the comforting dirt, which nevertheless was not quite comforting enough, and waited for a barrage to begin to fall. Nothing happened, however, and after a moment they began to put their heads up to look at the kicking man who still bucked and screamed.

"I dont think they can see us any better than we can see them," Welsh muttered, tight-lipped.

"I believe that's Private Jacques," Lt Band said in an interested voice.

The screaming had taken on a new tone, one of realization, rather than the start and surprise and pure fear of before. One of the aidmen got to him and with the help of two men from 2d Platoon tore open his shirt and got a syrette of morphine into him. In a few seconds he quieted. When he was still, the aidman pulled the hands loose and rolled him over. His belt off, his shirt up, he was looked over by the aidman, who then was seen to shrug with despair and reach in his pack and begin to sprinkle.

Behind the middle fold Bugger Stein was whitefaced, his lips tight, his eyes snapping open and shut behind his glasses. This was the first of his men he had actually seen wounded. Beside him Brass Band watched the same scene with a look of friendly, sympathetic interest on his face. Beyond Band Corporal Fife had raised up once to look while the man was still bucking and kicking and then lain back down sick all over; all he could think of was what if it had been him? It might easily have been, might still yet be.

"Stretcher bearers! Stretcher bearers!" Stein had suddenly turned back toward the hollow where two of the four groups had not yet departed with loads. "Stretcher bearers!" he yelled at the top of his lungs. One of the groups came on the run with their stretcher.

"But, Jim," Lt Band said. "Really, Jim, I dont—"

"God damn you, George, shut up! Leave me alone!" The bearers arrived out of breath. "Go get that man," Stein said pointing over the crest to where the aidman still knelt by the casualty.

The leader plainly had thought someone of the CP group here had been wounded. Now he saw his mistake. "But listen," he protested, "we already got eight or nine down there now that we're supposed to—We're not—"

"God damn it, don't argue with me! I'm Captain Stein! Go get that man, I said!" Stein bawled in his face.

The man recoiled, upset. Of course nobody was wearing insignia.

"But, Jim, really," Brass Band said, "he's not—"

"God damn you, all of you! Am I in command around here or not!" Stein was in a howling rage; and he was actually almost howling. "Am I Company Commander of this outfit or am I not! Am I Captain Stein or a goddamned private! Do I give the orders here or dont I! I said go get that man!"

"Yes, sir," the leader said. "Okay, sir. Right away."

"That man may die," Stein said more reasonably. "He's hit bad. Get him back to battalion aid station and see if they can't do something to save him."

"Yes, sir," the leader of the bearers said. He spread his hands palms up toward Stein absolving himself of guilt. "We got others that're hit bad, sir. That was all I meant. We got three down there might die any minute."

Stein stared at him uncomprehendingly.

"That's it, Jim," Band said from behind him soothingly. "Dont you see? Dont you think he ought to wait his turn? Isn't that only fair?"

"Wait his turn? Wait his turn? Fair? My God!" Stein said. He stared at both of them, his face white.

"Sure," Band said. "Why put him ahead of some other guy?"

Stein did not answer him. After a moment he turned to the leader. "Go and get him," he said stiffly, "like I told you. Get him back to battalion aid station. I gave you an order, Private."

"Yes, sir." The leader's voice was stony. He turned to his men. "Come on, you guys. We're goin over there after that guy."

"Well what the hell're we waitin for?" one of them snarled toughly. "Come on, Hoke. Or are you afraid of gettin that close to the shooting?" It was a ridiculous remark under the circumstances. The leader plainly wasn't afraid of going.

"You shut up, Witt," he said, "and let me alone."

All of them were squatting. The man he had addressed stood up suddenly. He was a small, frail-looking man, and the US helmet shell, which on Big Queen looked so small, looked like an enormous inverted pot on his small head and almost hid his eyes. He marched up to where Welsh half reclined.

"Hello, Firs' Sarn't," the small man said with a rapacious grin.

Only then did Stein, or any of the rest of the C-for-Charlie men for that matter, recognize that this Witt was their Witt, the same that Stein and Welsh had combined to transfer out before the division left for combat. All of them were astonished, as Witt obviously meant for them to be. Corporal Fife especially. Fife, still lying flat with the phone to his ear, sat up suddenly, grinning.

"By God! Hello, Witt!" he cried delightedly.

Witt, true to his promise of a few days before, passed his narrow eyes across the Corporal as if he did not exist. They came to rest on Welsh, again.

"Hi, Witt," Welsh said. "You in the medics now? You better get down."

Stein, who had felt guilty for having transferred Witt when he knew how badly Witt wanted to stay, even though he still felt he had done what was best for his company, said nothing.

Witt ignored Welsh's cautioning. He remained standing straight up. "Naw, Firs' Sarn't," he grinned. "Still in Cannon Comp'ny. Only, as you know, we aint got no cannons. So they've put us to work pushin boats up and down the river and as stretcher bearers." He inclined his head. "Who we goin after over there, Firs' Sarn't?"

"Jacques," Welsh said.

"Old Jockey?" Witt said. "Shit, that's too bad." His three companions had already gone on and were now running downhill beyond the crest of the fold and Witt turned to follow them. But then he turned back and spoke directly to Bugger Stein. "Please, sir, can I come back to the company? After we get Jockey back to battalion? I can slip away easy. They'll give Hoke another man. Can I, sir?"

Stein was flattered. He was also confused. This whole thing of the stretcher bearers and Jacques was getting out of hand, taking too much of his attention from the plan he had been just about to conceive. "Well, I—" he said and stopped, his mind blank. "Of course, you'll have to get someone's permission."

Witt grinned cynically. "Sure," he said. "And my rifle. Thank you, sir." He turned and was gone, after his mates.

Stein tried to reorganize the scattered threads of his thought. For a moment he stared after Witt. For a man to want to come back into a forward rifle company in the midst of an attack was simply incomprehensible to him. In a way, though, it was very romantic. Like something out of Kipling. Or Beau Geste. Now, what was it that he had just about had figured out?

Close to Stein, as Bugger's orders about the phone demanded he be, Corporal Fife had lain back down flat with his phone and shut his eyes. Even though he knew that Witt's gesture of ignoring him had to do with their argument of a few days back, he could not help taking it as contempt and disgust for his present cowardice—as if Witt with one glance had looked inside his mind. When he reopened his eyes, he found himself looking into the white face of little Bead a few feet away, eyes popeyed with fright, blinking almost audibly, like some overgrown rabbit.

"Dale!" Bugger called. "Now, look," he said, marshaling his mind.

Charlie Dale crawled closer. When he first returned from his mission, he had made himself stand upright quite a while, but when the mortar shell exploded wounding Jacques, he had flattened himself. Now he compromised by squatting. Bugger had been just about to tell him something, perhaps send him on another mission, when Jacques got hit and then the stretcher bearers came. Dale could not help feeling a little piqued. Not at Jacques of course. He couldn't be mad at Jockey really. But he might have picked himself a better time to get shot up. But those goddam stretcher bearers from Cannon Company and that goddam bolshevik Witt, they certainly could have taken less of the Company Cmander's valuable time. Especially when he was about to tell Pfc Dale something very important maybe. For Dale this was the first chance that he had had in a long time for talking to the Company Cmander personally like this, for being free of that goddam order-giving Storm and his cheating cooks, first chance to not be tied to that goddam greasy sweating kitchen cooking masses of food for a bunch of men to gorge their guts on, and Dale was enjoying it. He was getting more personal attention than he had ever had from this outfit, at last they were beginning to recognize him, and all he had to do for it was carry a few messages through some light MG fire that couldn't hit him anyway. Gravy. Not far off he could see fucking Storm lying all flattened out beside Sgt Welsh, and looking this way. Squatting, Dale put a respectful expression on his face and listened to his commander intently. An inarticulate, secret excitement burgeoned in him.

"I've got to know how 3d Platoon is doing," Bugger was telling him. "I want you to go and find out for me." He described the position and told him how to get there. "Report to Lt Gore if you can find him. But I've got to know if they occupied that grassy ridge, and I've got to know as soon as possible. Get back as soon as you can."

"Aye, aye, sir," Dale said, his eyes pleased.

"I want both you and Doll to stay with me," Bugger said. "I'll
have further work for both of you. You've both been invaluable."

"Yes, sir," Dale smiled. Then, unsmiling, he looked over at
Doll, and found Doll to be studying him equally.

"Now, go!"

"Right, sir." He snapped out a tiny little salute and took off,
running bent over along the low area behind the fold, his rifle
slung across his back, his Thompsongun in his hands. He did not
have to go far. At the corner where the hollow met the draw in
front of Hill 209, he met a man from 3d Platoon already on his
way back with the news that 3d Platoon had occupied the lefthand
grassy ridge without firing a shot and were now digging themselves in there. Together they returned to Stein, Dale feeling a
little cheated.

Stein had not waited for Dale's return. Gradually his plan had
shaped itself in his mind, even while he was talking to Dale.
Whether 3d Platoon had occupied the lefthand ridge made little
difference to it. They could provide more covering fire, and that
would help, but it was not essential, because this movement had
to do with the squad-size group of 1st Platoon men who had
made it in under the machineguns, into the thicker grass at the
foot of the righthand ridge. That righthand ridge was obviously
going to be the trouble spot, the stumbling block. With the squad-
sized group already there plus two more squads from 2d Platoon
Stein wanted to make a sort of double-winged uphill frontal attack whose center would hold and whose ends would curl around
and isolate the main strongpoint on the ridge, wherever it was.
The remainder of 2d Platoon could fire cover from the third fold,
and Stein thought the rest of 1st Platoon—the remnants, he
amended sourly—could fire cover along the flank from their advanced position in their holes. With this in mind he had already,
after Charlie Dale's departure, sent Doll back down into that
inferno beyond the third fold, now temporarily quiet, where 1st
Platoon still clung precariously to the dirt of their holes, sweating.
Doll had only just left when the stretcher bearers came back with
Jacques. Stein found he could not resist the desire to look at him.
Neither could anybody else.

They had laid him on his stomach on the stretcher. The aidman had a gauze compress over the wound, but it was apparent that there was a long glancing hole in the small of Jacques's back. His face hung over the side of the stretcher, and his half-closed eyes, dulled of intelligence by the morphine and by shock, held only a peculiar questioning look. He appeared to be asking them, or somebody, why?—why he, John Jacques, ASN so-and-so, had been chosen for this particular fate? Somewhere a stranger had dropped a metal case down a tube, not knowing exactly where it would land, not even sure where he wanted it to land. It had gone up and come down. And where did it land? On John Jacques, ASN so-and-so. When it had burst, thousands of chunks and pieces of knife-edged metal had gone chirring in all directions. And who was the only one touched by one of them? John Jacques, ASN so-and-so. Why? Why him? No enemy had aimed anything at John Jacques, ASN so-and-so. No enemy knew that John Jacques, ASN so-and-so, existed. Any more than *he* knew the name, character and personality of the Japanese who dropped the metal case down the tube. So why? Why him? Why John Jacques, ASN so-and-so? Why not somebody else? Why not one of his friends? And now it was done. Soon he would be dead.

Stein forced himself to look somewhere else. At the tail, off end of the stretcher he saw Witt, who, being shorter, had to strain more to keep his end up level. Thinking about Doll and 1st Platoon, Stein was just about to send someone after Sgt. Keck, the new commander of 2d Platoon, when Charlie Dale and the messenger returned.

Doll had gone back reluctantly. He had not intended, when he first came back, to set himself up as a troubleshooting messenger to dangerous areas for Bugger Stein. Truthfully, he did not really know why he had done it. And now he was hooked. Also, he was angered at the easiness of Charlie Dale's mission when compared to the hardness of his own. Any damn fool could go *back,* after stretcher bearers, or even forward when he had a covered route all the way. For himself, he did not know how he was going to accomplish his job. Whyte was dead, Grove dead or badly wounded, and that left the command of the platoon to Skinny

Culn, the platoon guide. If he was not hit or dead too. Sgt Culn was a round, red-faced, pugnosed, jovial Irishman of 28, an old regular who ought to be all right leading the platoon. But Doll had no idea where to find him. The only man whose whereabouts Doll knew was Big Queen. This meant that he would have to hunt, maybe even run from hole to hole, looking, and down there Doll did not relish that idea. He'd like to see Dale do it.

Before going, he lay behind the crest of the third fold amongst the 2d Platoon and raised his head to look down into the low area where he must go. The 2d Platoon men nearby, cheeks pressed to the earth, stared at him with indifferent, sullen curiosity. He was aware that his eyes were narrowed, his nostrils flared, his jaw set. He made a handsome picture of a soldier for the 2d Platoon men who watched him without liking. Out in front one of the medics was helping back a fat man who had been shot through the calf and was groaning audibly. Doll felt a sort of amused contempt for him; why couldn't he keep his mouth shut? Once again the sick excitement had taken hold of him and gripped him by the belly, making his crotch tingle and his heart pound and paralyzing his diaphragm so that he breathed slower and slower and slower, and even slower still, until his essence and being ran down and seemed to stop in an entranced totality of concentration. Then he was up and running. He ran bent over and at half speed and exposed to the world, the same way he had run up out of there. Some bullets kicked up dirt to right and left. He zigged and zagged. In ten seconds' time he was back down flat in his little depression already calling breathlessly for Queen and wanting to laugh out loud. He had known all along he'd make it. A burst of MG fire tickled the rim of his hole and whined away, showering him with dirt.

But the getting here was only the beginning. He still had to find Culn. And the muffled information which came to him from Big Queen down in his hole was that Culn was somewhere over on the right; at least Queen had seen him there before the charge. But when Doll rolled over and called off to his right, the man who should have been, must *be* somewhere there, did not answer. A great soft lump of fear had risen in Doll's throat as he talked. He tried now to swallow it, but it remained. This was the situation he had been dreading back at the third fold before taking off. He was going to have to run down the line of holes looking for Culn.

All right then goddam them. He would show them. He'd do it, do it standing on his head. And then let's see what that little punk Dale could do. He was Don Doll and nobody was going to kill him in this war. The sons of bitches. Once again that great, strange stillness which he got, and which affected his breathing, came over Doll, blanketing out everything, as he prepared to get up. In his pants his balls tingled acutely. It was exactly the same feeling he used to get as a kid when something like Christmas got him excited. Let's see their faces and Bugger Stein's when he came back out of this.

In the fact, Stein had almost completely forgotten about his messenger to the 1st Platoon. The stress of newer developments claimed him. With the return of Charlie Dale and the good news about 3d Platoon, he decided not to send for Keck but to go to him. There, behind the third fold with 2d Platoon, he could both mount the attack he planned and observe it. With this in mind he had sent George Band with Sgt Storm and the cook force back around the covered route to join 3d Platoon. Band was to assume command and be prepared to attack the righthand ridge if Stein's attack succeeded. Band, with his weird bloodthirsty grin, constant neat advice and cool calm interest in the wounded, had been getting on Stein's nerves more and more, and this was a good way to get rid of him and at the same time make him useful. Then he put in a call to Col Tall, Battalion Commander.

More and more things had been getting on Stein's nerves, more and more increasingly. In the first place he could never be sure that what he did was right, mightn't have been done better and with less cost in some other way. He felt that way about the attack he was preparing to mount now. In addition there was his own nervous fear and apprehension, which kept eating into his energy more and more. Danger flickered and blinked in the air like a faulty neon tube. Whenever he stood up he might be struck by a bullet. Whenever he moved a few feet he might be moving under a descending mortar shell. Hiding these apprehensions from his men was even more fatiguing. Also, he had already finished off one of his two canteens of water, and was a third through the other, without ever having allayed his thirst. And in addition to all of this that was wearing him down there was something else coming increasingly to attention, and that was inertia. His men would do what he told them to if he told them explicitly and specifically. Otherwise they would simply lie with their cheeks pressed to the ground and stare at him. Except for a few volunteers like Dale; and Doll. Initiative may have been the descriptive word for the Civil War; or enthusiasm. But apparently inertia was the one for this one.

Stein had already talked to Tall about the Japanese evacuation of the lefthand grassy ridge, and had informed him that it was being occupied by C-for-Charlie's 3d Platoon; so he was dumbfounded when the Colonel began to shout at him over the sound power phone that he was too far to the right. He was not even given an opportunity to explain his proposed attack. The sound power phone was a great invention for explanations and one-sided conversations, because the listening party could not speak until the other turned it over and released the button; but somehow Tall seemed able to make this work for him, while Stein could not do the same.

"But I dont understand. What do you mean too far to the right? I told you they've evacuated the lefthand grassy ridge. And my 3d Platoon's occupied it. How can I be too far to the right? You agreed to attack from the right across our front. Over."

"God damn it, Stein!" the Col's cold thin angry voice cried. "I'm telling you your left flank's exposed." Because of the phone Stein could not protest that it wasn't, and the Col went on with rhetoric. "Do you know what it is to expose your left flank? Did you ever read in a tactics manual about exposing your left flank? Your left flank is *exposed*. And damn it, you've got to *move* down there. You're not moving! Over!"

The moment for protesting was past, lost while Tall's thumb depressed the button. Stein could only defend, harassed fury burning in him. "But God damn it, Colonel, that's why I called you! I'm trying to! I'm preparing to attack the righthand grassy ridge right now." He stopped, forgetting to say 'over', and there was a long silence. "Over," he said. "God damn it."

"Stein, I told you you're too far right already," the Col's voice came from the faroff areas of safety. "You're sideslipping to the right alla time. Over."

"Well, what do you want me to do? You want me to withdraw the rest of my company to the lefthand grassy ridge, too? Over." That, he knew, would be insane.

"No. I've decided to commit the reserve company on your left—with orders to attack. Orders to attack, Stein, you hear? orders to attack. You stay where you are. I'll have Baker Company's commander send your reserve platoon back to you. Over."

"Do you want me to go ahead with my attack?" Stein asked, because it wasn't plain from what he'd heard. "Over."

"What else?" the Col's thin, outraged voice piped at him. "What else, Stein? You're not supposed to be down there on a goddamned asshole vacation. Now, get cracking!" There was a pause and Stein could hear electrical whinings and what sounded like polite mumblings. He heard one distinct, respectful "Yes, sir" in Tall's voice. Then the Colonel's voice came back on again, much kinder now, more jovial. "Get cracking, boy! Get cracking!" Tall said heartily. "Over and out."

Stein came back to himself to find himself looking into the wide, nervous eyes of Fife. He handed him the phone. Well, that was that. He had not even got to explain his attack plan, and he would have liked to because once again he could not be sure that he was right. But the big brass had arrived at the phone station, obviously. There was no point in trying to call back while Tall had those people clustered around him.

Yes, the big brass. The observers. Today they even had an Admiral. Stein had a sudden and unholy, heartfreezing picture, which transfixed him for a moment, bulge-eyed, of an identical recurrence up there now of the scene he himself had witnessed on Hill 207 two days ago. The same harassed, apprehensive Battalion Colonel with field glasses; the same diffident, but equally apprehensive little knot of eagles and stars peering over his spiritual shoulder; the same massed mob of pawns and minor pieces craning to see like a stadium crowd; all were up there right now, going through the identical gyrations their identical counterparts had gone through two days ago. While down below were the same blood-sweating Captains and their troops going through theirs. Only this time he himself, he Jim Stein, was one of them, one of the committed ones. The committed ones going through their exaggerated pretenses of invoking the cool calm logic and laws of the science of tactics. And tomorrow it would be someone else. It was a horrifying vision: all of them doing the same identical thing, all of them powerless to stop it, all of them devoutly and proudly believing themselves to be free individuals. It expanded to include the scores of nations, the millions of men, doing the same on thousands of hilltops across the world. And it didn't stop there. It went on. It was the concept—concept? the fact; the reality—of the modern State in action. It was so horrible a picture that Stein could not support or accept it. He put it away from him, and blinked his bulging eyes. What he had to do right now was get his Company Hq over behind the third fold with Keck and the 2d Platoon.

From the top of the third fold there was really very little to see. Stein and his sergeants lay behind the crest and looked as they talked. In front of them perhaps a hundred yards away the waiting grassy ridge rose, apparently devoid of life. Behind it at some distance the upper reaches of The Elephant's Head, their real objective, rose still higher. The stony open ground, thinly grassed, fell gently in a rolling motion for fifty yards, then leveled out.

Tactically Lt Whyte (whose body still lay just beyond the crest) had served no good purpose at all with his charge, Stein saw immediately. Whyte's platoon, situated further to the left where the white eyeballs and sweating faces of 2d Platoon now lay watching Stein, had rolled forward in a long wave not directed at either ridge but with its ends lapping against both, while the main strength bulged out into the open center which served only to funnel the fire from both ridges and the Hill itself. It couldn't have been handled worse.

But that was that. This was this. Stein's problem now as he saw it, his first problem anyway, was the getting of his men from the comparative safety of here down that fucking outrageous bareass slope to the comparative safety of the foot of the ridge, where they would be defiladed from the MGs and protected from the mortars by their closeness to the Japanese. Once they were there—But getting them there—

Stein had already decided to use only two squads of his 2d Platoon, augmented by the men already hiding down there. He was not sure this was enough, and he had not got to discuss it with Col Tall, but he did not want to commit more men until he had some idea of what was against him. He had also decided how to choose the two squads. In fact, he had given more thought to this than to the other. He was obsessed by a feeling of moral culpability about choosing which men to send in. Some of them would surely die, and he did not want to choose which ones. Rather than do that he decided simply to take arbitrarily the first two squads on the right of the line (they were the closest), and thus let Luck or Chance or Fate or whatever agency ran the lives of men do the choosing. That way no agent of retribution could hold him responsible. Lying on the slope, he told Keck which ones he wanted. Keck, who certainly would know, who always knew just where his men were, nodded and said that that would be McCron's and Beck's squads, the 2d and the 3d. Stein nodded back, feeling sorry for them. McCron the motherhen, and Milly Beck the martinet. John Bell was in McCron's squad.

But before he could do anything with his two squads he must, Stein felt, know more about the men already down there. They were already there, and wouldn't have to run the gauntlet, but what sort of shape were they in? Were any of them wounded? Did they have a noncom with them? Was their morale unbroken? Stein felt he had to know, and the only way to find out was to send somebody. He sent Charlie Dale.

It was an extraordinary performance. The little man licked his lips in their mean, dull grin, hitched up his rifle and Thompsongun, and nodded his head. He was ready to go. Stein, who had never liked him, and didn't like him now, watched him go with a growing admiration which only increased his dislike. He went dogtrotting and unblinking (the thick set of his back made you know he was not blinking) in a straight line down the open slope toward the grassy ridge. He ran bent over at the waist in that peculiar fashion everybody instinctively adopted, but he did not zig or zag. Nothing touched him. Arriving, he dived into the thicker grass and disappeared. Three minutes later he reappeared, and came dogtrotting and unblinking back. Stein could not help wondering what he thought about, but would not ask.

Charlie Dale would have been pleased to have been asked. But he really did not think much of anything. He had been told that all Japs had bad eyes and wore glasses and were poor marksmen, anyway. He knew nothing could hit him. Going down, he concentrated his eyes and all his attention on the foot of the ridge. Coming back, he concentrated on a spot at the crest of the fold. The only thing he really thought about or felt was a querulous irritation that Storm and the other cooks had been sent off to the 3d Platoon and so weren't here to see him. This, and the fact that after he had completed one or two more of these things, he ought to be able to move into a rifle platoon as at least a corporal or perhaps even as a sergeant, and in this way get out of the kitchen without having to become a private. This had been his secret plan from the beginning. And he had noted that casualties among the noncoms were already pretty heavy.

Dale arrived back at the third fold a hero. In its way it was quite a feat, what he had done. Even from the crest of the fold it was possible to see the amount of MG and rifle fire which had been hitting the ground all around him. Everybody who had not wanted to go, and would not have gone, was pleased with him; and Dale was pleased with himself. Everyone within reach slapped him on the back as he made his way to Stein to make his report, which was that they were all okay down there, that their morale was unimpaired, but that they did not have a noncom with them. They were all privates.

"All right," Stein said, still lying beside Keck on the reverse slope. "Now, listen. They haven't got a noncom with them, and I can't send anybody here away from his own squad. If you want to go back down there with the others when they go, I'll make you an acting sergeant right now, and you'll be in command of that extra squad. Do you want to do that?''

"Sure," Dale said at once. He made his mean grin and licked his lips. "Sure, sir.'' He bobbed his head on his perpetually hunched shoulders, and his expression changed to one of patently false humility. "If you think I'm capable, sir. If *you* think I can do it.''

Stein looked at him with distaste, not very well concealed. But it was concealed enough for Charlie Dale's acumen.—Or was it? "Okay," he said. "I make you acting sergeant. You'll go down with the others.''

"Aye, sir," Dale said. "But dont you have to say hereby?''

"What?''

"I said: Dont you have to say hereby? You know, to make it official.'' In some slow-stirring, labyrinthine depth of his animal's mind Dale seemed to be suspicious of Stein's honesty.

"No. I dont have to say hereby. Hereby what? I dont have to say anything but what I've said. You're an acting sergeant. You'll go down with the others.''

"Aye, sir," Dale said and crawled away.

Stein and Keck exchanged a glance. "I think I better go down, too, Cap'n," Keck said. "Somebody should be in charge down there.''

Stein nodded, slowly. "I guess you're right. But take care of yourself. I need you.''

"I'll take care of myself as good as anybody can around here,'' was Keck's humorless answer.

Around them the tension over the attack was beginning to mount and be felt. It showed plainly on the faces of 2d Platoon, white-eyed and sweating, and all turned toward the little group of leaders like a row of sunflowers turned toward the sun. On the left the first elements of the 3d Platoon had reappeared in the low between the second and third folds and were making their way toward Stein running bent over at the waist, the others following strung out behind them. Over the top of the second fold behind him another, lone figure came hurrying toward Stein, also running bent over at the waist. It was Witt returning, this time with

his rifle and some extra bandoliers. Everything seemed to be concentrating. The moment of truth, Stein thought and looked at his
watch, which said 12:02. Moment of truth, shit. My God, could it
have been that long? It seemed like only seconds. And yet it
seemed like years, too. It was at this moment that Pfc Doll—or
his fate for him—chose to return from his hazardous mission to
1st Platoon.

Doll came running up the slight slope at about the middle of
the 2d Platoon, dove over the crest and fell, then scrambled along
the reverse slope to where Stein was, to report. He had found Sgt
Culn. But arriving at the knot of leaders he collapsed, sobbing for
breath for almost a minute. There was no giggling this time, and
no arch display of insouciance. His face was drawn and strained,
the lines beside his open mouth deeply etched. He had run along
the uneven line of holes calling for Skinny Culn, with fire being
put down all around him. Men had looked up at him from their
holes with startled disbelief on their faces. His body, abetted by
his imagination, had quickly reached the point where it was
threatening to disobey him. Finally three holes in front of him a
hand and arm had shot into the air, the hand describing the old
circular hand-and-arm-signal for 'Gather here.' Doll had pulled
up to find Culn lying placidly on his side and grinning up at him
ruefully, his rifle hugged against his chest. "Come right in,"
Culn said; but Doll had already dived. The hole wasn't big
enough for two men. They had huddled together in it while Doll
brought Culn up to date on the casualties, told him Stein's plan,
told him 1st Platoon's part in it. Culn had scratched his reddish
stubble. "So I got the platoon. Well, well. Okay, tell him I'll try.
But you tell Bugger we're sort of de-morale-ized down here, as it
says in the field manuals. But I'll do the best I can." Seconds
later Doll had been back behind the third fold in what seemed to
him to be enormous safety, and then reporting to Stein. He made
his report proudly.

Doll did not know what kind of reception he had expected from
them, but it was not the one that he got. Charlie Dale had already
returned before him, and from a tougher mission, and with much
less display of nerves. 3d Platoon was in the act of arriving, and

had to be taken care of by Stein. And the mounting tension of the
coming attack made everybody rather preoccupied, anyway. Bugger listened to his report and nodded, gave him a pat on the arm
as one might toss a fish to a trained seal after its act, and dismissed him. Doll had no choice but to crawl away, his bravery
and heroism ignored and unappreciated. Wondering that he was
still alive, he ached to tell somebody how narrowly he had escaped death. And then, as he sat down and looked up, there
adding salt to his wounds was Charlie Dale, sitting nearby and
grinning a rapaciously superior grin at him. While he sat and
stared back at him, Doll was forced to listen to little Private Bead,
lying beside him, recount the tale of Dale's exploit.

Nor was Dale all. Witt, the mad volunteer, the crazy sentimental Kentuckian who wanted to come back to a rifle company
under fire, had been crouching behind Doll all during Doll's report, waiting his own turn at Stein. Now he reported too and
when Stein briefly explained the impending attack to him, he
immediately asked permission to go along. Stein, unable to hide
his stunned disbelief entirely, nodded his agreement and sent Witt
over to Milly Beck's squad. It was this final straw, this blow in
the face by Fate, added to the knowledge that Charlie Dale was
going—and as an acting sergeant yet, which made Doll open his
mouth and speak up. As much a reflex as the yell of a man
pricked with a knife, Doll heard his voice. With horror he listened
to himself asking, in a clear, bell-like, resolute, confident tone, if
he could not go along himself. When Stein said yes and sent him
to McCron's squad, he crawled away biting the inside of his lip so
hard that it brought tears to his eyes. He was wishing he could do
worse: bang his head up and down on a rock; bite a whole chunk
out of his arm. Why did he do things like this to himself? Why
did he?

There was nothing to keep them now. Everything was arranged. They could get on with it any time. Stein and Keck lay
side by side behind the little crest, with 1st Sgt Welsh lying beside them in a flat-faced, uncommunicative silence, and looked it
over one more time. Stein had placed 3d Platoon about thirty
yards behind and below them on the slope, in two echelons of two

squads each; they were to be ready to attack and exploit any advantage which arose. He had sent word back to his mortar section to raise their fire further up the ridge. He had his one remaining machine gun placed behind the crest of the third fold. Off to the left on the lefthand grassy ridge a lot of fire was being put forth but Stein did not see any of B-for-Baker moving. As he watched, two Japanese mortar rounds landed and went up, there. It was impossible to tell if they hurt anyone.

"I think we better send them down in bunches of three or four, at irregular intervals," he said turning his head to Keck. "When they're all there, space them out. Advance them by rushes, or in a line. Use your own judgment.—I guess you might as well go."

"I'll take the first bunch down myself," Keck said huskily, staring down the slope. "Listen, Cap'n," he said, looking at Stein, and at Brass Band who had just come up, "there's somethin I wanted to tell you. That guy Bell is a good man. He's pretty steady. He helped me get going and get the platoon out of that hole we were in after that charge." He paused. "I just wanted to tell you."

"Okay. I'll remember." Stein felt an unnamable, nigh-unbearable anguish that he could not do anything about. It forced him to look away down the slope. Beside him Keck started to crawl off.

"Give them hell, Sergeant!" George Band said cheerily. "Give them hell!"

Keck paused in his crawl long enough to look back. "Yeh," he said.

The two squads, with their three extra men, had more or less separated themselves from the other half of the platoon. The most of them, in their bodily attitudes and in their faces, resembled sheep about to be led to the slaughter pens in Chicago. They waited. Keck had only to crawl to them and instruct them. "Okay, you guys. This is it. We're goin down in groups of four. No point in goin by rushes, only make a better target stopped. So run all the way. We aint got any choice. We're picked, and so we got to go. I'll take the first bunch myself to show you how easy it is. I want Charlie Dale with me. Dale? So you can organize them guys that's down there. Let's move out."

He started to crawl to the jumpoff point just beyond the knot of officers and CP men, and it was here that the first case of overt cowardice (if it could be called that, and if S/Sgt Stack could be omitted) occurred in C-for-Charlie. A big, beautifully muscled man named Sico, an Italian draftee from Philly with some five months service, suddenly sat down in his tracks and began to hold his stomach and groan. It blocked the line behind him and when somebody called, the ones in front stopped also. Keck crawled back to him. His squad sergeant, Beck the martinet, crawled over to him too. Beck was very young for a martinet, but he was a very good one. The rifles of his squad had been the most perfect at inspections since he came into the company with six years service and immediately got promoted. Withal, he still was not really mean, only stern. He was not very bright at anything else or even interested, but soldiering was his code. Right now he appeared deeply ashamed that anything like this could happen to any man in his squad, and because of this, furious.

"Get up, God damn you, Sico," he said in his stern, command voice. "Or I'll kick you so hard in that stomach you'll really be sick."

"I can't, Sergeant," Sico said. His face was drawn up grotesquely. And his eyes were puddles of terror, bottomless, anguished, and a little guilty. "I would if I could. You know I would. I'm sick."

"Sick, my foot," said Beck, who never swore much, and for whom the phrase God damn you was inordinately strong.

"Hold it, Beck," Keck said. "What is it, Sico?"

"I dont know, Sergeant. It's my stomach. Pains. And cramps. I can't straighten up. I'm sick," he said, looking at Keck appealingly out of the dark, tortured holes of his eyes. "I'm sick," he said again, and as if to prove it suddenly vomited. He did not even try to bend over and the vomit burped up out of him and ran down over his fatigue shirt onto his hands which held his belly. He looked at Keck hopefully, but appeared ready to do it again if necessary.

Keck studied him a moment. "Leave him," he said to Beck.

"Come on.—The medics will take care of you, Sico," he said to Sico.

"Thank you, Sergeant," Sico said.

"But—" Beck began.

"Dont argue with me," Keck said, already crawling away.

"Right," Beck said, and followed.

Sico continued to sit and watched the others pass. The medics did indeed take care of him. One of them, the junior, though he looked much like his shyfaced, bespectacled senior, came and led him back to the rear, Sico walking bent over in pain with his hands holding his stomach. He groaned audibly from time to time and now and then he gagged, but apparently did not feel it necessary to vomit more. His face was haunted-looking and his eyes tormented. But clearly nobody would ever convince him he had not been sick. Whenever he looked at the C-for-Charlie men he passed, it was appealingly, a certain unspoken request for understanding, for belief. As for the others, they looked back noncommittally. None of their faces held contempt. Instead, under the white-eyed sweating pucker of fear, there was a hint of sheepish envy, as if they would have liked to do the same but were afraid they could not bring it off. Sico, who could undoubtedly read this look, apparently got no comfort from it. He tottered on, helped by the junior medic, and the last that C-for-Charlie ever saw of him was when he hobbled out of sight beyond the second fold.

In the meantime Keck's men had begun their gauntlet-running. Keck led off with Dale and two other men. Each squad sergeant, first Milly Beck then McCron, supervised the jumpoff of his men in groups of four. All of them made it down safely except two. Of these one, a Mississippi farmer 'boy' of nearly forty named Catt, about whom nobody in the company knew anything for the simple reason that he never talked, was killed outright. But with the other something really bad happened for the first time in the day.

At first they thought the second one was dead too. Hit running, he had fallen, bounced hard, and lain still like the Mississippian. So that was that. When a man was hit and killed outright, there was nothing anyone could do. The man had ceased to exist. The living went right on living, without him. On the other hand, the wounded were evacuated. They would live or die someplace else. So they too ceased to exist to the men they left behind, and could be forgotten also. Without a strong belief in a Valhalla, it was as good a way to handle the problem as any, and made everybody feel better. But this was not to be the case with Pvt Alfredo Tella of Cambridge, Massachusetts, who, as he liked jokingly to say, 'had not gone to Harvard, but he had dug many a cesspool underneath its ivy-covered walls.'

Actually, Tella did not begin to yell, at least not loud enough to be heard by Bugger Stein's CP, until after Keck had framed and then carried out most of his attack. And by that time lots of other things were happening.

For the moment, there was still nothing much to be seen from the top of the fold. Two new bodies lay on the slope, and that was all. Keck and his running men had dived headfirst into the taller grass and apparently disappeared from the face of the earth. The yammering of the cortex of Japanese fire had ceased. Quiet—at least, a comparative quiet, if one disregarded the racketing and banging which still hung and jounced everywhere high in the air—reigned over the grassy ridge. On the third fold they lay and waited, watching.

Unfortunately, the Japanese heavy mortars, still firmly seated on the heights of The Elephant's Head, had seen the forward movement of American troops, too. A mortar round exploded in the low between the folds. That one hurt nobody, but more followed. Mortar shells began exploding their fountains of terror, dirt and fragments along the rearward slope every minute or so, as the Japanese gunners fingered the area searching American flesh. It was not a barrage, but it was very nerve-racking, and it wounded some men. Because of it, only a very few, Stein, Band and Welsh among them, actually saw Keck's attack. Most were as flat to the ground as they could get.

Stein felt it was his duty to watch, to observe. Anyway, there was very little choice as to cover. There were no holes here, and one flat place was as good as another. So he lay, only his eyes and helmet above the crest of the fold, and waited and watched. He could not escape a distinct premonition that quite soon a mortar shell was going to land squarely in the center of his back. He did not know why Band had decided to watch too, but suspected that it was in the hope of seeing some new wounded, though he knew this was unfair. And as for Welsh, Stein could not even imagine why this flatfaced, expressionless man should want to expose himself to watch, especially since he had not said a single word to anyone since offering his Thompsongun to Keck. The three of them lay there while a mortar shell blew up somewhere behind them, then a minute later another, then almost a minute later still another. There were no screams with any of them.

When they finally did see men, it was about a third of the way up the ridge. Keck had crawled his men that far unseen. Now they rose in a line, which bellied downhill somewhat in the center like a rope bellying of its own weight, and began to scamper uphill firing as they went. Almost immediately the Japanese fire began to hammer, and at once men began to fall.

If Pvt Alfredo Tella of Cambridge Mass had begun to yell before this, no one had heard him. And in the intensity of the action and of watching, no one was to hear him until it was over.

In fact, it did not last long. But while it did, many things happened. Arriving in the defiladed area, Keck had first turned his attention to organizing the disorganized group of privates already there, and sent Dale to do that. Then he himself lay in the grass directing the others off to the right as they arrived. When the line was formed, he gave the order to crawl. The grass which was about chest high here had a matted, tangled underlayer of old stems. It choked them with dust, tied up their arms and feet, made it impossible to see. They crawled for what seemed an eternity. It required tremendous exertion. Most of them had long since used up all of their water, and it was this as much as anything in Keck's mind when he passed the word to halt. He judged they were about half way up the slope, and he didn't want them to start passing out on him. For a moment as Keck lay gathering his will power he thought about their faces as they arrived and dived into the grass down below: whites of the eyes showing, mouths open and drawn, skin around the eyes pinched and tight. They had all arrived terrified. They had all arrived reluctant. Keck felt no sympathy for them, any more than he felt sympathy for himself. He was terrified too. Taking a deep breath he stood straight up in the grass yelling at them: "Up! Up! Up! Up and *GO!*"

From the top of the fold they could take the operation in at a glance, and follow its progress. This was not so easy on the ridge itself. But John Bell standing rifle in hand and trying to shoot and run in the thick grass was able to see several important things. He was, for instance, the only man who saw Sgt McCron cover his face with his hands and sit down weeping. When they had first stood up, the fury of the Japanese fire had struck them like a wind-tormented hailstorm. The Japanese had been smart and had waited, conserving their fire till they had targets. Four men of McCron's squad went down at once. On the right a young draftee named Wynn was shot in the throat and screamed, "Oh, my God!" in a voice of terror and disbelief as a geyser of blood spurted from his neck. Ridiculously like a rag doll he fell and disappeared in the grass. Next to him Pfc Earl, a little shorter, was caught in the face, perhaps from the same burst. He went down without a sound, looking as if he'd been hit in the face with a tomato. To Bell's left two other men tumbled, yelling with fear that they were killed. All this was apparently too much for McCron, who had clucked over and mothered this squad of his for so many months, and he simply dropped his rifle and sat down crying. Bell himself was astonished that he himself was not already struck down dead. He only knew, could only think one thing. That was to keep going. He had to keep going. If he ever wanted to get back home again to his wife Marty, if he ever wanted to see her again, kiss her, put himself between her breasts, between her legs, fondle, caress, and touch her, he had to keep going. And that meant he had to keep the others going with him, because it was useless to keep going by himself. It had to stop. There had to be a point in time where it ended. In a cracked bellow he began to harangue the remainder of McCron's 2d Squad. In back of and a little below him off in the center as he looked behind, he saw Milly Beck leading his men in a fury of snarling hatred which shocked Bell numbly: Beck who was always so controlled and almost never raised his voice. Still below him yet came Keck, roaring and firing Welsh's Thompsongun uphill. A silly phrase came in Bell's mind and he began to yell at the other men senselessly. "Home for Christmas! Home for Christmas!"

Keep going. Keep going. It was a ridiculous thought, a stupid idea in any case and he would wonder later why he had it. Obviously, if he wanted to stay alive to get home, the best thing to do would have been to lie down in the grass and hide.

It was Charlie Dale on the far left who saw the first emplacement, the first live one any of them had ever actually seen. Far enough left to be beyond their flank, it was a one-gun job, a simple hole dug in the ground and covered over with sticks and kunai grass. From the dark hole he could see the muzzle spitting fire at him. Actually, Dale was probably the calmest of the lot. Imaginationless, he had organized his makeshift squad, and found them eager to accept his authority if he would simply tell them what to do. Now he urged them on, but not bellowing or roaring like Keck and Bell. Dale thought it looked much better, was far more seemly, if a noncom did not yell like that. So far he had not fired a shot. What was the point, when there were no targets? When he saw the emplacement, he carefully released his safety and fired a long burst with his Thompsongun, straight into the hole twenty yards away. Before he could release the trigger the gun jammed, solidly. But his burst was enough to stop the machinegun, at least momentarily, and Dale ran toward it pulling a grenade from his shirt. From ten yards away he threw the grenade like a baseball, wrenching hell out of his shoulder. The grenade disappeared through the hole, then blew up scattering sticks and grass and three rag dolls and upending the machinegun. Dale turned back to his squad, licking his lips and grinning with beady pride. "Come on, you guys," he said. "Let's keep it moving."

They were almost done with it. Off to the right of center Pfc Doll and another man discovered a second small emplacement simultaneously. They fired a clip apiece into its hole and Doll grenaded it, keeping up his unspoken competition with Charlie Dale, even if he wasn't an acting sergeant. Wait'll he hears about that, he thought happily, because he didn't know that Dale had got one too. But the happiness was shortlived, for Doll and everybody else, as they ran on. Knocking out two one-gun emplacements made no appreciable difference in the volume of the Japanese fire. MGs still hammered at them from seemingly every quarter of the globe. Men were still going down. They still had not located any main strongpoints. Directly in front of them thirty yards away a rock outcropping formed a four-foot ledge which extended clear across their front. Instinctively everyone began to run for that, while behind them Keck, gasping, bellowed the useless order: "That ledge! Head for that ledge!"

They dived in behind its protection pellmell, all of them sobbing audibly with exhaustion. The exertion and the heat had been too much. Several men vomited. One man made it to the ledge, gurgled once senselessly, then—his eyes rolling back in his head—fainted from heat prostration. There was nothing with which to cover him for shade. Beck the martinet loosened his belt and clothes. Then they lay against the ledge in the midday sun and smelled the hot, summer-smelling dust. Insects hummed around them. The fire had stopped.

"Well, what're we gonna do now, Keck?" someone asked finally.

"We're gonna stay right here. Maybe they'll get some reinforcements up to us."

"Ha! To do what?"

"To capture these goddam fucking positions around here!" Keck cried fretfully. "What you think?"

"You mean you really want to go on with it?"

"I dont know. No. Not no uphill charge. But they get us some reinforcements, we can scout around and maybe locate where all these goddam fucking MGs are. Anyway, it's better than going back down through that. You want to go back down?"

Nobody answered this, and Keck did not feel it necessary to elaborate. By counting heads they found that they had left twelve men behind them on the slope killed or wounded. This was almost a full squad, almost a full third of their number. It included McCron. When Bell told him about McCron, Keck appointed Bell acting sergeant in his place; Bell couldn't have cared less. "He'll have to look out for himself, like the rest of the wounded,'' Keck said. They continued to lie in the hot sun. Ants crawled on the ground at the foot of the ledge.

"What if the Japs come down here in force and throw us off of here?'' somebody asked.

"I dont think they will,'' Keck said. "They're worse off than we are. But we better have a sentry. Doll.''

Bell lay with his face against the rock facing Witt. Witt lay looking back. Quietly in the insect-humming heat they lay and looked at each other. Bell was thinking that Witt had come through it all all right. Like himself. What power was it which decided one man should be hit, be killed, instead of another man? So Bugger's little feeling attack was over. If this were a movie, this would be the end of the show and something would be decided. In a movie or a novel they would dramatize and build to the climax of the attack. When the attack came in the film or novel, it would be satisfying. It would decide something. It would have a semblance of meaning and a semblance of an emotion. And immediately after, it would be over. The audience could go home and think about the semblance of the meaning and feel the semblance of the emotion. Even if the hero got killed, it would still make sense. Art, Bell decided, creative art—was shit.

Beside him Witt, who was apparently not bothered by any of these problems, raised himself to his knees and cautiously stuck his head up over the ledge. Bell went on with his thinking.

Here there was no semblance of meaning. And the emotions were so many and so mixed up that they were indecipherable, could not be untangled. Nothing had been decided, nobody had learned anything. But most important of all, nothing had ended. Even if they had captured this whole ridge, nothing would have ended. Because tomorrow, or the day after, or the day after that, they would be called upon to do the same thing again—maybe under even worse circumstances. The concept was so overpowering, so numbing, that it shook Bell. Island after island, hill after hill, beachhead after beachhead, year after year. It staggered him.

It would certainly end sometime, sure, and almost certainly—because of industrial production—end in victory. But that point in time had no connection with any individual man engaged now.

Some men would survive, but no *one* individual man *could* survive. It was a discrepancy in methods of counting. The whole thing was too vast, too complicated, too technological for any one individual man to count in it. Only collections of men counted, only communities of men, only *numbers* of men.

The weight of such a proposition was deadening, almost too heavy to be borne, and Bell wanted to turn his mind away from it. Free individuals? Ha! Somewhere between the time the first Marines had landed here and this battle now today, American warfare had changed from individualist warfare to collectivist warfare—or perhaps that was only his illusion, perhaps it only seemed like that to him because he himself was now engaged. But free individuals? What a fucking myth! *Numbers* of free individuals, maybe; *collectives* of free individuals. And so the point of Bell's serious thinking finally emerged.

At some unspecified moment between this time yesterday and this time today the unsought realization had come to Bell that statistically, mathematically, arithmetically, any way you wanted to count it, he John Bell could not possibly live through this war. He could not possibly go home to his wife Marty Bell. So it did not really make any difference what Marty did, whether she stepped out on him or not, because he would not be there to accuse her.

The emotion which this revelation created in Bell was not one of sacrifice, resignation, acceptance, and peace. Instead, it was an irritating, chaffing emotion of helpless frustration which made him want to crawl around rubbing his flanks and back against rocks to ease the itch. He still had not moved his face from the rock.

Beside him Witt, still kneeling and peering out, yelled suddenly. Simultaneously Doll yelled too from down at the other end.

"Something's comin!"

"Something's comin! Somebody's comin at us!"

As one man the line behind the ledge swept up and forward, rifles ready. Forty yards away seven pot-headed, bandylegged, starved-looking Japanese men were running down at them across an ungrassed area carrying hand grenades in their right hands and bayoneted rifles in their left. Keck's Thompson, after his firing of almost all its ammo on the way up, had finally jammed, too. Neither gun could be unstuck. But the massed riflefire from the ledge disposed of the seven Japanese men quickly. Only one was able even to throw; and his grenade, a dud, landed short. At the same moment the dud grenade should have exploded, there was a loud, ringing, halfmuffled explosion behind them. In the excitement of the attack and defense they continued to fire into the seven bodies up the slope. When they ceased, only two bodies continued to move. Aiming deliberately in the sudden quiet, Witt the Kentuckian put a killing round into each of them. "You never can tell about them tricky suicidal bastards," he said. "Even when they're hit."

It was Bell who first remembered the explosion behind them and turned around to see what had caused it. What he saw was Sgt Keck lying on his back with his eyes closed, in a strangely grotesque position, still holding the ring and safety pin of a hand grenade in his right hand. Bell called out, and rushing to him, they rolled him over gently and saw that there was nothing they could do for him. His entire right buttock and part of his back had been blown away. Some of his internal organs were visible, pulsing busily away, apparently going about their business as if nothing had happened. Steadily, blood welled in the cavity. Gently they laid him back.

It was obvious what had happened. In the attack, perhaps because his Thompsongun was jammed, but at any rate not firing his rifle, Keck had reached in his hip pocket to pull out a grenade. And in the excitement he had gotten it by the pin. Bell, for one, experienced a dizzying, near-fainting terror momentarily, at the thought of Keck standing and looking at that pin in his hand. Keck had leaped back from the line and sat down against a little dirt hummock to protect the others. Then the grenade had gone off.

Keck made no protest when they moved him. He was conscious, but apparently did not want to talk and preferred to keep his eyes closed. Two of them sat with him and tried to talk to him and reassure him while the others went back to the line, but Keck did not answer and kept his eyes shut. The little muscles at the corners of his mouth twitched jerkily. He spoke only once. Without opening his eyes he said clearly, "What a fucking recruit trick to pull." Five minutes later he stopped breathing. The men went back. Milly Beck, as the senior noncom present, was now in command.

Stein had watched the silly little Japanese counter-attack from the top of the third fold. The seven Japanese men had come out from behind a huge outcrop, already running and already too close to the Americans for Stein to dare tell his one MG to fire. The counter-attack was doomed to failure anyway. What made them do it? Why, if they wanted to throw Stein's platoon off the ridge, did they not come in force? Why just seven men? And why come across the open ground? They could have slipped down through the grass until they were on top of Keck and thrown the grenades from there. Were those seven men doing all that on their own, without orders? Or were they some kind of crazy religious volunteers who wanted into Nirvana, or whatever it was they called it? Stein did not understand them, and had never understood them. Their incredibly delicate, ritual tea service; their exquisitely sensitive painting and poetry; their unbelievably cruel, sadistic beheadings and torture. He was a peaceful man. They frightened him. When the riflefire from the platoon took care of the seven so easily, he awaited a second, larger attack, but knowing somehow intuitively that one would not come, and he was right.

Stein had not thought anyone was wounded in the little attack, so he was surprised when the men all clustered around one figure on the ground. On the ridge they were slightly above his own height here, now, and at this distance—more than two hundred yards—it was impossible to tell who it was. Hoping desperately that it was not Keck, he called to Band to give him back his glasses, focused them, and saw that it was. Almost immediately a rifle bullet whooshed past him only inches from his head. Startled wide-eyed, he jerked down and rolled over twice to his left. He had forgotten to shield the lenses, and they had glinted. This time he cupped them with his hands, verified that it was Keck dead, then saw that Sgt Beck was looking at him—or anyway toward him—and making the Old Army hand-and-arm signal for "Converge on me." He wanted reinforcements?! Thirty-five yards behind Stein another mortar shell exploded and somebody yelled. Again he ducked.

Exertion, nervous exhaustion, and fear were wearing Stein down. When he looked at his watch, he could not believe it was after one. Suddenly he was ravenous. Putting down the glasses, he got out a bar of D Ration and tried to munch it but could not get it down because his mouth was so dry from lack of water. He spat most of it out. When he looked again with the glasses, Beck was again making his hand-and-arm signal. As he watched, Beck stopped and turned back to the ledge. Stein cursed. His little three-squad attack had failed, bogged down. They had not been nearly enough men. Stein very seriously doubted if he even had that many men. He had just watched two full platoons of B-for-Baker on the lefthand ridge come running back ftom a failed attack up the Bowling Alley in an attempt to outflank the right-hand grassy ridge. And Beck wanted reinforcements!

That whole fucking outrageous ridge was one giant honeycomb of emplacements. It was a regular fortress. He himself was fast nearing the limbo of total mental exhaustion. It was hard to try and act fearless for your men when you were actually full of fear. And Beck wanted reinforcements!

Stein had lain and watched Keck lead his three pitiful little squads up that goddamned ridge with tears in his eyes. Beside him George Band had lain and watched eagerly through the glasses, smiling toughly. But Stein had choked up, cried enough moisture so that everything blurred and he had to wipe his eyes out quickly. He had personally counted every one of the twelve to go down. They were his men, and he had failed in his responsibility to each one who fell. And now he was being asked to send more after them.

Well, he could give him the two remaining squads of 2d Platoon. Pull them back out and put the reserve 3d Platoon up on the crest to fire cover. That would work all right. But before he did it, he intended to talk to Col Tall and get Tall's opinion and assent. Stein simply did not want that responsibility, not all alone. Rolling over, he motioned to Corporal Fife to bring him the telephone. God, but he was *bushed*. It was just then that Stein first heard from down in the little valley the first thin, piping yells.

They sounded insane. What they lacked in volume, and they lacked a great deal, they more than made up in their penetrating qualities, and in their length. They came in a series, each lasting five full seconds, the whole lasting thirty seconds. Then there was silence under the high-hanging, jouncing racket of noise.

"Jesus!" Stein said fervently. He looked over at Band, whom he found looking back at him with squinted, dilated eyes.

"Christ!" Band said.

From below, high and shrill, the series of yells came again. They were not screams.

Stein was able to pick him out easily with the glasses, which brought him up very close, too close for comfort. He had fallen almost at the bottom of the slope, seventy-five or eighty yards, not far from the other one, the Mississippian Catt, who—seen through the glasses—was clearly dead. Now he was trying to crawl back. He had been hit squarely in the groin with a burst of heavy MG fire which had torn his whole belly open. Lying on his back, his head uphill, both hands pressed to his belly to hold his intestines in, he was inching his way back up the slope with his legs. Through the glasses Stein could see blue-veined loops of intestine bulging between the bloodstained fingers. Inching was hardly the word, since Stein estimated he was making less than half an inch per try. He had lost his helmet, and his head thrown back on his neck, his mouth and his eyes wide open, he was staring directly up at Stein as if he were looking into a Promised Land. As Stein watched, he stopped, laid his head flat, and closing his eyes he made his series of yells again. They came to Stein's ears faintly, exactly in the same sequence as they had before. Then, resting a second and swallowing, he yelled something else.

"Help me! Help me!" Stein heard. Feeling sick and dizzy in

the area of his diaphragm, he lowered the glasses and handed them to Band.

"Tella," he said.

Bank looked a long time. Then he too lowered the glasses. There was a flat, scared look in his eyes when he looked back at Stein. "What're we gonna do?" Band said.

Trying to think of some answer to this, Stein felt something touch him on the leg. He yelped and jumped, fear running all through his body like quicksilver. Whirling around, he found himself staring downslope into the fear-ridden eyes of Corporal Fife, who was holding out to him the telephone. Too upset even to be sheepish or angry, Stein waved him away impatiently. "Not now. Not now." He began to call for a medic, one of whom was already on his way. From below the insane series of yells came again, identical, unchanging.

Stein and Band were not the only ones to have heard them. The entire remainder of the 2d Platoon lying along the crest of the fold had heard them. So had the medic who was now running bentover along the slope to Stein. So had Fife.

When his commander waved him away with the telephone, Fife had collapsed exactly where he was and flattened himself as low to the ground as he could get. The mortar shells were still falling at roughly one-minute intervals; sometimes you could hear their fluttery shu-ing sound for two seconds before they hit; and Fife was completely terrorized by them. He had lost the power to think reasonably, and had become a piece of inert protoplasm which could be made to move, but only when the proper stimuli were applied. Since making up his mind that he would do exactly what he was told, but exactly that and no more, he had lain exactly where he had been until Stein called him for the telephone. Now he lay exactly where he had dropped and waited to be told to do something else. This gave him little comfort, but he had no desire to see or do more. If his body would not work well, his mind could, and Fife realized that by far the great majority of the company were reacting like himself. But there were still those others who, for one reason or another of their own, got up and walked about and offered to do things without being told first.

Fife knew it, because he had seen them—otherwise he wouldn't have believed it. His reaction to these was one of intense, awed hero worship composed of about two-thirds grinding hate, and shame. But when he tried to force *his* body to stand up and walk around, he simply could not make it do it. He was glad that he was a clerk whose job was to take care of the telephone and not a squad noncom up there with Keck, Beck, McCron and the others, but he would have preferred to be a clerk at Battalion Hq back on Hill 209, and more than that a clerk at Regiment back down in the coconut groves, but most of all a clerk at Army Hq in Australia, or in the United States. Just above him up the slope he could hear Bugger Stein talking with the medic, and he caught the phrase "his belly blown open." Then he caught the word "Tella". So it was Tella who was yelling down there like that. It was the first concrete news Fife had had of anyone since the two dead lieutenants and Grove. He pressed his face to the dirt sickly, while Bugger and the medic moved off a few feet for another look. Tella had used to be a buddy of his, for a while at least. Built like a Greek god, never very bright, he was the most amiable of men, despite his career in life as a honeydipper in Cambridge Mass. And now Tella was suffering in actual reality the fate which Fife all morning had been imagining would be his own. Fife felt sick. It was so different from the books he'd read, so much more *final*. Slowly, in trepidation at even raising it that far, he lifted his head a fraction off the dirt to peer with pain-haunted, fear-punctured eyes at the two men with the binoculars.

They were still talking.

"Can you tell?" Stein asked, anxiously.

"Yes, sir. Enough," the medic said. He was the senior one, the more studious looking. He handed the glasses to Stein and put back on his spectacles. "There's nothing anybody can do that'll help *him*. He'll be dead before they can ever get him back to a surgeon. And he's got dirt all over his bowels. Even sulfa won't fix that. In these jungles?"

There was a pause before Stein spoke again. "How long?"

"Two hours? Four, maybe? Maybe only one, or less."

"But, God *damn* it, man!" Stein exploded. "We can't *any* of us stand it that long!" He paused. "Not counting him! And I can't ask you to go down there."

The medic studied the terrain. He blinked several times behind his glasses. "Maybe it's worth a try."

"But you said yourself nobody could do anything to help him."

"At least I could get a syrette of morphine into him."

"Would one be enough?" Stein asked. "I mean, you know, would it keep him quiet?"

The medic shook his head. "Not for long." He paused. "But I could give him two. And I could leave him three or four for himself."

"But maybe he wouldn't take them. He's delirious. Couldn't you just, sort of, give them all to him at once?" Stein said.

The medic turned to look at him. "That would kill him, sir."

"Oh," Stein said.

"I couldn't do that," the medic said. "I really couldn't."

"Okay," Stein said grimly. "Well, do you want to try it?"

From below the set, unchanging series of yells, the strangely mechanical cries of the man they were talking about, rose up to them, precise, inflexible, mad, a little quavery toward the end, this time.

"God, I hope he dont begin to cry," Stein said. "God *damn* it!" he yelled, balling a fist. "My company won't have any fighting spirit left at all if we dont do something about him!"

"I'll go, sir," the medic said solemnly, answering the question of before. "After all, it's my job. And after all, it's worth a try, isn't it, sir?" he said, nodding significantly toward the spot where the series of yells had now ceased. "To stop the yells."

"God," Stein said, "I dont know."

"I'm volunteering. I've been down there before, you know. They won't hit me, sir."

"But you were on the left. It's not as bad there."

"I'm volunteering," the medic said, blinking at his Captain owlishly.

Stein waited several seconds before he spoke. "When do you want to go?"

"Any time," the medic said. "Right now." He started to get up.

Stein put out a restraining arm. "No, wait. At least I can give you some covering fire."

"I'd rather go now, sir. And get it over with."

They had been lying side by side, their helmets almost touching as they talked, and now Stein turned to look at the boy. He could not help wondering whether he had talked this boy into volunteering. Perhaps he had. He sighed. "Okay. Go ahead."

The medic nodded, looking straight ahead this time, then sprang up into a crouch, and was gone over the crest of the fold.

It was all over almost before it got started. Running like some fleeting forest animal, his medic's web equipment flopping, he reached the damaged Tella, swung round to face him up the hill, then dropped to his knees, his hands already groping at the pouch which held his syrettes. Before he could get the protective cap off the needle, one MG, one single MG, opened up from the ridge stitching across the area. Through the glasses Stein watched him jerk straight up, eyes and mouth wide, face slack, not so much with disbelief or mental shock as with sheer simple physiological surprise. One of the objects which had struck him, not meeting bone, was seen to burst forth through the front of him puffing out the green cloth, taking a button with it and opening his blouse a notch. Stein through the glasses saw him jab the now-bared needle, whether deliberately by design or from sheer reflex, into his own forearm below the rolled up sleeve. Then he fell forward on his face crushing both the syrette and his hands beneath him. He did not move again.

Stein, still holding the glasses on him, waited. He could not escape a feeling that something more important, more earthshaking should happen. Seconds ago he was alive and Stein was talking to him; now he was dead. Just like that. But Stein's attention was pulled away before he could think more, pulled away by two things. One was Tella, who now began to scream in a high quavery babbling falsetto of hysteria totally different from his former yells. Looking at him now through the glasses—he had almost forgotten him entirely in watching the medic—Stein saw that he had flopped himself over on his side, face pressing the dirt. Obviously he had been hit again, and while one bloodstained hand tried to hold in his intestines, the other groped at the new wound in his chest. Stein wished that at least they had killed him, if they were going to shoot him up again. This screaming, which he ceased only long enough to draw sobbing breath, was infinitely more bad than the yells for everyone concerned, both in its penetration and in its longevity. But they were not firing more now. And as if to prove it deliberate a faint faraway voice called several times in an Oriental accent, "Cly, Yank, cly! Yerl, Yank, yerl!"

The other thing which caught Stein's attention was something which caught the corner of his eye in the glasses as he lay looking at Tella and wondering what to do. A figure emerged from the grass on the righthand ridge plodding rearward across the flat and began to mount the forward slope of the fold. Turning the glasses on him, Stein saw that it was his Sergeant McCron, that he was wringing his hands, and that he was weeping. On his dirty face two great white streaks of clean skin ran from eye to chin accentuating the eyes as if he were wearing the haunting makeup of a tragic actor in some Greek drama. And on he came, while behind him Japanese MGs and smallarms opened up all across the ridge, making dirt puffs all around him. Still he came on, shoulders hunched, face twisted, wringing his hands, looking more like an old woman at a wake than an infantry combat soldier, neither quickening his pace nor dodging. In a kind of incredulous fury Stein watched him, frozen to the glasses. Nothing touched him. When he reached the top of the fold, he sat down beside his Captain still wringing his hands and weeping.

"Dead," he said. "All dead, Capn. Every one. I'm the only one. All twelve. Twelve young men. I looked after them. Taught them everything I knew. *Helped* them. It didn't mean a thing. Dead."

Obviously, he was talking only of his own twelve-man squad, all of whom Stein knew could not be dead.

From below, because he was still sitting up in the open beside his prone Captain, someone seized him by the ankle and hauled him bodily below the crest. To Corporal Fife, who had seen the

vomiting Sico go and who now lay looking up at McCron with
his own fear-starting eyes, there was some look not exactly sly
about his face but which appeared to say that while what he was
telling was the truth, it was not all the truth, and which made Fife
believe that like Sico McCron had found his own reasonable excuse. It did not make Fife angry. On the contrary, it made him
envious and he yearned to find some such mechanism which he
might use with success himself.

Stein apparently felt somewhat the same thing himself. With
only one further look at the handwringing, still weeping, but now
safe McCron, Stein turned his head and called for the medic.

"Here, sir," the junior medic said from immediately below
him. He had come up on his own.

"Take him back. Stay with him. And when you get back there,
tell them we need another medic now. At least one."

"Yes, sir," the boy said solemnly. "Come on, Mac. That's it.
Come on, boy. It'll be all right. It'll all be all right."

"You dont understand that they're all dead," McCron said
earnestly. "How can it be all right?" But he allowed himself to
be led off by the arm. The last C-for-Charlie saw of him was
when he and the medic dropped behind the second fold, now
seventy-five to a hundred yards behind them. Some of them were
to see his haunted face in the Division's hospital later, but the
company as a whole saw him no more.

Stein sighed. With this last, new crisis out of the way and taken
care of, he could turn his attention back to Tella. The Italian was
still screaming his piercing wailing scream and did not seem to
show any indication that he was ever going to run down. If it kept
on, it was going to unnerve them all. For a fleet second Stein had
a lurid romantic vision of taking up his carbine and shooting the
dying man through the head. You saw that in movies and read it
in books. But the vision died sickly away, unfulfilled. He wasn't
the type and he knew it. Behind him his reserve platoon, cheeks
pressed to earth, stared at him from their tense, blank, dirty faces
in a long line of white, nerve-racked eyes. The screaming seemed
to splinter the air, a huge circular saw splitting giant oak slabs,
shivering spinal columns to fragments. But Stein did not know

what to do. He could not send another man down there. He had to give up. A hot unbelieving outraged fury seized him at the thought of McCron plodding leisurely back through all that fire totally unscathed. He motioned furiously to Fife to hand him the phone, to take back up the call to Colonel Tall which Tella's first screams had interrupted. Then, just as he was puckering to whistle, a large green object of nature on his right, a green boulder topped by a small metallic-colored rock, rose up flapping and bellowing. Taking earthly matters into its own hands, it bounded over the crest of the fold growling guttural obscenities before Stein could even yell the one word, "Welsh!" The First Sergeant was already careering at full gallop down into the hollow.

Welsh saw everything before him with a singular, pristine, furiously crystal clarity: the rocky thin-grassed slope, mortar- and bullet-pocked, the hot bright sunshine and deep cerulean sky, the incredibly white clouds above the towering highup horseshoe of the Elephant's Head, the yellow serenity of the ridge before him. He did not know how he came to be doing this, nor why. He was simply furious, furious with a graven, black, bitter hatred of everything and everybody in the whole fucking gripeassed world. He felt nothing. Mindlessly, he ran. He looked curiously and indifferently, without participation, at the puffs of dirt which had begun now to kick up around him. Furious, furious. There were three bodies on the slope, two dead, one alive and still screaming. Tella simply had to stop that screaming; it wasn't dignified. Puffs of dirt were popping up all around him now. The clatterbanging which had hung in the air at varying levels all through the day had descended almost to ground level, now, and was aimed personally and explicitly at him. Welsh ran on, suppressing a desire to giggle. A curious ecstasy had gripped him. He was the target, the sole target. At last it was all out in the open. The truth had at last come out. He had always known it. Bellowing "Fuck you!" at the whole world over and over at the top of his lungs, Welsh charged on happily. Catch me if you can! Catch me if you can!

Zigzigging professionally, he made his run down. If a fucking nut like McCron could simply walk right out, a really bright man like himself in the possession of his faculties could get down and back. But when he skidded to a stop on his belly beside the mutilated Italian boy, he realized he had made no plans about what to do when he got here. He was stumped, suddenly, and at a loss. And when he looked at Tella, an embarrassed kindliness came over him. Gently, still embarrassed, he touched the other on the shoulder. "How goes it, kid?" he yelled inanely.

In mid-scream Tella rolled his eyes around like a maddened horse until he could see who it was. He did not stop the scream.

"You got to be quiet," Welsh yelled, staring at him grimly. "I came to help you."

It had no reality to Welsh. Tella was dying, maybe it was real to Tella, but to Welsh it wasn't real, the blueveined intestines, and the flies, the bloody hands, the blood running slowly from the other, newer wound in his chest whenever he breathed, it had no more reality for Welsh than a movie. He was John Wayne and Tella was John Agar.

Finally the scream stopped of itself, from lack of breath, and Tella breathed, causing more blood to run from the hole in his chest. When he spoke, it was only a few decibels lower than the scream. "Fuck you!" he piped. "I'm dying! I'm dying, Sarge! Look at me! I'm all apart! Get away from me! I'm *dying!*" Again he breathed, pushing fresh blood from his chest.

"Okay," Welsh yelled, "but goddam it, do it with less noise." He was beginning to blink now, and his back to crawl, whenever a bullet flipped up dirt.

"How you going to help me?"

"Take you back."

"You can't take me back! You want to fucking help me, shoot me!" Tella screamed, his eyes wide and rolling.

"You're off your rocker," Welsh yelled in the noise. "You know I can't do that."

"Sure you can! You got your pistol there! Take it the fuck out! You want to help me, shoot me and get it over with! I can't stand it! I'm scared!"

"Does it hurt much?" Welsh yelled.

"Sure it hurts, you dumb son of a bitch!" Tella screamed.

Then he paused, to breathe, and bleed, and then he swallowed, his
eyes closed. "You can't take me back."

"We'll see," Welsh yelled grimly. "You stick with old Welsh.
Trust old Welsh. Did I ever give you a bum steer?" He was aware
now—he knew—that he wouldn't be able to stay much longer.
Already he was flinching and jerking and jumping uncontrollably
under the fire. Crouching he ran around to Tella's head and got
him under the armpits and heaved. In his own arms Welsh could
feel the body stretch even before Tella screamed.

"Aaa-eeeee!" The scream was terrible. "You're killing me!
You're pulling me apart! Put me down, goddam you! Put me
down!"

Welsh dropped him quickly, by simple reflex. Too quickly.
Tella landed heavily, sobbing. "You son of a bitch! You son of a
bitch! Leave me alone! Leave me alone! Dont touch me!"

"Stop that yelling," Welsh yelled, feeling abysmally stupid,
"it aint dignified." Blinking, his nerves already fluttering like
fringe in a high wind now and threatening to forsake him, he
scrambled grimly around to Tella's side. "All right, we'll do it
this way, then." Slipping one arm under the Italian's knees and
the other under his shoulders, he lifted. Tella was not a small
man, but Welsh was bigger, and at the moment he was endowed
with superhuman strength. But when he heaved him up to try and
carry him like a child, the body jackknifed almost double like a
closing pocketknife. Again there was that terrible scream.

"Aaa-eeeee! Put me down! Put me down! You're breaking me
in two! Put me down!"

This time Welsh was able to let him down slowly.

Sobbing, Tella lay and vituperated him. "You son of a bitch!
You fucker! You bastard! I told you leave me alone! I never ast
you to come down here! Go away! Leave me alone! You shiteater!
Stay away from me!" And turning his head away and closing his
eyes, he began his desperate, wailing, piercing scream again.

Five yards above them on the slope a line of machinegun bullets slowly stitched itself across from left to right. Welsh happened to be looking straight at it and saw it. He did not even
bother to think how all the gunner had to do was depress a de-

gree. All he could think about now was getting out of here. And yet how could he? He had come all this way down here. And he had not saved Tella, and he had not shut him up. Nothing. Except to cause more pain. Pain. With sudden, desperate inspiration he leaped across the prostrate Tella and began rummaging in the dead medic's belt pouches.

"Here!" he bellowed. "Tella! Take these! Tella!"

Tella stopped screaming and opened his eyes. Welsh tossed him two morphine syrettes he had found and began to attack another pouch.

Tella picked one up. "More!" he cried when he saw what they were. "More! Gimme more! More!"

"Here," Welsh yelled, and tossed him a double handful he had found in the other pouch, and then turned to run.

But something stopped him. Crouched like a sprinter at the gun, he turned his head and looked at Tella one more time. Tella, already unscrewing the cap from one of the syrettes was looking at him, his eyes wide and white. For a moment they stared at each other.

"Goodby," Tella cried. "Goodby, Welsh!"

"Goodby, kid," Welsh yelled. It was all he could think of to say. For that matter, it was all he had time to say, because he was already off and running. And he did not look back to see whether Tella took the syrettes. However, when they were able to get to him safely later in the afternoon, they found ten empty morphine syrettes scattered all around him. The eleventh remained stuck in his arm. He had taken them one after the other, and there was an at least partially relaxed look on his dead face.

Welsh ran with his head down and did not bother to zigzag. He was thinking that now they would get him. After all of that, that run down, all that time down there, *now* they would have to get him, on the way back. It was his fate, his luck. He knew that they would get him now. But they didn't. He ran and ran and then he fell headlong over the little crest and just lay there, half dead from exhaustion, Tella's wild face and bulging blue intestines visible behind his closed eyes. Why in the Name of Foolish Bastardly God had he ever done it in the first place? Sobbing audibly for breath, he made himself a solemn unspoken promise never again to let his screwy wacked-up emotions get the better of his common sense.

But it was when Bugger Stein crawled over to him to pat him on the back and congratulate and thank him, that Welsh really blew his top.

"Sergeant, I saw the whole thing through the glasses," he heard, feeling the friendly hand on his shoulder. "I want you to know I'm mentioning you in Orders tomorrow. I'm recommending you for the Silver Star. I can only say that I—"

Welsh opened his eyes and found himself staring up into the anxious Jewish face of his Commander. The look in his eyes must have stopped Stein, because he did not finish.

"Captain," Welsh said deliberately, between ebbing sobs for breath, "if you say one word to thank me, I will punch you square in the nose. Right now, right here. And if you ever so much as mention me in your fucking Orders, I will resign my rating two minutes after, and leave you to run this pore, busted-up outfit by yourself. If I go to jail. So fucking help me."

He shut his eyes. Then as an afterthought he rolled over away from Bugger, who said nothing. As a second afterthought, he got to all fours and crawled away, off to the right, by himself. Shutting his eyes again, he lay in the sun-tinged dark, listening to the mortars that were still dropping every couple of minutes, groaning over and over to himself his one phrase of understanding: "Property! Property! All for fucking property!" He was terribly dry, but both his canteens were bone empty. After a while he took out the third one and took one precious swallow of its precious gin without opening his eyes.

The lack of water was getting to everyone. Stein was thirsty, too, and his canteens were as empty as Welsh's. And Stein had no gin. In addition, he still had his call to put through to Colonel Tall at Battalion CP. He was not looking forward to it, and Welsh's reaction just now in crawling away from him like that was not especially heartening or confidence inspiring. Slowly he crawled back to Fife and the sound power phone. He understood that his crazy First Sergeant, mad or not, wanted to be alone. He must be terribly wrought up. After having just helped a mutilated man to kill himself? And not even counting the danger to himself, to Welsh. His reaction was quite normal. But in spite of that, just for a moment, when Welsh had opened his eyes with that look and had said what he did, Bugger Stein could not escape a fleeting impression that it was because he Stein was Jewish. He thought he had gotten over all that sort of stuff long ago. Years and years ago. He made a grim inward smile. Both because of what he had just thought, and because of what he thought next: It was that fucking infuriating outrageous Anglo-Saxon Tall, with his cropped blond head and young-old boyish face, and his tall spare soldierly frame. West Point, class of '28. Whenever Stein was forced by the duties of his military life to have contact with that commanding gentleman, Stein always somehow came away from it made doubly aware of being of Jehovah's Own, a Jew. He motioned to Fife to give him the phone.

When Stein took the phone, he received the extraordinary impression that his arm, his whole body, was too tired, too weak, to lift the almost weightless little tin instrument to his ear. Astonished, he waited. Slowly the arm came up. Already worn out, the affair of Tella's death had taken more out of him than he realized. How long could he go on? How much longer could he watch his men being killed in agony like this without ceasing to function entirely? Suddenly, for the first time, he was terribly afraid that he might not be able to cut it. This fear, added to the already heavy burden of simple physical fear for himself, seemed almost too much of a load to bear, but it jerked a renewed energy up out of some deep in him. He whistled into the mouthpiece.

Scattered around him, as he whistled and waited, the mixed remnants of his CP force plus a smattering of 2d and 3d Platoon men lay huddled to earth, watching him with white eyes and those drawn in-turned faces, as if all were looking to him and hoping he could in some way get them out of this bind, this mess, so that they might go on living. Stein could grin, and did, at the looks on the faces of Storm and his cook force, which seemed to say clearly that they had had their fill of this volunteering for combat, that if they ever got out of this one they would most certainly never do it again. They were not alone in it, either. Supply Sergeant MacTae and his clerk wore the same look.

Stein did not have long to wait; almost before his whistle had ended the phone was answered on the other end, and it was Colonel Tall himself, not any communications clerk. It was not a long conversation, but in a way it was one of the most important conversations in Stein's life up to now. Yes, Tall had seen the little three squad attack, and had thought it fine. They had made a good lodgment. But before Stein could say anything further, he demanded to know why Stein had not already followed it up and exploited it? What was the matter with him? Those men should be reinforced immediately. And what were they doing? Tall could see them through his glasses, just lying there behind that ledge. They should be already up and out and at work cleaning out those emplacements.

"I dont think you understand what's going on down here, Sir." Stein said patiently. "We're taking a lot of fire down here. We've had heavy casualties. I was planning to reinforce them right away, but something bad happened. We had a man—" he did not actually hesitate or gulp over the word, but he wanted to gulp— "gutshot out on the slope, and he caused quite a bit of upset. But that's taken care of now, and I'm planning to reinforce now." Stein swallowed. "Over?"

"Fine," Colonel Tall's voice said crisply, without his former enthusiasm. "By the way, who was that man who ran out on the slope? Was that what he was doing? The Admiral—Admiral Barr—saw him through the glasses; the Admiral couldn't tell for sure but thought he had gone out to help someone. Was that it? The Admiral wants to recommend the man for something. Over."

Stein had listened wanting suddenly to laugh hysterically. Help him? Yes, he had helped him all right. Boosted him right on off the old cinder and out and away. "There were two men who went out, Sir," he said. "One was our senior medic. He was killed. The other," he said, remembering what he now thought of as his conspiratorial promise to Welsh, "was one of the privates. I dont know which one yet, but I'll find out. Over." And fuck you. And the Admiral.

Fine. Fine, fine. And now, Tall wanted to know, what about those reinforcements? Stein went on to lay out, while the mortars continued to search unabated along and around the fold, his little plan of bringing his reserve platoon forward to this slope, while sending the remaining two squads of 2d Platoon up with the other three—other two now, rather, after casualties—up on the ridge. "I lost Keck, you know, too, Colonel. Up there. He was one of my best men," he said. "Over."

The answer he got was an unexpected outburst of official fury. Two squads! What the hell did he mean, two squads! When Tall said reinforcements, he meant reinforcements. Stein should throw every man he had in there, and should do it now. Should have done earlier, as soon as the lodgment was made. That meant commit the reserve platoon and all. And what about Stein's 1st Platoon? They were lying on their fat asses down there doing nothing. Stein should move them by the flank in to the ridge, should get a man down there to them right now with orders to attack—attack around the left of the ridge. Send his reserve platoon to attack around the right. Leave the 2d Platoon there to hold and press the center. An envelopment. "Do I have to give you a ten cent lesson in infantry tactics while your men are getting their ass shot off, Stein?" Tall howled. *"Over!"*

Stein swallowed his wrath. "I dont think you fully understand what's going on down here, Colonel," he said more quietly than he felt. "We've already lost two officers dead, and a lot of men. I dont think my company alone can take that position. They're too well dug in, and have too much firepower. I formally request, Sir, and I have witnesses, to be given permission to make a patrol reconnaissance around to the right of Hill 210 through the jungle. I believe the entire position can be outflanked by a maneuver there in force." But did he? Did he really believe that? Or was he only grasping at straws? He had a hunch, that was the truth. He had a real hunch but that was all. There had been no fire from there all day. But was that enough? "Over," he said, trying to muster all his dignity—then blinked and ducked down flat, as a mortar shell went up roaring ten yards away along the little crest and somebody screamed.

"NO!" roared Tall, as if he had been waiting fuming, dancing a little dance of frustration at the other end, until he could push *his* button and speak *his* piece into this maddening one-way phone. "I tell you, *no!* I want a double envelopment! I order you, Stein, to attack, and attack now, with every available man at your disposal! I'm sending B-for-Baker in too on your left! Now, *AT-TACK*, Stein! That's a direct order!" He paused for breath. "Over!"

Stein had heard himself talking of "formally request" and "have witnesses" with a sort of astonished, numb disbelief. He had not really meant to go that far. How could he be sure that he was right? And yet, he was sure. At least, reasonably sure. Why had there been no firing from down there, then? In any case, he had now either to put up or shut up. His heart suddenly up in his throat, he said formally, "Sir, I must tell you that I refuse to obey your order. I again request permission to make a patrol reconnaissance in force around to the right. The time, Sir, is 1321 hours 25 seconds. I have two witnesses here listening to what I've said. I request, Sir, that you inform witnesses there. Over."

"Stein!" he heard. Tall was raging. "Dont pull that guardhouse lawyer shit with me, Stein! I know you're a goddamned lawyer! Now shut up and do like I said! I didnt hear what you just said! I repeat my order! Over!"

"Colonel, I refuse to take my men up there in a frontal attack. It's a suicide! I've lived with these men two and a half years. I won't order them all to their deaths. That's final. Over." Someone was blubbering now not far away along the crest, and Stein tried to see who it was and couldn't. Tall was stupid, ambitious, without imagination, and vicious as well. He was desperate to succeed before his superiors. Otherwise he could never have given such an order.

After the little pause, Tall's voice was cool, and sharp as a razorblade. "This is a very important decision you're making, Stein. If you feel that strongly, perhaps you have reason. I'm coming down. Understand: I'm not rescinding my order to you, but if I find there are extenuating circumstances when I get down there, I'll take that into account. I want you to hold on there until

I get there. If possible, get those men up on the ridge out and moving. I'll be there in" he paused "ten or fifteen minutes. Over and out."

Stein listened unbelieving, mentally stunned, feeling scared. To Stein's knowledge, which he knew was not universal but nevertheless, no Battalion Commander had come forward with his fighting troops since this battle started and the division entered combat. Tall's inordinate ambition was a Regimental joke, and he certainly had every bigshot on the island here today to perform for, but Stein still had not anticipated this. What had he expected, then? He had expected, if he made his protest strong enough, to be allowed to make his patrol in force and test the right before having to face a necessity of this frontal attack,—even though he knew it was a little late in the day now for that kind of an operation. And now he was really scared. It was almost funny, how even lying here terrified and half-expecting to be dead at any moment, his bureaucratic fear of reprimand, of public embarrassment was stronger than his physical fear of dying. Well, at least as strong.

Well, he had two things to do, while he waited for Tall. He must see about that man who was wounded a moment ago. And he must get the other two squads of 2d Platoon up there on the ridge to Beck and Dale.

The wounded man proved to be little Pfc Bead from Iowa, Fife's assistant clerk, and he was dying. The mortar round had exploded five yards away from him on his left, sending a piece probably no bigger than a silver dime into his left side after tearing its way through the triceps muscle of his upper left arm. The chunk out of his arm would never have killed him though it might have crippled him a bit, but blood was pouring from the hole in his side into the compresses somebody had stuck on it, and from the soaked gauze dripping down to stain the ground. When Stein arrived, trailed by the wide-eyed Fife with the telephone, Bead's eyes were blank and he spoke just barely above a whisper.

"I'm dying, Captain!" he croaked, rolling his eyes toward Stein. "I'm dying! Me! *Me!* I'm dying! I'm so scared!" He closed his eyes for a moment and swallowed. "I was just laying there. And it hit me right in the side. Like somebody punched me. Didn't hurt much. Doesn't hurt much now. Oh, Captain!"

"Just take it easy, son. Just take it easy," Stein said in a kind of fruitless, bootless anguish.

"Where's Fife?" Bead creaked, rolling his eyes. "Where's Fife?"

"He's right here, son. Right here," Stein said. "Fife!" He himself turned away, feeling like an old, old, useless man. Grandfather Stein.

Fife had stopped behind the Captain, but now he crawled closer. There were two or three others clustered around Bead. He had not wanted to look; at the same time he could not convince himself of the reality of it. Bead hit and dying. Someone like Tella, or Pvt Jockey Jacques, was different. But Bead, with whom he had worked so many days in the office, in the orderly room. Bead, with whom he had—His mind balked away from that. "I'm here," he said.

"I'm dying, Fife!" Bead told him.

Fife could not think of anything to say, either. "I know. Just take it easy. Just take it easy, Eddie," he said, repeating Stein. He felt impelled to use Bead's first name, something he had never done before.

"Will you write my folks?" Bead said.

"I'll write them."

"Tell them it didn't hurt me much. Tell them the truth."

"I'll tell them."

"Hold my hand, Fife," Bead croaked then. "I'm scared."

For a moment, a second, Fife hesitated. Homosexuality. Fagotism. Fairies. He didn't even think them. The act of hesitation was far below the level of conscious thought. Then, realizing with horror what he had done, was doing, he gripped Bead's hand. Crawling closer, he slid his other arm under his shoulders, cradling him. He had begun to cry, more because he suddenly realized that he was the only man in the whole company whom Bead could call friend, than because Bead was dying.

"I've got it," he said.

"Squeeze," Bead croaked. "Squeeze."

"I'm squeezing."

"Oh, Fife!" Bead cried. "Oh, Captain!"

His eyes did not go shut but they ceased to see.

After a moment Fife put him down and crawled away by himself, weeping in terror, weeping in fear, weeping in sadness, hating himself.

It was only five minutes after that that Fife himself was hit.

Stein had followed him when he crawled away. He obviously did not fully understand Fife's weeping. "Lie down somewhere for a little bit, son," he said, and briefly patted his back. He had already taken the sound power phone from Fife when he sent him up to Bead, and now he said, "I'll keep the phone for a few minutes myself. There won't be any calls coming in for a while anyway, now," he said with a bitter smile. Fife, who had listened to the last call to Tall, had in fact been one of Stein's two witnesses, knew what he meant, but he was in no condition or mood to make any answer. Dead. Dead. All dead. All dying. None left. *Nothing* left. He had come unstrung, and his unnerving was the worse because he was helpless, could do nothing, could say nothing. He must stay here.

The mortar rounds had continued to drop at random points along the fold with strict regularity, all during the time it had taken Bead to die, all during the time after. It was amazing how few men they actually wounded or killed. But everyone's face wore that same vague-eyed, terrorized, in-drawn look. Fife had seen an abandoned, yellowdirt hole a few yards off to his right and he crawled to this. It was hardly even a hole, really. Someone had scooped out with his hands, bayonet or entrenching tool a shallow little trough perhaps only two inches below the surface. Fife crouched flat in this and put his cheek to the mud. Slowly he stopped weeping and his eyes cleared, but as the other emotions, the sorrow, the shame, the selfhatred seeped out of him under the pressure of self-preservation, the fourth component, terror, seeped in to replace them until he was only a vessel completely filled with cowardice, fear and gutlessness. And that was the way he lay. This was war? There was no superior test of strength here, no superb swordmanship, no bellowing Viking heroism, no expert marksmanship. This was only numbers. He was being killed for numbers. Why oh why had he not found and taken to himself that clerkish deskjob far in the rear which he could have had?

He heard the soft "shu-u-u" of the mortarshell for perhaps half a second. There was not even time to connect it with himself and frighten him, before there was a huge sunburst roaring of an explosion almost on top of him, then black blank darkness. He had a vague impression that someone screamed but did not know it was himself. As if seeing some dark film shown with insufficient illumination, he had a misty picture of someone other than himself half-scrambling, half-blown to his feet and then dropping, hands to face in a stumbling, rolling fall down the slope. Then nothing. Dead? Are we, that other one, is I? am he?

Fife's body came to rest rolling in the lap of a 3d Platoon man, who happened to be sitting up, his rifle in his lap. Tearing itself loose, it scrambled away on elbows and knees, hands still to the face. Then Fife returned to it and opened its eyes and saw that everything had become a red flowing haze. Through this swirling red he could see the comic, frightened face of the 3d Platoon man whose name was Train. Never was there a less likely, less soldierly looking soldier. Long fragile nose, chinless jaw, pipsqueak mouth, huge myopic eyes staring forth in fright from behind thick glasses.

"Am I hit? Am I hit?"

"Y-yes," Train mumbled. "Y-you are." He also stuttered. "In the head."

"Bad? Is it bad?"

"I c-can't tell," Train said. "Y-you're b-bleeding from your h-head."

"Am I?" Fife looked at his hands and found them completely covered with the wet red. He understood now that peculiar red haze. It was blood which flowing down through his eyebrows had gotten in his eyes. God, but it was *red!* Then terror blossomed all through him like some ballooning great fungus, making his heart kick and his eyes go faint. Maybe he was dying, right now, right here. Gingerly he probed at his skull and found nothing. His fingers came away glistening red. He had no helmet and his glasses were gone.

"I-it's in the b-back," Train offered.

Fife probed again and found the tornup spot. It was in the center of his head, almost at the peak.

"H-how d-do you f-feel?" Train said fearfully.

"I dont know. It dont hurt. Except when I touch it." Still on hands and knees Fife had bent his head, so that the blood flowing into his eyebrows now dripped to the ground instead of into his eyes. He peered up at Train through this red rain.

"C-can you w-walk?" Train said.

"I-I dont know," Fife said, and then suddenly realized that he was free. He did not have to stay here any more. He was released. He could simply get up and walk away—provided he was able—with honor, without anyone being able to say he was a coward or courtmartialing him or putting him to jail. His relief was so great he suddenly felt joyous despite the wound.

"I think I better go back," he said. "Dont you?"

"Y-yes," Train said, a little wistfully.

"Well—" Fife tried to think of something final and important to say upon such a momentous occasion, but he failed. "Good luck, Train," he managed finally.

"Th-thanks," Train said.

Tentatively Fife stood up. His knees were shaky, but the prospect of getting out of here gave him a strength he might not otherwise have had. At first slowly, then more swiftly, he began to walk rearward with his head bent and his hands to his forehead to keep the still flowing blood from getting in his eyes. With each step he took his sense of joyous release increased, but keeping pace with it his sense of fear increased also. What if they got him now? What if they hit him with something else now just when he was free to leave? As much as he could, he hurried. He passed a number of 3d Platoon men lying prone with those terror-haunted, inward-looking faces, but they did not speak and neither did he. He did not take the longer route back the way they had come, over the second and first folds, but took the direct one, walking straight along the hollow between the folds to the forward slope of Hill 209. Only when he was halfway up the steep slope of Hill 209 did he think of the rest of the company, and pausing he turned and looked back to where they lay. He wanted to yell something to them, encouragment or something, but he knew that from here they could never hear him. When several sniper bullets kicked up dirt around him, he turned and pressed on to come over the crest and down into the crowded Battalion aid station on the other side. Just before he breasted the crest, he met a party of men coming down from it and recognized Colonel Tall. "Hold on, son," the Colonel smiled at him. "Dont let it get you down. You'll be back with us soon." At the aid station he remembered his one nearly full canteen and began to drink greedily, his hands still shaking. He was reasonably sure now that he would not die.

When Fife got hit, Bugger Stein had just crawled away from him. Fife had crawled one way and Stein the other, to instruct the two remaining squads of 2d Platoon to advance and reinforce Beck and Dale on the grassy ridge. He might just as easily have crawled along with Fife and so have been there when the mortar-shell landed. The element of chance in it was appalling. It frightened Stein. Anyway he was dead-beat tired and depressed, and scared. He had watched Fife stagger bloodily to the rear, but there was nothing he himself could do because he was already in the midst of instructing the two squads from 2d Platoon about what they were to do when they got to the ridge, and what they were to tell Beck—which was, mainly, that he was to get his ass out and moving and try to knock out some of those machineguns.

None of them in the two squads looked very happy about their assignment, including the two sergeants, but they did not say anything and merely nodded tensely. Stein looked back at them earnestly, wishing there was something else, something important or serious, he could tell them. There wasn't. He told them good luck and to go.

This time, as he had the last, Bugger watched their run down through his glasses. He was astonished to see that this time not one man was hit. He was even more astonished, when he watched through the glasses as they worked their way up through the grass to the little waisthigh ledge, to see that here no one was shot down, either. Only then did his ears inform him of something they ought to have noticed earlier: the volume of the Japanese fire had diminished considerably since Sergeant Welsh's run down to aid the mutilated Private Tella. When he raised his glasses to the ledge itself, as he did immediately, even before the first of the newcomers began to arrive, Stein was able to see why. Only about half of Beck's little two squad force was visible there. The rest were gone. On his own hook, without orders, Beck obviously had sent part of his group off raiding and, apparently, with some success. Lowering his glasses, Stein turned to look at George Band, who by now had appropriated glasses of his own somewhere (Stein remembered Bill Whyte's father had presented him with a fine pair as a parting gift), and who now was looking back at Stein with the same astonished look on his face that Stein knew he himself wore. For a long moment they simply looked at each other. Then, just as Stein was turning to the newly arrived replacement medics to tell them he thought they might cross over to pick up the wounded with some degree of safety now, a cool, calm voice behind him said, "Now, Stein!" and he looked up to see Colonel Tall his Battalion commander walking leisurely toward him carrying beneath his arm the unadorned little bamboo baton he had carried there ever since Stein had known him.

What Bugger Stein and Brass Band could not know was that Sergeant Beck the martinet had, on his own initiative, knocked out five Japanese machinegun emplacements in the last fifteen or twenty minutes, all at the cost of only one man killed and none wounded. Phlegmatic, sullen, dull and universally disliked, an unimaginative, do-it-like-the-book-says, dedicated professional of two previous enlistments, Milly Beck came to the fore here as perhaps no one else including his dead superior, Keck, could have done. Seeing that no reinforcements were immediately forthcoming, framing his dispositions exactly as he had been taught in the small units tactics course he had once taken at Fort Benning, he took advantage of the terrain to send six men around to the right of the ledge and six to the left under his two acting sergeants, Dale and Bell. The rest he kept with himself in the center readied to fire at whatever targets of opportunity turned up. Everything worked. Even the men he kept with himself were able to knock down two Japanese who were fleeing from the grenades of his patrols. Dale and his men on the left accounted for four emplacements and returned untouched. Finding the little ledge totally unguarded, they were able to crawl into the midst of the Japanese position and drop grenades from the ledge down into the rear doors of two covered, camouflaged emplacements they spotted below them; the other two emplacements, on the uphill side, were more difficult but by bypassing them and crawling up alongside they were able to pitch grenades into the apertures. Not a single one of them was even fired at. They returned led by the grinning Dale licking his lips and smacking his chops over his success. The importance of their accomplishment was cut down by at least fifty percent the firepower which could be directed from the left of the ridge down upon the 1st Platoon or into the flat which their reinforcements later crossed in safety.

Bell on the right was not so lucky, but he discovered something of great importance. On the right the ledge slowly graded upwards, and after bypassing and grenading one small emplacement below them Bell and his group came upon the main Japanese strongpoint of the whole position. Here the ledge ended in a twenty foot rock wall which further on became a real cliff and was impassable. Just above this rock wall, beautifully dug in and with apertures in three directions, was the Japanese strongpoint. When the lead man climbed out above the ledge to detour around the rock wall, he was riddled fatally by at least three machineguns. Both Witt the volunteer Kentuckian and Pfc Doll were in Bell's party, but neither of them happened to be the lead man. This distinction was reserved for a man named Catch, Lemuel C Catch, an oldtime regular and drunkard and a former boxing friend of Witt's. He died immediately and without a sound. They pulled his body down and retreated with it, while all hell broke loose firing just above their heads, but not before—further back along the ledge—Acting Sergeant Bell got a good look at the strongpoint so he could describe it.

Why he did it even Bell himself never knew. Most probably it was sheer bitterness and fatigue and a desire to get this goddamned fucking battle over with. Bell at least knew that at the very least an accurate, eyewitness description of it might prove valuable later on. Whatever the reasons, it was a crazy thing to do. Halting his men thirty-five to forty yards back from the rock-wall where Catch had died, Bell told them to wait and indulged himself in his crazy desire to look too. Leaving his rifle, holding a grenade in one hand, he climbed up the little ledge and poked up his head. The Japanese firing all had stopped now, and there was a little scrub on the lip of the ledge here, which was why he chose it. Slowly he climbed up, led on by whatever insane, mad motive, until he was out in the open, lying in a tiny little defiladed place. All he could see was the unending grass, rising slowly along a hillock which stuck up out of the ridge. Pulling the pin, he heaved the grenade with all his strength and ducked down. The grenade fell and exploded just in front of the hillock, and in the cyclone of MG fire which followed Bell was able to count five guns in five spitting apertures which he could not see before. When the firing ceased, he crawled back down to his men, obscurely satisfied. Whatever it was that made him do it, and he still didn't know, it made every man in his little group look at him admiringly. Motioning them on, he led them back down and around the ledge until the company's main position at the third fold hove into view. From there on it was easy to get back. Like Dale's group, they did not see or hear a single Japanese anywhere near the ledge. Why the ledge, which was the real key to the whole position on the ridge, had been left totally unguarded by riflemen or MGs, no one ever found out. It was lucky for both groups, as well as for Beck's minuscule little attack plan, that it was unguarded. As it was, they had cleaned out all the Japanese below the ledge and established a real line, and had changed the situation. That they changed the entire situation almost exactly at the precise moment Colonel Tall walked on the field was one of those happenstantial ironies which occur, which are entirely unpredictable, and which seem to be destined to dog the steps of certain men named Stein.

"What are you doing lying down there where you can't see anything?" was the next thing Tall said. He himself was standing upright but, because he was ten or twelve yards away, only his head and the tips of his shoulders, if anything of him at all, showed above the crest. Stein noticed he apparently had no inclination to come closer.

Stein debated whether to tell him that the situation had changed. Almost in the last few seconds before his arrival. But he decided not to. Not just yet. It would look too much like an excuse, and a lame one. So instead he answered, "Observing, Sir. I just sent the other two squads of my 2d Platoon forward to the ridge."

"I saw them leaving as we were coming along," Tall nodded. The rest of his party, Stein noted, which included three privates as runners, his personal sergeant and a young Captain named Gaff, his Battalion Exec, had decided that it might be just as well to be lying down flat on the ground. "How many of them were hit this time?" Right to the point, it was.

"None, Sir."

Tall raised his eyebrows under the helmet which sat so low on his small, fine head. "None? Not one?" A mortar round mushroomed exploding dirt without hurting anybody somewhere along the rearward slope of the third fold, and Tall coming forward to where Stein lay permitted himself to squat on his haunches.

"No, Sir."

"That doesn't sound much like the situation you described to me over the sound power." Tall squinted at him, his face reserved.

"It's not, Sir. The situation's changed." Stein felt he could honorably tell it now. "In just the last four or five minutes," he added, and detested himself.

"And to what do you attribute the change?"

"Sergeant Beck, sir. When I last looked, half of his men had disappeared. I think he sent them off to try and knock out some emplacements, and they seem to have succeeded."

From somewhere far off a machinegun began to rattle and a long line of bullets struck up dirt twenty-five yards below them on the forward slope. Tall did not change his squatting position or alter his voice. "Then you got my message to him."

"No, Sir. I mean, yes, Sir, I did. It went forward with the two new squads. But Beck had already sent his men off before they got there. Some time before."

"I see." Tall turned his head and squinted his blue eyes off at the grassy ridge in silence. The long line of MG bullets came sweeping back from Stein's left, this time only fifteen yards below them. Tall did not move.

"They've seen you, Sir," Stein said.

"Stein, we're going over there," Tall said, ignoring his remark, "all of us, and we're taking everybody with us. Do you have any more formal complaints or demurrers?"

"No, sir," Stein said lamely. "Not now. But I reiterate my request to take a patrol down into the jungle on the right. I'm convinced it's open down there. There hasn't been a shot fired from there all day. A Jap patrol could have enfiladed the hell out of us from there with very little trouble. I was anticipating it." He pointed away down the hollow between the folds to where the tree tops of the jungle were just barely visible, while Tall followed his gaze.

"In any case," Tall said, "it's now too late in the day to send a patrol down there."

"A patrol in force? A platoon? With an MG? They could make a perimeter defense if they didn't get back before dark."

"Do you want to lose a platoon? Anyway, you're emptying your center. We dont have A-for-Able in reserve, Stein. They're off on your right rear fighting their own fight. B-for-Baker is our reserve, and they're committed on your left."

"I know that, Sir."

"No, we'll do it my way. We'll take everybody over to the ledge. We may be able to take that ridge before nightfall."

"I think that ridge is quite a way from being reduced, Sir," Stein said earnestly, and adjusted his glasses, the four fingers on the frame above, the thumb below.

"I dont think so. In any case, we can always make a perimeter defense for the night there. Rather than withdraw like yesterday." The conference was over. Leisurely Tall stood up to his full height. Again the MG in the distance rattled, and a swishing line of bullets struck the ground a few feet from him as Stein ducked, the bullets seeming, at least to Stein, to go whining off all about Tall's feet and between his legs. Tall gave the ridge one contemptuous amused look and started walking down the rearward slope still talking to Stein. "But first I want you to get a man down there to your 1st Platoon and move them by the flank over to the ridge. They are to take up position behind the ledge and extend the left flank from Beck's left. As soon as a man reaches your 1st Platoon safely, I'll sound power Baker to move out, and then we'll move."

"Yes, Sir," Stein said. He was unable to keep his teeth from grinding, but his voice was level. Slowly, very slowly, because he was reluctant, he too stood up to his full height also, then followed Tall down the slope. But before he could give an order young Captain Gaff, who had been lying prone not far away, had already crawled up to them.

"I'll go, Sir," he said to Tall. "I'd like to. Very much."

Tall gazed at him fondly. "All right, John. Go ahead." With strong fatherly pride he watched the young captain move away. "Good man, my young Exec," he said to Stein.

There was really no need for the glasses this time. 1st Platoon wasn't all that far away. Standing upright, their heads just showing above the crest, Tall and Stein watched Gaff zigzag his way professionally down into the shellhole area on the main flat to the left of the grassy ridge. Stein had told him roughly where to find Skinny Culn, now platoon commander by attrition. In a few moments men began moving to the right in rushes, by twos and threes.

"All right," Tall said. "Give me the sound power." He spoke into it at length. "Okay," he said. "Now *we'll* go."

Around them, as if sensing something or other was in the wind, the men began to stir.

Whatever else Stein could find to say about him, and Stein could find plenty, he nevertheless had to admit that with Tall's arrival on the battlefield a change for the better had come over everything and everybody. Partly of course the change was due to Beck's feat, whatever that was exactly. But it could not all be that, and Stein had to admit it. Tall had brought with him some quality that had not been here before, and it showed in the faces of the men. They were less in-drawn looking. Perhaps it was only the feeling that after all in the end not everybody would die. Some would live through it. And from there it was only a step to the normal reaction of ego: *I* will live through this. Others may get it, my friends right and left may die, but I will make it. Even Stein felt better, himself. Tall had arrived and taken control, and had taken it firmly and surely and with confidence. Those who lived would owe it to Tall, and those who died would say nothing. It was too bad about those ones; everybody would feel that; but after all once they were dead they did not really count anymore, did they? This was the simple truth, and Tall had brought it with him to them.

The whole thing was evident in the way Tall handled the move forward. Striding up and down in front of the prone 3d Platoon, his little bamboo baton in his right hand, tapping it lightly against his shoulder as he frowned in concentration, he explained to them briefly what he planned to do, and why, and what their part in it must be. He did not exhort them. His attitude said quite plainly that he considered any exhortation to be cheating and trickery and he would not indulge in it; they deserved better than that; they must do what they must do, and do it without any chauvinistic pleading from him; there would be no jingoism. When the move was completed and both 1st and 3d Platoons were installed behind the ledge to the left and right of the 2d, only two men had been wounded and these lightly, and everybody knew they owed this to Colonel Tall. Even Stein felt the same way.

But having got them that far, it was evident that even Tall was not going to get them very much further. It was now after three-thirty. They had been out here since dawn, and most of them had not had any water since mid-morning. Several men had collapsed. Nerves frayed by being almost constantly under fire and without water, many more were hysterically close to collapse. Tall could see all this himself. But after taking the reports of Beck, Dale and Bell, he wanted to have, before dark, one more go at reducing the strongpoint on the right.

The little assemblage of officers and noncoms around the Colonel now included those of B-for-Baker. When Charlie Co was making its move to the ledge, Baker on Tall's telephoned orders had made its third attack of the day. Like the others it too had failed, and in the confusion half of Baker had overlapped Charlie's 1st Platoon on the left and hung there. In returning the rest had tumbled in and stayed there also, so Tall had sent for their leaders, too.

"That strongpoint is obviously the key to the ridge," he now said to the whole of them. "Se—uh—*Sergeant* Bell here is quite right." He gave Bell a sharp look and went on, "From their knob there our little brown brothers can cover the whole of the flat rising ground in front of our ledge from our right clear over to Baker on the left. Why they left the ledge unguarded I have no idea. But we must exploit it before they see their error. If we can reduce that big bunker, I see no reason why we can't take the whole ridge before nightfall. I'm asking for volunteers to go back there and knock it out.

Stein, hearing for the first time this news about a further attack, was so horrified he could hardly believe his ears. Surely Tall must know how depleted and worn out they all were. But Stein's impetus to argue with Tall had worn out, especially in front of over half the Battalion officers.

To John Bell, squatting with the others, it was all once again like some scene from a movie, a very bad, cliché, third rate war movie. It could hardly have anything to do with death. The Colonel still remained fully upright, still paced back and forth with his bamboo baton as he talked, but Bell noted that he carefully remained far enough back down the slope so that his head did not show above the ledge. Bell had also noted the hesitation and then italicized pronunciation when Tall applied the title Sergeant to himself. This was the first time Bell had ever met his Colonel, but there was no reason to assume Tall did not also know his story. Everybody else knew it. Perhaps it was this, more than anything else, which made him say what he said.

"Sir, I'll be glad to go back again and lead the way for a

party." Was he mad? He was angry, he knew that, but was he insane as well? Ah, Marty!

Immediately, off to Bell's right, another voice piped up. Hunchshouldered, grapplehanded, crackfaced, Acting Sergeant Dale was making his bid for future fame, future sinecures, future security from army kitchens. For whatever it was that drove him. Bell did not know.

"I'll go, Colonel, Sir! I want to volunteer!" Charlie Dale stood up, made three formal paces forward, then squatted again. It was as if Dale, the liberated cook, did not believe his offer legal without the prescribed three paces forward. From his squat he glanced all around, his beady little eyes bright with something. To Bell the effect was distastefully ludicrous, laughable.

Almost before Dale had squatted, two other voices were added. Behind Bell, from among the privates and within the remnant of his own little patrol group, Pfc Doll and Private Witt came forward. Both sat down, much closer to Bell than to Dale who still squatted by himself. Bell felt impelled to wink at them.

Pfc Doll, who was still outraged over the success of Charlie Dale's patrol as against their own, was startled by Bell's wink. Why the fuck would anybody want to wink? From the moment he spoke and started to move forward Doll had felt his heart in his throat again, making his eyes swim dizzily. Moving his tongue in his mouth was like rubbing two damp pieces of blotting paper together. He had had no water for over four hours, and thirst had become so much a part of him that he could not remember ever having been without it. But this other was extra, this blotting paper in his mouth was the thirst of fear, and Doll recognized it. Was Bell ridiculing him? He essayed a small cold guarded smile at Bell.

Witt on the other hand, sitting relaxed to the left of Doll and a little nearer to Bell, grinned and winked back. Witt was at ease. He had made up his mind, when he first volunteered himself back into the old company this morning, to go through with it all the way. And that was what he intended to do. When Witt made up his mind, it was made up, and that was that. As far as he was concerned this volunteer mission was only another little chore to be got through and done by a few men of talent like himself. He had enough confidence in himself as a soldier to be pretty sure he could take care of himself in any situation requiring skill; and as for accidents or bad luck, if one of those caught him, well, it caught him, and that was that. But he didn't believe one would, and in the meantime he was sure he could help out, perhaps save a lot of his old buddies—some of whom, like that punk kid Fife, had not even wanted him to come back in the outfit. But Witt wanted to help, or save as many of them as he could, even Fife if it had happened like that.

Then, besides all of this, Witt had acquired considerable respect and admiration for Bell earlier, on the patrol when Bell pulled his stunt of exposing himself like he had. Witt, who had been a corporal three times and a sergeant twice during his career, could appreciate intelligence and courage in a man. And, despite the fact that he was chary of his personal endorsements, he now liked Bell. Witt felt that, like himself, Bell had the qualities of real leadership. Together they might do a lot, help, or save, a lot of guys. He liked Bell exofficer or not. So he grinned and winked back his feeling of kinship, before turning his attention back to Tall, whom Colonel or not he did not like.

The Colonel had had no chance to speak, his volunteers had been coming so thick and fast. He now had four. And before he could say anything to the four, he acquired three more in rapid succession. A rather elderly, Calvinistic-looking 2d Lieutenant, who might well have been a Chaplain but was not, presented himself from amongst the B Company officers. A B Company sergeant followed him. Then Tall's own Exec, young Captain Gaff, put in his two cents and offered his services.

"I'd like to lead the party, Colonel," he said.

Tall held up his hand. "That's enough, that's enough. Seven is plenty. In the terrain you'll be working more men would only hinder you, I think. I know many more of you would like to go, but you'll have to wait for another opportunity."

Captain Stein, hearing this, peered at this Commander closely through his glasses, and was amazed to see that Tall was in deadly earnest and not joking at all. He was not even being ironic.

Turning to Gaff, Tall said, "All right, John. It's your baby. You'll be in command. Now . . ."

Professionally, he laid out their operation for them. Succinctly, efficiently, missing no smallest detail or advantage, he planned their tactics. It was impossible not to admire both his ability and his command of it. Stein for one, and he was sure he was not alone, was forced to admit that here in Tall was a talent and an authority which he himself just simply did not possess.

"Almost certainly you will find the bunker guarded by smaller MG posts around it. But I think it is better to ignore these and go for the strongpoint itself if you possibly can. The little posts will fall of themselves if the big one is taken; remember that.

"That's all, gentlemen," Tall said with a sudden smile. "Noncoms return to your positions, but I want the officers to remain. Synchronize watches with me, John. Give Dog Co—oh—twelve minutes before you radio your first call. It should take you that long to get there."

As the little assault party crawled off to the right along the ledge, Colonel Tall was already on the sound power phone to contact Battalion. Captain Stein, squatting with the officers who had been told to stay and looking over at his own waterless exhausted men behind the ledge, could not help wondering just how far uphill they would be able to attack, even if the strongpoint fell? Thirty yards maybe? before they collapsed? The assault party disappeared around the corner of the hillside. Stein turned his attention back to Tall and the little group of company officers, of whom only six remained now out of ten. And as the assault party approached the spot where Bell earlier had exposed himself, Colonel Tall was already explaining to his officers his auxiliary plan, should the assault on the bunker fail. If that happened, Tall wanted to effect a surprise night attack. Of course that would mean setting up a perimeter defense first, so they should be prepared. Because Tall had no intention of withdrawing tonight as 2d Battalion had done yesterday. He himself would stay with the Battalion. In the meantime of course there was always the chance, the off chance, that the assault party would succeed.

John Bell, crawling along in the lead of the little seven-man assault group, did not concern himself with whether the attack could succeed. He kept thinking only that he had volunteered to *lead a party back*. He had not volunteered to be a fighting part of it. But no one except himself had paid the slightest attention to this nicety of phrasing. Now here he was, not only leading them as point, but expected to fight with them, and unable to back out without looking cowardly, schmucky. Pride! Pride! What stupid foolish things it forced us to do in its goddam fucking name! He kept his eyes glued on that changing point where the ledge disappeared around the curve of the hillside. It would be just his goddamned luck to find the Japanese had suddenly decided to correct their fault and put some men down here to cover this ledge. He as the point would be the first big fat target. Irritably, he glanced back to motion the others to come on and in doing so discovered something strange. He no longer cared very much. He no longer cared at all. Exhaustion, hunger, thirst, dirt, the fatigue of perpetual fear, weakness from lack of water, bruises, danger had all taken their toll of him until somewhere within the last few minutes—Bell did not know exactly when—he had ceased to feel human. So much of so many different emotions had been drained from him that his emotional reservoir was empty. He still felt fear, but even that was so dulled by emotional apathy (as distinct from physical apathy) that it was hardly more than vaguely unpleasant. He just no longer cared much about anything. And instead of impairing his ability to function, it enhanced it, this sense of no longer feeling human. When the others came up, he crawled on whistling over to himself a song called *I Am An Automaton* to the tune of *God Bless America*.

They thought they were men. They all thought they were real people. They really did. How funny. They thought they made decisions and ran their own lives, and proudly called themselves free individual human beings. The truth was they were here, and they were gonna stay here, until the state through some other automaton told them to go someplace else, and then they'd go. But they'd go freely, of their own free choice and will, because they were free individual human beings. Well, well.

When he reached the spot where he had crawled out above the

ledge he stopped and sending Witt ahead to guard, pointed the place out to Captain Gaff.

Witt, when he crawled out to take the point—or post rather, it was, since they were no longer moving—did think he was a man, and did believe he was a real person. As a matter of fact, the question had never entered his head. He had made his decision to volunteer himself back into the old outfit, and he had made his decision to volunteer for this thing, and he was a free individual human being as far as he was concerned. He was free, white and twenty-one and had never taken no shit off nobody and never would, and as the prospect of action got closer and closer he could feel himself tightening all up inside with excitement, exactly like he used to do in the coal strikes back in Bloody Breathitt. The chance to help, the chance to save all his friends that he could, the chance to kill some more goddam fucking Japanese, he would show that fucking Bugger Stein who had had him transferred out as a malcontent. Standing on his knees out away from the ledge, he held his rifle ready with the safety off. He had not shot squirrel all his life for nothing, he had not made High Expert on the range for the past six years for nothing, either. His only fear was that something might open up back there where Captain Gaff was trying to make up his mind, while he was out here on point—on post, rather—and could not get into it. Well, they would know soon enough.

And Witt was right. They did know soon enough. After he had been shown the spot, young Captain Gaff, who if he was nervous at all hid it to perfection, decided to crawl out for a look himself and after he returned, decided that this was as good a spot to observe the fire as any. The only trouble was that the tiny low place with its thin short brush cover was too low to allow him to drag the walkie-talkie up there above the ledge. "Any of you guys know how to operate this thing?" he asked. Bell was the only one who did. "Okay, you stay below the ledge and I'll call down the data to you from up above," Gaff said. First though he would call them and set up the coordinate himself. Then he explained his plan. Once the 81s had plastered the place as much as they were able, he and his trusty band would crawl out along the low place until they formed a line, then they would try to crawl as close as they could through the grass before throwing their grenades. "Okay?" Bell's automatons all nodded their heads. "Okay. Then here we go."

Gaff crawled out into the low place before the first shells arrived. They could hear their soft shu-shu-shu coming almost straight down before they hit, then the hillside exploded into smoke and flame and noise. Only about fifty yards from the bunker, they were showered with a rain of dirt, chips of rock and small pieces of hot metal. Someone had motioned Witt in against the wall of the ledge, and they all clung to it with their faces pressed against the sharp rock and their eyes closed, cursing with hatred the goddamned fucking mortarmen because they might drop a short round, though they didn't. After fifteen minutes of this, during which Gaff constantly yelled down changes of range, Gaff finally yelled down, "Okay! Tell them to stop!" Bell did. "I think that's enough!" Gaff yelled down. "Whatever damage they can do, they've done by now." Then, as the command was executed back there far away, the mortars stopped falling in a silence that was almost as devastating as the noise had been.

"Okay," Gaff called much more softly, "let's go!"

If they were under any hopeful illusion that the mortar barrage had smashed and flattened every Japanese in the strongpoint, they were straightened out on this point right away. As the elderly, morose, Calvinistic-looking 2d Lieutenant from B-for-Baker climbed out first, he foolishly climbed straight up exposing himself to the waist, whereupon a Japanese machinegunner immediately shot him three times through the chest. He fell down flat on his face in the little trough, as he should have been in the first place, and hung there, his legs dangling straight down against the ledge in the faces of those behind him. Gingerly, and as gently as they could, they pulled him back down behind the ledge. Stretched out on his back with his eyes shut and breathing shallowly, he looked more morose than ever. He did not open his eyes and put both hands up over his damaged chest and went on breathing shallowly, sour-visaged, Calvinistic, his blue jowls shining darkly in the late afternoon sun.

"Well, whadda we do now?" Charlie Dale snarled. "We can't take him with us."

"We'll have to leave him," Witt said. He had just come up.

"You can't leave him here," the Baker Company sergeant protested.

"Okay," Dale snarled. "He's from your company. *You* stay with him."

"Nah," the Baker Company sergeant said. "I didn't volunteer for this thing just to sit with him."

"I should have been a Chaplain," the dying man said in a faint voice without opening his eyes. "I could have, you know. I'm an ordained minister. I never should have fooled around with Infantry. My wife told me."

"We can leave him and pick him up on the way back," Bell said. "If he's still alive."

"You boys want to pray with me?" the Lieutenant said, his eyes still closed. "Our Father Who art in Heaven, Hallowed be Thy Name."

"We can't, Sir," Dale interrupted politely. "We got to get going. The Captain's waitin on us."

"All right," the Lieutenant said, still without opening his eyes. "I'll do it myself. You boys go ahead. Thy Kingdom come, Thy Will be done, on earth as it is in Heaven. Give us this day our daily . . ."

As they climbed out one by one on their faces and bellies so as not to make the same mistake he made, the faint voice droned feebly on. Dale went first, Witt immediately behind him.

"The son of a bitch," Witt whispered when they were both in the trough behind the thin fragile screen of leaves. "I wish he had of been a Chaplain. They've seen us now. They know we're here. It's going to be hell."

"Yeh, fuck his goddam prayin," Dale said, but he did not say it with much force. He was too busy looking all around everywhere, eyes wide with tension.

Bell was the last to go, but he stopped at the ledge feeling he ought to say something, some word of encouragement, except what did you say to a man dying? "Well, good luck, Sir," he managed finally.

"Thanks, son," the Baker Company Lieutenant said without opening his eyes. "Which one are you? I dont want to open my eyes if I can help it."

"I'm Bell, Sir."

"Oh, yes," the Lieutenant said. "Well, if you get the chance, maybe you can say some little prayer for my soul. I dont want to embarrass you. But it certainly can't do my soul no harm, can it?"

"Okay, Sir," Bell said. "Goodby."

As he climbed out, pressing his face and chest as hard into the dirt of the trough as he could, the faint voice went droning feebly on, repeating some other kind of prayer now which Bell had never heard and didn't know. Automatons. Religious automatons, irreligious automatons. The Business and Professional Automatons Club, Chaplain Gray will give the benediction. Yes, siree. The dirt tasted very dusty in his mouth that was pressed to it.

Captain Gaff, the Battalion Exec, had crawled completely to the end of the trough and out beyond the tiny little brush screen, a matter of twenty or thirty yards.

"Is he dead?" he asked when the others reached him. They were now strung out single file one behind the other in the trough.

"Not yet," Dale whispered from immediately behind him.

Out here beyond the little screen of brush they were more in the open, though the trough still hid them, but here the grass was much thicker than back near the ledge, and it was here that Gaff had decided to make his move. They were to turn their little line by its right flank, he informed Dale and Witt behind him, and told them to pass it back, and on his signal begin to crawl, out of the trough and through the grass, toward the bunker. They were not to fire or throw their grenades until he gave the signal. He wanted to get as close to the bunker as possible without being seen.

"Actually," he pointed out to Dale behind him, "we could go straight on here. You see? After that little open space we would be behind that little rise, and I think we could maybe crawl all the way around behind them."

"Yes, sir," Dale said.

"But I dont think there's that much time."

"Yes, Sir," Dale said.

"That would take at least another hour of crawling," Gaff said earnestly. "And I'm afraid it's too near dark."

"Yes, Sir," Dale said.

"What do you think?" Gaff said.

"I agree with you, Sir," Dale said. No fuckin officer was goin to get Charlie Dale to take no responsibility for what the officer done.

"Has everybody behind been informed?" Gaff whispered.

"Yes, Sir."

Gaff sighed. "Okay. Let's do it."

Slowly Gaff snaked his belly over the lip of the trough and off into the grass, dragging his rifle by the muzzle rather than cradling it, so as not to disturb the grass more than absolutely necessary. One by one the others followed.

For John Bell it was like some insane, mad nightmare which he could remember having had before. His elbows and feet fell through holes in the mat of old dead stems, catching and holding him. Dust and seeds filled his nose and choked him. Stems whipped his face. Then he remembered: it was that crawl up through the grass to the ledge with Keck. It really had happened to him after all. And Keck was dead now.

None of them ever knew what set them off. One moment they were crawling along in utter silence, each man totally alone and separate and out of contact with the others, and in the next machinegun fire was whipping and slashing over and around and all about them. No one had fired, no one had thrown a grenade, no one had shown himself. Perhaps one nervous enemy had seen some grass move and had fired, thus setting them all off. Whatever it was, they now lay in a storm of fire, separated and cut off from contact with each other, unable to take concerted action. Each man put his head down and huddled to the ground, praying to gods or godlessnesses that he might keep on living. Contact was lost and with it all command and control. Nobody could move. And it was in this static situation of potential total loss that Pfc Don Doll came forward as hero.

Sweating, lying pressed flat in an ecstasy of panic, terror, fear and cowardice, Doll simply could not stand it any longer. He had had too much this day. Wailing over and over in a high falsetto the one word "Mother! Mother!", which fortunately nobody at all could hear, least of all himself, he leaped to his feet and began to run straight at the Japanese emplacement, firing his rifle from his hip at the one embrasure he could see. As if startled beyond reasonable expectation, most of the Japanese fire stopped suddenly. At the same moment Captain Gaff, released from his own temporary panic, leaped up waving his arm and bawling "Back!" With him in the lead the rest of the assault force ran for the trough and their lives. Meanwhile Doll charged on, wailing his incantation:

"Mother! Mother!"

When his rifle was empty, he threw it at the embrasure, drew his pistol and began firing that. With his left hand he tore a grenade from his belt, stopped firing the pistol long enough to pull the pin with one finger, and lobbed the grenade over onto the camouflaged roof of the emplacement, which he could now see clearly since it was only about twenty yards away, and where the grenade exploded uselessly and without effect. Then, continuing to fire the pistol, he charged on. Only when the pistol ceased to fire for want of ammunition did he come to his senses and realize where he was. Then he turned and ran. Luckily for him, he did not turn back toward the others but simply ran blindly off to the right—though he would deny this later. In that direction the curving ledge was only ten yards away, and he reached it before the mass of the Japanese fire, which by now as if getting over its start had commenced again, could find him and cut him down.

From behind him as he ran the ten yards a dark round fizzing object arched over his head and fell a few feet in front of him. Automatically Doll kicked at it with his foot as if placekicking a football and ran on. It bounced away a few yards and exploded in a cloud of black smoke which knocked him down. But when he fell he found that there was nothing under him; he had fallen over the ledge. His foot stinging painfully, he bounced to the foot of the ledge at almost the exact spot where Private Catch had been killed, landed with a bonejarring thud, then rolled another twelve yards further down the hillside before he could get himself stopped. For a while he just lay in the grass, breathing in groans, bruised, sore, the wind knocked out of him, half-blinded, thinking dully of almost nothing. This one had not been like his other experiences: the zig-zag run back from 1st Platoon, then the return to find Skinny Culn, not like the charge up the ridge with Keck. This one had been horrible, totally and completely horrible, without any relieving qualities or graces. He devoutly hoped he would never have even to think of it again. When he looked at his shoe, he found a neat little slit a sixteenth of an inch long just above the ankle bone. Where the fuck was he, anyway? He knew where he was, but was he alone? What had happened to the others? Where were they? At the moment all he could think about was that he wanted to be with people, so he could put his arms around somebody and they could put their arms around him. With this in mind he got up, climbed to the ledge and ran gasping back along it till he came to the trough, where he almost ran headon into the others, all sitting against the rock and gasping breathlessly. Only one of them, the Sergeant from Baker Company, had been hurt, and he had had his shoulder smashed by an MG bullet.

"Doll," Captain Gaff gasped, before Doll could apologize, make excuses or explain away what he had done, "I'm personally recommending you to Colonel Tall for the Distinguished Service Cross. You saved all our lives, and I never saw such bravery. I shall write the recommendation myself, and I shall pursue it. I promise you."

Doll could hardly believe his own ears. "Well, Sir, it wasn't nothin," he gasped modestly. "I was scared." He could see Charlie Dale looking at him with a kind of hate-filled envy from where he leaned gasping against the ledge. Ha, you fucker! Doll thought with a sudden explosion of pleasure.

"But to have the presence of mind to remember that the ledge was ten yards off there to the right," Gaff gasped, "that was wonderful."

"Well, Sir, you know, I was with the first patrol," Doll said and smiled at Dale.

"So were some of these others," young Captain Gaff said. He was still breathing heavily but beginning to get his breath back. "Are you okay? You're not hurt?"

"Well, Sir, I dont know," Doll smiled, and proceeded to show them the tiny slit in his boot.

"What's that from?"

"A Jap handgrenade. I kicked it away." He bent to unlace the shoe. "I better look." Inside he found the little piece of metal, which had slipped to the bottom of his shoe like a pebble, but in actual truth he had not even felt it during the run back along the ledge. "Hunh!" he lied, laughing. "I thought I had a rock in my shoe." It had struck his anklebone just above its peak and cut it slightly; it had bled a little into his sweat-wet sock.

"By God!" Gaff exclaimed. "It's only a scratch, but by God I'm recommending you for the Purple Heart, too. You might as well have it. But you're all right except for that?"

"I lost my rifle," Doll said.

"Take Lieutenant Gray's," Gaff said. He looked around at the others. "We better be getting back. And tell them we couldn't take the objective. Can a couple of you drag Lieutenant Gray?" Gaff turned to the Baker Company sergeant. "You all right? Think you can make it?"

"I'm all right," the Baker Co sergeant said with a grin that was more a pained grimace. "It only hurts when I laugh. But I want to thank *you!*" he said, turning to Doll.

"Don't thank me," Doll said, and laughed shyly, brilliant eyed, with a new magnanimity born of his sudden recognition. He had forgotten all about wanting to put his arms around somebody, or have them put their arms around him. "But what about you? Are you going to be all right?" He looked down at the bloody hand from which blood dripped slowly as the arm hung useless against the sergeant's side, and suddenly he was scared again.

"Sure, sure," the sergeant said happily. "I'm out of it now. I'll be going back. I hope I'm crippled a little."

"Come on, you guys," Captain Gaff said. "Let's move. You

can talk it over later. Dale, you and Witt drag Lieutenant Gray. Bell, you help the sergeant. I'll take the walkie-talkie. Doll, you rearguard us. Them little brown brothers, as the Colonel likes to call them, are liable to send some people down here after us, you know.''

And thus arranged the little party made its way back. The Japanese sent no one after them. Gaff with the radio, Bell and the B-for-Baker sergeant behind him, then Dale and Witt dragging the dead lieutenant's body by its two feet, with Doll bringing up the rear, they did not make a very prepossessing sight as they came crawling around the corner into view of the Battalion. But Gaff had been talking to them on the way back.

"If we do get another chance at it tomorrow, I think we can take it," he said, "and I for one am going to volunteer for the assignment. If we crawl on across that open space and get behind the little rise, we can come around in behind them and come down on them from above. That's what we should have done today. From above like that we can put the grenades to them easier than hell. And that's what I'm going to tell the Colonel.''

And strangely enough, there was not one of them but who wanted to go back with him—excepting of course the Baker Company sergeant who of course could not go. Even John Bell wanted to go, just like all the others. Automatons all. What was it? Why? Bell did not know. What was this peculiar masochistic, self-destructive quality in himself which made him want to get out in the open and expose himself to danger and gunfire as he had that first time at the trough? Once as a child—(once? many times, and in many different ways, but this one particular time when he was fifteen, and the memory assailed him now so strongly that it was as if he were actually there, living it again)— once he had gone for a tramp in one of the Ohio woods outside his town. This particular woods had a cliff and a cave, if you could call a hole four feet deep in the rock a cave, and up above the cliff there was more woods for about fifty yards which ended at a gravelled country road. Across the gravel road farmers were working in their fields. Hearing their voices and the snorts and jingles of their horses and harness, he had a strange sweet secre-

tive excitement. Peeking through the screen of leaves that marked
the end of the wood, he could see them, four men in overalls and
rubber boots standing beside the fence, but they could not see
him. A lot of cars used this gravelled country road, too. One of
the cars, with a man and three women in it, stopped to talk to the
four men, and Bell suddenly knew what he was going to do. In a
sweet, hot rush of visceral excitement he retreated through the
trees almost all the way back to the clifftop and began to take off
his clothes. Naked as the day he was born in the warm, rich June
air, sporting a throbbing erection, he crept like an Indian back to
the screen of leaves, the twigs and old leaves crunching noise-
lessly under his bare feet, leaving his clothes and his sandwiches
back there behind him because that was all part of it: his clothes
must be far enough away so that he could never reach them in
time if he were caught or seen, otherwise it was cheating; and
standing just behind the leaf screen, where he could see them and
the expressions on all their faces, trembling violently in his excitement and excitation, he masturbated. Crawling along behind
Captain Gaff beneath a ledge on Guadalcanal, helping along the
wounded sergeant beside him, John Bell stopped and stared,
transfixed by a revelation. And the revelation, brought on by his
old memory, and which he was forced to face, was that his volunteering, his climb out into the trough that first time, even his
participation in the failed assault, all were—in some way he could
not fully understand—sexual, and as sexual, and in much the
same way, as his childhood incident of the gravelled road.

"Ouch!" said the sergeant beside him. "God damn it!"

"Oh! I'm sorry!" Bell said.

He had not thought of that episode in a long time. When he had
told that one to his wife Marty, it had excited her too, and they
had gone rushing off to bed together to make love. Ahhhhh,
Marty! The silent cry was like an explosion wrung involuntarily
from his bowels.

Covertly Bell with his new knowledge looked around at the
others. Were their reactions sexual too, then? How to know? He
couldn't tell. But he knew that he himself, as had all the others
said too, would be volunteering to go back again tomorrow if the

chance arose. Partly it was an esprit de corps and a closeness of comradeship coming from having shared something a bit tougher than the rest. Partly it was Captain Gaff whom he liked and respected more and more all the time. And partly, for him at least, it was that other thing, which he could hardly name, that thing of sexuality. Could it be that with the others? Could it be that *all* war was basically sexual? Not just in psych theory, but in fact, actually and emotionally? A sort of sexual perversion? Or a complex of sexual perversions? That would make a funny thesis and God help the race.

But whether or not Bell could discover in his comrades anything about their sexual involvement, and he couldn't, he could read something else in their faces. That spiritual numbness and sense of no longer feeling human which he had become aware of in himself on the way up, was growing apace on all their faces. Even Gaff who had only been up here with them for a couple of hours was showing a bit of it now. So Bell was not alone. And when they crawled, limping and licking their wounds, back into the midst of the Battalion, which was already beginning to take on the look of a permanent, organized position, which indeed it was, or was soon to become, he was able to note the same ahumanness in many other faces, some more than others, all of them almost precisely measurable in direct ratio to what the owner of the face had been through since dawn today. Next to his own little assault group, those who had made the first crossing with Keck showed it the most.

It was getting very close to dark. In their absence, they found most of Charlie had on Colonel Tall's orders already dug themselves in a few yards back from the ledge. As it turned out, their little battle had been heard and interpreted correctly as a failure, and because of this B-for-Baker had been ordered to pass below and to the rear of Charlie, curving their flanks uphill to join and thus completing the defensive circle, and were now busily at work digging their holes for the night. There was to be no withdrawal. Holes for themselves, the little assault force, were already being dug for them, also on Colonel Tall's orders.

And as it also turned out, as they found out almost immediately, they *were* going to get a chance at the bunker again tomorrow. Colonel Tall made this plain to them as soon as he took Captain Gaff's report. Colonel Tall's plan for a night attack, about which they knew nothing and of which they heard with astonishment, had been vetoed by the Division Commander. But at least, Colonel Tall said, he had made the offer. Anyway, he agreed with Captain Gaff's tactical interpretation completely. He shook hands with Doll first because of his recommendation for the DSC, then with each of the others, excepting of course Lieutenant Gray, who was already on his way back to Hill 209 on a stretcher. Then, tucking his bamboo baton under his arm, he dismissed the enlisted men and turned to a dispositions discussion about tomorrow with the officers.

Colonel Tall's plan, which he had devised after receiving the news of the rejection of his proposed night attack, was one calculated to take account of every contingency, and it utilized—as Bugger Stein was quick to note—Stein's suggestion of today to explore the right for the possibility of a flanking maneuver. Before dawn Stein was to take his C-for-Charlie Company (less the men with Gaff) back across the third fold and move down the hollow to the right into the jungle which had been so quiet today. Unless he encountered very heavy resistance, he was to push on to the top of the Elephant's Head from the rear. "That Elephant's Trunk is one hell of a fine escape route for our brown brothers," smiled Colonel Tall. If Stein could get astride of it higher up where the slopes were steeper, perhaps they could bottle up the whole force. Meantime, Baker would be moved by Captain Task up to the ledge, where he would wait the reduction of the strongpoint by Captain Gaff's assault force to begin his uphill frontal attack. "I'm giving you the roundabout flanking movement, Stein, because it was your idea in the first place," said Colonel Tall. Perhaps, but only perhaps, and then even only to Stein, there was a veiled double meaning in the slightly thin way Tall said it.

"That Bell," Colonel Tall said after the discussion of his plan was over. He looked off to where he had thoughtfully placed the assault force near to Gaff's hole and his own. "He's a good man." This time the unspoken meaning was clear to every officer present, since they all knew, and they knew Tall knew, about Bell's past as an officer.

"He sure is!" young Captain Gaff put in with boyish enthusiasm, and without reservation.

"In my company I have always found him an excellent soldier," Stein said when Tall glanced at him.

Tall said no more, and so neither did Stein. He was willing enough to let well enough alone. Stein had increasingly found himself put by Tall into the position of a guilty schoolboy who had failed his exam, although the Colonel had never said anything to him openly or directly. Slowly the talk among the officers drifted back to the outlook for tomorrow as they squatted in the center of the position. It was almost quiet now; the high racketing which had hung in the air all day had ceased some time ago, and only sporadic riflefire was heard now in the distance. Both sides lay waiting and breathing.

And as the twilight deepened, that was the way they remained: the little knot of officers in the center discussing the prospects and possibilities of tomorrow, the men in the holes around the circle checking and cleaning their weapons: the Battalion at the end of its first real day of real combat: neither successful nor unsuccessful, nothing decided, exhausted, growing numb-er. Just before full dark the officers parted and went to their own holes to lie down and wait with the men for the expected Japanese night attack. Perhaps the worst thing was that now one could no longer smoke. That, and the shortage of water. A few more men had collapsed during the late afternoon and been carted away like the wounded, and many more remained on the verge of collapse. Fear was a problem too, more in some, less in others, according to how far the ahuman numbness had advanced in each. John Bell was not afraid at all now, he found. Wait until the shooting started, to get scared.

They were paired off of course in each two holes, one man to guard, one to sleep; but nobody slept very much. Quite a few men, spending their first night outside their own lines, fired at shadows, fired at everything, fired at nothing, revealing their positions; but the expected Japanese night attack did not develop, though they did manage to cut both companies' sound power phone lines. Probably they were too weak and too sick to attack. And so the Battalion lay and waited for the dawn. Along about two o'clock John Bell suffered another malarial attack of chills and fever like the one he had had two days before on the road, except that this one was much worse. At its worst he was shaking so uncontrollably that he would have been of no use to anybody if the Japanese had attacked. And he was not alone. First Sergeant Welsh, clutching his precious musette bag containing the leatherbound Morning Report book in which for tomorrow he had already recorded in the dusk all of the personnel changes of today: "KIA; WIA; Sick;"—suffered his first malarial attack, which was worse than Bell's second one, though neither knew it about the other. And there were others.

One man who had to shit did his business in the corner of his hole cursing hysterically, and spent the rest of the night trying to keep his feet out of it. To have gotten out of your hole was worth your life with this bunch.

CHAPTER 5

Billions of hard, bright stars shone with relentless glitter all across the tropic night sky. Underneath this brilliant canopy of the universe, the men lay wide awake and waited. From time to time the same great cumuli of the day, black blobs now, sailed their same stately route across the bright expanse blotting out portions of it, but no rain fell on the thirsting men. For the first time since they had been up in these hills it did not rain at all during the night. The night had to be endured, and it had to be endured dry, beneath its own magnificent beauty. Perhaps of them all only Colonel Tall enjoyed it.

Finally, though it was still black night, cautionary stirrings and whispers sibilated along the line from hole to hole as the word to move out was passed. In the inhuman, unreal unlight of false dawn the grubby, dirtyfaced remnants of C-for-Charlie sifted from their holes and coagulated stiffly into their squads and platoons to begin their flanking move. There was not one of them who did not carry his cuts, bruises or abrasions from having flung himself violently to the ground the day before. Thick fat rolls of dirt pressed beneath the mudcaked fingernails of their hands, greasy from cleaning weapons. They had lost forty-eight men or just over one-fourth of their number yesterday in killed, wounded or sick; nobody doubted they would lose more today. The only question remaining was: Which ones of us? Who exactly?

Still looking dapper although he was now almost as dirty as themselves, Colonel Tall with his little bamboo baton in his armpit and his hand resting on his rakishly lowslung holster, strode among them to tell them good luck. He shook hands with Bugger Stein and Brass Band. Then they trudged away in the ghostly light, moving away eastward back down the ridge to face their new day while thirst gnawed at them. Before dawn lightened the area, they had crossed back over the third fold—where they had lain so long in terror yesterday, and where the familiar ground now looked strange—and had traversed the low between the folds to the edge of the jungle where they were hidden, where Col Tall would not let them go yesterday, and where not a single Japanese was in sight. Approaching it cautiously with scouts out, they found nobody at all. A hundred yards inside the jungle they discovered a highly passable, much used trail, its mud covered with prints of Japanese hobnailed boots, all pointing toward Hill 210. As they moved along it quietly and without trouble, they could hear the beginning of the fight on the ridge—where they had left the previously four, but now five volunteers with Captain Gaff.

Tall had not waited long. B-for-Baker now manned the line of holes behind the ledge. Tall sent them forward to the ledge itself, and as soon as it was light enough to see at all, sent the middle platoon forward in an attack whose objective was to wheel right in a line pivoted on the ledge so that they would be facing the strongpoint. This would place them in a position to aid Gaff.

But the middle platoon's move was not successful. MG fire from the strongpoint, and other hidden points nearby, hurt them too badly. Four men were killed and a number of others were wounded. They were forced to return. That was the noise of the fight C-for-Charlie heard; and its failure left everything up to Gaff and his now five volunteers. They would have to take the strongpoint alone. Tall walked over to them where they lay.

This fifth volunteer with Gaff was Pfc Cash, the icy-eyed taxidriver from Toledo with the mean face, known in C-for-Charlie as "Big Un." Earlier, before C-for-Charlie moved out, Big Un had come up to Tall in the dark and in a ponderous voice had asked to be allowed to stay behind and join Gaff's assault group. Tall, who was not used to being approached by strange privates anyway, could hardly believe his ears. He could not even remember ever having seen this man. "Why?" he asked sharply.

"Because of what the Japs done to them two guys from 2d Battalion three days ago on Hill 209," Big Un said. "I aint forgotten it, and I want to get myself a few of them personally before I get knocked off or shot up without getting a chance to kill some. I think Capn Gaff's operation'll be my best oppratunity."

For a moment Tall could not help believing he was being made the victim of some kind of elaborate and tasteless hoax, perpetrated by the wits of Charlie Company who had sent this great oaf up to him deliberately with this stupid request for personal, heroic vendetta. 1st Sgt Welsh, for one, had a mind capable of such subtle ridicule.

But when he looked up (as he was forced to do; and Tall was by no means a small man) at this huge, murderous face and icy, if not very intelligent eyes, he could see despite his flare of anger that the man was obviously sincere. Cash stood, his rifle slung not from one shoulder but across his back, and carrying in his hands one of those sawed-off shotguns and bandolier of buckshot shells which some fool of a staff lieutenant had had the bright idea of handing out for "close quarter work" the night before the attack—which meant that Cash had hung onto the damned thing all through the danger of yesterday. Tall thought they had all been thrown away. A sudden tiny thrill ran through Tall despite himself. The brute really was big! But his own reaction made him even more angry.

"Soldier, are you serious?" he snapped thinly. "There's a war on here. I'm busy. I've got a serious battle to fight."

"Yes," Big Un said, then remembering his manners added, "I mean: Yes, sir: I'm serious."

Tall pressed his lips together. If the man wanted to make such a request, he should know he was supposed to go through channels: through his Platoon Leader and his Company Commander to Gaff himself; not come bothering the Battalion Commander with it when the Battalion Commander had a battle to fight.

"Dont you know—" he began in frustration, and then stopped himself. Tall prided himself on being a professional and such requests for personal vendetta offended and bored him. A professional should ignore such things and fight a battle, or a war, as it developed on the ground. Tall knew Marine officers who laughed about the jars of gold or gold-filled Japanese teeth some of their men had collected over the campaign, but he preferred to have nothing to do with that sort of thing. Also, though his protégé Gaff had lost two men yesterday evening, they had decided between them that the experience and the knowledge of the terrain gained by the survivors more than made up for the adding of two green replacements who would probably be more liability than help. Still . . .

And anyway, here this great oaf still stood, waiting dumbly, as though his wishes were the only ones in the world, and blocking Tall's path with his huge frame so Tall could not see anything that was going on.

After biting the inside of his lip, he snapped out coldly, "If you want to go with Captain Gaff, you'll have to go talk to him about it and ask him. I'm busy. You can tell him that I dont object to your going. Now, God damn it, *go away!*" he yelled. He turned away. Big Un was left holding his shotgun.

"Yes, Sir!" he called after the Colonel. "Thank you, Sir!" And while Tall had continued with getting C-for-Charlie moving, Cash had gone in search of Gaff.

Big Un's cry of thanks after the Colonel had not been without his own little hint of sarcasm. He had not been a hack pusher all his life not to know when he was being deliberately snubbed by a social better, high intelligence or low. As far as intelligence went, Big Un was confident he could have been as intelligent as any— and more intelligent than most—if he had not always believed that school and history and arithmetic and writing and reading and learning words were only so much uninteresting bullshit which took up a man's time and kept him from getting laid or making an easy buck. He still believed it, for his own kids as well as for himself. He had never finished his first year of high school and he could read a paper as well as anybody. And as for intelli-

gence, he was intelligent enough to know that the Colonel's statement about not objecting was tantamount to acceptance by Gaff.
In fact, all the time he was talking there to the Colonel, Big Un
had intended to tell Gaff that, anyway. Now he could tell him
truthfully.

So, in the still dark predawn, Gaff and his four volunteers were
treated to the awesome spectacle of Big Un looming up over them
through the dark, still clutching his shotgun and bandolier of
shells which he had clung to so dearly all through the terror of
yesterday in his US-made shellhole among the 1st Platoon. Stolidly and without excitement, Big Un made his report. As he had
anticipated, he was immediately accepted—although Gaff, too,
looked at his shotgun strangely. All he had left to do was find
Bugger Stein and report the change, then come back and lie down
with the others to wait until B Company's middle platoon made
its attack and it was their own turn. Big Un did so with grim
satisfaction.

There was little for them to do but talk. During the half hour it
took the middle platoon of B Company to fail and come tumbling
and sobbing back over the ledge with drawn faces and white eyes,
the six of them lay a few yards back down the slope behind B's
right platoon which in addition to holding the right of the line
along the ledge was also acting as the reserve. It was amazing
how the longer one lasted in this business, the less sympathy one
felt for others who were getting shot up as long as oneself was in
safety. Sometimes the difference was a matter of only a very few
yards. But terror became increasingly limited to those moments
when you yourself were in actual danger. So, while B's middle
platoon shot and were shot, fought and sobbed thirty yards away
beyond the ledge, Gaff's group talked. Cash the new addition
more than made his presence felt.

Big Un himself did very little of the talking, after explaining
his reason for wanting to come with them, but he made himself
felt just the same. Unslinging his rifle, he arranged it and the
shotgun carefully to keep their actions out of the dirt, and then
simply lay, toying with the bandolier of shotgun shells and slipping them in and out of their cloth loops, his face a stolid, mean

mask. The slingless shotgun was a brandnew, cheap-looking automatic with its barrel sawed off just behind the choke and a five shell magazine; the shot shells themselves were not actually buckshot at all, but were loaded with a full load of BB shot capable of blowing a large, raw hole clear through a man at close range. It was a mean weapon, and Cash looked like the man to use it well. Nobody really knew very much about him in C-for-Charlie. He had come in as a draftee six months before and while he had made acquaintances, he had made no real friends. Everybody was a little afraid of him. He kept to himself, did most of his drinking alone, and while he never offered to challenge anybody to a fight, there was something about his grin which made it plain that any challenges he received would be cheerfully and gladly accepted. Nobody offered any. At six foot four and built accordingly, in an outfit where physical fighting prowess was considered the measure of a man's stature, nobody wanted to try him. Except for Big Queen (over whom he towered by five inches, though he did not weigh as much) he was the biggest man in the company. There were those who were not above trying slyly to promote this battle of the giants between Big Un and Big Queen, just to see who *would* win; and many bets might have been taken, except that nothing ever came of it. Curiously enough, the nearest Big Un ever came to having a real friend was Witt the Kentuckian who hardly came up to his waist, and who used to go on pass with him before Witt was forcibly transferred. This turned out to be because in Toledo Big Un had known and admired so many Kentuckians who had come up north to work in the factories, and had liked their strong, hardheaded sense of honor which showed itself in drunken brawls over women or fistfights over particular prize seats at some bar. But now, today, he did not even speak to Witt beyond a perfunctory grunt of greeting. The rest of them watched him and his shotgun curiously. Despite the fact that they were now seasoned veterans of this particular assault and could look down on Big Un from this height of snobbery, they were all somehow a little reluctant to try it.

John Bell, for one, had forgotten all about the Japanese torture

killing of the two George Company men three days before. It was
too long ago and too much had happened to him since. When Big
Un recalled it with such surprise to them all, Bell found it didn't
really matter so much any more. Guys got killed, one way or
another way. Some got tortured. Some got gutshot like Tella.
Some got it quick through the head. Who knew how much those
two guys suffered, really? Only themselves; and they no longer
existed to tell it. And if they no longer existed, it didn't either and
was no longer important. So what the fuck? A wall existed between the living and the dead. And there was only one way to get
over it. That was what was important. So what was all this fuss
about? Bell found himself eyeing Big Un coolly and wondering
what his real angle was, behind all this other crap. The others in
the little group obviously felt the same way, Bell noted, from the
peculiar looks on their faces; but nobody said anything. Thirty-
five yards away beyond and above the little protective ledge the
middle platoon of Baker still fired and fought and now and then
yelled just a little bit. If Bell was any judge by the sound of it,
what was left of them would be coming back pretty quickly. A
rough fingernail of excitement picked at his solar plexus when he
thought what this would mean soon for himself. Then, suddenly,
like a bucket of cold water dashed in his face, his own supreme
callousness smashed into his consciousness and shook him with a
sense of horror at his own hardened brutality. How would Marty
like being married to this husband, when he finally did get home?
Ah, Marty! so much is changing; everywhere. Therefore, when
the middle platoon of B did come rolling and tumbling and cursing and sobbing back over the ledge with their white eyeballs in
their faces and their open mouths, Bell watched them with an
anguish which was perhaps out of all proportion even to their
own.

How the others in the assault group felt about the return of the
platoon, Bell could not tell. From their faces they all, including
Cash, seemed to feel the same cool, guarded callousness he himself had just been feeling, and now was so desperately wanting
not to feel. The Baker Company men lay against the ledge staring
at nothing and seeing nobody and breathing in long painful gasps

through their parched throats. There was no water to give them and they needed water badly. Though the day was not yet really hot, they were all sweating profusely, thus losing even more precious moisture. Making a noise like a battery of frogs in a swamp two of them rolled up their eyeballs and passed out. Nobody bothered to help them. Their buddies couldn't. And the assault group only lay and watched them.

This lack of water was becoming a serious problem for everybody, and would be more of one as the glaring equatorial sun mounted, but whatever the reason—though there was plenty of it in the rear—no water could be got this far forward to them. Curiously enough, it was little Charlie Dale the insensitive, rather than Bell or Don Doll, who voiced it for all of them in the assault group. Imaginative or not he was animal enough to know what his belly told him and be directed by it. "If they dont get us some water up here soon," he said loud enough to be heard by everybody in the vicinity, "we aint none of us going to make it to the top of this hill." Abruptly, he rolled over to face the looming shape of Hill 209 in their rear and began to shake his fist at it. "Dirty Fuckers! Dirty bastards! Pig bastards! You got all the fucking water in the world, and you drinking ever fucking drop of it, too! You aint lettin any of it get past you up to us, are you! Well you better get some of it up here to your goddam *fightin men*, or you can take your goddam fucking battle and shove it up your fat ass and lose it!" He had yelled this much of his protest, and it verberated off along the ledge where nobody, least of all the middle platoon of B, paid any attention to it. The rest of it tapered away into an intense, unintelligible mutter which, as Colonel Tall now sauntered toward them from his command hole baton in hand, became a respectful and attentive silence.

The Colonel whose walk was leisurely and erect—as straight up as he could get, in fact—condescended to squat while he talked in a low serious voice to Gaff. Then they were off and crawling again along the by now so familiar ledge—familiar to the point of real friendliness almost, John Bell thought, which could be a bad trap if you believed it—as it curved away out of sight around the hill's curve, Gaff in the lead.

Bell crawled around Charlie Dale in the second spot and touched the Captain on the behind. "You better let me take the point, Sir," he said respectfully.

Gaff turned his head to look at him with intense, crinkled eyes. For a long moment the two, officer and ex-officer, looked honestly into each other's eyes. Then with an abrupt gesture of both head and hand Gaff admitted his small error and signaled Bell to go on past him. He let one more man, Dale, pass him and then fell into the third spot. When Bell reached the point where the trough began and Lieutenant Gray had died, he stopped and they all clustered up.

Gaff did not bother to give them any peptalk. He had already explained the operation to them thoroughly, back at the position. Now all he said was, "You all know the job we've got to do, fellows. There's no point in my going over it all again. I'm convinced the toughest part of the approach will be the open space between the end of the trough here and the shoulder of the knob. Once past that I think it won't be so bad. Remember that we may run into smaller emplacements along the way. I'd rather bypass them if we can, but we may have to knock some of them out if they block our route and hold us up. Okay, that's all." He stopped and smiled at them looking each man in the eyes in turn: an excited, boyish, happy, adventuresome smile. It was only slightly incongruous with the tensed, crinkled look in his eyes.

"When we get up to them," Gaff said, "we ought to have some fun."

There were several weak smiles, very similar to his own if not as strong. Only Witt's and Big Un's seemed to be really deep. But they were all grateful to him. Since yesterday all of them, excepting Big Un, had come to like him very much. All last evening, during the night, and again during the predawn movements, he had stayed with them except during his actual conferences with Colonel Tall, spending his time with them. He kidded, cajoled and boosted them, cracking jokes, telling them cunt stories about his youth at the Point and after, and all the kooky type broads he had made—had in short treated them like equals. Even for Bell who had been one it was a little thrilling, quite flattering to be treated as an equal by an officer; for the others it was moreso. They would have followed Gaff anywhere. He had promised them the biggest drunk of their lives, everything on him, once they got through this mess and back down off the line. And they were grateful to him for that, too. He had not, when he promised, made any mention about 'survivors' or 'those who were left' having this drunk together, tacitly assuming that they would all be there to enjoy it. And they were grateful for that also. Now he looked around at them all once more with his boyish, young adventurer's eager smile above the tensed, crinkled eyes.

"I'll be leading from here on out," he said. "Because I want to pick the route myself. If anything should happen to me, Sergeant Bell will be in command, so I want him last. Sergeant Dale will be second in command. They both know what to do.

"Okay, let's go." It was much more of a sigh than a hearty bellow.

Then they were out and crawling along the narrow, peculiarly sensed dangerousness of the familiar trough, Gaff in the lead, each man being particularly careful of the spot where the trough opened out into the ledge and Lieutenant Gray the preacher had absentmindedly got himself killed. Big Un Cash, who was new to all this, was especially careful. John Bell, waiting for the others to climb out, caught Charlie Dale staring at him with a look of puzzled, but nonetheless hateful enmity. Dale had been appointed Acting Sergeant at least an hour before Bell, and therefore should have had the seniority over him. Bell winked at him, and Dale looked away. A moment later it was Dale's turn to go, and he climbed out into the trough without a backward look. Only one man, Witt, remained between them. Then it was Bell's own turn. For the—what was it? third? fourth? fifth time? Bell had lost track—he climbed out over the ledge and crawled past the thin screen of scrub brush. It was beginning to look pretty bedraggled now from all the MG fire which had whistled through it.

In the trough ahead with his head down Charlie Dale was thinking furiously that that was what you could always expect from all goddam fucking officers. They hung together like a pack of horse thieves, busted out or not. He had broke his ass for them

all day yesterday. He had been appointed Acting Sergeant by an
officer, by Bugger Stein himself, not by no fucking platoon sergeant like Keck. And about a hour before. And look who got
command? You couldn't trust them no further than you could
throw them by the ears, no more than you could trust the government itself to do something for you. Furiously, outraged, keeping
his head well down, he stared at the motionless feet of Doll in
front of him as if he wanted to bite them off.

Up ahead Gaff had waited, looking back, until they were all
safely in the trough. Now there was no need to wait longer. Turning his head to the right he looked off toward the strongpoint, but
without raising his head high enough to see anything above the
grass. Were they waiting? Were they watching? Were they looking at this particular open spot? He could not know. But no need
in spotting them a ball by exposing himself if they were. With one
last look back directly behind him at Big Un Cash, who favored
him with a hard, mean, gimleteyed grin that was not much help,
he bounced up and took off with his rifle at high port, running
agonizingly slowly and pulling his knees up high to clear the
matted kunai grass like a football player running through stacks
of old tires. It was ludicrous to say the least, not a dignified way
to be shot, but not a shot was fired. He dived in behind the
shoulder of the knob and lay there. After waiting a full minute he
motioned the next man, Big Un, to come on. Big Un, who had
moved up, as the others had moved up behind him, took right off
at once running in the same way, his rifle pounding against his
back, the shotgun in his hands, his helmet straps flapping. Just
before he reached the shoulder a single machinegun opened up,
but he too dived to safety. The machinegun stopped.

The third man, Doll, fell. He was only about five yards out
when several MGs opened up. They were watching this time. It
was only twenty or twenty-five yards across, the open space, but
it seemed much longer. He was already breathing in ripping
gasps. Then his foot caught in a hole in the mat of old grass and
he was down. Oh, no! Oh, no! his mind screamed at him in panic.
Not me! Not after all the rest that's happened to me! Not after all
I've lasted through! I won't even get my medal! Blindly, spitting

grass seeds and dust, he clambered up and staggered on. He only had ten yards more to go, and he made it. He fell in upon the other two and lay sobbing for breath and existence. The bright, washed sun had just come up over the hills in the east.

By now in the early morning sunshine and stark shadows all the MGs from the strongpoint were firing, hosing down the trough itself as well as the open space. Bullets tore over the heads of Charlie Dale, Witt and Bell in bunches which rattled and bruised the poor thin little bushes. It was now Dale's turn to go, and he was still furious at Bell. "Hey, wait!" Bell yelled from behind him. "Wait! Don't go yet! I got an idea!" Dale gave him one hate-filled contemptuous look and got to his feet. He departed without a word, chugging along solidly like a little engine, in the same way he had gone down and come back up the slope in front of the third fold yesterday. By now a sort of semi-path had been pushed through the grass, and this aided him some. He arrived behind the shoulder and sat down, apparently totally unmoved, but still secretly angry at Bell. Nothing had touched him.

"You must be out of your mind!" Captain Gaff shouted at him.

"Why?" Dale said. Maliciously, he settled himself to see what fucking Bell would do now. Heh heh. Not that he wanted him to get hurt, or anything.

Bell demonstrated his idea immediately. When he and Witt had crawled to the end of the trough, the MGs still firing just over their heads, Bell pulled the pin on a grenade and lobbed it at the strongpoint. But he did not throw it straight across; he threw it into the angle formed by the ledge and the trough, so that it landed in front of the bunker but further back much closer to the ledge. When the MGs all swung that way, as they did immediately, he and Witt crossed in safety before they could swing back. Clearly the three of them could have done it just as easily, and when he threw himself down grinning in the safety behind the shoulder, Bell winked at Charlie Dale again. Dale glowered back. "Very bright," Gaff laughed. Bell winked at Dale a third time. Fuck him. Who did he think he was? Then suddenly, after this third wink, like some kind of a sudden stop, Bell realized the fear he had felt this time had been much less, almost none at all, negligible. Even when those bullets were sizzing just over his head. Was he learning? Was that it? Or was he just becoming inured. More brutalized, like Dale. The thought lingered on in his head like an echoing gong while he sat staring at nothing, then slowly faded away. And so what? If answer is yes, or if question does not apply to you, pass on to next questionnaire. What the hell, he thought. Fuck it. If he only had a drink of water, he could do anything. The MGs from the strongpoint were still hosing and belaboring the empty trough and its poor straggly bushes as the party moved away.

Gaff had told them that he thought the rest of the route would be easier once they were past the open space, and he was right. The terrain mounted steeply around the knob which jutted out of the ridge and up here the mat of grass was not quite so thick, but now they were forced to crawl. It was next to impossible to see the camouflaged emplacements until they opened up, and they could not take any chances. As they moved along in this snail's way, sweating and panting in the sun from the exertion, Bell's heart—as well as everybody else's—began to beat with a heavier pulse, a mingled excitement and fear which was by no means entirely unpleasant. They all knew from yesterday that beyond the knob was a shallow saddle between the knob and the rock wall where the ledge ended, and it was along this saddle which they were to crawl to come down on the Japanese from above. They had all seen the saddle, but they had not seen behind the knob. Now they crawled along it, seeing it from within the Japanese territory. They were not fired upon, and they did not see any emplacements. Off to the left near the huge rock outcrop where the seven Japanese men had made their silly counterattack early yesterday, they could hear the tenor-voiced Japanese MGs firing at Baker Company at the ledge; but nothing opened up on them. When they reached the beginning of the saddle, sweating and half-dead from the lack of water, Gaff motioned them to stop.

He had to swallow his dry spittle several times before he could speak. It had been arranged with Colonel Tall that the commander of Baker's right platoon would move his men along the ledge to the trough and be ready to charge from there at Gaff's whistle signal, and because of this he unhooked his whistle from his pocket. The saddle was about twenty or twenty-five yards across, and he spaced them out across it. Because of the way it fell the strongpoint below was still invisible from here. "Remember, I want to get as close to them as we can before we put the grenades to them." To Bell's mind, overheated and overwrought, the Captain's phraseology sounded strangely sexual; but Bell knew it could not be. Then Gaff crawled out in front of them, and looked back.

"Well, fellows, this is where we separate the men from the boys," he told them, "the sheep from the goats. Let's crawl." He clamped his whistle in his teeth and cradling his rifle while holding a grenade in one hand, he commenced to do so.

Crawling along behind him, and in spite of his promise of a big beerbust, everything paid for by him, Gaff's volunteers did not take too kindly to his big line. Shit, I could have done better than that myself, Doll thought, spitting out yet another grass seed. Doll had already entirely forgotten his so near escape crossing the open space, and suddenly for no apparent reason he was transfixed by a rage which ranged all through him like some uncontrollable woods fire. Do not fire until you see the red of their assholes, Gridley. You may shit when ready, Gridley. Damn the torpedoes, full crawl ahead. Sighted Japs, grenaded same. There are no atheists in foxholes, Chaplain; *shit* on the *en*emy! He was—for no reason at all, except that he was afraid—so enraged at Gaff that he could have put a grenade to him himself right now, or shot him. On his left, his major competition Charlie Dale crawled along with narrowed eyes still hating all officers anyway and as far as he was concerned Gaff's final line only proved him right. Beyond Dale, Big Un Cash moved his big frame along contemptuously, his rifle still on his back, the fully loaded shotgun cradled in his arms; he had not come along on this thing to be given dumb slogans by no punk kid officers—sheeps and goats my ass, he thought and there was no doubt in his hard hackpusher's mind about which side he would be on when the count came. Witt, beyond Big Un and himself the extreme left flank, had merely spat and settled his thin neck down into his shoulders and set his jaw. He was not here for any crapped up West Point heroics, he was here because he was a brave man and a very good soldier and because his old outfit C-for-Charlie needed him—whether *they* knew it or not; and Gaff could spare him the conversation. Slowly, as they crawled, the extreme left of the strongpoint came into view fifty yards away and about twenty yards below them.

On the extreme right of the little line John Bell was not thinking about young Captain Gaff at all. As soon as Gaff had made his bid for an immortal line Bell had dismissed it as stupid. Bell was thinking, instead, about cuckoldry. Why that subject should come into his mind at a time like this Bell didn't know, but it had and he couldn't get rid of it. Thinking about it seriously, Bell discovered that under serious analysis he could only find four basic situations: sad little husband attacking big strong lover, big strong lover attacking sad little husband, sad little husband attacking big strong wife, big strong wife attacking sad little husband. But always it was a sad little husband. Something about the emotional content of the word automatically shrunk all cuckolded husbands to sad little husbands. Undoubtedly many big strong husbands had been cuckolded in their time. Yes, undoubtedly. But you could never place them in direct connection with the emotional content of the word. This was because the emotional content of the word was essentially funny. Bell imagined himself in all four basic situations. It was very painful, in an exquisitely unpleasant, but very sexual way. And suddenly Bell knew—as well and as surely as he knew he was crawling down this grassy saddle on Guadalcanal—that he was cuckold; that Marty was stepping out, was sleeping with, was fucking, somebody. Given *her* character and *his* absence, there was no other possibility. It was as though it were a thought which had been hanging around the borders of his mind a long time, but which he would never allow in until now. But with one man? or with several? Which did one prefer, the one man which meant a serious love affair? or the several which meant that she was promiscuous? What would he do when he got home? beat her up? kick her around? leave her? Put a goddamned grenade in her bed maybe. Ahead of him the entire strongpoint was visible by now, its nearer, right end only twenty-five yards away, and only a very few yards below their own height now.

And it was just then that they were discovered by the Japanese.

Five scrawny bedraggled Japanese men popped up out of the ground holding dark round objects which they lobbed up the hill at them. Fortunately only one of the five grenades exploded. It lit near Dale who rolled over twice away from it and then lay huddled as close to the ground as he could get, his face turned away. None of its fragments hit him, but it made his ears ring.

"Pull and throw! Pull and throw!" Gaff was yelling at them through the noise of the explosion, and almost as one man their six grenades arched at the strongpoint. The five Japanese men who had popped up out of the ground had by now popped back down into it. But as the grenades lit, two other, unlucky Japanese popped up to throw. One grenade lit between the feet of one of these and exploded up into him, blowing off one of his feet and putting him down. Fragments put the other one down. All of the American grenades exploded.

The Japanese with his foot off lay still a moment then struggled up to sit holding another grenade as the blood poured from his severed leg. Doll shot him. He fell back dropping the ignited grenade beside him. It did not go off.

"Once more! Once more!" Gaff was yelling at them, and again six grenades arched in the air. Again all of them exploded. Doll was a little late getting his away because of the shot, but he got it off just behind the others.

This time there were four Japanese standing when the grenades lit, one of them carrying a light MG. The exploding grenades put three of them down, including the man with the Nambu, and the fourth, thinking better of it, disappeared down a hole. There were now five Japanese down and out of action in the little hollow.

"Go in! Go in!" Gaff cried, and in a moment all of them were on their feet running. No longer did they have to fret and stew, or worry about being brave or being cowardly. Their systems pumped full of adrenaline to constrict the peripheral blood vessels, elevate the blood pressure, make the heart beat more rapidly, and aid coagulation, they were about as near to automatons without courage or cowardice as flesh and blood can get. Numbly, they did the necessary.

The Japanese had shrewdly taken advantage of the terrain to save themselves digging work. Behind the holes into the emplacements themselves was a natural little low area where they could come out and sit in cover when they were not actually being shelled, and it also served as a communication trench between the holes. Now in this hollow the scrawny, bedraggled Japanese rose with rifles, swords and pistols from their holes to meet Gaff and his crew. At least, some of them did. Others stayed in the holes. Three tried to run. Dale shot one and Bell shot another. The third was seen to disappear in a grand broadjump over the edge of the rockface where it fell clear, sixty or eighty feet to the jungle treetops below. He was never seen again and no one ever learned what happened to him. The others came on. And Gaff and his troops, the Captain blowing his whistle shrilly with each exhalation of breath, ran to meet them, in clear view of Baker Company at the ledge until they passed out of sight into the hollow.

Big Un killed five men almost at once. His shotgun blew the first nearly in two and tore enormous chunks out of the second and third. The fourth and fifth, because the gun was bucking itself higher each time he fired, had most of their heads taken off. Swinging the empty shotgun like a baseball bat, Big Un broke the face of a sixth Japanese man just emerging from a hole, then jerked a grenade from his belt, pulled the pin and tossed it down the hole after him into a medley of voices which ceased in the dull roaring boom of the constricted explosion. While he struggled to unsling the rifle from his back, he was attacked by a screaming officer with a sword. Gaff shot the officer in the belly from the hip, shot him again in the face to be positive after he was down. Bell had killed two men. Charlie Dale had killed two. Doll, who had drawn his pistol, was charged by another screaming officer who shouted ''Banzai!'' over and over and who ran at him whirling his bright, gleaming sword around his head in the air. Doll shot him through the chest so that in a strange laughable way his legs kept right on running while the rest of him fell down behind them. Then the torso jerked the legs up too and the man hit the ground flat out with a tremendous whack. Doll shot him a second time in the head. Beyond him Witt had shot three men, one of them a huge fat sergeant wielding a black, prewar U.S. Army cavalry saber. Taking the overhead saber cut on the stock of his rifle, cutting it almost to the barrel, Witt had buttstroked him in the jaw. Now he shot him where he lay. Suddenly there was an enormous quiet except for the wailing chatter of three Japanese standing in a row who had dropped their weapons. There had been, they all realized, a great deal of shouting and screaming, but now there was only the moans of the dying and the hurt. Slowly they looked around at each other and discovered the miraculous fact that none of them was killed, or even seriously damaged. Gaff had a knot on his jaw from firing without cheeking his stock. Bell's helmet had been shot from his head, the round passing through the metal and up and around inside the shell between metal and fiber liner and coming out the back. Bell had an enormous headache. Witt discovered he had splinters in his hand from his busted riflestock, and his arms ached. Dale had a small gash in his shin from the bayonet of a downed and dying Japanese man who had struck at him and whom he subsequently shot. Numbly, they stared at each other. Each had believed devoutly that he would be the only one left alive.

It was clear to everyone that it was Big Un and his shotgun which had won the day, had broken the back of the Japanese fight, and later when they discussed and discussed it, that would remain the consensus. And now in the strange, numb silence— still breathing hard from the fight, as they all were—Big Un, who still had not yet got his rifle unslung, advanced snarling on the three standing Japanese. Taking two by their scrawny necks which his big hands went almost clear around, he shook them back and forth gaggling helplessly until their helmets fell off, then grinning savagely began beating their heads together. The cracking sound their skulls made as they broke was loud in the new, palpable quiet. "Fucking murderers," he told them coldly. "Fucking yellow Jap bastards. Killing helpless prisoners. Fucking murderers. Fucking prisoner killers." When he dropped them as the others simply stood breathing hard and watching, there was no doubt that they were dead, or dying. Blood ran from their noses and their eyes were rolled back white. "That'll teach them to kill prisoners," Big Un announced, glaring at his own guys. He turned to the third, who simply looked at him uncomprehendingly. But Gaff jumped in between them. "We need him. We need him," he said, still gasping and panting. Big Un turned and walked away without a word.

It was then they heard the first shouts from the other side, and remembered they were not the only living. Going to the grassy bank they looked out over and saw the same field they themselves had tried to cross last evening. Coming across it at a run, the platoon from Baker was charging the strongpoint. Back beyond them, in full view from here, the other two platoons of B had left the ledge and were charging uphill, according to Colonel Tall's plan. And below Gaff and his men the first Baker platoon charged on, straight at them, yelling.

Whatever their reason, they were a little late. The fight was already over. Or so everyone thought. Gaff had been blowing his whistle steadily from the moment they first had gone in right up to the end of the fight, and now here came the heroes. Preparing to wave and cheer ironically and hoot derision at their 'rescuers,' Gaff's men were prevented by the sound of a machinegun. Directly below them in one of the apertures, a single MG opened up and began to fire at the Baker Company platoon. As Gaff's men watched incredulously, two Baker Company men went down. Charlie Dale, who was standing nearest to the door of the embrasure which was firing, leaped over with a shocked look on his face and threw a grenade down the hole. The grenade immediately came flying right back out. With strangled yells everyone hit the dirt. Fortunately, the grenade had been thrown too hard and it exploded just as it fell over the lip of the rockface, where the broadjumping Japanese had also disappeared, hurting nobody. The MG below continued to fire.

"Look out, you jerk!" Witt cried at Dale, and scrambled to his feet. Pulling the pin on a grenade and holding it with the lever depressed, he grabbed his rifle and ran over to the hole. Leaning around the right side of it, holding his rifle like a pistol in his left hand with the stock pressed against his leg, he began to fire the semi-automatic Garand into the hole. There was a yell from below. Still firing, Witt popped the grenade down the hole and ducked back. He continued to fire to confuse the occupants. Then the grenade blew up with a dull staggering roar, cutting off both the scrabble of yells and the MG, which had never stopped firing.

Immediately, others of the little force, without any necessity of orders from Gaff, began bombing out the other four holes using Witt's technique. They bombed them all, whether there was anyone in them or not. Then they called to the Baker Company platoon to come on. Later, four Japanese corpses were found huddled up or stretched out, according to their temperaments, in the small space Witt had bombed. Death had come for them and they had met it, if not particularly bravely, at least with a sense of the inevitable.

So the fight for the strongpoint was over. And without exception something new had happened to all of them. It was apparent in the smiling faces of the Baker Company platoon as they climbed up over the emplacement leaving five of their guys behind them in the kunai grass. It was apparent in the grinning face of Colonel Tall as he came striding along behind them, bamboo baton in hand. It showed in the savage happiness with which Gaff's group bombed out the empty bunkers using Witt's safety technique: one man firing while another tossed the grenades. Nobody really cared whether there was anyone in them or not. But they hoped there were hundreds. There was a joyous feeling in the safety of killing. They slapped each other on the back and grinned at each other murderously. They had finally, as Colonel Tall was later to tell newsmen and correspondents when they interviewed him, been blooded. They had, as Colonel Tall was later to say, tasted victory. They had become fighting men. They had learned that the enemy, like themselves, was killable; was defeatable.

This feeling had an enormous effect on everyone. It was evident in the other two Baker Company platoons in the way they were now pushing their attack uphill, as Colonel Tall pointed out when he came striding and grinning up to congratulate Captain Gaff.

"Look at them move!" he said from the top of the embankment after they had shaken hands. "And we owe it all to you, John. When they saw you make that attack of yours, and win! It was like you had put their hearts back into them. Well, let's have a look around here, now."

There were, it was discovered after a full count, twenty-three Japanese down on the ground of the little hollow. They lay scattered around in various positions and postures. Of these five had been knocked out by the grenade shower and two had been shot trying to run. Of the twenty-three most were dead, several were still in process of dying, and a few though badly hurt looked as if they might live. To Gaff and his group, following the Colonel around, it seemed that the number should be considerably higher. They seemed to remember hundreds. But in discussing it it was found that at least four Japanese had been 'killed' twice by different men. Even so it was a goodly number. Especially when one remembered they were only six in the attacking force, and once again the miracle that none of them were killed seemed incredible. Partly this was because the Japanese had come out in uncoordinated small groups. But mostly, once again, it was attributed to Big Un and his shotgun, not only for having killed five men so quickly but also for the obvious shock value it had had upon the rest of the Japanese. Big Un himself did not take—as yet—any pleasure in this new fame, although the men from the B Company platoon watched him with heroworshiping eyes. He prowled back and forth and around the single remaining prisoner like a loose wolf trying to get at a caged victim. His shotgun was broken, but now he had his rifle unslung. He appeared to be waiting hopefully for the Japanese to make any move for which he could kill him legitimately.

The prisoner himself looked as though he were not capable of escaping anywhere, even if there had been no one around to watch him. Filthy and emaciated, he had a bad case of dysentery and was continually indicating to his Baker Company guards that he had to relieve himself. This he did through a system of signs and pantomime. Then he would squat beside his two dead companions and strain his miserable bowels, all the time eyeing Big Un. He had already messed his pants a couple of times apparently, during the fighting when he could not go outside, and he stank so badly he could be smelled a couple of yards away. All in all he was a pretty sorry spectacle.

However, if anything about this sorry specimen moved Big Un, Big Un did not show it in his tough, mean face. Neither did anybody else, including Colonel Tall—although Tall immediately marked the peculiarity of the two dead prisoners.

It was easy enough to see. They lay side by side forming, with the third, still-living one, a little line quite apart from the rest. Their two helmets lay just beside them, and except for the blood running from their noses they showed no signs of injury or wounds.

"What happened here?" Tall murmured to Gaff. He had already turned away in disgust from the smelly, still-living one.

Gaff only raised his eyebrows, as if he didn't know either. He did not want actually to lie to the old boss, but neither did he want to rat on his gang. He had acquired an intense loyalty for them which almost brought tears to his eyes when he thought of it.

Tall turned back to the dead ones. They were about as sorry-looking, and as smelly, as the live one. He could read well enough what had happened, but he could not understand the method. They should have had their heads bashed in, or been bayoneted, or shot. He didn't like this sort of thing, but on the other hand one had to make allowances for men in the heat of combat. But how had it been done? "Some sort of explosive concussion?" he said to Gaff; "but there aren't any fragment wounds." He had not expected Gaff to answer, and Gaff didn't; he shrugged. "Well," Tall said smiling and loud enough to be heard all around, "a dead brown brother is one brown brother less, isn't it?" Eventually the real story of how it happened would get back to him anyway, he was sure of that.

"Take good care of that one, men!" he called to the Baker Company guards. "G-2 will want him. There should be someone around before long."

"Aye, aye, Sir, yeah," one of them grinned; "we'll take care of him." With his rifle muzzle he reached out and poked the prisoner, who was squatting and crapping again, and tipped him over backward into his own mess. The men around all laughed, and the prisoner scrambled back to his feet and began to try patiently to clean himself with handfuls of grass. He appeared to expect this kind of treatment and looked as if he were only putting in time, waiting for them to shoot him. Tall turned away again. He had not meant to cause that reaction, but the Baker Company man (really hardly more than a boy really) had, because of his remark about dead brown brothers, misinterpreted him. He walked away followed by Gaff. Across the hollow a Baker Company man had just finished kicking one of the wounded Japanese resoundingly in the ribs. It sounded as though someone had just punted a football out of the hollow down the hill. The wounded Japanese man simply stared back at him with acquiescent, pain-dulled, animal eyes.

"Don't do that, Soldier!" Tall called at him sharply.

"Okay, Colonel, Sir, if you say so, Sir," the man answered cheerfully. "But he would of killed me in a minute if he'd had the chance."

Tall knew that was true enough and he did not answer. Anyway, he did not want to jeopardize the new toughness of spirit which had come over the men after achieving success here. That spirit was more important than whether or not a few Jap prisoners got kicked around, or killed.

"I think we've wasted about enough time here," he said loudly, with a grin for the men.

"Sir," Gaff said tentatively from behind him, and Tall turned around. "Sir, I've got a few recommendations for decorations I'd like to turn in to you."

"Yes, yes," Tall grinned. "Of course. We'll get everything for all of them that we can. But later. In the meantime I want you to know I'm personally recommending you for something, John. Perhaps," he said and leaning forward, took Gaff lightly by his lapel to whisper: "Perhaps even—the Big One."

"Well, thank you, Sir. But I dont feel I really deserve that."

"Oh yes you do. However, *getting* it for you will be another problem. But it would be a big thing for the Battalion, and for Regiment too, if you did get it." He let go the lapel and straightened. "But in the meantime, I think we better get moving out of here. I think the best way to proceed is to move right back up the saddle you came down, rather than trying to circle the knob on the left. From the top we can debouch out and extend our line left to hook up with the other platoons. Would you like to take command?"

"Yes, Sir."

"Get Lieutenant Achs, then. He's around here somewhere."

"Sir," Gaff said hesitantly; "I dont like to sound depressing or be a wet blanket or anything like that, but what about water? If we dont—"

"Dont worry about water!" Tall said sharply, but then he smiled. "John, I dont want anything to break up this attack of ours, now that we've got it started. As for water, I've already taken care of that. We'll have *some* water by—" he looked at his watch, and then at the sky—"in a couple of hours. I've arranged for that. But we can't stop now to wait for it."

"No, Sir."

"If some of the men pass out, they'll just have to pass out," Tall said.

"Yes, Sir."

"If any of them ask you about water, tell them what I said. But dont bring it up yourself. Dont mention it unless they ask you."

"No, Sir. But they could die from it, you know. From heat prostration."

"They could die from enemy fire, too," Tall said. He looked around himself, at them. "They're all tough boys." He looked back at Gaff. "Okay? Now, come on."

Together with the lieutenant, Achs, from Baker Company, they began to round up the men who were still staring curiously at the various dead Japanese. "You'll see plenty more of those," Tall told them. "At least I hope you will. Come on." Most of the dead men's equipment, he noted, had already been appropriated for souvenirs, along with their wallets and the contents of their pockets, and two of Gaff's volunteers—Doll and Cash—now carried the sheathed 'Samurai sabers' of the two officers. Tall would have liked one of those himself, but he had no time to think about that now. There was too much else to occupy him at the moment. Tall was more worried about the lack of water than he had let Gaff know. It was all very well to say some of the men might have to pass out, or even die, from heat prostration. But if enough of them passed out, he was going to be left without an attack. No matter how much spirit and heart they had recently acquired, or what he himself might do. They were going to have to have some water, and he had done the only thing about it that he knew to do.

An hour before—back when Gaff and his group were making their crawl—Tall had sent out another patrol. Only, the irony of this patrol was that it had gone rearward. Looking for water. Because both sound powers were cut, he had intended to send back a runner to tell them the water situation was reaching critical. But because he had sent back at least two runners yesterday, and had telephoned again and again, all of it the same message, the idea had come to him to send a 'patrol' instead. And once the patrol idea was in his mind, he decided to go ahead with it and carry it through all the way. He sent his own personal Battalion Hq sergeant and all three of his runners he had left, all of whom carried pistols, of course. Their orders were to proceed rearward as far as they had to go to find water and bring it back with them. They were not even to report in to the Regimental Commander. They were to cross the ridge of Hill 209 away from the command post and travel rearward along the basin until they found people with water and when they found it they were to take it, at gunpoint if necessary. Each man could carry two full jerrycans, Tall decided; that would be hard on them, but under the circumstances they would have to do it. They were to proceed back as fast as their strength would let them, resting only when they had to. If anyone tried to take any water from them, they were to fight for it. These were harsh orders. And the cruel irony which had forced him to send an armed patrol to the rear into his own lines all ready to fight, was not lost upon Tall's sense of propriety. But he had to do it. Anyway, he did not think it would ever come to the actual shooting point; nobody back there was going to argue with his boys once they drew their pistols; but even if it did go to the shooting point he did not intend to lose everything now. He was convinced the Japanese position was now broken. All they had to do was keep going and they would have Hill 210 by noon. And the remarkable spirit which had ballooned in everybody when the strongpoint fell had to be taken advantage of before some other event occurred to sap its strength. To have his battalion relieved in defeat now, or even to have them reenforced by troops from the reserve regiment if they stalled before reaching the top, was more than Tall could support unless he was absolutely forced to. This was a chance Tall had waited for all his professional life. He had studied, and worked, and slaved, and eaten untold buckets of shit, to have this opportunity. He did not intend to lose it now, not if he could help it. He only hoped that C-for-Charlie was proceeding according to schedule also, and that Stein would not chicken out on him now, and the thinking of this thought, and worrying suddenly about them now, gave him a sudden new idea. An inspiration almost, even.

"I want a runner!" he called out suddenly to the assembling men. It would be, he thought immediately, better to send them one of their own, and he turned in mid-stride and addressed himself to the Charlie Company volunteers who, having no assigned stations with the Baker Company platoon, were all hanging around their new paternal hero, Captain John Gaff.

"I want one of you men to make your way back to C Company. It—"

"I'll go, Sir!" Witt said immediately. "I want to go! Let me go, Sir!"

"It will be a tough job. You'll have to go back over the third fold and make your way to the jungle and then follow them from there," Tall said. "But I think it's very important. I want them to know what we've accomplished here. Tell them everything we've done. The strongpoint is taken. And we're moving uphill and nothing's stopping us. We're going all the way. And we want them to meet us there."

"Aye, aye, Sir!" Witt said. "I can do it. Dont worry about me, Colonel."

"I think you can, son," Colonel Tall said and patted him on the back. "I know they haven't got any water. But, by God! tell them when they meet us we'll have all the goddamned water they can drink for them!"

"Aye, Sir!" Witt cried.

Tall saw John Gaff looking at him with astonished, disbelieving eyes. Tall stared back at him with a flat gaze until Gaff remembered himself and disguised his face. But Tall daren't have winked. "All they can drink," he repeated solemnly, and now stared Witt in the eyes. "Okay. That's all, son," he said. "Go."

Witt did, loping.

"Now, you men!" Tall said. "Are we going up this hill, or aren't we?"

The speed and power with which they moved was more than even Tall had hoped for. Within ten minutes and only two casualties they had hooked up with the other two platoons of B and the whole line was bowling along uphill as Tall earlier had hoped it would be yesterday. The Japanese they found in the various emplacements which they were forced to take, and which literally honeycombed the ridge, were almost without exception the same starved-looking, sick, emaciated types they had found at the strongpoint; only now and then did they find one or two like the fat sergeant Witt had killed who looked fresh and healthy. None survived. They found the Japanese themselves had very little water either, and the water they did have the Americans were afraid to drink because of the lack of proper sanitation.

The water, when it finally came, came much sooner than Tall had expected. Even so, it appeared to arrive in the last possible moment before complete collapse. B Company plus Gaff and volunteers had stalled just a hundred yards short of the end of the ridge, where three widely dispersed single MGs (the like of which they had already taken easily many times today) held up the entire line. And it was impossible to make them move. More and more men were passing out, fainting in the dry dusty morning sun heat. Tall had first planned to set up his CP on top the knob above the

former strongpoint, and did do it. But the speed with which the
line moved on soon forced him to move if he wanted to see and
direct anything. Wounded were left where they fell. And the dead,
about whom nobody could do anything anyway, were too. With
only two privates to assist him as runners Tall moved forward to
the vicinity of the big rock outcrop from which the little Japanese
counterattack had come yesterday. And it was from this vantage
point that he saw his water 'patrol' approaching with their jerrycans. Motioning for haste, he descended himself with his two
privates to help carry. His Hq sergeant and three runners were
almost unconscious with exhaustion and the climb. They had only
had to draw their pistols once, which was when they actually took
the water; nobody argued with them. Tall cajoled them, wheedled
them, personally helped carry. Somehow, they arrived. The water
was kept in comparative safety behind the rock outcrop, and the
men came back in shifts. After a half a canteen cup of water at
the outcrop and a ten minute rest on the line, three separate
groups took the three machineguns with only five or six casualties, and they moved on. Once again his line, his own private,
living, loving line was moving. If he didn't get an eagle and a
regiment out of this by damn, nobody would ever get one. If only
C-for-Charlie and Bugger Stein as his men liked to call him were
fulfilling their part of the plan.

At first Tall had kept back four of the eight full cans. Then he
had withheld two. He had not forgotten his promise to Charlie
Company, but finally he was down to one can. Trembling, shaky
men sloshed water over the edges of the cups in trying to pour for
each other. In the enormous excitement many men got more than
just a half a cup, many got full ones and overfull ones. In the end
the eighth can went, too. Tall was sorry that he would have no
water for Charlie when they met them at the top of the hill, truly
sorry, but today there was something that was more important,
counted more than water, and that was victory.

In spite of that, Tall did everything he could for them, little
help though it probably would be. "Sergeant James," he told his
beaten Hq sergeant as the line moved forward over the demolished MGs, and he himself prepared to move forward in their

wake. "Sergeant James, I have a further sacrifice to ask of you. I want you to go back once more." Sergeant James appeared to groan though it was actually inaudible, but Tall went on. "You know the Regimental Commander pretty well. I want you to go back to the CP on Hill 209 and attach yourself to him. I want you to make it plain to him how badly we need water up here. Don't let him out of your sight. Stay with him every minute. Remind him of it all the time. If any general officers are there, or should any general officers come around, so much the better. That's the time to tell him the loudest. But I want him to know how badly we need water. I want water at the top of Hill 210 at the same time we get there, or failing that as soon after as possible. I want the Regimental Commander to know that even if we take it, we may not be able to hold it without water."

As he continued to talk, his sergeant's face had changed from a groaning look to a surprised smile, and finally to an open grin: He was going to get to spend the next few very important hours haranguing the Regimental Commander in appreciably greater physical safety than existed here. He would have to be a little careful, because the Old Man could be ornery, but James knew the Great White Father's idiosyncrasies pretty well and was sure he could take care of himself, as Tall well knew.

"Well, it's a hard job, Sir, but I'll do the best I can," the sergeant grinned.

Tall watched him walk away. Then he turned back to his runners and private soldier aides. He had to pick out a site for a new CP further up. He had done the best he could for C-for-Charlie. He only hoped they were doing the best they could for him.

C-for-Charlie Company in the fact had no need of Colonel Tall's solicitude. They did not even have need of the runner Witt he had sent after them to pep them up. They had had a little firefight of their own, in which they demolished a four-man heavy MG outpost with only one casualty, and they were moving along quite well. Whether some of the excitement of the fight on the hill had seeped down to them through the humid air, whether the mere survival of yesterday had stiffened them into veterans, whether the progressive numbness they all felt had finally sub-

merged their fear, whether their own successful little firefight had
sparked them to enthusiasm, they now passed along the ample
trail with alacrity and dispatch. After the firefight they left the
wounded scout, who was not too upset by this, alone along the
trail where Witt later found him. Although they had no water, it
was shady in the jungle, not like the fierce dusty heat on the
ridge; and in that murky humidity it seemed that their dehydrated
bodies actually sucked in moisture through their pores out of the
air, even while they sweated. Witt, as he trailed cautiously along
behind them, discovered the same unexpected relief.

Witt had sustained the powerful emotion of his leavetaking
from Colonel Tall. All across the long traverse from the old position on the third fold to the jungle's edge, he kept thinking with
fierce sentiment about what great, wonderful guys they all were.
The Colonel, Captain Gaff who was not too high-toned to treat an
EM like an equal, Bell, Doll, Dale, Big Un, Keck (now dead),
Skinny Culn. The truth was Witt had never really much liked
Colonel Tall until today. A cold fisheye of an intellectual text-
book soldier, had been Witt's opinion. But now he had to admit
he had been wrong. As far as Witt was concerned the most important qualification of an officer was whether he really had the
interests of his men at heart, and Tall had proved that today. The
truth was, Witt loved them all, passionately, with an almost sexual ecstasy of comradeship. Even Bugger Stein and Welsh came
under the magnanimous aura of his warm affection today. As well
as everybody else in *the company*. Which was why he had volunteered just now to go back to them: perhaps his experience and
knowledge could help, and he could save somebody. These were
his thoughts all the way across the traverse from the third fold and
it was only afterwards, after he had entered the jungle and found
the trail, that he had any second thoughts and first doubts about
the matter.

He had followed them in from the edge easily enough by the
trampled swath of undergrowth they had chopped down or walked
over, but at the trail the swath stopped. He had checked all around
to make sure. This left him two choices, right or left along the
trail, and certainly they would not have turned right away from

Hill 210. So he had struck off left along the trail confidently, if cautiously. The green gloom under the tall jungle giants was eerie. His feet slipped in the mud. He had not known what he expected to find, but he supposed it was that they would be dug in along here somewhere, engaged in a firefight trying to force their way to the hill. Instead, all he heard was silence punctuated by rustles and crackles and the whistles of them crazy birds. Setting his jaw against the nervous chill which crept up his back, he moved along with his rifle ready and it was then that his first doubt hit him. He remembered that Bugger Stein had wanted to come down here yesterday on the theory that this spot was undefended, and that Colonel Tall had refused. His doubts were reenforced when he met the wounded 3d Platoon scout, a man named Ash, who grinned at him from the side of the trail.

"I'd of had you, Kaintuck, if you was a Jap—long ago!"

"They leave you here?"

"I would of slowed them up. I dont really mind. Medic fixed me up before they left. I got plenty of ammo and Welsh left me his pistol. They'll be somebody along for me evenshully." He seemed about three-fourths drunk from shock, morphine and the pain of his bandaged wound, which he displayed for Witt. "Right in the knee. I'm out of this war for good, I think, Witt. But what the hell're *you* doin down here?"

Witt explained about his message, and about the water.

"That's good," Ash said. "But they better hurry if they want to beat old C-for-Charlie."

"How's the company doin, you think?"

"Fine! I aint heard a shot fired since they left here. I dont think there's anything back in here except that one heavy MG we got up the way, which you will see when you pass it. And we owe it all to old Bugger Stein. He wanted to bring us back down around here yesterday. If he had of, we'd of saved ourselves a lot of good men."

"I know."

"Well, give all them boys my best up there."

"You can come with me if you want. I'll help you along."

"Nah, it's nice and quiet and peaceful here. Anyway I'd slow you up. Somebody'll be along for me."

"I'll remind them."

"Okay," Ash said drunkenly.

Witt left him not feeling much about him one way or the other. It was just one of them things that happened to guys. He passed the destroyed machinegun and its four dead Japanese, who looked more like bundles of dirty old rags than dead people. But then they all did, including your own side, unless it was a face you happened to know personally. He kicked the helmeted head of one who lay half out in the path, and the head rolled back and forth. At the first bend of the trail he turned back and waved. Ash did not see him because he was grinning drunkenly at the trees across the trail. He would die, C-for-Charlie would find out a long time later, of gangrene after a year in a General Hospital and a series of successive amputations which did not arrest the infection.

After the second bend the trail began to mount noticeably uphill as it curved away and around to the right. Cutting around back of Hill 210, the Elephant's Head, to meet the open rising ground of the Elephant's Trunk, Witt decided. The escape route. He trudged on, occasionally slipping in the slanting mud, keeping his eyes out for snipers in the trees. But he saw nothing, nothing at all. There was nobody anywhere, and he could not help thinking again of Colonel Tall and yesterday. Ash had said it pretty well: If Bugger had of brought them down here yesterday, they'd of saved themselves a lot of good men. Men like Keck, men like Tella, men like Grove, and Wynn, and his old buddy Catch, and Bead, and Earl. Not a one of whom Witt had been able to save. And why was that? After all his big talk to himself? Hell, he couldn't be everyplace at once! What did Tall and those others expect of him? He couldn't do it all, could he? Not to mention them two punk lieutenants dead. A deep, angry bitterness filled Witt at the impossibility of even his experience and knowledge being able to handle such a snafu operation. It was a bitterness so deep and so angry that it was totally inarticulate even inside his own head in his thoughts. And its object was Colonel Tall. He was ashamed of the bullshit he had eaten from the hand of Tall so short a time ago, embarrassed by the emotion he had felt crossing the traverse, and this made him even angrier. If it wasn't for Bugger Stein, whom he had once disliked but had changed his mind about, he would for two cents after delivering his message turn right around and walk back to Hill 209 and report back in to Cannon Company. He was free, white and twenty-one and from Kentucky, and he didn't have to take this shit. This was his state of mind when he finally came upon the rear guard of C-for-Charlie, and it was a strange experience to find himself suddenly once again—as he had just been before—among so many enthusiastic men.

Everyone Witt talked to felt the same thing: it was a shame Bugger had not been allowed to bring them down here yesterday. But none of them, apparently, took it quite as seriously as Witt. And anyway, nothing could disrupt their enthusiasm for their new position.

Stein had placed them in three lines across the open space of The Elephant's Trunk, and they were now in the process of beginning to move up it. 3d Platoon who had suffered the least yesterday had the first line, 1st Platoon had the second, and 2d Platoon which had suffered most had the third. Behind them was the Company Hq with MacTae and Storm and his cooks, and last was the little rear guard Witt had encountered first. So far they had received no fire, and everyone looked elated. They had outflanked the enemy with scarcely a shot and entered his rear, and now they sat athwart his escape route. For the first time they had something like the upper hand, and they did not mean to let go of it.

Down below, the long skinny ridge which everybody now referred to simply as "The Trunk" had gentle side slopes, allowing the jungle to encroach more deeply on the open ridge; but up above the side slopes steepened, forcing the jungle back and widening the open space in the center. The whole thing was about two hundred and fifty yards long. A little over halfway up the side slopes steepened until they became impassable to troops, and Stein had made this his first objective. A line here, with both ends anchored on cliffs, could not be outflanked by fleeing Japanese. It could even be dug in and defended, once it was reached. And Stein's forward 3d Platoon reached it without firing a shot, at about the same time Witt came up with his message. The second line composed of the 1st Platoon was fifty yards behind them. All this in itself seemed incredible to Stein: apparently the Japanese had no outposts up there at all. From here he could see his own men when they were standing up, and standing himself he waved them on furiously. He watched 3d Platoon rush forward another twenty-five or thirty yards and 1st Platoon move up to take over their position. All of them disappeared in the grass. Not far in front of Stein his battered tough old, and now favorite, 2d Platoon kneeled formed in two staggered lines so each man could fire, commanded by Buck Sergeant Beck the old martinet, and now Stein motioned them forward to close up the gap. One more such move would put 3d Platoon over the top, and he wanted the other two to be as close as they could to give aid. He loved them all, he thought suddenly, all of them, even the ones he didn't much like. No man ought to have to go through an experience like this—not even the ones who enjoyed it. It wasn't normal. Or was it that it was just too *goddam* fucking normal? He watched 2d Platoon run up bent over at the waist in that ridiculous posture which gave a sense of security but aided nobody. Thirty yards behind 1st Platoon they disappeared in the grass, and he sank back down himself to find Witt kneeling beside him.

When he had delivered his message about the strongpoint and the water Stein nodded, debating whether to send a runner up with the news; it ought to provide added incentive, especially about the water. His tongue felt like sandpaper on the roof of his mouth. He himself had not had any water since—? he could not remember. Deciding in favor, he motioned for the last of his little clerks, the middle-aged draftee Weld, and sent him forward with the information and orders to 1st and 2d Platoons to move up behind the 3d to a distance of twenty yards. When the 3d moved, they were both to move forward and occupy the vacated positions. If 3d was not stopped, they were to move forward again and join it. Then he turned to Witt and grinned out of his dirt-blackened, stubbled face. "It looks like we're in luck today, Witt."

Witt could have thrown his arms around his commander and kissed him on his dirt-crusted, stubbled cheek in an ecstasy of loving comradeship. Except that it might have looked faggoty, or get taken the wrong way. Emotions were coursing through Witt today that he had never known existed in him in his life. He was, he found strangely enough, really very happy.

"How did it go with the strongpoint?" Stein asked him. He had some minutes to wait anyway.

Witt told him a little bit about it, about Big Un Cash and his shotgun—and about his own big fat Jap sergeant, shyly. He showed him his rifle.

"How many did they get altogether?"

"About thirty-five," Witt said, batting his lashes in a shy, abashed embarrassment he could not control.

"Thirty-five!"

"But more than ten of those was bombed out in the bunkers. Seven was knocked out beforehand, and Big Un got six with his shotgun. That only left around nine. I only got three myself."

"Pretty damn good job. Okay, why dont you stay here with us and have yourself a rest?"

"I ruther be with the company, Sir," Witt said, then added hastily: "I mean, you know, with the platoons. I always feel like maybe I could help somebody, you know? Maybe *save* somebody." It was the first time he had ever told anyone his secret.

Stein stared at him quizzically, and Witt cursed himself. He had learned long ago in his life never to tell anybody anything about what he really felt, what had made him do it now? Stein shrugged. "Okay. Report to Beck then. He needs noncoms badly. Tell him I just appointed you Acting Sergeant."

"But I'm not even in the compny, Sir, officially."

"We'll worry about all that later."

"Aye, Sir." Witt crawled away.

"If you hurry," Stein called softly, "you can get there before we start. I won't signal for a couple of minutes." Motioning to the Hq and the rearguard, he moved them forward.

But he never did signal. Before he could, they had been discovered. But they were discovered in the most delicious way any infantryman ever can be. A party of fourteen or fifteen unprepared Japanese, all packing portions of dismantled heavy mortars they were carrying to the rear and safety, came over the crest. Needless to say, none of them survived. 3d Platoon took them from right, left and center. Stein was on his feet as soon as the first shot was fired and saw most of them go down.

They had left all of their weapons platoon back with Colonel Tall except for one machinegun. Stein had placed it on the extreme left flank of the 3d Platoon in the first line with orders to fire when they heard him blow four short blasts on his whistle. Now, with his lungs crammed full of air, his mouth open, his head pushed back and his whistle moving in his hand to his mouth, he heard the MG open up, anticipating him. He exhaled, and watched them put a covering fire down all along the crest, which was much less a sharp line from where they crouched than from where he watched, as 3d Platoon led by Al Gore leaped to its feet and rushed the crest. It was almost exactly like the G Company charge against the crest of Hill 209 which Stein had witnessed from the basin, and for an insane moment Stein thought he was back there and that none of all this had happened yet. He had to blink his eyes to bring himself out of it. But this wasn't G Company's charge against Hill 209, these were his men, this his company, and also this charge was, apparently, successful. His MG was answered only by a very weak scattering of riflefire. It continued to fire until to go on would endanger 3d Platoon, then Stein saw its crew—without any orders or suggestions from him—pick it up and run it up over the crest. Two men carried the gun on its tripod and the other two staggered along behind with all the ammo boxes. It disappeared over the crest. 3d Platoon disappeared over the crest. The MG began firing again. 1st Platoon was moving up to replace the 3d. 2d Platoon was moving up to replace the 1st. "Go on! Go on!" Stein heard his own voice bellowing. "Dont stop now!" He knew nobody could hear him but he could not stop it, and he could not stop waving his arms. Nevertheless, almost as if they actually could hear him, 1st Platoon led by S/Sgt Skinny Culn hesitated only a moment at 3d Platoon's old position, then themselves charged on up and disappeared over the crest, from which was now coming the sound of a great amount of American smallarms fire and very little of the Japanese. "Hot damn! Hot damn!" Stein kept yelling over and over. 2d Platoon, much farther down the slope, was still toiling toward the 1st Platoon's old position where the impassable side slopes began, and Stein suddenly realized that he did not want them to go over the crest, too.

"Come on! Come on!" he yelled at the men around him. "We got to get up there!" And he started off through the grass running.

At just that moment something which sounded like a Japanese grenade, but which must have been one of the smaller knee mortars, exploded among the dispersed Hq group. Except for Stein almost everyone hit the dirt, but Stein ran on. He stopped long enough to turn around and bellow at them insanely, waving his arms, then went on running. No more of the objects fell, and slowly the others got up. Only one of them had been hurt by it, and this was Storm the mess sergeant. A tiny fragment not much bigger than a pinhead had entered the back of his left hand between the fingerbones but had not come out on the other side. Storm stared at the little blue-rimmed hole which was not bleeding, flexed his hand and heard something grate, then ran numbly on after the others beyond whom Stein was already thirty yards in the lead. Storm could not associate the puncture with the explosion. They didn't seem to have anything to do with each other. Grimly he ran to catch up. Everything everywhere seemed to be ungovernable chaos with the firing, the shouts and the breathless running.

Stein had moved the Hq and rearguard up to within forty yards of 2d Platoon before the action started so abruptly. Even so, he would never know how an essentially puny, windless man like himself made it to them, but he did. A few yards beyond 1st Platoon's old position he caught them, ran right on through them and out in front. Bracing himself he turned, his arms spread wide and his carbine clutched at the balance in one hand.

"Hold it! Hold it!" he sobbed. When they had stopped, he shouted back down to the Hq and rearguard being led on by

George Band and Sergeant Welsh. "Keep your distance! Keep your distance! Twenty yards! Form a line there!"

When they were all stopped and into position, he assumed command himself and led them forward to within twenty yards of the crest. He did not want his reserve rushing pellmell and disorganized over that crest until he knew what was going on, until he knew whether he would have to hold them back to cover a retreat. The sound of the firing had become somewhat muffled, as if the shooters had moved on some distance, and its volume had diminished. There seemed very little of the sharper crackle of the Japanese weapons. Stein advanced alone by himself until he could see over the crest. What he saw was a scene which would stay with him the rest of his life.

His two bloodthirsty platoons had burst into what was clearly a bivouac area. The tall jungle trees, by whatever logic of their own, had climbed up out of the gulches and established themselves here on this crest. These were the trees which had been visible from the low area before the ridge all day yesterday. The Japanese had cleared out all the small trees and undergrowth so that what was taking place here now was taking place in the cool-looking sundappled shade of the big trees as though in some park. The only thing that was not like a park was the gluey mud which was everywhere on the ground. In this pretty, natural setting Stein's two platoons in small disorganized groups were shooting and killing Japanese in what appeared to be carload lots. Stein saw one group pass a sicklooking Japanese man standing unarmed with his hands in the air, whereupon, as soon as they had passed, the Japanese lowered his arms and reached inside his shirt for something. A man in another group ten yards away shot him immediately. As he fell, the unignited grenade rolled from his hand. Stein saw another man (it looked like Big Queen but he couldn't be sure) advance upon a Japanese man who was grinning desperately with his hands high in the air, push his rifle which carried no bayonet to within an inch of the grinning face and shoot him in the nose. Stein could not help laughing. Especially at the thought of those widened eyes slowly crossing themselves in despair as they focused on the advancing muzzle. Harold

Lloyd. There were no tents visible, but there were surface shelters of branches and sticks which the Japanese had made themselves, and there were underground dugouts. The first were being shot to pieces or knocked apart with riflebutts. The underground shelters were being bombed out with grenades. Stein saw at a glance there would be no way of getting these men organized for quite some time. On the other hand they were not in any major danger requiring his reserve. They had the upper hand, and they were exercising it. A crazy sort of blood lust, like some sort of declared school holiday from all moral ethics, had descended on them. They could kill with impunity and they were doing it. The sweating terrors and suffering of yesterday, the enthusiasm over their undetected advance from the rear, the massacre of the fifteen unprepared Japanese at the crest, all had contributed to their ebullient mood and there was no stopping them till they wore it out—even if it would be safe to do so, which Stein didn't think it was because of the possibility of counterattack. This was not to say that there were not some of them being killed and wounded by the Japanese. There were, and not just a few. But the others, those who were not killed or wounded, didn't give a good goddamn about that.

Off to the left of this disorganized scene was the only bit of sensible organization Stein could see. His one machinegun which he had seen get run up over the crest was set up to cover the horseshoe-shaped forward slope which composed the left flank and rear of his two platoons as they worked their way right around the curving crest. Several thoughtful riflemen had foregone the shooting jamboree to place themselves as cover guards for the MG. All of them were now firing forward downhill whenever any of the Japanese in the forward positions attempted to come back to help their friends, and while there were not many of these Stein nevertheless saw immediately where an organized platoon could be of great service. Because it was down this way that Colonel Tall and B Company were still fighting their way up from the ridge. Immediately Stein turned to go back over the crest and get them moving. As he did so, he was nearly knocked down by a bull-roaring figure which slammed past him from the killing fest on the right, bent to seize the rifle and bandoliers of a dead compatriot—(Pfc Polack Fronk the dead one was, of his 3d Platoon, Stein realized vaguely)—and then went huge-chested and still roaring back into the melee. Big Queen, of course. There was blood dripping from the biceps of his huge left arm in the torn shirt. A khaki GI handkerchief had been knotted around it. Stein went on.

It was indeed Big Queen whom Stein had seen shoot the grinning Japanese in the nose. That had been his seventh. A few seconds after that his rifle had jammed itself irretrievably. Quite apart from the fact that it was exceedingly dangerous to go on fighting in this kind of a fight with a rifle that wouldn't shoot, it infuriated Queen beyond speech to think of being left out of the fun at this late date, and he had run rearward hunting the first loose rifle he could find. He was, Queen realized happily, quite a sight: a blood-dripping mad roaring bull, and he knew he made quite a picture. All this was because a delicious thing had happened to Queen today. He had discovered that, after all, he was not a coward. All day yesterday he had lain in that fucking US-made shellhole under the mortars, completely unnerved and terrorstricken into helplessnes. He had lain there like that until Captain Gaff had come down to order 1st Platoon over to the ridge. He had even, he thought with shame, ordered Doll to stay put and not carry his message back to Stein. What if Doll ever told anybody about that? But, big, strong and tough or not, that was what Queen had done. Because being big, strong and tough could not help you with enemy mortars. For that something else was required. And Queen had found that he did not have it. He had been reduced again to essentially the same puniness he had suffered from all during his early childhood when every kid in the neighborhood could beat him up if they could only catch him. He was sure, after he got his growth, that nothing like that could ever happen to him again, and so all day yesterday had become a horrible, unspeakable nightmare. He had hardly spoken a word to anybody since, except when necessary, to hide what he really felt.

But today all that had gone away. The compounded excitement of the secret march to the Japanese rear, the successful reduction

of the MG on the trail, plus the undiscovered move up to the top
of The Trunk, and then the joyous wholesale destruction of the
startled Japanese mortar carriers, had created an elation in him
which allowed him to move his body as easy as anything. And
with the others, running the last few yards to the top of the crest,
he hadn't been scared at all. He had led his squad with abandon.
And when he burst over into the disorganized bivouac area and
saw what was going on there, he knew with a savage joy that
*some*body was going to *pay* for what the fuckers had done to him.
The reason there was no bayonet on his rifle was because he had
forgotten it in the excitement. But after watching two men get
shot while trying to extricate their bayonets from the filthy
squirming bastards stuck on them, he decided it was better not to
have one anyway. He had been hit within almost the first fifteen
seconds after cresting the ridge. It hadn't hurt him at all. The
bullet had passed through the fleshy part of his upper arm, leaving a clean hole. He knotted a handkerchief around it using his
teeth and ran laughing and bellowing on. Before his piece
jammed he had killed seven, four of them with their hands up.
And now, bowling his way along roaring through the various
groups to the front like some flesh and blood tank, he arrived
back in time to shoot a Japanese officer who rising from a hole
had run at them screaming to die for his Emperor whirling his
sword on high. Queen tore the scabbard from him, jammed the
sword in it, stuck it all in his belt and rushed on.

"Queen's back!" he heard someone holler. "Big Queen's here
again! Old Queen's back!" He would never tell. If Doll told, he
would lie.

"Show me them Japs!" Queen bellowed.

Stein found his 'old veteran' 2d Platoon sturdily waiting exactly where he had left it, kneeling and leaning on their rifles.
Letting them continue to wait, he held a short 'Officers Call'.
There were only himself and Band actually; but he had Beck
commanding the Platoon, and Sergeants Welsh and Storm from
the Hq. Storm kept flexing his hand.

"I been wounded!" he said grinning sillily. "I been
wounded!"

"Okay," Welsh sneered. "So you'll get a Purple Heart."

"You fucking A," Storm said. "And dont you forget to put me in."

When he had them quiet, Stein explained his tactic to them. They would go over the crest in a sort of echelon of squads, bear left and then move straight on down. The MG would move further left to cover them. They were to search out any emplacements which had not been abandoned. They were under no circumstances to pause at, or have anything to do with the bivouac area. "This position's busted wide open," he said. "There's nothing left to do but clean it up. But Colonel Tall and Baker Company are obviously being held up down there. We're going to break it open for him from behind." He paused. "Any questions?"

Nobody had any questions. They all nodded their heads that they understood. Then Storm suddenly said:

"Captain, when can I go to the rear?"

The other four all turned to look at him.

"I mean, you know, I been wounded," Storm grinned. He raised his hand and flexed it for them. Nobody said anything.

"You mean you want to go right now?" Stein said.

"Sure!"

"Well, which way do you prefer to go? Do you want to go back down through the jungle by yourself? Or would you rather go straight on down the front of the hill?"

Storm didn't answer this for a moment and appeared to be thinking. "I see what you mean," he said finally. He raised his hand again and flexed it and looked at it. "I guess I better wait till we knock out those emplacements between us and Baker Company, hunh?"

Stein didn't say anything, but grinned at him. Storm grinned back. "Ah jest hope Ah don' git shot durin' 'is lil ol' operation," he said putting on his best Texas accent. He looked at his hand again and flexed it. It still wasn't bleeding and it didn't hurt him but they could all hear it grate. "I sure hope it's a big serious delicate medical operation to get that thing out of there," he said.

"Okay. Everybody know what he's supposed to do, now?" Stein said.

They all went back to their groups. Beck, imitating his predecessor Keck, had asked permission to take the first squad down
himself. He led off while the machinegun changed its position,
and slowly they spread out over the descending grassy hillside
which yesterday from the valley had looked so high and so far
away and so terrifyingly unattainable. Far below them they could
see the ridge where they had spent last night.

All in all it was a much easier job than any of them had expected. The hillside was honeycombed with riflepits and MG emplacements, and it was obviously the Japanese commander's
intention to sell it very dearly. But now, having heard such great
enemy firing in their rear, the Japanese began to come up out of
their holes and surrender, sick, haggard, beaten-looking men, obviously terrified at the treatment they expected to receive at the
hands of their enemy. Those who made the mistake of coming up
with weapons in their hands were taken care of immediately by
the machinegun or by the rifles of the platoon. The others, who
came out empty-handed and hands up, were socked, punched,
beaten, prodded, and hammered with riflebutts, but rarely—only
in a few instances, say, six or seven—were they actually killed.
But nobody liked them very well, that was the truth. Many of the
holes were already silent and empty, abandoned by men who had
rushed back to fight at the bivouac. If their silence seemed suspicious at all, these were bombed out with grenades without further
ado. But only much further down the hill was there anything like
a real fight. Led by Beck and Witt, a group attacked two large
emplacements which were still firing at Colonel Tall's men, who
were trying to creep close enough to get at them. The MGs were
silenced from behind. A few riflemen in pits nearby elected to
shoot it out with rifles and died. B-for-Baker poured in through
the gap, and the main fight was over and the mopping up began.
Several Japanese committed suicide by holding grenades to their
bellies, but not very many. 2d Platoon C-for-Charlie had suffered
four casualties, of which one was dead.

The mopping up proved to be a pretty big operation in itself.
There were still many unreduced emplacements scattered across
the hillside, and many Japanese preferred to die rather than be

captured. Some were too sick even to surrender, and simply sat by their guns firing them until they were killed. But first before all this could be taken care of, there had to be the reunion.

Stein was standing with Band, Beck and Welsh when Colonel Tall came striding along behind the Baker Company platoons, bamboo baton in hand, and smiling happily like a politician who has just received the confirmation of his election. Acting Sergeant Witt, who had been standing not far off, backed away and then disappeared.

A 2d Platoon man standing not far from Stein on the scorching hot sunburnt hillside a few minutes before had suddenly gargled like some sort of deathrattle and fallen flat on his face in a dead faint. He was not the first, nor was he the last. Someone had rolled him over and loosened his shirt and belt, and placed his sweat-and-snot-stained GI handkerchief over his face for protection. He still lay there and at the moment when Colonel Tall came up Stein was thinking about water. His own mouth was so parched he could hardly swallow, and he had already seen that there could be no water for them amongst the men with Tall, because nobody was carrying any cans. Water was what he wanted to know about most, but when Tall shook hands with him and made his congratulations, he waited politely until the amenities were over. Afterwards, he would often wonder why he had? Perhaps it was simply because he just was not that type of man?—not very forceful, really? He did notice that when Tall shook his hand, the Colonel's smiling face underwent a peculiar subtle change which could no longer be called truly pleasant. John Gaff, who was coming along right behind the Colonel, looked at him strangely too, when he grinned and shook hands.

"Well, Stein, we did it, son! We did it!" Tall said, and slapped him on the back—rather sadly, Stein thought. He did not remember the Colonel ever having called him 'son' before.

There was further handshaking with Band and the sergeants. When the chortling was over he asked about the water.

"I'm sorry about that, Stein!" the Colonel smiled. "But there wasn't a damn thing I could do. I had four cans for you—half of the eight cans my boys brought me. But the men were so excited,

so wrought up, so thirsty, so . . ." He spread his hands. "They
spilled about half of it, I guess. To get half a cup apiece." Tall did
not look guilty, simply resigned to life.

There was heavy firing still going on all around them. But they
were all of them used to that by now.

"But you said you'd have all the water for us we could drink
when we got here," Stein said, much too mildly, he thought, once
the words were out.

"And we will!" Tall smiled. "If you'll look down there, you'll
see them coming. When I saw what was happening, I sent James
back to harangue the Regimental Commander, the Division Commander, the Commanding General—any and everybody he could
get his hands on, and the more stars the better."

Stein turned automatically to look. Far below toiling along the
valley, where he and his men had lain in such fear and terror
yesterday, he could just make out a long snakelike line working
slowly toward them. If he looked at it directly, it disappeared; he
had to glance at it from the corner of his eye.

"That's the result," Tall said cheerfully from behind him.
"And they'll have rations as well as water, Stein! Now I think we
ought to see about getting a line organized along the crest. And
get this mopping up operation organized a little better. What do
you think about the possibilities of a counterattack, Stein?"

The last sentence was noticeably sharper and Stein turned back
quickly, in time to catch again on Tall's face that same odd look:
smiling, but underneath not smiling at all. Gaff only looked unhappy.

"We found no signs of any enemy at all, Sir," he said, then
forced himself to add for accuracy: "except one four-man heavy
MG which we reduced." He tried very hard to make his voice
completely factual, and not give any double entendre sound to it.
No triumph. But then his ego got the better of him. "What about
the wounded, Sir? You didn't bring any medics with you?"

"Stretcher parties should be along with the rations," Tall said;
in his steely voice. "You don't have any company medics?"

"One, Sir. The other's dead."

"We had three with us," Tall said. "But they've been kept

busy with our own casualties. I suspect that we've sustained more casualties than *you* have today.'' He peered at Stein.

"Shall we have a look at that crest line, Sir?'' Stein said.

"I'll let you do that,'' Tall said. "I'll see to this mopping up exercise.''

"Yes, Sir,'' Stein said, and saluted. "Beck! Welsh!'' He left George Band with the other officers.

The blow fell late that afternoon. Stein could not honestly say he had not anticipated it. C-for-Charlie's 1st and 3d Platoons, having effectively cleaned out the bivouac area and captured a number of heavy mortars as well as two 70 mm field guns, were placed into a line along the crest they had captured and which covered the dangerous Elephant's Trunk. B-for-Baker plus Charlie's 2d Platoon, organized by Colonel Tall, had continued with the mopping up. Once they had finished, and it took them the best part of the day, 2d Platoon went into reserve behind the 1st and 3d. Baker Company moved into the crest line on the right of Charlie with one of its own platoons as its reserve. Notable in the midst of all this activity was the arrival of the water, and rations, which suspended everything for a half hour. It was when all this had been accomplished, and the fierce sun heat was beginning to abate and prelude the first signs of evening, that Colonel Tall called Stein off to himself in the former Japanese bivouac area back down behind the crest.

"I'm relieving you of your command, Stein,'' he said without preamble. His face, that face, that young-old Anglo-Saxon face, so much younger looking and so much handsomer than Stein's, was set in stern lines.

Stein could feel his heart suddenly beating in his ears, but he did not say anything. He thought about how he had handled that move up The Trunk today. But of course a lot of that *had* been luck.

"George Band will take over for you,'' Tall said when Stein didn't answer. "I've already told him. So you won't have to.'' He waited.

"Yes, Sir,'' Stein said.

"It's a hard thing to do,'' Tall said, "and a difficult decision to make. But I just dont think you'll ever make a good combat officer. I've thought it over carefully."

"Because of what happened yesterday morning?" Stein said.

"In part," Tall said. "In part. But it's really something else. I dont think you're tough enough. I think you're too soft. Too soft-hearted. Not tough-fibered enough. I think you let your emotions govern you too much. I think your emotions control you. As I said, I've thought it over carefully."

For no reason Stein found himself thinking of young Fife, his clerk who got hit yesterday, and of his run-ins with him, and how he himself used to think of Fife. He had said to the G-1 that he thought Fife too neurotic, too emotional to make a good infantry line officer. Perhaps that was the way Tall thought of him? That was strange. But what would his father the ex-World War I Major say to this? He still did not say anything, and suddenly the schoolboy feeling came over him again, the sense of guilt and of being dressed down. He could not shake it. It was almost laughable.

"In a war people have to get killed," Tall said. "There just isn't any way around it, Stein. And a good officer has to accept it, and then calculate the loss in lives against the potential gain. I dont think you can do that."

"I dont *like* to see my men get killed!" Stein heard himself saying hotly in defense.

"Of course not. No good officer does. But he has to be able to face it," Tall said. "And sometimes he has to be able to *order* it."

Stein didn't answer.

"In any case," Tall said sternfaced, "it's my decision to make, and I've already made it."

Stein was studying his own reactions. There was, he found, a quite strong desire to describe for the Colonel the actions he had accomplished today: the long march, the taking of The Trunk, how he had come to Tall's aid and broken open a way in for him—and then to point out that yesterday, as if Tall didn't know it, was the first time he had ever really been under real fire, point out that today he had been much less concerned about seeing his men killed. Perhaps that was what Tall wanted him to say, in order to allow him to keep him? Or perhaps Tall didn't want, did not intend to keep him in any case? But Stein didn't say it. Instead, he grinned suddenly and said something else. He could feel it was a pretty stiff grin. "In a way, it's almost a compliment then, isn't it, Colonel, sort of?"

Tall stared at him exactly as though he had not heard what he said, or that if he had it did not apply to anything at all, and went on with what he obviously had already prepared to say. Stein did not feel like saying it again. Anyway, he was not sure—in fact, he did not *believe*—that what he had just said was true. He believed, with Tall, the opposite. It was no compliment.

"There's no point in making a scandal," Tall went on. "I dont want it in the records of the Battalion while I commanded it, and there's no point in your having it put down against you on your records. This has nothing to do with cowardice or inefficiency. I'm going to let you apply for reassignment to the Judge Advocate General's Corps in Washington for reasons of ill health. You're a lawyer. Have you had malaria yet?"

"No, Sir."

"Doesn't matter, really. I can fix that. Anyway, you probably will have it. Also I'm recommending you for the Silver Star. I will recommend it in such a way that it will definitely not be refused."

Stein felt an instinctive, angry desire to protest the medal, and half-raised his hand. But then he let it drop. What the hell? What difference did it *really* make? And in Washington. Stein liked Washington.

Tall from behind his stern, set, expressionless face had noted the half-raised hand of protest. "You might as well have the Purple Heart, too," he said.

"Why?"

Tall looked him over. "Well, for one thing," Tall said expressionlessly, "I notice a pretty deep scratch on your left cheek from hitting those goddamned fucking rocks back there yesterday." He raised his hand. "And if that's not enough, I also note a couple of blood streaks from scratches on your hands, underneath all that goddam fucking mud." He stared at Stein expressionlessly.

Stein suddenly wanted to weep. He didn't know why, really.
Perhaps it was because he could no longer even dislike Tall. Not
even Tall.

And if you couldn't dislike even Tall . . . "Aye, aye, Sir," he
said evenly, affecting boredom.

"I think it's best if you go back right away, with the next batch
of wounded and prisoners," Tall said expressionlessly. "It's no
good for you to keep hanging around. The quieter we keep this
thing the better it will be for all."

"Aye, Sir," Stein said, and saluted, and turned away. He suddenly saw himself in his imagination with tears in his eyes, stumbling, a broken man. But that was pretty cornball. And his eyes
were quite dry. To go to Washington? He could not really say he
minded that. God, what legends! The war had made it the biggest,
roaringest, richest, most exciting boomtown in the nation. And all
for paperwork. A group of stretcherbearers were preparing to
make the descent down to where the jeeps were finally making
their way forward on the short forward slope of Hill 209, and
Stein headed for them.

He stared a long time at Hill 209's short forward slope. That
was where just yesterday they had moved forward into enemy
territory, and now it was no longer dangerous. Men swarmed
along it. So this was it. The long-awaited, soul-illuminating experience of combat. Stein could not find it any different from working for one of the great law offices, or *any* of the huge
corporations. Or for government. Like the Soviets. A little more
dangerous to life and limb, but no different in its effect upon the
reward-haunted, ax-fearing spirits of the workers. When the
stretcher party was ready, he went with them, helping with the
stretchers over the rough places when it was necessary. What did
Tall really think of him? Or did he think nothing at all?

The word got around quickly. In spite of Tall's wish to keep it
quiet, all of C-for-Charlie—and for that matter, the entire Battalion—knew that C Company's commander had been relieved
within fifteen minutes after Stein had left. In C-for-Charlie it
made many of the men and noncoms very angry, but it was
Acting Sergeant Witt who first thought of the idea of raising a

deputation to go and protest. Many were in favor of the idea, but asked who would they protest to? To Brass Band, the new commander, or to Shorty Tall himself? It seemed a sort of slap in the face to protest to Band. On the other hand to protest to Shorty was inconceivable, since he would undoubtedly throw them all in the can for even daring to think of such a thing in the first place. In the end it all tapered away to nothing but bitter mumble. But if the others were willing to assuage their consciences this way, Witt who was very angry did not feel he could let it go at that.

Witt had already had one bad run-in today. When he had so wisely and delicately retired from proximity to the reunion of Tall and Stein, (he too had seen that there was no water), he had gone off a ways on the hillside to sit down by himself and rest. He was exhausted. And terribly dry. It was here, as he simply sat numbly staring emptily off down the hill, that Charlie Dale the ex second cook, who had come through with Gaff and the other volunteers in the B Company platoons, sought him out to complain.

The stocky Dale with his perpetually hunched shoulders and powerful long arms marched himself up stolidly, directly in front of the sitting Witt and stood himself there lumpishly to have his say. He had his rifle in his hands.

"I got somethin I want to tell you, Witt," he growled.

Witt's mind, such as it was at the moment, was far, far away. "Yeah?" he said somnambulantly. "What's that?"

"You shouldn't ought to talk to me like you did," Dale growled authoritatively, "and I dont want you to do it any more. That's an order."

"What?" Witt said, coming more awake at the tone of voice. "What? When?"

"Back there at the strongpoint this morning. You remember, Witt."

"What did I say?"

"You called me a jerk when I tossed that grenade down that one hole and that Jap tossed it back out. That's no way to talk to me. I'm a noncom now, and it aint dignified. In any case," he said, a phrase he had picked up from listening to Gaff and Stein, and then repeated it with relish. "In any case, I'm orderin you not to do it no more."

Witt looked as if he had been stung by a mad bee. Not angry. Mad. "Arngh, come off it, Charlie," he snarled. "I knew you when you was a lousy second cook. And a not very good one at that. I aint takin any orders from you. You can shove them acting stripes up your ass."

"You called me a jerk."

"Well, you are a jerk!" Witt shouted, scrambling to his feet. "A jerk! A jerk! A jerk! And what's more, you're stupid! You should of known better than to—And anyway, I'm an acting sergeant too myself! Stein made me this morning! Now, peel off!" He was still furious about Tall's having made such an ass of him this morning, and now here this ass was trying to give him stupid orders. "Jerk!" he shouted again insanely.

Dale appeared perplexed by the information that his enemy was now also an acting sergeant. "I'm not a jerk," he said calmly. "And you wasn't no acting sergeant when you done it. And anyway, I was made before you so I still outrank you. And I aint scared of you." Then his voice softened as he thought of a new thing. "Besides, it just dont look good in front of the men, Witt," he said as if they were two Majors bellying up to the Officers' Club bar.

"Men, my ass! Men, my ass!" Witt shouted. He bent and picked up his rifle and held it in both hands across the front of him the way a man holds a two-ended weapon. The bayonet wasn't on it. "Charlie Dale, I never hit nobody without I warn them first. That's my policy. Well, I'm warning you. Get away from me and stay away. If you ever say another word to me, I'll belt your fucking head in. And I can whip your ass!"

"I think I can whip you," Dale said in his phlegmatic way.

"Then have a *go!* Have a *go!*"

"No, there's too much work to do around here right now. The mopping up's just starting. I dont want to miss that."

"Anything you want!" Witt yelled. "Knives, bayonets, fists, riflebutts, shooting!"

"Fists'll do," Dale said narrowly. "I dont want to kill you—"

"You couldn't!"

"—and I know you been a boxer," Dale went on calmly. "And all that shit. I can still whip you."

"Yeah?" Witt advanced on him raising his riflebutt as if to stroke him in the side of the head with it, but Dale backed off. He raised his own rifle, which was bayoneted, into fighting position.

"Maybe I couldn't whip you," Dale decided. "But you'll know you been in a fight, buddy."

"Come on! Come on!" Witt cried. "Talk! Talk! Talk!"

"There's too much serious work to do," Dale said, "right now. I'll try you later, buddy." He turned and walked away.

"Any time!" Witt had yelled after him, and then sat back down, his rifle across his knees. He was trembling with a cold rage. Whip him! There wasn't a man his size in the Regiment who could whip him. And he doubted there was anybody in the Regiment who could whip him at bayonet fighting. As for shooting, he had been high gun in every Regiment he served with for the past six years. Don't look good in front of the men. Jesus!

Now, he had decided, he had two people in the Battalion to hate: its Commander and Charlie Dale.

Witt had not, what with all the mopping up fighting of the afternoon, retained his mood of supreme, disgusted fury; but it had come back over him soon enough as soon as the news of Stein's disgrace had reached him and he tried to organize a protest. These guys were all slobs, that was the truth. And this Battalion was going to hell on a sled. Band! For Company Commander? Witt believed he knew how to recognize a Company Commander, and Brass Band was no Company Commander. For that matter, neither had Stein been one. He had only just become one in the last two days, and look what happened! Now they were kicking him out. As the possibility of an organized protest slowly dwindled away into grumbling, just as slowly Witt gradually realized what he was going to do. He just didn't want to be in this shitty battalion any more. Not without Stein. A cold, implacable Kentuckyness came over him, pulling his sharp chin down into his thin neck and setting his narrow shoulders stolidly. He reported himself to the new Company Commander at the CP shortly before dusk.

That goddamned Welsh was there, of course. Brass Band was sitting six feet away from him, eating the last of a can of C ration meat-and-beans.

"Private Witt requests permission to speak to the Company Commander," Witt said to the Sergeant. Band looked up from his meat-and-beans with those eager, screwball eyes of his. But he didn't say anything. And Witt did not let his eyes waver from the Sergeant.

Welsh stared at him grimly. Then he turned his head. "Sir, Private Witt requests permission to speak to the Company Commander," he snarled.

"Okay," Band said, and smiled his eager smile. He took a last bite of his meat-and-beans, threw away the can, licked off his spoon and put it in his pocket. He was wearing no helmet. Witt, like everybody else in the two companies, knew that Band had had his helmet shot off his head by a Japanese coming up out of a hole, during the mopping up work. The bullet had gone in the left side at about the temple making a small, neat hole, and had come out the back making a large, jagged hole. Band who had not been knocked down had spun and shot the Jap. The battered helmet now lay beside him on the ground. Witt marched over to him and saluted.

"Sit down, Witt, sit down. Make yourself com-*fort*-able," he said in a jocular, cavalier way. "But you're not 'Private' Witt anymore; you're 'Acting Sergeant' Witt. I heard Captain Stein when he made you this morning." He bent and picked up the helmet. "Have you seen my helmet, Witt?"

"No, Sir," Witt said truthfully.

Band pulled the dented fiber liner out of it and displayed it. Then he stuck his finger through the bigger hole and waggled it at Witt. "That's something, isn't it, hunh?"

"Yes, Sir," Witt said.

Band threw the helmet aside, after putting back in the liner. "I never knew these things ever really protected anybody," he said.

"I'm going to keep this, the shell anyway, and take it home with me when I get another."

Witt suddenly thought of John Bell who had had the same thing happen to him at the strongpoint, and for a moment was intensely sorry to be leaving him, and the others. They were a good bunch, that assault group. Except for Charlie Dale.

"But I said sit down, Witt, sit down," Band smiled.

"I prefer to stand, Sir," Witt said.

"Oh?" Band's eager smile disappeared. "All right, Witt. What was it you wanted, Witt?"

"Sir, I want to tell the Company Commander that I am returning to my old outfit, Cannon Company of this Regiment," Witt said. "The reason I wanted to tell the Company Commander was so that if the Company Commander noticed I wasn't around, he would know why."

"Well that isn't necessary, Witt. I think we can arrange to have you transferred," Band said amiably. He laughed. "Dont worry about being AWOL. You've been a pretty valuable man the last couple of days, you know."

"Yes, Sir," Witt said.

"You know, we're short of noncoms. Tomorrow I intend to make all the temporary ranks permanent."

A bribe. Witt could smell Welsh watching with supreme disgust. "Yes, Sir," he said.

Band's eyes suddenly narrowed above his still smiling mouth. "You still want to go." He sighed. "All right, Witt. I guess there's really no way I can stop you officially. And anyway I wouldn't want a man in my command who didn't want to serve under me."

"It's not that, Sir," Witt lied. Because it was. At least partly. "It's that I dont want to serve in a battalion"—he deliberately did not mention Colonel Tall—"that does to guys what this battalion did to Captain Stein."

"Okay, Witt." Then he smiled that smile again. "But I feel that's not up to us to judge. Every army is bigger than any single man in it."

Preachin's. "Yes, Sir," Witt said.

"That's all, Witt," Band said. Witt saluted, Band returned it, and Witt turned away.

"Oh, Witt!" Band said softly. Witt turned back. "Perhaps you'd like a letter to present to your Company Commander in Cannon Company attesting to where you've been the past two days. If you would, I'd be glad to write one for you."

"Thank you, Sir," Witt said impassively.

"Sergeant," Band said, "write me a letter saying To Whom It May Concern that Witt has been with this organization the past two days in the thick of the fighting and has been recommended for decorations."

"I aint got no typewriter," Welsh said disgustedly.

"Dont argue with me, Sergeant!" Band shouted. "Write the letter! Take this sheet of paper and write the letter!"

"Aye, Sir," Welsh said. He took the sheet Band handed him from the inherited musette of Stein. "Weld!" The middleaged little draftee came running. "Take this paper and go over to that stump and write me a letter. I want it printed. You got a pen?" he barked.

"Yes, Sir!"

"You know what to put in the letter?"

"Yes, Sir!" Weld said. "Yes, Sir!"

"Okay. Move! And don't call me Sir, fuckface. You fucking draftee."

Welsh sat down and folded his arms and looked at both of them, Witt and Band. Then suddenly he grinned his crazy, mad, furry-eyed grin at both of them. Somewhere in that labyrinthine mind of his, he was obviously lumping them together and letting them know it. Witt didn't care, but he didn't like Band any better than Welsh did. Or than he liked Welsh himself, for that matter. There was something obscene and too soft about the way the Lieutenant acted.

When the letter was written and signed—it took only a few moments—Welsh handed it over. But when Witt took hold of it, Welsh suddenly clamped his thumb and forefinger together, not letting it go. When Witt exerted some pressure, Welsh held on, grinning that stupid insane grin down into his face. But when

Witt let go and was just dropping his arm, Welsh let go too, and the paper almost fell to the ground. Witt had to catch it. Welsh didn't say a word. Witt turned away.

"There's no need to go now, Witt," Band called from behind him. "It's practically dark. You can wait till tomorrow."

"I aint afraid of the dark, Lootenant," Witt said to him, but staring hard at Welsh. He left. He was angry at himself for wanting the letter. He should of left it, or refused it in the first place. He didn't really need it. Screw them all, the cheap bastards. Not a one of them had lifted a finger to help poor old Stein. And if Band thought he could buy off Bob Witt with a sergeantcy, or an offer to stay overnight and maybe reconsider, he didn't know his guy. As for hiking back to Hill 209 through the dark, he could do that standing on his head. And he did.

It was only a few minutes after Witt left the C-for-Charlie CP that Colonel Tall sent out from his own Headquarters CP the letter that he had spent the last two hours drafting. He was not really satisfied with it, the style was both too florid and too hard at the same time, but he wanted to get it out to be read to the men before it got too dark. He much would have preferred to make the Battalion a personal address, but with them on the line that was impossible. So he had had his clerks make two handwritten copies for each company. He spoke of the victory, of course, in glowing terms. But mainly what he wanted them to know was that he had secured for the Battalion a week's rest off the line. (He had spent the best part of half an hour arguing about it with both Regiment and Division, as soon as the sound power phone lines were laid.) His Battalion had sustained the highest casualties in the Division, and had captured the toughest objective. They would be relieved late tomorrow by a battalion of the Division's reserve regiment. Tall hoped to hear a few cheers from the line when this was read to them, and in the gathering dusk as he stood off from his CP by himself to listen, he was not disappointed. The other thing he wanted to tell them was that there would be a personal inspection of the line tomorrow by the Division Commander. It was because of this inspection that they could not be relieved sooner. Tall expected to hear some groans about this and, he noted smiling to himself, he was not disappointed here either. He flattered himself that he knew pretty well how enlisted men worked—he ought to after fifteen years—and the news of the week's relief much more than offset any natural irritation over the inspection.

The inspection began at ten-thirty. This was because the Division Commander was spending the morning going over the battle-ground down the hill with his staff. But long before ten-thirty the Division Press Officer was up on the line going over the area, checking, arranging, changing, setting up camera angles—and searching. He was a big, bluff, open sort of man, a Major, who had been an All-America tackle during his years at The Point. He found what he was searching for in the person of Private Train, the stutterer, upon whose lap young Coporal Fife had fallen after being hit with his mortar shell.

There had been a number of 'Samurai Sabers' taken during the two days. Queen (now evacuated), Doll and Cash each had one. So did several others in both companies. But it was left by fate to Train (through no particular fault of his own, it must be said) to take the only real jewel-encrusted sword like the ones they had all read about in the papers for so long. Train, more from exhaustion and to catch a breather than anything else, had stumbled into one of the stick shanties along the crest for a moment, and had found it lying on the mud floor.

This particular sword had a sort of false hilt of dark wood chased with a lot of gold and ivory, in addition to its beautifully made leather hilt cover. It was not an especially secret mechanism, and later when Train took it off, he found jewels—a couple as large as his thumbnail—embedded in the steel tang. Rubies, emeralds, some small diamonds. The false wooden hilt had been cunningly carved inside to fit perfectly together over the protuberances of the stones. The whole sword was a beautiful piece of workmanship. It must have belonged to at least a general, Train's wide-eyed buddies told him when he showed it—though, however, they said, 2d Lieutenants were known to carry such swords when they were family heirlooms.

The sword caused a great deal of excitement in the Battalion,

its value being variously estimated at everything from $500 up to
$2000. And it was this sword which the Division Press Officer
was seeking, in addition to doing the rest of his duties. He did not
know it belonged to Train, but he knew it was somewhere in
C-for-Charlie. Rumor of it had penetrated far to the rear, and the
Press Officer had had a brilliant idea when he heard about it. He
went straight to Lieutenant Band when he arrived. After thinking
a moment, Band sent him to Train. He thought that must be the
one. He hadn't seen it himself, or paid much attention. But that
must be the one. It was.

"This is it!" the Press Officer cried excitedly when Train
showed it to him. "This is the one! Son, you're a very lucky man!
You know what you're going to do? You're going to present this
sword to the General when he makes his inspection!"

"I-I a-am?" Train said.

"You sure are! Why, I'll have your face in every movie theater
across the whole of the United States that shows newsreels!
Think of that! What do you think of that? *Your* face!"

Train gulped beneath his sharp-edged, dangling, pickle nose.
"W-Well, I-I k-kind of thought I'd l-like to k-keep it, M-Major,
S-Sir," he said timidly.

"Keep it!" the Major roared. "Whatever for! What the hell
for! What would you do with it!"

"W-Well, y-you know. N-Nothing r-really. J-Just k-keep it,"
Train tried to explain. "F-For a s-souvenir, l-like."

"Dont be silly!" the Major bellowed. "In the first place, you'd
probably lose it before this war is over! Or sell it! The General
has a marvelous collection of bizarre and antique weapons! A
piece like this belongs in a collection like his!"

"W-Well—"

"And think what a newsreel shot it will make," the Major
hollered. "The General comes up! You give him the sword! You
draw it and you show him how to take the false hilt off! Then you
give it back to him! He puts the hilt back on! He shakes your
hand! General Bank shakes your hand! And we'll record your
voice! You'll say, 'General Bank, I'd like you to have this Japanese sword I took!' Or something like that! Think of it! Think of

that! You'll have *your* face, and *your* voice, in every movie theater across the nation! Maybe even your family will see you!"

"W-Well," Train said with timid regret, "if you r-really think it's the b-best th-thing to—"

"Think it!" the Major trumpeted. "Think it! I, personally—personally! can guarantee you that! It's something you'll never regret! Wait until your family writes you they have seen you!" He shook his hand. "Now, give me the sword! I want to look at it some more! Have to figure out the best angle to photograph it, you know! I'll give it back to you just before the General takes it! Thank you,—uh,—uh, Train?"

"Y-Yes, S-Sir," Train said. "Frank P."

"You go ahead with your work here, and I'll see you later on!" the Major shouted.

With the sword, the Press Officer came back down to the little CP where Welsh and Band were still working on their casualty listings. They all looked at it. But the Press Officer was scratching his head and didn't look very happy.

"What a face," he said. "I guess I never saw a more goddamned un-soldierly-looking face in my whole life. With that nose. And no chin. And he would have to stutter." He looked up. "You suppose I could get another, slightly better looking type to do the actual presentation?" He looked at both of them.

"I suppose not," the Press Officer said, answering himself. "But, God." Then he brightened. "I suppose in one way it'll really look even more democratic, won't it? A little rear-rank pipsqueak like that. Yeah, I guess it'll even be better, in a way."

It was, in fact, the highlight of the whole camera-recorded inspection tour, the movie cameras grinding, the General smiling, shaking Train's hand, Train smiling. The still cameras got it all the first time, but the movie cameras had to shoot their sequence over a second time because Train was so nervous at speaking to a General that he stuttered more than usual. But the second time he was better.

There was some muttered comment and bitter grumbling in the C-for-Charlie platoons, about Train letting himself be talked into giving his trophy away like that. Several of his friends told him he

was stupid. Train tried to explain that it did not appear that he had
had much choice. And anyway, if the General really wanted it
that bad . . . His friends shook their heads in disgust.

But nobody really cared very much. They were all too excited,
and too relieved, to be getting a chance to go back off the line. As
soon as the Division Commander had passed on to the B Company line, they began getting their stuff together to make the
move.

The march back, over that terrain where they had lain so long
in such fear and trembling the last two days, and which now was
so peaceful, was strange to everyone. And they all felt a bit numb.

CHAPTER 6

As soon as they were bivouacked the interminable accounts began. Everybody had at least three stories of personal, hair-raising escape from death to tell, and at least two stories of personal, exciting Jap-killing. Only in the last two days of their week off, when they began to think about going back up there a second time, did they begin to stop talking about the first time.

It was interesting to watch the gradual diminution of the universal numbness which afflicted everyone. In most of them the numbness required about two days to go away. By the third day nearly all of them had become almost the same personalities they had been before. But John Bell, for one,—who watched this denumbnification process with more self-interest than most—could not help wondering if any of them could ever really become the same again. He didn't think so. Not without lying, anyway. Perhaps long years after the war was done, when each had built his defenses of lies which fitted his needs, and had listened long enough to those other lies the national propaganda would have distilled for them by then, they could all go down to the American Legion like their fathers and talk about it within the limits of a prescribed rationale which allowed them selfrespect. They could pretend to each other they were men. And avoid admitting they had once seen something animal within themselves that terrified them. But then, most of them were doing that right now. Already.

Including him. Bell had to laugh, and then was terrified because he had. At any rate, it was those first two days of numbness which set the pattern for the entire week of 'rest'. Rest!?

They came down from the hills and out of the jungle with their haunted faces and pooldeep, seadark eyes, lugging every ounce of booty they could carry and looking more like Bowery scavengers than soldiers. Japanese pistols, rifles, helmets, belts, pouches, swords and sabers, and even one machinegun: Privates Mazzi and Tills, in addition to carrying the buttplate and mortar tube on their backs, plus their other souvenirs, transported between them a heavy caliber Japanese MG, tripod and all, which had escaped the notice of the Ordnance people largely because Mazzi and Tills had hidden it. Tills had found it first and Mazzi had offered to go in on the carrying for half, thus patching up their friendship. They had hopes of getting a whole case of Australian scotch for such a rare item, and they staggered in with it into the bivouac area near-dead from fatigue.

The bivouac which had been assigned C-for-Charlie was on top of a small, bare hill in some trees, just on the northern edge of the airfield which spread itself out below them. As a result, they were able almost every afternoon to lie out on their backs in the sun with their shirts off and watch the Japanese light bombers come in from the north to bomb the field. Because of their hill's position, the bombbay doors were always open before the bombers reached them, and once they were even able to see a Japanese face peering down at them. Twice the bombs were released directly over their heads, which was spinechilling fun and perfectly safe. And each time after the bombers had passed, they could jump up and watch the effects down on the field, for which they had a perfect grandstand seat. The first day the raid scared the living hell out of everybody: to be killed by an aerial bomb after what they'd been through? but after they understood, it became their daily—or almost daily—double feature: first the planes themselves, and then the effect on the field. Several times they were able to see American planes exploded and burning. Air Corps men fighting gasoline fires, now and then some actual wounded and dead, and if nothing else there were always the exploded holes in the metal matting of the airstrip which had to be repaired before planes could take off. Altogether it made a very entertaining spectacle to be seen almost every day. But despite the greatness of the bivouac's daytime entertainment facilities, there was something else about it of even greater importance due to its proximity to the airfield. This was the souvenir trade. For which they had come down from the hills prepared.

Every afternoon after the daily raid—if there was one, and usually there was—the whole of C-for-Charlie would descend en masse to the field, spread out over the undamaged or least damaged areas of it, and begin the bargaining. While prices had become more or less stabilized, they were not absolutely fixed and it was possible if you had an item some Air Corps man particularly wanted, to get higher than the normal going rate. The Air Corps men could and would pay higher because it was they who imported the booze. Every day a plane flew in from Australia with Air Corps Generals' supplies such as milk, meat and cheese, and the crews of these flights, known universally as the "Milk Run", stuffed every available bit of space with bottles or cases of Scotch. Consequently it was pointless to bargain with the ground troops or service forces, all of whose whiskey ultimately came from the Air Corps, and who even if they did not drink it themselves had to be extremely close with it—pointless at any rate if you could get to the airfield easily, and C-for-Charlie could.

A silk battle flag, preferably bloodstained, was always worth at least three Imperial quarts. A rifle on the other hand would hardly bring a pint. A helmet if it bore the officer's gold or silver star and was in good condition might bring one Imperial quart. Pistols were especially in demand. There were two types of Japanese pistols. One, cheaper and blighter, was modeled on some European popgun pistol and would bring three Imperial quarts; the other, heavier and better made, was copied from the German Luger and had the Luger's elbow-type slide action. This one was much rarer and apparently for officers and would bring four, five or even six Imperial quarts. A typical, *normal* 'Samurai saber' was always worth five Imperial quarts at least, and the better grade ones with gold and ivory chasing could bring as high as nine Imperial quarts. A jewelled one you could set your own price on, but they were unknown in the ordinary market. In addition to these solid staples there were other things. The thick leather belts with their old-fashioned leather ammo pouches, for example, which the Air Corps men liked to wear for pistol belts. Also a lot of the Air Corps men wanted Japanese photographs and wallets. The photos with Japanese writing on them were worth more than those without, and the photos of the soldiers themselves, or of groups of soldiers, were worth more than the photos of wives or girlfriends—unless of course they were pornographic. A certain amount of pornographic photos did turn up from time to time and were worth a lot. Money of course was practically meaningless to everyone except the crews of the "Milk Run" planes who could spend it in Australia, and men who had it but no souvenirs to trade were known to pay as high as fifty dollars for one Imperial quart of Scotch.

Into this already existing market C-for-Charlie charged eagerly with all its hard-earned leathergoods and hardware. The other three companies of the Battalion, for some reason of Army logic no one even attempted to understand, had been bivouacked at other sites, all of them far down at the other end of Red Beach in the coconut groves. For them it was an all-day job to get to the airfield and back, and even that was only possible if they got up at dawn to start hitching their rides. They had no choice but to sell most of their plunder on the cheaper ground-troops-and-service-forces market around them. But C-for-Charlie prospered.

On top the little hill above the airfield the drinking began before breakfast. They would crawl out of their netcovered cots, have a good stiff jolt of Australian Scotch, wash up at the trough, have another jolt, then report with mess gear to the kitchen tent which was now being run by First Cook Land in the absence of Storm who was in the hospital. Beside almost every bed there stood an Imperial quart. Breakfast was the only rollcall of the day by order of Shorty Tall, and after that they were on their own. Some might descend to the Air Corps with some plunder in the morning, but most preferred to sit in the tents or in the sun with their shirts off drinking from their Imperial quarts and refighting the great battle. Sometimes there was beer for a chaser, taken in from an outfit of Naval Seabees stationed at the field who apparently had endless amounts of it to trade for souvenirs. Almost everyone put away at least an Imperial quart a day, many quite a bit more. They were all young, and except for the malaria which everybody had at least a touch of by now, probably in the best physical condition of their lives. They could handle it. Besides, they were veterans. Blooded veterans. And they never intended to forget it—or let anybody else forget it, either. If some of them drank enough to get sick or pass out, they simply sat down or lay down wherever they were and slept it off until they felt like waking up and drinking some more. There were a number of drunken fistfights. After a midday dinner at which they consumed straight whiskey in the same way a European takes wine with his meals, they would drink more and wait for the rather tough spectator-sport of the afternoon light bomber raid. Then, when the airfield was safe, though sometimes burning, they would swagger toughly down with their souvenirs for the afternoon trading period. The Air Corps men who bought their objects must have hated them as much as they hated the Air Corps. In the night, after a meal of fried Spam and dehydrated potatoes, they would sit out on the open hillside drinking more and smoking cautiously in cupped hands and watch the spectacle of the night airraids, which because they bombed the coconut groves never bothered them on their hill.

They were, of course, undergoing the worst mental shock of their young lives, excepting perhaps only a few who had survived bad automobile accidents. As the blessed numbness receded, the unbelievability of each man's death to himself returned to ridicule and plague each one who had ever thought that. They talked much in the nights too, though more drunkenly, as they watched with malicious relish the nocturnal raids. The dead of their great battle were always spoken of with a sort of awed wonder. The wounded when they were spoken of at all, was spoken of in terms of as to just how far along that long line of stops between here and the States each man's wound would carry him: Division Forward Hospital here, Division Rear Hospital on Esperito Santo,

Naval Base Hospital No. 3 on Ephate, Noumea in New Caledonia, New Zealand, Australia, home. Hardly anyone spoke of his
own potential death next week. They were tough veterans; that
much had been explained to them, and they sought desperately to
carry out the role—not only because they were egotistically proud
of it, but also because there wasn't any other role. It was while in
this state that on the evening of the fourth day they looked up
drunkenly to find Mess Sergeant Storm and Corporal Fife were
returned to them from the—"from the dead" was the only way
they could honestly think of it; or, at least, "from the gone." The
safely gone.

Storm and Fife were the first wounded to be returned to C-for-
Charlie, and as such they were objects of extreme curiosity. Everybody crowded around them. Everyone in the company who
had not been hurt beyond the normal minor bruises and cuts
carried the small, nagging guilt of a well man who through no
fault of his own has not suffered. They pressed drinks on the two
returnees and asked them questions. Fife's head wound had
turned out to be totally superficial and with no fracture, and after
six days of observation he had been released for duty despite the
fact that he had lost his glasses. He now sported a small patch on
the shaved part of his head which he had been told he could leave
off after three days. Storm's hand had been examined by several
doctors who asked him if he could use it. When he said yes, he
had been assigned a bed in a tent where he sat ignored by everyone for five days until an orderly came and told him he could go
back to duty. They had done nothing to his hand at all. They had
not even put a bandage on it, and now there was a small scab over
the tiny blue-edged hole. It still grated when he flexed it, and it
still hurt him.

So that was it, and here they were. They were tough fuckers,
those doctors in Division Hospital, was the opinion of the returnees. They were not letting anybody get out of anything if they
could possibly help it. Apparently Division policy was to send
everybody back to their outfits who could crawl, so the Division
Commander could get this fight over with and secure the island
and his reputation. Even the very worst of the malaria cases were

not being admitted. Instead, they were given a double handful of atabrine and sent back to their outfits. The shit, the returnees said, had apparently hit the fan.

And so, borne on the wings of hospital gossip, in the mouths of Storm and Fife, the first real sense of the true imprisonment of combat reached the newly blooded veterans of C-for-Charlie. Storm and Fife had had nothing to do for some days except join in the unbelievably intense discussions among the wounded about who would be evacuated and who wouldn't, and they brought that intensity back to C-for-Charlie with them. It was easy to see, when you looked at it from one point of view, that all prisoners were not locked up behind bars in a stone quadrangle. Your government could just as easily imprison you on, say, a jungle island in the South Seas until you had done to its satisfaction what your government had sent you there to do. And when one considered it—as all the wounded had—this matter of evacuation might well be actually and in fact a life and death matter. So a new element darkled in their already darkling mood: a somber, deep-rooted bitterness which would grow and grow until it would make of them—those who survived—the tough, mean, totally cynical infantry fighters which their leaders fondly on sentimental grounds already believed they were, and which all of them, everybody, hated the Japanese for being. And in this dark mood they plied Storm and Fife, their first two returnees, with Australian whiskey and with questions about the wounded; and while Storm and Fife got drunk they explained that So-and-so would certainly make it out but would just as certainly die, that So-and-so and So-and-so would be evacuated at least as far as Australia and perhaps to the States, that these three would never make it further back than Noumea, and that So-and-so and So-and-so would never make it off The Rock any more than they themselves had. It was quite a long cataloging, but neither of them minded much what with the whiskey.

Storm and Fife had talked together quite a lot in the hospital. There was little else to do once the doctors had made their rounds, and Fife had turned to Storm as a sort of father or older brother in his sharp despair at finding that his head wound was not serious. Not only was it not serious, it was not even semi-serious, and it certainly would never get him evacuated. When Fife learned this, he was almost beside himself with terror, fear and disappointment. He had wanted to lie down on the ground of the doctor's examination tent and beat his fists in the mud there.

When Fife first had walked away from the battle streaming his blood, the only thought or emotion he had was a wild joy that he was wounded and could leave, plus a nagging desire to get behind Hill 209 where he could not be hit again and maybe killed. He could not remember anything else until he got to the bottom of the forward slope of Hill 209, where he saw something which stopped him. On the steep slope, which was thinly scattered with pieces of abandoned equipment including two rifles, lay an abandoned stretcher. On it lay a boyish looking soldier who was dead. The boyish soldier's eyes and mouth were closed, and one hand and arm hung outside the stretcher. His other hand, which was inside the stretcher, was submerged to the wrist in an astonishing amount of drying, almost jellylike blood which all but filled the cavity made by his buttocks in the canvas. Standing like an oaf and staring at this sight, Fife realized the man had been hit a second time while they were trying to carrying him out. But it was that hand submerged to the wrist in his own blood which distressed Fife the most, and he had an impulse to go over and pluck it out for him and wipe it off. But he hesitated. On the other hand, what if it was already stuck there? That might be even more terrible. Fife suddenly wanted to cry. Suddenly he wanted to shout at the whole world of men: "Look what you *human beings* have done to this boy who might have been me? Yes, *me,* you *human beings!*" He was brought to his senses by a rifle bullet which struck and whined away a few yards from him, and he turned away. He tried to run, but the slope was too steep. He could only plod. He thought he saw a few other rifle bullets strike dirt near him. In any case the damage had already been done—by that boyish looking dead man in the stretcher—and when he reached the aid station he was blubbering.

They treated him very well at the Battalion aid station. But there seemed to be thousands of people running around everywhere, all shouting at one another in confusion. He sat with a line of grimy, bleeding, groaning men on the hillside, mopping the blood from his forehead whenever it began to drip. All Fife wanted most in the world was simply not to go back down below. He had done nothing heroic, nor even anything normally brave, but these men here thought him heroic. In fact, he had not even done what he considered to be his normal duty. But he was not going to tell anybody that.

When a doctor finally got to him, he swabbed it and probed at it and then shook his head. "I can't tell. You never can tell with these." He began wrapping a turban of bandage around Fife's head. "Dont walk. You mustn't walk. Wait for the stretcherbearers to take you," he said, and an orderly attached a colored tag to Fife's jacket.

"Hear me?" the doctor said. "Dont walk. Answer me." He leaned over and looked into Fife's eyes and then snapped his fingers in front of them. "I said dont walk."

"Yes, Sir," Fife said. He had been far away, concentrating intensely to see if he could feel whether he was dying. And anyway, he didn't think such a simple instruction required an answer.

"Good," the doctor said. "Now dont forget." He moved away.

Fife was carted away by four beat-looking stretcherbearers. Even in the hot day the blanket felt good because he was cold. Hell, if he couldn't walk he was a cinch to be evacuated to Australia. When the bearers were resting for the last and steepest climb to where the jeeps could come he sat up and said, "Listen, fellows. I can make it all right. You guys should be carrying somebody who's hit worse than me." He was pushed back down by a roughly gentle hand. "You just take it easy, Mack. Let us worry about the carryin." Good guys, good guys. He relaxed cozily. This was the destiny he had been born to carry, and he had always known it. He would never have to go back there, and it hadn't really been bad at all. Not like with some of the guys, like Keck and McCron and Jacques and little Bead.

But at Regimental aid station he had found it was not going to be at all as easy as all that. After the jeep ride with the three other stretcher cases hung from the pipe and angle-iron frame, he was carried into the tent where the four doctors were working on four separate tables. Each doctor had a second table beside him on which a man waited, making a total of eight tables in the tent. Fife was put on the only vacant one, and saw he had drawn old Doc Haines, the Head Regimental Surgeon. Red-headed, grizzled and bald with a big paunch, Doc Haines worked with an unlit stub of a cigar in his mouth, grunting to himself from time to time. On Sick Call back before the war Fife had made a father figure out of old Doc Haines, as had many others, and momentarily Fife's eyes fogged up again. The man old Doc was working on was a young man with a slim, handsome, well-muscled back except for the fact that there was a hole the size of the mouth of a water tumbler just beneath his right shoulderblade. He sat on the edge of the table while Doc Haines working his cigar butt back and forth in his mouth cut loose strips of skin and flesh from the edge of the hole with tweezers and a pair of surgical scissors. The hole fascinated Fife and he could not take his eyes off it. Very slowly blood would well up in it until it overflowed in a slow-moving, thick, dark rill down the handsome back. When it had nearly reached his waist, Doc Haines would casually wipe it right back up to the hole again with a gauze swab and go on cutting. Frustrated but undaunted, it would prepare itself to start again. When he had finished tidying the hole to his satisfaction, Doc bandaged it and slapped the boy lightly on his good shoulder. He grinned with his much-wrinkled eyes.

"Okay, son. Lay down there till they come for you. If there's any more stuff in there, they'll take it out back there. In any case, I've given you the best-looking cunt between here and Melbourne. Orderly!" he bawled around his cigar stub in his raspy voice, "bearers."

The boy as he lay down grinned a silly drunken morphine grin, but he did not say anything. Fife suddenly felt that he had returned to the world of men, but he felt he had returned as a stranger. Doc Haines came over to him.

"Wait. Dont tell me. It's—" he grinned. "It's—Fife, isn't it? C-for-Charlie Company."

"Yes, Sir, Doc," Fife grinned.

"I remember you from when you went up to Post Hospital for that appendectomy that time. How did that ever turn out? Everything all right now?" He didn't give Fife time to answer. "What have we here now? Head wound, hunh? Can you sit up?"

Fife wanted to shout at him that he was not the same Fife, and that it was not the same, that this was not an appendectomy, but he swallowed it. "I'm not that Fife," he said wanly instead.

"Yeah. We none of us are," Doc Haines grinned. "Can you sit up?"

"Sure!" Fife said eagerly, "sure!" and heaved himself up and was immediately dizzy.

"Easy. Take it easy. You've lost a little blood there. Now, let's have a look-see," he said, and with his tongue pushed the cigar butt from the right side to the left.

Efficiently he went to work, removing the turban, probing the wound with his fingers. "This'll hurt a little bit now," he said, and colored lights danced before Fife's eyes as old Doc pushed a metal probe into it.

Doc Haines said softly, "Just one more time now," and again a spiral turban of velvet-colored light engulfed Fife's head.

"You're lucky. It isn't fractured. You may have, I think, what we call a greenstick fracture, which is a sort of crack like, but not a break. In any case, there's no foreign objects inside. In a week or so you'll be all ready to go again." Having given his opinion, he came around in front of Fife.

"Then,—you dont think I'll be evacuated," Fife said. "Or anything like that."

"I wouldn't hardly think so," old Doc said. Quite suddenly his smile disappeared from around the cigar butt in it. His eyes got flatter, as if some veil had fallen over them.

"Then I can walk all right now," Fife said desperately. "Now."

"Do anything you like," old Doc Haines said. "Except you should take it easy for a day or two."

"Thanks, Doc," Fife said bitterly.

"This battle'll be over in a day or two, you know," Doc Haines said. Without dropping his eyes he suddenly reached up and rubbed his stubby fingers in his grizzled fringe.

Fife got up off the table onto his feet. Somehow he had known all along that this would be the answer. And all that about it being his destiny to get out had been horseshit he'd fed himself. He felt a little shaky in the knees. "Sure, and as soon as this one's over there'll be another one. Right away after." From his blood-caked face he grinned, feeling it draw his cheeks. He knew he made a good picture of a wounded man anyway.

Old Doc Haines stared back at him obdurately now. "I didn't make the rules, son," he said. "I just try to live by them."

"Did you ever try dying by them?" Fife grinned. Then suddenly he felt ashamed and when Doc Haines didn't answer he said quickly, "It's not your problem. If a guy aint hurt bad enough to evacuate, you can't evacuate him, can you?" But it came out bitter. He paused, ashamed again. "I better go now. You're busy." On the other table, the one where the boy with the hole in his back had been, the waiting table now, a man lay groaning with his eyes closed, one arm and shoulder bloody in their bandages and badly mangled. The whole thing had only taken a very few seconds, really, and he hadn't kept him waiting long. Fife tottered out past him. Perhaps he tottered a little more than he really needed to. "Good luck, son," old Doc Haines called after him, and Fife waved his hand without looking back. He felt very wounded, and quite pleased with himself for having carried it all off so well.

It was on the jeep ride back to Division Hospital that Fife saw, for the first time in a very long time, the young Captain who was the Regimental S-1, and who had once turned down—or sent back to Bugger, anyway—Fife's application for OCS Infantry. He was standing with a bunch of other staff officers beside the road, and he recognized Fife or Fife would never have noticed him. He did not, of course, know Fife's name. But he did recognize his face beneath all the bandages and dried blood, and, after he was hailed, Fife thought that was pretty good for an officer on the Regimental staff. After all, one could not expect to be known by name to everyone in the world.

Fife was riding beside the driver, now that he had been reclassified as "walking wounded," and there were four litter cases hanging on the frame behind them. The young Captain, whose name Fife knew—and in fact, would never forget for the rest of his whole life (however long that might be)—left the group when he saw Fife and came toward them.

"Hey! Aren't you from Charlie Company?"

"Yes, Sir." A sudden emotion blossomed and burst in Fife like some miniature explosion, a perfect little miniature of the explosion which had caused his own wound, perhaps. "Yes, Sir! I sure am!" He was very aware of how wounded he looked. And the Captain couldn't know he would not be evacuated.

They were back down off the hills now, back in the mud of the jungle, though they hadn't yet crossed the river, and the jeep was moving slower than a man could walk, so that the Captain as they came toward him could turn and walk alongside.

"How's it going up there?"

"Terrible!" Fife cried. "Just terrible!"

"Well." It was obviously not the answer the S-1 had expected.

"They're knocking the shit out of us!" Fife cried maliciously.

"How's Lt Whyte making out?"

"Dead!"

The young S-1 Captain recoiled a little as if he had been struck, his eyes disturbed. "How about Lt Blane?"

"Dead!"

The S-1 had chosen to ask about the only two injured officers, as Fife had suspected he would, since he knew he was friends with them. The Captain had stopped following now, and was standing motionless beside the road. All the others in the gossiping group had turned and were listening too.

"Keck's dead!" Fife cried. "Grove's dead! Spain" (the other rifle platoon sergeant) " 's wounded!"

"Well what about Captain Stein," the S-1 called. "We were good friends, you know."

Fife swung himself around in the jeep seat to yell it back to him. "He was all right when I left! But he's probly dead too by now!"

The Captain didn't answer. Fife swung back around in the seat, strangely satisfied—in a grinding, unsatisfied, miserable kind of way. The fuckers, never getting shot at, and with their shitty private club kind of atmosphere which they copied so carefully from the fucking British. Did they ask about anybody except officers?

There were several other small triumphs on the way down, as when groups of rear-area troops stopped their work to stare at the jeep and its cargo with widened eyes and Fife would flash them all a wolfish grin out of his blood-caked face. But through all of these, despite his enjoyment of the role, there was still the grinding misery of his knowledge that it was only an act, that he was not in fact the future evacuee whom all of the wide-eyed rear-area troops so obviously envied. Suddenly, for no apparent reason, he began to blubber again. The driver, in a guilty, eyes-intent-upon-the-road silence, mercifully did not say anything to him, and finally he got himself stopped.

At the Division Hospital he was put in a hastily erected eight-man pyramidal tent with three others, none of whom knew each other or him, and they all sat around groaning or sighing to themselves in silence. Slowly the tent filled up, until two new cots were added in the center alongside the pole making a total of ten wounded. None of them saw a doctor that evening, though there were plenty of orderlies running around helping them, and when it came time for evening chow those of them who could walk lined up in the familiar coconut trees for their ration of the fried Spam and dehydrated potatoes served in the tin compartmentalized hospital plates. After the meal there was a great deal of searching through the milling throng in the late light while each man tried to find members of his own outfit. Fife was able to find four members of C-for-Charlie but none of them had any later news of the company than he himself had. After that they all sat around smoking cautiously and waiting for the night air raids. When the mosquitoes finally drove them all back to their tents long after the raids had ceased, he did not even try to sleep but lay mulling over and over the events of the day and his bad luck at getting a head wound. It would have been difficult to sleep anyway because in his own tent or in one of the tents nearby someone woke up every few minutes screaming or with a loud strangled yell. The one time he did doze off, he woke up yelling too.

Fife's interview with the doctor next day was short and succinct. After probing his head, making the colored lights dance again, he came around in front to tell him with a big, pleased grin that not only was it not fractured, it was not even a greenstick fracture—only a big gouge in Fife's thick, tough, American skull. He seemed to expect Fife to share his pleasure with him, and the physical toughness of American skulls seemed to be important to him. Lt Col Roth (Fife had heard him so addressed by an orderly) was a big meaty man with beautiful, perfectly silver, wavy hair (which matched his silver oak leaves) and the heavy, wellpadded face of a very successful bigcity doctor. He had a deep, heavy, authoritarian voice and eyes of cold blue steel—"eyes of steel" which, Fife thought with a cold inward infantryman's sneer, he would like to see looking at the business end of a bayonet and see how they looked. He had been hoping desperately they would find him worse than Doc Haines had predicted, and he guessed this and his despair showed in his face, but he tried to hide it from this man.

"That's fine, Sir," he said. "But, you see, I lost my glasses."

"You what?" Col Roth said, his steel eyes widening and getting more steely. "You lost what?"

"My glasses. When I was hit." Fife was aware of the half-guilty, three-quarters-anguished look on his own face, but he had worn glasses since he was five, and he could just barely make out the facial features of someone ten feet away, and he did not intend to stop now. "I can't see to do hardly anything without them." He deliberately did not say Sir.

Col Roth made no attempt to conceal his contempt and disdain. He did not shout the word coward, but he looked as though he would like to. "Soldier, we've got badly wounded men dying all over the place here. What do you expect me to do about your glasses?"

"Well, I won't be any good to anybody without them," Fife

said. He did not ask the obvious followup question. But then there was no need to.

Col Roth had stepped behind him and was rather roughly putting a small compress bandage on his head with adhesive tape.

"What's your name again, Soldier?" he asked ominously.

"Fife, Sir. Corporal Geoffrey P," Fife said, feeling that now the paperwork of bureaucracy would eventually and inevitably descend upon him and mark him forever—which of course was what Eyes of Steel wanted him to think.

"Well, Corporal," Col Roth said coming around in front again and not hiding his contempt, "you'll have several days to recuperate and convalesce here before you go back to your outfit. I'm going to forget all about this. You must know as well as I that we have no facilities here for making glasses. I dont like malingering, or malingerers. But we need soldiers, even the worst kind. If we have the time, we'll try and give you an eye examination and send to Australia for glasses for you. However, they may be a long time reaching you," he said with a distasteful smile. "That's all. You may go."

Fife saw that he had a choice. He could go on protesting about his eyes and take the consequences or he could shut up and accept the insult, and something about the ponderous selfsatisfied setmindedness of Eyes of Steel warned him not to press. "Yes, Sir. Thank you, Sir," he said getting up and trying to put all his hatred in his eyes. He left without saluting. Only when he was outside did he begin to brood over the possibility that if he had gone on protesting this Lt Col might actually have shipped him out, and that he had let himself be talked down. Later that same day, strolling around the hellish, moaning compound looking for someone from the company who was new and could give him news, he found Storm sitting on a cot staring glumly at the blue-edged hole in the back of his hand.

The Division Forward Hospital had been set up at the junction of two of the main thoroughfares of mud in the coconut groves so that the ambulances and jeeps from the front could get to it easier. Unfortunately, no one had noticed or considered important the fact that this junction was no more than six or eight hundred yards from the seaward side of the airfield, the prime target of the airraids; and while the hospital was never once hit by bombs, perhaps reenforcing the opinion of the planners, no statistical inquiry was ever made concerning the wear and tear on the nerves of the patients, all of whom had been wounded at least once. Despite this constant source of complaint, the hospital was well equipped and functioned very well under the circumstances. The installation consisted of two large three-masted circustype tents capable of holding upwards of a hundred men plus smaller tents for operating and treatment, plus now as an emergency measure a large number of pyramidal tents due to the unexpectedly high incidence of casualties. It was in one of the big dim circustype tents that Fife, who could not bear sitting in his own hastily erected, whopper-jawed, out-of-plumb pyramidal tent, came upon Storm.

Fife was overjoyed to see him. Despite his own current, very serious problems. Having been in the Company Headquarters himself, Fife had associated with Storm and his kitchen force more than he had with most of them in the company. And Fife had always felt that Storm liked him—at least, anyway, Storm *had* protected him from Welsh on several occasions.

Storm for his part was glad to see Fife, too. For one thing he had been sure back up there, watching Fife walk away with all that blood running out of him, that Fife would be dead soon, and that his walking away was only one of those last gasp reflexes that headless chickens sometimes display in dying. Also Fife was the first C-for-Charlie man Storm had seen since entering this miserable, groaning hellhole of the damned which the Army called a hospital. And right now any familiar face was welcome, in this buzzing, susurrus, crowded, haunted place. He had never much cared for Fife one way or the other, never much paid him any attention, but now he began pouring out all the news of the company Fife wanted to hear: what had happened on the rest of the first day after Fife had left, what had happened on the second day. But when Storm told him they had taken The Elephant's Head before noon on the second day—today—it was clear to him that Fife found it very hard to believe, if not impossible. And he was right. Fife himself could remember only total and complete holocaust, Armageddon, and he had expected them all to be dead—or at least ninety percent of them—before they ever got to the top of that hill. And he said as much. Nevertheless it was true, Storm said glumly inspecting his hand, and the casualties for the second day when added to the 25% of the first day still only made up a grand total of one-third of the company. This was, Storm felt and so did most of the guys, because Bugger Stein had taken them down around behind them and outflanked and surprised the position.

"But he wanted to do that the first day!" Fife said remembering suddenly with terror the third fold and the phone he'd held for Stein.

"I know." Then Storm went on to tell him how Bugger had been relieved by Shorty Tall.

Fife was properly incensed, or at least he tried to be. He was watching Storm and listening, blinking his eyes and nodding at the proper moments, but it was clear to Storm he hardly saw or heard anything Storm did or said. Probably he was still preoccupied with being wounded. Storm didn't blame him for that, but it was like talking to a dead man.

Storm had had some traumas and rude awakenings of his own, but being wounded was not one of them. And neither was Stein's relief by Colonel Tall. Storm had predicted that one to himself with pinpoint accuracy. As for being wounded, in his case that was such a little thing and counted for so very little that it hardly mattered. The explosion of the knee mortar—if that was what it was, and everybody said so—had not been close enough to shake him up, and the entry of the fragment had not hurt the slightest bit. Storm's traumas came from other things. Chief among them was the feeling that he was letting the company down by coming back down here with this hand. And next in line to that was the way he and the others in the party he had come down with had treated the Jap prisoners they had brought down with them. His rude awakening was an awakening to the fact that he did not want any part of any more combat, here or anywhere.

Storm had killed four Japs up there today during the breakthrough to Tall and the mopping up afterward, and had enjoyed every one of them. Only one of the four had had even the remotest chance of killing him, and that was all right with Storm too. That was fine. But his four Japs, each one of whom he remembered distinctly, were the only things that he had enjoyed during the whole four days C-for-Charlie had spent at the front. He had been scared shitless all the rest of the time. And the pageant, the spectacle, the challenge, the adventure of war they could wipe their ass on. It might be all right for field officers and up, who got to run it and decide what to do or not do. But everybody else was a tool—a tool with its serial number of manufacture stamped right on it. And Storm didn't like being no tool. Not, especially, when it could get you killed; and fuck organization. Combat was for foot sloggers and rifle platoons, and he was a messergeant. He felt sorry, and perhaps even a little guilty, to have left the company and come back down here with his 'wounded' hand. But for a sensible man that was the only thing for it and that was all there was to it. If this hand didn't get him clean away from this fucking island, he would go back to being a messergeant. He would cook hot food for them and get it to them—if he could. But he would not carry it himself. That, the carriers could do. A lot of people were going to come out of this war alive, more than got killed, and Storm intended to be one of them if he possibly could. Why, even that trip down from up there—which he should have been very pleased over, should have enjoyed immensely—had been ruined by those Jap prisoners they had had to bring down with them.

He had come down with the next party to leave after the one Bugger Stein left with. Stein's party was the last of the stretcher parties, and most of the walking wounded cases had gone down long before. A few like himself and Big Queen had elected to stay till the mopping up was finished. There were seven of these, four from Baker Company three from C-for-Charlie, and with four unwounded men they were told off to act as guards to a party of eight prisoners—half of the total number taken. In this way Tall could free more unwounded men to remain up on the line for the anticipated night counterattack.

It was great to be leaving with a night counterattack expected (though Storm felt a momentary sharp thrust of guilt) and everything went off well at the start. Queen's flesh wound in his left upper arm was beginning to stiffen up, and he was not as chipper and energetic as he had been during the fighting at the bivouac. But just before leaving he roused himself to brightness again. "I'll be back!" he cried in his bull voice. "I'll be back! It'll take more than a little old flesh wound to keep me from comin back to old C-for-Charlie! I dont care where they send me! I'll be back if I have to stowaway on a replacement boat!" A few C-for-Charlie men who were watching the departure grinned and waved and cheered, and Brass Band who was there came over to shake hands with Queen—with unnecessary showiness, Storm felt. Storm had no idea why Big Queen had elected to stay behind for the mopping up when he could have gone down earlier. As for himself, he had stayed because he was already planning to parlay this hand wound into an evacuation, if he could, which would take him as far back from this Rock as he could milk out of it; and he wanted to leave a good impression on his old outfit when he left it perhaps forever.

The eight Japanese prisoners were a sorry, sicklooking lot. Feeble, stumbling, they shambled along appearing to be totally benumbed by their experiences, and looking as though they would not have had the energy or the will to escape even if they were guarded by just one GI. All of them were suffering from dysentery, jaundice and malaria. Two of them (just why, no one ever learned) were stark bareass naked, and it was one of these who finally collapsed and caused all the serious trouble. When Big Queen came over to kick him to his feet, he just lay vomiting and shitting at the same time, leaving two yellow trails of liquid behind him as each kick slid him sideways a few feet further down the path. Half-starved, his ribs and shoulder bones showing starkly through his sick-looking yellow skin, he looked more like some lower grade type of animal and really did not appear to be worth saving. Neither did the other seven, who now squatted on their haunches in patient numb resignation under the eyes of their guards. Some Lieutenant who spoke a little Japanese had learned from them that they had all been living off lizards and the bark off of trees for the past couple of weeks. On the other hand, the party was under the strictest personal orders from Colonel Tall to see that all of these men got back to Regimental Intelligence alive for questioning.

Queen, though stiffening badly and still bleeding, was still chipper enough to enjoy booting and clubbing his charges down the trail with hysterical joyousness whenever they fell behind, and the rest of the party had joined in the fun. Now Queen gave his considered opinion.

"I say shoot the fucker," he grinned, growling. "Look at him."

"You know Ol' Shorty ordered us to get them all back alive," someone else said.

"So we'll say he tried to escape," Queen said.

"Him?" someone said. "Look at him."

"So who'll see him?" Queen said.

"I'm with Queen," someone else said. "Remember what they did to our guys on the Bataan Death March."

"But Shorty gave us *personal* orders," the first man said. He was the corporal in charge of the four unwounded guards. "You know damn well he's gonna check up if one turns up missin. What if he has Intelliegence ask these other guys what happened to their buddy? I dont want to get in no trouble, that's all."

"Well, it's either that or carry him," Queen said with finality. "I'm not about to carry no fuckin Jap all the way back to Hill 209. Are you? Anyway, I outrank you. I'm a sergeant. I say kill him. Look at him. Be doin the poor fuck a favor." He looked around at the others.

"The corprl's right," Storm said, putting in for the first time. He had been thinking it all over, pros and cons. "Shorty's sure to check up if one is missin. If we shoot him or lose him, he'll be on our ass like a bullwhip, spittin and bitin. Might even court-martial us." He did not add that he was a S/Sgt, and thus outranked Queen.

Queen stared down at the Japanese man, then shrugged and grinned ruefully. "Okay. I guess you're right," he said goodnaturedly. "It looks like we carry him." He slapped his great palms together. "All right then! Come on! I'll take a leg! Who wants the rest of him?"

Storm, who wisely had already considered this problem, too, and decided he preferred vomit to feces, moved over to him and took an arm. Two of the other wounded got hold of the other arm and leg, and with Queen comically in command and calling the movements for them like a coxswain of a crew shell hollering "Stroke!", the party moved off down the trail again.

Queen's goodnatured surrender to wisdom, plus his comical commands about portaging the sick Japanese, had put them all back into the high humor of their departure. Whooping and hollering they descended the steep hillside in a sort of nonsensical hysteria of cruel fun, slipping and sliding, one or another of them falling from time to time, and all of them except the four portagers who had all they could take care of, booting or shoving their seven walking prisoners to make them keep up. "Hey, Jap," one of them cried once. "Come on, Jap! Tell the truth! Aint you glad you dont have to fight no more now? Hunh? Aint you?" The Japanese he had addressed, who obviously did not understand a word, bobbed and bowed and nodded his head smiling numbly. "See there!" cried the guard. "I told you! They dont want to fight no more than we do! What's all this Emperor shit?" "Just you dont give him your loaded rifle," laughed another, "and then see how much he want to fight." Queen soon caught on to the fact that he had made a mistake by taking a leg to carry. Both of the men on the sick man's legs had difficulty keeping out of the way of the jets of yellow liquid the nude Japanese kept squirting as they bobbled him along down the steep hillside, and Queen goodnaturedly chided Storm for being smart enough to take an arm without letting him in on the idea. Then he had an idea of his own. "Let's bump him a little," he said as they came to a rock. "Maybe we can *knock* the shit out of him, hunh? Or, at least, enough of it to make him stop till we get him down." Swinging him in unison, they bumped his behind against the rock and made him squirt, all of them laughing uproariously. The other Japanese bobbed and grinned, because they too had gotten the idea by now.

Nevertheless, the bumping did little good. He kept right on
squirting as they continued to carry him down. Conscious enough
to blink his open eyes from time to time, he was too far gone, too
near out, to control his bowels, and when his head hit the ground
from time to time it did not even make him flinch. They would
bump him against every rock they came to as they went on down,
and then go on. When they delivered him to Regimental Hq, a
doctor was called and went to work on him immediately. It was
interesting to note that Big Queen passed out two minutes later on
his way down the reverse slope and rolled the rest of the way
down into the Battalion aid station, causing great consternation.

Storm on his hospital cot with his head in his hands (he had
given up trying to talk to the dead face of Fife in front of him)
remembered everything in a state of agonized numbness which
try as he would, he could not pull himself back up out of. His
whole soul seemed anesthetized as if shot with a massive hypo of
some powerful drug. This scared him, but he could not shake it.
How long ago had it been? that all that had happened? Only a
couple of hours. And laughing. They all laughed. Storm didn't
care about those Japs. All those Japs had coming to them everything they got and more. That didn't bother him. But it had all
been done in that state of numbness, he could see that now. Not
only him but the other guys, too. Maybe even the Japs too. Storm
had always thought of himself as a decent man. Sure, he had been
rough on KPs and cooks in his time, to make them work. Had
even beat up a couple, when he had to. But he did not believe in
kicking a man when he was down, taking advantage of a weak
person, or stealing from the poor. That was his code and he had
always tried to live by it. Now he had to face the possibility that
maybe he wasn't so decent after all. And not only that, he who
had always believed in never letting a friend down, was here
preparing to try and use his hand to get him out of the company,
out of the Battalion, out of the whole fucking combat zone. And
what was more, he knew it was the only sane thing to do.

"Well what about your hand there?" Fife said hollowly from
in front of him. The silence had gone on and on, and Fife had
been thinking about himself again. To have gone through all that:

the explosion, the blacking out, the pain, the blood, the fear, and then to find out that it all really meant nothing. He had suffered all the terror, fear and agony of being killed in action and had not gained a thing from it. Fife felt he must talk to somebody about it, but he did not see how he could come out and boldly admit to someone he was that much of a coward.

Storm had raised his head and was now staring at Fife with dark, haunted eyes. "Since you aint a doctor I guess I can tell you the truth," he said, and looked down at it glumly in his lap. He raised it and flexed it and they both could hear it grate. "I got a pretty solid hunch it aint ever gonna get me off this Rock," Storm said.

"They've already told me that about my head wound," Fife said.

Around them in the big, dim tent in the hot afternoon air orderlies stirred and moved quietly about on the mud floor, and here and there men groaned from within their bandages.

"I *can* move it. And it don't really hurt *too* bad," Storm said glumly. "But I aint got any *strength* left in it."

Two orderlies and a doctor came hurrying down the aisle between the cots past them and one of the orderlies said in a matter-of-fact voice, "I think he's had it, Sir." They stopped at a cot eight beds further up.

"But you never thought you were going to die with it," Fife said. "Did you?"

Storm looked up at him. "No. No, I never thought that with it."

"I did."

Up the way the doctor was fussing over the man on the cot. Then he stood up. "Okay," he said to the orderlies in a strangely angry voice. "Get the meat board and blankets and get him out of here. We need the fucking beds. How about Number 33?" An orderly said, "About twenty minutes or a half hour, Sir, I think." The doctor snapped, "Call me." They all left along the aisle in the high, dim, hot-aired tent.

"I really did," Fife said.

"Yeah, I remember it. I was layin not far from you. You looked pretty bad then."

"And nothing," Fife said bitterly. "Nothing! Not a fucking thing. Not even a fracture."

"It's just tough luck," Storm said sympathetically.

"And I'm worried about losing my glasses," Fife said. "I can't really see very well without them, you know."

"Did you tell them that?"

"They laughed."

After a while, Storm said, "I'll tell you one thing, Fife. Whether I get off The Rock with this" (he raised his hand) "or not. I dont have to go back up there to the front with the compny, and I'm not going to. I'm a Messergeant. I aint even supposed to be up there. Me and my cooks'll get the kitchen as close as we can, and I'll get them guys up hot meals every time I can. But fuck this volunteering shit. They got them hot meals coming to them—if they can get them. But that's all. No more volunteer fightin. I aint required to, I aint supposed to be, and I aint."

"What about me? I'm the Forward Echelon clerk. I got to go."

"I'm sorry," Storm said.

"Yeah." There didn't seem to be anything else left to say. Fife still had not got said what he had been trying to say, nor had he come anywhere near it. How did you go about telling someone you were a coward? How you had never thought you would be a coward, but it had turned out that you were?

"I'm a coward," he said to Storm.

"So am I," Storm said immediately. "And so is everybody who aint a fucking goddam fool."

"Some of the guys aint. Witt, and Doll, and Bell. Even Charlie Dale."

"Then they're fools," Storm said without hesitation.

"You dont understand," Fife began, but a sleeping man near them began to scream and then woke up. Fife jumped up and ran over to him and patted his shoulder. "Jerry. Jerry," the man said, then "Oh!" when he saw Fife. After a moment he sighed and said, "It's okay." Fife came back.

"I mean *really* a coward," he said.

"What did you think I meant?" Storm said.

"But with you it's different."

"No it aint."

"I mean, I didn't want to be a coward."

"Well, I didn't want to be one either, I guess," Storm said. "But I am." He flexed his bad hand and it grated. "Thank God I dont have to go back up there, that's all."

"But I do," Fife said.

"I'm sorry," Storm said again. And it was clear that he was sorry. But his tone pointed out that even while he was sorry, all that really had nothing at all to do with him. Still, Fife felt better. Storm took being a coward so much more in his stride somehow, and it made Fife feel less unmanly. Also, Fife had learned another thing. While Storm had said he was sorry and had meant it, this still had nothing to do with Fife and changed nothing. His belly-grinding misery remained exactly the same. And he could see now that it would be the same with everybody else he talked to.

"Maybe I could come to work for you in the kitchen," Fife said suddenly. "I mean, since Dale will be making line sergeant, you'll have a vacancy, won't you?"

"Yeah, I guess. Can you cook?"

"No, but I can learn."

"Well, but there's already a lot of guys in the compny who can already cook. If you can get the Compny Commander to move you to the kitchen force, I'll accept you."

"Brass Band? He would never let me go. And anyway I could never make myself ask him."

"It's the best I can do."

"Yeah," Fife said, twisting his neck from side to side and peering around the big tent. "I know, I know."

It had been a silly idea anyway, and he didn't bring it up again. He could never become a cook. It was a coward's pipedream, and he couldn't blame Storm for that. The grinding envy he felt for Storm's good luck in having a means by which to avoid going back up with the company was huge and bitter and enormously covetous. But in spite of that he kept coming back around to Storm every day, and they spent a lot of time together. It was

better than lying miserable and depressed in his own little overheated, badly pitched tent. Together they were able to find six
other C-for-Charlie men scattered around the compound, five of
whom could walk. Every day this little group would gather at
Storm's bunk to talk, pay a visit to the bedfast man, secure for
themselves a sunny spot in the cocopalms where they sat with
their shirts off and spent the rest of the day discussing their possibilities of being evacuated. It was absolutely impossible to find
anything at all to drink, but every night there was an openair
movie which they attended in a body to look nostalgically at the
glittering, free, sophisticated life of Manhattan, Washington and
California which they were fighting for but which none of them
had ever seen outside of the films. Films like "The Story of
Vernon and Irene Castle" with Fred Astaire and Ginger Rogers.
Invariably the airraids interrupted these showings, and in five
days Storm and Fife saw parts of five films without ever seeing
the end of one, but that didn't really matter much since all of
them had seen them all years ago. After the airraids, they would
sit up smoking and talking about possible evacuations. Nobody
wanted to go back to C-for-Charlie.

It was Storm who organized the expedition to visit Bugger
Stein. Regimental Rear Echelon Headquarters was only a short
piece down the road, and Storm had learned from some courier or
some old buddy of his at Regiment that Stein was staying there
while waiting to be shipped out. So one afternoon, after discussing it, the group of seven walkables simply walked off with Storm
in the lead to pay their respects to their Company Commander
whom they had once hated but now admired, and tell him
goodby. There were no guards or fences to stop them like there
would have been in a civilized camp hospital, and they simply
walked off through the sunblazing hot sweltering afternoon. After
all, where was anybody going to run away to on this fucking
island, that they needed guards?

Stein was at work in his little tent sorting what few papers he
had, when his guests arrived and took him by surprise. He had
only just learned that he would be going out tomorrow to New
Zealand by plane. He had a bloodstained battleflag, a Luger-type

pistol, two officers' collar insignias, and sundry photographs and leather articles as souvenirs to prove he had been here, and his personal baggage waited ready on the floor around him. Stein had spent the last three days hunting down that baggage. The Regimental Commander had kindly given him the use of a jeep, though he could not now allow him a driver of course under the circumstances, he said. Stein had enjoyed driving around the island by himself. At the company's old bivouac near the airfield, where they had packed and laced down in the tents their "A" and "B" bags, he had found another outfit encamped there, with their own tents pitched in their own, to him entirely strange, formation. Not a trace of C-for-Charlie remained. After that, he had driven from the Matanikau through Lunga Point and the bustling welter of supply dumps to the far end of Red Beach twice, asking questions and hunting the C-for-Charlie cache. He finally found it not too far from the company's old original first bivouac, half-in half-out of a little spur of jungle. Stein had no idea who might have done all this work of loading and unloading bags, striking and re-pitching tents, but they must have worked at it the whole five days of the battle. He spent one entire afternoon sweltering in the hot bright sun or sweating in the humid jungle shade looking through the tents for his own two bags, but he had enjoyed it—largely because he was alone—and now he was ready to go whenever they told him.

This thing of preferring to be alone had grown on him steadily over the four days since he had come down. The second evening—after his first full day down here below—he had decided to brazen it out, and had gone over to the Regimental 'Officers Club' for a drink after supper. After all, officially (and even unofficially), the way Tall had laid it out to him, it was not supposed to be a stigma.

The 'Club', which was the Regimental Commander's idea, was really no more than an ordinary kitchen fly draped in mosquito netting with a knockup bar made out of crates at which the Regimental Commander's personal sergeant served. There were camp chairs and one camp table for poker. For after dark there was a blacked out tent right next to it to which they could adjourn.

Normally the staff and rear echelon officers were the only ones here to use it, but that night because Tall had secured 1st Battalion a week's relief most 1st Battalion officers were almost certain to be there too. They would be talking that relaxed, amiable chitchat conversation about tactics which helped all of them himself included to keep up the pretense of sanity. But he should have known better, and after that first time he did not go back. It just wasn't worth it; the gain in pride just wasn't worth the cost in energy. And, unaccountably, when he started doing it, he found he preferred being alone.

It was not that they were nasty to him. Nobody snubbed him. Nobody refused to speak to him. It was just that unless he spoke first, nobody seemed able to find anything to say to him. And that took energy—from both sides. There were several little groups of them sitting around when he first came through the netting. He had the distinct impression that at least one group had been talking about him. Lt Col Tall was the center of another group, one which Stein sensed had very definitely *not* been talking about him. Tall nodded and smiled pleasantly with his lined, young-looking, handsome face, but at the same time he very deftly gave the impression that he thought Stein should not have come here. Stein had walked nodding and helloing straight to the bar and leaning on its structure of crates ordered a drink. He drank it there alone. But during his second Fred Carr, the Regimental S-1 and Stein's old drinking buddy from the Officers Club back home, got up from his group and came over looking strange and unhappy. Because they had not seen each other since before the battle they shook hands and Fred stood and talked to him a while, mostly about the extraordinary encounter he had had with young Corporal Fife (Stein recognized who it was, though Carr didn't know his name) coming down in a jeep wounded. Carr's talk was rushed and nervous, but Stein appreciated the gesture in an objective way. A little later Captain John Gaff came in looking pretty drunk, though obviously nobody cared about that with Johnny Gaff, and he too came over and talked to Stein at the bar, mostly about yesterday's mopping up operation and how well it had gone. He too, like Fred Carr, looked unhappy and finally excused himself. Gaff then joined Colonel Tall. Stein who was on his fourth drink now signed for them, all of which money went into the Regimental Officers' Fund by order of the Regimental Commander, and left. After that he bought a bottle and kept it on the little camp table in his tent. He liked to sit in the little tent whose two ends had been opened up and covered with netting and watch it get dark in the coconut groves. He never bothered to close the tent down and black it out so he could have a light, and when the planes came over he would sit quietly in the dark without any fear and listen to the bombings, having a small drink from time to time. He was not at all afraid. Of course the whiskey helped, though he never got drunk, and he kept a bottle on the little camp table all the time. In fact, there was one there when the seven wounded C-for-Charlie-ites came crowding into the tent to say goodby to him, and Stein seized it and offered them all a drink thinking that not so long ago he would never have dared do such a thing for fear that it might impair discipline.

There was only one glass in the tent so they all took it straight from the neck of the bottle. They all drank greedily, and Stein suddenly realized that whatever medicines they had been dosed with at the hospital whiskey was not one of them. Bending to his baggage, he hauled out the three bottles he had intended to take with him on the plane and gave them to them. He could easily get more before he left. When they tried to thank him, he only smiled a sad little selfdeprecating half-smile.

They were all talking at once, all babbling away together, and Stein felt curiously detached from them. The upshot of what they wanted to say was that they wanted to thank him for saving the company with his flanking move, that they were all sorry to see him go, that they thought he had gotten a rotten deal. Stein merely smiled and moved his head depreciatingly. He was not at all sure himself that they were right. And anyway it didn't matter. He didn't care. He was glad to be going.

"We ought to all go and make a protest!" Fife cried, almost with tears in his eyes. "All go in a body and—"

"For what?" Stein smiled and shook his head. "What good

would it do? Anyway, I want to go. You wouldn't want to take away my chances of getting evacuated, would you?''

No, they chanted in unison, Jesus Christ no. They wouldn't want to do that.

"Then leave it alone. Let it lay like it is.''

When they had left, he stood in the door of the tent and sadly watched them struggle off with their whiskey, unshaven, dirty, still in the mudslicked fatigues from the battle, each one sporting his clean white bandage somewhere on his person—except for Storm and McCron: Storm's hand had never been bandaged, and McCron's wound was inside. Then he went back inside and poured himself a drink.

He would never know. That was the truth. And that was the hell of it. Perhaps the Japanese had had that jungle line on the right fully covered during the first day, and had only moved their men away later, in the night. Even if the jungle had been open, a patrol in force with a platoon, as he suggested, would have been no good. One platoon could never have taken that bivouac area alone. And it *was* too late in the day to send an entire company. Certainly, the right should have been reconnoitered thoroughly before making an attack plan calling for a frontal attack. But he had not suggested that himself the day before and neither had Tall or anybody else. So where did that leave you?

But none of that was the basic problem, was it? He had been too hasty, certainly, in refusing Tall's order to attack, and he should have stalled and waited till he found out what Beck could do on the Ridge. The basic problem was something else. And Stein didn't know the answer to that either. The question was: Had Stein refused Tall's order really because he was afraid for his men, because so many of his men were being killed? Or had he refused Tall's order because he was afraid for himself, afraid *he* might be killed? Nobody had ever suggested such a thing or even hinted at it. But Stein didn't know. He had pondered and pondered it in those nights when he sat alone in the little sleeping tent and listened to the airraids, and he just didn't know. Perhaps it had been some of both. But if it had been both, then which had been the stronger impulse? Which had really dictated his decision? He just didn't know. And if he didn't know now, he would never know. It would remain with him, unsolved. That was something to live with, but on the other hand Stein found he no longer gave a damn what his father the World War I Major thought. Men changed their wars in the years that followed after they fought them. It was that old thing about "I'll-believe-your-lies-about-you, if-you'll-believe-my-lies-about-me." History. And Stein knew now his father had lied—or if not lied, had augmented. And Stein hoped he would never do that. He might, but he hoped not.

But as for the rest, he no longer cared. A lot of people were going to live through this war, many more than got killed in it, and Stein intended to be one of those if he could. Washington. Women. The fat boom town. With his campaign ribbons and medals he ought to make out pretty well. He could do a lot worse. And even if rumor followed him, nobody was going to say anything to him about it because it was all part of the great conspiracy. And as long as you played ball with the conspiracy . . . the great conspiracy of history . . .

Stein knew something else that he had not told the C-for-Charlie delegation of wounded, and that was that Captain Johnny Gaff would not be going back up on the line with the Battalion when they went. Gaff had been recommended for the Congressional Medal of Honor, and he was now too valuable to send back up. Under Colonel Tall's auspices, the recommendation had already been signed by the Division Commander and sent forward to CINCSWPA by cable. In a week or so it ought to be back from Washington, and in the meantime Johnny Gaff was being flown to Esperito Santo to act as aide to the General Commanding. Stein fully expected to meet him in Washington someday, during one of his bond selling tours. Maybe they'd get drunk together. Anyway, Gaff's line about "This is where we separate the men from the boys, the sheep from the goats." had been quoted in full in the cable.

While the delegation of C-for-Charlie wounded had babbled their silly, idiotic, childish ideals about 'fair play to Stein,' Stein had exchanged with Storm—who said almost nothing—an incredible, astonishing look of secret knowledge, and had been shocked to realize that Storm knew what he knew. It was not something that could be admitted aloud, or even acknowledged privately, but it was a look of full and complete understanding. Storm, like him, knew that many many more people were going to live through this war than got killed in it; that as soon as it was over all the nations involved would start helping each other and be friends again, except for the dead. And Storm—like him— meant to be one of the ones who lived if he possibly could. And Storm, like him, did not feel at all guilty. Stein finished his drink and sat down again to wait—for tomorrow and the plane. As he sat, the first chills and fever of his first malaria session attacked him and began playing on him like on a musical instrument. He sat tasting these physical sensations, grinning to himself.

It was on the way back to the hospital with the other six casualties and the three bottles of whiskey that McCron took another of his fits. He had been very quiet since leaving Bugger Stein's tent, a sign which usually presaged one of his attacks, but nobody had paid any attention because of the happy windfall of whiskey and their love-warm conversation about Stein. Consequently, no one was prepared for it when McCron suddenly threw himself down in the mud at the edge of the road and began to weep, whimper and howl, biting his clenched knuckles and staring over at them with the wild eyes of a rabid animal, while he curled himself up into the tightest ball his body could make. While they rushed to him and tried to straighten him out and soothe him, he screamed at them half in incomprehensible gibberish, half in lucid phrases. When they first stood up Wynn screamed "Oh my God!" in a voice of terrible recognition with the blood spurting a foot from his throat, and had gone down. Nineteen. Only nineteen. Next to him Earl went down in silence because his face had been torn open to a mass of red. He was twenty. Further to the left the other two Darl and Gwenne had gone down too yelling "I'm killed! I'm killed!" All of them at once, in a matter of seconds. And then the others. All the others. He had tried to help them. He had tried to protect them. I tried. I tried.

Finally they got him to stop screaming and got his body straightened out, which last they had learned by experience helped to quiet him more than anything. But he was still weeping and whimpering and went on biting his now bloody knuckles, and they knew also from experience that this stage usually went on a long time. It was either carry him, or stay here with him until they missed supper chow. So they carried him. Slowly the weeping and knuckle biting stopped until he was only drawing long shuddering sobs through his clenched fists pressed against his mouth. By the time they had almost reached the compound he was all right enough to say in a thick voice, "Gimme a drinka whiskey," which they stopped and did, then had one themselves, and then went on in to eat. They were all of them sure McCron would be evacuated any day now. They were also sure that with his haggard face and haunted eyes he would feel guilty about going the rest of his life, though none of them would have. He was in fact evacuated the day after the visit to Stein. Two days later Fife and Storm were sent back to the company together.

The first thing they both noticed, during that first evening of cataloging the hits, runs and errors of evacuation for the nonwounded who had not had their advantages, was that everybody in the old outfit was sporting a beard. In the hospital everybody was clean-shaven. Almost the first thing the orderlies did after getting them settled in was to come around with a dollar Gillette and a blade (which they later carried off to another bed, but brought back every day) and insist that everybody shave. Those incapable of shaving themselves, the orderlies shaved for them. So Fife and Storm with their smooth faces immediately noticed the beards first of all. It seemed to apply to everyone in the company except the officers. They were not very big beards— after all it was only eleven days since they had first departed on the march up to the line, and fifty per cent of them were too young to raise much of a beard anyway—but it seemed to be very important to everyone. But when Storm and Fife asked about it nobody seemed to know quite why. It was just something which had swept through the company like a fad and, they learned later, the same thing had happened in the rest of the Battalion. It was not a protest against anything. It was not a time device or a vow, as if they had promised not to shave till the whole island was captured. It was not even a manliness game: no display of 'tough virility'. It was just that everyone—rightly or wrongly (John Bell, whom Fife and Storm also saw, thought wrongly though he had a beard)—felt he was a different person from the man who had gone up on the line ten days ago; and the beards seemed to symbolize, seemed to make material, this change. Storm and Fife, of course, immediately stopped shaving.

There were other changes in the company besides the beards— as Fife, especially, found out soon enough. They drank and talked a long time that night, and so wound up sleeping drunk with borrowed blankets on the floors of somebody else's tents, but when Fife reported to the orderly room tent the next morning, he found he was out of a job.

There had been an almost wholesale number of promotions in the company: Skinny Culn replaced Grove as platoon sergeant of 1st Platoon; Beck of course replaced Keck as platoon sergeant of 2nd Platoon; Sergeant Field, Pfc Doll's old squad sergeant in 1st Platoon, had replaced S/Sgt Spain as platoon leader of 3rd Platoon. And after that it went right on down the line: Charlie Dale had made squad sergeant; Doll had made squad sergeant; John Bell had made squad sergeant; and so had a number of others. And as for the orderly room, the middleaged little draftee Weld had been made corporal and was now Welsh's Forward Echelon clerk. He had two privates for assistants, just as Fife himself had once had, and one of them turned out to be Pfc Train, the stutterer, in whose lap Fife had fallen after being hit, he who had found and then given away the jewelled sword.

It was strange what a little authority and a couple of stripes could do to a man. When Fife came in, Weld was sitting behind Fife's old field desk, punching away at Fife's old typewriter with a pencil behind his ear, and ordering his two assistants around as if they were a full Army Corps. Fife had always thought of little old Joe Weld as the meekest of men. Now Weld looked up at him with a coldeyed smile floating on his middleaged face, said calmly "Oh hello there Fife." He was obviously not about to turn loose of his newly acquired status if he could help it.

The two new assistant clerks, Train and the other one—a young draftee named Crown, both looked at Fife with deeply guilty looks on their faces and said nothing. Mad Welsh of course was sitting behind his own field desk, working. While Fife stood, he continued to work. Finally he looked up. He must have known already that Fife had returned with Storm from the hospital, but he showed no surprise, pleasure, warmth or even simple kindliness on his crazy, black-Welsh face.

"Well what do you want, kid?" he said brusquely, as if Fife had never been away. Then he smiled his crazy, slyeyed, sadist's grin.

"I came back from the hospital and I'm supposed to report in," Fife said furiously. But his anger could not even begin to overcome in him his sense of lostness, war terror, terrible aloneness. This orderly room had been his sanctuary.

"Okay," Welsh said. "So you've reported."

"What's Weld doing at my desk, punching my typewriter?" Fife demanded.

"*Corporal* Weld is my Forward Echelon clerk. Them other two punk assholes there are his assistant runners. Here, Fuckface!" Welsh barked and held out a paper to Weld. "Take this over to MacTae in supply."

"Right, Sarge!" Weld barked back. He got up and took the paper and turned around, throwing out his meager chest. "Train! Here!"

"*I said TAKE it!*" Welsh shouted.

"Right, Sarge!" Weld barked. He left.

"Aint he an asshole?" Welsh grinned at Fife.

"But you knew I was coming back from the hospital!" Fife said. "You knew I was—"

"Knew you were comin back! How the hell would I know you were comin back? I got a company to run here. You think it can wait for you? If you'd had any fucking guts or brains, you'd of got yourself evacuated off this Rock and back to the United States with a wound like you had. If I'd of been—"

"You can't do this to me, Welsh!" Fife cried. "By God you can't! You can't take and—"

"I can't, can't I!" Welsh bellowed. He stood up and leaned his knuckles on the desk. "Look around you! It's done. It was done while you were in the hospital waiting to be evacuated." He grinned his furry-eyed grin. "You can't blame me if you didn't have guts or brains enough to—"

"God damn you, I notice you didn't make anybody Mess Sergeant in Stormy's place!" Fife shouted.

"Storm asked me to wait because he thought he might be comin back," Welsh said, grinning insolently. He sat back down. Corporal Weld had sneaked back in and sat himself down at Fife's old desk to listen.

It was exactly like a hundred others of their furious battles and insulting arguments, and for a moment in the heat of it Fife forgot the reason for it. But then his heart sank, because he was no longer Welsh's clerk. He would never have believed, whatever their internecine fights, that Welsh would not have stood up for him and backed him up when it came to losing his job as clerk. But apparently Welsh was not going to, and had no intention of doing so.

"God damn you, Welsh! God damn you, you son of a bitch!" he spluttered.

Fortunately, Brass Band came through the tent flap at just that moment, and Welsh leaped up to shout "Attention!" at the top of his lungs while himself, the two frightened assistant clerks, Weld and Fife all snapped to.

"You don't have to call attention every time I come in, Sergeant," Band said benignly, "I've told you that." Welsh merely stared at him. Band looked at Fife. "Well! Hello there, Fife! So you're back with the old outfit. Glad to have you back aboard. At ease! Rest! Rest! By the way, Fife, have you seen my helmet?"

Fife could hardly believe his ears. He was still in the throes of bitterly cursing Welsh. Band went behind his own desk and produced for Fife's inspection his fractured helmet shell which that Japanese had put a bullet through. Fife listened to him in silence with increasing astonishment and indignation. He felt he deserved a *certain* amount of respect and prestige for being a wounded man. After all, none of these guys had been wounded. And here was this silly ass telling him this story about something that had not even hurt him. When Band finished the tale of his adventure, Fife was so furious he could hardly trust himself to speak.

At his own desk First Sergeant Welsh had taken a deep breath and blown it out and sat back down to his work. For himself, Welsh was just as glad Band had come in. Or he might *really* have lost his temper. He was getting damn tired of forever teaching punk asshole kids that to the world, the war, the nation, the company, none of them meant a goddam thing; that they were spendable like dollarbills; that they could all die day by day and one by one and it wouldn't mean a goddam fucking thing to anybody as long as there were replacements. *Who* the *fuck* did he think he *was?* Did he think he *meant anything* to this company? Welsh took in another deep, selfpitying breath and blew it out. Now he was angry. That hurt look on the punk's face when he came in and saw Weld made Welsh insanely furious. What did Fife expect him to *do* for him? The punks were all learning now—and Oh did it *hurt!* This week back off the line was good enough for that, was excellent for that: Shorty Tall and his bright ideas: time enough to get drunk good; time enough to talk; time enough to think about themselves and their impossible, ridiculous position. Time enough to reflect that this war was only starting, time enough to realize—or remember!—that behind every company like them stood at least ten companies stretching all the way back to Washington and dedicated with much less danger to getting them up there all equipped to do their dangerous work. Oh yes they were learning! They were learning now, but without appreciation, what Welsh had known and appreciated all along. Even Storm had not known that. But Welsh had.

First Sergeant Welsh had come down from the hills at the head of his company with the same drawn, haunted face and wrinkled, too bright eyes they all wore, but unlike them he had come down triumphant—triumphant, and without a souvenir except an iron contempt for the souvenirs the rest of them all carried. He was triumphant because everything had turned out exactly as he had expected and anticipated, thus leaving him with no real shock or trauma: men got killed mostly for statistical reasons, as he had anticipated: men fought well or badly about like they would have fought for women or other Property, as he had expected. The only thing that really bothered him was that dumb punk ass Tella. But he had thought that all out carefully, and had realized that some penancemaking, selfdestructive thing in his nature which had made him go after Tella would almost certainly make him liable to other such acts in future, and had accepted that. As for his contempt of souvenirs, he had never yet had to resort to such sophomoric methods to obtain his booze, and he certainly was not about to start now. In the first place he liked gin. These punks could have their whiskey. He could drink whiskey if he had to, but as long as he could get gin he meant to have it, and if his former source of gin had removed or transferred he would find another—and he didn't need no souvenirs to do it. He had marched along loosely through the dust under the sun, and through the mud under the jungle, chanting to himself his secret rune of "Property. Property. All for Property," while his company struggled along behind him loaded down and gasping; about the only sane man left in the outfit, he figured. And at that moment he was just about right. When they got down he had shaved every day and had not tried to grow a stupid beard, and no one had dared say a word to him about it because he had had a moustache for years.

From now on the punks could take care of themselves.

Behind him Welsh heard Fife say to Band with a heavy, furious irony: "Well now that's remarkable, Sir! I wish I could have seen my helmet. I bet it was torn up more than yours even. I was hit in the head, you know. But I never saw it."

Fife's voice was shaking with fury, and Welsh grinned to himself. Everybody in the company was sick to puking of Band's helmet. But when Fife turned to look over at him for corroboration, Welsh set his eyes like two rocks and stared right through him. Welsh had had his own run-ins with Brassass the last few days since he took over the company, but he had taken care of them himself and the punk could do the same.

Band had bent and was putting the helmet shell carefully away. He had only the shell there now because he had taken to wearing the scratched, dented liner at formations and around the camp. "Yes. It's too bad you couldn't have kept it so you could take it home with you for a souvenir like I'm doing."

"I was thinking of other things," Fife said, "Sir. At the time."

Band had straightened back up and was still smiling, but his eyes and smile did not have quite their customary eager look. "I suppose you were." He turned to Welsh. "Well, Sergeant?"

"There's nothing much new, Sir." Welsh's own series of petty clashes with Band had come to a head two days ago when, having been rebuked for not being properly respectful to the company officers, Welsh had said quietly, "Sir, you can have my stripes and my job whenever you want them." He had meant it, and Band knew he meant it. "Sergeant, dont ever get the idea you're indispensable," Band had said narrowly. "Sir, nobody knows better than me just exactly how dispensable every man in this company is," Welsh had countered, and that had ended it. Band had got himself off the hook by reminding him not to forget it, and he had not asked for the stripes and job.

Now Band said, "Well, that's good news." Suddenly, wearing his eager smile, he clapped his hands together and rubbed their palms briskly and said in his best schoolteacher voice, "Well then! Corporal Fife! I guess we better decide what to do about you, then, Fife. Hunh?" He did not wait for anyone to answer. "Since Weld here is now Corporal and clerk, we can't very well demote him back to private. Neither can we have two clerks. Also, since Weld is a good bit older and in less good physical shape than Fife, as well as being considerably less well-trained, I dont see how we can send him off to take second command of a rifle squad. . . ."

All Fife's anger ran down out of him like water as he realized the trend Band was taking, and he decided, too late, that he could have been much nicer about Band's helmet. Terror ballooned in him as he remembered that hellish exposed slope up there, the exploding mortar round, the dead boy on the stretcher.

". . . Soo—How would you like to become second in command of a top-rated rifle squad, Fife?" Band said cheerily. "Sergeant Jenks's squad of the 3d Platoon has no corporal."

Even in his sudden fear Fife did not see, Band having put it as
he had, that there was any other answer he could give except to
say Yes, he would like that. But he was saved from having to say
it by Welsh.

"Sir, Sergeant Dranno back at Rear Echelon has been devilling
me to give him someone to help him. He's had a lot of work over
casualties since this action. And he's gonna have a lot more."
Welsh stared at Band. "Fife here has more clerical knowledge
than anybody in the company except for Dranno."

"All right! There you are!" Band gave Fife his curiously bland
smile. "Now you have a choice, Fife! Which do you prefer?"

"I'll work for Draino," Fife managed to say lamely.

"All right!" Lt Band said cheerily, with that smile. He swung
in his chair toward Welsh. "When do you want him to leave,
Sergeant?"

"Hell," Welsh said. "Today."

"There you are, Corporal," Band smiled. "Okay. You can
go."

Fife got as far as to pack. Pack?! All he had to do was put his
messkit spoon in one pocket, his extra pair of socks in another,
buckle on his new riflebelt, pick up his new rifle. The Imperial
quart of Australian whiskey he had managed to wrangle from the
new magnanimity of the newly promoted Sgt Doll (which he
hated), he would carry in his hand. But then the rebellion came.
All of his fury returned, his fury at Band, his fury at Welsh, his
fury at the world. Fuck them. Fuck them all. With it came back
also that tragic sense of sorrow and loss he had felt so strongly on
the evening in the jungle beside the trail before they were to go
into battle the next morning. He was alone. There was nobody in
the world who gave a damn whether he lived or died. So be it. He
would die alone then. He knew what he felt was unrealistic; he
knew he would regret it immediately; he was sure he was signing
his own death warrant; but in spite of the fear and terror which
filled him in equal parts with and right alongside of the fury and
sorrow, he would not go back there to work for Draino. He would
show these bastards. He would show them all. With a curiously
selfgrinding, selfcastigating hatred of everything but most of all

himself, he rejected Welsh's goddamn charity. He unpacked. Had Welsh tried to keep him in the orderly room? Had Welsh tried to get him back *for* the orderly room? He returned to the orderly room tent to tell them that he had changed his mind, that he intended to stay. When Welsh heard him, his face turned so red it appeared his whole head would explode like a bomb with furious rage, but he said not a word in front of Band. Band himself gave Fife a curiously sharp, not truly pleased look which when Fife left the tent made Fife feel he had been actually and actively seduced. But it was too late now. He moved in with Jenks's squad. As he had anticipated, he immediately regretted what he had done. The only real pleasure he got out of it was Welsh's face.

Sergeant Jenks—he who as Corporal Jenks had once fought with fists with Pfc Doll back in the old days—had only been made Sergeant since the battle, when his own squad leader was killed in the fight at the Japanese bivouac. He was a dark, lean, tall, long-torsoed, short-legged man from Georgia who spoke little and took his rank and his soldiering seriously as jobs. He made Fife welcome with few words and went about his business, which at the moment was serious drinking, and that night Fife got drunk with Jenks's squad and 3d Platoon instead of with Storm and the Headquarters gang; but he never did feel part of them.

It was on that same night that Private Witt paid them his angry, drunken visit. And so it was from Witt, whose Cannon Company outfit was bivouacked at Regimental Rear Echelon Headquarters, that C-for-Charlie learned for the first time that Captain Johnny Gaff had been recommended for the Medal of Honor, and that he had been evacuated to Esperito Santo for safekeeping. Witt naturally first looked up his old buddies from Gaff's 'assault force' for some drinking, and it was to them he told the story. But it soon spread like wildfire through the whole company, and there was a big laugh about it. Because, naturally, everybody knew that Gaff had never looked up his little 'assault force' to pay off that big drunk he had promised them, everything paid for by him. It was a bitter laugh. Witt himself waxed drunkenly eloquent about the treachery of any man who could use them as Gaff had and then shuck them off like a wornout fatigue blouse. Gaff had bug-

gered them all in the ass, was Witt's opinion and he thought they
all ought to admit it. But the rest of them tried to laugh it off, as
the company in general had. Gaff was the final bitter sauce on the
bitter meat all C-for-Charlie had been masticating without appe-
tite for most of this past week. Neither, as far as Witt or anybody
else could find out, had Gaff recommended Doll for the Distinguished Service Cross he had promised personally to recommend
him for. Sergeant Doll—who now could remember clearly how
he had shrewdly saved the group by deliberately drawing the
Japanese fire knowing the ledge was ten yards off to the right—
tried to laugh this off too, but he found it a little harder to do than
the others did. As far as medals were concerned, from what any
of them could find out, nobody from C-for-Charlie had been recommended for any medals at all so far. Except of course for Gaff.

"If you can count him!" John Bell laughed drunkenly. "After
all, he was the Battalion Exec. He was never in C-for-Charlie."
Bell found the whole thing sourly, indigestibly amusing: the bitter, cold-Spam of knowledge; the mastication of it; the sauce of
Gaff and medals.

But this was about the only thing Bell found amusing. There
had been one mail call, a big one, during the past week and Bell
had received six letters from his wife. This was the first mail call
they'd had since first boarding the transports, and Bell did not
think six seemed like too huge a number. Of course, a lot of them
could have got shunted aside on other ships or delayed. Couldn't
they? Anyway, in the light of his revelatory knowledge which had
come to him up there in the saddle above the Japanese strongpoint, Bell strove to read between the lines for signs. Had this
batch seemed colder? Or was he only reading that into them? As
he always did when this sort of mood came over him he got up,
holding his Imperial quart by the neck, and walked off by himself
away from the others. Drunkenly he sat down on the hillside and
sat looking out over the darkened shape of the island toward the
sea in the half-moonlight. The airraids had already come and
gone, but there were no fires burning. Of course, back home . . .
back home . . . there were always so many more opportunities
for—what was it?—love partners—wasn't that what they called it

in all the psych courses back at State?—sure, that was it—than there were here on this beautiful, Godforsaken place. But he had to believe in her. If he couldn't believe in Marty, he couldn't believe in anything now. With a half-erection from thinking about her he got up and came back to find Witt holding forth again— with much laughter, but bitterly—about Gaff.

"Why dont you transfer back into old C-for-Charlie?" he asked suddenly of Witt. "You know you'd like to. And you only got tomorrow and tomorrow night. Left."

"Me? Not me!" Witt whooped. "I won't never come back in this Battalion long as Shorty Tall commands it. No, sir. Much's I might like to. If Tall ever gits promoted, or shipped out . . . But not now. As matter fact, I ought be movin long ratt now, for I contamnated," Witt cried, and got up swaying. Suddenly, in great giant strides, he began leaping off down the steep hillside, an Imperial quart in each hand, while his voice came back to them with the diminishing tone of a train whistle moving away from the listener: "Airraids over, think I take a look down there see they do any damage, then I meander on home to dear ol' Cannon Company, see if . . ." He had already disappeared from sight long since, but his voice kept coming back to them, then there was a crash and a loud "Owwwww!"

Several of them had already been on their feet starting to follow and stop him. When they reached him, they found him lying on his side grinning foolishly.

"I slipped," Witt said, peering up at them owlishly. A rock had gashed his cheek, and while he still grasped the necks of both Imperial quarts firmly, only one of the bottles was still whole. The other had broken out from under his grasp so that he now held only the jagged empty neck.

"You can't go back there anyway tonight!" Bell hollered at him. "You fool! You'll get your ass shot off by some triggerhappy sentry!"

"I guess yore ratt," Witt said. He allowed himself to be led docilely back up to the others. "But at fuckin Shorty Tall better stay way fum me, at son of a bitch, or I punch his fuckin haid in!'' he yelled once, struggling to get his arms loose. But after that he was quiet.

The next morning he left considerably chastened with a bandaid on his cheek, obviously reluctant to go. But no amount of persuasion could talk him into just staying and coming with them, not as long as Colonel Tall commanded the Battalion. So that night—the last night—they got drunk by themselves, without Witt.

There was plenty of whiskey left, and now most men carried three canteens instead of two: two for water, one for whiskey. The whiskey they could not take, as well as the remaining unsold souvenirs, was left with Sergeant MacTae and his supply clerk and Storm and his cooks, none of whom were volunteering to go up this time, and who promised to keep it all for them until they got back. And the last Storm saw of them was the last man of the last platoon who, just before he dropped over the crest of the hill, stopped and turned back and yelled plaintively: ''Goddam you, you take care of my whiskey now!''

As they began the long march up Privates Mazzi and Tills were again no longer speaking. They had sold their heavy Jap MG for a fair price, and had split the take, but one night giggling drunk Tills had told the tale of Mazzi's fright over the mortar shells that first day in the midst of his brave talk. Mazzi had stomped away back to his hep friends from New York in the 1st Platoon, saying he had got from Tills all he wanted anyway, which was half of the machinegun. Later he told other people he would have requested transfer out of the Weapons Platoon were it not that rifle platoons were so dangerous. Now they marched along back into combat side by side, one carrying the buttplate, the other carrying the tube, staring straight ahead and not saying a word to each other. Both men, like many others, had had their first serious attack of malaria during the week of rest.

CHAPTER 7

Everything looked changed. Behind Hill 209 things had been
tidied up and civilized. Camp sites had appeared, and the old jeep
track had been regraded and leveled until it was passable to other
vehicles. Hiking, C-for-Charlie regarded all of this with interest.
Beyond Hill 209, where they had fought and been terrorized on
the second and third folds a week ago, puptents were now
pitched. On the side ridge where Keck had led his three squads up
through the grass and later died of his own mistake, laughing men
were bivouacked. The brushy hollow where 2d Battalion had been
caught and mortared so badly the first day was now a bustling
Message Center. And the new jeep track, with the Engineers still
working on it, passed between the left and righthand grassy
ridges across the flat and on up the Bowling Alley onto Hill 210,
The Elephant's Head. As they swung along it, raising dust and
winded but stepping out smartly because they were being
watched by people they now thought of as rear area troops, C-for-
Charlie was the lead company of the Battalion and it was their
pride that they had effected all these changes they were noting,
even though they hadn't done the work. Because they had done
the killing.

This triumph did not last long. Under the shade of the tall
jungle trees along the line that followed the crest of Hill 210, the
relief went off smoothly. The company they were relieving had

been patrolling the past week and had lost two dead and five hurt. But they had not fought any major battles like The Dancing Elephant, and this showed in their admiring faces as they watched C-for-Charlie come up and take over. C-for-Charlie only glared back dourly. There was, they had learned immediately from the men they were relieving, a patrol scheduled for this afternoon. The attack itself was scheduled for tomorrow at dawn.

The march up had been fun, but it had brought them right back here, they suddenly realized, back here where everything counted.

Colonel Tall, however, was not with them today. Colonel Tall, the grapevine had it, was just in the process of being promoted. Nobody in the Battalion had seen him this morning when the march began, and he had not shown up at the rendezvous point by the river where the four companies met. By that mysterious process which nobody understood but which always seemed to know everything about Regimental (and even Division) events before they began to take place, rumor said that Tall was going away to command the detached sister regiment fighting in the mountains, whose CO was so ill from malaria that he could no longer command. This brought sour smiles to the lips of malaria sufferers in the Battalion, most of whom were running consistent temperatures of 104+ during their attacks. Another thing that brought laughter was the comprehension that Old Shorty was being promoted because of *their* exploits and *their* shed blood, was being, because of this reputation, jumped in over the Exec of the detached regiment with the temporary rank of full colonel. Nobody really cared very much that he was leaving. They were much more concerned with what his successor was going to be like, and with their forthcoming afternoon patrol.

With regard to the patrol there was, five hundred yards to their front, one more unjungled hill, a small one, rising out of the jungle all alone. This had been named "The Sea Slug". Since the one bright young staffer had succeeded in nicknaming The Dancing Elephant and making it stick, there had been a rash of names proposed for just about every hill remaining to be taken, by just about every bright young aide who had access to the aerial photos. Naming hills had become a game and a great lark. The

Sea Slug, a fat slightly curving ridge really, was so called because of a fanshaped series of ravines spreading out from its inland end, thus resembling the cluster of antennae-tentacles protruding from the head of the sea slug, or sea cucumber as it is more often called. This Sea Slug had been reconnoitered twice by patrols of the 3d Battalion to its seaward or tail end, which was the closer and easier approach; but both times they had been driven back by heavy MG and mortar fire. Apparently it was heavily defended. C-for-Charlie's patrol was to come at it from the inland or head end, against the fanshaped series of ravines, to see if it was less heavily defended there because of the harder terrain. They were also, if time permitted, to do some chopping work on the trail to enlarge it for tomorrow's big attack. 1st Lt George C Band, smiling his unfocused, somehow indecent smile, made the decision that Skinny Culn's 1st Platoon would do the patrol.

Tactically, they were told, The Sea Slug was useless except as an outpost, and as a jumping off point for the major push against the next big hill mass: the Hills 250-51-52-and-53 area, now known in the Division Plans Bureau as "The Giant Boiled Shrimp." But the Division Commander and the general commanding wanted it because its open length, angling forward, was a perfect approach route to The Giant Boiled Shrimp hill mass. Culn's patrol, like the others, was being given a walkie-talkie man to call back firing data to the mortars and artillery.

They ate first, picking out of the open cases cans of meat-and-beans or hash or stew according to preference and sitting down with them around on the hillside or on watercans. Then they filled their canteens and moved out, moving slowly, even reluctantly, down the open space of The Elephant's Trunk toward the same jungle trail which just a week ago they had climbed up from. At the bottom they disappeared into the leaves.

Up above, the rest of the company watched.

Despite fighting experience this was C-for-Charlie's first combat jungle patrol. Open hill fighting taught nothing about that. All of them had moved through enough jungle on foot to know what to expect. The jungle was eerie. Dripping trees, disturbed birds squawking, the sounds of their own breath in the green air, their feet squishing in the trail's mud, gloom. Ahead of them the trail branched. Theirs, the left one, immediately narrowed to a track just wide enough for men to walk in single file. It was known to take them in the direction of The Sea Slug hill. Hemmed in by wild bananas, papaya, huge looping lianas, and plants which dangled great fleshy red penises in their faces, they moved along this narrow space, announced ahead by the birds, trying to move quietly and failing, fighting down feelings of claustrophobia, and halting frequently while Culn and the green new Lieutenant took compass readings. Far enough back to be out of earshot the two rearmost squads did some feeble chopping at the trail with machetes which changed nothing. Four hours later they were back with one dead, two wounded, and faces which had aged twenty years.

The dead man was a little known and essentially friendless draftee named Griggs. He came first (after the Lieutenant and Culn) ported by four men bellyupward, his arms legs and head aflop and all dangling downward. Mortar fragments had hit him in the chest. He was placed on the hillside off by himself to wait for the medics to come cart him off, basically resented by everyone because he reminded them they might have been in his place. Of the two wounded who came right behind him one had had his thigh torn wide open by a big mortar chunk; he hobbled along on one foot between two men, groaning and sighing and occasionally weeping. The other one had gotten a piece of mortar shell through his neck and now wore a high gauze collar as he staggered along with his arm around still another man. A group of fresh men from the company took them over and got them started for the aid station while the rest of the patrol dropped down weary and shaky wherever they could on the hillside. They looked like men who had done their day's work and felt entitled to rest, but resented that they were being underpaid for the type work they did without hope of ever correcting it. Only Culn and the Lieutenant, after seeing them all in through the line, did not sit down and instead went to collect Band and go make their report to Battalion.

The Lieutenant would have preferred to sit down. He did not, however, feel he could do that as long as Culn didn't. He kept darting looks at Culn. Of them all Culn was the only one this afternoon who had kept his normal disposition, which in Culn's case was a sunny, happy, smiling one. The Lieutenant, whose name was Payne and who was still pale and stiff faced, would have attributed this to Culn's superior experience if he had not noticed that all of the others he saw reacted more like himself than they did like Culn. Right now, as they tramped along the side of the hill, Culn was whistling pleasantly a song which Payne had heard before somewhere and which he believed was called *San Antonio Rose*. Once he stopped whistling long enough to look over and smile cheerily and wink. Finally Payne could stand it no longer.

"Would you mind stopping that damned whistling, Sergeant!" he said, much sharper than he had originally intended.

"Okay, Lieutenant," Culn said amiably. "If you say so."

And he did stop. But he went on humming the notes silently to himself under his breath. There was no malice in him toward Lt Payne; he was whistling because he felt good. Skinny Culn was an amiable, easygoing sort of man, willing to live and let live, usually laughing, but he was also a careful, well grounded soldier with nine years service. That was the way he had run his patrol, and he had been nice to the new lieutenant—who, if the Irish truth be known, knew as much about that sort of patrol as he himself did, which was nothing. Culn had waited four years and had reenlisted and shipped over to get command of this platoon—which platoon his predecessor Grove, now predeceased, and with whom he had been good drinking buddies, had also reenlisted to keep, thereby frustrating Culn. But that was all in the game. In the end only Grove's death and the war had given it to him. Being a good Irish Catholic, if a lax one, Skinny could look upon that without guilt or horror as a sort of personal responsibility passed from Grove to him from beyond the grave. Certainly he did not intend to lose it now, either by having it shot out from under him, or having himself yanked off the top of it for some reckless swashbuckling or other. He also did not intend to lose it by antagonizing the officer who thought he led it. The reason he felt good was because he was alive and undamaged, and had before him the prospect of an easy safe afternoon and evening of loafing and banter before tomorrow, and maybe even a few drinks. It was highly possible that Brass Band would offer them both a good stiff snort when they reported to him. Culn had noticed that Band had taken good care of himself with the liquor situation, which he could more easily do, having a dogrobber orderly who had carried his personal bed roll up here for him. Walking along, he almost caught himself whistling the song again, but stopped himself just in time. They walked on.

"Didn't you feel *any*thing up there?" Payne asked finally in a strong voice, darting him another look and then looking away straight ahead. *"Out* there?"

"Feel?" Skinny said. "Yeah, I guess I felt scared. Once there, anyway. Durin the worst of the mortars." He smiled cheerfully at Payne as though now he knew what Payne's trouble was, which angered Payne.

"Well, you didn't look it, Sergeant," Payne said.

"You dont really know me very well yet, Lootenant," Culn grinned. But he was suddenly angry. He felt his rights were being infringed upon by Payne. He had plenty of feelings, but he didn't have to talk about them. He was not a cog in a machine, whatever Payne thought.

"But when those men were hit!" Payne said. "One died! They were in your platoon!" He was less pale now, away from the casualties, but his face was still stiff.

Culn smiled at him carefully. Payne sounded as if he had known this platoon for years. "Lootenant, I think we done pretty good. And got off pretty lucky. With them treebursts comin in on us like they were," he said cheerfully. "It ought to of been lots worse, see? And as for feeling," he said kindly, "the Service nor nobody pays me any extra 'Feeling Pay' for feeling. Like they pay flyers 'Flight Pay' for flyin. So I figure I aint required to feel. I figure I won't feel any more than's just absolutely necessary. The minimum feeling. Tomorrow's likely to be really rough, Lootenant. Did you know that?"

Payne did not answer this. His face looked like a stormcloud and even stiffer than before, and Skinny worried that he had gone too far. Nervously (why antagonize him?), to soften his statement, he chuckled and looked over at Payne and grinned and winked. He saw gratefully that in front of them a little uphill Brass Band had come out of his command post to greet them. Payne saw it too, and looked away in that direction recomposing his face. The CP had been located in one of the old Japanese stick shanties in the shade of the big trees just down behind the crest. Band now stood in front of it. Band was smiling at them proudly.

He did offer them a drink. A good stiff one, at his suggestion. They took it straight from the beautiful, lovely White Horse bottle. And then Band had one himself. George Band did not see why he should not indulge himself in a few little luxuries if they were available without too much trouble, since he was now Company Commander. Jim Stein, memory of whom was fading swiftly day by day, would have considered that highly immoral. But Band didn't see it that way at all. He had told off his new clerk Corporal Weld and Weld's number one assistant Train that between them he wanted his bedroll carried up on the march, and into it he had packed six bottles of the best, in addition to his canteens. As it had turned out, they would be leaving here tomorrow and he would have to leave both bedroll and whiskey to somebody, but they might very well have spent a week here before beginning the new attack. In any event he would have one good night's sleep out of it, and it hadn't really been too much extra work for his two clerks. If 1st/Sgt Welsh could use them as personal slaves, so could the Company Commander certainly. Like his men, Band had been drinking rather more heavily since the week of 'rest' began. He had another one out of the bottle before putting it away and turned his attention to his new lieutenant, Payne.

He watched Payne's pale, stiff face while they made their report, and decided things might be working out. When they had finished the report, he said, "Well, we better go along to Battalion and tell them all. The new Commander's arrived, I think." Band was thinking privately that maybe this new commander might very well offer them all a drink, and Culn was thinking the

same thing. "You're sure everything's been done for the
wounded?" Band added piously. Both men nodded.

Actually there really wasn't very much to do for them and
everybody knew it. They had crossed over into that Other Realm.
They had taken their sulfa pills. The medic on the patrol had
given them each a syrette of morphine. There was nothing the
group who helped them down to the aid station could do for them
except give them water and a shot of whiskey. The one with the
leg wound kept groaning and weeping and wailing over and over
in a child's voice, "Goddam, it *hurts!* It *hurts!*" Quite a large
group walked them down, many more than were needed. It was as
if they thought they could give the two wounded comfort in sheer
numbers, and at the same time satisfy their own curiosity. Also, it
was a welcome relief from the boring duty of having to stay in the
holes on the line. The group hung around the aid station watching
while the doctors worked on them and shipped them out swiftly
on a stretcher carrying jeep. Neither of them would ever come
back, and the general opinion seemed to be that they were the
both of them pretty goddamned lucky. The man with the leg
wound, when the doctor unwrapped it to have a look at it,
screamed with pain. His name was Wills. The other man's larynx
was damaged and he could not talk at all. The tiny mortar fragment had gone completely through his neck and come out the
other side without hitting any major nerves or blood vessels.
Once they were gone, waving feebly back from the jeep, there
was no more point in hanging around and the group walked back
up to the position together. One of these was Corporal Fife, newly
of the 3d Platoon, and another was Buck Sergeant Doll.

Fife had done nothing to help either of the wounded, and indeed had not wanted to get close enough to them to touch them.
But he could not resist coming along and watching them with
obscene fascination from the outskirts of the group between the
heads of those who clustered around them. He remembered in
detail his own trip back to the aid station, was haunted by it and
by the fact that he could have been hit again and killed at any
moment. Also, he could not forget the bloodstained trip down to
the beach in the jeep, knowing all the time that no matter how bad

it looked his wound was not as serious as he had hoped it was. Fife had nightmares about this trip now every night, sometimes waking up screaming sometimes not, but always in a cold sweat of fear and panic the essential essence of which was a feeling of complete entrapment. Trapped in every direction no matter where he turned, trapped by patriotic doctors, trapped by longfaced crewcut infantry Colonels who demanded the willingness to die, trapped by Japanese colonial ambitions, trapped by chic grinning S-1 officers secure in their right to ask only after other officers, trapped by his own government and its faceless nameless administrators, trapped by Stein and his increasingly sad face, trapped by 1st/Sgt Mad Welsh who wanted only to laugh at him. In the dream all these came in on him in an insane jumble of shrieks and accusations while they sat waiting in the middle distance positive that he would prove them all right and show himself to be yellow. Even when he drank himself to sleep those nights after getting out of the hospital during the week of 'rest', the nightmare or one of its variations came. Sometimes it was bombers and polyglot faces laughing down at him from the bombbay doors as they released their loads on him: they had trapped him into bravery and killed him. Either way he lost. Naturally, he was somewhat upset by watching the two wounded being handled and cared for. And yet he could not *not* watch. The worst thing was the element of chance which came into it. The most perfect, most perfectly trained soldier could do nothing to protect against, or save himself from, the element of chance. As he walked away back up the hill, Fife did not feel it was safe, could not trust himself, even to speak. To anyone. And naturally, it was then that newly promoted Sergeant Doll chose to come over and talk to him.

Doll, in fact, thought he had interpreted correctly the painful look on Fife's face, and that was why he came over. Since making sergeant, a new and powerful sense of paternal responsibility had blossomed in Doll. It applied mainly to his own squad, but it could be extended to every rank below his own in the company. Before being promoted Doll had never realized what a marvelous thing it was to help other people or what sheer pleasure it could give you. When noncoms used to want to help him out with something, he hated them and thought they were pompous. But now he understood it. Fife was the only man who had been wounded and returned to the company, if you left out Storm in the kitchen who wasn't combat. Doll thought he could understand what a violent shock it must be to get hit and find you were not invulnerable. But all it really needed was a return of confidence, and Doll thought he could help. He had confidence enough for damn near everybody. He had it because he never thought about being wounded or killed. Take tomorrow: by this time tomorrow they were certain to be in it up to their ass; but did he think about that? What was the good of that?

Doll, when he'd been promoted, had requested transfer to the 2d Platoon and a squad there. His own former Squad Leader in 1st Platoon, Sgt Field, had been promoted to Staff and made Platoon Sgt of 3d Platoon; but Doll had asked expressly not to be given his own old squad. He explained to Brass Band that this was because he didn't think it would look good if he was jumped from Pfc to Sgt over the squad's former Corporal, who by rights should (and did) get the rating. Also, he said he wanted to be with the rest of the old Hill 210 'Assault Force', all of whom except for Witt were now noncoms in the 2d Platoon. All this sounded good, and Band immediately accommodated him. But the real reason Doll didn't want to take his own old squad was that he was afraid that there his new authority might be questioned or even laughed at. He could smile at that now. But he was a lot more sure of himself now than he had been a week ago.

There had been a few bad moments when he first began to use his new authority. For instance, one morning at the single formation they had every day during the week off, when the platoon had straggled untidily into its long single line, Doll had stood out in front of them and harangued and harangued them to dress up their line, shouting and cursing, and getting almost no results, though they bobbed and shuffled and looked at each other. It went on like that, with him shouting louder and louder, until finally one of the oldtime squad leaders—a guy who had been one a long time but would never get promoted beyond it—had stepped up, simply called them to attention, then given them the command,

"Dress right, Dress!" In seconds the line was perfect, and the whole platoon was grinning at Doll who was standing there with his mouth hung open. The only thing was to grin with them and laugh it off, and Doll did. But for hours afterwards his ears burned whenever he thought of it. But bad incidents like that had been few, and he had his heroisms with the assault force working for him. His squad admired him for that. And he had done other things, like taking on himself more than his share of the dirty jobs instead of passing them out to the guys in the squad. It was astonishing how great his protective sense had grown once he knew they'd accepted him as their leader. And right now, hiking back up the hill to the position, Doll felt that same overwhelming all-pervasive protective feeling for poor Fife. They had used to talk together a lot out in front of the messhall or the orderly room, back in the old days.

He came over wearing a broad, easy grin.

"Pretty rough go, hunh, Fife? Pretty tough row to hoe for both of them."

"Yeah," Fife managed to get out in a small voice. He could not associate this heroic personage with the Doll he had used to know back in peacetime. Asshole or not, he *had* done all those things. And this put him as far away from Fife as if Fife had never met him before, or as if Doll came from another planet.

"I dont know which was the worse really," Doll said. "That leg wound probly hurt more right now, at the moment. But the throat wound's liable to cause more serious trouble later on. Anyway, they both out of it."

"Yeah," Fife said gloomily. "If they dont die of infection. Or get killed in an air raid before they get shipped out."

"Hey! You sound pretty gloomy! Sure, I guess there always is that possibility." Doll paused. "How you makin out in Jenks's squad, Fife?" Both of them remembered Doll's long, monumental fistfight with Jenks.

"All right," Fife said guardedly.

Doll raised his eyebrow, his old prewar gesture. "Because you dont seem very happy."

"Happy enough under the circumstances."

"Old Jenks is kind of a cold fish. Or I always thought so, anyway," Doll grinned. "Not an understanding guy."

"I guess he's a good enough squad leader," Fife said guardedly. He wished Doll would go away and leave him alone.

"Then you're happy in his squad?"

"It dont make much difference whether I am or not, does it?"

"Because," Doll went on. "Because I aint got no corporal in my squad, you know. A Pfc acting. But Band never made him for some reason. Dont like him maybe? Anyway I thought if you weren't happy in Jenks's squad maybe I might put in a word to Band to get you transferred to mine. We're a pretty leathery crew now—we aint green,—but I could help you out at first and show you a few things. The Welshman played a pretty dirty trick on you." He suddenly wanted to put his arm around Fife, but refrained. " 'Course I spose he couldn't help it, since he didn't know you was comin back."

For the first time Fife's eyes lit up a little. "Could you do that?" he asked. "*Would* you?"

"Well, sure," Doll said. He was a little startled at the direction the conversation had taken him. But he *could* do it. And, now, he had every intention of it. "You want me to do it?"

"Yeah," Fife said huskily, his eyes shining out suddenly from deep within his tormented face. "Yeah, I would."

"Okay. I'll go and see him and—" Doll hesitated. He had started to say: *and come tell you what he says later*. But that sounded too unsure, and as if he had to *ask* Band. Instead, he said: "—and come pick you up later." He slapped Fife on the back.

They had reached the top now, where the rest of the company—in and out of their holes—were waiting for the news from the aid station. Fife watched Doll go off in the direction of the CP and then turned off toward 3d Platoon and his own squad—of which, he reminded himself, he was still second in command. A new, but deeprooted cynicism attacked him and told him not to get his hopes up. But he put it down, at least somewhat. It would be great to have someone to look after him and take care of him, somebody he could trust as a friend. He wouldn't mind taking the

orders of somebody like that. And Doll *had* done all those things.
He knew infantry in-fighting well now, and could teach Fife the
ropes. But more than that it was having somebody he could depend on, somebody who was a mentor and a protector and also a
friend. Fife suddenly wondered what Doll would say if he knew
about what had happened between himself and little Bead. He
shuddered. Well, he was never going to tell anybody about that.
Nobody in the world. Not even his wife, when he got married
someday.

It was getting on toward dark. Fife sat on the edge of his hole
and waited for Doll to come back and collect him. Naturally, he
didn't tell anybody. He was superstitious about hexing it, and too
it would be too embarrassing if it didn't come off. Not far away
the taciturn closedfaced Jenks was assiduously and expressionlessly cleaning his rifle. Fife continued to sit. When the near dark
had grown into full black night with only the farflung tropical
starscape lighting it, he knew Doll wasn't coming. Nobody dared
leave his hole after dark. The new, deeprooted cynicism came
back making him smile bitterly in the dark. Who knew why?
Maybe Band said no. Or maybe he didn't even go to Band even.

Fife settled himself in the mudslick bottom of his hole. In a
way he ought to be glad. 2d Platoon had become the company
troubleshooters. They were going to lead off in the attack tomorrow. Did he want to be in that? It was just that he did not appreciate the talkative Jenks. He did not sleep much. The one time he
did drop off, the nightmare woke him with a cry which he automatically stifled before he was even fully awake.

Fife was not the only one who slept little. Up and down the line
many others had the same hollow in the pit of the stomach, the
same nervous tingling in the balls, and quiet conversations passed
the time of night between holes while men smoked guardedly into
cupped hands. They knew now that it was always like this the
night before an attack. Skinny Culn had not been able to resist
telling around the story of his little run-in with the new lieutenant
Payne (who of course had immediately been nicknamed The
Pain) and this was one of the more appreciated topics. Skinny's
self-quoted remark about not being paid feeling pay for feeling

like flyers were paid flight pay for flying went from hole to hole
with an appreciative snort until everyone in C-for-Charlie knew
it. Everything considered it was as good a philosophy as any for
this kind of life and everyone who heard it decided immediately
to adopt it. Skinny's other quote was also taken up: *Whatever
They say, I'm not a cog in a machine.* It had been a thought, not a
statement aloud to The Pain, but it said for everybody what they
all felt fiercely and needed to believe. They took it to themselves,
and applied it to their own particular situations, and they believed
it. They were not cogs in a machine, whatever *anybody* said. Only
one man looked into it deeper than that. And he didn't look far,
because he had troubles of his own.

Sgt John Bell was having another bad attack of malaria, and he
was about to have a nightmare himself. His nightmare was not
recurrent, like Fife's. He had never had it before. And when it
was over, he hoped he never had it again. The malaria had hit him
shortly before dark. It went along slow for an hour or so. But
when the chills, sweats and fever started to take him in their
regular as clockwork intervals of ever rising intensity, he had
gotten to thinking about his wife and her lover. And to speculat-
ing about what kind of a guy he was. Because he was sure she
had one. Ever since that day in the grassy trough above the
strongpoint when they had started to crawl. Nothing in her batch
of warm, loving letters during the week off tended to make him
think any differently. Sure, they were warm. But, in there between
those lines, his hunger to see sexual hunger in her, through her
letters, went completely unfed.

But what kind of guy? A civilian? Would she go with some
local guy they had both known all their lives? Or a serviceman.
Both Wright and Patterson Fields were right there outside Dayton. Officer? Enlisted man? There would be thousands of Air
Corps guys crawling over Dayton, all hungry. He would certainly
be a sensitive type, one who could honestly sympathize with her
when she felt bad about what she was doing to John. The next
thing Bell knew, that one word J-o-h-n was echoing down long
high hollow sky corridors and he was in a maternity hospital
delivery room. How he knew it was a maternity delivery room, he

couldn't say. Movies, maybe. But he recognized many objects. He was dressed in white gown, white cap and gauze mask. Then they wheeled Marty in. "You have to push," the doctor said in a kindly tolerant voice as if to a child. "I'm pushing!" Marty cried in a child's brave voice. "I'm pushing! I'm trying!" And she was. Her rectum had come out until it looked like a doughnut. Bell loved her. "But only when it hits you," the doctor smiled. He was actually bored. Then he turned to Bell, hands held straight up from the elbows fingers spatulate beside his face in the rubber gloves, speaking through the gauze. "We're going to knock her out. She's having a little trouble and I'm going to have to take it." Bell could see he was smiling behind the gauze. "Nothing to worry about." He turned back to the table where they had strapped her legs in the stirrups and her arms down and where the anesthetist now had her. Bell sat on a stool a few feet behind the doctor who sat on his own stool. Strangely, at least half his mind was occupied with showing the doctor he wasn't going to faint. He also knew that he was dreaming.

The head came first, facedown. Deftly, the doctor turned it over and swabbed out the nostrils. Then he eased the shoulders out, twisting it sideways. When it was out to the waist it began to wail in a feeble voice and the doctor swabbed it some more, and it was then that Bell realized that it was black. Coal black. The doctor went on working happily, easing the hips out, the young nurse with her hair tied up hovering smiling at the presence of new life, and Bell sat aghast in horror, embarrassed, disbelieving, and strangely acquiescent, and watched the coal black baby come lasciviously the rest of the way out of the beautiful, beautifully white, shaved crotch of his wife.

The color contrast was strangely gorgeous, oddly satisfying, suddenly very sensual. And more bluntly painful than anything Bell had ever felt in his life.

Now it will stop, he thought, now it will stop and I and me we can both wake up. But it didn't. And he had to stay there, watching, and trying to wake up and failing. How should he act? Bell looked down at it, still struggling feebly in its effort to escape being out in the cold, cold world living on its own. When he looked back up, both nurse and doctor were smiling at him expectantly. Marty was still out, still unconscious, on the table. So she couldn't know yet. Had she suspected? The doctor began to work on her again, the finishing up work. The nurse was still smiling at Bell. The anesthetist was smiling at him too, from behind his bottles and gear. A new life had happened. What should he do, say? Had they none of them noticed that it was black? Or didn't they care? Should he pretend? The worst thing was that he was sexually excited, sexually hot. And very embarrassed. But when he looked back down, he saw that it wasn't black it was Japanese. He could tell because it wore a tiny, bent up Imperial Army forage cap, with a tiny, baby iron star.

Bell woke up with a ringing cry that he had not learned to smother like Fife had learned, because he wasn't used to nightmares.

"I can't see anything! I can't see anything!" the awake sentry in the next hole cried in panic. "I can't see anything!"

"Dont shoot!" Beck called back, from further off. "Dont shoot anyway! Wait! Dont anybody fire!"

"It was me, it was me," Bell mumbled to them, his ears burning red. He was covered in freezing sweat, and now he had a raging high fever. After a moment he rubbed his hand over his face. "I had a nightmare."

"Well for fuck's sake try and keep it to yourself," the sentry called. "You scared the living shit out of me."

Bell mumbled inaudibly, slid a little further down in the slippery hole bottom, and tried to compose himself. Every bone in his body ached monstrously and separately. His head felt as if it might actually begin to boil the blood passing through it at any moment. His hands were so weak he could not clench them into fists to save his life, and bright hot geometric patterns danced before his eyes in semi-delirium. All that was the fever. But the other remained too, and the horror it had brought. Feebly, because that was the only way his heated brain could think, Bell tried to analyze it. He could understand the Japanese part readily enough. Sure. But why a *black* baby? Neither he nor Marty had ever had any racial prejudices, or pro segregation ideas.

Searching through his feverish brain, Bell remembered something Marty had told him once, before they were married. They were walking across the campus in Columbus, returning from a rendezvous in the apartment of married friends who let them use it afternoons for their love making. It was early fall. The leaves had been turning fast, and were just beginning to fall. They had been holding hands as they walked. Marty had turned to him, eyes smiling coquettishly, and wearing a slight flush of confession, and had said suddenly: "I'd love to have a black baby. Once. Sometime." The remark had thrilled Bell. Intuitively he understood exactly what she meant, and also why she'd said it. Though he couldn't have put it into words, any more than she. It was, first, a crack in the face at social convention which they both hated. It was a compliment to him, also, that she would let him in on the inside of this particular fantasy. But there was more than that. And the only word for that part of it he could give, was the 'sexual esthetic' of it. He had been pleased she'd told him and at the same time furious with her. He had squeezed her hand and said: "Well, you'll have to let me watch the conception of it." And intuitively she had understood what he meant, too. She had colored deeply and said: "But I happen to be in love with *you.*" And they had turned in their tracks and gone back to the living-room rug of the apartment, which was as far as they had gotten, even though both of them missed a class. They had been married that same year, he remembered. Or was it the next year? No, it was the next year.

Bell shifted in the wet hole, burning up with fever. Had that ancient exchange, lost and forgotten in the grabbag of memory, come back to plague him now? But why now and not before? Dull and halfclosed, his eyes stared at the forward rim of the slit trench, only slightly less dark than the surrounding blackness. He was willing to do anything in order not to go back to sleep and risk having that dream again. The whole thing was as clear, as real to him as if it had really, actually happened, only ten minutes ago. But why had he been sexually excited? Why that? Something licked at his mind lightly and he caught at it. The lascivious sensuality of knowing, of being sure, of having proof. Perhaps

that was why so many men thinking of their wives, hated other
races. Because nobody wanted to know he was cuckold. Everybody preferred the painful doubt to the sensual luxury of knowing
for sure. But if the baby was another color, there was no— . . .
Bell felt himself slipping into a waking daydreamnightmare of
watching the conception of the black baby, and stopped himself
in terror, and just in time.

And from that he learned something else. Or thought he did:
what he might desire in masochistic fantasy, for the luxurious
pain of knowing for sure, he could almost certainly kill her for, in
the reality—simply because he could never admit to himself the
desire he had, never, never. Suddenly he began to laugh, hysterically in the fever, but carefully stifling the sound. Cocks and
cunts! Cocks and cunts! Who cared who fucked who? When he
got himself stopped from laughing, he found to his surprise that
he was crying, weeping. He could feel the malaria beginning to
recede.

Naturally, he was glad when the next hole passed on the story
about Skinny Culn and The Pain. Not only did the conversation
keep him awake and away from that nightmare, it also helped him
stop thinking. The philosophy? Sure, it was fine. Skinny's philosophy of not feeling except for feeling pay. Bell snorted like the
rest, and embraced it. But when the next hole passed him on the
other quote, his mind balked and went blank. "Sure, sure," he
said automatically, "of course." Not cogs in a machine? Not
cogs in a machine? What did they think they were then? Their
wanting and needing to believe that was pathetic, shocked him
into re-examining the other one: the philosophy. And when he
did, he found he saw it entirely differently. Not feel? Not feel? No
feeling without Feeling Pay? No caring without Caring Pay?
What was happening to them? And to himself? Bell's watch read
3:05 on its luminous dial. Two hours to go, then.

The artillery began almost exactly at dawn. This time it continued for over two hours. 105s blasted The Sea Slug in its entirety,
and the jungle immediately surrounding it. The 155s occupied
themselves with the much bigger hill mass of The Giant Boiled
Shrimp further on, and invisible from here. The 155 rounds

arched shushing high overhead from invisible guns to invisible target. On The Sea Slug terrified, pathetic birds rose squawking in white clouds at every 105 jungle burst. The men of 1st Battalion stood out in the open on the hill and watched the display, reluctantly waiting the order to move. When it came, they moved out along the same route the patrol had taken, C-for-Charlie (due to a request by Band) in the lead, with 2d Platoon as their spearhead.

It was still almost black night in the jungle. Only when they reached the blasted area around The Sea Slug did any light serious enough to see by filter down to them. 1st Platoon's chopping work yesterday had done no good at all. They could not afford the time or attenuation of going single file now. Men scrambled along through the underbrush on both sides of the trail, tripping over vines and roots, getting their hands and faces scratched and torn, chopping with machetes when they had to. After a hundred yards of this everybody was so exhausted they had to stop and break.

It was when they reached the beginning of the blasted area that they received their first fire. There was now somewhat less than a hundred yards to go. It was amazing how slightly the artillery barrage had affected the jungle. There was a little more light, you could see a little further ahead, and there was some new looking deadfall. That was all. Sgt Beck had told off Doll's squad to act as point squad of 2d Platoon, and Doll had immediately decided to take the point man position himself. It was Doll who stopped them when he saw the first blast signs.

Doll had in fact not gone to Lt Band at all the night before about Fife. On his way up to the CP he had suddenly found himself angry at Fife for the way Fife had somehow tricked him into offering to take him into the squad. He had had no intention of doing that when he first went over to Fife, but Fife had somehow conned him into it. If there was anything Doll did not like, it was being tricked or conned into something. He preferred an honest approach. Angrily, Doll had stopped off to talk to Skinny Culn for a minute. He of course did not mention Fife. When he left Culn's hole, Doll was decided.

And he still felt the same way today as he moved along at the head of his squad with two grenades hooked in his belt. It would hardly have been fair to his Pfc acting, would it? Whatever else, Doll's squad came first. That was why he took more than his share of the dirty jobs, like taking this point himself today, for his point squad: he wanted them to know it. And now when he turned around to tell the man behind to pass the word back to Beck that he thought they were approaching destination, Doll grinned at him reassuringly. It was just then that the machinegun somewhere in front of them opened up with its stuttery voice.

As one man, the platoon dived off the trail into the leaves, some on one side, some on the other. Doll himself, who had caromed off a treetrunk in his blind leap through the leaves, found himself landing squarely on top another man, a young Pfc from his own squad named Carol Arbre. Already lying on his stomach on the jungly ground while Doll was still bouncing half-stunned off his tree, Arbre had not entertained the idea of having someone light on his back; and now Doll, his crotch pressed tightly to the juncture of Arbie's already powerfully-clamped-together buttocks, sprawled on top of him in the classic position of buggery. A rather girlishly-built, girlish-looking young man, who was continually having his bottom felt in joke or perhaps not in joke, Arbre had been forced throughout his Army career to protest furiously against such indignities. People could not believe, given his girlish build, that he was not homosexually inclined. Now he turned his head back over his shoulder to peer at Doll, red with embarrassment and frowning furiously, and said in a choked voice: "You git off of me like that!"

Doll, still a little stunned from running headlong into the tree, required several seconds to collect his scattered wits. At the same time, stunned as he was, he was not unaware of his crotch pressed to the now-even-more-tightly-pressed-together buttocks of Arbre beneath him. Shaking his head a few times, he rolled off one full circuit to the right, using his riflebutt to keep the muzzle out of the dirt and still have it ready in front of him. And it was just then that they heard the too swift, murderously soft shu-shu sound they knew so well and mortar rounds began to land and explode around and among them. But despite the mortars, within Doll the memory—of his crotch pressed to the (if the truth had to be told) rather sweet, girlish buttocks of Carrie (of course they called him Carrie) Arbre—lingered.

The mortars kept on coming. Doll heard a couple of men yell somewhere behind him. Still out of breath and a little groggy from running into the tree, he tried to think what to do. He was pleased to note, to realize suddenly, that the numbness he had felt during the last stages of the big battle last week, was now coming back over him swiftly—had in fact been growing in him unnoticed since their departure from Hill 210. It left his mind clear, and cool, suffused with a grinning bloodthirstiness. It spread all through him, making a solid impenetrable layer between himself and the choking fear which would not allow him to swallow as he hugged the ground. He could not tell exactly how far the MG (it had now been joined by another one somewhere else) was from him. He debated whether it was worthwhile trying to crawl uphill to it with one or two men and some grenades to see if they could get close enough to throw. He was pulled from this revery by someone vigorously jiggling his left foot behind him. He looked around. Sgt Beck had crawled up from the rear of the platoon.

Beck, when Doll first halted the column, had immediately taken another compass reading, allowing his own new lieutenant, Tomms, to pretend to help: after all, that cost him nothing. The largely inaccurate map they had was not to be trusted very far. They had Culn's and Payne's descriptions from yesterday, but Beck was always instinctively suspicious of other people's explications. He preferred his own two eyeballs, and he was already (even before the message from Doll could have reached him, which it never did because of the MG) pretty sure they were quite close to The Sea Slug. When the mortars started dropping in, he had decided to go forward to find out why Doll had halted them *before* the machinegun.

Beck too, like Doll, was surprised to find that the old, peculiar numbness was right there, already waiting, and that it had quickly taken him over leaving the rest of him, the best of him, free to act. It was a good thing to know. Apparently it came quicker with practice. No feeling without Feeling Pay! He too felt murderously bloodthirsty. Make them pay, was what his head told him. If you can. If you can make them. Everybody knew the mortars were coming from somewhere on The Giant Boiled Shrimp, and as he crawled forward Beck stopped off by the walkie-talkie man Band had thoughtfully given him and told him to radio back for fire on The Shrimp.

"Tell them to throw every-fucking-thing they got," he snarled. "Piss on the cost of ammo. Tell them cover the whole damned area! Shut them mortars up!"

Behind him Beck heard a man scream up through the sound flower of a mortar round. It was hardly so much a scream as a guttural, surprised, infuriated "Hagh-ah-ah-*ah!*" Beck pressed on, tripping and treading on members of his platoon as well as on jungle vines. Well, this was it. They were in it for sure now. He was pleased to note that he wasn't scared—just afraid. What a fucking, shiteating war. He *would* have to get the platoon after the goddam war started. A platoon used to be gravy.

As soon as Doll looked around at the jiggling of his foot, Beck tried to smile at him. "What's the situation?"

There was a drawn, wrinkle-eyed look on everybody's face, including his own. Everybody had crowsfeet today.

Doll seemed surprised to see him. "I dont know. I dont think they is any."

"Why'd you halt us?"

Doll pointed to the ground. "We were gettin into the blast area, and it begins to get a lot steeper here."

"I think you were right. You probly saved us a couple guys from that MG." He paused. "Well, what the hell do we do now? Why the hell dont Band get up here?"

Beck was thinking out loud to himself more than speaking to Doll, and Doll hesitated before he spoke. "Screw Band! Lissen, Milly," he said, using one noncom's prerogative of intimate address to another. Beck's first name was Millard. "I think we can knock out that MG. See how far he's firin over our heads here?"

Beck didn't mind the intimate address. He squinted uphill through the growing smoke. "You think you can?"

"I think we're deefalaided here. If I take two guys with three four grenades apiece, I think we can crawl up and knock him out and move on in." He gestured. "Out of this crap." When the mortar rounds weren't actually going off, his voice sounded preternaturally loud.

Milly Beck debated. Band should have arrived by now. "Okay. But wait'll I get the platoon into position. Pick two guys. Them squads should of been up by now without me telling them." Turning his head rearward, Beck began to roar, waving his right arm. He was sure nobody could see him. But it made him feel better. "Bell's squad up on the right! Dale's squad up on the left! Make a line, make a line! You assholes! Load and lock! Prepare to fire cover!"

Behind them somebody else screamed with startled pain as he was hit. While Beck continued to roar, Doll looked over his squad, his whole face grinning. The bloodthirstiness was growing to a dull blood roar in his ears, almost drowning even the mortars. "You," he said, pointing. "And you." Then he realized the second man he had chosen was the fawneyed Arbre. "No, not you," he said; "you," and picked another. It was instinctively done, without thinking, but even so he was a little surprised at himself. Arbre was as good a soldier as the next man. He could carry his weight. "Everybody take five grenades." Arbre was staring at him strangely. Doll grinned back at him. On right and left the two squads were moving up. Thorne's, the fourth squad, was coming up as reserve.

"Okay?" Doll said.

"Okay," Beck said huskily. "Let's get the fuck *out* of this."

Doll wasn't really sure they were defiladed. The gunner could probably depress if he wanted. But he gambled and took them forward on their feet, instead of crawling. But they had not gone ten yards when there were screams up above, the explosions of several grenades, and the machinegun stopped. Then voices in English with unmistakable American accents yelled down at them. "Hold your fire! Hold your fire! This is 3d Battalion! Hold fire, 2d Battalion!" Doll was suddenly so frustrated that he bit his lip till tears came in his eyes. He had had himself all primed. And now nothing. Adrenaline and emotion surged through him unreleased leaving him lightheaded.

Seconds later the mortars stopped. An unearthly silence fell, deathly, weird, mentally unmanageable as yet. It was over. At least temporarily. Men strove to adjust themselves to the silence and to the idea that they were not going to be dead yet for a while. There were surprisingly few yells or screams from the wounded, only a few low moans. The two new company medics, who were never as well liked as the two nowdead originals, but who were gaining, moved among them. They were all getting pretty old pro there, Sgt Beck thought, listening and feeling proud.

"Well, shall we get on up there?" he said aloud. He stood up. Other men around him stood up. It was then that Lt Tall George Band appeared, picking his way among the men who had not yet gotten up.

"What's the situation, Beck?" he asked.

"3d Battalion seems to be in full control on The Sea Slug, Sir."

"Why did the mortars stop?"

"I dont know for sure, Sir. Maybe the artillery stopped them. I radioed back for fire."

"Good work. All right, let's go up and have a look." Adjusting his steelrimmed spectacles, Band started off without looking back. He headed for Doll and his two men, who were now standing up holding or wearing all their extra, unused grenades. Beck stood staring after him wanting to curse, but Band did not know this. "You men look like Christmas trees!" he called to Doll in a jocular voice as he clumped along. "Where the hell you going dressed up like that?"

It was a mistake, a mistake from start to finish. Perhaps it was a serious mistake. But Band was not aware of it. He clumped on past Doll heading uphill, pushing his way over the artillery damaged undergrowth. Slowly, in ones and twos, the men began to follow him—except for Beck, who stayed a minute to check on his four wounded: a thing he might not have done or bothered with, had Band not gone on.

Why had Band done it? Nobody knew. Nobody knew exactly

why it was a mistake either. Another man could have done and said the same things Band did and said and it would not have been a mistake. But in Band's case it was one. Everyone present who saw and heard it, marked it down jealously in their little private mental notebooks of references which they just as jealously would not forget. And those who had not seen or heard it were informed by the others, and marked it down just as jealously in their own jealous notebooks. They had not all that quickly forgotten Capt James Bugger Stein, whom they subsequently had heroized out of all reasonable proportion; Bugger had been for them, they believed. And Band knew nothing about it at all, never suspected.

George Band had enjoyed himself immensely during the mortar bombardment—in much the same way Doll had. He had lain with most of the rest of the company back out of range and had felt like weeping when the wounded yelled. He had not gone forward into the fire because his place was back where he could direct the other platoons if they were needed. He really wanted to be up there with them, but he knew it was not his job. But this did not preclude his sharing the emotions which he knew Beck and Doll and the others must be feeling.

Band had also enjoyed himself immensely the night before, with the new Battalion Commander from the other regiment. In fact, his capacity for enjoying himself immensely had increased enormously, out of all proportion, with the simple routine act of becoming a Company Commander. He had always known he would make it, and last night after Payne and Culn had reported, been given a drink, and were dismissed, the new Colonel had asked him to stay a bit. The new Colonel had had a correspondent with him all during the day before and had gleaned from him two bottles of Time-&-Life-bought scotch, one of which he now broke out for just the two of them: Grand MacNeish! He and Band had several snorts of it together. The new Colonel was quite pleased with the results of the patrol, especially Culn's voluntary lingering under the mortars to put rifle and BAR fire into The Sea Slug's enemy MGs. "Make them think a bit anyway," was his retort. "If they're smart," he smiled. "I mean, if they know their tactics they'll withdraw." He smiled again. "I mean, it can only be an outpost for them. Their main defensive line has to be the hill mass of The Giant Boiled Shrimp." He and Band had one more quick snort. It was then that Band offered his company to lead off the Battalion for tomorrow. The new Colonel accepted smiling, nodding his big graying handsome head appreciatively; he had already heard about C-for-Charlie. It was the best scotch Band had tasted in he did not know when. He arrived back at the company just as it fell full dark, peacefully content. Band had always known he would get the command. And as he bedded down for the night in the little Japanese shanty, he dwelt upon it.

He would do for them what Stein could never have done; because he loved them. He *really* loved them. Not with sentimentality like Stein, but with full, tragic cognizance of what voluntary sacrifices would be demanded of them and of himself too. You simply could not treat them equal as men, as Stein had tried. It had to be a stern paternal love relationship, because they were children and did not know their own minds or what was best for them. They had to be disciplined and they had to be ordered. Band had two children of his own. And in his high school classes back home he had treated his students the same way, too. But he could not feel for any of those children back there, students or real ones, what he felt for these children here. How could he, when he had not shared with those the terrible, horrible, brave experiences he had shared with these ones here? A great, warm, paternal, each-child-hugging love brimmed in him. Filled with a sure awareness of the things he and they would accomplish together out of the depth of their more-than-mated love, Band had dropped blissfully off to sleep, not at all disturbed by—more, even relishing—the rocks and knobs of dirt which stuck him in the various parts of his back through the canvas stuffing of his bedroll.

That had been last night. And now, as he climbed the slopes of The Sea Slug to meed 3d Battalion at 7:40 the next morning, after a mortar pummeling that had wounded four men of his best platoon, and some others, he still felt the same way about them. He would do anything in the world for them. Behind him his men followed, much more interested in the terrain they were getting a first look at, than in what their present commander might ever do for them.

"Jesus!" Sgt Doll said to Sgt Beck. "Am I glad 3d Battalion did get there first!"

"Yeh," Beck said, out of breath. "So'm I."

What they saw was a series of fingerlike ridges thirty-five to forty feet high, rocky, steep, totally bare, with narrow, bare, ten to twenty foot draws between them. These were on the left. To have scaled them under Japanese fire was more than the toughest wished to contemplate. But on the right was a long, steep grassy slope devoid of cover for at least fifty yards. To have gone up this into MGs would have been to invite being mown like Nebraska wheat. The Japanese had even cut multiple fire lanes in the waist-high grass. Lucky. Lucky.

Band shook hands with the commander of 3d Battalion's L Company, an old drinking pal of his and Stein's who had reduced the position, and whose men were standing all around getting back their breath. 2d Platoon, and then the others following, mingled in with them, talking and smoking. But this time there was no evidence of competition, no digs or wisecracks about being late or who got there first.

L had not suffered badly: five men hit, one of them killed. Two of them by the first machinegun further back the ridge, three by the mortars which had hit them at the same time they hit C-for-Charlie. They had found only two MGs on the entire Sea Slug ridge, both suicide crews left behind to hold up the advance apparently. All had preferred to die. But there was evidence that there had been many more. The Japanese had pulled back apparently late yesterday, or last night.

What did all this mean? Neither L Company and its commander nor Band and C-for-Charlie had any idea. Both had expected a much tougher fight. Each would radio back the development to his respective battalion and carry on with his mission unless told otherwise. They decided to leave it like that. When they did radio, they were both told to carry on as planned.

L Company's orders were to cross to and attack the open

ground of The Giant Boiled Shrimp hill mass as soon as The Sea
Slug was taken. C-for-Charlie's were to dig in and hold The Sea
Slug against counterattack for an approach route. It was still not
yet eight o'clock in the morning. "I'm not at all sure you've got
the easier job," L Company's commander smiled as he shook
hands with Band before leaving. "Not if they find we're using
this ridge as an approach route and decide to turn loose those
mortars again." With a grim chill those men of Charlie who
heard him thought he might very well be right.

Band put them to work right away. He chose for them the most
advanced, most susceptible part of The Sea Slug ridge. Behind
them Baker and Able were beginning to come up and spread out
rearward from their flanks. As they dug, I-for-Item and K-for-
King came up along the ridge and passed through them, I to take
the left flank of the attack up the open ground of The Shrimp,
twice as big as The Dancing Elephant in area, K to follow them
as reserve 2d Battalion, they said, provided 3d was able to move
on into the wider areas, was to follow them soon after and join in
the attack.

This was not, however, the way it worked out in the reality.

Digging and sweating grimly in the growing heat of the day,
1st/Sgt Welsh was the first man in the company to finish his hole,
and he only demanded a very little help from his three clerks.
After all, they had to dig Band's hole and the new Exec's, before
they could start on their own. Sitting in his, and staring off at the
high ground of The Elephant's Head where they had come from,
Welsh was made to think of one of those sixteenth century bath-
tubs he had seen pictures of. Because of the slope, the rear of it
rose to his ears while in the front it was two feet deep and halfway
up his shins. (This was less than the required three feet but Welsh
had cheated, and fuck them.)

Welsh suddenly envisioned himself sitting here with a big fat
cigar in his face, a sponge in one hand and a longhandled brush
in the other, enjoying this remarkably beautiful view. Which nobody else in the world had a right to look at, or pang! you're
dead! Welsh hated cigars and people who smoked them. But a
cigar seemed proper in his vision all the same. He would soap

and soap. And scrub and scrub. Not to get clean so much. He never minded being dirty. But because the view and the bathtub demanded it. Behind him his three clerks chattered at their digging like crazy birds, and Welsh had a momentary impulse to get up and boot them all three in the ass.

Welsh had taken a terribly dangerous chance yesterday when they moved out from the weekold vacation bivouac. He had filled two of his three canteens with gin, leaving only one for water. It was a desperate gamble heh heh but now it was paying off. Fuck water! He could get by without water. And with two shots inside his skin now he could look at the world again. It was really a beautiful world he thought looking off toward the distant magnificence of The Elephant's Head. Where so many men had died and so many others had sickened. Fuck all that! Beautiful. Especially from a filled sixteenth century bathtub. He wiggled his toes in his stickywet socks. Ought to change, but the other pair was already stiff as boards in his pocket. Calmly he puffed on his imaginary cigar.

You guys! You guys! Welsh wanted to holler, listening to his three new clerks jabbering like three Japs behind him. You don't know how to appreciate nothin'. Of them all he was, he was convinced, the only one left who really understood it. Home, family, country, flag, freedom, democracy, the honor of the President. Piss on all that! He didn't have one of them, yet he was here, wasn't he? And from choice, not necessity, because he could easily have gotten himself out of it. At least, *he* under*stood* himself. The truth was, he liked all this shit. He liked being shot at, liked being frightened, liked lying in holes scared to death and digging his fingernails into the ground, liked shooting at strangers and seeing them fall hurt, liked his stickywet feet in his stickywet socks. Part of him did. In a way he was sorry about young Fife, though. Fife, in a rifle platoon!?

Of all the company including officers, Welsh was perhaps the only one as far as he knew who had never yet felt the combat numbness. He had heard them talk about it, during the week off, and had listened. He understood that it was the saving factor, and sensed the animal brutality that it brought with it. But he had not

yet had the experience. He did not know whether this was because life had already made him numb like that years ago and he
had never realized it, whether his foreknowledge of what to expect plus his superb natural intelligence heh heh had made him
immune to it, or whether it was just that the combat itself had
never yet gotten quite tough enough to freeze up his particular
brand of personality. There were times, moments, when Welsh
realized that he was quite mad. Like: Three cherries on the same
stem = George Washington. Two no, never. Three yes, always.
Who would understand that if he told them? If he *dared* tell them.
He still hated cherries to this day and could not eat them, though
he loved the taste of them. Typically, when his malaria had gotten
much worse during their week's vacation, he had told nobody
about it and had hidden it with a kind of secret glee. And he never
was going to tell anybody. He didn't know why. It was all part of
this silly game they pretended was adult and mature, that was all.
He would go till he dropped in his tracks or some dumb Jap shot
him and they could bury him while he laughed. But he did feel a
little sorry about Fife. Not a lot, of course. After all, when some
ass got himself shot up bad enough to go to the hospital and get
himself evacuated forever, and then didn't have the gumption or
guts to follow it through, what the fuck could you do with him?

Welsh settled down in his hole. He had an intuition they were
going to have a pretty easy day of it. To prove him wrong, it was
just exactly then that the walkietalkie man somewhere close behind him called out he had a message for Band from the new
Colonel ordering 1st Battalion to move out immediately in support of 3d Battalion on The Shrimp, Band to call back confirmation. Band came running from somewhere down the line, and
Welsh got wearily up from his hole. He was aware that once again
he had screwed himself. If he had waited a half hour to start
instead of pitching in to get done, he would not have had to dig at
all. He grinned mirthlessly.

More men had not finished digging than had finished, like
Welsh. One of these was young Corporal Fife on the other, forward slope of the narrow little ridge. Here the fall was less steep
than on the rearward slope where Welsh was, but it still required a

considerable digging job to make a creditable hole. Fife had attacked it disheartedly with his inadequate little shovel. It seemed
an insuperable job, and yet at the same time he knew he must
make a good job of it because 3d Platoon had been placed on the
forward slope, beside the 2d Platoon who held the apex of the
angling ridge. Any counterattack must come right at him. As he
dug, Fife was thinking about Fife somewhat the same as Welsh
was—but differently. Fife was *sure,* absolutely and positively
sure, that *nothing* he did could ever have gotten him evacuated.
Not even if he had kept after them and persisted about his lost
glasses. He paused digging and squinted off toward the (for him)
blurred bulk of Hill 210 trying to see just how bad his eyes really
were. He did not know if his eyes would see what they were
supposed to see to save him. But he suspected not. Between half-
hearted stabs with his shovel, he peered off anxiously squinting at
The Elephant's Head, checking and rechecking his bad eyes.
When the news to stop digging bulleted itself down the line, he
threw down his shovel with a great sigh of relief. Then he realized what that meant, and irrational panic seized him.

Fife had lain with the 3d Platoon along the trail, and just back
out of range, while 2d Platoon had taken their beating this morning. One or two rounds hit quite near him. The terror for mortars
which he now carried was so great it was indescribable in words,
even to himself. Every round that he heard fall had to hit him
squarely on that spot where his neck joined his shoulders. After
the barrage he had a severe neck ache which lasted more than an
hour. Now in his panic at having to leave The Sea Slug and move
forward, he did not know if he could actually shoot and kill
another human being or not, even if he had to. To save himself.
And more, he did not know whether even if all that part did go
well, did work right, it would make any difference and he
mightn't get killed anyway. Killed! Dead! Not alive anymore! He
didn't think he could face it. God, he had already been wounded
once, hadn't he? What did they want from him? He wanted to sit
down and cry, and he couldn't. Not in front of the company.

In the fact, the company probably would not have noticed if
Fife had sat down and cried. They were all too engrossed in

thinking about their own bad luck as they fell in in their squads
and platoons. And it really wasn't anybody's fault, that was the
worst thing. The reason, as Band found out when he radioed his
confirmation call, and as the rest of them found out by word of
mouth gossip seconds later, was simply that they happened to be
closest and somebody was needed right away. Old 1st Battalion
got the shitty end of the stick in every sense. Wearily, though
more in the morale sense than the physical, they gathered their
gear together and prepared to do, once more, the necessary.

It was just at this point that another man in the company was
wounded. This was a tall, quiet buck sergeant Squad Leader from
Pennsylvania in the 3d Platoon whose name was Potts. Potts's
squad had been the linkup of the 3d Platoon with John Bell's
squad of the 2d. Potts and Bell and two others were standing out
in the open by their holes on The Sea Slug, looking out toward
The Giant Boiled Shrimp across the jungle that separated them.
They were discussing the advance and what they might expect to
find over there, and trying to see The Shrimp which from here
was only a vague indistinct mass of brown. Bell, who happened to
be standing with his back to The Shrimp at that particular moment and looking at Sgt Potts who was talking, saw the whole
thing. One moment Potts was talking away. In the next there was
a loud "Thwack!", and immediately after the shrill whine of a
bullet ricochetting away. Potts, who was looking straight at Bell
and wearing no helmet, stopped in midword and stared at Bell
crosseyed as if thoughtfully trying to see something on the end of
his own nose. Then he fell down. A red spot had appeared in the
center of his forehead. Potts immediately sat back up, still staring
out at the world crosseyed, then fell back down again. By this
time Bell was to him, but Potts was out, unconscious, those
crossed eyes mercifully closed. Bell could see that on his forehead an inchlong groove had been cut—or burned rather, was
perhaps the better word, since it did not bleed. Beneath it he
could see the white, undamaged bone of Potts's skull. A spent
ricochet from somewhere on The Shrimp, traveling flatways instead of by the point, had passed beside Bell's head and struck
Potts square between the eyes and gone screaming on its way.

Laughter beginning to make spasms in his diaphragm and bubble up into his throat despite himself, Bell knelt and brought him around by gently slapping his cheeks and chafing his hands. Potts was perfectly all right. Laughing so hard they could hardly see where they were going through the tears, the three of them helped him back to Battalion Aid Station which was just setting up on The Sea Slug, and where the doctor, laughing also, put a patch over the cut and gave Potts a handful of aspirin. Until the moment of departure he lay on his back resting with his helmet over his face because of his headache, assured of his Purple Heart. Potts did not think it was at all funny, and complained bitterly about his headache the rest of the day. Everybody else roared with laughter whenever it was mentioned. It put the company in a good mood to begin the incredible, unbelievable march they did not yet know they were going to make.

In the future annals of the Regiment (and the Division) it would be known forever as "The Race" or the "Grand Prix." Sometimes it was referred to also as "The Long End Run." C-for-Charlie was to become and remain one of its foremost elements. In the maps of the Division history (all drawn very much later) the "Long End Run" would be shown with red and blue arrows to be the logical development of a situation and its equally logical followthrough. The truth was that at the time nobody anywhere really knew what the situation was. As 1st Battalion led by C-for-Charlie came up out of the jungle and moved around the left side of Hill 250, the Shrimp's Tail, the only evidence of any Japanese was a honeycomb of deserted, well camouflaged emplacements which several men stumbled over and fell into. It was clear to everyone it should have been an expensive battle. But where were the Japanese? Why had they left? Slowly and cautiously, they deployed on the left of 3d Battalion in the flat open ground and probed on. Two hours and two thousand yards later they arrived worn out and waterless on the forward slope of Hill 253, The Shrimp's Head, without having suffered a casualty.

It really wasn't all that easy. On their right L Company had had a fire fight with twenty or thirty Japanese on top of Hill 251, a long narrow ridge projecting into the jungle which corresponded to one of The Shrimp's Feet, finally destroying them with their company mortars from the other end of the ridge. Moving along down below, C-for-Charlie could watch the whole action. Far back on Hill 250 they could see Dog Company busily setting up its heavy mortars. It was very quiet in the bright sunshine. There was tough going in the crotchhigh grass. But at least they could walk standing up. Here and there men shook themselves and settled their shoulders as if to indicate this wasn't so bad after all; but nobody dared voice the feeling, for superstitious fear that all hell would break loose immediately after.

2d Platoon had again been chosen by Brass Band to be lead platoon, so it was they who were out in front as skirmishers. Beck the martinet had cursed and complained about this to his squad leaders (who agreed with him) but so far had said nothing to Band. Beck himself had switched his point squad, putting Bell's squad out in front, and when they deployed had placed Doll's squad on Bell's right in the safest place, letting the other two, Thorne's and Dale's, go to the open left flank. It was in this position, as they walked slowly forward through the tough grass with their rifles held at a low port in tired arms, that Pfc Carrie Arbre left his position and sidled over until he was beside his squad leader. Arbre had seemed to be avoiding Doll, or so Doll thought, ever since the two episodes of this morning. Doll waited.

"Can I talk to you private a minute, Doll?"

"Sure, Carrie."

As they talked both of them kept their eyes moving to left and right as they moved ahead, looking for emplacements, looking for Japanese.

Arbre frowned, but he had long ago given up trying to make anyone stop calling him Carrie. "I just wanted to ast you why you changed yore mind about pickin me to go with you, back there today."

A person always expected that Arbre, because of his girlish shyness and sensitive look, would be more educated than most but in fact he wasn't. He had not gone as far in high school as Doll. Doll had nearly graduated.

"Well, I don't know, Carrie," he said. "It was just something that hit me. A sort of sudden instinct. Or something."

"Well, I can sojer as well as the next man. I carry my weight."

"I know that. Course you do. Course you can." By a momentary inspiration Doll was moved to put his arm around Arbre's thin shoulders which in the shower always looked so much narrower than his wide, lean, woman's hips, but he did not do it because he didn't want to let go of his rifle with one hand. They walked ahead through the tough grass. "If I was to analyze it, like I'm tryin to do now, I'd say it was just because I wanted to look out for you and protect you." Doll felt his heart beat suddenly, as a brilliant idea came to him.

"I dont want nobody to look out for me," Arbre said beside him sullenly. "I dont need any protection."

"Everybody needs help, Carrie," Doll said. He turned his head for a second to smile at him, and when he did Arbre turned to look at him, a strange enigmatic expression on his face as if he knew something he was not saying, or as if he knew something Doll was not saying and perhaps did not even know. They both turned back and began looking for emplacements again.

"I want to live through this fucking war as much as anybody," Arbre said. "I didn't want to go up there with you." He moved on ahead, slumpshouldered and narrowchested, with that same strange halfsoft, halfhard, almost apologetic look. "I guess I do need help. I mean, all of us." With that he turned and moved away, still looking as if he knew something extra.

Doll spared a quick look after him wondering what the hell all that had been about, watching those girlishly goodlooking hips. Then he turned back to the business at hand, shifting his rifle a little, wondering how the hell much longer this walk was going to go on like this. Momentarily he wondered nervously if anybody had noticed the two of them together. Well, what if they did? Everybody knew Doll liked broads. When the hell *was* something going to happen around here?

It was just then that three bedraggled, scarecrowlooking Japanese men burst out of the jungle brush ahead of them on the left and ran toward them chattering and wailing and waving their hands and arms high in the air, skittering and stumbling along in the stony grass. Doll threw up his rifle and fired, his face a mask of grim satisfaction. So did others, and the three were shot down before they had gotten twenty yards. Then the sunny morning silence returned. In it, the lead platoon watched and listened. Then they moved on. Ahead of them now not too far away was the hill of The Giant Boiled Shrimp's Head. Behind them, as the column moving forward passed the three corpses, hardly anybody even bothered to look down at them. Their wallets had already been taken.

Like Doll, Buck Sergeant Squad Leader Charlie Dale was one of the men in 2d Platoon who had fired first and definitely gotten one of the three Japanese. Dale had never believed in giving no Jap no chance anyway, and after fighting them for ten days now believed in it even less. Like that one that tried to grenade Big Queen on The Elephant's Head at the Jap bivouac after surrendering first. They just didn't have no conception of honor or honesty. Grinning smugly, Dale ran forward to them through the grass. His particular one's wallet contained nothing of any value except a picture of some Jap broad, which wasn't much. She wasn't even naked. But he kept it anyway because he was getting quite a collection of them now. The wallet he threw away. It was falling apart from jungle rot. Somebody—Doll, in fact—found one of those small, individual soldier's battleflags on one of them, but Dale's didn't have anything. Some crappy luck. He didn't even have any gold teeth when Charlie opened his mouth.

During their week off, with part of his loot, Dale had traded for a pair of electrician's pliers. These now reposed in his hip pocket with a supply of Bull Durham sacks. If damned Marines could have collections of gold teeth worth a thousand dollars Charlie Dale could by God have one. And this would have been his first chance to use the pliers—except the bastard had to go and not have any. And before he could look over the other two corpses, the order to move out came, which order Dale obeyed swiftly because Brass Band that asshole was close enough to be watching him. And Dale had evolved for himself a new, grandiose plan. Cursing savagely with regret, he led his squad off.

Dale's plan was a simple one. He had watched the promotions list with a shrewd and careful eye that went far beyond his own sergeantcy. He knew that that fool schoolteacher Band liked him. And he was convinced that Sergeant Field, Doll's old squad leader, had been promoted to Platoon Guide of 1st Platoon simply to get him out of the way. If anything happened to Skinny Culn now, Dale was convinced he could bullshit Teacher Band into promoting himself into the job of platoon sergeant of 1st Platoon. Also, the Platoon Guide of 3d Platoon was a pretty wishywashy type character. For that matter, Fox, the new platoon sergeant of 3d Platoon was no very great shakes himself. It might be even possible to live to see him replaced without him even getting wounded or killed.

So there were a couple good chances. And Charlie Dale had decided he wanted a platoon. He had gotten a squad and a sergeantcy when he wanted one, just like he planned it. What was to stop him from doing the same thing with a platoon? Just as easy. He meant to watch for some opportunity where he could handle two or three squads in some little action all by himself, and let Band see it. Ahead of him the ground steepened and he shifted his rifle slightly, changing his plodding pace to a lighter, more alert one, and narrowed his eyes. He was sure asshole Band would jump him up over everybody the first chance that offered.

And he was right. Band would have. Band had watched him during the shooting of the three Jap *camaraden*. He was aware Dale was not the most intelligent man in his company, that his physical courage sometimes took on the look of sheer insanity; and he personally did not much care for the sadistic cruelty Dale displayed now and then, he thought with a smile. But in a war everything had to be used that was useful. He had almost given Dale the 3d Platoon during the mass promotions. Now he wondered if he hadn't been wrong, too overcautious.

During the long walk forward from Hill 250 across the flat, Band had moved his Company Hq forward in the column. He was reasonably positive nothing much would happen on the low ground; and he wanted to keep an eye on his men out in front, and on any developments. Now as they approached Hill 253—

The Shrimp's Head—he ordered 2d Platoon into a double column of squads, the better to maneuver the steepening slopes, and allowed 3d and 1st Platoons to pass through ahead of the Hq into close support. They were still unfired upon. L Company had caught up to them on the right after their little fire fight, and had signalled they would go around the right side of the big hill while C-for-Charlie went around the left. This was fine with Band. He held back his Hq and Weapons Platoon near the foot while his rifle platoons explored for resistance, unaware that his two best platoon sergeants Culn and Beck were silently cursing him under their breath for not being up front with them and for hanging back whenever the possibility of danger came up. After a half hour's work, the two companies met on the forward slope without having fired a shot and Band brought his Hq and Weapons up, as did the L Company commander.

It was a perfectly proper maneuver Band had executed, holding back his Hq. L Company's Commander had done the same thing. But both Beck and Culn could not help wondering why Tall George had moved his Hq forward in the column down there on the flat, where there obviously wasn't going to be any danger, and where it also was not needed. What kind of cheap display was that? Perhaps they were both being a little touchy. But Beck was still mad at him for leaving 2d Platoon out in front after their casualties on The Sea Slug; and both men remembered how he had waited to come forward on The Sea Slug until after the mortars stopped. It was one more thing both of them chalked up in their little mental notebooks while Band shook hands with L Company's commander again.

Everybody knew they had now reached the point where they had taken so much ground they were in serious danger of overextending themselves. That was the main problem now. The men stood around waiting to see what their commanders would decide. They were also about out of water. Item and Baker, equally dry, had stationed themselves around on the reverse slope of the big hill. Their commanders came up to join the conference. Still further back, K-for-King and A-for-Able had spread out along both edges of the open ground facing the jungle to cover the flanks; but their lines covered less than a quarter of the distance back to The Shrimp's Tail. A counterattack coming in behind them in force could cut off both Battalions, and it was still only eleven thirty in the morning. Nobody wanted the responsibility of deciding whether to stay or go on. It was decided that L and C, as lead companies, would both radio their respective Battalion CPs for instructions.

Band, for his part, when he finally got through, found as much if not more confusion back on The Shrimp's Tail as there was here on The Shrimp's Head. The new Exec (replacing Capt John Gaff) was the biggest man Band could find to talk to. Col Spine the new Commander was off at an emergency conference with the Regimental Commander and the other Battalion Commanders. The Division Commander was on his way up from Hill 214 personally to meet with them and take personal command himself. In the Exec's voice, in spite of the whistles and static, Band could detect the same elation and excitement that he himself had felt as they proceeded up the length of The Shrimp without meeting resistance. Water? It was at this very moment being started to them by native carrier; they should get it in half to three quarters of an hour. Also, 2d Battalion was already on its way down the face of Hill 250 with orders to extend the lines of King and Able rearward. Beside Band, Mad Welsh checked and confirmed this for him through the late Lt Whyte's handsome binoculars which Band handed him. In addition, the Exec said, the other regiment was in the process of being pulled bodily by battalions from the line of The Dancing Elephant and sent forward here, leaving the line undefended on orders of the Division Commander and the General Commanding. They were going all out. It might be a big break: a major breakthrough following right on the heels of a general withdrawal. Or it might be some sort of a trap.

"I know," Band said thinly.

He really ought to see what was going on back here! Then: Do? What should they do? That was when the pause came. The Exec did not want the responsibility of deciding, either. He didn't know what they were supposed to do, he said lamely. The Colonel should be back with orders in an hour or so. Maybe even less.

"Time's a-wasting," Band said. He felt the thin humorous contempt and superiority of a combat person for a rear area person. He listened disdainfully as the Exec told him if he would wait, if he would not break contact, the Exec would try to get the Colonel. The conference was only fifty yards or so away, and he would take the walkietalkie man with him. Would he wait? Band waited. As he waited, he could feel his eyes narrowing, his neck lengthening as his stance straightened, his jaw setting, his mouth compressing, a combat man against the hillside. He stared rearward toward The Giant Boiled Shrimp's Tail, toward where the brass was.

When the orders came, they came not in the voice of the 1st Battalion Exec, but from the person of the Regimental Commander himself. That mottlefaced, whitehaired old drunkard with the huge paunch was taking on himself the responsibility of ordering both Battalions to go on, immediately. The Division Commander had already received permission from the General Commanding to change the division's boundary on the right. The plan was for 3d Battalion to turn right from The Shrimp's Head and attack toward the beach over a series of more or less connected, open hills. The objective was to reach the beach at the village of Bunabala (which high command had not expected to reach for weeks, or months) splitting the Japanese Army and cutting off the Japanese still holding out against the beach division. Band whistled silently. This was quite some objective, for one battalion—or even for two battalions. As if in answer, the Exec went on that, of course, they would be reinforced as soon as practicable by 2d Battalion and the other regiment.

1st Battalion on the other hand, the Exec said, and Band nodded because he thought he already knew, was to turn right also, but in a wider sweep, on the outside of 3d Battalion, to protect their flank. They were, uh, in an image, to run blocking interference for 3d Battalion who would be carrying the ball. But as they would have no series of connected open hills over which to maneuver, their situation would be somewhat different. They would find on the map a series of widely separated small hills some distance to the left of 3d Battalion's route. These, which came out into the coconut groves just to the left Bunabala, were their objectives. They were to take them, leaving just enough men to hold each one, and move on—finally to Bunabala, where they would turn left to protect the rear of 3d Battalion fighting on the right. As soon as their water, rations and stretcherbearers reached them, they were to move out. As to future water, they would have to find that for themselves on the way. There were several creeks and some waterholes on the map adjacent to their route. They had water purifying pills, didn't they? Band said that they did. Okay, that was all, and good luck, the Exec said excitedly. Band was about to switch over, thank him drily and sign off, when the Exec called him.

There was one other thing. "What? What, sir?" Band heard him say dimly, then: "The Regimental Commander says you may find yourself being cut off from your own lines. Certainly 1st and 3d Battalions will be cut off from each other. But within your Battalion your companies may even find themselves cut off from each other." The Exec spoke slowly, as though the Regimental Commander was giving it to him sentence by sentence. "Therefore," he said, "you are to consider yourselves operating as independent commands, except where communication is possible. Okay? Over."

Band's mouth was suddenly dry with excitement. "Roger," he said calmly. "Over and out." When he hung up the instrument, his eyes behind his spectacles were brighter than they had ever been. Independent commands! Operating as independent commands!

The Exec had said earlier that Col Spine would try to keep up with them as closely as was practicable, but Band knew what that meant. It meant Spine would be at least as far back as the front of 2d Battalion or the other regiment, as they moved up to consolidate.

L Company's commander had received substantially the same dope, with one exception. Their Colonel commanding was going with them. Band and the L Company commander shook hands once again.

C-for-Charlie watched L Company take off. There was a nervous, strangely excited feeling in the air now. It was impossible to tell which battalion had drawn the easier assignment. The front slope of The Shrimp's Head fell away gently to the right of their own axis of advance, thus creating The Shrimp's long Face and little Beard which showed up so plainly in the aerial photos. The last elements of L Company crossed the Beard and disappeared into the jungle as C-for-Charlie watched.

Band called a council of his officers and all first-three-graders. Independent commands! He smiled his small smile. When they had all arrived, he told them, "It looks like maybe the whole thing has been blown wide open. Nobody—in our sector anyway—can find the Imperial Japanese Army. Our orders are to keep pushing ahead until we do find them, and then hit them to see how strong they are. If possible, we're to aid 3d Battalion in the capture of Bunabala. This may be a breakthrough and we may be able to cut them off. Okay, men, let's get it to movin. We got a lot of walkin to do." He dismissed them and they started back to their units. He was pleased with his speech. He was pleased with squatting here and making such a speech, in this hot sweltering bright morning sunshine on a dusty mountain slope with the jungle all around below them on this island of Guadalcanal, far off in the tropical South Pacific sea. Independent commands! Band was absolutely certain that his company anyway, for one, was going to be there for the capture of Bunabala.

It was essentially a new word to the company. It had cropped up in a few conversations long, long ago back down on the beach, before combat. The Marines had once sent an illfated expedition to try to capture it. Now Bunabala ran through the company from squad to squad like wildfire and, of course, was immediately changed by somebody to Boola Boola. It was, they knew, a village situated on the beach in the coconut groves. Up to today Boola Boola had been a distant mirage, a nonexistent-in-the-future town they would someday have to attack and take. Now it was, excitingly, their immediate objective.

Their stretcherbearers, rations and water arrived. Nobody carried packs now, but two cans of C ration could be carried in the hip pockets. Almost everybody, for the first time since leaving the rest bivouac, decided to drink down, give away, or pour out their remaining whiskey and refill the second canteen with water. Welsh was one of the few exceptions. He kept his two canteens of gin. Then, equipped as well as they could hope to be, they prepared to move out.

It was just at this point, while the final hitching and settling and stamping was going on, that Milly Beck the martinet and former squad sergeant, now an equally conscientious platoon leader, came to Band with a deeply frowning face and a request that his platoon be put in company reserve. "My boys've had it tougher than any of the other platoons, Lootenant. Including The Elephant's Head. They've had more casualties, and are more under strength. They deserve a break now."

"Did you ask Lieutenant Tomms about this?" Band said, adjusting his glasses to peer at him.

"Him?" Beck said in his stolid direct way. "No. What's he know about any of it?"

"That's true," Band said. He did not like this kind of request. But Beck was scrupulously fair—in his dumb way—and what was more important, he was good at his job. Band thought in silence, pushing at the bridge of his glasses with his middle finger.

"It aint fair to leave my boys out there all the goddam time," Beck added in the silence, as if that made it conclusive.

Afterward Band thought he might have acceded to the request if Beck had not spoken just then. Now, instead, he jerked his head up to stare at him. "Fair? What's not fair? What's fair got to do with it? No," he said. "I'm afraid I'll have to deny your request, Sergeant. Your platoon is the best I've got. They've got more experience, they're tougher, they know how to handle themselves better. They belong out in front."

"Is that an order then, Sir?" Beck growled, staring at him.

"I'm afraid it is, Sergeant."

"In other words, the more of us get killed gettin experience, the more of us *got* to get killed usin it."

Band felt it was time to pull rank, but he did not do it bluntly or brutally. "As I said, fair has nothing to do with it," he said crisply. "Unfortunately. In a war everything useful has to be used. And here it is me who decides what is most useful where." He made his eyes steely behind his steel spectacles. "Any other questions, Sergeant Beck?"

"No, sir." Beck growled it, furiously.

"Then that's all."

"Aye, aye, Sir!" Beck saluted, did an accurate aboutface, and marched away at attention at a solid 120 per. It was the only way left him of showing his disapproval. "My platoon!" he bawled. "Off and on!"

Poor man, Band thought, smiling his small smile. He was sorry. Still, he thought he had handled it pretty well. "Sergeant!" he called, on a sudden whim.

Beck swung around. He was only about fifteen feet away. Nobody else was near them. "I want to tell you something, Sergeant," Band said, smiling behind his spectacles.

"Sir?"

"Do you know why C-for-Charlie is the Battalion's lead company today in this attack? It's because I volunteered us for it to the new Battalion Commander."

"You what!" Beck cried in disbelief, and crouched almost as if to charge him.

Band raised his eyebrows, and waited. Beck was too old a hand not to know what that meant. *"Sir!"* he added chokingly.

"That's right," Band smiled. "And do you know why I did? It was because I felt C-for-Charlie with its superior combat experience would be more useful there. To Regiment, to the Division, to the attack. To everybody." He continued to smile, hoping it would sink in.

Slowly, Beck drew himself up to attention, his eyes completely filmed over. "Is that all, Sir?" he said distantly, and with dignity.

"That's all, Sergeant."

For answer Beck saluted, aboutfaced and went on. "My platoon!" he bawled again. "Off and on!"

Sadly, Band watched him go.

This time Beck put Dale's squad in front as point. He saw no reason why Band's being a chicken shit must make him one too.

And this time there was grumbling in the platoon over being first again. Wherever Beck heard it, he cursed them roundly and furiously. He was brooking no argument in his platoon. First Dale's squad disappeared into the leaves, then the other three. Then came 3d Platoon, followed by the Company Hq, then 1st Platoon, then Weapons. As they disappeared one by one, Baker Company moved around to the front of the hill to form up and follow them.

While C-for-Charlie, ignored by Baker who were worried only about themselves and quite glad of their number two spot, was cautiously beginning its first 1000 yard jungle trek, at least two of its partisans were doing everything in their power to catch up with it. Mess Sergeant Storm and Acting-P.F.C. Witt, unknown to each other, and for different reasons, were both doing their best to find the company.

If C-for-Charlie was not thinking of Witt, and had not thought about him since the night he had run drunk off the side of the mountain, Witt had nevertheless been thinking about them all the time. There was true anguish in his implacable Kentucky heart when he learned they had been moved from reserve up into the attack this morning and he knew he could not be with them because of his vow. At the time he learned it, he was back on Hill 209 carrying watercans and rationboxes. Cannon Company—still thought of as an outfit of bums, misfits and deadbeats, and still without their cannons—had been pressed into service as supply porters this time, instead of as stretcherbearers, and were carrying supplies between Hill 209 and Hill 214, The Elephant's Forelegs. It was because of this that Witt had not heard about Colonel Tall's promotion. It was not until noon, when he returned from another pack trip to Hill 214 and overheard some Regimental Hq clerks talking about Tall's raise in salary, that he found out. He immediately got his rifle and some bandoliers and sneaked off, heading for Hill 214 along the jeep road. He had only been made Acting-P.F.C. two days ago—Acting because all ranks were Acting in Cannon Company, which had never yet been given an official TO—and now he was sure to lose his rating. On the other hand, he had been an Acting-Sergeant in C-for-Charlie for two days. Laughing happily over all of this, he traversed the brand

new jungle road between Hill 214 and The Sea Slug, and found
Maynard Storm and his entire kitchen all set up on the open
ridge, at just about the same time that C-for-Charlie was captur-
ing its first undefended hill off in the midst of the jungle sea.

Storm was having his own troubles. Back at the hospital, when
he had sworn to remain a mess sergeant and stay the hell off the
front lines, he had also sworn to feed his pore, bleeding outfit at
least one hot meal a day if it was at all humanly possible. To this
end, back at the empty bivouac where MacTae the supply sergeant was the only other person of authority left and who certainly didn't mind, Storm had commandeered both company
jeeps, loaded them with his cooks, stoves and supplies and had
taken off at dawn to feed C-for-Charlie, only to find them already
gone when he arrived at The Elephant's Head. They were, he was
informed, on The Sea Slug digging in as Regimental reserve.
Patiently doubling back and taking the other road he arrived at
The Sea Slug (after considerable argument with the Provost Mar-
shal's MPs guarding the new jungle section) only to find them
gone again. 2d Battalion was already moving into their holes.
And here he was stumped. He could not go any farther. Even
jeeps could not move to The Shrimp's Tail until the Engineers
made a road, and all supplies were being carried by native porters. Even when there was a road, he was told, other transport
would have priority, like ammo, cold rations, water. Modern war,
after first wounding him, had finally caught up with Storm in his
work. Modern war didn't give a damn whether Storm fed his
company hot food or not. Modern war couldn't care less about a
solitary company mess, trying to get far enough forward to give
its outfit hot food and fucking up the highway priorities, and
nobody was going to help him. And it had become an obsession
with Storm to feed his outfit at least one hot meal a day. Only in
that way could he relieve himself of the guilts he felt for not
being with them. And now all he could do was sit here with one
thumb up his ass and the other in his mouth like some baby. A
lesser man would have broken and wept. Storm cursed with tears
in his eyes.

On the other hand, Storm's cooks were all glad. None of them had liked this crazy idea anyway. It was too dangerously near the firing. He had forced them to come here and try this goofy scheme over their collective objections. They didn't even have any KPs to do the dirty work. And now they watched their near tearful leader maliciously and whispered among themselves that maybe now he would let them go home to the bivouac. Finally one of them got up nerve enough to go and ask him this. Storm delivered him such a left hook in the side of the head that it knocked him down and his head rang for two hours. While he worked. Because Storm had immediately put them all to work.

He did not know exactly when the idea came to him. It was a simple enough connection. Here all around him were men hungering for hot food, and here he was with the stoves and supplies to fix it. So he had set up his kitchen on some nearly level ground ten yards from the main ridge. The stoves were unloaded and fired up, his cooks told off for their various shifts, the skillets put to sizzling on the ranges, and Storm was open for business. He had brought more than enough food in the two jeeps to feed the company three hot meals a day for a week. It might be a long battle. By that calculation, he could feed six companies two hot meals a day for almost two days. Or, if he . . . He stopped counting and went back to work. By the time Witt arrived he had fed the two companies of the 2d Battalion holding The Sea Slug one hot meal apiece before they moved out, and had served another hot meal to the one company of the sister regiment which had relieved them. Then he had gotten an even better idea, when a strange company had marched by heading for The Giant Boiled Shrimp.

Coming up from the jungle road back to Hill 214, the sight to these men of a foreign company mess sitting by the trail with stoves aglow and skillets sizzling had caused their eyes to bug out. Several of them had broken ranks and rushed over, only to burn their hands on the slices of hot Spam as they ran to fall back in. Storm had brought lots of bread. Now he broke it out. He also posted a sentry at the mouth of the jungle road to Hill 214. When this man signaled, the cooks on shift started frying all the Spam they could handle. The cooks not on shift sliced the bread and

then did the serving, passing out along the column with armloads
of hot fried Spam sandwiches while Storm roared and hollered
and clapped his hands like pistol shots like some football coach to
pep them up. They could not feed every single man like that,
there wasn't the time, but now and then—though rarely—an understanding company commander suddenly decided to call a ten
break on The Sea Slug. And there were enough outfits moving
across The Sea Slug now, heading for The Shrimp, to keep Storm
occupied. Then there would be the evening meal to prepare for
this stranger company here. His cooks stared at him as if he'd
gone mad, but he didn't care. Fuck all that! Fuck everything!
Feed men!

However, every now and then, he would think of C-for-Charlie,
all those faces that he knew so well passing slowly in review
before his eyes. Then he would know that it didn't mean anything, what he was doing, didn't help at all, was worthless to him.
And then that look, whether of rage, frustration, guilt or pain, or
all four, would come back over his face. Modern war. You
couldn't even *pretend* it was human. Then he would plunge back
in.

This comic routine, this emotional strophe and antistrophe, was
what he was doing when Witt came up the road alone, a solitary
figure, humping along under his combat pack with slung rifle and
bandoliers, thin and frail looking, his peanut head sunk deep into
his helmet shell, Witt the Kentuckian, Witt who hated niggers
because they all wanted to vote. Even if one told him he didn't
want to vote, Witt would not believe him. He would simply have
to be lying. From beneath the shell, in shadow, his hard implacable eyes peered out like the eyes of some ferretlike animal.

There was a great deal of handshaking. The kitchen had not
seen Witt since the night he tried to run down the mountain. A
huge meal was prepared for him. Storm fed him all the fried
Spam, dehydrated mashed potatoes, and stewed dehydrated apples his small belly could hold. Storm broke out an Imperial
quart.

"What the hell are you doin up here? Like this? All by yourself."

"I'm headin back to the company," Witt said, wiping his mouth with the back of his hand.

"You're what?!"

Witt grinned. "Goin back. Shorty Tall got promoted yesterday."

"You must be out of your mind," Storm said.

Witt's helmetshadowed eyes turned slowly in their sockets to stare at him. "No I aint."

"In the first place nobody knows where they are. They're way to hell and gone off on their own someplace. They're not even on The Giant Boiled Shrimp anymore."

Witt nodded. "I can find them. Somebody's got to know."

"The last dope we had here said that all companies of both 1st and 3d Battalions have been authorized to act as independent commands. You know what that means."

"Sure. They probably out of contact."

"You must be off your rocker."

"Why?" Witt said. "It's the company, aint it? They must of left a trail. And Tall's promoted, aint he?" He looked straight at Storm out of his black Kentucky eyes.

Storm stared back. "Have a nuther drink," he said.

"Thank you, I will," Witt said politely. Then he smiled his shy smile. "It's good to see you, Stormy. But what are you doin up here feeding all these strangers?"

"I tried to catch up to the company, but we missed them. And these guys was here." Storm shrugged lamely. "I figured I might as well feed somebody."

"Well, I guess it's a good deed," Witt said. "It was good for me, anyway."

"Angh," Storm said and shrugged again. He looked around the ridge. "For two cents I'd go with you."

Witt got up. "Come on along."

"But I don't know what these dumbasses would do if they didn't have me around to take care of them," Storm said.

"We'd have some fun."

"The truth is," Storm said, "I dont like to get shot at."

"Everybody to his own taste," Witt said. Then he grinned. "I think I like it. But honestly I wouldn't be doin this if it wasn't the old company, I guess.''

They left it at that. Witt was well aware of the effect his odyssey was creating, and he was openly proud of himself. He hung around talking and having a couple more drinks so that he did not get away heading for The Shrimp, shtumping along in solitary splendor, until just after four, which was just about the time that C-for-Charlie unaided captured their second undefended hill.

Storm watched him until he disappeared from sight going down into the jungle toward The Shrimp behind some native porters at the front end of The Sea Slug ridge. Witt was not aware of this because he was too proud to let himself look back, but he could not help wondering if some of them weren't watching. Because of having to stop and ask directions so often from so many people who could tell him nothing or only the vaguest rumors, he had to cover almost every foot of The Giant Boiled Shrimp and it was a quarter to five in the afternoon of the next day when he finally reached The Shrimp's Head and had pointed out to him the trail 1st Battalion had taken. This was almost precisely the same moment that C-for-Charlie was beginning its attack against Hill 279, its fourth, which was defended by a platoonsized body of Japanese.

It was a tough fight and, curiously enough, a boring one. For almost everybody. One man, however, it was not boring for, and this was Corporal Geoffrey Fife, newly of 2d Squad, 3d Platoon, because during it Fife killed his first Japanese.

Most of them could not even remember how many hills they had captured and passed. Everything ran together in one long stumbling breathless rush of green leaves and ropy lianas interspersed with blazing sunshine on bare knobs and dustysmelling masses of kunai grass. Somewhere in the midst of this a night passed. Band, though he told no one, still meant to be in on the capture of Boola Boola (as even he was calling it, now) and he had pushed them so hard that by the time they occupied their third undefended hilltop the next morning they were more like seven hundred yards ahead of Baker instead of the proper two, and everybody including himself was in a stupor of exhaustion which could no longer be the whiskey they had gulped down at The Shrimp because that had long since been sweated out of them. Twice they had run out of water and had had to search off the trail with the map for the marked waterholes. It was at the second of these that Big Un Cash was killed by a light Nambu. So that, while they mightn't remember the hills, nobody forgot that particular waterhole.

It was located off the main trail on a little side trail which the Japanese had cleverly hidden by leaving a thick screen of undergrowth at its mouth between it and the big trail. They had to search for it until they began to doubt the map or else their own understanding of it. It was defended by five starving Japs with rifles and that one Nambu. This was between the second and third undefended hills, in the morning. Finally somebody stumbled blindly into the side trail. It led downhill into a deep hollow where a muddy stinking pool had been formed by springs. The jungle hid it forever from the sun. Green scum floated on its surface. In spite of that it looked good. Sgt Thorne's squad of 2d Platoon was point squad at the time. Cash (who had been made Corporal after The Dancing Elephant and had requested 2d Platoon) had been assigned to Thorne's squad as second in command. When Thorne's squad took over from Dale's, he had placed himself in front as point man and had been there since.

The five Japanese had planned their defense cleverly, given their poor circumstances, and had hidden themselves and their little camp behind some downed trees directly across from the side trail so they could fire enfilade on it. They were obviously a suicide group, left behind to take with them in death as many Americans as they could get, but they got only Cash. He was perhaps ten yards in front of the second man as they came down to the pool. He fell forward on his face in the mud hit through the hips, crotch and lower groin by the first burst of fire. Everybody else scattered. Dale's and Bell's squads worked around to the right and left while two BAR men under Doll kept the Japanese pinned, and grenaded most of them. Two survivors who stood up were shot and fell into the pool. The two squads met in the center and assured themselves nobody was left. Then they came back for

Cash. He was conscious and had managed to turn himself over and wipe some of the mud off his face.

The two dead men bleeding pink, dissolving streams into the pool did not keep them from filling their canteens. It ran out into the muddy water from their bodies only a little way, and then swirling diluted itself into invisibility. "Everybody's got to drink a little enemy blood in his lifetime some time or other," Charlie Dale growled cheerfully, whereupon two men vomited, but filled their canteens nevertheless. *"You* can't see it, but it's *there!"* Dale sang. He was told to shut up by several men and the watergetting work went on, men standing around vigorously shaking their canteens up and down to dissolve the purifying pills, while the two medics did what they could for Cash.

After filling their canteens, a small group explored the little Japanese camp for booty and discovered there the first evidence any of them had seen of cannibalism. They had all heard rumors, but this was no rumor. A dead Japanese man, who apparently had died from artilleryinflicted chest wounds, had been strung up from a branch by his heels and strips of flesh about two inches wide had been cut from his buttocks, lower back and thighs. Apparently they had carried him back this far from The Shrimp before he died, and then they had utilized him. The charred remains of the little campfire where they had cooked him was only a few feet away. All five of the other corpses were ragged, filthy dirty, near shoeless, and starved looking. They obviously had been given little or no rations to sustain them, and curiously enough nobody was very shocked or horrified by the cannibalism. In this mad jungle world of mud, perpetual wet, gloom, green air, stink, and slithering animal life, it seemed far more normal than not normal. Carrie Arbre poked at one of the evenly cut strip wounds with his bayonet and giggled. "He still looks pretty fresh." "Maybe he was good," Doll grinned. "Anybody want to try some?" somebody else said. When he heard about it, Brass Band came over to have a look with the new Exec, a longnosed, mean, and meanlooking, Italian 1st Lieutenant named Creo. Charlie Dale found two gold teeth in the head of one corpse. He was finding out that not nearly as many Japanese had gold teeth as he had been led to believe.

The two medics had propped Cash up against the bole of a tree where he leaned his head back and kept both hands between his legs. Sgts Thorne and Bell had somehow gotten themselves tacitly designated to sit up with him. Thorne, of course, was his squad leader and should have been there. But John Bell never did figure out why the hell he should have been stuck with the job. Big Un was bleeding to death internally and they all knew it. It took him about fifteen minutes.

"You guys write my old lady, will you?" he growled toughly, raising his head to look at them. "Dont forget. I want her to know I died like a man."

"Sure, sure," Thorne said. "But nobody's gonna haf to write your old lady. You'll come out of this. We got stretcherbearers with us, remember? Battalion Aid Station's movin up all the time. They'll have you back to the docs in no time."

Big Un had laid his head back against the trunk. "Bullshit," he said. "Dont bullshit me." Then he said, "I'm cold."

The four men sat looking at him with the sweat streaming from them in rivulets. "There, there," Bell said. "Just take it easy."

"You guys dont forget to write my old lady I died like a man," Big Un said. Then he sighed, first sign of the approaching breathlessness of massive hemorrhage. "You'd think there wouldn't be any of them here, though, would you? When there wasn't any on either one of them hills. What was it old Keck said? *What a fucking recruit trick to pull.*" He raised one arm to rub at his face with his sleeve. "This fuckin mud on my face," he said. "This fuckin mud on my face."

Bell sacrificed his one remaining handkerchief and wet it in the pool to clean his face for him. This somehow seemed to make him feel better. "Just dont forget to write my old lady I died like a man."

"Just take it easy," Bell said. "Dont talk like that. You'll make it out of this."

Big Un raised his head again. "Horse shit," he said. "I'm

bleedin to death inside." He looked at one of the medics. "Aint I?"

The medic nodded dumbly.

"See? Maybe it's just as good. I'm all shot up on the crock. What if I couldn't fuck any more? Just dont forget to write my old lady I died manly."

"Sure, sure," Thorne said. "I'll write her. Just take it easy."

When the breathlessness really hit him, they knew it wouldn't be too long. "Christ, I'm cold!" he gasped. "Freezin!" The last thing he said, from somewhere down there inside the breathlessness, was, "Dont—forget—write—oldlady—diedlike—aman." He went on gasping for almost another full minute before he finally stopped.

The four men stood up.

"You going to write his wife?" Bell asked.

"Fuck no!" Thorne said. "I dont know his old lady. That's the Compny Commander's job, not mine. You out of your mind? I aint no good at writin letters."

"But you told him you would." Bell looked back down at him who was no longer Big Un, no longer anything.

"I tell them anything when they're like that."

"Somebody ought to do it."

"Then you write her."

"I didn't tell him I would."

Charlie Dale came over to them. "All over?" Thorne nodded. "Yeah."

A detail buried him at the edge of the main trail, and jammed his rifle in the ground with his helmet on it and one dogtag tied to the triggerguard. Nobody had a blanket to wrap him in, but it was better than leaving him to be eaten by rats or whatever it was lived in this undergrowth. Once they had covered his face and bare hands first, it wasn't so hard to fill in the hole over the rest of him.

They put up an arrow sign for B Company to show the water.

Then they went on to find the third hill (if it was the third hill) unoccupied, too. This was early afternoon.

But not the fourth. If it was the fourth.

It was Band who decided to go on and not wait for Baker to catch up. He still had his mind on Boola Boola for the next day, and the next hill was only four hundred yards off by the map. Actually it turned out to be nearer to six hundred yards when they got there, and this time they had to chop trail. Up to now they had been able to follow old trails. This too took its toll, as well as the normal exhaustion of having pressed on so hard, and they arrived at Hill 279 eight men short, all of whom had been left stretched out along the trail in varying states of collapse, with orders to come on when they could, or wait and be picked up by the patrol Band had left back on the third, if it was the third, hill for Baker Company.

It was just before leaving this next to last, third, fourth, or fifth hill that Sgt Beck came to Band again with a request that his 2d Platoon be allowed to relinquish the point to somebody else. Again Band refused him, but he promised that tomorrow—in the morning at least, Band amended quickly—Beck's platoon could go into reserve. So it was once again the 2d Platoon which was in the lead when the company received fire. This time, John Bell's squad was the point squad.

It was the most—in fact, it was the *first*—boring situation, and fight, that any of them could remember. That any fight at all could be boring was incredible, but it was true.

They had been listening hard, as they chopped their way along, hoping there would not be any fight at all and they could move right in, and they had not heard or seen anything at all. Then a man in Bell's point squad hollered and went down as machine-guns and rifles opened up on them. They were about fifty yards from the top of Hill 279 and open ground. The others in the point squad scattered and spread out. The second squad moved into line on the first squad's left. The prolonged burst had ceased for several seconds. Now a second came. The wounded man lay crying and moaning. The third squad spread out on the first's right. The tense-faced men lay and looked at each other and up the hill. All this had been without any orders, without a word spoken. Everybody knew his job. Sgt Beck (trailing behind him the new lieutenant, Tomms) crawled up with the fourth squad, Thorne's, which

now had no real second in command. Beck, with his hand, held
them there in reserve position. A medic pushed past Beck to get
to the wounded man who still writhed and cried out piteously on
the ground. Behind them directed by Brass Band the 3d Platoon
was already scrambling, but in the noise seeming to glide,
through the dense undergrowth on a tangent which would bring
them into line on 2d Platoon's left. 1st Platoon under Skinny
Culn and his new lieutenant, The Pain, was moving up to spread
out in company reserve. One MG section each from Weapons was
on its way to the two front platoons. And the two mortar sections
were flat on their faces. The whole thing had taken maybe forty-
five seconds since the first shot. Everybody was scared—naturally—but they were also very tired. It would have to happen to
them now at the end of the day. Also, the combat numbness had
been advancing in all of them since yesterday morning. It was
hardly even exciting, and the half hour's battle which followed
was hardly more exciting.

The upshot of it was that they kept drifting left trying to find a
hole. And that was the form the battle took. It was soon clear
there would be no counter-attack. Band overestimated the enemy
force at just under a company. He sent 1st Platoon around to the
left of 3d Platoon, but they found no hole either. The three platoons hid behind trees and the huge tree roots and fired back with
no appreciable effect. It was tiring, uninspired, nervousmaking
work which everybody wanted to get over and done with; but the
Japanese defended their little hill expertly and toughly. Two more
men had been wounded now, and with their crying and moaning
added their small but important bit to the general noise. Finally
Band decided on a frontal attack. A charge. It was the only thing
he could think of, since his mortars could not fire because of
overhead obstruction.

In front of 3d Platoon was a gently sloping depression up onto
the hilltop which seemed to present a sort of psychological entrance channel. So 3d Platoon was given the rather dubious honor
of making the charge. They wouldn't just charge, of course. They
would work their way forward as far as they could, then give them
a grenade shower, and rush. The MGs and the other two platoons

would give them fire support and be prepared to join them as soon as they were in. Lt Al Gore, a thin, hollowcheeked, anguish-faced young man, and Sgt Fox, a heavier, hollowcheeked, anguish-faced man, crawled forward to have a look. They would go in two waves of two squads each.

Corporal Fife, as he got himself ready in Jenks' squad which would be in the first wave, could hardly believe this was happening to him. Somehow he had always thought he would be spared this experience, that somehow something would always intervene to prevent him having to face Japanese in close proximity with bayonets or knife. He was not at all sure that he could kill somebody who was looking right at him. As they started the crawl under the fire the other two platoons were trying to draw away from them, his teeth were chattering and he was shaking like a leaf from head to foot with terror and lack of confidence.

Earlier, when the first fire had opened on them, wounding and breaking the arm of that man in Bell's squad, Fife's squad had been directly behind 2d Platoon. While the others were starting their quick move to the left, Fife had simply frozen, standing there crouched in his tracks unable to move, until Jenks had to yell at him irritably to "Come on, damn it! Get to movin!" After that he was able to move, but his mind simply would not function and he could not think about anything. He knew this sort of thing could get you killed, but that did not help him. And anyway you could get killed in a lot of ways, in just about any way at all in fact. This thing about all the ways you *could* get killed had been with him ever since his own wounding, and now its sheer unreckonability unnerved him. The cries and moans of the hurt man unnerved him further. Why couldn't he keep his mouth shut? Fife had. This was not just another day's work to him like it apparently was to Jenks. And also Jenks had never been hit. Getting hit made you realize that you—. . .

He had tried to do better, helping Jenks herd the squad, pretending he was not unnerved, that he was not thinking of all the unreckonable ways to get killed. But his performance was at best mechanical. And the worst thing in his mind was that he might not be able to kill some Japanese or other who confronted him, and who, therefore, would kill him.

And the same thing was in his mind now as they crawled. Suddenly, for no real reason, he found himself remembering that young, foolish, innocent, gullible Corporal Fife, that total stranger, who once had stood forth in the dawn on Hill 209 and had stretched out his arms willing to be killed for mankind, and the love of mankind. Well, fuck mankind, that bunch of 'honorable' animals. Piss and shit on them. That was what they deserved.

They were on their feet before the grenade shower had even exploded. They ran uphill, hollering and yelling. Fife scampered along with them, panting and sweating. Nothing touched him. On his right the usually imperturbable Jenks let out a long, shrill, screeching, quavering rebel yell. Three men went down hollering in the rush. Nothing touched Fife. Then they were in. The second two squads were right behind them. Fife had no trouble shooting. When he first saw those scrawny, tattered, scarecrow yellow men firing their rifles and MGs intently, he could hardly believe it and felt astonished. When he saw one Japanese in a hole whirl with a grenade in his hand and stare at him wide-eyed, he shot him through the chest and watched him fall, the phrase repeating itself over and over in his mind happily that "I can kill, too! I can! Just like everybody! I can kill, too!" Then he looked around for more targets and saw a Japanese running, trying to make the jungle. Head down, arms pumping, he ran in total despair like a man on a too-swift treadmill which was carrying him backward. Fife led him just a hair and shot him through the left side just below the armpit, shouting with elation as the man tumbled with a yell just feet away from the jungle and safety. Then it was all over. 2d and 1st Platoons were pouring in on both sides of them.

A number of the Japanese—maybe half—had got out, running and diving into the jungle leading to their own rear. If such a term as rear applied, in this crazy campaign. The rest, including the two or three who tried to surrender, were shot out of hand by tense-faced, nerve-racked men who wanted no fucking nonsense. The whole thing had lasted just under half an hour. They were all exhausted, by the long trailchopping jungle trek, by the difficult maneuvering through the dense undergrowth, by the fight itself. Now all they had left to do, as soon as they got their breath back, was to get rid of the corpses and make a perimeter defense and dig in for the night. C-for-Charlie had lost two dead and six wounded. The Japanese had lost twenty-three dead. There were no Japanese wounded. But some might have escaped with the others.

Standing with the others of his platoon as they panted and sweated and slowly came back to themselves, or presumed to, Corporal Geoffrey Fife ex-company clerk was astonished to realize that he had personally killed two Japanese. He did not, like most of the others, take part in the poking and looking and souvenirhunting because the corpses made him feel queasy and vaguely guilty. But he watched. Was this the way they'd done it at The Elephant's Head? And when Charlie Dale whipped out his pliers and Bull Durham sacks and began yanking gold teeth, Fife had to turn away. A few others appeared to view Dale's toothpulling with distaste, but nobody said anything, and nobody looked as upset as Fife felt. And this upset Fife even more. Don Doll, for instance, was watching Dale and grinning broadly. What was wrong with him? If the rest of the guys could be this tough, why couldn't he be? He had killed two, hadn't he?—one of whom had been looking straight at him.

Taking himself in hand, he made himself turn back and watch. He even grinned a little. Doll was grinning. So Fife grinned too. Casually—much more casually than he actually felt—he made himself walk over to one of the cadavers and look at it. He thought of sticking his bayonet in it, to show he didn't give a damn, but he was afraid that would look too affected. So instead he squatted, taking the stragglybearded greasy chin in his hand, and turned the head so he could look directly into the face. The eyes were still open and a tiny thin trickle of blood had run out of the halfopen, mutilated mouth where Dale had worked on it. Fife gave it a push and stood up and walked away. That ought to show them! He had a strong impulse to wipe his hand vigorously on his pantsleg, but he resisted it. Instead he started getting out his entrenching tool off his belt because soon they'd have to start digging, that much was for sure.

Fife was quite right. That was the next major chore that faced them, before they themselves could face the night. Digging. Their neverending, universal digging. Sweating and panting with exhaustion, digging. Like last night. And almost every night in the world. And sometimes two or three times in the day. A place to lay your head. Three by three by seven, slit trench. Only the very lucky ever inherited another outfit's holes. Nobody dug the round deep foxholes here because there weren't any tanks. Here the home was the slit trench. There might not be any atheists in foxholes, John Bell thought with a grim smile, like that dumb Catholic Chaplain in the Philippines said, because nobody here dug foxholes. But he knew a lot of them in slit trenches, and getting more and more every day.

A detail was sent to complete the remaining fifty yards of trail. A patrol was sent back to collect the stragglers and inform Baker where they were. The wounded went out with the patrol. Of the six wounded, only three were litter cases. This meant that one of the four litter teams could stay with the company. Replacement litter teams were to be requested and sent forward, in the morning, perhaps shuttled up from Baker. Everything done, Brass Band decided not to call Battalion. He had not called them last night. After all, they had told him he was an independent command. Independent command! And he was well within the schedule, and even ahead of it.

It was about a half hour after dark—when both of the patrols, and all of the stragglers, were back safely inside the perimeter defense—that the men awake in the section of holes overlooking the trail, heard themselves hailed from the trail in a strong Kentucky accent.

"Charlie Compny! Charlie Compny! Hold your fahr! It's Witt! It's Witt! Acting-P-F-C Witt!" the voice added in a burst of sly humor, "of Cannon Compny!"

It was indeed Witt. He had walked the last six hundred yards alone in the dark from B-for-Baker's position on the next hill back. He had found A-for-Able first, gone on, stopped to read the dogtag on the triggerguard of Big Un's rifle, reached B-for-Baker where they gave him the password, decided to come on despite their best advice, and here he was. Hardly anyone was asleep yet, and there was a great deal of backslapping, laughter, and hand-shaking. The first thing he wanted to know was what was the new Battalion Commander like. Everybody was overjoyed to see him, to know that he would have searched them out like this just to be with them. Everybody included Brass Band, who with his insipid smile had only just then decided to place outside the perimeter the roadblock which he had decided the company's position needed.

Witt of course volunteered for it immediately.

Everybody had wondered why the Japanese had decided to defend Hill 279 and not the others. The answer, which also showed on the map had anyone thought about it, was just on the other side of the hill. Following a usually dry river bed toward the coconut groves and the beach, one of the two major north-south trails across the whole island passed through the jungle just under the shoulder of Hill 279. Beaufort Trail, much further on ahead, and this one here called Dini-Danu in the native tongue but im-mediately renamed Ding Dong Trail by the Americans, were the only means of moving across the island. It was known that the Japanese used them both to march across their skimpy reenforce-ments landed from fast destroyers on the other side of the island, and it was because of this fact that Tall George Band decided to throw a block across it. He wanted to deny the Japanese any reenforcements that he could for the battle of Boola Boola tomor-row. He had received no orders about Ding Dong Trail one way or the other, from Battalion or from Regiment, but he was con-vinced that he could help in this way.

Witt was the first man to volunteer for it, though he had, he said, serious reservations about the whole idea. John Bell was the second, though he could not have told anybody why. The third was Charlie Dale, who still had in mind his plot for getting a platoon, and whose nose had been put out of joint by Witt's dramatic return. Dale, however, was disallowed by Band, who said two noncoms were enough, and who thereby probably saved his life because Witt and Bell were the only two to survive the mission.

The rest of the volunteers were Pfcs and privates. A couple of men from Bell's squad volunteered because their leader was going. A man named Gooch, an oldtime Regular and boxing buddy of Witt, volunteered because he was a good friend of Witt and wanted to talk to him. Band wanted two BARs so Bell's BAR man volunteered. Then Charlie Dale's BAR man volunteered to go with Witt. They were twelve Pfcs and privates in all. All of them died.

Originally Band had thought to send his entire 'Old Vet' 2d Platoon, but had thought better of it and asked for volunteers when he remembered Beck's protests. In a way it was lucky, because from what happened it was pretty clear that a platoon would have done no more good than the fourteen men Band later decided to send, though more of them certainly would have survived. Band did not yet know that most of his company was already calling him by his new nickname The Glory Hunter behind his back, or that the majority of his higher sergeants already knew from Beck that he had volunteered the company to be lead company. If he had, it probably would not have influenced his decision. Witt did not yet know any of this, either. If he had, it would certainly have made him protest about the roadblock even stronger. As it was, it was strong enough to astonish Band.

"I want to go," Witt said, when he first volunteered. "But I want to make it plain that I think the whole thing is a pretty bad idea. If they come through there like in any strength at all, Lootenant, they going to knock that roadblock to hell and flinders even if it's a whole platoon. We couldn't hold them. But I want to go."

Band was staring at him in amazement from behind his spectacles. He had only just finished making him Acting Sergeant again a moment before. "You dont have to go, Sergeant Witt," he said thinly. "If you dont want to. Others will volunteer."

"No, I want to go," Witt said. "If somethin bad happens, I want to be there so maybe I can help. Besides, nothin bad may happen at all."

But as it turned out, there wasn't much he could do to help. Or anybody. They were had cold turkey. The only thing that saved him himself was that he was sitting over on the far left end with Gooch, Gooch who later died silently in his arms so as not to give him away. They had been talking about the last Regimental boxing season. Gooch had just missed making Department bantam champion, winding up as runnerup, and he was explaining to Witt again his excuses for this failure. That was when it hit them.

So there they were, twelve Pfcs and privates and two sergeants, one of them Acting. All normal men in a normal situation, all normal soldiers, who had accepted a normal commission to do a normal job, and death came for them in a normal way—except that nobody dies normally. Not to himself, at least. But the normality of it was what was so grotesque—afterwards, to both of the survivors. Death came for them in the form of a .31 cal machine-gun strapped to the back of a perfectly normal Japanese soldier.

Actually their tactical situation was not a bad one. They had come down the hill in the faint moonlight, explored the trail carefully for several hundred yards (at great danger to everybody), and—Witt and Bell conferring—chosen themselves the best spot available. They picked a place where the sandybottomed dryriverbed narrowed to a gulch so thin that only one man or at the most two could squeeze through it at a time. Thirty yards in front of this, on the downhill, seaward side, they spread themselves out behind a couple of downed saplings which really offered only psychological comfort, both BAR men prominently displayed. One man was told off to watch the other, seaward approach, but they all knew, somehow, that if anything came it would come from inland. Witt was over on the far left, and John Bell was on the right though not as near the nine foot bank.

What they saw, by that faint moonlight, was one man plodding along with a heavy load on his back. He must have seen them at the same instant because he fell to his hands and knees as he came through the narrow opening. The BARs killed at least one man behind him, maybe more. But it did not help, because there were many, many men behind the first one to pull the trigger of the MG on his back with which he hosed down the widening draw before him. It was like being fired at in an empty swimming pool. For the Japanese, it was fish in a barrel. Bullets ricocheted everywhere, catching on the rebound people they had missed the first time around. Japanese machine-guns, at least at this period of the war, were noted for the fact they did not have built into their tripods the ability to traverse. The veteran company in front of C-for-Charlie's roadblock solved this problem admirably, simply by having the man who wore the gun twitch his shoulders back and forth.

The thing that saved John Bell was that he saw what was happening and was on his feet three seconds before the men around him, hollering "Run! Run!" as he sprinted for the bank. That, and luck. He made it over, into the undergrowth. Two men immediately behind him fell clawing at the bank, riddled through head, trunk and legs like some kind of strange living sieves used in some mad hospital for screening blood. None of the others got even that far. And all it was was simply one sole machinegun strapped to the back of a smart veteran Japanese who wiggled his shoulders.

Witt, on the other hand—and on the other side—saw nothing and was simply lucky. Having Gooch shot out from under him almost in midword so to speak, he leaped for the other bank just behind him in blind panic. In that second the gun swung the other way. Sheer luck. And so there he lay. He had kept his rifle in his hand by blind instinct, but now he could not fire it without muzzle blast getting him found and killed. He lay and counted one hundred and thirty Japanese pass, biting his fingers and weeping real tears because he had no grenades. Just one, even one grenade. He could have caused incalculable damage in that closed space. But Cannon Company had not been issued grenades, and he had not thought to borrow some up above on the hill. In the faint moonlight he watched them pass, able to see in the brighter patches here and there faces which were not the starved, haunted faces of the men who had held the hill. This was apparently an entire company of veteran troops from somewhere who had been landed lately as reenforcements.

How Gooch, in his condition, made it up the bank, and then found him, he would never know. Nor did Gooch tell him. All he did was whisper "Please! Please!", twice like that, hurt all over as he was, and then Witt held his fingers to his lips. Gooch understood and nodded, and said no more. Witt cradled his head against him to try and show him how sorry he was, and so the best bantamweight the Regiment had ever had died in his arms as he watched the Japanese company file past. A couple of the C-for-Charlie men had lain moaning in the riverbottom, but the first elements of the Japanese column immediately shot these with pistols. And Witt lay thinking one grenade. One grenade, just one grenade.

All normal men. All out on a fairly normal mission. And now all dead.

John Bell on the other side of the dryriverbed had no grenades either. He had divested himself of everything except his rifle and one bandolier for lightness' sake. But he knew, later, that even if he had had grenades he would never have stopped to use them. For the first time in this war, hysterical panic had taken him over. For him, too, the funny thing was the feeling of how normal it had all been, normal—and easy. Like a terrified jungle animal, he crawled away stealthily through the undergrowth, cunning and crafty, always uphill, always toward the company—and safety. Safety, safety. He did not care if anyone else was left alive or not. It would return often to haunt him later. It took him over half an hour to make the five minute climb. Nobody ever said a word to him about it, including Witt. Some things—unfortunately, usually only the most extreme—everybody understood.

In the morning they went down for the bodies. But before that had happened Witt had gone back to Cannon Company.

It was more than an hour before he could get back up the hill to C-for-Charlie's perimeter. It took a half hour for all the Japanese troops to pass. And after that, since Gooch was dead now anyway and there was no hurry, he waited almost another half hour to make sure they had left no rear point or booby trappers. But they hadn't. He was almost afraid to move enough to peep around and look. Finally, he sprinted across, stepping carefully among the bodies of the American dead. When he got back inside the company, he went straight to Band who was squatting by, and still questioning, Bell.

"I ought to kill you!" Witt said in a voice that was higher than he had meant it to be.

The longnosed, mean, and meanlooking, Italian Exec, who was standing near Band, pulled down with his carbine and covered him. Witt laughed at him.

"Dont worry!" He turned back to Band. "You're a lowlife, nogood, worthless, ignorant, stupid, legbreaking, shiteating bastard! You just got twelve men shot to hell and killed for nothin. Abso-lootly *nothin!* I hope yore happy! I love this compny better'n anything, but I wouldn't serve in no outfit commanded by a son of a bitch like you! If they ever kill you or get rid of you, I might come back."

He still had his rifle with him, and with this speech he slung it, turned his back on them to express his outrage, picked up the rest of his gear, and he left. He hiked the six hundred and fifty yards back through the night jungle, back to Baker Company, as he had earlier hiked it forward. At Baker, he paused just long enough to borrow some water and tell the story of the roadblock fiasco, and then went on. He did not get killed. Before daylight he was back with Cannon Company, which had been moved forward to The Shrimp's Head to carry more rations and water, and where when he reported his section sergeant said only "Christ! You? I thought you'd been knocked off," and rolled over and went back to sleep.

"I had every right and every reason in the world to shoot him down," the longnosed, mean, and meanlooking, Italian Exec said after he had left. "Like a dog!"

"No, you did right. I think he was a bit hysterical from what he went through," Band murmured. Band had not moved and was still squatting, by Bell. He was blinking slowly behind his steel-rimmed spectacles.

"I should have shot him," the Italian Exec said, bitterly. "He threatened his own Company Commander!"

"No, no. It's all right," Band murmured. He went on blinking slowly behind his glasses.

Over on the other side of the perimeter Sergeants Skinny Culn and Milly Beck looked at each other.

"Well?" Culn said.

Beck shrugged. "He's still the Company Commander."

Back with the officers Bell finished telling them his story for the second time. "I guess we better wait till morning," Band murmured. He was still blinking slowly behind his glasses.

It was a pretty sorry sight. Two had been shot in the back of the head with pistols as they lay in the sand. The dryriverbed seemed to be strewn with all of them. One other, like Gooch, had managed to creep up the bank without the Japanese seeing him, and had crawled off a few yards to die, alone, in the underbrush. They carried them all back up the hill and buried them with the two men from yesterday. It made quite a little cemetery. They did all this as soon as there was the faintest light to see by, and they hurried with it as much as they could. Band, who still blinked slowly behind his glasses from time to time when he addressed someone directly, was still pushing hard to make Boola Boola.

The Japanese had taken every weapon and every bit of ammunition they could find down in the draw. Luckily, one of the men to die directly behind Bell against the bank had been a BAR man, who accidentally had tossed his weapon ahead of him up into the undergrowth as he fell. That one was found. But it was with one BAR short—as well as being short twelve more Pfcs and privates—that they started off for Boola Boola just as the sun came up out of the sea, beautifully and gloriously, on the third morning of the attack. On the other hand, they now had the Ding Dong Trail all the way and would have no chopping work to do except possibly for those hills they would have to take along the way. B-for-Baker came up just as they were moving out, bringing new stretcher bearers. Then it was the jungle all over again for C-for-Charlie. Hours and hours. Heat.

They captured two undefended hills, leaving a squad on each to wait for Baker and Able, and emerged from the jungled foothills into the coconut groves at noon, just as 3d Battalion eight hundred yards away on the right was beginning its two company

attack against Boola Boola. Band immediately started them over
that way, moving them in a column of platoons.

He should have rested them. They looked like a ragged, taggle-
assed wrath of God, locusts and adders, descending upon a hap-
less countryside, and that was what they were. They were also
beat. That jungle somehow took more out of a man than any other
kind of physical endeavor. The coconut groves around them now
looked exactly like the ones they had been bivouacked in, back
over there on the other side, eons ago, and at the same time they
looked entirely different, because this was enemy country now,
not American. Band kept them moving. The sounds of 3d Battalion's fight on the right grew louder. But long before they got
there they were spotted and brought under fire. This time they had
mortars against them, the big ones. The haggardfaced men
hugged the ground and looked sweating across at each other with
white eyes. But Band kept them moving, in rushes and small
groups. A halfmad schoolteacherish gleam in his eye behind his
steel spectacles, he could think of nothing but being in on the
battle of Boola Boola. Actually, the mortar fire was nothing like
as bad, nowhere had the character of a real barrage, as on The
Dancing Elephant. The Japanese were fading fast. But it still hurt
men. Finally they made contact.

Band had told the Baker Company commander Captain Task
earlier in the morning that he was going to push hard, and now he
was more than half a mile in front of Baker which had not yet
emerged from the jungle. Captain Task, in turn, had told Band
that he had talked to Battalion who were worried about Charlie
Company because they had not heard from them. They had somehow already heard about the roadblock fiasco and were worried
also about his losses. Band had begun to blink slowly at Task, a
thing which Task perhaps noticed or perhaps did not notice, Band
couldn't tell, and had answered that his losses had been negligible, twenty-one men, to be exact, which was nothing for the job
they had accomplished. Now he pushed his people even harder,
remembering this peculiar, strange conversation. He knew that in
war, as in everything else, it was *results* which counted. And he
did love this company, desperately, passionately.

He had told his two squads he left behind on the two undefended hills to come on as quickly as they could, once they were
relieved by Baker or Able. Naturally they did not. They did not
arrive on the field until Baker Company itself did, which was too
late to get hurt.

But in spite of their absence, and the absence of the twelve
dead at the roadblock, the company succeeded.

The Japanese had two concentric lines of defense around Boola
Boola. These were about a hundred yards apart, and both were
clearly visible and well entrenched. Apparently they were determined to make some sort of stand here, and Band came in against
the left of the semicircle while 3d Battalion was attacking the
right. Actually, 3d Battalion had had to split its attack. Driving in
to split the Japanese clear to the beach, they had had to wheel two
of their companies right to attack an even larger Japanese force
cut off there, so that in fact only one company was attacking the
village, in what was really a holding attack instead of an allout
effort at conquest. Band of course knew nothing of this. While his
2d and 3d Platoons reenforced by the two machineguns probed at
the lines trying to find a hole, he withdrew his mortars far enough
back so that they could fire, telling one off to fire for the first line
and the other to hit at the second. In spite of the fact that they
were attacked on the ground by a wandering squad of Japanese
who had no business being there, they laid down good fire.

This went on until the mortar sections had used up every round
of their ammunition. But then suddenly they were in, running
hard but cautiously slow through the short grass between the long
lines of coconut trees, leaping emplacements like the ones they
had once looked at with awe and wonder, gasping and weeping
and once in a while dying. They did not know that this sudden
breakup was all due to the right having crumbled before Item
Company's attack. Nor did they care. Corporal Fife scampered
along with Jenks's squad shooting every Japanese he could see,
filled with both terror and elation to a point where he could not
separate one from the other. Then Jenks went down with a loud
squawk and a rifle bullet through the throat, and Fife had the
squad for himself, and the responsibility, and found he loved it,

and all of them. John Bell, his panic of last night gone, ran
leading his squad and yelling them on, but mainly watching
coolly to keep the casualties down. Don Doll ran grinning with
his rifle in one hand and his pistol in the other, and when the
pistol was empty he let it hang and bounce from its rope lanyard
and began using the rifle. They were in. They were in. When they
began to come into the village proper, they found the majority of
the Japanese killing themselves with grenades, guns or knives,
which was just as well because most of those who did not were
shot or bayoneted. In all, only eighteen prisoners were taken.

When it was all over, they began shaking hands with the guys
from Item Company, grinning at each other out of blackdirty
faces. A few men sat down and wept. Charlie Dale garnered many
gold teeth, and an excellent chronometer which he later sold for a
hundred dollars. Coming on a Japanese sitting dejectedly on a
doorstoop with his head in his hands, this beautiful watch sticking
out like a big diamond on his wrist, Dale shot him through the
head and took the watch. This was almost the only loot taken.
Quartermaster people arrived in what seemed like only seconds
later, and began claiming everything. Also, almost everyone was
too tired, too beat and exhausted, to care about loot. Later, of
course, they would all regret it.

They attacked up the beach all the next day. They were relieved
the day after. New, clean, smoothfaced, jollylooking troops from
a totally new division relieved them and were to push the attack
on toward Kokumbona up the coast. The Imperial Japanese Army
was reputed to be in full retreat. At least as important as this was
the fact that they did not have to walk home this time but were
picked up by trucks which drove them back along the coast road
sitting staring numbly at each other and at the peacefulooking
sun-dappled shade of the wheeling groves, with the bright sea and
the sound of the surf only a few yards away.

CHAPTER 8

Band was relieved three days later.

But before that happened the whole of C-for-Charlie had gotten blind, crazy drunk in a wild mass bacchanalian orgy which lasted twenty-eight hours and used up all the available whiskey, and Band—partly because of this great drunken rout—learned finally what his command that he loved so really thought of him. The honor for this development had to be given to, of all people, Private Mazzi the hep Bronxite of the Weapons Platoon.

The orgy itself was incredible. And it only stopped at all when it was discovered in drunken panic, like in some mad, fearridden, delirium tremens nightmaredream, that there was not a single Imperial quart, not a single *drop* of whiskey left anywhere in C-for-Charlie.

The scene was the coconut groves, where the new bivouac was this time. They were hardly down out of the trucks when the bottles, left behind here so long ago by different men and cataloged so carefully by Storm, were out and being utilized. MacTae and his clerk, in an excess of guilty love and aided by Storm and his disgruntled cooks who had returned from The Sea Slug when their stores ran out, had pitched all of the company's pyramidal tents at the new site, and had even set up the cots in them complete with their blankets and mosquitobars. The kitchen fly was up and the stoves were lighted. All the weary warriors had to do was clamber down and start drinking seriously, as soon as they could draw their marked bottles from Storm's locked chests.

All of them were a little bit mad. The combat numbness, with its stary eyes and drawn faces, had not yet left them and would not, this time, for a much longer period than last time. This led John Bell to theorize privately that, given a sufficient number of times up on the line after each of which it took longer to lose it and recover, combat numbness might possibly perhaps become a permanent state. Meanwhile, at the orgy, almost everybody vomited one or more times. Several men got down on their hands and knees, in the moonlight shining tranquilly down into the beautiful if deadly coconut groves, and bayed the moon like wolves or hounds. Another group of ten or twelve divested themselves of all clothing and, bareass nude, ran tripping and dancing like Martha Graham students across the open field beside the bivouac to swim in the Matanikau in the moonlight. There were at least nine fist fights. And Don Doll tried to seduce Carrie Arbre.

But the climax, the high point of all of it, was when Mazzi decided to beard Tall George Band in his den and tell him what he thought of him. What his outfit thought of him.

He was egged on to do it by Carni, Suss, Gluk, Tassi, and the rest of his Greater New York buddies. They were all sitting drinking in the tent of Carni, where Carni lay in bed drinking too but knocked nearly out with an especially bad malaria attack which had hit him on the way home in the trucks. Home? They were talking, naturally, about the campaign. Band had pushed them far too hard. Band had taken dangerous chances. Band had not needed to take them into Boola Boola at all where they were not even needed and which was not even their assignment. And, of course, The Glory Hunter should never have tried to set up that disastrous roadblock. Everybody was busy knocking Band, when Mazzi growled at them they ought to tell Band himself and what was the good of sitting around here yacking about it. Carni, droopyeyed and slackfaced from the fever, and who was the leader of the little Greater New York group of hep guys if it could be said to have a leader at all, looked over at him and asked in a voice hollow with fever and cynicism why the hell didn't he do it himself then? Yeah, somebody else said, why didn't he? Yeah, Suss added, why not? all he had to lose was that Pfc he might hope to get on the next promotions list because, Suss grinned, while it was certainly safer in the Weapons Platoon, the chances for rapid advancement there were correspondingly much more limited.

Mazzi got up drunkenly. "All right, by God I will!" he announced.

He marched out of the tent and staggered off through the cocopalms toward Band's Hq tent, only falling down once. The others followed him at a distance sniggering happily, content to let him take the dangerous chance alone. All, that is, except Carni who could not get out of his bed.

Mazzi might not have done it if he had not been drunk, or if what happened to him at Boola Boola had not happened. But there raged in him such a despair, hatred, and unredeemable misery that, uninhibited by the alcohol, he no longer cared one way or the other what he did except that the worse it was the better. It had had to be that fucking goddamned Tills! So far Tills had not told anybody, but that did not mean that he wouldn't. Mazzi was convinced that he would. After all, when somebody hated you as much as Tills hated him, how could they help telling? Especially when you had been showing them up for what they were all their lives? Whenever he thought about it it made his asshole twitch and his stomach burn.

During the Boola Boola attack, when the mortar sections had been counterattacked by that wandering squad of Japanese, they had been caught off guard. There weren't supposed to be any Japanese around there. Finally they had been compelled to run. Their mission was not to engage in a longrange firefight with a squad of Japanese strays; it was to lay mortar into Boola Boola. The Japanese, firing down the lanes of cocopalms, showed no inclination to come on in and close with them, and appeared content to stay back off in safety and try to pick them off. Behind them on their right not far away was a small tongue of jungle undergrowth. With two men slightly wounded, on hectic orders from Lt Fullback Culp in the smoke, noise and confusion (the

Japanese mortars were still laying in searching rounds here and there trying to find them) they dismantled and ran for this refuge in a long uneven sweating line. They were to meet, reassemble and set up again on the other side of it. And this was when, Mazzi thought for the tenthousandth miserable time, that it had happened.

Buttplate in one hand and carbine in the other, running somewhere near the right end of this line, Frankie Mazzi swung around backward to crash through the facewhipping screen of leaves. Once through, he swung to turn face front again, and suddenly felt himself speared, caught, and then held. He knew what it was, but he couldn't think clearly enough to do anything about it. Some *thing* had grabbed hold of his ammo belt near his right hipbone. Unable to believe it, plunging and cursing and listening to rifle bullets snickerwhack through the brush around him, he remained tethered, still holding buttplate in one hand and carbine in the other. If he had dropped one, he might have been able to get himself loose and then pick it back up, but he could not think of this except far off dimly. Eyes wide and glaring, his mouth a cavern of teeth, he pushed and jerked eternally in a timeless world whose only measurable moments of sane, live time, coming like erratic red flashes of some mad beacon at sea at night, were the unevenly spaced clicksnaps of bullets through the undergrowth. And there he remained, buttplate and carbine still senselessly in hand. And he knew he would still be there when they came for him, shot him, cooked him, and ate him.

Two men from the section had pushed past him running hurriedly and obliviously, and he had begun to call in a feeble, moronic, plaintive voice the same word over and over. "Help!" Even to his own ears it sounded ridiculously hopeless. "Help!" he keened feebly. "Help! Help!"

It was Tills who came back for him. Eyes glaring wildly also, running hurriedly in a crouch, he had run up, surveyed the scene, and freed him. Mazzi had been pushing and plunging forward all this time. Tills merely shoved him backward two feet and the snag came free. Then they were both running in a crouch, the bullets still slitherclacking around them in the brush. Once Tills glanced over at him, made a liplifting mock of a grin, spat brown from the quid in his jaw, and ran on. By the time they could see sunlight on the other side the bullets had stopped. When they came out into the bright, eyebeating light, they could see the others about thirty yards away already setting up, resetting the bubble levels. They pushed on toward them going slower now, Tills with his carbine slung still carrying the mortar tube in both arms like a baby, Mazzi still with buttplate in one hand and carbine in the other. Someone waved at them to hurry.

"Just don't think it makes me like you any better," Mazzi said sullenly.

"Done thank ut makes *me* lack *yew* any butter," Tills snarled. Mazzi was certain he would tell.

And now, as he stood drunkenly before the Hq tent of Glory Hunter Band, he was still just as certain. Everybody would know and laugh about his ignominy. It made his belly grind with cramps.

"Come out, you son of a bitch!" he shouted wildly for his preamble. From the blacked out tent just the faintest hint of light crept out to the waiting men outside. Inside the tent nothing seemed to move.

"I said *come out,* you cowardly shiteater! Come out and find out what the men in your outfit think of you, Band! You want to know what we think of you? They call you Glory Hunter Band! Come on out and volunteer us for somethin else! C'mon out and ged some more of us killed! You gonna make Captain for takin us into Boola Boola, Glory Hunter? How many medals you gonna ged for that roadblock, Glory Hunter?"

Other men had begun to gather around too now, their grinning teeth white in the bright moonlight. Aware of them, Mazzi raged on, marching back and forth and swinging his skinny arms, compounding insult and profanity with great artistry into an ever higher rising house of cards of his imagination. Twice there were quietly muffled cheers from the grinning men in the bright moonlight. However, nobody else came forward. But there were the gurgles of whiskey bottles.

"You're a *prick,* Band! A schmuck! C'mon out and I'll take

you myself! Everybody in this outfit hates your guts! Did you know that? How does it feel, Band, how does it feel?''

Finally the light in the tent went out. Then the flap was thrown back and Band stood in the doorway leaning on his hand on the canvas. He swayed ever so slightly, was about as drunk as they were, and a bottle dangled from his other hand. On the back of his head was the mutilated helmet with the big hole in it he had saved ever since the last day on The Dancing Elephant and personally had shown to almost every man in the outfit. The bright moonlight struck him square in the face, glinting on the steel rims of his spectacles, from behind which his lensenlarged eyes stared out at them blinking that queer slow blink of his. He said nothing. Behind him was visible the dark, mean, and meanlooking, picklenosed Italian Exec, once again holding his carbine.

"You think that fucking helmet makes any goddam difference?'' Mazzi screamed. "You think anybody cares about that fucking goddam helmet?''

Band continued to say nothing. He looked at Mazzi—and out at the rest of them—squarely, looking them levelly in the eyes, but still blinking that strange slow blink he had acquired, which was not unlike that of some kind of somnambulist.

Slowly the men began to drift away awkwardly. The fun was gone. "Let's git back to some ser-yous drinkin,'' somebody muttered. Soon there was nobody left except the loyal little group of Greater New Yorkers, as Mazzi raved on.

"You think that fucking hero helmet means anything alongside all the good dead men that are really *dead?*'' Mazzi screamed.

"Come on, Frankie!'' Suss whispered.

Mazzi jerked his arm loose. "And that's what we think of you!'' he summed up, yelling. "And so courtmartial me!'' And he stalked off proudly.

They congratulated him, his tight little Greater New York clan, all the way back to the tents, crowding around him to slap his back and shake his hand, forming a sort of comet of helmets with a diminishing tail and him as the hard core head. Mazzi kept chuckling happily. "I sure got him told,'' he said to each one who came up. "I sure got him told.'' Other men kept drifting up

out of the moonlit night shadows, bottles in hand, to add their
drunken applause. Now that Band's silent slowblinking face was
no longer before them, the fun had come back. "And he never
said one word back," Mazzi chuckled. Then suddenly he saw
Tills's mocking, liplifting face square in front of him and was
startled into a new hollow apathy.

"I sure got him told," he chuckled hollowly to still another
well-wisher.

"You sure did!" said his new satellite Gluk.

Tills spat brown out of the side of his grin. He had changed
some too, since the first weeks. "You never got nobody tole
nothin," he snarled grinning. "Nothin a tall. And I know."
Mazzi felt completely hollow.

He needn't have. Tills told the story. During the course of the
long orgiastic night and the drunken day that followed until the
whiskey ran out, Tills buttonholed just about every man in
the company and told him the story of Mazzi snagged, panicked,
and helpless. Everybody laughed, but they laughed without malice and there was no ridicule. Mazzi was a hero. As this dawned
on him slowly over the next couple of days, Mazzi was able to
forget his hollow despair and become condescending again, even
to Tills.

There were other repercussions of the nightanddaylong baccha-
nal. The worst one was a general one affecting everybody, which
was not so much that they ran out of whiskey and had to stop, as
it was the realization, as they slowly sobered up, that there was no
more whiskey to be had because they had not brought any loot
back from Boola Boola. This time they had not staggered in
loaded down with Japanese weapons, gear and memorabilia. How
to get whiskey then? It took on the appearance of catastrophe. Of
course, there were a few in C-for-Charlie who didn't drink. A
couple of these were uneducated Baptist ministers from the
South. Two others were metalminded C.P.A.'s who had somehow
gotten mistakenly entangled with the Infantry. And there were
some others. But all of them knew enough to keep their mouths
shut and not chortle when the horror became apparent, because
none of them really wanted to get beaten up.

But there were other, personal reverberations of the twenty-eight hours' orgy, too. For instance, Corporal Fife. Corporal Fife was now Sergeant Fife, squad leader of 2d Squad 3d Platoon. Jenks was dead, shot square through the larynx, dying as taciturn and uncommunicative as he had lived—though perhaps this was due to the nature of his wound—and Fife had been promoted his successor on the field by The Glory Hunter. More important, Fife was now sure he had become a real soldier. He did not yet know that as the combat numbness (with which he had not been around long enough before to have any experience) receded, he would come to revise this opinion. One of the nine fist fights that took place that night was Fife's.

Fife had started the night sitting around gulping down whiskey with Don Doll and some of the men from both of their squads. And he didn't want to be with anyone else. He felt a fiercely paternal, protective love for each man in his squad, now that it was his squad. And his squad reciprocated with the same son-to-father love for him, now that their Jenks was gone. It was a truism, Fife thought profoundly, that everybody in a war had to have some father-son love relationship of mutual adoration, or the war just couldn't go on. He was feeling pretty cocky, as the whiskey quiet grew inside his numbed and splintered nerves. But he had saved at least two of them once apiece, and at least three of them had saved him. He had killed eight Jap bastards on the crazy rush into Boola Boola, four of them unarmed and setting. And he had been knocked down twice by mortar. He had found out that he was really much braver than he'd thought, and this gave him real joy. It wasn't so hard to be a real soldier at all. It was really very easy. All you had to do was do it, whatever it was. He treated Doll as an equal now and Doll could lump it. But Doll now also treated him as an equal. He did not hold it against Doll any more that he had not made him Corporal of his squad that time.

But there was one thing that still rankled him, and that was the way that fucking son of a backbiting bitch Joe Weld had treated him in the orderly tent that day that he and Storm came back from the hospital. This he had not forgotten, or forgiven. Stealing his job like a sneak thief. And then acting so goddam fucking holier-thanthou. Rage fumed in him with the whiskey.

They had picked themselves a nice spot not far from their own tent, right on the edge of the groves where it opened up into the open field that led to the river. It was one of the few nice grassy spots that wasn't hummocky, and sitting under the tall rustling cocopalm in the moonlight they could look across the field to the river and the trees beyond. They drank and talked about one bit of action or another that had happened during their three days' battle for the village. All of them had nearly passed out at least once during the long, hard, hot marches, and their sorenesses were only just now beginning to appear.

Not far away up the line was the tent where the Company Hq personnel slept, and there was a group sitting out there, too. Fife suddenly got up, in midsentence of somebody or other who was talking, and walked up that way without saying a word to anybody. Joe Weld and Eddie Train the stutterer whose lap Fife had once landed in in terror and the new kid Crown were sitting out drinking with two of the cooks. They were talking about the hardest march, which they believed to be the one from The Shrimp's Head on to Hill 279. The clerks were telling the cooks! Fife sauntered up to them mouth pursed, tongue rubbing slowly over his teeth, his arms dangling. He went up to within three feet of Weld and stopped, stood there saying nothing. It was almost a minute before anybody seemed to notice him and his silence.

"Oh—uh, hello there, Fife," Weld said in the condescending voice he had used ever since that day. Before that he had been the meekest lamb. "We were just—"

"*Sergeant* Fife to you, *Corporal*," Fife said. "And dont ever call me anything else!"

Weld looked startled, behind his glasses. Then his look of start turned into a placating smile. "Well, I guess you really earned the title, Sergeant," he said unctuously. "The hard way. And I for one sure dont—"

"Dont asskiss me, you cheap fuck," Fife said.

"Now. Now, see here," Weld said, scrambling to his feet. "I never done—"

He did not get to finish because Fife stepped in and knocked him down without a word—without a sound, in fact, except for the smack of his fist on the cheekbone.

"Hey!" Weld said from the ground. "Hey! I was just sitting here drinking and talking and minding my own—"

"Get up, cheap fuck! Get up, job stealer! Get up, officer ass!" Fife cried. "Get up, and I'll knock you down again." First nearby, then further off in the background he heard uncaringly the happy cries of "Fight! Fight! Hey, fight!" and the sound of men's feet running.

"Sure," Weld said bitterly, crouching on one knee. "Sure. And it's easy for you. I'm twenty years older'n you. I'm old enough to be—"

"You're not! It's fifteen years!" Fife cried insanely. "I read it in your Service Record! You're a man in the prime of life!"

"Who's half your size," Weld said. He had taken off his glasses cautiously and was holding them carefully out to one side while watching Fife. "You could of broke my glasses," he said accusingly. "And I couldnt get new ones. H-here," he said to Train. "Take my glasses. Watch my glasses, will ya?"

"I-I'm w-watchin m-my own d-damn g-glasses," Train said. He had already taken his own off and put them carefully away in their case at the first signs of violence, and was now peering around him like some anxious owl. But he took Weld's.

"I dont want to fight you," Weld said. "I didn't steal your job. It was Lt Band and The Welshman who made me Corporal. Nobody knew you was comin back. I dont want to fight you, Fife," he repeated slyly. "I just want—" He didn't finish. Instead, he made a wild lunging leap for Fife's middle, to grapple.

It didn't succeed. Joyously, because he was sure this unsporting treacherous act of Weld's proved his whole thesis about Weld's having dirtied his honor, Fife stepped in again and lefthooked him. This time it was more accurate, and on the jaw. It sent Weld rolling away wildly to the ground, where he propped himself on his elbows shaking his head. When he rolled over to sit up, Fife dived on him.

It was as though a sudden scrambled lightning bolt of happy

maleness and joyous masculinity had split Fife's skull, blinding
him with glory. On top of the groggy Weld on the ground, he
cuffed and pummeled. Growling and cursing high in his throat
and crying "Job stealer!" over and over, he punched with both
fists and total abandon at the face below him. Beneath him Weld
gasped and whimpered and rolled around trying to get loose.
Finally they pulled him off of him.

"Lemme go! Lemme go!" Fife yelled breathlessly.

Somebody helped Weld up. His nose was broken and bleeding.
Both eyes were puffed almost shut. Blood ran from his mouth
between his broken lips but it was impossible to tell whether he
had lost any teeth; however, later it was found that he had not. He
was still groggy and he looked bewildered.

Fife, standing unheld now and in command of himself again,
though breathing hard, stared at him feeling both happiness and
consternation at the destruction he had caused. He was proud of
himself, but he hadn't really meant to hurt anyone.

"And I'll show you the same thing next time," he said senselessly, rubbing his fist.

Train and Crown took the swaying Weld by the arms to lead
him away.

"Hey!" Fife called. "Hey! Dont do that! Don't go! Come on
and let's have a drink. No hard feelings!"

From ten yards away Weld stopped and looked back at him. He
was weeping and at the same time trying not to. "You—You—"
he choked. He seemed to be searching his fuddled head for the
very worst thing he could think of to call Fife. "You *clerk,* you!"
he cried. He turned away, and the three of them went on.

Fife stared after him, stricken, momentarily deeply touched by
the strange appellation Weld had chosen to call him after searching so hard: clerk: the very thing he himself was. But he was also
still proud of himself. "Okay," he said, and shrugged elaborately. "So be a jerk." He turned to the two cooks who had
already backed off away from the whole thing. "Either one of
you guys want some of it?" he grinned. Both of them, though
they were both bigger than Fife, shook their heads in silence.

He walked back down with Doll, his old combat buddy who

had, however, only come up for the last few moments of the fight.
Around them the men were beginning to disperse now that it was
over. But only moments later there were more cries of "Fight!
Hey, fight!" from some other direction, and they all began to run
that way. Fife and Doll did not go with them, Fife because he had
already been a principal and was sated for the moment, Doll
because of whatever private reasons of his own. They walked on
back toward their grassy spot through the moonlit groves, Fife
rubbing his bruised hands, Doll congratulating him. Fife, who
was preoccupied with himself at the moment, did not notice the
strange pained look on Doll's face, or the odd strained way he
spoke. If he had, he would never have guessed the reason. Doll
had only just learned—only a few minutes before—that at least
one man in C-for-Charlie believed he Don Doll was an active,
practicing homosexual. A real fairy.

The man was Carrie Arbre.

When Fife had gotten up and so abruptly walked away, several
of the little group had noticed it and somebody had said that Fife
looked like he was looking for action. When the cries of "Fight!
Fight!" began to come from up by the Hq tent, one of Fife's new
squad had chortled "I bet that's Fife!" and they all jumped up
and started up there. Doll however had stayed behind. So had
Carrie Arbre, and Doll had suddenly felt his heart pounding excitedly. Just the two of them.

"Aint you goin up to watch the fight, Carrie?" he said.

"I never cared much for watchin fist fights," Arbre said in his
soft drawl. "But aint you goin?"

"I'm too tired. And too comfterble," Doll said, trying to keep
the blood pounding in his throat from making him sound choked.
He settled himself more against the tree. Arbre was lying
stretched out on his elbow only two feet away on his right. Doll
was very aware of his nearness.

A strange thing had happened to Doll during the fighting for
Boola Boola. He had discovered, to his intense surprise, that he
wanted to make love—make physical love—to Carrie Arbre. It
had been early in the attack, when they were still probing to find a
way in through the two defense lines in the coconut groves, and at

the time when they were still taking a lot of heavy mortar. Doll
had crawled back from his squad to where Band, Beck and Lt
Tomms were conferring, to find out what was going on. He had
started to crawl back up to the squad, and was almost there, when
the searching of the mortars passed their way again. He lay,
sweating, and pressed himself as close to the ground as he could
get. It was unbelievable, the intensity of concentration with which
his ears listened in all the racket for that faint, twoseconds'long,
fluttering *shu-shu-shu* which marked the near ones. Twice he was
bounced around by close ones. Eyes open, he lay gritting his teeth
and trying to make his mind blank. Ten yards in front of him
behind the crest of a tiny rise which ran across through the flat-
ness of the groves he could see Arbre doing the same thing, and
with some of that same intensity of concentration with which his
ears listened for the mortars his eyes concentrated themselves
upon that beautiful ass. That beautiful girl's ass. Sweating blood,
or feeling as if he were, he lay and stared at it until it became his
own, his possession. And he knew from some heretofore un-
reached depth within himself that he wanted to make love to it—
physical, gentle, fondling, sexual love. Finally the still searching
mortars passed on, but what had happened to Doll did not pass on
with them.

And after all, why couldn't he? He knew lots of oldtimer regulars who had their punks, their "boys", back in peacetime. He
could do a lot for Arbre. Protect him from the worst missions.
Get him made Corporal of the squad finally. Get him a squad
sergeantcy even, if he ever got the platoon himself. And what
about the Navy? They didn't call candy "pogeybait" for nothing.
If he wanted to pogey Arbre and look after and adopt him, that
didn't make *him* homosexual. It only made Arbre homosexual, if
he accepted it—as Doll was certain Arbre would accept it. Why
else had Arbre talked to him so strangely that time going up The
Shrimp's Head? Arbre was offering to make a deal. Crawling on
back up to the squad after the mortar passed, Doll remembered
again deliciously that time when he had accidentally fallen on
Arbre's back, back there on The Sea Slug ridge.

And he remembered it again now, sprawled back against the

coconut tree in the gossamer moonlight, with Arbre only two feet away from him.

It wouldn't make him queer, it would only make Arbre queer. Which was all right with Doll, he didn't mind that, he was liberal. What Doll wanted was a relationship. There were lots of queer Cooks and Bakers and such, coke sackers, sock tuckers, and cork soakers, all around on the island, and everybody knew about them. But you had to stand in line. It was like standing in line out on the street for those upstairs whorehouses in Honolulu when the Division had passed through. And Doll didn't want that. He wanted a girl of his own.

Cautiously, after taking a big bolstering drink, his right hand set the bottle down and came to rest by accident on Arbre's ankle. Trying to control his heavy breathing, he waited. Arbre didn't move, or say anything.

"Sure is one hell of a beautiful night out," Doll said, a little hoarsely.

"Sure is," Arbre said in his sweet, girl's voice. Doll suddenly loved him. He really did need somebody to look after him and take care of him, the poor kid.

Suddenly, by its own volition and without him knowing it, Doll realized his hand had worked its way up Arbre's pantsleg along his hairless shin to his hairless knee. He let it stay there.

"Be a great night for lovemakin," he said chokingly. "Back home."

"Sure would," Arbre said sweetly. Then suddenly he moved. His hands came down from behind his head to his crotch and began unbuttoning his fly. "Come on," he said.

Doll was aghast. Arbre had misinterpreted everything. He was reasonably sure Arbre could not see his face, but he himself could feel it from inside and knew it had frozen itself into a sickly look. It was a couple of seconds before he could force it into a stiff smile. He snatched his hand back as if it had been burned by something.

Arbre was going ahead with what he was doing. "Come on," he said softly. "Come on. I won't tell."

Doll forced himself to laugh, loudly, and got up.

"Ah, come on," Arbre said. "Look at it. I know what you want. I promise I'll never tell a soul."

"Listen. Dont forget I'm still in charge of this squad," Doll growled in a low, truly murderous tone. "Watch your step." Then, in a much more normal tone, too normal under the circumstances, he felt, he said, "I think I'll go and see how that fight up there's makin out."

Arbre didn't answer him. Maybe he was just catching on to what Doll had really intended. "Why, you son of a bitch!" Arbre said, after a moment. Doll heard it but he was already gone. Let the bastard sit on it, he thought furiously. His whole head was suffused in such a rosy red blush that it must look black in the moonlight, he thought. And so *that* was what Arbre meant by his ambiguous remarks up on The Shrimp's Head! He thought that Doll wanted to—And that Doll would make him Corporal and take—God! Doll thought painfully, how could anybody think that about—

And walking back down with Fife after the fight he blushed deeply again, thinking about it. No wonder his voice sounded strained. When they arrived back at the grassy spot, Arbre was still there. "Hello, Carrie," he said in a flat, cold voice. "Hi, Doll," Arbre answered in the same tone. "You should of seen the fight," Doll said airily. And then they all sat down to do some more serious drinking, Doll perhaps doing the most serious drinking of them all.

But if Doll was doing the most serious drinking at that particular moment, there were others who did as much or more during the rest of the night and the drunken day that followed. And when the whiskey ran out at four the next afternoon, there was real consternation everywhere. There was not a single piece of loot from Boola Boola to trade to the Air Corps for more.

When Band was relieved a day and a half later, the liquor problem still had not been solved and it concerned the company much more than Band's removal. A number of solutions had been put forward, most of them in desperation: silent theft in the night; armed robbery of the Air Corps at open gunpoint; the trading off of Governmentowned company equipment such as weapons and stoves and blankets; a companyrun cartel which would supply the raw materials to and collect the finished product from certain Kentucky and Tennessee personnel of the outfit who knew how to make moonshine from back home. None of these were really feasible. Night theft simply would not supply enough; armed robbery and the trading of company equipment would certainly eventually get everybody caught. And moonshine was out because not only were the raw grains impossible to come by, the steel "worms" so necessary to Kentucky or Tennessee distillation of spirits could not be located and stolen anywhere on the island. When the longnosed, mean, and meanlooking Italian Exec and new temporary Company Commander Johnny Creo made a speech about how he was going to tighten this outfit up and the things that had been going on in it were going to cease, nobody paid the slightest attention. They had a more serious problem and anyway, everyone knew that nobody as green and inexperienced as Johnny Creo was going to stay in command of their company very long.

Nobody really knew, or cared, what The Glory Hunter's sentence was, or how it was arrived at and brought about. Actually, it was the Regimental Commander himself, The Great White Father, who gave Band the Word, not Col Spine the Battalion Commander as had been the case with Jim Stein and Tall. Band could not help feeling that that was at least a step up.

He marched into the whitehaired old drunkard's presence in good order, at a solid one twenty per with his glasses and their steel rims gleaming. He wore a clean uniform and his shoes and bars were shined. Band did not know how he knew, but he did. There was always gossip, and you could always read things in the faces of your equals around the mess or the club. He was convinced in his own mind that everything he had done was right and proper and valid, that he had in fact—rather than making any mistakes—contributed strongly to the success of the whole operation after The Giant Shrimp's Head. What his men might think was one thing, they didn't have the overall view. This was different.

The old Colonel hummed and hawed. Rumor also had it that he

was making Brigadier soon, on the strength of this campaign. The handsome, distinguishedlooking Col Spine was there. So was full Colonel Grubbe the Regimental Exec, a New Englander from Newport who bore a startling resemblance to the longpicklenosed, mean, and meanlooking Johnny Creo, C-for-Charlie's Exec. So were the other Battalion Commanders there. But it was Old Whitehair who did the talking.

The upshot of what he had to say was that Band had committed two serious faults, the two of them together serious enough to have set the campaign for Guadalcanal back by a whole week, maybe more. One was his continued radio silence, his what Old Whitehair could only deem deliberate and persistent refusal to contact his Headquarters. This was inexcusable. The second was a fault of grand tactics, for which he could hardly be held responsible; but he should have turned left coming out of the jungle. He should have ignored Boola Boola, which was Item Company's job, and swung left up the coast in an effort to roll up the Jap line which at that particular moment was up in the air and totally confused. Had he done so, Baker and Able would have followed him, and the other companies pressing over the Hill 279 trail would have followed them, to form a line in real strength. Had that happened, they might now have Kokumbona and Tassafaronga in their hands, together with the entire Japanese Army on Guadalcanal. Had Band maintained his proper radio contact he would have been informed of this. Both Battalion and Regiment had tried and tried to call him all that morning for this very reason.

Band took it like a man. He recognized that almost everything the whitehaired old drunkard said was absolutely true, drunkard or not. But there were bigger minds than his behind this tactical strategy. He did not point out that, since they *were* in contact with Baker Company by walkietalkie, they might have ordered Baker to swing left, leaving him—however erroneously—in Boola Boola. He contented himself with saying only that he had been told he was functioning as an independent command. *Independent command!*

"Ah!" the old Colonel smiled through stained teeth, pouncing like a falcon. "Yes! *Yes! 'When communication was impossible',* I think my phrase was. In your case communication was not only possible, it was easy. No excuse. There's no excuse."

The verdict was that he should be taken hence, delivered to another company in another regiment, and remain there till dead. He would *not* go as a Company Commander. Would he remain an Executive Officer? or would he be demoted to a platoon? No, he would remain as Company Exec. But he must not, the old man said, uhh, expect any promotion through attrition—or for any other reason. There would be an eye on him there certainly, watching him. There would be no official disgrace. But war was teamwork, Old Whitehair said, softly pounding his fist in his other palm. Teamwork, teamwork, *teamwork.* Any Army was a team. A regiment was a team. A company, platoon, squad—all were *teams.* No one single man had a right to do anything. Not in war. Team, team, *team!* Too many lives depended upon every point. He need not go back to his outfit. His things were already being packed for him by his former orderly on orders from Lt Creo the new temporary Commander. And so George Band, too, passed from the life of C-for-Charlie, and was never seen or heard of again. As he saluted, withdrew, and walked across the mud of the Regimental area erect and undestroyed, he was absolutely certain that he had done nothing wrong, not one single, solitary thing, since taking command of the company and his conscience did not bother him. It was ironic he felt that *had* he done as Old Whitehair wanted and turned left, the casualties among his troops who so misunderstood and disliked him would have been 50% higher.

Meanwhile back at the bivouac C-for-Charlie was still trying desperately to solve its liquor shortage. Liquor, as almost all of C-for-Charlie saw it, was their only hope. Slowly as each day passed the hectic situation of the Regiment which pertained when they were relieved was becoming more organized, more clarified, more controlled. Work detail rosters were already beginning to come in, curtailing the free time available to search for a large and easily accessible source of alcohol. Soon training schedules, drill periods, and physical fitness schedules would be coming in also, curtailing it even further. It was becoming a vicious circle. And nobody could come up with a source of alcohol. The infrequent shipments of Aqua Velva at the PX simply would not provide enough. Nobody had enough cash money left now to buy more than one or two Imperial quarts at the most. Only Mad Welsh, grinning sardonically, was able to carry on, continue tapping his private, secret source for gin. And not only did they have all of this to plague them, they now found that the combat numbness was beginning to leave them, and as it did they became afraid of the air raids again.

John Bell calculated that this time it took the average man more than six full days to lose the combat numbness—as against the two days required after The Dancing Elephant. In reality this campaign, though longer, was not nearly as tough in either fire power or casualties as The Dancing Elephant. Bell could only conclude that the thing was cumulative. Cumulative or not, as it left them the air raids began to scare them again. Actually, the air raids were not nearly as dangerous now; and they themselves were in a much better position now than they had ever had. North of the Matanikau here, they were more than two miles from the air field.

It didn't make any difference. And anyway, the Japanese were executing more nuisance personnel raids now than they were attacks against the air strip, and were liable to drop their loads anywhere along the island.

Not one single man in C-for-Charlie had believed he would ever again be afraid of these puny air raids once he got back off the line, but when a man in a nearby company had his jaw taken off as he lay on his bunk by an unexploded dud antiaircraft shell, a number of men in C-for-Charlie rather shamefacedly began to dig themselves slit trenches outside their tents. To be killed in one of these silly, asinine air raids after all the combat they had lived through? It was an ironic flick of God which no one could face. Soon they would be back in the dull, mudhaunted, airraidfear-ridden routine of life they had lived before—B.C., as some wit said: Before Combat. A source of liquor simply had to be found.

Then one morning at Reveille Pfc Nellie Coombs the sharpy
card dealer fell down twice, dead drunk.

When the same thing happened two more days in a row, a
group of vigilantes was formed among the noncoms to shadow
him to his source. This proved to be an old cracker tin covered
with a cheesecloth, sitting in a sunny place in the tongue of jungle
near the bivouac and surrounded by buzzing millions of insects.
Nellie, like many of the other oldtimer regulars, had served in
both the Philippines and Hawaii before the war, when a private's
pay could afford only the homemade bootleg mess made by the
natives out of fruit and called 'swipe'. He had utilized this knowledge to steal some gallon cans of cherries and peaches and put it
up with yeast, sugar and water to ferment in the sun. The scout
shadowing him, who happened to be Sgt Beck, came back drunk
to report that the stuff tasted awful but it certainly was potent.
Wow! Why Nellie Coombs had decided to keep his treasure find
completely to himself nobody knew. It was just his secretive way.
But immediately raids were organized to steal tins of crackers and
cans of fruit from the ration dumps, which were simply loaded
with them. Finally a true source had been found! A source that
would never run out. Balance had been achieved, and at last they
could sit out again at night drinking, and laugh drunkenly at the
air raids.

1st Lt Johnny Creo, of course, had no idea what had happened
to his outfit, or where they were getting it. Nor did anyone tell
him: the conspiracy was complete.

The word spread like wildfire. Companies all around C-for-
Charlie began putting up their own crackertin mash, and passed
the technique on to those around them. After all, there was no
point in keeping it a secret since there was enough for all. One
thing the American Army was *never* going to run out of was
canned fruit. As often happened with humanity when in need of a
great innovation or invention, it was found that several experi-
menters working at widely separated points had made the same
discovery at almost exactly the same moment. From these centers
the great news spread like wavelets on a pond until they overlapped and everybody knew. When two men somewhere became

blind and partially paralyzed from some sort of lead poisoning caused by the crackertins, everybody switched to five and ten gallon wooden picklekegs and the courageous, experimental work went right on. It was found that if the picklekegs were left unscrubbed, the sour flavor left in the wood helped to cut the horrible sickly sweet taste of the fruit.

It was at just about this time—when C-for-Charlie was trying out its first series of picklekeg mashes—that Acting-P.F.C. Witt of Cannon Company showed up again. He was coming back around to ask for transfer back into his old outfit. He had just learned that Brass Band no longer commanded it. He got drunk with the boys that night on the new picklekeg swipe.

Naturally Johnny Creo wanted nothing to do with him. And Witt never did learn that it was Fullback Culp who saved the day for him and made his transfer possible. When Culp heard that Creo was not going to put through the request for transfer, he accosted the new Commander in his orderly tent and sent the clerks out, Weld with his broken nose still all taped up.

"Lissen, Johnny," he said earnestly. "I been with this compny longer than you have, and I know them better than you do. If you ever have to lead this outfit in combat, you'll wish to hell you had Witt with you!"

Creo compressed his thin lips beneath his longpicklenose. "I stood by and heard him *threaten* his own Company Commander!"

"Balls to that!" Culp snarled. "Sure. And I for one dont blame him. You dont understand these guys. Remember I been through more combat with them than you have, too. I was around there on The Elephant's Head when Witt went in with that assault force. I tell you you're makin a serious mistake if you dont take him back. You're denyin yourself one of the best potential platoon leaders you'll ever get a chance at."

"I dont want that kind of man in my outfit," Creo said thinly.

The Fullback hooted. "Next thing you'll be tellin me you're a liberal and you dont want him in your outfit because he hates Negroes! This is war, man! War! I know you outrank me and can put me down for what I'm sayin. But I dont care. You got to

listen.'' And listen he made him. He continued to argue with all
the same force and outrageous vitality that he had once used on
Jim Stein to argue the raid on the Marines for those Thompsonguns, and in the end he beat him down by sheer energy. Finally Creo agreed. It was almost the last act of any consequence
Culp was to perform in C-for-Charlie. Two days later he blew
most of his right hand off fishing.

It was not the first expedition to the Matanikau for fish to
augment the eternal diet of Spam, dehydrated mashed potatoes,
and canned fruit. Three times during the two weeks they had been
back off the line they had done it, and each time Storm had
created them such a massive fishfry that it made the more
fragileminded weep for home. This time they took only three
grenades with them because two were usually enough. It was
strictly prohibited of course, which was why they always went just
after dawn. Certain highranking officers had thoughtfully brought
their fly and baitcasting rods with them to Guadalcanal. Culp and
his boys were not after sport but the greatest volume of fish in the
shortest possible time, and for this grenades were perfect. Somebody—Skinny Culn, it was—threw the first one. Three swimmers
were already waiting nude on the bank, to make the collection
before the current could carry them off. A minute after the under-
water explosion maybe fifty fish were floating bellyupward on the
slowly moving stream.

"Two ought to do it! I'll throw the next one!" The Fullback
cried excitedly. "Further upstream!" He walked a few yards that
way. Then he pulled pin and threw. Everybody was laughing and
talking excitedly. Half a second out of his hand the grenade exploded in mid air. Some lady defenseplant worker in sexy blue-
jeans had been talking to her neighbor on the assemblyline about
her new dress or new lover and mismeasured her fusecutting.

He was lucky he wasn't killed. He was unconscious, of course.
Two fingers were completely gone and two dangled by shreds of
skin. In the rosy dawn light they got a tourniquet on the arm and
tied the whole hand up in a bundle in somebody's handkerchief
so as not to tear off the two fingers. Then they got him started for
the hospital in an improvised stretcher made of two buttoned up

fatigue blouses with poles through the arms. Two swimmers stayed behind to gather the fish. On the way they commandeered a jeep. At the hospital the doctor told them that their prompt action might possibly save the two fingers. But they were all old hands at First Aid by now. It was the very least they could do for The Fullback. When he finally woke up, Culp grinned groggily. "I never felt a thing!" he said proudly. "Didn't hurt at all!" His hand was already in a big wire frame that looked like a huge glove. Next day he was flown out to New Zealand.

Before he left The Fullback told Culn and Beck what he had done about Witt. "But you guys got to make him make Witt sergeant. He never will by himself. I was saving that till later."

"He can't," Skinny Culn said. "Make or break anybody. I got a good friend at Regimental S-1 told me Charlie's TO is froze on ranks till they make him permanent or give us a new permanent commander."

"I see," Culp said. "You get around, dont you? Well, maybe it'll work out then." He sighed. "Well, maybe I'll see you guys in some hospital or other, hunh?" he grinned. So The Fullback, that perennial collegeboy, was out too now. They would sorely miss his kindly, honest, insipid sanity.

It took three weeks for Witt's transfer to go through. Then the tiny Kentuckian showed up toting his "A" and "B" bags and everything else he owned, grinning from ear to ear. He was immediately promoted to sergeant by the new Company Commander, Captain Bosche, who had saved a spot for him.

Bosche was not the only thing that had happened to them during those three weeks. Though perhaps in a way he was the most important. Certainly he left his personal mark on everything else that did happen to them. But at least as important as Bosche was the new training schedule. The new training schedule arrived even before Bosche did, and the essence of it was amphibious training.

There had been rumors that they were going to Australia for training and regroupment like the 1st Marine Division had. Even the most hopeful knew better that first day they were carried out in the Channel in landing craft and brought back in to practice a landing. They were not going anywhere except north, to New Georgia. When this became clear, there was a marked increase in the amount of swipe consumed by the company.

The training continued without letup, and when Bosche arrived he at once made it even tougher. Rifle ranges had been built on the island, and they worked at them day after day, firing and firing, sweating under the hot sun without shade. There were practice marches every two or three days. The mortar and MG sections—under their new lieutenant replacing Culp—were given enormous practice firings, and with *live* ammo. No expense was being spared. Only the nights—of sitting out in the moonlight drinking the horrible tasting swipe and talking, the thinking about women—remained unchanged.

When Bosche first arrived to take over from Johnny Creo, he immediately made a speech about the swipe.

He was a tough little guy, maybe thirtyfive, tightly packed into his tailormade khakis. He wore a tight little belly that appeared at least as hard as the flat abdominals of most athletes. His brass belt buckle shone like a star. On his left breast was sewn a whole flock of ribbons amongst which were immediately noticeable a Silver Star and a Purple Heart with cluster. He had been wounded twice. He had seen action at Pearl Harbor. He was not a West Pointer. He had, instead, learned his soldiering the hard way, which was by experience. He was coming to them from one of the regiments of the Americal Division. This was his first command as a full-fledged captain.

"I've certainly seen as much, probably more, combat than you guys have. I dont like war. But we've got it and it's here. On the other hand, I can't say I dislike *every*thing about it.

"Now I know you men are making and drinking this goddam swipe. That's okay by me. Any man in an outfit of mine can get as drunk as he wants to every night, as long as he's ready—and in shape—to make Reveille and carry out any assignment he is given. If he can't do that, he's gonna have trouble, and from me. Personal."

He paused here and looked them over where they stood clustered around the jeep he had clambered up on.

"I dont much like this word team. It's creepin into everything. It's not a Regiment any more, it's a Regimental Combat Team. Okay. I dont much like it, but I'll use it when I have to. So we're a team."

With this admission he paused once more, this time for dramatic emphasis.

"But I prefer to think of myself as a family man. And that's what we all are here, whether we like it or not. A family. I'm the father, and,"—he paused again—"I guess that makes Sergeant Welsh here the mother." There was some laughter. "And whether you guys like it or not, that makes all of you the children in this family. Now a family can only have one head, and that's the father. Me. Father is the head, and mother runs it. That's the way it's gonna be here. If any of you guys want to see me about anything, anything at all, you'll find I'm available. On the other hand, I'm gonna be busy makin a living for this family, so if it's not important, maybe mother can handle it. That's all, except for one more thing.

"We're into training now, as all of you know. You all know what *kind* of training it is, too. Well, I'm going to make this training just as tough on everybody as I possibly can. Including me. No matter how tough I make it, it can't be as tough as combat. As you all well know. So, expect it. And that's all.

"—Except for one more thing.

"I want you to know that as long as you guys back *me* up, I'll back *you* up. All the way, and with any-body. With any outfit, and any army. Japanese, American, or what have you. You can count on that." He paused again. "And now that's really all." The tough little guy had not smiled once, even at his own jokes.

Everybody liked him. Even Welsh seemed to like him. Or, if not like, at least respect him. Which from Welsh was quite a lot. Anyway, he had to be better than Glory Hunter Band or Johnny Creo. And so this was the man who was going to take them up to New Georgia. Only John Bell, standing somewhere way at the back, had any suspicions, and Bell was not at all sure that these did not come more from himself than from Captain Bosche. After all, what could you ask of a man? Certainly no more than Bosche had offered. And if he lived up to and carried out his promises, you could ask nothing more. But Bell suffered a sudden impulse to laugh out loud insanely and call out at the top of his voice: *"Yes, but what does it all MEAN?"* He was able to restrain it. Bell had had seventeen letters from his wife in the last three weeks, all of them loving, but he could not escape a feeling that she had maybe written them all at once in a great burst of energy on the same day, sealed, stamped and addressed them, and stacked them on her desk where she would not forget to mail one every couple of days. He had done that once with his parents, when he was in college. Anyway, Bosche's speech was certainly better than the one they had to hear a couple of days later.

Two days after Bosche arrived in C-for-Charlie the campaign for Guadalcanal ended. The last Japanese were either killed, captured or evacuated by their own people, and the island was secured. This date happened to coincide with the Regimental Commander's promotion to Brigadier. More to celebrate this than the ending of the campaign, they were given a day off from training. It was supposed to be a party—a beerburst given and paid for by the Colonel. Unfortunately, the beer was hot, and it turned out that there was slightly less than a can per man. Perhaps this influenced the general reception of the Colonel's speech.

He was pretty well oiled, of course. All of the higher officers sitting on the platform of planks and sawhorses were. They had been celebrating the promotion. And The Great White Father had never been noted for being much of an afterdinner speaker. When introduced, he got up swaying slightly under his mottled red face and said in his drill voice: "You men got this star for me!" He touched it on his shoulder. "Now I want you to go out and get one for Colonel Grubbe, too!" Then he sat down. There were no cheers.

Col Grubbe, who though a New Englander nevertheless closely resembled the longnosed, mean, and meanlooking Johnny Creo, contented himself with saying he only hoped he made as good a commander as his predecessor and to point the matter up asked for a cheer for the new General. This time there were a few indulgent, ironic ones. John Bell, though he could not speak for the others, went away wanting to vomit out of sheer rage and anger or maybe it was the hot beer. The next day he was made a platoon sergeant by Bosche.

There were promotions dropping like propaganda leaflets all over. Once Bosche had arrived and been installed, the TO was unfrozen and he could make whoever he wanted to fill the vacancies of the last battle. True to his own estimate of his character as given in his speech, he allowed himself to be advised by his platoon sergeants. This time the casualties had been much less high than at The Dancing Elephant. Not counting the twelve men dead at The Glory Hunter's roadblock, there were only seven men dead in the company, making a grand total of nineteen. The wounded were also correspondingly light, only eighteen in all. Of these, seven were sergeants. An interesting statistical sidelight on The Battle for Boola Boola, and on all of the fighting done in the coconut groves those two days, was that there was an enormously greater percentage of leg wounds than normal. This was attributed to the fact that the Japanese were so starved and weak at this point that they could not raise their rifles high enough to aim any higher. True or not, more than half of C-for-Charlie's wounded were leg wounds. One of these was Platoon Sergeant "Jimmy" Fox of the 3d Platoon, and it was the 3d Platoon which Captain Bosche gave to John Bell. The other platoon vacancy was not due to casualties at all, and came as an odd strange surprise to almost everybody. On an order coming all the way down from the Division Commander himself, but which must have been largely controlled and handled by Regiment, Sgt Skinny Culn was given a field commission as a 2nd Lieutenant. It was almost the first, it *was* the first, experience any of them (excepting John Bell) had had to do with the crossing or breaking of the officer caste system. Their Old Army was breaking up under the pressure of war and grinning with pleased embarrassment, Culn packed to leave and be sworn in and assigned to another Regiment. His 1st Platoon was given by Bosche to Charlie Dale the ex-Second Cook, who now had one whole quart mason jar full of gold teeth as the beginning of his collection. Beck of course remained in charge of the 2d Platoon. But his platoon guide second in command was

out because of a wound at Boola Boola. His place was given to
Buck Sergeant Don Doll, who was promoted to Staff to replace
him. And all down the line others moved up to replace the promoted.

Through it all, through everything, the training went right on.
Green replacements were beginning to pour into the island and
get themselves apportioned out. For the first time in a long time
C-for-Charlie found itself almost back at strength. These new
ones were assigned to squads and incorporated in the range firings, small units' tactics problems, the simulated landings. "Cannon Fodder" they were called, as C-for-Charlie itself had once
been called, and they watched men like Beck and Doll and Geoffrey Fife with the same awe with which Beck and Doll and Fife,
themselves now bearded, had once watched the bearded Marines.
They were not, however, to remain bearded long.

In a way it was sort of sad. Their beards, since they first started
to nurture them in the week after The Dancing Elephant, were
precious status symbols. They symbolized the comparative freedom of the frontline combat infantryman, when compared with
the tighter, more disciplined, 'garrison' type life of the rear area
troops. Even the thinnest most straggly nineteenyearold beard was
worn proudly by its grower as the symbol of a combat man. Now,
on orders from the Division Commander, these were being taken
from them. As the fighting with its attendant excitement and hysteria faded—that same fighting which they were so proud of having done, and felt they deserved some credit for—as this faded,
they were being forced back into the tighter discipline of garrison
living, just as if they were real garrison troops who had never
fired a shot in anger. In fact, it was like living in garrison, now:
Saturday inspections, crappy training every weekday, work and
fatigue details, Sundays off. Everybody knew the training was
mostly bullshit, that when they got up there again next time nothing would happen like it was supposed to in the training manuals,
and all this fucking training would be useless. The only thing
really worthwhile was the range firing practice, at which they
were teaching these incredibly badly trained replacements how to
shoot their rifles; but the rest was crap. And now their beards.

After a few late night meetings and passionate swipe-inspired speeches, it was decided to make a formal protest to Captain Bosche. Milly Beck, as the senior platoon sergeant now, was delegated to carry the message. It would be the first time they would see Bosche in action with his you-back-me-up-I'll-back-you-up declaration.

"You know this trainin is mostly horseshit, Captain," Milly told him earnestly. "It aint gonna mean a fuckin damn thing when we get up there again. We—"

"No, Sergeant Beck," Bosche said, rubbing his always immaculately and smoothly shaven, little fat round jaw. "Let me make it plain that I dont agree with you there at all."

"Well, Okay, Captain. Like you say, you probly seen more combat than we have. But we still think it's bullshit. Except for the range firin, a course. But we've gone right on and done ever bit of it, and nobody's goofed off and nobody's complained. We've backed you up on it right down the line."

"I know you have, Sergeant," Bosche said.

"Well, now they want to take away our beards. That's nothin but just plain, lowdown, dirty pool. We—"

"Unfortunately, there happens to be in Army Regulations a paragraph which specifically states that beards will not be worn in the Army. I think it dates back to the Cavalry and Indians Wars. The Division Commander has seen fit to invoke that particular Regulation. I don't see that there's a damn thing I can do about it."

"Well, will you write him a letter of protest for us?" Milly Beck asked earnestly. "We—"

"You know you can't go around writing letters of protest like that in the Army, Sergeant," Bosche said evenly. "When I get an order from a superior, I have to obey it just like you do."

"I see," Beck said. "Then you won't write the letter for us?"

"I dont see how I possibly can. I can't."

"Okay." Beck scratched among his own tangled growth and thought for a moment. "Well, what about mustaches, Captain?"

"The order says nothing about mustaches. As far as I know, there is nothing in Army Regulations which says an enlisted soldier cannot wear a mustache. In fact, I think there is somewhere a paragraph specifically permitting it.''

"I know," said Milly Beck. "I mean, I think there is, too. I think I've seen it. But you won't write the letter for us about the beards? How much they mean to us?''

"I would," Bosche said simply. "I'd be glad to. But I simply can't. My hands are tied.''

"Okay, Sir. Aye aye," Beck said and saluted.

And that was all he had to bring back and report. In the first test of his you-back-me-up-I'll-back-you-up policy Bosche, it was decided, had come off a little less well than his promise. He was, it appeared, just like everybody else in this world, and no titan at all. If just one officer, one Company Commander, had seen fit to write the Division Commander about the importance of beards, maybe the Division Commander would have rescinded the order. No Company commander did. Almost overnight, beards disappeared from Guadalcanal, except for a few New Zealand Pioneer outfits, and some small US Marine units who had never seen any combat anyway. But the mustaches stayed. The only way left to protest the loss of beards now was to grow the most ridiculous, outlandish mustaches possible, and those who had sufficient face hair tried. And the training went right on.

The sense of doom was growing now. Nobody really wanted to go up to New Georgia, not even the swashbucklers. Doll and Fife had become bosom buddies since the night of Fife's fight, and they discussed the thing privately. Fife found himself oppressed by a deep and penetrating sense of the doom growing everywhere within the Division. This on the other hand did not bother Doll at all and, while he admitted that he really did not want to go, he found certain things exciting and intriguing about going up to New Georgia.

"We got it and it's here," he said. "There aint a fucking damn thing we can do about it. So there it is. And there's certain things about combat that I find enjoyable.

"Do you believe there's any life after death?" he asked after a moment.

"I dont know," Fife mumbled. "Certainly not like all the

churches say anyway. The Japs believe if they die fighting they go straight to heaven forever. How primitive can you get? I just dont know. That's the truth.''

"Well, I dont know either," Doll said. "But sometimes I can't help wondering about it.

"Let's go down to the dump and get some canned fruit," he grinned after a pause.

This was one of their favorite pastimes, ever since the making of swipe had started. The two of them had, in effect, become the canned fruit suppliers for the whole of C-for-Charlie. There was, Fife knew, something deathlike about it. He was not like Doll. And yet he always went. It was like biting on your own wound.

They would swagger up, hands resting on their holster flaps. They were swashbucklers. Fife had a pistol too now, come by at Boola Boola where he had taken it off a dead American he had found lying facedown with his toes turned in or was it out? They really were swashbucklers, and Fife loved it. Because for these few moments he could believe he was what the new cannonfodder thought he really was. A soldier? a pirate? anyway, a swashbuckler. The moment he found out about the swipe making, the General Commanding had ordered armed guards posted on all the ration dumps. They had orders to shoot to kill. That was what made it fun.

So they would walk up. The armed guard would be sitting way up there up on top, rifle in hand, and he would always be a cannonfodder. What you gonna do with that gun, bud? one of them would say. Shoot me or somethin like that? Nobody who was really hep called it a piece or arm any more. Usually they would be shouted at. By the cannonfodder. There would be threatening gestures. Somebody, some wit, in the company made up a word for the especially weak ones, which was cannonmudder. They would simply stand and look at him, hands resting on their holster flaps. Then they would take what they wanted and walk away, turning their backs disdainfully. Nobody was ever shot. But Fife was not like Doll. And he knew it.

When he first realized it, it was that bad time after the combat numbness left them and they had not yet found out about the swipe. He had never believed that he could be terrified by any of these puny piddling little air raids again, but he was. And Doll obviously was not. Fife had thought the combat numbness was a new state of mind. And when it went away and left him again a quivering mass of jelly, he was not prepared. He was forced to face once again the same fact he had faced before, which was that he was not a soldier. He was right back where he started. It took every ounce of courage he could muster to continue sitting under the cocopalm drinking and not run dive into his slit trench during the air raids. He could do it and he did but it cost him more than it did other people, like Doll. So he was forced to face up once again to the same old fact he had always known. He was a coward.

Perhaps it was that, that knowledge, which made him take advantage of the loophole when it appeared and Old MacTae the young supply sergeant told him he should. Of course, everybody who possibly could was taking advantage of the loophole. Even Doll tried to take advantage of it, but he was so disgustingly healthy that there was nothing at all he could do. The loophole was the recently discovered fact that Division hospital had relaxed the sternness of their evacuation policy.

It all started with Carni, Mazzi's hep pal from Greater New York in the 1st Platoon. Almost everybody except a few like Doll now had malaria in the company. But Carni had it so bad that he really could not function. Day after day he went on sick call with it, was handed a handful of atabrine, and came back to lie on his bunk totally incapacitated. And now, because of the atabrine, he had yellow jaundice to boot. Then one day he did not come back from sick call. Two days later they were informed he had been evacuated.

He was the first. Immediately almost everybody who had any malaria at all went on sick call. Unfortunately it helped almost no one. But slowly, over the weeks, first one then another of the honestly serious cases began to disappear and not come back from sick call. They were being sent, for the present moment anyway,—or so rumor had it—to either Naval Base Hospital No. 3 on Ephate in the New Hebrides, or to New Zealand. Naturally

New Zealand was better, and there was much anguish in almost every outfit at the thought of friends getting drunk and laid in Auckland New Zealand. Ephate had only one small town in which there was nothing except natives who tried to sell souvenir handcarved boats to everybody and to each other.

Then Stormy Storm got himself evacuated, and the lid was off. Storm was unique in that he was the first man any of them knew who got evacuated for a plain physical disability rather than for some disease like malaria or jaundice. His physical disability was his wounded hand. Having nothing else to utilize, and being one of those who obviously were never going to get sick with anything and would therefore have to stay and watch his friends leave him one by one, Storm decided to try with his bad hand again since they were loosening everything up so. To his astonishment, and everybody else's, he was examined by exactly the same doctor who had sent him back to duty during The Dancing Elephant, and was this time evacuated. The doctor did not even remember him. When Storm made the hand grate for him and told his story, he clucked his tongue and said someone had been seriously wrong in sending him back. What Storm really needed was an operation, and he was sending him to New Zealand because his hand would be in a cast for several months. The people there might even send him Stateside. But he should never have been sent back to duty. Storm, naturally, did not tell him who had done it. Almost everybody in the company came by to say goodby to him in the hospital where he was smoking cigars, eating well and enjoying himself since he was not at all sick.

And with Storm's success, just about everybody tried to get into the act. In one month and two weeks after Carni was evacuated for malaria, over 35% of the old C-for-Charlie—the men who had ridden back in the trucks from Boola Boola—had managed to get themselves evacuated for one thing or another. Many many more had tried and failed, and a few who knew they had no chance had not tried at all. And one man had been offered evacuation and had refused it.

Who else could it be but The Welshman, Mad Eddie Welsh the First Sergeant? His malaria, unlike John Bell's malaria which had

leveled off as a medium bad case, had gone on getting worse like
Carni's malaria had. When he was found in a dead faint one day
slumped across his desk with indelible pencil still in hand, he was
carried up to Division hospital and ordered evacuated. He came
to to find himself in a small section reserved for first three grad-
ers, in a bunk right next to that of Storm. The colored ticket for
evacuation was already attached to his bed foot.

"Aha, you fink bastard!" he bellowed. "So it was you who got
me hauled up here!" His crazy eyes glinted with an insane fever-
ishness. Storm could not tell whether it was the fever of the
malaria, or simply Welsh's personality.

"Knock off, First Sarn't," Storm, who was smoking a cigar,
said cautiously. "I'm a patient here like you, and I'm bein
shipped out like you."

"You'll never get away with it!" Welsh roared. "You'll never
beat *me* out of my job, Storm! I'm too smart! Anyway, while
you're okay in the kitchen, you got no head for Administration! I
know you!"

Storm, knowing him, simply could not believe he was delirious. From down the aisle the frail young 2d Lt doctor who ran the
ward came running with a wardboy.

"Now you just take it easy, Sergeant," he said. "You've got a
temperature of a hundred and five and two tenths."

"You're in cahoots with him!" Welsh hollered.

For answer the Lt shoved him back on his pillow and put a
thermometer in his mouth, at which point Welsh bit the thermometer in two, threw it on the floor, leaped out of bed and ran out the
tent flap and back to his company. He did not die, as the Lt
predicted he would; and he continued to recommend to everybody, smiling his sly, mad smile, that they try their damnedest to
get themselves evacuated while there was still time.

Into the midst of all this activity, like some ghost from another
world, Buck Sgt Big Queen suddenly returned. True to his word,
he had stowed away on a ship coming to Guadalcanal. Due to
some quirk, he had not been sent to Ephate or New Zealand, but
to a hospital in New Caledonia, which meant that if he *was* sent
back to duty he would not be sent to his old outfit but to some

new Division in New Guinea. On the other hand, the doctors there—because the bullet had taken a large bone chip out of his upper arm and left that arm slightly impaired—had offered to send him back to the States to become a combat instructor for draftees. Queen had refused to accept either alternative and finally had gone AWOL and stowed away on a boat heading here and aboard which, when he told his story, he was treated like a prince the rest of the voyage. But now, seeing what he had come back to, he was stunned. This was not his old outfit: Culn gone, and an *Officer*? Charlie Dale, an *ex-cook!* the Platoon Sgt of 1st Platoon? Jimmy Fox gone? Jenks dead? Stein relieved? Pvt John Bell a Platoon Sgt, too! Fife the clerk a combat squad leader? Pfc Don Doll a Platoon Guide? Queen, who because of his absence was still only a Buck Sgt squad leader, could not accept it. It was too much for him. After two days of drinking swipe and reminiscing, he reported back to the hospital complaining about his crippled arm and was at once shipped out to New Zealand.

Nobody seemed to know just why the doctors were doing all this. They had been so tough while the campaign was going on. Now, though, men who came back said the doctors smiled at them, asked them what was wrong with them, and even helped them describe and elaborate their symptoms if they had trouble talking. Apparently none of this was Division policy, which was as tough as ever. Apparently the doctors themselves had decided the veterans of the campaign had suffered enough, and had taken it upon themselves to help oldtimers get evacuated if it was at all medically possible. Almost without exception no green replacements were ever evacuated; only oldtimers.

Fife, when it came his turn to try and utilize this marvelous loophole, did not really expect much to come of it. In fact, it was MacTae who talked him into going. Fife had had a bad ankle ever since a high school football accident had torn some ligaments which made the ankle susceptible to going out of place on him. He had learned to anticipate in such a way as to take most of his weight off it before it went all the way out. Also, on most marches and during the campaign, he kept it taped up with a basketweave bandage he had learned from the old family doctor who had treated it originally. But he rarely thought about it. All of this had become as much a part of his normal life as his bad teeth, or bad eyes. Then one day, walking to noon chow with MacTae who happened to be passing, it had gone out on him again from stepping wrong on a halfdried mud rut. He had leaped to take the weight off it, but only partially succeeded. The pain was exquisite.

"Why, you're white as a sheet!" MacTae said. "What the hell happened to you there?"

Fife shrugged and explained. It didn't hurt after the first minute if he was careful to set his foot down absolutely straight.

MacTae looked excited. "Well, have you been up to the docs with it? You haven't? Really? Why, you're out of your everlovin mind! You can get evacuated on that!"

"You really think so?" Fife had never considered it.

"Sure!" MacTae said excitedly. "I know guys who got shipped out on a lot less than that."

"But what if they turn me down?"

"So what of you got to lose? You won't be any *worse* off than you are now, will you?"

"That's true."

"Man, if I had somethin like that, I'd be up there like a shot! Trouble with me, I'm so sickeningly healthy I aint *never* gonna get myself shipped out!"

"You really think so?"

"I wouldn't hesitate a second!"

Largely because of MacTae's enthusiasm, Fife went. He was still as unsure of himself about most things as he used to be, now that he had rediscovered his cowardice. But there were other things about him which had changed. Fistfighting, for instance. The old Fife had abhorred fistfights, largely because he was afraid of losing. The new Fife adored them, and had had six or eight more fights since his beating up of Corporal Weld. He no longer cared deeply whether he won or lost, as he used to. Every bump he gave, and every bump he took, caused in him an immense sense of release from something or other. And he was not afraid to tackle anybody. All this showed up in his first encounter with

Witt, after the Kentuckian's transfer went through. Witt had been back two days and drunk both nights, and Fife had had one fight, before they actually ran into each other face to face. When they did, Fife went up to him and smiled and stuck out his hand. Squinting his eyes and putting his head a little on one side and grinning, he said, "Hello, Witt. Or are you still not speakin to me?" Witt had grinned back and taken the hand. He seemed to sense some change he liked. "No. I guess I'm talkin to you now." "Because if you're not, I thought we might as well have it out right here and now," Fife grinned. Witt nodded, still grinning. Apparently he had seen the fight. "Well, we could do that. I think I could still take you. But you got a pretty good right hand there. If you tagged me with that right hand, you might could whup me. Awys pervided I couldn't keep away from it, a course." "There aint really no need though," Fife grinned, "now. Since you're talking to me. Is there?" "Not really," Witt said. "What do you say we have a slug of swipe instead?" Cynically, they did. And it was this quality—of cynicism, or whatever the hell you called it—that worked for him when he went up to the hospital on sick call after MacTae suggested it.

When his turn in the line came and they called him into the examining tent, he saw that the examining doctor was Lt Col Roth—that same big, meatylooking, wavywhitehaired, pompous Lt Col Roth who had examined his head wound and been so contemptuous to him about his lost glasses. As far as Fife was concerned, that blew it. Only, this time Lt Col Roth smiled. "Well, soldier, and what's your trouble?" he said, smiling in a sort of conspiratorial way. It was obvious that he did not recognize Fife. And that was the way Fife played it.

The climactic moment for Fife did not come till later. He told his story and showed his ankle. The ankle was still swollen. Lt Col Roth examined it carefully, twisting it this way and that until Fife winced. It certainly *was* a bad ankle, he said. He did not see how anybody could march, and fight in rough terrain, on something like that. How long had Fife had it? Fife told him the truth, then went on to tell him about the basketweave bandage and how he always carried tape with him. Lt Col Roth whistled admiringly, then looked at Fife sharply.

"Then how come you decided to report to hospital with it *now?*" the Colonel said sharply.

It was Fife's moment, and in some dim way he knew it. But his reaction was entirely instinctive. Instead of looking guilty, or even pleading, he gave Lt Col Roth a cynical, guarded smile. "Well, Colonel, it seems to be bothering me a lot more lately," he said, and grinned.

Roth's lips twitched, and his eyes glinted, and then the same identical cynical, conspiratorial smile passed across his own face fleetingly. He bent and manipulated the ankle again. Well, it would need an operation, that much was certain, and that would mean several months in a cast. Was Fife prepared to spend several months in a plaster cast?

Fife grinned guardedly again. "Well, if it will help it, Sir—I guess I am."

Lt Col Roth bent his head again. It might never be all right, he said, but perhaps it could be helped. Those ligament and tendon operations were ticklish things. There was an orthopedics man, a top man, at Naval Base Hospital No. 3 on Ephate, who really enjoyed doing that kind of ticklish job of surgery. After that, Fife would be shipped on to New Zealand, if he had to spend that long in a cast. And after that—Roth shrugged, and again his eyes glinted. He turned to the orderly. "Admit this man for evacuation," he said.

Fife was afraid to believe it, lest something happen to change it. Just like that. Just like that, and he was out. Out! *Out!* Saying nothing, he bent and began putting on his sock and boot.

As he was going out the flap, Roth called him. When he turned back, the Colonel said, "You're a Sergeant now, I see."

"Sir?" Fife said.

Roth grinned. "You were a Corporal before, weren't you? What happened about those eyeglasses of yours? Nothing? Well, when you get down there, mention it to them. They'll fix you up with new ones."

It didn't make any sense. Why would he be one way one time

like that, and then the exact opposite the next? Was this Lt Col Roth, who carried in his hands the decision between certain life and probable death for simple infantrymen, was this man prey to the changeabilities and vagaries of emotion like that? Like everybody else? The thought was terrifying. He had three days to wait for the next hospital ship. (Only serious cases and emergencies were being flown out.) They were three days of misery and sadness. Because now that he was sure he was going, now that he was definitely safe, Fife wondered if he really ought to go? Should he not just skip out of the hospital and go back to C-for-Charlie, like Welsh had done? He tried hard to keep his mind on the sensible, sane MacTae. But the question stayed.

He took it up with Welsh himself, finally, when the First Sergeant came up to the hospital bringing personal gear for somebody else who was shipping out.

"So you finally makin it out, hunh, kid?" Welsh leered at him when he saw him, his black eyes glinting contemptuously.

"Yeh," Fife said sadly. He couldn't help feeling melancholy. "But I been thinkin, First. Maybe I ought to stay?"

"You what!" Welsh snarled.

"Well, yes. I mean, you know, I'm gonna miss the company. And it's—it's sort of like running out. In one way."

Welsh leered at him in silence, his mad eyes gleaming. "Sure, kid. I think if you feel like that, you oughta come back."

"You think so? I thought I might slip out of here tonight maybe."

"You should," Welsh said, and then grinned his slow, sly grin. "You wanta know somthin, kid?" he said softly. "You want to know why I got you busted out of the orderly room that time? You thought it was because we thought you weren't coming back, didn't you?" Before Fife could answer, he said, "Well, it wasn't. It was because you were such a lousy fucking bad clerk, *I HAD to do it!*"

If he could have Fife would have hit him, he was so furious. He *knew* he was not a bad clerk. But he was lying on his bunk and before he could get up Welsh was gone, down the aisle and out through the flap. He did not even look back. Fife did not see him again. He did not slip out that night, and the hospital ship left the next day. He felt sad, but when the landing craft carried them out to the big ship he did not feel guilty. He was glad to leave such hate-filled people. It was a fine, sunshiny day.

It was on that same day that Sgt John Bell got the letter he had been waiting for from his wife. They had just broken from the morning training exercise for noon chow, and Corporal Weld came around with a batch of new mail. Actually, it was one of a batch of three. As he always did, Bell arranged them by postmark date and read the oldest first. So he did not read the new letter until last. When he opened it and saw how it began *(Dear John,* it said), he knew what it was, and that it was in fact a Dear John letter. Messkit, ringed lid, and handleopened canteen cup all dangling impotently from one hand together, he walked away by himself with it. *Dear John.* The others always began with *Darling* or *Dearest* or *Beloved,* or some such other of that phony shit. She *had* been doing it. She had been *doing* it. And him he had not touched a single soul, not once, since he had left. Superstitious fool bastard, thinking that would help or make any difference! He was ravenously hungry from the morning workout, but he knew he couldn't eat anything. He was sick all over. His legs were shaky and his hands and arms were shaky. He sat down on a cocopalm log with it.

When he finally could, he read it carefully and sanely instead of jumping jerkily around in it. It was carefully and sanely written. All the necessary information was there. The guy was an Air Force Captain at Paterson. She had fallen deeply in love with him. He was a scientific researcher in aerodynamics, and would therefore never be sent overseas. She wanted a divorce to marry him. She knew that he, Bell, could refuse to give her one. But she was asking him anyway—out of the memory of what they had had together. The war looked as though it might go on forever. And God only knew what was going to happen to the world afterward. She had fallen deeply in love, and she wanted that love while she could have it. She thought he would understand. And in between all this necessary information were sandwiched the repeated requests, pleas, for forgiveness. Oh, it was all there. It was sane and

sensible and calm and even sad. It was proper and it was reasonable. It was even prim. What was *not* there was any information
about what they did together. How they went to bed. What they
did in bed. What other things they did. Not one word about how
he compared to Bell. That, of course, was all private now, between her and the guy. That was something Bell could never be
admitted to. But he could imagine. Worse, he could remember.
Why, from the letter you'd think they didn't even have any sex
together at all, it was so prim and proper and polite and distant.
Come on, I used to fuck you, Baby! He sat with it, shaken all over
and, as a professional soldier, quite ready to die. Marty! Marty!

He couldn't eat anything. And during the afternoon exercise he
was something less than his normal competent self. "What's the
matter with you?" Buck Sgt Witt, who was now one of his squad
leaders, said, "You lost yore taw?" When they were back and
dismissed, he went off into the tongue of jungle by himself and
tried to evoke that translucent, so realistic image of his wife
which had come to him so many times and over so many places
on this island. He found he couldn't. He took the letter and went
to Captain Bosche.

"Yes? Come on in! What is it, Bell?" the Company Commander said. His hard, tight little belly was pressed to the edge of
his desk as he bent over his work. Bell handed him the letter
without a word. After all, this letter was such a formally proper
letter you could show it to anybody. You could show it to your
own mother.

The reaction he got from Bosche was astonishing, even to him
in his state of despair. As he read, the Captain's hands began to
shake until the letter rattled. His face became as white as a sheet
of his own memo paper with a rage so great that it seemed to
bunch his hard round little face into a tight hard round little ball
of such density it looked as though it could pulverize a granite
ball of equal size simply by falling on it. Somehow, in what
appeared to be slow degrees but was really very swiftly, Captain
Bosche got command of himself again. Bell had no idea why the
letter should affect him so.

"You know, of course, that you do not have to accede to this request," Bosche said in a hard thin voice. "Nor can your wife get a divorce or separation without your official permission."

"I know," Bell said, weakly.

"There is more. With a letter like this in your possession, you have the right to stop all allotments, all payments, all Government insurance policies." Bosche's voice was even harder.

"I didn't know *that*," Bell said.

"Well, you can," Bosche said. His little round jaw was as hard as a steel one.

"But I want to give it to her," Bell said tiredly. "I wanted to ask you if you would draft an official letter from you for me giving her the permission."

The Captain did not answer for a stunned second. "I dont understand you," he said stiffly. "Why do you want to do that?"

"Well, it's a little hard to explain," Bell said and paused. How to say it to him? If he didn't know. "Well, I guess it's just that what's the point of being married to a woman who doesn't want to be married to you?"

Captain Bosche's eyes had narrowed to slits, and with them he stared at Bell. "Well, there are all sorts of attitudes and opinions, I guess," he said profoundly. "That's what makes the world go round."

"Will you draft the letter for me, Sir?"

"I certainly will," Bosche said, and Bell turned to go.

"Oh, Bell!" he called, and when Bell turned back he was holding a sheaf of papers. "This came in yesterday, for you. I held it up a little because I wanted to write my own endorsement. Which is now written. I just thought that now might be a good time to give it to you. It's an order for a field commission appointing you a First Lieutenant of Infantry." He said it all flatly, but even then the slight emphasis on *First* Lieutenant could not be missed. He smiled. "Really?" Bell said. He felt silly.

Bosche grinned. "Really. I assumed that you would want to accept it, and I have already written my hearty endorsement."

"Can I think it over for a little while?"

"Of course," Bosche said promptly. "Take all the time you want. You've had several big things today. And if you want to change your mind about that other matter, that will be perfectly all right too.''

"Thank you, Sir.''

Outside, he sat down again upon the same cocopalm log. Or was this another one? It was hard to tell. Had she really calculated it all? written the letter in exactly the way which she knew would bring from him the type of reaction she wanted? Probably. She knew him well enough to do that, didn't she? She knew him well. Just as he knew her well. Well enough to know that what was going to happen with her would happen. And it happened, didn't it? People didn't stay married to each other that long without getting to know each other pretty well. Or did they never know each other at all? Bosche certainly wouldn't have given his wife permission to divorce, would he? Why had he reacted so strangely? Had the same thing maybe happened to him? The pain of transposing his own experience of making love with Marty into an imagined love-making between her and this other guy was too much to stand. He put his mind on his other problem.

The commission? *First* Lieutenant of Infantry! Smiling sadly, Bell decided he would probably do as little harm there as he would anywhere else. In the falling dark he rose to go and tell the Captain. The next day, the letter of permission to divorce drafted and signed, he packed and left to be sworn in and transferred. One more departure from old C-for-Charlie. When Bosche asked him to recommend his successor, Bell nominated Thorne from the 2d platoon because he felt Witt was inclined to be a little unpredictable if he got angry.

And so there they were. The remainder, filled up almost to capacity with new green men, was not at all the C-for-Charlie which had once landed on this island. It was a totally different organization, with a different feel altogether now. Three days after Bell left, the orders to move came down and everything was frozen again. No more transfers, no more promotions that could move a man out of the company, no more changes of any kind. The orders, marked TOP SECRET and known to everyone almost as soon as they arrived, stated that they should be prepared to move within ten days to two weeks. All training would cease upon receipt of this order and preparatory work for moving would be begun immediately. The orders did not say what destination the Division would be heading for.

Of course, they did not need to say. Everybody knew. Don Doll had become bosom buddies with his immediate superior Milly Beck, now that Fife was gone, and they discussed New Georgia. Doll was by common consent considered the best Platoon Guide in the company now, and was clearly the next in line for a platoon. Slender Carrie Arbre had been promoted to sergeant of Doll's old squad. He and Doll still spoke to each other with a carefully guarded stiffness.

One more thing, gift of a grateful nation, came to them before they left, and this was the medals. Cynically, they had forgotten all about them when they hadn't come through, but now here they came, complete with the citations. There was a presentation. Every member of Captain Gaff's little assault force on The Dancing Elephant received a Bronze Star or better. Big Un Cash's, of course, was posthumous. John Bell's was sent on to him. Skinny Culn, recommended for a Bronze Star by Bugger Stein, got one. Don Doll, recommended for a Distinguished Service Cross by Captain Gaff, received a Silver Star instead. Charlie Dale, recommended for a Distinguished Service Cross by both Stein and Glory Hunter Band for all his braveries during The Dancing Elephant, got a Distinguished Service Cross, the only one in the Battalion. There was some bitching about this, but—as some wit immediately said—it would look good with his collection of gold teeth. Everyone pretended medals didn't mean anything, but everyone who got one was secretly proud.

One last word of the legendary Captain Gaff reached them also, just two days before they left. A fairly recent copy of *Yank* Magazine somehow fell into the hands of a C-for-Charlie man, and in it was a full page photo of the former Battalion Exec. Dressed in his tailored dress ODs (it was winter back home), wearing his Medal of Honor on its ribbon around his neck, the Captain had been photographed for *Yank* while making a speech at a bond selling rally. The caption below the photo said that his by now world famous statement to his trusty little band of ex-

hausted but unbeaten volunteer Infantrymen on Guadalcanal
*(This is where we separate the sheep from the goats and the men
from the boys!)* had become a national slogan and was being
flown on bunting in letters a foot high all across the country,
while two song publishers had brought out patriotic war songs
using it for a title, one of which was succeeding and was now on
the Hit Parade.

They of course had to march to the beach, as no trucks happened to be available for them at the moment. Their route led
them past the new cemetery. Plodding along gasping in the airless
humidity and tripping over mud rolls and grass hummocks as
they were, the cemetery looked very green and cool. The area had
been well drained, and bluegrass had been planted on it. Big
sprinklers sent their long gossamer jets swirling through the air
above the crosses, and the white crosses were very beautiful in
their long even rows. Quartermaster men moved here and there on
its long expanse keeping it up and tending it.

Half a mile further on, passing a rusting wrecked Japanese
barge, they met a man eating an apple. Perched high up on the
prow of the wreck, he could look directly down on them as he
leisurely munched his apple. One apple. Somehow, by some incredible mistake in bills of lading and shipping tickets in quintu-
plicate, a gross oversight by some nameless but usually efficient
functionary, one fresh red apple had gotten sandwiched in
amongst all the cans and crates and boxes and cases of
precooked, dried and dehydrated foods, and hidden away in some
unsearched corner had stowed away overseas. By some unbelievably marvelous stroke of luck this man had gotten it and could sit
on the high prow of a wrecked barge eating it while they passed.
Had he known them, this stranger, he could have ticked off their
names as they passed below him in macabre review, their faces
twisted up at him to stare hungrily at his apple: Captain Bosche,
his officers, 1st/Sgt Eddie Welsh, Platoon Sergeants Thorne,
Milly Beck, Charlie Dale, S/Sgt Don Doll, Corporal Weld, Sgt
Carrie Arbre, Pfc Train, Pvt Crown, Pvts Tills and Mazzi, each
looking back and upward at him as they passed. But, of course,
he couldn't do this, since to him they were all strangers.

Mad Welsh, marching on behind the sturdy little figure of Captain Bosche, didn't give a fuck for apples. He had his two canteens of gin. Which was all he could carry this time, and he felt for them furtively. In his mind he was muttering over and over his old phrase of understanding: "Property. Property. All for property," which he had once said in rudimentary innocence arriving on this island. Well, this was a pretty good sized chunk of real estate, wasn't it? this island? He had known the combat numbness now—for the first time, at Boola Boola—and it was his calculated hope and belief that if pursued long enough and often enough, it might really become a permanent and mercifully blissful state. It was all he asked.

Ahead of them the LCIs waited to take them aboard, and slowly they began to file into them to be taken out to climb the cargo nets up into the big ships. One day one of their number would write a book about all this, but none of them would believe it, because none of them would remember it that way.

ABOUT THE AUTHOR

JAMES JONES was born in Robinson, Illinois, in 1921. His wartime experiences inspired some of his most famous works. He is the author of *From Here to Eternity, Some Came Running, The Pistol, The Thin Red Line, Go to the Widow-Maker, The Ice-Cream Headache and Other Stories, The Merry Month of May, A Touch of Danger, Viet Journal, WW II,* and *Whistle.* He died in 1977.

HB 01.15.2024 0953